JOHN MILTON: SELECTED PROSE

JOHN MILTON

SELECTED PROSE

New and Revised Edition

Edited by C. A. Patrides

University of Missouri Press
Columbia, 1985

Library of Congress Cataloging in Publication Data

Milton, John, 1608–1674.
John Milton: selected prose.

Rev. ed. of: Selected prose. 1974.
Bibliography: p.
I. Patrides, C. A. II. Title.
PR3569.P34   1985   824'.4   85–1027
ISBN 0–8262–0484–8

Cover art: Michelangelo, *Creation of the Sun, the
Moon, and the Planets*, from the Sistine Chapel

♾™ This paper meets the minimum requirements of
the American National Standard for Permanence of Paper
for Printed Library Materials, Z39.48, 1984.

for Marguerite

χαρὰ θεῶν

CONTENTS

TO THE READER

A Note on Method

If nature abhors a vacuum, so does the reader who must cope with passages torn from their context. In the present edition, therefore, the crucial Part II ("The Major Premises") provides the text of five prose works in full: *Of Education, Areopagitica, The Tenure of Kings and Magistrates, A Treatise of Civil Power*, and *The Readie and Easie Way to Establish a Free Commonwealth*. Two other works—*Of Reformation* and *The Doctrine and Discipline of Divorce*—could not in their entirety be accommodated within the space available to me, but in reducing them I have provided summaries of the sections omitted in order to preserve the continuity of each work. The lengthy treatise on systematic theology, *De doctrina christiana*, is necessarily represented in much condensed form and, of course, in translation; yet many of its premises and something of its style may be described even from so far afield.

Parts I and III appear to be mere extracts. Yet the selections in Part I ("Milton on Milton") constitute a unity if read in the light of the outline of Milton's life (pp. 11–14) and particularly the two early biographies by John Aubrey and Milton's nephew Edward Phillips (pp. 409–38); while Part III ("Extracts, Mainly on Literature") looks beyond these pages to Milton's total performance in poetry as in prose. So far, and perhaps only so far, the present edition has achieved its ambition adequately to represent Milton's "three species of liberty"—ecclesiastical, domestic, and civil (cf. p. 71)—by placing them within the context of both the seventeenth century and Milton's own life.

Acknowledgments

Milton's text is reprinted from *The Works of John Milton*, gen. ed. Frank A. Patterson (New York: Columbia University Press, 1931–1940), 20 vols.: permission to reprint was generously granted by the Columbia University Press and is gratefully acknowledged. I am also grateful to the University of Michigan Press for permission to reprint John Aubrey's "Milton" from *Aubrey's Brief Lives*, ed. Oliver Lawson Dick, 3d ed. (1960), pp. 190–203.

The preparation of this edition was substantially affected by the labors of the editors who preceded me in annotating Milton's prose, notably Merritt Y. Hughes (1957) and the several contributors to J. Max Patrick's edition (1967) and the Yale edition (see below). Their indispensable guidance is acknowledged with pleasure. But I should also like to express my gratitude to Professor Thomas Kranidas of the State University of New York at Stony Brook, who suggested several improvements to my Introduction; Professor Balachandra Rajan of the University of Western Ontario, who advised me on some of the selections included here; Professor William B. Hunter of the University of Houston and Dr. Gordon Campbell of the University of Leicester, who lent me their expert knowledge on the extracts from *De doctrina christiana*; the editorial staff of Penguin Books—the publishers of the first edition (1974)—who assisted me crucially during the inception of the present enterprise; and the editorial staff of the University of Missouri Press, who made it possible that a new and revised edition should now become available.

Abbreviations

The abbreviation "Columbia ed." refers throughout to the Patterson edition cited above; "Yale ed." refers to the *Complete Prose Works of John Milton*, gen. ed. Don M. Wolfe (New Haven: Yale University Press, 1953–1982, 8 vols. Other abbreviations are given below, pp. 439–40.

Ann Arbor   C.A.P.
Spring 1985

AN OUTLINE OF MILTON'S LIFE

within the context of contemporary events

[See further Milton's own account (below, pp. 66 ff.) and the biographies by John Aubrey and Edward Phillips (pp. 409 ff.)]

1603	Death of Elizabeth I; accession of James I. The Millenary Petition.
1604	The Hampton Court Conference. *Othello* first acted.
1605	The Gunpowder Plot. *King Lear* first (?) acted. Cervantes's *Don Quixote*, Part I, published (Part II in 1615).
1606	*Macbeth* and Jonson's *Volpone* first (?) acted.
1607	First successful English colony founded, in Virginia.
1608	December 9: Milton born in Cheapside, London.
1609	Spenser's *Faerie Queene*: 1st folio edition.
1610	Jonson's *Alchemist* first acted; also Shakespeare's *Winter's Tale*. Galileo reports on his telescopic view of the heavens.
1611	The King James ("Authorized") Version of the Bible published. Shakespeare's *Tempest* first (?) acted.
1614	Webster's *Duchess of Malfi* first (?) acted. Ralegh's *History of the World* published.
1615	George Villiers, later Duke of Buckingham, in favor.
1616	Death of Shakespeare.
1618	Ralegh executed. Bacon appointed Lord Chancellor. The Synod of Dort. The Thirty Years War begins.
1620	Settlement of first New England colony by the Pilgrim Fathers.
1620?	Milton attends St. Paul's School (to 1624).
1621	Bacon impeached. Donne appointed Dean of St. Paul's Cathedral.
1623	Shakespeare's plays: 1st folio edition.
1624	Cardinal Richelieu chief minister in France.
1625	Death of James I; accession of Charles I. Outbreak of the plague. Milton admitted to Christ's College, Cambridge.
1626	Death of Bacon.
1627	War with France (to 1629).

1628   Buckingham assassinated.

1629   Milton admitted to the B.A. Emigrations to New England (1629 ff.).

1631   Death of Donne.

1632   Milton admitted to the M.A. His poem "On Shakespeare" published in the 2d Folio of Shakespeare's plays.

1633   William Laud appointed Archbishop, defends conformity against mounting opposition. Death of Herbert. Poems of Donne and Herbert published.

1634   A Mask [Comus] performed (published 1637).

1636   Advent of Cambridge Platonism (1636 ff.).

1637   Descartes's Discourse of Method published. Death of Jonson.

1638   Milton embarks on a visit to France and Italy. Lycidas published in the Edward King memorial volume.

1639   First Bishops' War. Milton returns to London in the late summer.

1640   The Short Parliament; Second Bishops' War. The Long Parliament (to 1660); Laud and Strafford impeached.

1641   Strafford executed. Irish Rebellion. The "Grand Remonstrance" issued. Milton publishes three of his antiepiscopal pamphlets: Of Reformation (see pp. 77 ff.), Of Prelatical Episcopacy, and Animadversions.

1642   Milton publishes two more antiepiscopal pamphlets: The Reason of Church Government (see pp. 49 ff.) and An Apology for Smectymnuus (pp. 61 ff.). Parliamentary strength increases; Charles I raises his standard at Nottingham: the Civil War begins. Milton marries Mary Powell; she leaves him two (?) months later.

1643   The Westminster Assembly of Divines. The Solemn League and Covenant. Sir Thomas Browne's Religio Medici (authorized ed.) published. Milton publishes The Doctrine and Discipline of Divorce (see pp. 112 ff.).

1644   Parliamentary victory at Marston Moor. Milton publishes Of Education (see pp. 181 ff.), Areopagitica (pp. 196 ff.), and a second divorce pamphlet, The Judgment of Martin Bucer.

1645   Laud executed. The New Model Army formed; parliamentary victories at Naseby and elsewhere. Milton publishes the last two divorce pamphlets, Tetrachordon and Colasterion.

Mary Powell returns to him. First edition of *The Poems of Mr. John Milton* (the shorter poems).

1646   Birth of Milton's first daughter, Anne.

1647   Parliamentary army occupies London. Charles I is arrested; escapes.

1648   Second Civil War; Charles I is seized. Birth of Milton's second daughter, Mary.

1649   Charles I tried and executed; Charles II, proclaimed in Scotland, escapes to France in 1651. Monarchy and the House of Lords abolished. The Commonwealth established. The Irish Rebellion crushed by Cromwell. Milton publishes *The Tenure of Kings and Magistrates* (see pp. 249 ff.); appointed Secretary of Foreign Tongues to the Council of State (until 1659?); publishes *Eikonoklastes* ("The Image Breaker") in reply to *Eikon Basilike* ("The Royal Image"), attributed to Charles I.

1650   Milton's blindness progresses rapidly.

1651   Milton publishes *Pro populo anglicano defensio* (the so-called "First Defense of the English People") in reply to Salmasius's defense of Charles I (1649). Birth of Milton's only son, John. Hobbes's *Leviathan* published.

1652   End of the war in Ireland. Birth of Milton's third daughter, Deborah; death of his wife, Mary, and son, John.

1653   The Protectorate established under Cromwell.

1654   Milton publishes *Pro populo anglicano defensio secunda* ("The Second Defense of the English People": see pp. 66 ff.) in reply to Pierre du Moulin's attack on the Commonwealth (1652: the presumed author was Alexander More).

1655   Milton publishes *Pro se defensio* ("Defense of Himself") in reply to a personal attack by Alexander More (1654).

1656   Milton marries Katherine Woodcock.

1657   Marvell appointed Milton's assistant in the Secretaryship. Birth of Milton's fourth daughter, Katherine.

1658   Death of Milton's wife, Katherine, and daughter, Katherine. Death of Cromwell; the Protectorate passes to his son Richard.

1659   Milton publishes *A Treatise of Civil Power* (see pp. 296 ff.) and *Considerations touching the likeliest means to remove Hire-*

> *lings out of the Church*. Richard Cromwell obliged to abdicate; the Protectorate ends.

1660   Milton publishes *The Readie and Easie Way to Establish a Free Commonwealth* (see pp. 327 ff.). Charles II recalled by Parliament. The House of Lords restored. Milton imprisoned for a time; copies of his books burned by order of Parliament. The theaters, closed since 1642, reopened. The Royal Society founded.

1661   Louis XIV assumes full powers in France.

1662   The Act of Uniformity.

1663   Milton marries Elizabeth Minshull.

1665   Outbreak of the Great Plague (to early 1666).

1666   The Great Fire of London.

1667   *Paradise Lost* published.

1669   Milton's *Accedence Commenc't Grammar* published.

1670   Milton's *History of Britain* published.

1671   *Paradise Regained* and *Samson Agonistes* published jointly (2d ed., posthumously in 1680).

1672   Milton's *Artis logicae plenior institutio* ("A Fuller Institution of the Art of Logic") published.

1673   Milton's *Of True Religion, Heresy, Schism and Toleration* published. 2d enlarged edition of his shorter poems (1645).

1674   Bunyan's *Pilgrim's Progress* published (Part II in 1684). Milton's *Epistolae familiares et prolusiones* ("Letters and Prolusions") published. 2d enlarged edition of *Paradise Lost*.
        Death of Milton about November 8.

[Milton's posthumously published works include in particular *De doctrina christiana* (see pp. 359 ff.)]

INTRODUCTION
MILTON IN THE SEVENTEENTH CENTURY

he wrote 'Lycidas', 'Comus', 'Paradise Lost', and other Poems,
with much delectable prose; he was moreover an active friend to
Man all his Life, and has been since his death.

John Keats

I

HAS there been a vast conspiracy uncritically to foster on us Milton's prose? Do we not feel at times much as Dr. Johnson felt about Congreve's novel, that we would rather praise it than read it?

To be more precise: would we have read Milton's prose works had he not been the author of *Paradise Lost*? True, we are fully cognizant of the intrinsic merits of *Areopagitica*; but what comparable claim can be advanced for the embarrassing histrionics of the ecclesiastical tracts, the apparent narrowness of outlook in *The Doctrine and Discipline of Divorce*, the laborious defensiveness of *The Tenure of Kings and Magistrates*, or the depressing dullness of the Latin treatise on Christian doctrine? Keats may have thought that Milton—"an active friend to Man all his Life"—had written "much delectable prose."[1] But might not Dr. Johnson have been more perceptive in his austere judgment on Milton's political convictions? In his words,

Milton's republicanism was, I am afraid, founded on an envious hatred of greatness, and a sullen desire of independence; in petulance impatient of control, and pride disdainful of superiority. He hated monarchs in the State, and prelates in the Church; for he hated all whom he was required to obey. It is to be suspected that his predomi-

1. Letter to James Rice, 24 March 1818.

nant desire was to destroy rather than establish, and that he felt not so much the love of liberty as repugnance to authority.[2]

Dr. Johnson did not necessarily regard Milton as "an active friend to Man all his Life."

Shelley, on the other hand, praised exactly what Dr. Johnson had elected to denounce: "the sacred Milton was, let it be remembered, a republican, and a bold inquirer into morals and religion."[3] Wordsworth generalized even more. In 1802, adversely affected by the "vanity and parade" of England in contrast to the revolutionary zeal of France, he composed the celebrated sonnet beginning

> Milton! thou shoulds't be living at this hour:
> England hath need of thee.

He continued:

> Thy soul was like a Star, and dwelt apart;
> Thou hadst a voice whose sound was like the sea:
> Pure as the naked heavens, majestic, free.
> So didst thou travel on life's common way,
> In cheerful godliness; and yet thy heart
> The lowliest duties on herself did lay.

But to be aware of Milton's activities is to realize the extent to which Wordsworth like everyone else created Milton in his own image. Whether Milton's voice during the revolutionary period of the seventeenth century was consistently majestic is debatable; and whether always pure, doubtful. Cheerful godliness was in evidence only spasmodically, whenever he managed to rise above the smoke and stir of passionate controversies. Perennially embattled, he would have found Wordsworth's notion of his apartness "like a Star" a travesty of his

---

2. *Lives of the English Poets*, Everyman ed. (1925), I, 92–93. Edgar Allan Poe in 1845 firmly separated Milton's subject from Milton's style: "Independently of the subject-matter, his treatises are among the most remarkable ever written" (in *Selected Prose and Poetry*, ed. T. O. Mabbot [1951], p. 362).

3. Preface to *Prometheus Unbound* (1818–1819).

total commitment to the causes he had espoused throughout his life.

Shelley's view of Milton as "a bold inquirer into morals and religion" likewise defines tendencies latent not so much in Milton as in Shelley; while Dr. Johnson's judgment on Milton's republicanism is descriptive less of Milton's actual sentiments than of Dr. Johnson's obsessive partiality to the established order in Augustan England. To have hated monarchs in the State and prelates in the Church may have appeared dangerous to Dr. Johnson; but uncritically to have accepted either was, for Milton, unworthy of the dignity of man. As in *Paradise Lost* the Son of God reigns not so much by right of birth as by merit (III, 309), so in *The Tenure of Kings and Magistrates* sovereignty is reserved for the individual who is worthy of the consent of the governed. Variations on this theme abound, yet the ethical orientation of the central concept was never surrendered by Milton: "queen truth ought to be preferred to king Charles" (below, p. 74). Equally, however persuasive the rhetoric that claims Milton felt "not so much the love of liberty as repugnance to authority," it is imperative to recognize how insistently Milton held that nothing is "of more grave and urgent importance throughout the whole life of man, than is discipline." I quote from the paean to discipline at the outset of *The Reason of Church-Government* (1642). It continues:

What need I instance? He that hath read with judgement, of Nations and Common-wealths, of Cities and Camps, of peace and warre, sea and land, will readily agree that the flourishing and decaying of all civill societies, all the moments and turnings of humane occasions are mov'd to and from as upon the axle of discipline. So that whatsoever power or sway in mortall things weaker men have attributed to fortune, I durst with more confidence (the honour of divine providence ever sav'd) ascribe either to the vigor, or the slacknesse of discipline. Nor is there any sociable perfection in this life civill or sacred that can be above discipline, but she is that which with her musicall cords preserves and holds all the parts thereof together. Hence in those perfect armies of *Cyrus* in *Xenophon*, and *Scipio* in the Roman stories, the excellence of military skill was esteem'd, not by the not needing, but by the readiest submitting to the edicts of their commander. And certainly discipline is not only the removall of disorder, but if any visible shape can be given to divine things, the very visible shape and image of vertue, whereby she is not only seene in the regular gestures and motions of her heavenly paces as she walkes, but also makes the harmony of her voice audible to mortall eares. Yea the Angels themselves, in whom no disorder is fear'd, as the Apostle that saw them in his rapture describes [Rev. 7:1], are distinguisht and quaterniond into their celestiall Princedomes, and Satrapies, according as God himselfe hath writ his imperiall decrees through the great provinces of heav'n. The state also of the blessed in Paradise, though never so perfect, is not therefore left without discipline, whose golden survaying reed marks out and measures every quarter and circuit of new Jerusalem. Yet is it not to be conceiv'd that those eternall effluences of sanctity and love in the glorified Saints should by this meanes be confin'd and cloy'd with repetition of that which is prescrib'd, but that our happinesse may orbe it selfe into a thousand vagancies of glory and delight, and with a kinde of eccentricall equation be as it were an invariable Planet of joy and felicity, how much lesse can we believe that God would leave his fraile and feeble, though not lesse beloved Church here below to the perpetuall stumble of conjecture and disturbance in this our darke voyage without the card and compasse of Discipline.[4]

Yet Milton's celebration of discipline at the cosmic level does not terminate here. It reverberates across his prose and poetry, vesting man with that majesty of responsibility which is commensurate to his dignity as the favorite of God.

II

The best introduction to Milton's life and work are the autobiographical statements reprinted here, especially if read in the light of the two biographies by John Aubrey and Edward Phillips and the outline of the events surrounding Milton's activities.[5] The rest is commentary.

But commentary should suggest in particular the cumulative impressions registered by the more recent activities of our

---

4. *Works*, Columbia ed., III, 184–86; *Prose Works*, Yale ed., I, 750–53.
5. See below, pp. 409 ff., 411 ff.; cf. above, pp. 11 ff.

scholars. Yet as it is no less perilous to be categorical than impossible fully to represent the diversities of opinion, one development may be cited as providing testimony to the conclusions now laboriously arrived at. It concerns Milton's visit to the Continent from the spring of 1638 to the late summer of 1639, and the presence especially of five names among the numerous individuals he befriended: Hugo Grotius, Lucas Holstein, Pietro Frescobaldi, Antonio Malatesti, and Francesco Cardinal Barberini.

Grotius at the time of Milton's visit to Paris was Queen Christina's ambassador to the French court. Among his achievements he could already number *Adamus Exul* (1601), a play in Latin on the Fall of Man, but also a vast reputation as the founder of international law in *De jure belli ac pacis* (1625). Later, in Rome, Milton also befriended the learned Lucas Holstein, secretary and librarian to Cardinal Barberini, and later librarian of the Vatican.[6] Might Milton have discussed with Grotius the problems inherent in the literary treatment of the Fall of Man, and with Holstein the visual representations of the same subject by Raphael in the Stanze della Segnatura and especially by Michelangelo in the Sistine Chapel? Of these possibilities Milton himself is silent; yet his contacts with Grotius and Holstein are certainly significant, immediately because of their ready acceptance of Milton's company, and mediately because of the evolutionary nature of his plans for a major poem.

To credit the conventional view of Milton as a grim Puritan is to expect him fanatically to have eschewed the company of the representatives of Antichrist in Rome. On the contrary, his Florentine friends included the devout Frescobaldi, soon to become a prince of the Catholic Church; while in Rome he not only dined at the English Jesuit College but even entered the circle of the one man certainly to have been regarded as

---

6. See Milton's letter to Holstein in the Columbia ed., XII, 38–45, and the holograph discussed by J. McG. Bottkol in *PMLA* 68 (1953): 617–27.

anathema by any committed Puritan, Cardinal Barberini, prime minister and chief counselor to his uncle Pope Urban VIII. Milton was impressed as much by Barberini's "submissive loftiness of mind" as by the musical entertainments, which, performed at the theater recently completed (1632) in the Cardinal's palace, exhibited those exuberant elements that constitute the *grandiosità monumentale* of the baroque. It was the period of Rome's transformation by Borromini and Bernini.[7]

No less instructive is Milton's friendship with the Florentine Antonio Malatesti, author of *La Tina*, a cycle of fifty amusingly obscene sonnets in the baroque idiom. *La Tina* was dedicated to Milton. Yet the expected strictures of that grim Puritan never materialized; instead, on his return to England, he sent Malatesti his warm regards.[8]

What do Milton's encounters on the Continent reveal? Above all, I think, they reveal a developing catholic taste, since the five men referred to represent achievements not so much incompatible as mutually exclusive: Milton in France and Italy had been studying the nature of multiform reality. But even more significant is the authority with which Milton on his return home articulated his future expectations:

in the privat Academies of *Italy*, whither I was favor'd to resort, perceiving that some trifles . . . were receiv'd with written Encomiums, which the Italian is not forward to bestow on men of this side the *Alps*, I began thus farre to assent both to them and divers of my friends here at home, and not lesse to an inward prompting which now grew daily upon me, that by labour and intent study (which I take to be my portion in this life) joyn'd with the strong propensity of nature, I might perhaps leave something so written to aftertimes, as they should not willingly let it die. (below, p. 54)

7. On Frescobaldi, see Roland M. Frye in *MQ* 7 (1973):74–76; on Milton's visit to the Jesuit College: Leo Miller, *MQ* 13 (1979):142–46; and on Barberini: John Arthos, *Milton and the Italian Cities* (1968), pp. 53 ff., 69 ff.

8. Columbia ed., XII, 53; Yale ed., II, 765. *La Tina* has been translated by Donald Sears in *MS* 13 (1979):275–317.

Thus inspired, Milton extended the range of his activities spectacularly. For the first time he set down detailed outlines of several subjects for a major poem, even if, mindful less of Renaissance critical theory than of the practice of Grotius in *Adamus Exul*, the preferred form in each case is not an epic but a play—and in one particular instance a play on the Fall of Man under the title *Adam Unparadis'd*.[9] Shortly, too, Milton commenced writing in prose a number of works which by the end of his life were to include treatises on a vast range of subjects. He himself described them as labors of his left hand, yet they remain the most complete program actually carried out by any of the equally ambitious "universal men" of the English Renaissance. Reduced to its essentials, the program involved "three species of liberty": ecclesiastical, domestic, and civil (see p. 71).

III

By the middle of the 1640s royalists tended increasingly to lament the plight of "poore, miserable, distracted, almost destroyed *England*."[10] But to others—were they the majority?—the Civil War offered the opportunity to confirm the self-evident truth that England was favored of God. In a sermon delivered less than a year before the execution of Charles I, Paul Knell upheld the widespread persuasion that

we may compare with *Israel* for a fruitfull scituation, being neither under the torrid nor the frozen Zone, neither burned away with parching heat, nor benummed away with pinching cold, but seated in a temperate climate & a fertile soile; our folds are full of sheep, our rallies stand so thick with corne that we may laugh and sing. God hath also fenced us about, like the *Israelites* in the red sea with a wall of water, the waters are as a wall unto us on our right hand, and on our left. But especially God hath fenced us by his protection, salvation hath the Lord

9. The outlines are in the manuscript now in the library of Trinity College, Cambridge (reproduced in the Columbia ed., XVIII, 231–32).

10. John Harris, *Englands Out-cry* (1644), p. 1.

appointed for wals and bulwarks. He hath likewise gathered the stones out from us, he hath cast out the *Romish* rabble, and hath planted our Land with the choicest Religion, that of Protestants.[11]

Yet the Reformation was far from complete. The process initiated a century earlier by Luther was now threatened by the episcopalian or prelatical form of ecclesiastical government whose hierarchical structure and elaborate church services were in appearance, and plausibly in fact, extensions of Roman Catholicism. In the early 1640s one of the most vociferous attacks on episcopalianism was mounted by a group of five Presbyterians improbably signing themselves "Smectymnuus" (from the initials of their names: Stephen Marshall, Edmund Calamy, Thomas Young, Matthew Newcomen, William Spurstow). Arranged on the other side were in the main Archbishop James Ussher of Armagh and Bishop Joseph Hall of Norwich. Milton was perhaps drawn into the controversy by one of the Smectymnuans, Thomas Young, who was once his tutor. Five pamphlets later, in any case, Milton's initially enthusiastic commitment was displaced by wary disenchantment, even acerbic disquiet.

Milton's experience parallels that of several of his contemporaries, for example Henry More the Cambridge Platonist. More was a decade later to engage in a bitter controversy with Thomas Vaughan, the poet's brother; but his ambitious effort to curtail his antagonist's "preposterous and fortuitous imaginations" resulted first in Vaughan's abusive counterattack in *The Man-Mouse taken in a Trap*, then in More's bitingly satiric *Second Lash*, and finally in Vaughan's virulent attempt at a *Second Wash, or the Moore scour'd once more*! A badly shaken More sounding retreat concluded ruefully: "if ever *Christianity* be exterminated, it will be by *Enthusiasme.*"[12]

Idealism adjusted in the face of brutal reality was also the

---

11. *Israel and England Paralelled* (1648), p. 15. The sermon was delivered at Gray's Inn on 16 April 1648.

12. See *The Cambridge Platonists*, ed. C. A. Patrides (Cambridge, Mass., 1969), pp. 8–9.

lesson that embittered controversy impressed on Milton. His first tract, *Of Reformation touching Church-Discipline* (1641), combines a serene assurance that an appeal to reason would prove decisive with an apocalyptic persuasion that the Primal Reason could hardly fail to intervene on behalf of so just a cause as Milton's (below, pp. 77 ff.). The tract ends with a prolonged prayer that looks back to the denunciation of the corrupt clergy in *Lycidas* (1637) and ahead to the celebration of the eventual triumph of goodness in *Paradise Lost* (1667):

Thou therefore that sits't in light & glory unapproachable, *Parent* of *Angels* and *Men*! next thee I implore Omnipotent King, Redeemer of that lost remnant whose nature thou didst assume, ineffable and everlasting *Love*! And thou the third subsistence of Divine infinitude, *illumining Spirit*, the joy and solace of created *Things*! one *Tripersonall* GODHEAD! looke upon this thy poore and almost spent and expiring *Church*, leave her not thus a prey to these importunate *Wolves*, that wait and thinke long till they devoure thy tender *Flock*, these wilde *Boares* that have broke into thy *Vineyard*, and left the print of thir polluting hoofs on the Soules of thy Servants. (below, p. 108)

The fervent prayer concludes first with the consecration of Milton's personal aspirations to the service of the Divine Purpose and finally with the celebration of the beatific vision beyond the confines of time.[13]

But Milton's opponents were not impressed; and as their replies filled the air with barbarous dissonance, he tried again with a scholarly study *Of Prelatical Episcopacy* as well as with some satirical *Animadversions* (1641), and next with the rational and patient discourse entitled *The Reason of Church-Government urg'd against Prelaty* (1642). Frequently able to

---

13. The imagery of warfare in *Of Reformation*, often present in Milton's more militant prose works, has been noted frequently. See Theodore H. Banks, *Milton's Imagery* (1950), pp. 76–92; James H. Hanford, *John Milton: Poet and Humanist* (Cleveland, 1966), chap. V; and Joan Webber, *The Eloquent "I"* (Madison, 1968), pp. 204 ff. On the recurrent imagery of disease, consult Kester Svendsen, *Milton and Science* (Cambridge, Mass., 1956), chap. VI.

ascend from the immediate controversy to general principles, Milton once more relates his personal aspirations to the larger pattern by outlining his expectations and defining the role of the poet within a narrowly partisan society. Yet already Milton's reasonable tone is decreasingly in evidence. Enthusiasm—the "enthusiasm" of the fanatic, which Henry More would soon learn to fear—has intervened to sacrifice principles on the questionable altar of ephemeral abuse. Milton's opponents have now grown into a "whippe of Scorpions," else "a continuall *Hydra* of mischiefe, and molestation," or "unctuous, and epicurean paunches."[14] However, Milton's abusive vocabulary and devastating scorn were common to any number of his contemporaries who likewise opposed the Anglicans' lukewarm *via media* by "the language of zeal." The justification was apparently biblical: "because thou art lukewarm, and neither cold nor hot, I will spew [literally 'vomit'] thee out of my mouth" (Rev. 3:16).[15] Equally, however, the justification was broadly traditional—witness in particular Pascal's lengthy exposition of the way in which "mockery is sometimes the best way to bring men to their senses, and in that case is a righteous action."[16] Milton's view is not unlike Pascal's:

although in the serious uncasing of a grand imposture (for to deale plainly with you Readers, Prelatry is no better) there be mixt here and there such a grim laughter, as may appeare at the same time in an austere visage, it cannot be taxt of levity or insolence: for even this

14. These are only three of the phrases rather lovingly collected in the Yale ed. (I, 113) as testimony to Milton's "bitter hatred." But they should be judged in the light of the period's vocabulary in controversy. Well into the Restoration, for example, Andrew Marvell having written *The Rehearsal Transpros'd* (1672) was denounced in Samuel Parker's *Reproof* as: "Thou a Rat-Divine! thou hast not the Wit and Learning of a Mouse," etc.

15. See the indispensable study by Thomas Kranidas, "Milton and the Rhetoric of Zeal," *TSLL* 6 (1965):423–32.

16. *The Provincial Letters*, trans. A. J. Krailsheimer (Penguin Books, 1967), p. 165 (Letter XI, dated 18 August 1656).

vaine of laughing (as I could produce out of grave Authors) hath oft-times a strong and sinewy force in teaching and confuting; nor can there be a more proper object of indignation and scorne together then a false Prophet taken in the greatest dearest and most dangerous cheat, the cheat of soules.[17]

Later, in *Paradise Lost*, Milton would confine "blind Zeal" to the Limbo of Vanity (III, 452); yet he retained scorn, boldly asserting that it is deployed by God in his derisive attitude toward the vain pursuits of Satan (II, 188–91; V, 735–37; VIII, 75–79). Biblical precedent was again not far to seek: "The kings of the earth set themselves, and the rulers take counsel together, against the Lord. . . . He that sitteth in the heavens shall laugh: the Lord shall have them in derision" (Psalms 2:2–4). Embarrassed by the implications, biblical commentators often tried to evade the issue ("God laughs figuratively," Alexander Ross suggested nervously in 1652).[18] But the "ever-memorable" John Hales of Eton perceptively concluded,

It is a sport, and as it were a kind of recreation to God to discover false play, to wash off the colour and paint from disguised actions, and openly expose them to the laughter and scorn of Men and Angels.[19]

Another biblical precedent often invoked ("answer a fool according to his folly") was annotated by a commentator in 1638 thus:

Answer therefore such a foole lest hee thinke himself victorious, be-

---

17. From the Preface to *Animadversions* (Columbia ed., III, 107; Yale ed., I, 663–64). Milton's "grave Authors" are fully set forth by Pascal (pp. 164 ff. in the work cited in the previous note). Elsewhere Milton sought support in the origin and nature of satire: "a Satyr as it was borne out of a Tragedy, so ought to resemble his parentage, to strike high, and adventure dangerously at the most eminent vices among the greatest persons" (*An Apology for Smectymnuus*, in Columbia ed., III, 329; Yale ed., I, 916).

18. *Arcana Microcosmi* (1652), p. 177.

19. *Sermons preach'd at Eton*, 2d ed. (1673), p. 36. The first edition appeared posthumously in 1660.

cause there appeareth no one in the field against him. But if thou doe answer him, let it be *according to his folly*, and in such a manner as that it may declare his error and folly unto him, and that as it doth reproove him, for it may teach him the truth.[20]

Here as elsewhere, the consideration of Milton's activities in the light of seventeenth-century assumptions and practice should restrain our indecent haste to misconstrue as personal bias attitudes in fact widely upheld. More important aspects would then be readily apparent: that Milton's wary disenchantment after his last contribution to the controversy meaningfully testifies to vital experience gained; that such experience contributed greatly to his subsequent activities; and that it was a richly endowed poet who finally turned to *Paradise Lost*. To learn to temper "enthusiasm" and exorcize zeal are no mean achievements.

IV

Milton in the five anti-episcopal tracts is increasingly emotional, even hysterical; yet he should have lapsed into insensate incoherence after his next experience, when far more personally involved he lifted his pen in defense of divorce. Married to Mary Powell in 1642, he was abandoned by her before the year was out; and faced with the unlikelihood of a divorce unless adultery was proved, he launched four treatises including in particular *The Doctrine and Discipline of Divorce* (below, pp. 112 ff.). The four treatises should have been hastily prepared, ill considered, and highly partisan. Yet they are fully scanned, carefully wrought, and exceptionally liberal.

The background to *The Doctrine and Discipline of Divorce* is partly the vast Puritan literature on domestic conduct, partly the infinity of courtesy books, but especially the liberal tradition of Christian humanism emanating from Erasmus.[21] Had

---

20. Proverbs 26:5; as annotated by Michael Jermin, *Paraphrasticall Meditations, by Way of Commentarie, upon the Whole Booke of the Proverbs of Solomon* (1638), p. 598.

21. The Puritan literature is emphasized by Chilton L. Powell, *En-*

Milton been chained to the emotions that Mary Powell's departure must have aroused, he should have argued for divorce on the grounds of desertion. But he consciously chose the far more difficult and controversial task of pleading for divorce on the basis of mental incompatibility. Its "first protagonist in Christendom,"[22] he anticipated the more compassionate laws of our own day by three centuries. But the price he paid for this distinction was certainly high. Instantly denounced by a number of his shocked contemporaries, he remained tarnished in reputation until the end of his life.[23]

The violent reaction of Milton's contemporaries is understandable. For centuries the single valid ground for divorce had been adultery; and as this was taken to be the attitude of Christ himself (Matthew 19:9), its "flat contradiction" by Milton naturally horrified his contemporaries and obliged them to protest against his defense of divorce "for many other causes besides that which our Saviour only approveth, namely, in case of Adultery."[24]

---

glish Domestic Relations 1487–1653 (1917), pp. 147–48, and William and Malleville Haller, "The Puritan Art of Love," *HLQ* 5 (1941–1942):235–72; the courtesy books, by John Halkett, *Milton and the Idea of Matrimony* (New Haven, 1970); and the Christian humanist tradition, by V. Norskov Olsen, *The New Testament Logia on Divorce: A Study of Their Interpretation from Erasmus to Milton* (Tübingen, 1971).

22. Edward A. Westermarck, *Christianity and Morals* (1939), p. 385. One of the best studies of the treatises on divorce is by Halkett (previous note), to which I am indebted; but I have also drawn liberally on my own remarks in *Milton and the Christian Tradition* (Oxford, 1966), pp. 178–86.

23. See William Haller, *Tracts on Liberty in the Puritan Revolution* (1934), vol. I, appendix B, and the passages collected by William R. Parker, *Milton's Contemporary Reputation* (Columbus, 1940), pp. 73 ff., 170 ff. Cf. Milton's two sonnets, XI ("I did but prompt the age to quit their cloggs") and XII ("A Book was writ of late call'd *Tetrachordon*").

24. Thus Ephraim Pagitt, *Heresiography*, 3d ed. (1647), p. 150, and Daniel Featley, *The Dippers Dipt*, 5th ed. (1647), sig. A4.

Milton rested his case in part upon an appeal to the often used (and as often abused) "fundamentall law book of nature" (below, p. 147). Here as elsewhere the basic premise was the well-known idea that "the first and most innocent lesson of nature [is] to turn away peacably from what afflicts and hazards our destruction."[25] But existing laws of divorce, Milton protested, violate "the reverend secret of nature" by frequently forcing "a mixture of minds that cannot unite." Surely the spiritual aspect of marriage ought to take precedence over the physical? "In marriage," St. Thomas Aquinas had written, "the union of souls ranks higher than union of bodies." Humanists agreed. According to the widely respected Juan Luis Vives, "There canne be [no] maryage or concorde" where man and wife "agree not in wyll and minde, the whyche twoo are the beginning & seate of all amitie & friendship."[26] Therefore, as in *Paradise Lost* Raphael insists that where there is no love there can be no happiness but only gratification of the senses, mere bestiality (VIII, 579 ff., 621), so *The Doctrine and Discipline of Divorce* maintains, "Where love cannot be, there can be left of wedlock nothing, but the empty husk of an outside matrimony; as undelightfull and unpleasing to God, as any other kind of hypocrisie" (p. 140). God did not institute marriage "to remedy a sublunary and bestial burning," to have man and wife "grind in the mill of an undelighted and servil copulation" (pp. 144, 141).

God in the first ordaning of marriage, taught us to what end he did it, in words expresly implying the apt and cheerfull conversation [association] of man with woman, to comfort and refresh him against the evill of solitary life, not mentioning the purposes of generation till afterwards, as being but a secondary end in dignity, though not in necessity. (p. 124)

The generous compass of Milton's thesis was widened as he

25. *Tetrachordon*, in the Columbia ed., IV, 117.
26. St. Thomas, *Summa theologica*, III, lv, 1, trans. the English Dominican Fathers (1911–1925), and Vives, *The Office and Duetie of an Husband*, trans. Thomas Paynell (1550?), sigs. K8–K8v.

went on to comprehend his belief in the potentialities of "the divine and softening breath of charity." "Our Saviours doctrine," he affirmed in *Tetrachordon*, "is, that the end, and the fulfilling of every command is charity; no faith without it, no truth without it, no worship, no workes pleasing to God but as they partake of charity." [27] Charity is "a command above all commands," "the supreme dictate," "whose grand commission is to doe and to dispose over all the ordinances of God to man; that love & truth may advance each other to everlasting" (pp. 180, 135, 168). As the concluding sentence of *The Doctrine and Discipline of Divorce* has it, "God the Son hath put all other things under his own feet; but his Commandments hee hath left all under the feet of Charity."

Milton's treatises on divorce have twice reappeared in English literature, first in the surprising context of Farquhar's *The Beaux' Stratagem* (1707), and later as "the tragic machinery of the tale" in Hardy's *Jude the Obscure* (1895). [28] But we read *The Doctrine and Discipline of Divorce* not because of its influence on Farquhar or Hardy, much less as a venture in autobiography. It is above all a remarkable testimony to a man's ability so to transcend his towering passions as to formulate principles of universal validity. At once a plea for liberty and a protest against institutionalism, it warrants also Milton's right proudly to claim: "Let not England forget her precedence of teaching nations how to live" (p. 120).

V

A year later, in 1644, the precedence was further confirmed in *Of Education* and *Areopagitica* (below, pp. 181 ff., 196 ff.). The obvious differences between the two works forcefully re-

---

27. Columbia ed., IV, 96 and 135.
28. See M. A. Larson, "The Influence of Milton's Divorce Tracts on Farquhar's *Beaux' Stratagem*," *PMLA* 39 (1924) : 174–78. Milton's influence on Hardy has not yet been studied.

mind us how impossible it is to generalize on Milton's style. Each work possesses a style appropriate to the given occasion. *Of Education* in assuming the reader's familiarity with humanist educational theories does not argue; it posits. But *Areopagitica* in deploying a thesis contrary to received opinion displaces assertion by argument, and mere allegation by cogent analysis. The stylistic consequences are clearly to be observed. *Of Education* is authoritative in appearance, categorical in manner, and almost entirely devoid of rhetoric since its thesis is, as it were, self-evident. But *Areopagitica* advances cumulatively in a series of waves, until the gathered force of argument and rhetorical patterns overwhelms our reservations and commands our assent.

Of Education was, like the treatises on divorce, the direct result of Milton's experience. The experience was twofold: on the practical level, the education and instruction of his sister's two sons; and on the theoretical, the extensive discussions then under way concerning the methods of Comenius, the great Czech educational reformer who had visited England in 1641 possibly at the invitation of Parliament and who numbered among his English friends Samuel Hartlib, the recipient of Milton's address. Milton's participation in these discussions significantly assumed the form of a reiteration of the great ideals of Renaissance humanism. The vast compass of the educational scheme he endorses is by no means peculiar to him but displays the humanist aspiration to create the "universal man." The countless precedents include the idealistic vision that in Rabelais informs Gargantua's celebrated letter to Pantagruel (book 2, chap. 8); the all-encompassing nature of Vives's treatise *De disciplinis* in 1531; and, in England, Sir Philip Sidney's outline of a course of studies that extends from the Scriptures ("the foundation of foundations, the Wisdome of Wisdomes") to works on moral philosophy as on the art of war, and on geography as on history—the latter including all the major historians of ancient Greece, Rome, Byzantium, and Renaissance Europe! Milton like every humanist would have agreed with Sidney's disarming remark: "To me, the variety rather delights me, then confounds me."[29]

The program of studies outlined in *Of Education* is placed in *Areopagitica* within an even broader framework, the necessity of unlimited access to reading in order to exercise man's talents and issue in discrimination. The talents themselves, and man's ability to exercise them properly, are not called into question. Firm in his faith in man, Milton reserves the full weight of his ire against those who hubristically tamper with the individual's right to decide for himself. The emphasis is humanistic in general even while it is Protestant in particular: "Give me the liberty to know, to utter, and to argue freely according to conscience above all liberties" (below, p. 241). It is noteworthy that fifteen years later, in *A Treatise of Civil Power in Ecclesiastical Causes* (1659), the plea was voiced yet again, on that occasion more particularly on behalf of religious liberty.

Originality of argument need not be sought in *Areopagitica* for it will not be found. Commonplaces, indeed, abound; but they are commonplaces raised to the level of great literature. Bishop Joseph Hall, Milton's antagonist in the anti-episcopal tracts, rephrased a familiar notion thus: "ther can be but one truth: and that one Truth oft-times must be fetcht by peecemeal out of divers branches of contrary opinions."[30] But Milton's restatement is a touchstone of English prose:

Truth indeed came once into the world with her divine Master, and was a perfect shape most glorious to look on: but when he ascended, and his Apostles after him were laid asleep, then strait arose a wicked race of deceivers, who as that story goes of the *Ægyptian Typhon* with his conspirators, how they dealt with the good *Osiris*, took the virgin Truth, hewd her lovely form into a thousand peeces, and scatter'd

29. John Buxton, "An Elizabethan Reading List: An Unpublished Letter from Sir Philip Sidney," *TLS*, 24 March 1972, pp. 343–44. Vives's treatise is available in English, trans. Foster Watson (1913, reprint Totowa, N.J., 1971). The humanist burden of Milton's *Of Education* is most ably expounded by William R. Parker, "Education: Milton's Ideas and Ours," *CE* 24 (1962): 1–14.

30. *Holy Observations* (1607), p. 52.

them to the four winds. From that time ever since, the sad friends of Truth, such as durst appear, imitating the carefull search that *Isis* made for the mangled body of *Osiris*, went up and down gathering up limb by limb still as they could find them. We have not yet found them all, Lords and Commons, nor ever shall doe, till her Masters second coming; he shall bring together every joynt and member, and shall mould them into an immortal feature of lovelinesse and perfection. (below, p. 234)

The style *is* the work. It looks beyond Milton's other works— and other styles—to the only other classical oration in English literature, Sidney's *Defence of Poesie. Areopagitica* like the *Defence* weds style and argument in such a manner that, while style and structure reflect the practice of classical rhetoricians, the thesis appeals to the most liberal instincts in man. Milton has appreciated by now what he would later transmute into poetry, that rhetoric by itself may be put to perverse uses—witness its deployment by Satan in *Paradise Lost.* But rhetoric exerted on behalf of truth—the truth of moral precepts immemorially upheld—could so imprint a cause upon the consciousness of men as they should not willingly let it die.

VI

The liberty of the individual, threatened in Milton's time as in ours by a society militantly bent on conformity, was further defended by Milton in his several expressly political works. Whatever their nominal subjects, their one constant theme coincides with Blake's visionary denunciation of society's efforts to curtail the prerogatives of the individual ("One Law for the Lion and Ox is Oppression"). The fundamental principle of Milton's thought is lucidly stated: "No man who knows ought, can be so stupid as to deny that all men naturally were born free" (below, p. 255).

The Tenure of Kings and Magistrates (1649), published within two weeks of the execution of Charles I, could be read as a straightforward justification of regicide. As with the treatises on divorce, however, Milton ascends beyond the immediate

32

episode to formulate general principles, in this instance that free men having once entered into a voluntary contract with their governors may terminate it whenever tyranny is palpably in evidence. But *The Tenure* also attends to a development that was becoming increasingly apparent ever since the abolition of episcopacy in 1646: the tendency of the victorious Presbyterians "to sit the closest & the heaviest of all Tyrants, upon the conscience, and fall notoriously into the same sinns, wherof so lately and so loud they accus'd the Prelates" (p. 284). In the memorable words of a poem Milton wrote at this time, "*New Presbyter* is but *Old Priest* writ Large."[31]

As *The Tenure* yielded to the two *Defenses* of the republican regime (1651–1654), and they to *The Readie and Easie Way to Establish a Free Commonwealth* (1660), Milton's thinking appears to have become less flexible until in the latter work he endorsed government by a self-perpetuating grand council of the "worthiest" (below, pp. 327 ff.). But the wildest undulations in Milton's stated attitudes cannot obscure either his insistence that sovereignty may never be "transferrd, but delegated only," or his consistent and even exclusive opposition to rule by any single person, whether Charles I or Cromwell.[32] On the very eve of the monarchy's restoration he warned: "that people must needs be madd or strangely infatuated, that build the chief hope of thir common happiness or safetie on a single person," "corruptible by the excess of his singular power and exaltation" (pp. 336, 348). The sage conclusion of John Aubrey in his brief life of Milton is apposite:

Whatever he wrote against Monarchie was out of no animosity to the King's person, or owt of any faction or interest, but out of a pure Zeale to the Liberty of Mankind, which he thought would be greater under

31. "On the New Forcers of Conscience under the Long Parliament," the last line.

32. The thesis is persuasively argued by Merritt Y. Hughes, *Ten Perspectives on Milton* (New Haven, 1965), pp. 267–68. See also his essay "Milton's *Eikon Basilike*," in *Calm of Mind*, ed. Joseph Wittreich (Cleveland, 1971), pp. 1–24.

a free state than under a Monarchiall government.[33]

Not that the consistency of Milton's opposition to rule by any single person should mislead us into thinking that his political views remained static. Development there was, partly in the inevitable disillusionment when his great expectations for a radical reformation were shattered, but especially in the increasing realization that his apocalyptic entreaties for an external reformation—the rule of the saints exorcizing malefic prelates and authoritarian monarchs—should be preceded by an internal reformation, "a paradise within."[34]

Milton's political thought may also be approached by way of its opposition to that of Hobbes. After the appearance of Salmasius's royalist apologia in *Defensio regia* (1649) and Milton's reply in the first *Defense*—the *Pro populo anglicano defensio* (1651)—Hobbes wrote:

I have seen them both. They are very good Latin both, and hardly to be judged which is better; and both very ill reasoning, hardly to be judged which is worse.[35]

Milton's judgment of Hobbes was equally generous. It is reported by Aubrey:

His widowe assures me that Mr. T. Hobbs was not one of his acquaintance, that her husband did not like him at all, but he would acknowledge him to be a man of great parts, and a learned man. Their

33. *Brief Lives*, ed. Oliver L. Dick, 3d ed. (1960), p. 203; reprinted below, p. 414.
34. Cf. *Paradise Lost*, XII, 587. For an interpretation of Milton's development along the lines suggested, see Michael Fixler, *Milton and the Kingdoms of God* (1964). I have discussed the nature of Milton's apocalyptic emphases in "'Something like Prophetic Strain': Apocalyptic Configurations in Milton," in *The Apocalypse in English Renaissance Thought and Literature*, ed. C. A. Patrides and Joseph Wittreich (Ithaca, N.Y., 1984), chap. VIII.
35. *English Works*, ed. Sir William Molesworth (1839), VI, 368; quoted by Don M. Wolfe, "Milton and Hobbes: A Contrast in Social Temper," *SP* 41 (1944):410–26.

Interests and Tenets did run counter to each other.[36]

Hobbes was a materialist, Milton an idealist. Hobbes upheld determinism in a universe obedient to inflexible laws, Milton maintained that the liberty of man is an inalienable right granted by God in perpetuity. Hobbes espoused absolute authoritarianism, Milton vehemently rejected any doctrine that deprived man of his independence. The power of kings, argued Milton, is "derivative, transferr'd and committed to them in trust from the People, to the Common good of all" (below, p. 257). Hobbes would have agreed but for the crucial qualification "in trust." It measures the abyss dividing two mutually exclusive responses to the predicament of man.

Milton also divides from Hobbes—and indeed from every other political philosopher of the seventeenth century—in terms of style. The magniloquent voice of the epic poet is heard throughout the two *Defenses* beginning with the preface to the first:

I shall relate no common things, or mean; but how a most puissant king, when he had trampled upon the laws, and stricken down religion, and was ruling at his own lust and wantonness, was at last subdued in the field by his own people, who had served a long term of slavery; how he was thereupon put under guard, and when he gave no ground whatever, by either word or action, to hope better things of him, was finally by the highest council of the realm condemned to die, and beheaded before his very palace gate. I shall likewise relate (which will much conduce to the easing men's minds of a great superstition) under what system of laws, especially what laws of England, this judgement was rendered and executed; and shall easily defend my valiant and worthy countrymen, who have extremely well deserved of all subjects and nations in the world, from the most wicked calumnies of both domestic and foreign railers, and chiefly from the reproaches of this utterly empty sophister [Salmasius], who sets up to be captain and ringleader of all the rest. For what king's majesty high enthroned ever shone so bright as did the people's majesty of England, when, shaking off that age-old superstition which had long prevailed, they overwhelmed with judgement their very king (or rather him who

36. As above, note 33; also reprinted below, p. 414.

from their king had become their enemy), ensnared in his own laws him who alone among men claimed by divine right to go unpunished, and feared not to inflict upon this very culprit the same capital punishment which he would have inflicted upon any other.

As always in Milton, however, an apparently secular event is promptly placed within a metaphysical context. The preface to the first *Defense* continues:

Yet why do I proclaim as done by the people these actions, which themselves almost utter a voice, and witness everywhere the presence of God? Who, as often as it hath seemed good to his infinite wisdom, useth to cast down proud unbridled kings, puffed up above the measure of mankind, and often uprooteth them with their whole house. As for us, it was by His clear command we were on a sudden resolved upon the safety and liberty that we had almost lost; it was He we followed as our Leader, and revered His divine footsteps imprinted everywhere; and thus we entered upon a path not dark but bright, and by His guidance shown and opened to us. I should be much in error if I hoped that by my diligence alone, such as it is, I might set forth all these matters as worthily as they deserve, and might make such records of them as, haply, all nations and all ages would read. For what eloquence can be august and magnificent enough, what man has parts sufficient, to undertake so great a task? Yea, since in so many ages as are gone over the world there has been but here and there a man found able to recount worthily the actions of great heroes and potent states, can any man have so good an opinion of himself as to think that by any style or language of his own he can compass these glorious and wonderful works—not of men, but, evidently, of almighty God?[37]

The two *Defenses* like the five anti-episcopal tracts are intimately related to the point of view which, as we shall see, also pervades *The History of Britain*.

But the two *Defenses* and especially the third *Defense of Himself* (1655) are considerably marred by the frequently intemperate language which readers have often remarked, and as often deplored. Milton's earlier treatment of the bishops, indeed, pales before his personal attacks against both Salmas-

37. *Pro populo anglicano defensio*, trans. Samuel L. Wolff, in the Columbia ed., VII, 3 ff.

ius, the author of the *Defensio regia*, and Alexander More, the presumed author of the *Regii sanguinis clamor* (1652). But here Milton appears to have relied not only on the weapons furnished by the traditional forms of mockery we noted in Pascal; he also depended on classical precedents, particularly the vituperation which in Cicero among others is intimately related to the ethical orientation of one's opponents.[38] The resort to abuse, at any rate, never propelled Milton toward distortion. Whether immersed in the broad argument of *The Tenure* or in the narrow attacks on Salmasius and Alexander More, he remained throughout remarkably faithful to his sources.[39]

VII

We do not know when Milton composed *The History of Britain* or the controversial theological treatise *De doctrina christiana*. The former was published for the first time in 1670; the latter, following its discovery a century and a half after Milton's death, in 1825 (below, pp. 359 ff.).

The History of Britain may well have been written in the early 1640s. Edward Phillips, Milton's nephew, appears to have thought so, and at least one modern scholar places it even earlier.[40] But the work bears the mark of substantial revisions prior to its publication in 1670, most obviously in connection with the parallels Milton frequently and pointedly drew between the past and the present. Such "parallelism" was far from unknown during the Renaissance in England. Conditioned by Plutarch's *Parallel Lives*, historians fully shared the conviction articulated by Thomas Heywood in 1612 that "If

38. See Diane P. Speer, "Milton's *Defensio Prima*: Ethos and Vituperation in a Polemic Engagement," *QJS* 56 (1970): 277–83.

39. See Hughes (as above, note 32), chap. IX. Milton's charges against More have been largely substantiated: consult the studies by Kester Svendsen in *TSLL* 1 (1959): 11–29; *JEGP* 60 (1961): 796–807; and *Th' Upright Heart and Pure*, ed. A. P. Fiore (Pittsburgh, 1967), pp. 117–30.

40. As early as 1632–1638, according to Lloyd E. Berry, *RES*, n.s. 11 (1960): 150–56. For Phillips's view, see below, p. 430.

wee present a forreigne History"—or indeed the history of Britain—"the subject is so intended, that in the lives of *Romans*, *Grecians*, or others, either the vertues of our Countrymen are extolled, or their vices reproved."[41] Sir Walter Ralegh in the seventeenth century's most popular historical work, his monumental *History of the World* (1614), piously disclaimed any interest in reproaching the present through the past but wittily proceeded to leave the question wide open:

It is enough for me (being in that state I am) to write of the eldest times: wherein also why may it not be said, that in speaking of the past, I point at the present, and taxe the vices of those that are yet living, in their persons that are long since dead; and have it laid to my charge. But this I cannot helpe, though innocent. And certainly if there be any, that finding themselves spotted like the Tigers of old time, shall finde fault with me for painting them over a new; they shall therein accuse themselves justly, and me falsely.[42]

One spotted tiger, James I, promptly suppressed Ralegh's work because it appeared to be a veiled denunciation of his reign. Part of the "evidence" consisted of several comparisons of the early seventeenth century with the expired glories of the Elizabethan age. But even more crucial was Ralegh's unrelenting series of "parallels"—some intentional, some accidentally relevant—for instance the account of the great Queen Semiramis and her incompetent successor Ninias ("esteemed no man of war at all, but altogether feminine, and subjected to ease and delicacy").[43] King James knew well enough whom

---

41. *An Apology for Actors* (1612), sig. F3v. On Milton's parallel between the period after the Roman conquest and his own age, see William R. Parker, *Milton* (Oxford, 1968), I, 331 ff. The general tendency is set forth by Herschel Baker, *The Race of Time* (Toronto, 1967), pp. 28–34; and its relevance to dramatic literature, by David Bevington, *Tudor Drama and Politics: A Critical Approach to Topical Meaning* (Cambridge, Mass., 1968).

42. *The History of the World*, ed. C. A. Patrides (Philadelphia, 1971), pp. 19 and 80.

43. Ibid., pp. 19 and 179.

Ninias was supposed to represent!

Milton's endorsement of the same approach resides partly in his account of the usurpation of Britain by William the "outlandish Conquerer"—an obvious parallel to the restoration of the monarchy in 1660—but also in his more emphatic representations of sovereigns with a moral authority entirely lacking in Charles II, for instance that "mirror of Princes" Alfred the Great, whose life advanced "not idely nor voluptuously, but in all vertuous emploiements both of mind and body."[44] But the "lessons" of history also comprehended the traditional belief that historical events are a record of divine mercies and judgments. This expressly Christian view of history reappears in Milton's work mostly in connection with the periodic invasions of Britain, now firmly interpreted as so many judgments on a wayward nation:

when God hath decreed servitude on a sinful Nation, fitted by thir own vices for no condition but servile, all Estates of Government are alike unable to avoid it. God hath purpos'd to punish . . . according to his Divine retaliation; invasion for invasion, spoil for spoil, destruction for destruction.[45]

Even while embracing traditional beliefs, however, Milton passionately pursued "truth" in accordance with the highest ideals of humanist historiography. Fables like Britain's mythical origins were not eschewed, "be it for nothing else but in favour of our English Poets, and Rhetoricians, who by thir Art will know, how to use them judiciously"; yet even then Milton drew the line, firmly, at Arthur ("who *Arthur* was, and whether ever any such reign'd in *Britain*, hath bin doubted heertofore, and may again with good reason").[46] On the other hand, Britain's documented past since the Roman invasion was so diligently and constructively researched that Milton is now

44. Columbia ed., X, 315, 223, 220; Yale ed., V, 402, 292, 289.

45. Columbia ed., X, 198; Yale ed., V, 259. I discuss the background to this tradition in *"The Grand Design of God": The Literary Form of the Christian View of History* (Toronto, 1972).

46. Columbia ed., X, 3 and 127–28; Yale ed., V, 3 and 164.

generally regarded as "a judicious and conservative scholar."[47]
Style was made subservient to truth. In opposition to no less
an authority than Thucydides, he wrote:

I affect not set speeches in a Historie, unless known for certain to
have bin so spok'n in effect as they are writt'n, nor then, unless worth
rehearsal; and to invent such, though eloquently, as some Historians
have done, is an abuse of posteritie, raising, in them that read, other
conceptions of those times and persons then were true.[48]

The pursuit of truth also led Milton boldly to question
widely held beliefs, and even sacrosanct dogmas, in *De doctrina christiana*. He tampered with the doctrine of the Trinity,
denying the equality of the Father and the Son; he argued that
the soul dies with the body; and he claimed that polygamy is
not contrary to divine law. The work is richly embarrassing.

But it is embarrassing less because of its subject than because of the numerous flaws in its logical argument, and its
singularly dull style. In arguing against the doctrine of the
Trinity, for instance, Milton denied that the Father and the
Son are equal in "essentia" yet concurrently affirmed that
they participate with the Holy Spirit in one common "sub-
stantia," which in effect yields not unity but plurality—
tritheism within the Godhead! Stylistically, too, the treatise
might have been illumined by any number of outstanding precedents in manner equal to their great argument, for example
the imposing orations of St. Athanasius against the Arians.
But Milton preferred an arid style utterly devoid of literary
grace, "resting in the meere element of the Text"—to quote
what he himself had denounced as a pernicious habit in *The
Doctrine and Discipline of Divorce* (below, p. 125). The result
is quite inauspicious, for it involves among other infelicities
the improbable point that God the Father is greater than God
the Son in much the same way, and for precisely the same rea-

47. Harry Glicksman, "The Sources of Milton's *History of Britain*,"
University of Wisconsin Studies in Language and Literature 11 (1920):
105–44.
48. Columbia ed., X, 68; Yale ed., V, 80.

sons, that fathers are older than their sons![49] Was Milton—a poet, we recall with mounting despair—so totally unaware that "Father" and "Son" are only suggestive metaphors for the relations within the transcendent Godhead?

De doctrina christiana began to be compiled sometime after Milton's return from the Continent in 1639, as Edward Phillips testifies (below, p. 424); but there is evidence to suggest that it was being amended well into the 1650s, and possibly into the 1660s. Yet Milton never published it. Did he hesitate because aware of the furor its controversial arguments would have generated? Where totally committed, however, Milton utterly disregarded the possibility of the public's disapprobation, witness his bold publication of the treatises on divorce and the perilous reaffirmation of his republican convictions mere weeks before the restoration of the monarchy. It may be that he simply regarded De doctrina as incomplete, still seeking on his death a way out of the labyrinthine mazes he had entered in pursuit of "truth."

Stillborn though the treatise may be, it merits our scrutiny because Milton's achievement in prose cannot be divorced from his sporadic failures in the same medium. Moreover, the opportunity to compare the ideas expressed in De doctrina and Paradise Lost may not be bypassed. Obvious differences in mode of expression, and more subtle ones in intent, will not lead us to regard the treatise as a "gloss" upon the poem[50] but ought to clarify those vital issues which, boldly explored in De doctrina, were finally resolved only through the poetry of Paradise Lost.

49. Columbia ed., XIV, 313; Yale ed., VI, 264. Among other discussions of the treatise's theological implications, see the study by Dayton Haskin, S.J., and the several studies by Gordon Campbell (cited below, p. 460).

50. As Maurice Kelley has done in This Great Argument (Princeton, 1941). In opposition, see the arguments thematic as well as stylistic by William B. Hunter, J. H. Adamson, and myself, in Bright Essence (Salt Lake City, 1971). My own final remarks on the matter are in "Milton and the Arian Controversy," Proceedings of the American Philosophical Society 120 (1976): 245–52.

VIII

Milton's literary criticism is severely circumscribed, for he remarked on prose and poetry only occasionally, and sometimes almost accidentally. His brief remarks, extracted from their context, make an impressive if misleading collection;[51] but sustained statements are extremely rare, except where called for by the immediate occasion. Instances include his views on the aims of scorn (quoted earlier, pp. 24–25), the celebrated passage in *The Reason of Church-Government* on his personal aspirations and the nature of poetry generally (below, pp. 49–60), and of course the preface to *Samson Agonistes* (pp. 406–8).

The passage in *The Reason of Church-Government* and the preface to *Samson* are particularly meaningful in the light of seventeenth-century thought. Implicit in the first is the widespread fear that the abuse of poetry by inconsequential "poet-apes" (to borrow Sidney's term)[52] threatens not simply the art of poetry but, given Milton's idealistic view of the poet's mission, the very fiber of national life. Should the personal terms of Milton's utterance irritate us, it is well to remember that other Renaissance humanists display much the same vaulting pride in their achievements. But the personal "I" may also be regarded as an assumed persona expediting the transition from the particular to the general, from the merely personal to the expressly universal. In such a reading, the concluding statement on the office of the poet (p. 57) appears as a pronouncement of a poet-prophet, not unlike the dramatic peroration in Sidney's *Defence of Poesie*.

The preface to *Samson Agonistes* is similarly comprehensible within the context of seventeenth-century critical opin-

---

51. Ida Langdon's *Milton's Theory of Poetry and Fine Art* (New Haven, 1924).

52. From the peroration of his *Defence of Poesie*: "the cause why it [poetry] is not esteemed in Englande, is the fault of Poet-apes, not Poets." Cf. Ben Jonson's similar denunciation of "poetic apes," discussed by Leah Jones, *The Divine Science* (1940), pp. 22 ff.

ion. In appearance a merely personal defense of Milton's practice, it is in fact a "highly compressed treatment of complex
critical problems" involving the major issues of English neo-
classical criticism.[53] Incidentally, however, the preface also il-
lumines the omnipresent difference between Milton's poetry
and Milton's prose; for while the preface censures the mixture
of the tragic and the comic, the play itself reaches its crisis in
the introduction of the giant Harapha, who is a distant relative of the braggarts in Continental comic literature.[54]

The discrepancy—if indeed it is a discrepancy—has far-
reaching implications. If Milton's engagement with prose differs in kind from his engagement with poetry, we would be
well advised to hesitate before accepting the preface to *Samson* as entirely relevant to the play itself—or, further afield,
before equating the prose of *De doctrina christiana* with the
poetry of *Paradise Lost*. Milton's prose is after all unremit-
tingly multiform, as we noted earlier in connection with *Of
Education* and *Areopagitica* (p. 30). Vastly different in style
because vastly different in intent, *Of Education* and *Areopagitica* disarm any effort to generalize on Milton's prose. The
"total effect" of this prose has been said to depend "more on
an accumulation of convictions gained from individual sentences than on the logical progress of the argument through
the complete work."[55] But however accurate an observation
on Milton's polemical pamphlets, the statement misrepresents
the method and effect of the eminently logical *Doctrine and
Discipline of Divorce*, the fully sustained *Tenure of Kings
and Magistrates*, the relatively unemotional *Treatise of Civil
Power*, the serenely progressive *History of Britain*, or the re-
lentlessly unrhetorical *De doctrina christiana*. Only one gen-

53. See Annette C. Flower, "The Critical Context of the Preface to
Samson Agonistes," *SEL* 10 (1970) :409–23.

54. See D. C. Boughner, "Milton's Harapha and Renaissance Comedy," *ELH* 11 (1944) :297–306.

55. K. G. Hamilton, "The Structure of Milton's Prose," in *Language
and Style in Milton*, ed. R. D. Emma and J. T. Shawcross (1967),
chap. X.

eralization pertains to Milton's multiform prose, that it is distinguished by its impressively variable tonal range.

The multiformity of Milton's prose can best be defined negatively. Eschewing Senecan laconisms, it is not given to "Sentences by the Statute, as if all above three inches long were confiscat."[56] At the other extreme, it avoids also the stylistic extravagances that Milton enumerates in *Of Reformation* as

knotty Africanisms, the pamper'd metafors; the intricat, and involv'd sentences of the Fathers; besides the fantastick, and declamatory flashes; the crosse-jingling periods which cannot but disturb, and come thwart a setl'd devotion worse then the din of bells, and rattles.[57]

Milton's own prose advances along the path marked by Cicero and his imitators. "I cannot say," he once wrote in a rare understatement, "that I am utterly untrain'd in those rules which best Rhetoricians have giv'n, or unacquainted with those examples which the prime authors of eloquence have written in any learned tongue."[58] Yet the best precedent for the multiformity of his own prose Milton discovered not in "the prime authors of eloquence" but in the Bible. His claim deserves to be quoted at length:

Our Saviour who had all gifts in him was Lord to expresse his indoctrinating power in what sort him best seem'd; sometimes by a milde and familiar converse, sometimes with plaine and impartiall home-speaking regardlesse of those whom the auditors might think he should have had in more respect; otherwhiles with bitter and irefull rebukes if not teaching yet leaving excuselesse those his wilfull impugners. What was all in him, was divided among many others the teachers of his Church; some to be severe and ever of a sad gravity that they may win such, & check sometimes those who be of nature over-confident and jocond; others were sent more cheerefull, free, and still

56. For example, like the style of Milton's opponent Joseph Hall, the so-called "English Seneca" (*An Apology for Smectymnuus*, in the Columbia ed., III, 268, and the Yale ed., I, 873).

57. Columbia ed., III, 34; Yale ed., I, 568.

58. *An Apology for Smectymnuus*, in the Columbia ed., III, 362, and the Yale ed., I, 948–49.

as it were at large, in the midst of an untrespassing honesty; that they who are so temper'd may have by whom they might be drawne to salvation, and they who are too scrupulous, and dejected of spirit might be often strengthn'd with wise consolations and revivings: no man being forc't wholly to dissolve that groundwork of nature which God created in him, the sanguine to empty out all his sociable livelinesse, the cholerick to expell quite the unsinning predominance of his anger; but that each radicall humour and passion wrought upon and correct as it ought, might be made the proper mould and foundation of every mans peculiar guifts, and vertues. Some also were indu'd with a staid moderation, and soundnesse of argument to teach and convince the rationall and sober-minded; yet not therefore that to be thought the only expedient course of teaching, for in times of opposition when either against new heresies arising, or old corruptions to be reform'd this coole unpassionate mildnesse of positive wisdome is not anough to damp and astonish the proud resistance of carnall, and false Doctors, then (that I may have leave to soare a while as the Poets use) then Zeale whose substance is ethereal, arming in compleat diamond ascends his fiery Chariot drawn with two blazing Meteors figur'd like beasts, but of a higher breed then any the Zodiack yeilds, resembling two of those four which *Ezechiel* and S. *John* saw, the one visag'd like a Lion to expresse power, high autority and indignation, the other of count'nance like a man to cast derision and scorne upon perverse and fraudulent seducers; with these the invincible warriour Zeale shaking loosely the slack reins drives over the heads of Scarlet Prelats, and such as are insolent to maintaine traditions, brusing their stiffe necks under his flaming wheels. Thus did the true Prophets of old combat with the false; thus Christ himselfe the fountaine of meeknesse found acrimony anough to be still galling and vexing the Prelaticall Pharisees.[59]

The close relationship here said to exist between rhetoric and truth is emphasized throughout Milton's prose and poetry. In the *Apology for Smectymnuus*, for instance, Milton maintained,

true eloquence I find to be none, but the serious and hearty love of truth: And that whose mind so ever is fully possest with a fervent desire to know good things, and with the dearest charity to infuse

59. Ibid., in the Columbia ed., III, 312–14, and the Yale ed., I, 899–900.

knowledge of them into others, when such a man would speak, his words (by what I can expresse) like so many nimble and airy servitors trip about him at command, and in well order'd files, as he would wish, fall aptly into their own places.[60]

The principle, applied in *Paradise Lost*, issues in Milton's invitation that we discriminate sharply between Satan's seductive eloquence and his ambition to ruin man, a discrepancy amply confirmed in the harrowing episode involving the infernal trinity (II, 648 ff.). Satan's eventual reappearance in Book IX as the representative of corrupt eloquence (665–76) links with Christ's pointed contrast in *Paradise Regained* between the orators of Greece and the prophets of Israel:

> Thir Orators thou then extoll'st, as those
> The top of Eloquence, Statists indeed,
> And lovers of thir Country, as may seem;
> But herein to our Prophets farr beneath,
> As men divinely taught, and better teaching
> The solid rules of Civil Government
> In thir majestic unaffected stile
> Then all the Oratory of *Greece* and *Rome*.
> In them is plainest taught, and easiest learnt,
> What makes a Nation happy, and keeps it so,
> What ruins Kingdoms, and lays Cities flat;
> These onely with our Law best form a King.
>   (IV, 353–64)

The possession of a kingdom within which Milton's last poems persistently celebrate had been the aim of the poet himself many years since. As he wrote in 1642, "he who would not be frustrate of his hope to write well hereafter in laudable things, ought him selfe to bee a true Poem" (below, p. 62).

To what extent the poem has been realized will continue to be debated. But the aspiration itself commands respect.

---

60. As above, note 58. The passage is crucial to the anti-episcopal tracts because of Milton's insistent censure of the bishops' abuse of *language*. See Thomas Kranidas's discussion of Milton's "decorum" in *The Fierce Equation* (The Hague, 1965), chap. II(a).

I

MILTON ON MILTON

from

THE REASON OF CHURCH-GOVERNMENT
(1642)

[*The Reason of Church-Government urg'd against Prelaty* is the fourth and longest of Milton's anti-episcopal tracts (see above, p. 21). In the Preface to Book II, here reprinted in its entirety, he digressed to provide an idealistic account of his aspirations to contribute 'to Gods glory by the honour and instruction of my country'.

Dated 1641 on the title page (Old Style), the treatise was actually published early in 1642; the first edition was the only one to appear in Milton's lifetime. Source: the Columbia edition, III, 229–42; ed. Harry M. Ayres.]

How happy were it for this frail, and as it may be truly call'd mortall life of man, since all earthly things which have the name of good and convenient in our daily use, are withall so cumbersome and full of trouble if knowledge yet which is the best and lightsomest possession of the mind, were as the common saying is, no burden, and that what it wanted of being a load to any part of the body, it did not with a heavie advantage overlay upon the spirit. For not to speak of that knowledge that rests in contemplation of naturall causes and dimensions, which must needs be a lower wisdom, as the object is low, certain it is that he who hath obtain'd in more then the scantest measure to know any thing distinctly of God, and of his true worship, and what is infallibly good and happy in the state of mans life, what in it selfe evil and miserable, though vulgarly not so esteem'd, he that hath obtain'd to know this, the only high valuable wisdom indeed, remembring also that God even to a strictnesse requires the improvement of these his entrusted gifts,[1] cannot but sustain a sorer burden of mind, and more

---

1. Cf. the parable of the talents in Matthew 25:14–31, and Milton's sonnet XIX ('When I consider how my light is spent').

pressing then any supportable toil, or waight, which the body can labour under; how and in what manner he shall dispose and employ those summes of knowledge and illumination, which God hath sent him into this world to trade with. And that which aggravats the burden more, is, that having receiv'd amongst his allotted parcels certain pretious truths of such an orient lustre as no Diamond can equall, which never the lesse he has in charge to put off at any cheap rate, yea for nothing to them that will, the great Merchants of this world fearing that this cours would soon discover, and disgrace the fals glitter of their deceitfull wares wherewith they abuse the people, like poor Indians with beads and glasses, practize by all means how they may suppresse the venting of such rarities and such a cheapnes as would undoe them, and turn their trash upon their hands. Therefore by gratifying the corrupt desires of men in fleshly doctrines, they stirre them up to persecute with hatred and contempt all those that seek to bear themselves uprightly in this their spiritual factory: which they foreseeing, though they cannot but testify of Truth and the excellence of that heavenly traffick which they bring against what opposition, or danger soever, yet needs must it sit heavily upon their spirits, that being in Gods prime intention and their own, selected heralds of peace, and dispensers of treasure inestimable without price to them that have no pence, they finde in the discharge of their commission that they are made the greatest variance and offence, a very sword and fire both in house and City over the whole earth. This is that which the sad Phophet *Jeremiah* laments, *Wo is me my mother, that thou hast born me a man of strife, and contention.*[2] And although divine inspiration must certainly have been sweet to those ancient profets, yet the irksomenesse of that truth which they brought was so unpleasant to them, that every where they call it a burden. Yea that mysterious book of Revelation which the great Evangelist was bid to eat, as it had been some eye-brightning electuary of knowledge, and foresight, though it were sweet in his mouth, and in the learning, it was bitter in his belly; bitter in the denouncing.[3]

2. Jeremiah 15:10.
3. Cf. Revelation 10:9, 10.

Nor was this hid from the wise Poet *Sophocles*, who in that place of his Tragedy where *Tiresias* is call'd to resolve K. *Edipus* in a matter which he knew would be grievous, brings him in bemoaning his lot, that he knew more then other men.[4] For surely to every good and peaceable man it must in nature needs be a hatefull thing to be the displeaser, and molester of thousands; much better would it like him doubtlesse to be the messenger of gladnes and contentment, which is his chief intended busines, to all mankind, but that they resist and oppose their own true happiness. But when God commands to take the trumpet and blow a dolorous or a jarring blast, it lies not in mans will what he shall say or what he shall conceal. If he shall think to be silent, as *Jeremiah* did, because of the reproach and derision he met with daily, and *all his familiar friends watcht for his halting* to be reveng'd on him for speaking the truth, he would be forc't to confesse as he confest, *his word was in my heart as a burning fire shut up in my bones, I was weary with forbearing, and could not stay.*[5] Which might teach these times not suddenly to condemn all things that are sharply spoken, or vehemently written, as proceeding out of stomach, virulence and ill nature, but to consider rather that if the Prelats have leav to say the worst that can be said, and doe the worst that can be don, while they strive to keep to themselves to their great pleasure and commodity those things which they ought to render up, no man can be justly offended with him that shall endeavour to impart and bestow without any gain to himselfe those sharp, but saving words which would be a terror, and a torment in him to keep back. For me I have determin'd to lay up as the best treasure, and solace of a good old age, if God voutsafe it me, the honest liberty of free speech from my youth, where I shall think it available in so dear a concernment as the Churches good. For if I be either by disposition, or what other cause too inquisitive, or suspitious of my self and mine own doings, who can help it? but this I foresee, that should the Church be brought under heavy oppression, and God have given me ability the while to reason against

---

4. *Oedipus Rex*, ll. 316–17.
5. Jeremiah 20:8–10.

that man that should be the author of so foul a deed, or should
she by blessing from above on the industry and courage of faith
full men change this her distracted estate into better daie,
without the lest furtherance or contribution of those few talent
which God at that present had lent me, I foresee what stories
I should heare within my selfe, all my life after, of discourage
and reproach. Timorous and ingratefull, the Church of God i
now again at the foot of her insulting enemies: and thou
bewailst, what matters it for thee or thy bewailing? when time
was, thou couldst not find a syllable of all that thou hadst
read, or studied, to utter in her behalfe. Yet ease and leasure
was given thee for thy retired thoughts out of the sweat
of other men. Thou hadst the diligence, the parts, the
language of a man, if a vain subject were to be adorn'd or
beautifi'd, but when the cause of God and his Church was to be
pleaded, for which purpose that tongue was given thee which
thou hast, God listen'd if he could heare thy voice among
his zealous servants, but thou wert domb as a beast; from hence
forward be that which thine own brutish silence hath made
thee. Or else I should have heard on the other eare, slothfull
and ever to be set light by, the Church hath now overcom her
late distresses after the unwearied labours of many her true
servants that stood up in her defence; thou also wouldst take
upon thee to share amongst them of their joy: but wherefore
thou? where canst thou shew any word or deed of thine which
might have hasten'd her peace; what ever thou dost now talke
or write, or look is the almes of other mens active prudence
and zeale. Dare not now to say, or doe any thing better then thy
former sloth and infancy, or if thou darst, thou dost impudently
to make a thrifty purchase of boldnesse to thy selfe out of the
painfull merits of other men: what before was thy sin, is now
thy duty to be, abject, and worthlesse. These and such like
lessons as these, I know would have been my Matins duly, and
my Even-song. But now by this little diligence, mark what a
privilege I have gain'd; with good men and Saints to clame
my right of lamenting the tribulations of the Church, if she
should suffer, when others that have ventur'd nothing for her
sake, have not the honour to be admitted mourners. But if she

lift up her drooping head and prosper, among those that have something more than wisht her welfare, I have my charter and freehold of rejoycing to me and my heires. Concerning therefore this wayward subject against prelaty, the touching whereof is so distastfull and disquietous to a number of men, as by what hath been said I may deserve of charitable readers to be credited, that neither envy nor gall hath entered me upon this controversy, but the enforcement of conscience only, and a preventive fear least the omitting of this duty should be against me when I would store up to my self the good provision of peacefull hours. So lest it should be still imputed to me, as I have found it hath bin, that some self-pleasing humor of vain-glory hath incited me to contest with men of high estimation, now while green yeers are upon my head, from this needlesse surmisall I shall hope to disswade the intelligent and equal auditor, if I can but say successfully that which in this exigent behoovs me, although I would be heard only, if it might be, by the elegant & learned reader, to whom principally for a while I shal beg leav I may addresse my selfe. To him it will be no new thing though I tell him that if I hunted after praise by the ostentation of wit and learning, I should not write thus out of mine own season, when I have neither yet compleated to my minde the full circle of my private studies, although I complain not of any insufficiency to the matter in hand, or were I ready to my wishes, it were a folly to commit any thing elaborately compos'd to the carelesse and interrupted listening of these tumultuous times. Next if I were wise only to mine own ends, I would certainly take such a subject as of it self might catch applause, whereas this hath all the disadvantages on the contrary, and such a subject as the publishing whereof might be delayd at pleasure, and time enough to pencill it over with all the curious touches of art, even to the perfection of a faultlesse picture, whenas in this argument the not deferring is of great moment to the good speeding, that if solidity have leisure to doe her office, art cannot have much. Lastly, I should not chuse this manner of writing wherin knowing my self inferior to my self, led by the genial power of nature to another task, I have the use, as I may account it, but of my left hand. And though I shall be foolish in saying more to this purpose, yet since it will be such a folly, as wisest men going about to commit, have only confest and so committed, I may trust with more reason, because with more folly to have courteous pardon. For although a Poet soaring in the high region of his fancies with his garland and singing robes about him might without apology speak more of himself then I mean to do, yet for me sitting here below in the cool element of prose, a mortall thing among many readers of no Empyreall conceit, to venture and divulge unusual things of my selfe, I shall petition to the gentler sort, it may not be envy to me. I must say therefore that after I had from my first yeers by the ceaseless diligence and care of my father, whom God recompense, bin exercis'd to the tongues, and some sciences, as my age would suffer, by sundry masters and teachers both at home and at the schools, it was found that whether ought was impos'd me by them that had the over-looking, or betak'n to of mine own choice in English, or other tongue, prosing or versing, but chiefly this latter, the stile by certain vital signes it had, was likely to live. But much latelier in the privat Academies of *Italy*, whither I was favor'd to resort,[6] perceiving that some trifles which I had in memory, compos'd at under twenty or thereabout (for the manner is that every one must give some proof of his wit and reading there) met with acceptance above what was lookt for, and other things which I had shifted in scarsity of books and conveniences to patch up amongst them, were receiv'd with written Encomiums, which the Italian is not forward to bestow on men of this side the *Alps*, I began thus farre to assent both to them and divers of my friends here at home, and not lesse to an inward prompting which now grew daily upon me, that by labour and intent study (which I take to be my portion in this life) joyn'd with the strong propensity of nature, I might perhaps leave something so written to aftertimes, as they should not willingly let it die. These thoughts at once possest me, and these other. That if I were certain to write as men

6. See Milton's fuller account of his visit to the Continent, below, pp. 67 ff.; cf. Edward Phillips, pp. 415 ff.

buy Leases, for three lives and downward, there ought no regard be sooner had, then to Gods glory by the honour and instruction of my country. For which cause, and not only for that I knew it would be hard to arrive at the second rank among the Latines, I apply'd my selfe to that resolution which *Ariosto* follow'd against the perswasions of *Bembo*, to fix all the industry and art I could unite to the adorning of my native tongue;[7] not to make verbal curiosities the end, that were a toylsom vanity, but to be an interpreter & relater of the best and sagest things among mine own Citizens throughout this Iland in the mother dialect. That what the greatest and choycest wits of *Athens, Rome,* or modern *Italy,* and those Hebrews of old did for their country, I in my proportion with this over and above of being a Christian, might doe for mine : not caring to be once nam'd abroad, though perhaps I could attaine to that, but content with these British Ilands as my world, whose fortune hath hitherto bin, that if the Athenians, as some say, made their small deeds great and renowned by their eloquent writers, *England* hath had her noble atchievments made small by the unskilfull handling of monks and mechanicks.

Time servs not now, and perhaps I might seem too profuse to give any certain account of what the mind at home in the spacious circuits of her musing hath liberty to propose to her self, though of highest hope, and hardest attempting,[8] whether

---

7. So Ariosto (1474–1533) had expressed a preference for his native Italian – enacted in the *Orlando Furioso* – against the imitation of the ancients recommended by Pietro Bembo (1470–1547).

8. The celebrated remarks that follow are Milton's reflections on the epic, tragedy, and lyric poetry, in the light of Renaissance critical theories. The epic is considered to be either 'diffuse' (as in the case of the *Iliad*, the *Odyssey*, the *Aeneid*, and Tasso's *Jerusalem Delivered*) or 'brief' (as the Book of Job is here said to be, in line with Aristotle's notion of the 'short' epic in the *Poetics*, Ch. 26). With the remarks on tragedy, cf. the Preface to *Samson Agonistes* (below, p. 406). Lyric poetry is represented by the 'odes and hymns' (i.e. songs) of Pindar and Callimachus, but with Biblical precedents pointedly emphasized.

that Epick form whereof the two poems of *Homer*, and those
other two of *Virgil* and *Tasso* are a diffuse, and the book of
Job a brief model : or whether the rules of *Aristotle* herein are
strictly to be kept, or nature to be follow'd, which in them
that know art, and use judgement is no transgression, but an
inriching of art. And lastly what K[ing] or Knight before the
conquest might be chosen in whom to lay the pattern of a
Christian *Heroe*. And as Tasso gave to a Prince of *Italy* his choise
whether he would command him to write of *Godfreys* expe
dition against the infidels, or *Belisarius* against the Gothes, or
Charlemain against the Lombards; if to the instinct of nature
and the imboldning of art ought may be trusted, and that there
be nothing advers in our climat, or the fate of this age, it
haply would be no rashnesse from an equal diligence and
inclination to present the like offer in our own ancient stories
Or whether those Dramatick constitutions, wherein *Sophocles*
and *Euripides* raigne shall be found more doctrinal and exem
plary to a Nation, the Scripture also affords us a divine pastoral
Drama in the Song of *Salomon* consisting of two persons and
a double *Chorus*, as *Origen* rightly judges. And the Apocalyps
of Saint *John* is the majestick image of a high and stately
Tragedy, shutting up and intermingling her solemn Scenes and
Acts with a sevenfold *Chorus* of halleluja's and harping
symphonies: and this my opinion the grave autority of
Pareus commenting that booke is sufficient to confirm. Or if
occasion shall lead to imitat those magnifick Odes and Hymns
wherein *Pindarus* and *Callimachus* are in most things worthy
some others in their frame judicious, in their matter most an
end faulty: But those frequent songs throughout the law and
prophets beyond all these, not in their divine argument alone
but in the very critical art of composition may be easily made
appear over all the kinds of Lyrick poesy, to be incomparable.

9. This persuasion is not peculiar to Milton. Common to several
defenders of poetry during the Renaissance, it is also echoed in
Donne's assurance to his congregation that while Virgil is 'the
King of Poets', David remains 'a better *Poet* than *Virgil*' (*Sermons*
ed. E. M. Simpson and G. R. Potter, Berkeley, 1953–60, IV, 167)
Cf. *Paradise Regained*, IV, 331–64.

These abilities, wheresoever they be found, are the inspired guift of God rarely bestow'd, but yet to some (though most abuse) in every Nation: and are of power beside the office of a pulpit, to inbreed and cherish in a great people the seeds of vertu, and publick civility, to allay the perturbations of the mind, and set the affections in right tune, to celebrate in glorious and lofty Hymns the throne and equipage of Gods Almightinesse, and what he works, and what he suffers to be wrought with high providence in his Church, to sing the victorious agonies of Martyrs and Saints, the deeds and triumphs of just and pious Nations doing valiantly through faith against the enemies of Christ, to deplore the general relapses of King-doms and States from justice and Gods true worship. Lastly, whatsoever in religion is holy and sublime, in vertu amiable, or grave, whatsoever hath passion or admiration in all the changes of that which is call'd fortune from without, or the wily suttleties and refluxes of mans thoughts from within, all these things with a solid and treatable smoothnesse to paint out and describe. Teaching over the whole book of sanctity and vertu through all the instances of example with such delight to those especially of soft and delicious temper who will not so much as look upon Truth herselfe, unlesse they see her elegantly drest, that whereas the paths of honesty and good life appear now rugged and difficult, though they be indeed easy and pleasant, they would then appeare to all men both easy and pleasant though they were rugged and difficult indeed. And what a benefit this would be to our youth and gentry, may be soon guest by what we know of the corruption and bane which they suck in dayly from the writings and interludes of libidinous and ignorant Poetasters, who having scars ever heard of that which is the main consistence of a true poem, the choys of such persons as they ought to introduce, and what is morall and decent to each one, doe for the most part lap up vitious principles in sweet pils to be swallow'd down, and make the taste of vertuous documents harsh and sowr. But because the spirit of man cannot demean it selfe lively in this body without some recreating intermission of labour, and serious things, it were happy for the Common wealth, if our

Magistrates, as in those famous governments of old, would take into their care, not only the deciding of our contentious Law cases and brauls, but the managing of our publick sports, and festival pastimes, that they might be, not such as were autoriz'd a while since, the provocations of drunkennesse and lust, but such as may inure and harden our bodies by martial exercises to all warlike skil and performance, and may civilize, adorn and make discreet our minds by the learned and affable meeting of frequent Academies, and the procurement of wise and art-full recitations sweetened with eloquent and gracefull intice-ments to the love and practice of justice, temperance and forti-tude, instructing and bettering the Nation at all opportunities, that the call of wisdom and vertu may be heard every where, as *Salomon* saith, *She crieth without, she uttereth her voice in the streets, in the top of high places, in the chief concours, and in the opening of the Gates.*[10] Whether this may not be not only in Pulpits, but after another persuasive method, at set and solemn Paneguries, in Theaters, porches, or what other place, or way may win most upon the people to receiv at once both recreation, & instruction, let them in autority consult. The thing which I had to say, and those intentions which have liv'd within me ever since I could conceiv my self any thing worth to my Countrie, I return to crave excuse that urgent reason hath pluckt from me by an abortive and foredated dis-covery. And the accomplishment of them lies not but in a power above mans to promise; but that none hath by more studious ways endeavour'd, and with more unwearied spirit that none shall, that I dare almost averre of my self, as farre as life and free leasure will extend, and that the Land had once infranchis'd her self from this impertinent yoke of prelaty, under whose inquisitorious and tyrannical duncery no free and splendid wit can flourish. Neither doe I think it shame to covnant with any knowing reader, that for some few yeers yet I may go on trust with him toward the payment of what I am now indebted, as being a work not to be rays'd from the heat of youth, or the vapours of wine, like that which flows

---

10. Cf. Proverbs 1 : 20–21 and 8 : 2–3.

at wast from the pen of some vulgar Amorist, or the trencher fury of a riming parasite, nor to be obtain'd by the invocation of Dame Memory and her Siren daughters, but by devout prayer to that eternall Spirit who can enrich with all utterance and knowledge, and sends out his Seraphim with the hallow'd fire of his Altar to touch and purify the lips of whom he pleases: to this must be added industrious and select reading, steddy observation, insight into all seemly and generous arts and affaires, till which in some measure be compast, at mine own peril and cost I refuse not to sustain this expectation from as many as are not loath to hazard so much credulity upon the best pledges that I can give them. Although it nothing content me to have disclos'd thus much before hand, but that I trust hereby to make it manifest with what small willingnesse I endure to interrupt the pursuit of no lesse hopes then these, and leave a calme and pleasing solitarynes fed with cherful and confident thoughts, to imbark in a troubl'd sea of noises and hoars disputes, put from beholding the bright countenance of truth in the quiet and still air of delightfull studies to come into the dim reflexion of hollow antiquities sold by the seeming bulk, and there be fain to club quotations with men whose learning and beleif lies in marginal stuffings, who when they have like good sumpters laid ye down their hors load of citations and fathers at your dore, with a rapsody of who and who were Bishops here or there, ye may take off their pack-saddles, their days work is don, and episcopacy, as they think, stoutly vindicated. Let any gentle apprehension that can distinguish learned pains from unlearned drudgery, imagin what pleasure or profoundnesse can be in this, or what honour to deal against such adversaries. But were it the meanest under-service, if God by his Secretary conscience injoyn it, it were sad for me if I should draw back, for me especially, now when all men offer their aid to help ease and lighten the difficult labours of the Church, to whose service by the intentions of my parents and friends I was destin'd of a child, and in mine own resolutions, till comming to some maturity of yeers and perceaving what tyranny had invaded the Church, that he who would take Orders must subscribe slave, and take an oath withall, which unlesse he took with a conscience that would retch, he must either strait perjure, or split his faith, I thought it better to preferre a blamelesse silence before the sacred office of speaking bought, and begun with servitude and forswearing. How soever thus Church-outed by the Prelats, hence may appear the right I have to meddle in these matters, as before, the necessity and constraint appear'd.

from

AN APOLOGY FOR SMECTYMNUUS
(1642)

[Milton's five anti-episcopal treatises (see above, p. 21) terminate
with *An Apology against a Pamphlet call'd A Modest Confutation
of the Animadversions upon the Remonstrant against Smectymnuus*,
mercifully abbreviated in a later issue as *An Apology for Smectymnuus*. Stung by a personal attack, Milton replied in kind; yet the
passage reprinted here recalls the idealism that informs *The Reason
of Church-Government* (above, pp. 49 ff.).

The *Apology* was published in April 1642; the first edition was the
only one to appear in Milton's lifetime. Source: the Columbia
edition, III, 302–6; ed. Harry M. Ayres.]

I HAD my time Readers, as others have, who have good learning bestow'd upon them, to be sent to those places, where
the opinon was it might be soonest attain'd: and as the manner
is, was not unstudied in those authors which are most commended; whereof some were grave Orators & Historians; whose
matter me thought I lov'd indeed, but as my age then was, so
I understood them; others were the smooth Elegiack Poets,
whereof the Schooles are not scarce. Whom both for the pleasing sound of their numerous writing, which in imitation I found
most easie, and most agreeable to natures part in me, and for
their matter which what it is, there be few who know not, I
was so allur'd to read, that no recreation came to me better
welcome. For that it was then those years with me which are
excus'd though they be least severe, I may be sav'd the labour
to remember ye. Whence having observ'd them to account it
the chiefe glory of their wit, in that they were ablest to judge, to
praise, and by that could esteeme themselves worthiest to love
those high perfections which under one or other name they
took to celebrate, I thought with my selfe by every instinct
and presage of nature which is not wont to be false, that what

imboldn'd them to this task might with such diligence as they us'd imbolden me, and that what judgement, wit, or elegance was my share, would herein best appeare, and best value it selfe, by how much more wisely, and with more love of vertue I should choose (let rude eares be absent) the object of not unlike praises. For albeit these thoughts to some will seeme vertuous and commendable, to others only pardonable, to a third sort perhaps idle, yet the mentioning of them now will end in serious. Nor blame it Readers, in those yeares to propose to themselves such a reward, as the noblest dispositions above other things in this life have sometimes preferr'd. Whereof not to be sensible, when good and faire in one person meet, argues both a grosse and shallow judgement, and withall an ungentle, and swainish brest. For by the firme setling of these perswasions I became, to my best memory, so much a proficient, that if I found those authors any where speaking unworthy things of themselves; or unchaste of those names which before they had extoll'd, this effect it wrought with me, from that time forward their art I still applauded, but the men I deplor'd; and above them all preferr'd the two famous renowners of *Beatrice* and *Laura*[1] who never write but honour of them to whom they devote their verse, displaying sublime and pure thoughts, without transgression. And long it was not after, when I was confirm'd in this opinion, that he who would not be frustrate of his hope to write well hereafter in laudable things, ought him selfe to bee a true Poem, that is, a composition, and patterne of the best and honourablest things; not presuming to sing high praises of heroick men, or famous Cities, unlesse he have in himselfe the experience and the practice of all that which is praise-worthy. These reasonings, together with a certaine nicenesse of nature, an honest haughtinesse, and self-esteem either of what I was, or what might be, (which let envie call pride) and lastly that modesty, whereof though not in the Title page yet here I may be excus'd to make some beseeming profession, all these uniting the supply of their naturall aide together, kept me still above

---

1. Dante and Petrarch.

hose low descents of minde, beneath which he must deject and
lunge himself, that can agree to salable and unlawfull prosti-
utions. Next, (for heare me out now Readers) that I may tell
e whether my younger feet wander'd; I betook me among those
ofty Fables and Romances, which recount in solemne canto's
he deeds of Knighthood founded by our victorious Kings; &
rom hence had in renowne over all Christendome.[2] There I
ead it in the oath of every Knight, that he should defend to the
xpence of his best blood, or of his life, if it so befell him, the
onour and chastity of Virgin or Matron. From whence even
hen I learnt what a noble vertue chastity sure must be, to the
efence of which so many worthies by such a deare adventure
f themselves had sworne.[3] And if I found in the story afterward
ny of them by word or deed breaking that oath, I judg'd it the
ame fault of the Poet, as that which is attributed to *Homer*;
o have written undecent things of the gods.[4] Only this my
ninde gave me that every free and gentle spirit without that
ath ought to be borne a Knight, nor needed to expect the
uilt spurre, or the laying of a sword upon his shoulder to
tirre him up both by his counsell, and his arme to secure and
rotect the weaknesse of any attempted chastity. So that even
hose books which to many others have bin the fuell of wanton-
esse and loose living, I cannot thinke how unlesse by divine
ndulgence prov'd to me so many incitements as you have heard,
o the love and stedfast observation of that vertue which
bhorres the society of Bordello's. Thus from the Laureat
raternity of Poets, riper yeares, and the ceaselesse round of
tudy and reading led me to the shady places of philosophy, but
hiefly to the divine volumes of *Plato*, and his equal[5] *Xenophon*.
Where if I should tell ye what I learnt, of chastity and love, I
neane that which is truly so, whose charming cup is only
ertue which she bears in her hand to those who are worthy.

---

2. A reference to Spenser?

3. Hereafter the relevance of Milton's remarks to *Comus* (first
erformed in 1634, published in 1637) should be all too obvious.

4. Cf. Plato, *Republic*, 377e.

5. 'Contemporary with'? Or 'the equal of Plato as teacher' (as
ow and Sasek suggest, below, p. 452)?

The rest are cheated with a thick intoxicating potion which
certaine Sorceresse the abuser of loves name carries about; an
how the first and chiefest office of love, begins and ends i
the soule, producing those happy twins of her divine gene
ation knowledge and vertue, with such abstracted sublimities :
these, it might be worth your listning, Readers, as I may or
day hope to have ye in a still time, when there shall be n
chiding; not in these noises the adversary as ye know, barking a
the doore; or searching for me at the Burdello's where it ma
be he has lost himselfe, and raps up without pitty the sag
and rheumatick old *Prelatesse* with all her young *Corinthia
Laity*[6] to inquire for such a one. Last of all not in time, but
perfection is last, that care was ever had of me, with my earlie:
capacity not to be negligently train'd in the precepts of Christia
Religion: This that I have hitherto related, hath bin to shew
that though Christianity had bin but slightly taught me, yet
certain reserv'dnesse of naturall disposition, and morall disci
line learnt out of the noblest Philosophy was anough to keep m
in disdain of farre lesse incontinences then this of the Burdelle
But having had the doctrine of holy Scripture unfolding thos
chaste and high mysteries with timeliest care unfus'd, that *th
body is for the Lord and the Lord for the body*,[7] thus also
argu'd to my selfe; that if unchastity in a woman whom Sair
Paul termes the glory of man, be such a scandall and dishonou
then certainly in a man who is both the image and glory c
God, it must, though commonly not so thought, be much mo
deflouring and dishonourable.[8] In that he sins both against h
owne body which is the perfeter sex, and his own glory whic
is in the woman, and that which is worst, against the imag
and glory of God which is in himselfe. Nor did I slumber ove
that place expressing such high rewards of ever accompanyin
the Lambe, with those celestiall songs to others inapprehensibl

---

6. An allusion to Corinth's reputation for licentiousness.

7. 1 Corinthians 6:13.

8. 1 Corinthians 11:7: 'man ... is the image and glory of God
but the woman is the glory of the man.' Hence *Paradise Lost*, IV
299: 'He for God only, she for God in him.'

ut not to those who were defil'd with women,[9] which doubt-
esse meanes fornication: for mariage must not be call'd a
defilement. Thus large I have purposely bin, that if I have bin
ustly taxt with this crime, it may come upon me after all this
my confession, with a tennefold shame.

---

9. Cf. Revelation 14:1–5; also 19.

from

PRO POPULO ANGLICANO
DEFENSIO SECUNDA
(1654)

[Milton's *Second Defense of the People of England* was a reply, in
Latin, to his presumed antagonist Alexander More (see above, pp. 13,
37). Its ringing reaffirmation of Milton's dedication to the cause of
liberty encompasses the self-vindication reprinted here.

The *Second Defense* was issued several times after its first appearance in 1654, most often on the Continent. Source: the Columbia
edition, VIII, 113, 119–39; the Latin text, ed. Eugene J. Strittmatter;
trans. George Burnett (1809), revised by Moses Hadas.]

... Who and whence I am, say you, is doubtful. So also was it
doubtful, in ancient times, who Homer was, who Demosthenes.
The truth is, I had learnt to be long silent, to be able to forbear
writing, which Salmasius[1] never could; and carried silently in
my own breast what if I had chosen then, as well as now, to
bring forth, I could long since have gained a name. But I was
not eager for fame, who is slow of pace; indeed, if the fit
opportunity had not been given me, even these things would
never have seen the light; little concerned, though others were
ignorant that I knew what I did. It was not the fame of every
thing that I was waiting for, but the opportunity.

*

I was born at London, of respectable parents. My father was
a man of the highest integrity; my mother, an excellent
woman, was particularly known throughout the neighbour-
hood for her charitable donations. My father destined me from
a child for the pursuits of polite learning, which I prosecuted
with such eagerness, that after I was twelve years old, I

---

1. See above, p. 37.

arely retired to bed from my lucubrations till midnight. This
was the first thing which proved pernicious to my eyes, to the
natural weakness of which were added frequent headaches. But
as all this could not abate my instinctive ardour for learning, he
provided me, in addition to the ordinary instructions of the
grammar school, masters to give me daily lessons at home. Being
thus instructed in various languages, and having gotten no slight
taste of the sweetness of philosophy, he sent me to Cambridge,
one of our two national colleges. There, aloof from all profligate
conduct, and with the approbation of all good men, I studied
seven years, according to the usual courses of discipline and
of scientific instruction – till I obtained, and with applause, the
degree of master, as it is called; when I fled not into Italy, as this
foul miscreant falsely asserts, but, of my own free will, returned
home, leaving behind me among most of the fellows of the
college, who had shown me no ordinary attention, even an
affectionate regret. At my father's country house, to which he
had retired to pass the remainder of his days, being perfectly
at my ease, I gave myself up entirely to reading the Greek and
Latin writers; exchanging, however, sometimes, the country
for the town, either for the purchase of books, or to learn
something new in mathematics, or in music, which at that time
furnished the sources of my amusement. After passing five
years in this way, I had the curiosity, after the death of my
mother, to see foreign countries, and above all, Italy;[2] and having obtained permission of my father, I set out, attended by
one servant. On my departure, I was treated in the most friendly
manner by Sir Henry Wotton, who was long ambassador from
King James to Venice, and who not only followed me with
his good wishes, but communicated, in an elegant letter, some
maxims of the greatest use to one who is going abroad.[3] From
the recommendation of others, I was received at Paris with the
utmost courtesy, by the noble Thomas Scudamore, Viscount of
Sligo, who of his own accord introduced me, accompanied by

2. See also the account by Edward Phillips, below, pp. 420 ff.

3. Sir Henry Wotton (1568–1639), having served with distinction
as Ambassador to Venice, became Provost of Eton College in 1624.
He was the first to commend Milton's *Comus*. Cf. above, p. 19.

several of his suite, to the learned Hugo Grotius, at that time
ambassador from the queen of Sweden to the king of France, and
whom I was very desirous of seeing.[4] On my setting out for
Italy some days after, he gave me letters to the English merchants on my route, that they might be ready to do me any
service in their power. Taking ship at Nice, I arrived at Genoa;
and soon after at Leghorn and Pisa, thence to Florence. In this
last city, which I have always valued above the rest for the
elegance of its dialect and of its genius, I continued about two
months. Here I soon contracted a familiar acquaintance with
many persons eminent for their rank and learning, and regularly
frequented also their private academies – an institution which
deserves the highest commendation, as calculated to preserve at
once polite letters and friendly intercourse: for, the pleasing,
the delightful recollection I still retain of you Jacobo Gaddi, of
you Carolo Dati, Frescobaldi, Coltellino, Bonmatthei, Clementillo, Francini, and many others, no time will efface.[5] From
Florence I pursued my route to Sienna, and then to Rome; and
having been detained about two months in this city by its antiquities and ancient renown, (where I enjoyed the accomplished
society of Lucas Holstenius[6] and of many other learned and
superior men) I proceeded to Naples. Here I was introduced by a
certain hermit, with whom I had travelled from Rome, to John
Baptista Manso, Marquis of Villa, a man of the first rank and
authority, to whom the illustrious poet, Torquato Tasso,
addressed his book on friendship.[7] By him I was treated, while

---

4. Hugo Grotius (1583–1645), the eminent Dutch authority on
international law, had also written a Latin play on the Fall of Man,
the *Adamus Exul* (1601). Cf. above, p. 19.

5. The Florentines listed were demonstrably eminent in the period's
intellectual world; for details of their activities see the Yale edition,
IV, 616–17. Other individuals Milton met in Italy include Galileo
(see below, p. 228) and Malatesti (above, p. 20).

6. The German scholar Lucas Holstein (1596–1661) was librarian
to Francesco Cardinal Barberini from 1627, and librarian of the
Vatican from 1653. Cf. above, p. 19.

7. The reference is to Tasso's *Il Manso*. Giovanni Battista Manso
(1560–1640) in extending a welcome to Milton gained two tributes in

stayed there, with all the warmth of friendship: for he conducted me himself over the city and the viceregent's court, and more than once came to visit me at my own lodgings. On my leaving Naples, he gravely apologized for showing me no more attention, alleging that although it was what he wished above all things, it was not in his power in that city, because I had not thought proper to be more guarded on the point of religion. As I was preparing to pass over also into Sicily and Greece, I was restrained by the melancholy tidings from England of the civil war: for I thought it base, that I should be travelling at my ease, even for the improvement of my mind abroad, while my fellow-citizens were fighting for their liberty at home. As I was about to return to Rome, the merchants gave me an intimation, that they had learnt from their letters, that, in case of my revisiting Rome, the English Jesuits had laid a plot for me, because I had spoken too freely on the subject of religion: for I had laid it down as a rule for myself, never to begin a conversation on religion in those parts; but if interrogated concerning my faith, whatever might be the consequence, to dissemble nothing. I therefore returned notwithstanding to Rome; I concealed from no one, who asked the question, what I was; if any one attacked me, I defended in the most open manner, as before, the orthodox faith, for nearly two months more, in the city even of the sovereign pontiff himself. By the will of God, I arrived safe again at Florence; revisiting those who longed no less to see me than if I had returned to my own country. There I willingly stopped as many months as before, except that I made an excursion for a few days to Lucca; when, crossing the Apennine, I made the best of my way, through Bononia and Ferrara, to Venice. Having spent a month in getting a survey of this city, and seen the books shipped which I had collected in Italy, I was brought, by way of Verona, Milan, and the Pænine Alps, and along the lake Lemano, to Geneva. This city, as it brings to my recollection the slanderer More, makes me again call God to witness, that, in all these places where so much licence is given, I lived

his Latin poetry: the verse letter *Manso* and several lines in the pastoral elegy *Epitaphium Damonis* (235–55).

free and untouched of all defilement and profligate behaviour
having it ever in my thought, that if I could escape the eyes of
men, I certainly could not escape the eyes of God. At Geneva I
had daily intercourse with John Deodati, the very learned
professor of divinity.[8] Then, by the same route as before, I
returned through France, to my own country, after an absence
of a year and about three months. I arrived nearly at the time
that Charles, breaking the pacification, renewed the war, called
the episcopal war, with the Scots, in which the royal forces
were routed in the first engagement; and Charles, now finding
the whole English nation enraged, and justly, to the last degree
against him, not long after called a parliament; though not by
his own will, but as compelled by his necessities. Looking
about me for some place in which I might take up my abode,
if any was to be found in this troubled and fluctuating state of
affairs, I hired, for me and my books, a sufficiently spacious
house in the city. Here I returned with no delight to my
interrupted studies; leaving without difficulty, the issue of
things more especially to God, and to those to whom the
people had assigned that department of duty. Meanwhile, as
the parliament acted with great vigour, the pride of the bishops
began to lose its swell. No sooner did liberty of speech begin to
be allowed, than every mouth was open against the bishops.
Some complained of their personal vices, others of the vice of
the order itself. It was wrong, they said, that they alone
should differ from all other reformed churches; that it was
expedient the church should be governed by the example of
the brethren, and above all by the word of God. I became perfectly awake to these things; and perceiving that men were in
the right way to liberty; that, if discipline originating in religion
continued its course to the morals and institutions of the commonwealth, they were proceeding in a direct line from such
beginnings, from such steps, to the deliverance of the whole
life of mortal man from slavery – moreover, as I had endeavoured from my youth, before all things, not to be ignorant
of what was law, whether divine or human; as I had con-

8. Giovanni Diodati (1576–1649) was uncle to Milton's friend
Charles Diodati (1609?–38), the subject of the Epitaphium Damonis.

sidered, whether I could ever be of use, should I now be wanting to my country, to the church, and to such multitudes of the brethren who were exposing themselves to danger for the gospel's sake – I resolved, though my thoughts were then employed upon other subjects, to transfer to these the whole force of my mind and industry. Accordingly, I first wrote *of the Reformation of the English Church*, in two books, to a friend [below, p. 77 ff.]. Next, as there were two bishops of reputation above the rest, who maintained their own cause against certain leading ministers;[9] and as I had the persuasion, that on a subject which I had studied solely for the love of truth and from a regard to Christian duty, I should not write worse than those who contended for their own lucre and most iniquitous domination; to one of them I replied in two books, of which one was entitled *Of Prelatical Episcopacy*, the other *Of the Reason of Church Government* [above, pp. 49 ff.]; to the other, in some *Animadversions*, and soon after, in an *Apology* [above, pp. 61 ff.]; and thus, as was said, brought timely succour to those ministers, who had some difficulty in maintaining their ground against the bishops' eloquence : from this time too, I held myself ready, should they thenceforward make any reply. When the bishops, at whom every man aimed his arrow, had at length fallen, and we were now at leisure, as far as they were concerned, I began to turn my thoughts to other subjects; to consider in what way I could contribute to the progress of real and substantial liberty; which is to be sought for not from without, but within, and is to be obtained principally not by fighting, but by the just regulation and by the proper conduct of life.[10] Reflecting, therefore, that there are in all three species of liberty, without which it is scarcely possible to pass any life with comfort, namely, ecclesiastical, domestic or private, and civil; that I had already written on the first species, and saw the magistrate diligently employed about the third, I undertook the domestic, which was the one that remained.

---

9. The two bishops were James Ussher and Joseph Hall; the 'leading ministers', the five Smectymnuans (see above, p. 22).

10. Cf. the exchanges between Adam and Michael in *Paradise Lost*, XII, 383–404.

But as this also appeared to be three-fold, namely, whether the affair of marriage was rightly managed; whether the education of children was properly conducted; whether, lastly, we were to be allowed freedom of opinion – and elsewhere I explained my sentiments not only on the proper mode of contracting marriage, but also of dissolving it, should that be found necessary : and this I did according to the divine law which Christ has never abrogated; and much less has he given a civil sanction to any other, that should be of higher authority than the whole law of Moses [below, pp. 112 ff.]. In like manner I delivered my own opinion and the opinion of others concerning what was to be thought of the single exception of fornication – a question which has been also elucidated by our celebrated Selden, in his *Hebrew Wife*, published some two years after.[11] Again, it is to little purpose for him to make a noise about liberty in the legislative assemblies, and in the courts of justice, who is in bondage to an inferior at home – a species of bondage of all others the most degrading to a man. On this point, therefore, I published some books, and at that particular time, when man and wife were often the fiercest enemies, he being at home with his children, while she, the mother of the family, was in the camp of the enemy, threatening slaughter and destruction to her husband. I next treated, in one little work, of the education of children, briefly it is true, but at sufficient length, I conceived, for those, who apply themselves to the subject with all that earnestness and diligence which it demands – a subject than which there can be none of greater moment to imbue the minds of men with virtue, from which springs that true liberty which is felt within; none for the wise administration of a commonwealth, and for giving it its utmost possible duration [below, pp. 181 ff.]. Lastly, I wrote, after the model of a regular speech, *Areopagitica*, on the liberty of printing, that the determination of true and false, of what ought to be published and what suppressed, might not be in the hands of the few who may be charged with the inspection of books, men commonly without learning and of vulgar judgement, and by

---

11. John Selden's *Uxor Hebraica* was published in 1646.

whose licence and pleasure, no one is suffered to publish any
thing which may be above vulgar apprehension [see below, pp.
96 ff.]. The civil species of liberty, the last which remained,
I had not touched, as I perceived it drew sufficient attention
from the magistrate. Nor did I write any thing on the right of
kings, till the king, pronounced an enemy by the parliament,
and vanquished in war, was arraigned as a captive before
judges, and condemned to lose his head. But, when certain
presbyterian ministers, at first the bitterest foes to Charles, unable to endure that the independent party should now be
preferred to them, and that it should have greater influence in
the senate, began to clamour against the sentence which the
parliament had pronounced upon the king (though in no wise
angry at the deed, but only that themselves had not the execution of it) and tried to their utmost to raise a tumult, having
the assurance to affirm that the doctrine of protestants, that all
the reformed churches shrunk with horror from the atrocity of
such a sentence against kings – then indeed, I thought it behoved
me openly to oppose so barefaced a falsehood [see below,
pp. 249 ff.]. Yet even then, I neither wrote nor advised any
thing concerning Charles; but simply showed, in general, what
may be lawfully done against tyrants; adducing, in confirmation,
the authorities of no small number of the most eminent divines;
inveighing, at the same time, almost with the zeal of a preacher
against the egregious ignorance or impudence of those men,
who had promised better things. This book was not published
till after the death of the king, being intended rather to compose the minds of men, than to settle any thing relating to
Charles; that being the business of the magistrates instead of
mine, and which, at the time I speak of, had been already done.
These services of mine, which were performed within private
walls, I gratuitously bestowed at one time upon the church, at
another, upon the commonwealth; while neither the commonwealth nor the church bestowed upon me in return any thing
beyond security. It is true, that I gained a good conscience, a
fair repute among good men, and that the deeds themselves
rendered this freedom of speech honourable to me. Some men
however gained advantages, others honours, for doing nothing;

but no man ever saw me canvassing for preferment, no man ever saw me in quest of any thing through the medium of friends, fixed, with supplicatory look to the doors of the parliament, or clung to the vestibules of lower assemblies. I kept myself commonly at home, and supported myself, however frugally, upon my own fortune, though, in this civil broil, a great part was often detained, and an assessment rather disproportionate, imposed upon me. Having dispatched these things, and thinking that, for the future, I should now have abundance of leisure, I undertook a history of the nation from its remotest origin; intending to bring it down, if I could, in one unbroken thread to our own times.[12] I had already finished four books, when lo! (Charles's kingdom being reduced to a commonwealth) the council of state, as it is called, now first constituted by authority of parliament, invited me to lend them my services in the department more particularly of foreign affairs – an event which had never entered my thoughts! Not long after, the book which was attributed to the king made its appearance, written certainly with the bitterest malice against the parliament. Being ordered to prepare an answer to it, I opposed the *Iconoclast* to the *Icon*; not as is pretended, 'in insult to the departed spirit of the king', but in the persuasion, that queen truth ought to be preferred to king Charles; and as I foresaw that some reviler would be ready with this slander, I endeavoured in the introduction, and in other places as far as it was proper, to ward off the reproach. Next came forward Salmasius; and no long time, as More reports, was lost in looking about for some person to answer him, so that all, of their own accord, instantly nominated me, who was then present in the council. . . .

---

12. *The History of Britain*, first published in 1670, terminates with the accession of William the Conqueror.

II

THE MAJOR PREMISES

OF REFORMATION
TOUCHING CHURCH-DISCIPLINE
(1641)

[The first of Milton's anti-episcopal tracts (see above, pp. 21 ff.) is described on the title page as *Of Reformation touching Church-Discipline in England: and the Causes that hitherto have hindred it. Two Bookes, written to a Freind.*

The edition of the Spring of 1641 was the only one to appear in Milton's lifetime. The extracts reprinted here are from the Columbia edition (III, 1–79; ed. Harry M. Ayres).]

Sir,[1]

AMIDST those deepe and retired thoughts, which with every man Christianly instructed, ought to be most frequent, of *God*, and of his miraculous *ways*, and *works*, amongst men, and of our *Religion* and *Worship*, to be perform'd to him; after the story of our Saviour *Christ*, suffering to the lowest bent of weaknesse, in the *Flesh*, and presently triumphing to the highest pitch of *glory*, in the *Spirit*, which drew up his body also, till we in both be united to him in the Revelation of his Kingdome : I do not know of any thing more worthy to take up the whole passion of pitty, on the one side, and joy on the other : then to consider first, the foule and sudden corruption, and then after many a tedious age, the long-deferr'd, but much more wonderfull and happy reformation of the *Church* in these latter dayes. Sad it is to thinke how that Doctrine of the *Gospel*, planted by teachers Divinely inspir'd, and by them winnow'd, and sifted, from the chaffe of overdated Ceremonies, and refin'd to such a Spirituall height, and temper of purity, and knowledge of the Creator, that the body, with all the circumstances of

---

1. The unnamed recipient of Milton's address (cf. the full title in the headnote, above).

time and place, were purifi'd by the affections of the regenerate
Soule, and nothing left impure, but sinne; *Faith* needing not the
weak, and fallible office of the Senses, to be either the Ushers,
or Interpreters, of heavenly Mysteries, save where our Lord
himselfe in his Sacraments ordain'd; that such a Doctrine should
through the grossenesse, and blindnesse, of her Professors, and
the fraud of deceivable traditions, drag so downwards, as to
backslide one way into the Jewish beggery, of old cast rudiments, and stumble forward another way into the new-vomited
Paganisme of sensuall Idolatry,[2] attributing purity, or impurity,
to things indifferent, that they might bring the inward acts of
the *Spirit* to the outward, and customary ey-Service of the body,
as if they could make *God* earthly, and fleshly, because they
could not make themselves *heavenly*, and *Spirituall*: they
began to draw downe all the Divine intercours, betwixt *God*,
and the Soule, yea, the very shape of *God* himselfe, into an
exterior, and bodily forme, urgently pretending a necessity,
and obligement of joyning the body in a formall reverence,
and *Worship* circumscrib'd, they hallow'd it, they fum'd it,
they sprincl'd it, they be deck't it, not in robes of pure inno-
cency, but of pure Linnen, with other deformed, and fantastick
dresses in Palls, and Miters, gold, and guegaw's fetcht from
Arons old wardrope, or the *Flamins vestry*:[3] then was the
Priest set to *con his motions*, and his *Postures* his *Liturgies*,
and his *Lurries*,[4] till the Soule by this meanes of over-bodying
her selfe, given up justly to fleshly delights, bated her wing
apace downeward: and finding the ease she had from her
visible, and sensuous collegue the body in performance of
Religious duties, her pineons now broken, and flagging, shifted
off from her selfe, the labour of high soaring any more, forgot
her heavenly flight, and left the dull, and droyling carcas to

2. Milton claims that, because of Anglicanism, the Reformation
has lapsed into the codified ritualism of Judaism and the idolatrous
practices of Roman Catholicism ('Paganisme').

3. '*Arons* old wardrope' (cf. Exodus 28:2 ff.) is meant to describe
Judaic ritualism, and 'the *Flamins vestry*' the rituals enacted by
sacrificial priests ('flamines') in ancient Rome. Cf. previous note.

4. Set speeches.

plod on in the old rode, and drudging Trade of outward conformity. And here out of question from her pervers conceiting
of *God*, and holy things, she had faln to beleeve no *God* at all,
had not custome and the worme of conscience nipt her incred-
ulity hence to all the duty's of evangelicall grace instead of the
adoptive and cheerfull boldnesse which our new alliance with
God requires, came Servile, and thral-like feare: for in very
deed, the superstitious man by his good will is an Atheist; but
being scarr'd from thence by the pangs, and gripes of a boyling
conscience, all in a pudder shuffles up to himselfe such a *God*,
and such a *worship* as is most agreeable to remedy his feare,
which feare of his, as also is his hope, fixt onely upon the
Flesh, renders likewise the whole faculty of his apprehension,
carnall, and all the inward acts of *worship* issuing from the
native strength of the SOULE, run out lavishly to the upper
skin, and there harden into a crust of Formallitie. Hence men
came to scan the *Scriptures*, by the Letter, and in the Covenant
of our Redemption, magnifi'd the external signs more then the
quickning power of the *Spirit*, and yet looking on them through
their own guiltinesse with a Servile feare, and finding as little
comfort, or rather terror from them againe, they knew not how
to hide their Slavish approach to *Gods* behests by them not
understood, nor worthily receav'd, but by cloaking their Servile crouching to all *Religious* Presentments, somtimes lawfull,
somtimes Idolatrous, under the name of *humility*, and term-
ing the Py-bald frippery, and ostentation of Ceremony's,
decency.[5]

Then was Baptisme[6] chang'd into a kind of exorcism, and
water Sanctifi'd by *Christs* institute, thought little enough to
wash off the originall Spot without the Scratch, or crosse impression of a Priests fore-finger: and that feast of free grace,[7]

---

5. So Archbishop Laud had claimed to have striven 'for Decency
and an Orderly settlement of the Externall Worship of God' (see
Yale edn, I, 522–3).

6. One of the two sacraments (cf. next note) normally recognized
by Protestants. The ceremony to which Milton alludes is the Roman
Catholic practice of exorcism prior to the actual baptism.

7. The Lord's Supper.

and adoption to which *Christ* invited his Disciples to sit as
Brethren, and coheires of the happy Covenant, which at that
Table was to be Seal'd to them, even that Feast of love and
heavenly-admitted fellowship, the Seale of filiall grace became
the Subject of horror, and glouting adoration, pageanted about,
like a dreadfull Idol: which sometimes deceve's wel-meaning
men, and beguiles them of their reward, by their voluntary
humility, which indeed, is fleshly pride, preferring a foolish
Sacrifice, and the rudiments of the world, as Saint *Paul* to the
Colossians explaineth,[8] before a savory obedience to *Christs*
example. Such was *Peters* unseasonable Humilitie, as then his
Knowledge was small, when *Christ* came to wash his feet; who
at an impertinent time would needs straine courtesy with
his Master, and falling troublesomly upon the lowly, alwise,
and unexaminable intention of *Christ* in what he went with
resolution to doe, so provok't by his interruption the meeke
Lord, that he threat'nd to exclude him from his heavenly Portion, unlesse he could be content to be lesse arrogant, and
stiff neckt in his humility.[9]

But to dwell no longer in characterizing the *Depravities* of
the *Church*, and how they sprung, and how they tooke increase;
when I recall to mind at last, after so many darke Ages, wherein the huge overshadowing traine of *Error* had almost swept
all the Starres out of the Firmament of the *Church*; how the
bright and blissfull *Reformation* (by Divine Power) strook
through the black and settled Night of *Ignorance* and *Antichristian Tyranny*, me thinks a soveraigne and reviving joy
must needs rush into the bosome of him that reads or heares;
and the sweet Odour of the returning *Gospell* imbath his Soule
with the fragrancy of Heaven. Then was the Sacred BIBLE
sought out of the dusty corners where prophane Falshood and
Neglect had throwne it, the *Schooles* opened, *Divine* and
Humane Learning rak't out of the *embers* of *forgotten Tongues*,
the *Princes* and *Cities* trooping apace to the new erected
Banner of *Salvation*; the *Martyrs*, with the unresistable *might*

8. Colossians 2:8.
9. Cf. John 13:5–11.

of *Weaknesse*, shaking the *Powers* of *Darknesse*, and scorning the *fiery rage* of the old *red Dragon*.[10]

The pleasing pursuit of these thoughts hath oft-times led mee into a serious question and debatement with my selfe, how it should come to passe that *England* (having had this *grace* and *honour* from GOD to bee the first that should set up a Standard for the recovery of *lost Truth*, and blow the first *Evangelick Trumpet* to the *Nations*, holding up, as from a Hill, the new *Lampe* of *saving light* to all Christendome) should now be last, and most unsettl'd in the enjoyment of that *Peace*, whereof she taught the way to others; although indeed our *Wicklefs* preaching,[11] at which all the succeeding *Reformers* more effectually lighted their *Tapers*, was to his Countrey-men but a short blaze soone dampt and stifl'd by the *Pope*, and *Prelates* for sixe or seven Kings Reignes; yet me thinkes the *Precedencie* which GOD gave this *Iland*, to be the first *Restorer* of *buried Truth*, should have beene followed with more happy successe, and sooner attain'd Perfection; in which, as yet we are amongst the last: for, albeit in *purity* of *Doctrine* we agree with our Brethren; yet in Discipline, which is the *execution* and *applying* of *Doctrine* home, and laying the *salve* to the very *Orifice* of the *wound*; yea tenting and searching to the *Core*, without which *Pulpit Preaching* is but shooting at Rovers; in this we are no better then a *Schisme*, from all the *Reformation*, and a sore scandall to them; for while wee hold *Ordination* to belong onely to *Bishops*, as our *Prelates* doe, wee must of necessity hold also their *Ministers* to be no *Ministers*, and shortly after their *Church* to be no *Church*. Not to speake of those senceless *Ceremonies* which wee onely retaine, as a dangerous earnest of sliding back to *Rome*, and serving meerely, either as a mist to cover nakednesse where true *grace* is extinguisht; or as an Enterlude to set out the *pompe* of *Prelatisme*. Certainly it would be worth the while therefore and the paines, to enquire more particu-

---

10. Here as elsewhere Milton draws upon the imagery, and sometimes the phrasing, of the Book of Revelation.

11. John Wycliffe (1320?–84) was widely regarded by Protestants as the instigator of the Reformation in England. Milton expands the claim even further; but see also below, p. 236.

larly, what, and how many the cheife causes have been, that have still hindred our *Uniforme Consent* to the rest of the *Churches* abroad, (at this time especially) when the *Kingdome* is in a good *propensity* hereto; and all Men in Prayers, in Hopes, or in Disputes, either for or against it.

Yet will I not insist on that which may seeme to be the cause of GODS part; as his judgement on our sinnes, the tryall of his owne, the unmasking of Hypocrites; nor shall I stay to speake of the continuall eagernes and extreame diligence of the *Pope* and *Papists* to stop the furtherance of *Reformation*, which know they have no hold or hope of *England* their lost Darling, longer then the *government* of *Bishops* bolsters them out; and therefore plot all they can to uphold them, as may bee seene by the Booke of *Santa Clara* the Popish *Preist* in defence of *Bishops*,[12] which came out piping hot much about the time that one of our own *Prelats* out of an ominous feare had writ on the same *Argument*; as if they had joyn'd their forces like good Confederates to support one falling *Babel*.

But I shall cheifly indeavour to declare those Causes that hinder the forwarding of *true Discipline*, which are among our selves. Orderly proceeding will divide our inquirie into our *Fore-Fathers dayes*, and into *our Times*. HENRY the 8. was the first that rent this *Kingdome* from the *Popes* Subjection totally; but his Quarrell being more about *Supremacie*, then other faultinesse in *Religion* that he regarded, it is no marvell if hee stuck where he did. The next default was in the *Bishops*, who though they had renounc'd the *Pope*, they still hugg'd the *Popedome*, and shar'd the Authority among themselves, by their sixe bloody Articles[13] persecuting the *Protestants* no slacker then the *Pope* would have done. And doutles, when ever the *Pope* shall fall, if his ruine bee not like the sudden down-come of a *Towre*, the *Bishops*, when they see him tottering, will leave him, and fall to scrambling, catch who may, hee a Patriarch-

---

12. Possibly the *Apologia episcoporum seu sacri magistratus* (1640) by the Franciscan Sancta Clara, an English convert to Catholicism.

13. 'The Six Articles Act' which Henry VIII obliged Parliament to pass in 1539.

dome, and another what comes next to hand; as the French Cardinall of late, and the *See* of *Canterbury* hath plainly affected.[14]

In *Edward* the 6. Dayes, why a compleate *Reform* was not effected, to any considerate man may appeare. First, he no sooner entred into his Kingdome, but into a Warre with *Scotland*; from when the Protector[15] returning with Victory had but newly put his hand to repeale the 6. *Articles*, and throw the Images out of *Churches*, but Rebellions on all sides stir'd up by obdurate Papists, and other Tumults with a plaine Warre in *Norfolke*, holding tack against two of the Kings *Generals*,[16] made them of force content themselves with what they had already done. Hereupon follow'd ambitious Contentions among the *Peeres*, which ceas'd not but with the Protectors death, who was the most zealous in this point: and then *Northumberland* was hee that could doe most in *England*, who little minding *Religion*, (as his Apostacie well shew'd at his death), bent all his wit how to bring the Right of the *Crowne* into his owne Line. And for the *Bishops*, they were so far from any such worthy Attempts, as that they suffer'd themselvs to be the common stales[17] to countenance with their prostituted Gravities every Politick Fetch that was then on foot, as oft as the Potent *Statists* pleas'd to employ them. Never do we read that they made use of their Authority and high Place of accesse, to bring the jarring Nobility to *Christian peace*, or to withstand their disloyall Projects; but if a Toleration for *Masse* were to be beg'd of the King for his Sister MARY, lest CHARLES the Fifth should be angry; who but the grave Prelates *Cranmer* and

---

14. The 'French Cardinall' is Richelieu, who was said to have aspired to become patriarch of an independent Church of France. But 'the *See* of *Canterbury*' (i.e. Archbishop) was also said to have entertained ambitions involving a Patriarchate (see below, p. 225, Note 99).

15. Somerset.

16. Northampton and Warwick (later Northumberland); the latter managed to suppress a Catholic insurrection in Norfolk, and in time to oust Somerset.

17. Prostitutes.

Ridley[18] must be sent to extort it from the young King? But out of the mouth of that godly and Royall *Childe*, Christ himself return'd such an awfull repulse to those halting and timeserving *Prelates*, that after much bold importunity, they went their way not without shame and teares.

Nor was this the first time that they discover'd to bee followers of this World; for when the Protectors Brother, Lord *Sudley*, the Admirall through private malice and mal-engine was to lose his life,[19] no man could bee found fitter then Bishop *Latimer* (like another Doctor *Shaw*) to divulge in his Sermon the forged Accusations laid to his charge, thereby to defame him with the People, who else was thought would take ill the innocent mans death, unlesse the Reverend *Bishop* could warrant them there was no foule play. What could be more impious then to debarre the Children of the King from their right to the Crowne? To comply with the ambitious Usurpation of a Traytor; and to make void the last Will of HENRY 8. to which the Breakers had sworne observance? Yet Bishop *Cranmer*, one of the Executors, and the other *Bishops* none refusing, (lest they should resist the Duke of Northumberland) could find in their Consciences to set their hands to the disinabling and defeating not onely of Princesse MARY the *Papist*, but of ELIZABETH the *Protestant*, and (by the *Bishops* judgement) the Lawfull Issue of King HENRY.

Who then can thinke, (though these *Prelates* had sought a further *Reformation*) that the least wry face of a *Politician* would not have hush't them. But it will be said, These men were *Martyrs*: What then? Though every true Christian will be a *Martyr* when he is called to it; not presently does it follow that every one suffering for Religion, is without exception. Saint

---

18. Milton's adverse view of Archbishop Cranmer and Bishop Ridley is singular; later, he even dismisses their martyrdom under Queen Mary. The 'Royall *Childe*' is, of course, Edward VI.

19. He had mounted an abortive plot against his brother Somerset, the Protector, and Edward VI. Latimer was later to be burnt at the stake, together with Ridley (previous note). 'Doctor [Ralph] *Shaw*' had maintained in a sermon that the legitimate heir to the throne was Richard Gloucester, not Edward.

Paul writes, that *A man may give his Body to be burnt,* (meaning for Religion) *and yet not have Charitie* :[20] He is not therfore above all possibility of erring, because hee burnes for some Points of Truth.

Witnes the *Arians* and *Pelagians*[21] which were slaine by the Heathen for *Christs* sake; yet we take both these for no true friends of *Christ*. If the *Martyrs* (saith *Cyprian* in his 30. Epistle)[22] decree one thing, and the *Gospel* another, either the *Martyrs* must lose their Crowne by not observing the *Gospel* for which they are *Martyrs*; or the Majestie of the *Gospel* must be broken and lie flat, if it can be overtopt by the *novelty* of any other *Decree*.

And heerewithall I invoke the *Immortall* DEITIE *Reveler* and *Judge* of secrets, That wherever I have in this BOOKE plainely and roundly (though worthily and truly) laid open the faults and blemishes of *Fathers, Martyrs,* or Christian *Emperors;* or have otherwise inveighed against Error and Superstition with vehement Expressions: I have done it, neither out of malice, nor list to speak evill, nor any vaine-glory; but of meere necessity, to vindicate the spotless *Truth* from an ignominious bondage, whose native worth is now become of such a low esteeme, that shee is like to finde small credit with us for what she can say, unlesse shee can bring a Ticket from *Cranmer, Latimer,* and *Ridley;* or prove her selfe a retainer to *Constantine,* and weare his *badge.*[23] More tolerable it were for the *Church* of GOD that all these Names were utterly abolisht, like the *Brazen Serpent;*[24] then that mens fond opinion should thus idolize them, and the Heavenly *Truth* be thus captivated.

Now to proceed, whatsoever the *Bishops* were, it seemes they themselves were unsatisfi'd in matters of *Religion,* as they

---

20. I Corinthians 13:3.

21. The Arians had denied that the Son of God is equal to the Father; the Pelagians, that Grace has absolute primacy in man's salvation.

22. Not in fact St Cyprian's own epistle, but an address to him.

23. The Emperor Constantine the Great is here regarded as representative of the Catholic Church.

24. Cf. Numbers 21:9.

then stood, by that Commission[25] granted to 8. *Bishops*, 8. other *Divines*, 8. *Civilians*, 8. *common Lawyers*, to frame *Ecclesiasticall Constitutions*; which no wonder if it came to nothing for (as *Hayward*[26] relates) both their Professions and their Ends were different. Lastly, we all know by Examples, that exact *Reformation* is not perfited at the first push, and those unweildy Times of *Edward 6.* may hold some Plea by this excuse: Now let any reasonable man judge whether that *Kings Reigne* be a fit time from whence to patterne out the Constitution of a *Church Discipline*, much lesse that it should yeeld occasion from whence to foster and establish the continuance of Imperfection with the commendatory subscriptions of *Confessors* and *Martyrs*, to intitle and ingage a glorious *Name* to a grosse *corruption*. It was not *Episcopacie* that wrought in them the Heavenly Fortitude of *Martyrdome*; as little is it that *Martyrdome* can make good *Episcopacie*: But it was *Episcopacie* that led the good and Holy Men through the temptation of the *Enemie*, and the snare of this present world to many blameworthy and opprobrious *Actions*. And it is still *Episcopacie* that before all our eyes worsens and sluggs the most learned, and seeming religious of our *Ministers*, who no sooner advanc't to it, but like a seething pot set to coole, sensibly exhale and reake out the greatest part of that zeale, and those Gifts which were formerly in them, settling in a skinny congealment of ease and sloth at the top: and if they keep their Learning by some potent sway of Nature, 'tis a rare chance; but their *devotion* most commonly comes to that queazy temper of luke-warmnesse, that gives a Vomit to GOD himselfe.[27]

But what doe wee suffer mis-shapen and enormous *Prelatisme* as we do, thus to blanch and varnish her deformities with the faire colours, as before of *Martyrdome*, so now of *Episcopacie*? They are not *Bishops*, GOD and all *good Men* know they

---

25. Thirty-two authorities assisted Cranmer to revise ecclesiastical polity, but they failed to secure parliamentary approval.

26. Sir John Hayward, the Elizabethan historian, whose *Life and Raigne of King Edward the Sixt* is one of Milton's major sources.

27. Cf. the Introduction, above, p. 24.

are not, that have fill'd this Land with late confusion and violence; but a Tyrannicall crew and Corporation of Impostors,
that have blinded and abus'd the World so long under that
Name. He that inabl'd with *gifts* from *God*, and the lawfull and
Primitive choyce of the *Church* assembl'd in convenient number, faithfully from that time forward feeds his Parochial *Flock*,
ha's his coequall and compresbyteriall Power to ordaine *Ministers* and *Deacons* by Publique *Prayer*, and *Vote* of *Christs*
Congregation in like sort as he himselfe was ordain'd, and is a
true *Apostolick Bishop*. But when hee steps up into the Chayre
of *Pontificall* Pride, and changes a moderate and exemplary
House, for a mis-govern'd and haughty *Palace*, *spirituall Dignity*
for carnall *Precedence*, and *secular high Office* and *employment*
for the *high Negotiations* of his Heavenly *Embassage*, Then he
degrades, then hee *un-Bishops* himselfe; hee that makes him
Bishop makes him no *Bishop*. No marvell therfore if S. *Martin*
complain'd to *Sulpitius Severus*[28] that since hee was *Bishop* he
felt inwardly a sensible decay of those *vertues* and *graces* that
God had given him in great measure before; Although the same
Sulpitius write that he was nothing tainted, or alter'd in his
habit, *dyet*, or personall *demeanour* from that simple plainnesse
to which he first betook himselfe. It was not therfore that
thing alone which *God* tooke displeasure at in the *Bishops* of
those times, but rather an universall rottennes, and gangrene
in the whole *Function*.

From hence then I passe to Qu. ELIZABETH, the next *Protestant* Prince, in whose Dayes why *Religion* attain'd not a
perfect reducement in the beginning of her Reigne, I suppose the
hindring Causes will be found to bee common with some
formerly alleg'd for King EDWARD 6. the greennesse of the
Times, the weake Estate which Qu. MARY left the Realme in,
the great Places and Offices executed by *Papists*, the *Judges*,
the *Lawyers*, the *Justices* of Peace for the most part *Popish*, the
Bishops firme to *Rome*, from whence was to be expected the
furious flashing of Excommunications, and absolving the *People*

---

28. Sulpicius Severus (363–410) wrote among other things a hagio-
graphy of St. Martin by whom he had been converted.

from their Obedience. Next, her private *Councellours*, whoever they were, perswaded her (as *Camden*[29] writes) that the altering of *Ecclesiasticall Policie* would move sedition. Then was the *Liturgie* given to a number of moderate *Divines*, and Sir *Tho. Smith* a Statesman[30] to bee purg'd, and Physick't: And surely they were moderate *Divines* indeed, neither hot nor cold; and *Grindall*[31] the best of them, afterwards *Arch-Bishop* of *Canterbury* lost favour in the Court, and I think was discharg'd the government of his *See* for favouring the *Ministers*, though *Camden* seeme willing to finde another Cause: therefore about her second Yeare in a *Parliament* of Men and Minds some scarce well grounded, others belching the soure Crudities of yesterdayes *Poperie*, those Constitutions of EDW. 6. which as you heard before, no way satisfi'd the men that made them, are now establish't for best, and not to be mended. From that time follow'd nothing but Imprisonments, troubles, disgraces on all those that found fault with the *Decrees* of the Convocation, and strait were they branded with the Name of *Puritans*. As for the Queene her selfe, shee was made beleeve that by putting downe *Bishops* her *Prerogative* would be infring'd, of which shall be spoken anon, as the course of Method brings it in. And why the *Prelats* labour'd it should be so thought, ask not them, but ask their Bellies. They had found a good Tabernacle, they sate under a spreading Vine, their Lot was fallen in a faire Inheritance. And these perhaps were the cheife impeachments of a more sound rectifying the *Church* in the Queens Time.

From this Period I count to begin our Times, which, because they concerne us more neerely, and our owne eyes and eares can give us the ampler scope to judge, will require a more exact search; and to effect this the speedier, I shall distinguish such as I esteeme to be the hinderers of *Reformation* into 3. sorts, *Antiquitarians* (for so I had rather call them then *Anti-*

---

29. William Camden, the historian of Elizabeth's reign (*Annales*, 1615–27; also invoked below, p. 353).

30. Author of the celebrated *Commonwealth of England* (1583).

31. Edmund Grindal (1519–83).

quaries, whose labours are usefull and laudable) 2. *Libertines,* 3. *Politicians.*[32]

.   .   .   .

Now Sir, for the love of holy *Reformation,* what can be said more against these importunat clients of Antiquity, then she her selfe their patronesse hath said. Whether think ye would she approve still to dote upon immeasurable, innumerable, and therfore unnecessary, and unmercifull volumes, choosing rather to erre with the specious name of the Fathers, or to take a sound Truth at the hand of a plain upright man that all his dayes hath bin diligently reading the holy Scriptures, and therto imploring *Gods* grace, while the admirers of Antiquity have bin beating their brains about their *Ambones,* their *Diptychs,* and *Meniaia's?*[33] Now, he that cannot tell of Stations, and Indictions;[34] nor has wasted his pretious howrs in the endles conferring of Councels and Conclaves that demolish one another, although I know many of those that pretend to be great Rabbies[35] in these studies have scarce saluted them from the strings, and the titlepage, or to give 'em more, have bin but the Ferrets and Moushunts of an Index: yet what Pastor, or Minister how learned, religious, or discreet soever does not now bring both his cheeks full blown with Oecumenical, and Synodical, shall be counted a lank, shallow, unsufficient man, yea a dunce, and not worthy to speak about *Reformation* of *Church Discipline.* But I trust they for whom *God* hath reserv'd the honour of Reforming this Church will easily perceive their adversaries drift in thus calling for Antiquity, they feare the plain field of the Scriptures; the chase is too hot; they seek the dark, the bushie, the tangled Forrest, they would imbosk: they

---

32. The lengthy section here omitted demonstrates, with evidence provided from a variety of sources, that the 'Antiquitarians' hindered the Reformation by falsifying the record to ensure for bishops a position of unwarranted authority.

33. Elaborate pulpits, wax writing tablets, and prayers for feasts.

34. Places of devotion, and periods of fifteen years in papal documents. (Each of the two words could also mean 'fast'.)

35. i.e. rabbis.

feel themselvs strook in the transparent streams of divine Truth, they would plunge, and tumble, and thinke to ly hid in the foul weeds, and muddy waters, where no plummet can reach the bottome. But let them beat themselvs like Whales, and spend their oyl till they be dradg'd ashoar: though wherfore should the Ministers give them so much line for shifts, and delays? Wherfore should they not urge only the Gospel, and hold it ever in their faces like a mirror of Diamond, till it dazle, and pierce their misty ey balls? maintaining it the honour of its absolute sufficiency, and supremacy inviolable: For if the Scripture be for *Reformation*, and Antiquity to boot, 'tis but an advantage to the dozen, 'tis no winning cast: and though Antiquity be against it, while the Scriptures be for it, the Cause is as good as ought to be wisht, Antiquity it selfe sitting Judge.

But to draw to an end; the second sort of those that may be justly number'd among the hinderers of *Reformation*, are Libertines, these suggest that the Discipline sought would be intolerable: for one Bishop now in a Dioces we should then have a Pope in every Parish. It will not be requisit to Answer these men, but only to discover them, for reason they have none, but lust, and licentiousnes, and therfore answer can have none. It is not any Discipline that they could live under, it is the corruption, and remisnes of Discipline that they seek. Episcopacy duly executed, yea the Turkish, and Jewish rigor against whoring, and drinking; the dear, and tender Discipline of a Father; the sociable, and loving reproof of a Brother; the bosome admonition of a Friend is a *Presbytery*, and a Consistory to them. 'Tis only the merry Frier in *Chaucer* can disple them.

> Full sweetly heard he confession
> And pleasant was his absolution,
> He was an easie man to give pennance.[36]

And so I leave them: and referre the political discourse of Episcopacy to a Second Book.

---

36. *The Canterbury Tales*: General Prologue, ll. 221-3.

THE SECOND BOOK.

Sir,

IT is a work good, and prudent to be able to guide one man; of larger extended vertue to order wel one house; but to govern a Nation piously, and justly, which only is to say happily, is for a spirit of the greatest size, and divinest mettle. And certainly of no lesse a mind, nor of lesse excellence in another way, were they who by writing layd the solid, and true foundations of this Science, which being of greatest importance to the life of man, yet there is no art that hath bin more canker'd in her principles, more soyl'd, and slubber'd with aphorisming pedantry then the art of policie; and that most, where a man would thinke should least be, in Christian Common-wealths. They teach not that to govern well is to train up a Nation in true wisdom and vertue, and that which springs from thence magnanimity, (take heed of that) and that which is our beginning, regeneration, and happiest end, likenes to *God*, which in one word we call *godlines*, & that this is the true florishing of a Land, other things follow as the shadow does the substance: to teach thus were meer pulpitry to them. This is the masterpiece of a modern politician, how to qualifie, and mould the sufferance and subjection of the people to the length of that foot that is to tread on their necks, how rapine may serve it selfe with the fair, and honourable pretences of publick good, how the puny Law may be brought under the wardship, and controul of lust, and will; in which attempt if they fall short, then must a superficial colour of reputation by all means direct or indirect be gotten to wash over the unsightly bruse of honor. To make men governable in this manner their precepts mainly tend to break a nationall spirit, and courage by count'nancing open riot, luxury, and ignorance, till having thus disfigur'd and made men beneath men, as *Juno* in the Fable of *Iö*,[37] they deliver up the poor transformed heifer of the Commonwealth to

---

37. Beloved of Zeus, Io was transformed into a heifer to protect her from Hera's (Juno's) jealousy; but Hera set the herdsman Argus to watch her, and when he failed in his mission, the goddess sent a gadfly that drove Io through the world.

be stung and vext with the breese, and goad of oppression under the custody of some *Argus* with a hundred eyes of jealousie.[38] To be plainer Sir, how to soder, how to stop a leak, how to keep up the floting carcas of a crazie, and diseased Monarchy, or State betwixt wind, and water, swimming still upon her own dead lees, that now is the deepe designe of a politician. Alas Sir! a Commonwelth ought to be but as one huge Christian personage, one mighty growth, and stature of an honest man, as big, and compact in vertue as in body; for looke what the grounds, and causes are of single happines to one man, the same yee shall find them to a whole state, as *Aristotle* both in his ethicks, and politiks,[39] from the principles of reason layes down; by consequence therfore, that which is good, and agreeable to monarchy, will appeare soonest to be so, by being good, and agreeable to the true wel-fare of every Christian, and that which can be justly prov'd hurtfull, and offensive to every true Christian, wilbe evinc't to be alike hurtful to monarchy: for *God* forbid, that we should separate and distinguish the end, and good of a monarch, from the end and good of the monarchy, or of that, from Christianity. How then this third, and last sort that hinder reformation,[40] will justify that it stands not with reason of state, I much muse? For certain I am, the *Bible* is shut against them, as certaine that neither *Plato*, nor *Aristotle* is for their turnes. What they can bring us now from the Schools of *Loyola* with his Jesuites,[41] or their *Malvezzi* that can cut *Tacitus* into slivers and steaks,[42] we shall presently hear. They alledge 1. That the Church government must be conformable to the civill politie, next, that no forme of Church government is agreeable to monarchy, but that of Bishops. Must

---

38. Argus (previous note) is said to have had eyes all over his body.

39. Cf. *Ethics*, I, 9, and *Politics*, VII, 2.

40. i.e. the politicians (above, p. 89).

41. St. Ignatius Loyola (1491–1556) was the founder of the Society of Jesus.

42. The learned Virgilio Malvezzi's *Discourses upon Cornelius Tacitus* was to be translated into English a year after Milton's treatise was published.

Church government that is appointed in the Gospel, and has chief respect to the soul, be conformable, and pliant to civil, that is arbitrary, and chiefly conversant about the visible and external part of man? this is the very maxim that moulded the Calvs of *Bethel* and of *Dan*, this was the quintessence of *Jeroboams* policy, he made Religion conform to his politick interests, & this was the sin that watcht over the Israelites till their final captivity.[43] If this State principle come from the Prelates, as they affect to be counted statists, let them look back to *Elutherius* Bishop of *Rome*,[44] and see what he thought of the policy of *England*; being requir'd by *Lucius* the first Christian King of this Iland to give his counsel for the founding of Religious Laws, little thought he of this sage caution, but bids him betake himselfe to the old, and new Testament, and receive direction from them how to administer both Church, and Commonwealth; that he was *Gods* Vicar, and therefore to rule by *Gods* Laws, that the Edicts of *Cæsar* we may at all times disallow, but the Statutes of *God* for no reason we may reject. Now certaine if Church-government be taught in the Gospel, as the Bishops dare not deny, we may well conclude of what late standing this Position is, newly calculated for the altitude of Bishop elevation and lettice for their lips. But by what example can they shew that the form of Church Discipline must be minted, and modell'd out to secular pretences? The ancient Republick of the Jews is evident to have run through all the changes of civil estate, if we survey the Story from the giving of the Law to the *Herods*, yet did one manner of Priestly government serve without inconvenience to all these temporal mutations: it serv'd the mild Aristocracy of elective Dukes, and heads of Tribes joyn'd with them; the dictatorship of the Judges, the easie, or hard-handed Monarchy's, the domestick, or forrain tyrannies, Lastly the Roman Senat from without, the Jewish Senat at home with the Galilean Tetrarch, yet the Levites had some right to deal in civil affairs: but seeing the Evangelical precept[45] forbids Church-

---

43. I Kings 12:26–33.

44. According to Bede's *Church History* (I, 4), Pope Eleutherius was instrumental in the conversion of King Lucius.

45. Cf. I John 2:15–17.

men to intermeddle with worldly imployments, what inter-weavings, or interworkings can knit the Minister, and the Magis-trate in their several functions to the regard of any precise correspondency? Seeing that the Churchmans office is only to teach men the Christian Faith, to exhort all, to incourage the good, to admonish the bad, privately the lesse offender, pub-lickly the scandalous and stubborn; to censure, and separate from the communion of *Christs* flock, the contagious, and in-corrigible, to receive with joy, and fatherly compassion the penitent, all this must be don, and more then this is beyond any Church autority. What is all this either here, or there to the temporal regiment of Wealpublick, whether it be Popular, Princely, or Monarchical? Where doth it intrench upon the temporal governor, where does it come in his walk? where does it make inrode upon his jurisdiction? Indeed if the Min-isters part be rightly discharg'd, it renders him the people more conscionable, quiet, and easie to be govern'd, if otherwise his life and doctrine will declare him. If therfore the Constitution of the Church be already set down by divine prescript, as all sides confesse, then can she not be a handmaid to wait on civil commodities, and respects: and if the nature and limits of Church Discipline be such, as are either helpfull to all political estates indifferently, or have no particular relation to any, then is there no necessity, nor indeed possibility of linking the one with the other in a speciall conformation.

Now for their second conclusion, *That no form of Church government is agreeable to Monarchy, but that of Bishops,*[46] although it fall to pieces of it selfe by that which hath bin sayd: yet to give them play front, and reare, it shall be my task to prove that Episcopacy with that Autority which it challenges in *England* is not only not agreeable, but tending to the destruc-tion of Monarchy.[47]

.   .   .   .

... the fall of Prelacy, whose actions are so farre distant from *Justice*, cannot shake the least fringe that borders the royal

---

46. Cf. the celebrated dictum of King James I, 'No bishop, no king'.

47. The 'proof' is duly provided in several pages here omitted.

canopy: but that their standing doth continually oppose, and lay battery to regal safety, shall by that which follows easily appear. Amongst many secondary, and accessory causes that support Monarchy, these are not of least reckning, though common to all other States: the love of the Subjects, the multitude, and valor of the people, and store of treasure. In all these things hath the Kingdome bin of late sore weak'nd, and chiefly by the Prelates. First let any man consider, that if any Prince shall suffer under him a commission of autority to be exerciz'd, till all the Land grone, and cry out, as against a whippe of Scorpions, whether this be not likely to lessen, and keel the affections of the Subject. Next what numbers of faithfull, and freeborn Englishmen, and good Christians have bin constrain'd to forsake their dearest home, their friends, and kindred whom nothing but the wide Ocean, and the savage deserts of *America* could hide and shelter from the fury of the Bishops.[48] O Sir, if we could but see the shape of our deare Mother *England*, as Poets are wont to give a personal form to what they please, how would she appeare, think ye, but in a mourning weed, with ashes upon her head, and teares abundantly flowing from her eyes, to behold so many of her children expos'd at once, and thrust from things of dearest necessity, because their conscience could not assent to things which the Bishops thought *indifferent*. What more binding then Conscience? what more free then *indifferency*? cruel then must that *indifferency* needs be, that shall violate the strict necessity of Conscience, merciles, and inhumane that free choyse, and liberty that shall break asunder the bonds of Religion. Let the Astrologer be dismay'd at the portentous blaze of comets, and impressions in the aire as foretelling troubles and changes to states: I shall beleeve there cannot be a more illboding signe to a Nation (*God* turne the Omen from us) then when the Inhabitants, to avoid insufferable grievances at home, are inforc'd by heaps to forsake their native Country. Now wheras the only remedy, and amends against the depopulation, and thinnesse of a Land within, is

---

48. It has been estimated that over 20,000 Englishmen left for New England during the period 1629–40 alone.

the borrow'd strength of firme alliance from without, these Priestly policies of theirs having thus exhausted our domestick forces, have gone the way also to leave us as naked of our firmest, & faithfullest neighbours abroad, by disparaging and alienating from us all Protestant Princes, and Commonwealths,[49] who are not ignorant that our Prelats, and as many as they can infect, account them no better then a sort of sacrilegious, and puritanical Rebels, preferring the *Spaniard* our deadly enemy before them, and set all orthodox writers at nought in comparison of the Jesuits, who are indeed the onely corrupters of youth, and good learning; and I have heard many wise, and learned men in *Italy* say as much. It cannot be that the strongest knot of confederacy should not dayly slak'n, when Religion which is the chiefe ingagement of our league shall be turn'd to their reproach. Hence it is that the prosperous, and prudent states of the united Provinces,[50] whom we ought to love, if not for themselves, yet for our own good work in them, they having bin in a manner planted, and erected by us, and having bin since to us the faithfull watchmen, and discoverers of many a Popish, and Austrian complotted Treason, and with us the partners of many a bloody, and victorious battell, whom the similitude of manners and language, the commodity of traffick, which founded the old Burgundian league betwixt us, but chiefly Religion should bind to us immortally, even such friends as these, out of some principles instill'd into us by the Prelates, have bin often dismist with distastfull answers, and somtimes unfriendly actions: nor is it to be consider'd to the breach of confederate Nations whose mutual interest is of such high consequence, though their Merchants bicker in the East Indies,[51] neither is it safe, or warie, or indeed Christianly, that the *French* King, of a different Faith, should afford our neerest Allyes as

49. Especially the Dutch, who had rightly suspected Charles I of collusion with Spain.

50. i.e. of Holland, which England had already sustained, just as the Dutch had themselves alerted Elizabeth of the 'complotted Treason' to depose her.

51. The Dutch East India Company had obliged English traders to retire from the Spice Islands and other areas.

good protection as we.[52] Sir, I perswade my selfe, if our zeale to true Religion, and the brotherly usage of our truest friends were as notorious to the world, as our *Prelatical Schism*, and captivity to *Rotchet Apothegmes*,[53] we had ere this seene our old Conquerours, and afterward Liege-men the *Normans*, together with the *Brittains* our proper Colony, and all the *Gascoins* that are the rightfull *Dowry* of our ancient Kings,[54] come with cap, and knee, desiring the shadow of the *English* Scepter to defend them from the hot persecutions and taxes of the *French*. But when they come hither, and see a Tympany of *Spanioliz'd Bishops* swaggering in the fore-top of the State, and meddling to turne, and dandle the *Royall Ball* with unskilfull and *Pedantick palmes*, no marvell though they think it as unsafe to commit Religion, and liberty to their arbitrating as to a Synagogue of Jesuits.

But what doe I stand reck'ning upon advantages, and gaines lost by the mis-rule, and turbulency of the *Prelats*, what doe I pick up so thriftily their scatterings and diminishings of the meaner Subject, whilst they by their seditious practises have indanger'd to loose the King one third of his main Stock; what have they done to banish him from his owne Native Countrey? but to speake of this as it ought would ask a Volume by it selfe.

Thus as they have unpeopl'd the Kingdome by expulsion of so many thousands, as they have endeavor'd to lay the skirts of it bare by disheartning and dishonouring our loyallest Confederates abroad, so have they hamstrung the valour of the Subject by seeking to effeminate us all at home. Well knows every wise Nation that their Liberty consists in manly and honest labours, in sobriety and rigorous honour to the Marriage Bed, which in both Sexes should be bred up from chast hopes to loyall Enjoyments; and when the people slacken, and fall

---

52. In 1632 the Dutch had been offered an alliance against Spain by Richelieu.

53. A reference to the Anglican predilection for apophthegms – possibly including James's own (above, p. 94, Note 46).

54. Until its capture in 1451, Gascony had been claimed by England.

to loosenes, and riot, then doe they as much as if they laid
downe their necks for some wily Tyrant to get up and ride.
Thus learnt *Cyrus* to tame the *Lydians*,[55] whom by Armes he
could not, whilst they kept themselves from Luxury; with one
easy Proclamation to set up *Stews*, dancing, feasting, & dicing
he made them soone his slaves. I know not what drift the
Prelats had, whose Brokers they were to prepare, and supple us
either for a Forreigne Invasion or Domestick oppression; but this
I am sure they took the ready way to despoile us both of *man-hood* and *grace* at once, and that in the shamefullest and un-godliest manner upon that day which Gods Law, and even
our own reason hath consecrated, that we might have one day
at least of seven[56] set apart wherein to examin and encrease our
knowledge of God, to meditate, and commune of our Faith, our
Hope, our eternall City in Heaven, and to quick'n, withall,
the study, and exercise of Charity; at such a time that men
should bee pluck't from their soberest and saddest thoughts,
and by *Bishops* the pretended *Fathers of the Church* instigated
by publique Edict, and with earnest indeavour push't forward
to gaming, jigging, wassailing, and mixt dancing is a horror to
think. Thus did the Reprobate hireling Preist *Balaam* seeke to
subdue the Israelites to *Moab*, if not by force, then by this
divellish *Pollicy*, to draw them from the Sanctuary of God to
the luxurious, and ribald feasts of *Baal-peor*.[57] Thus have they
trespas't not onely against the *Monarchy of England*, but of
Heaven also, as others, I doubt not, can prosecute against them.

I proceed within my own bounds to shew you next what
good Agents they are about the Revennues and Riches of the
Kingdome, which declares of what moment they are to *Mon-archy*, or what availe. Two Leeches they have that still suck,
and suck the Kingdome, their Ceremonies, and their Courts.
If any man will contend that Ceremonies bee lawfull under the
Gospell, hee may bee answer'd otherwhere. This doubtlesse
that they ought to bee many and over-costly, no true *Protestant*

55. Cf. Herodotus, I, 155.

56. Milton adds his voice to the swelling chorus for the preserva-tion of the Sabbath.

57. Numbers 22–25.

will affirme. Now I appeale to all wise men, what an excessive wast of Treasury hath beene within these few yeares in this Land not in the expedient, but in the Idolatrous erection of Temples beautified exquisitely to out-vie the Papists, the costly and deare-bought Scandals, and snares of Images, Pictures, rich Coaps, gorgeous Altar-clothes: and by the courses they tooke, and the opinions they held, it was not likely any stay would be, or any end of their madnes, where a pious pretext is so ready at hand to cover their insatiate desires. What can we suppose this will come to? What other materials then these have built up the *spirituall* BABEL to the heighth of her Abominations? Beleeve it Sir right truly it may be said, that *Antichrist* is *Mammons* Son. The soure levin[58] of humane Traditions mixt in one putrifi'd Masse with the poisonous dregs of hypocrisie in the hearts of *Prelates* that lye basking in the Sunny warmth of Wealth, and Promotion, is the Serpents Egge that will hatch an *Antichrist* wheresoever, and ingender the same Monster as big, or little as the Lump is which breeds him. If the splendor of *Gold* and *Silver* begin to Lord it once againe in the Church of *England*, wee shall see *Antichrist* shortly wallow heere, though his cheife Kennell be at *Rome*. If they had one thought upon *Gods glory* and the advancement of Christian Faith, they would be a meanes that with these expences thus profusely throwne away in trash, rather *Churches* and *Schools* might be built, where they cry out for want, and more added where too few are; a moderate maintenance distributed to every painfull Minister, that now scarse sustaines his Family with Bread, while the *Prelats* revell like *Belshazzar*[59] with their full carouses in *Goblets*, and *vessels* of *gold* snatcht from *Gods Temple*. Which (I hope) the Worthy Men of our Land will consider. Now then for their COURTS. What a Masse of Money is drawne from the Veines into the Ulcers of the Kingdome this way; their Extortions, their open Corruptions, the multitude of hungry and ravenous Harpies that swarme about their Offices declare sufficiently. And what though all this go not oversea? 'twere

58. Cf. Matthew 16:6 ('beware of the leaven of the Pharisees and of the Sadducees').

59. Daniel 5:1–5.

better it did; better a penurious Kingdom, then where excessive wealth flowes into the *gracelesse* and injurious hands of common sponges to the impoverishing of good and loyall men, and that by such execrable, such irreligious courses.

If the sacred and dreadfull works of holy *Discipline*, *Censure*, *Pennance*, *Excommunication*, and *Absolution*, where no profane thing ought to have accesse, nothing to be assistant but sage and Christianly *Admonition*, brotherly *Love*, flaming *Charity*, and *Zeale*; and then according to the Effects, Paternall *Sorrow*, or Paternall *Joy*, milde *Severity*, melting *Compassion*, if such Divine *Ministries* as these, wherin the Angel of the *Church* represents the Person of *Christ Jesus*, must lie prostitute to sordid Fees, and not passe to and fro betweene our Saviour that of free grace redeem'd us, and the submissive Penitent, without the truccage of perishing Coine, and the Butcherly execution of Tormentors, Rooks, and Rakeshames sold to lucre, then have the Babilonish Marchants of *Soules* just excuse. Hitherto Sir you have heard how the *Prelates* have weaken'd and withdrawne the externall Accomplishments of Kingly prosperity, the love of the People, their multitude, their valour, their wealth; mining, and sapping the out-works, and redoubts of *Monarchy*; now heare how they strike at the very heart, and vitals.

We know that *Monarchy* is made up of two parts, the Liberty of the subject, and the supremacie of the King. I begin at the root. See what gentle, and benigne Fathers they have beene to our liberty. Their trade being, by the same Alchymy that the *Pope* uses, to extract heaps of *gold*, and *silver* out of the drossie *Bullion* of the Peoples sinnes, and justly fearing that the quick-sighted *Protestants* eye clear'd in great part from the mist of Superstition, may at one time or other looke with a good judgement into these their deceitfull Pedleries, to gaine as many associats of guiltines as they can, and to infect the temporall Magistrate with the like lawlesse though not sacrilegious extortion, see a while what they doe; they ingage themselves to preach, and persuade an assertion for truth the most false, and to this *Monarchy* the most pernicious and destructive that could bee chosen. What more banefull to *Monarchy* then

Popular Commotion, for the dissolution of *Monarchy* slides ptest into a *Democraty*; and what stirs the Englishmen, as our wisest writers have observ'd, sooner to rebellion, then violent, nd heavy hands upon their goods and purses? Yet these devout *Prelates*, spight of our great Charter, and the soules of ur Progenitors that wrested their liberties out of the *Norman* ripe with their dearest blood and highest prowesse, for these many years have not ceas't in their Pulpits wrinching, and praining the *text*, to set at nought and trample under foot all he most sacred, and life blood Lawes, Statutes, and Acts of *Parliament* that are the holy Cov'nant of Union, and Marriage betweene the King and his Realme, by proscribing, and confiscating from us all the right we have to our owne bodies, goods and liberties. What is this, but to blow a trumpet, and proclaime a fire-crosse to a hereditary, and perpetuall civill warre. Thus much against the Subjects Liberty hath been assaulted by them. Now how they have spar'd Supremacie, or likely are hereafter to submit to it, remaines lastly to bee consider'd.

The emulation that under the old Law was in the King toward the *Preist*, is now so come about in the Gospell, that all the danger is to be fear'd from the *Preist* to the *King*. Whilst the *Preists Office* in the Law was set out with an exteriour lustre of Pomp and glory, Kings were ambitious to be *Preists*; now *Priests* not perceiving the heavenly brightnesse, and inward splendor of their more glorious *Evangelick Ministry* with as great ambition affect to be Kings; as in all their courses is easie to be observ'd. Their eyes ever imminent upon wordly matters, their desires ever thirsting after wordly employments, in stead of diligent and fervent studie in the Bible, they covet to be experts in Canons, and Decretals, which may inable them to judge, and interpose in temporall Causes, however pretended *Ecclesiasticall*. Doe they not hord up *Pelfe*, seeke to bee potent in *secular Strength*, in *State Affaires*, in *Lands, Lordships*, and *Demeanes*, to *sway* and carry all before them in *high Courts*, and *Privie Counsels*, to bring into their grasp, the *high*, and *principall Offices* of the Kingdom? have they not been bold of late to check the *Common Law*, to slight and brave the indiminishable Majestie of our highest Court the Law-giving and

Sacred *Parliament*? Doe they not plainly labour to exemp
Churchmen from the *Magistrate*? Yea, so presumptuously as t
question, and menace *Officers* that represent the *Kings Perso*
for using their Authority against drunken *Preists*? The cause o
protecting *murderous Clergie-men* was the first heart-burnin
that swel'd up the audacious *Becket* to the pestilent, and odiou
vexation of *Henry* the second. Nay more, have not some o
their devoted Schollers begun, I need not say to nibble, bu
openly to argue against the Kings *Supremacie*? is not the Cheif
of them[60] accus'd out of his owne Booke, and his *lat*
Canons to affect a certaine unquestionable *Patriarchat*, inde
pendent and unsubordinate to the Crowne? From whenc
having first brought us to a servile *Estate* of *Religion*, an
Manhood, and having predispos'd his conditions with the *Pope*
that layes claime to this *Land*, or some *Pepin* of his own creat
ing,[61] it were all as likely for him to aspire to the *Monarch*
among us, as that the *Pope* could finde meanes so on the sudde
both to bereave the Emperour of the *Roman Territory* with th
favour of *Italy*, and by an unexpected friend out of *France*
while he was in danger to lose his *new-got Purchase*, beyon
hope to leap in to the faire *Exarchat* of *Ravenna*. A good whil
the *Pope* suttl'y acted the *Lamb*, writing to the Emperour, my
Lord *Tiberius*, my Lord *Mauritius*, but no sooner did this hi
Lord pluck at the Images, and Idols, but hee threw off hi
Sheepes clothing, and started up a Wolfe, laying his pawes upo
the Emperours right, as forfeited to *Peter*. Why may not wee a
well, having been forewarn'd at home by our renowned *Chaucer*
and from abroad by the great and learned *Padre Paolo*,[62] from
the like beginnings, as we see they are, feare the like events

---

60. Archbishop Laud.

61. In an earlier section here omitted, Milton had mentioned how
Chilperic – 'the rightfull K[ing] of *France*' – had been dethroned 'by
Papall sentence' in favour of Pippin. The service was repaid whe
Pippin won Ravenna for the Pope.

62. On Chaucer, see above, p. 90. 'Padre Paolo' is Paolo Sarpi
author of *The Historie of the Councel of Trent* (translated int
English in 1620), elsewhere described by Milton as 'the great un
masker of the *Trentine* Councel' (below, p. 205).

Certainly a wise, and provident King ought to suspect a *Hier-archy* in his Realme, being ever attended, as it is, with two such greedy Purveyers, Ambition and Usurpation, I say hee ought to suspect a *Hierarchy* to bee as dangerous and derogatory from his Crown as a *Tetrarchy* or a *Heptarchy*. Yet now that the *Prelates* had almost attain'd to what their insolent, and un-bridl'd minds had hurried them; to thrust the Laitie[63] under the despoticall rule of the *Monarch*, that they themselves might confine the *Monarch* to a kind of Pupillage under their *Hier-archy*, observe but how their own *Principles* combat one an-other, and supplant each one his fellow.

Having fitted us only for peace, and that a servile peace, by lessening our numbers, dreining our estates, enfeebling our bodies, sowing our free spirits by those wayes as you have heard, their impotent actions cannot sustaine themselves the least moment, unlesse they rouze us up to a *Warre* fit for *Cain* to be the Leader of; an abhorred, a cursed, a Fraternall Warre. ENGLAND and SCOTLAND dearest Brothers in *Nature*, and in CHRIST must be set to wade in one anothers blood; and IRELAND our free Denizon upon the back of us both, as occa-sion should serve:[64] a piece of Service that the *Pope* and all his Factors have beene compassing to doe ever since the *Reforma-tion*.

But ever-blessed be he, and ever glorifi'd that from his high watch-Tower in the Heav'ns discerning the crooked wayes of perverse, and cruell men, hath hitherto maim'd, and infatuated all their damnable inventions, and deluded their great Wizzards with a delusion fit for fooles and children : had GOD beene so minded hee could have sent a Spirit of *Mutiny* amongst us, as hee did betweene *Abimilech* and the *Sechemites*,[65] to have made our Funerals, and slaine heaps more in number then the miser-able surviving remnant, but he, when wee least deserv'd, sent

63. i.e. Parliament.

64. Laud was decidedly in favour of the war against Scotland; and Strafford had urged Charles I to deploy the Irish army against the English. Even as Milton was writing, however, both men were already imprisoned : Strafford was executed in 1641, Laud in 1644.

65. Judges 9.

out a gentle gale, and message of peace from the wings of those his Cherubins, that fanne his Mercy-seat. Nor shall the *wisdome*, the *moderation*, the *Christian Pietie*, the *Constancy* of our Nobility and Commons of *England* be ever forgotten, whose calme, and temperat connivence could sit still, and smile out the stormy bluster of men more audacious and precipitant, then of solid and deep reach, till their own fury had run it selfe out of breath, assailing, by rash and heady *approches*, the impregnable situation of our Liberty and safety, that laught such weake enginry to scorne, such poore drifts to make a *Nationall Warre* of a *Surplice Brabble*, a *Tippet-scuffle*, and ingage the unattainted Honour of *English* Knighthood, to unfurle the streaming *Red Crosse*,[66] or to reare the horrid *Standard* of those fatall guly Dragons for so unworthy a purpose, as to force upon their *Fellow Subjects*, that which themselves are weary of, the *Skeleton* of a *Masse-Booke*. Nor the *Patience*, the *Fortitude*, the *firme Obedience* of the Nobles and People of *Scotland* striving against manifold Provocations, nor must their sincere and moderate proceedings hitherto, be unremember'd, to the shamefull Conviction of all their Detractors.

Goe on both hand in hand O NATIONS never to be disunited, be the *Praise* and the *Heroick Song* of all POSTERITY; merit this, but seeke onely *Vertue*, not to extend your Limits; for what needs? to win a fading triumphant *Lawrell* out of the *teares* of *wretched Men*, but to settle the *pure worship* of *God* in his Church, and *justice* in the State. Then shall the hardest difficulties smooth out themselves before ye; *envie* shall sink to hell, *craft* and *malice* be confounded, whether it be homebred mischeif, or outlandish cunning : yea, other Nations will then covet to serve ye, for Lordship and victory are but the pages of *justice* and *vertue*. Commit securely to true *wisdome* the vanquishing and uncasing of craft and suttletie, which are but her two runnagates :[67] joyn your invincible might to doe worthy, and Godlike deeds, and then he that seeks to break your union, a cleaving curse be his inheritance to all generations.

---

66. i.e. of St. George, in the English standard.
67. Runaway servants.

Sir, you have now at length this question for the time, and as my memory would best serve me in such a copious, and vast theme, fully handl'd, and you your selfe may judge whether Prelacy be the only Church-government agreeable to MONARCHY. Seeing therfore the perillous, and confused estate into which we are faln, and that to the certain knowledge of all men through the irreligious pride and hatefull Tyranny of Prelats (as the innumerable, and grievous complaints of every shire cry out) if we will now resolve to settle affairs either according to pure Religion, or sound Policy, we must first of all begin roundly to cashier, and cut away from the publick body the noysom, and diseased tumor of Prelacie, and come from Schisme to *unity* with our neighbour Reformed sister Churches, which with the blessing of *peace* and *pure doctrine* have now long time flourish'd; and doubtles with all hearty *joy*, and *gratulation*, will meet, and welcome our Christian *union* with them, as they have bin all this while griev'd at our strangenes and little better then separation from them. And for the Discipline propounded, seeing that it hath bin inevitably prov'd that the natural, and fundamental causes of political happines in all goverments are the same, and that this Church Discipline is taught in the Word of *God*, and, as we see, agrees according to wish with all such states as have receiv'd it, we may infallibly assure our selvs that it will as wel agree with Monarchy, though all the Tribe of *Aphorismers*, and *Politicasters* would perswade us there be secret, and misterious reasons against it. For upon the setling hereof mark what nourishing and cordial restorements to the State will follow, the Ministers of the Gospel attending only to the work of *salvation* every one within his limited charge, besides the diffusive blessings of *God* upon all our actions, the King shall sit without an old disturber, a dayly incroacher, and intruder; shall ridde his Kingdome of a strong sequester'd, and collateral power; a confronting miter, whose potent wealth, and wakefull ambition he had just cause to hold in jealousie: not to repeat the other present evills which only their removal will remove. And because things simply pure are inconsistent in the masse of nature, nor are the elements or humors in Mans Body exactly *homogeneall*, and hence the best founded Common-wealths, and least barbarous have aym'd at a certaine mixture and temperament, partaking the severall vertues of each other State, that each part drawing to it selfe may keep up a steddy, and eev'n uprightnesse in common.

There is no Civill *Government* that hath beene known, no not the *Spartan*, not the *Roman*, though both for this respect so much prais'd by the wise *Polybius*,[68] more divinely and harmoniously tun'd, more equally ballanc'd as it were by the hand and scale of Justice, then is the Common-wealth of *England*: where under a free, and untutor'd *Monarch*, the noblest, worthiest, and most prudent men, with full approbation, and suffrage of the People have in their power the supreme, and finall determination of highest Affaires.[69] Now if Conformity of Church *Discipline* to the Civill be so desir'd, there can be nothing more parallel, more uniform, then when under the Soveraigne Prince *Christs* Vicegerent using the *Scepter* of *David*, according to *Gods Law*, the *godliest*, the *wisest*, the *learnedest* Ministers in their severall charges have the instructing and disciplining of *Gods people* by whose full and free Election[70] they are consecrated to that holy and equall *Aristocracy*. And why should not the Piety, and Conscience of *Englishmen* as members of the Church be trusted in the Election of Pastors to Functions that nothing concerne a *Monarch*, as well as their worldly wisedomes are priviledg'd as *members* of the *State* in suffraging their Knights, and Burgesses to matters that concern him neerely? And if in weighing these severall Offices, their difference in time and qualitie be cast in, I know they will not turn the beame of equall Judgement the moity of a scruple. Wee therfore having already a kind of Apostolicall, and ancient *Church* Election in our State, what a perversnesse would it be in us of all others to retain forcibly a kind of imperious, and stately Election in our *Church*? And what a blindnesse to thinke that what is

---

68. Cf. Polybius, *Histories*, VI, 48.

69. The limitations here imposed on the monarchy anticipate Milton's argument in *The Tenure of Kings and Magistrates* (below, pp. 249 ff.).

70. As urged by the Presbyterians.

already Evangelicall as it were by a happy chance in our *Politie*, should be repugnant to that which is the same by divine command in the Ministery? Thus then wee see that our Ecclesiall, and Politicall choyses may consent and sort as well together without any rupture in the STATE, as Christians, and Freeholders. But as for honour, that ought indeed to be different, and distinct as either Office looks a severall way, the Minister whose *Calling* and *end* is spirituall, ought to be honour'd as a Father and Physitian to the Soule (if he be found to be so) with a *Son*-like and *Disciple*-like reverence, which is indeed the dearest, and most affectionate *honour*, most to be desir'd by a wise man, and such as will easily command a free and plentifull provision of outward necessaries, without his furder care of this world.

The Magistrate whose Charge is to see to our Persons, and Estates, is to bee honour'd with a more elaborate and personall Courtship, with large Salaries and Stipends, that hee himselfe may abound in those things wherof his legall justice and watchfull care gives us the quiet enjoyment. And this distinction of Honour will bring forth a seemly and gracefull Uniformity over all the Kingdome.

Then shall the Nobles possesse all the Dignities and Offices of temporall honour to themselves, sole Lords without the improper mixture of Scholastick, and pusillanimous upstarts, the *Parliament* shall void her *Upper House* of the same annoyances,[71] the Common, and Civill *Lawes* shall be both set free, the former from the controule, the other from the meere vassalage and *Copy-hold* of the *Clergie*.

And wheras *temporall Lawes* rather punish men when they have transgress't, then form them to be such as should transgresse seldomest, wee may conceive great hopes through the showres of Divine Benediction, watering the unmolested and watchfull paines of the *Ministery*, that the whole Inheritance of God will grow up so straight and blamelesse, that the Civill Magistrate may with farre lesse toyle and difficulty, and far more ease and delight steare the tall and goodly *Vessell* of the

---

71. i.e. of the twenty-six bishops sitting in the House of Lords.

Common-wealth through all the gusts and tides of the Worlds mutability.[72]

.   .   .   .

O Sir, I doe now feele my selfe inwrapt on the sodaine into those mazes and *Labyrinths* of dreadfull and hideous thoughts, that which way to get out, or which way to end I know not, unlesse I turne mine eyes, and with your help lift up my hands to that Eternall and Propitious *Throne*, where nothing is readier than *grace* and *refuge* to the distresses of mortall Suppliants: and it were a shame to leave these serious thoughts less piously then the Heathen were wont to conclude their graver discourses.

Thou therefore that sits't in light & glory unapproachable, *Parent* of *Angels* and *Men*! next thee I implore Omnipotent King, Redeemer of that lost remnant whose nature thou didst assume, ineffable and everlasting *Love*! And thou the third subsistence of Divine Infinitude, *illumining Spirit*, the joy and solace of created *Things*! one *Tri-personall* GODHEAD! looke upon this thy poore and almost spent, and expiring *Church*, leave her not thus a prey to these importunate *Wolves*, that wait and thinke long till they devoure thy tender *Flock*, these wilde *Boares* that have broke into thy *Vineyard*, and left the print of thir polluting hoofs on the Soules of thy Servants. O let them not bring about their damned *designes* that stand now at the entrance of the bottomlesse pit expecting the Watchword to open and let out those dreadful *Locusts* and *Scorpions*, to *re-involve* us in that pitchy *Cloud* of infernall darknes, where we shall never more see the *Sunne* of thy *Truth* againe, never hope for the cheerfull dawne, never more heare the *Bird* of *Morning* sing. Be mov'd with pitty at the afflicted state of this our shaken *Monarchy*, that now lies labouring under her throwes, and struggling against the grudges of more dreaded Calamities.

O thou that after the impetuous rage of five bloody Inundations, and the succeeding Sword of intestine *Warre*, soaking the

---

72. In approximately ten pages here omitted, Milton argues in favour of furthering at once the 'Divinely-warranted *Reformation*'.

Land in her owne gore, didst pitty the sad and ceasles revolution of our swift and thick-comming sorrowes when wee were quite breathlesse, of thy *free grace* didst motion *Peace*, and termes of Cov'nant with us, & having first welnigh freed us from *Antichristian* thraldome, didst build up this *Britannick Empire* to a glorious and enviable heighth with all her Daughter Ilands about her, stay us in this felicitie, let not the obstinacy of our halfe Obedience and will-Worship bring forth that *Viper* of *Sedition*, that for these Fourescore Yeares hath been breeding to eat through the entrals of our *Peace*; but let her cast her Abortive Spawne without the danger of this travailling & throbbing *Kingdome*. That we may still remember in our *solemne Thanksgivings*, how for us the *Northren Ocean* even to the frozen *Thule* was scatter'd with the proud Ship-wracks of the *Spanish Armado*, and the very maw of Hell ransack't, and made to give up her conceal'd destruction, ere shee could vent it in that horrible and damned blast.

O how much more glorious will those former Deliverances appeare, when we shall know them not onely to have sav'd us from greatest miseries past, but to have reserv'd us for greatest happinesse to come. Hitherto thou hast but freed us, and that not fully, from the unjust and Tyrannous Claime of thy Foes, now unite us intirely, and appropriate us to thy selfe, tie us everlastingly in willing Homage to the *Prerogative* of thy eternall *Throne*.

And now wee knowe, O thou our most certain hope and defence, that thine enemies have been consulting all the Sorceries of the *great Whore*,[73] and have joyn'd their Plots with that sad Intelligencing Tyrant that mischiefes the World with his Mines of *Ophir*, and lies thirsting to revenge his Navall ruines that have larded our Seas;[74] but let them all take Counsell together, and let it come to nought, let them Decree, and doe

---

73. i.e. the Catholic Church, here identified – as was common among Protestants – with the 'whore' of Revelation (17:1, 19:2).

74. The 'Tyrant' is Spain, her activities sustained by the gold mined in South America ('*Ophir*' is the Biblical equivalent in I Kings 10:11), and aimed at cancelling the defeat of the Armada (1588) already referred to. The 'damned blast' is the Gunpowder Plot (1605).

thou Cancell it, let them gather themselves, and bee scatter'd, let them embattell themselves and bee broken, let them imbattell, and be broken, for thou art with us.

Then amidst the *Hymns*, and *Halleluiahs* of *Saints* some one may perhaps bee heard offering at high *strains* in new and lofty *Measures* to sing and celebrate thy *divine Mercies*, and *marvelous Judgements* in this Land throughout all AGES; whereby this great and Warlike Nation instructed and inur'd to the fervent and continuall practice of *Truth* and *Righteousnesse*, and casting farre from her the *rags* of her old *vices* may presse on hard to that *high* and *happy* emulation to be found the *soberest*, *wisest*, and *most Christian People* at that day when thou the Eternall and shortly-expected King shalt open the Clouds to judge the severall Kingdomes of the World, and distributing *Nationall Honours* and *Rewards* to Religious and just *Commonwealths*, shalt put an end to all Earthly *Tyrannies*, proclaiming thy universal and milde *Monarchy* through Heaven and Earth. Where they undoubtedly that by their *Labours, Counsels*, and *Prayers* have been earnest for the *Common good* of *Religion* and their *Countrey*, shall receive, above the inferiour *Orders* of the *Blessed*, the *Regall* addition of *Principalities, Legions*, and *Thrones*[75] into their glorious Titles, and in supereminence of *beatifick Vision* progressing the *datelesse* and *irrevoluble* Circle of *Eternity* shall clasp inseparable Hands with *joy*, and *blisse* in over measure for ever.

But they contrary that by the impairing and diminution of the true *Faith*, the distresses and servitude of their *Countrey* aspire to high *Dignity, Rule* and *Promotion* here, after a shamefull end in this *Life* (which *God* grant them) shall be thrown downe eternally into the *darkest* and *deepest Gulfe* of HELL, where under the *despightfull controule*, the trample and spurne of all the other *Damned*, that in the anguish of their *Torture*

---

75. The angels, Milton wrote elsewhere, are 'quaterniond into thir celestiall Princedomes, and Satrapies' (quoted above, p. 18) – but not according to the *nine*fold hierarchy upheld by Catholics, which Milton like most Protestants rejected as unwarranted by the Bible (cf. *Paradise Lost*, V, 601, 840).

shall have no other ease then to exercise a *Raving* and *Bestiall Tyranny* over them as their *Slaves* and *Negro's*, they shall remaine in that plight for ever, the *basest*, the *lowermost*, the *most dejected*, most *underfoot* and *downe-trodden Vassals* of *Perdition*.

THE DOCTRINE AND DISCIPLINE
OF DIVORCE

(1643; revised 1644)

[The first of Milton's treatises on divorce (see above, pp. 26 ff.) is described on the title page as *The Doctrine and Discipline of Divorce: restor'd to the good of both sexes, from the bondage of Canon Law, and other mistakes, to Christian freedom, guided by the Rule of Charity. Wherein also many places of Scripture, have recover'd their long-lost meaning. Seasonable to be now thought on in the Reformation intended.* The present condensed version excludes, from Book I, Chapters VIII and XIV; and from Book II, Chapters II–XVI.

First published in 1643, the treatise was much revised in 1644; two more editions were issued a year later. The Yale edition provides the text of both 1643 and 1644 (II, 222–356); the Columbia edition reprinted here provides the revised text of 1644 (III, 367–511, with textual notes in 525–85; ed. Chilton L. Powell and Frank A. Patterson).]

TO THE PARLAMENT OF ENGLAND, WITH
THE ASSEMBLY.

If it were seriously askt, and it would be no untimely question, Renowned Parlament, select Assembly, who of all Teachers and Maisters that have ever taught, hath drawn the most Disciples after him, both in Religion, and in manners, it might bee not untruly answer'd, Custome. Though vertue be commended for the most perswasive in her *Theory*; and Conscience in the plain demonstration of the spirit, finds most evincing, yet whether it be the secret of divine will, or the originall blindnesse we are born in, so it happ'ns for the most part, that Custome still is silently receiv'd for the best instructer. Except it be, because her method is so glib and easie, in some manner like to that vision of *Ezekiel*,[1] rowling up her sudden book of implicit knowledge, for him that will, to take and swallow down at pleasure; which proving but of bad nourishment in the concoction, as it was heedlesse in the devouring, puffs up unhealthily, a certaine big face of pretended learning, mistaken among credulous men, for the wholsome habit of soundnesse and good constitution; but is indeed no other, then that swoln visage of counterfeit knowledge and literature, which not onely in private marrs our education, but also in publick is the common climer into every chaire, where either Religion is preach't, or Law reported : filling each estate of life and profession, with abject and servil principles; depressing the high and Heaven-born spirit of Man, farre beneath the condition wherein either God created him, or sin hath sunke him. To persue the Allegory, Custome being but a meer face, as Eccho is a meere voice, rests not in her unaccomplishment, untill by secret inclination, sheè accorporat her selfe with error, who being a blind and Serpentine body without a head, willingly accepts what he wants, and supplies what her incompleatnesse went seeking. Hence it is, that Error supports Custome, Custome count'nances Error. And these two betweene them would persecute and chase away all truth and solid wisdome out of humane life, were it not that God, rather then man, once in many ages, cals together the prudent and Religious counsels of Men, deputed to represse the encroachments, and to worke off the inveterate blots and obscurities wrought upon our mindes by the suttle insinuating of Error and Custome : Who with the numerous and vulgar train of their followers, make it their chiefe designe to envie and cry-down the industry of free reasoning, under the terms of humor, and innovation; as if the womb of teeming Truth were to be clos'd up, if shee presume to bring forth ought, that sorts not with their unchew'd notions and suppositions. Against which notorious injury and abuse of mans free soule to testifie and oppose the utmost that study and true labour can attaine, heretofore the incitement of men reputed grave hath led me among others; and now the

---

1. Ezekiel 2:9 ff.

duty and the right of an instructed Christian cals me through the chance of good or evill report, to be the sole advocate[2] of a discount'nanc't truth: a high enterprise Lords and Commons, a high enterprise and a hard, and such as every seventh Son of a seventh Son does not venture on. Nor have I amidst the clamor of so much envie and impertinence, whether to appeal, but to the concourse of so much piety and wisdome heer assembl'd. Bringing in my hands an ancient and most necessary, most charitable, and yet most injur'd Statute of *Moses*:[3] not repeald ever by him who only had the authority, but thrown aside with much inconsiderat neglect, under the rubbish of Canonicall ignorance: as once the whole law was by some such like conveyance in *Josiahs* time.[4] And hee who shall indeavour the amendment of any old neglected grievance in Church or State, or in the daily course of life, if he be gifted with abilities of mind that may raise him to so high an undertaking, I grant he hath already much whereof not to repent him; yet let me arreed[5] him, not to be the foreman of any mis-judgd opinion, unlesse his resolutions be firmly seated in a square and constant mind, not conscious to it self of any deserved blame, and regardles of ungrounded suspicions. For this let him be sure he shall be boorded presently by the ruder sort, but not by discreet and well nurtur'd men, with a thousand idle descants and surmises. Who when they cannot confute the least joynt or sinew of any passage in the book; yet God forbid that truth should be truth, because they have a boistrous conceit of some pretences in the Writer. But were they not more busie and inquisitive then the Apostle commends, they would heare him at least, *rejoycing, so the Truth be preacht; whether of envie or other pretence whatsoever*:[6] For Truth is

---

2. Not an exaggeration: Milton is the 'first protagonist in Christendom' of the case about to be presented (cf. Introduction, above, p. 27).

3. Deuteronomy 24:1 (quoted fully below, p. 129). Milton will insistently argue that this text was not abrogated by Christ, despite Matthew 5:32 (see below, Note 85).

4. On the 'conveyance' (furtive carrying off), see 2 Kings 22 and 23.

5. Advise.   6. Cf. Philippians 1:18.

as impossible to be soil'd by any outward touch, as the Sun beam. Though this ill hap wait on her nativity, that shee never comes into the world, but like a Bastard, to the ignominy of him that brought her forth : till Time the Midwife rather then the mother of Truth, have washt and salted the Infant, de-clar'd her legitimat, and Churcht the father of his young *Minerva*, from the needlesse causes of his purgation.[7] Your selves can best witnesse this, worthy Patriots, and better will, no doubt, hereafter : for who among ye of the formost that have travail'd in her behalfe to the good of Church, or State, hath not been often traduc't to be the agent of his owne by-ends, under pretext of Reformation. So much the more I shall not be unjust to hope, that however Infamy, or Envy may work in other men to doe her fretfull will against this discourse, yet that the experience of your owne uprightnesse mis-interpreted, will put ye in mind to give it free audience and generous con-struction. What though the brood of Belial,[8] the draffe of men, to whom no liberty is pleasing, but unbridl'd and vagabond lust without pale or partition, will laugh broad perhaps, to see so great a strength of Scripture mustering up in favour, as they suppose, of their debausheries; they will know better, when they shall hence learne, that honest liberty is the greatest foe to dishonest licence. Arfd what though others out of a waterish and queasy conscience because ever crasy and never yet sound, will rail and fancy to themselves, that injury and licence is the best of this Book? Did not the distemper of their own stomacks affect them with a dizzy megrim,[9] they would soon tie up their tongues, and discern themselves like that *Assyrian* blasphemer[10] all this while reproaching not man but the Al-mighty, *the holy one of Israel*, whom they doe not deny to

---

7. 'Churching', the Anglican ritual of thanksgiving for women after childbirth, is linked to the generation of Minerva from the head of Jupiter.

8. The Old Testament frequently describes the enemies of the Lord as the children of Belial.

9. Severe headache.

10. King Sennacherib of Assyria. Cf. 2 Kings 19 : 22.

have belawgiv'n[11] his owne sacred people with this very allowance, which they now call injury and licence, and dare cry
shame on, and will doe yet a while, till they get a little cordiall
sobriety to settle their qualming zeale. But this question concerns not us perhaps: Indeed mans disposition though prone
to search after vain curiosities, yet when points of difficulty
are to be discusst, appertaining to the removall of unreasonable wrong and burden from the perplext life of our brother, it
is incredible how cold, how dull, and farre from all fellow
feeling we are, without the spurre of self-concernment. Yet if
the wisdome, the justice, the purity of God be to be cleer'd from
foulest imputations which are not yet avoided, if charity be
not to be degraded and trodd'n down under a civil Ordinance,
if Matrimony be not to be advanc't like that exalted perdition,
writt'n of to the *Thessalonians, above all that is called God,*[12] or
goodnesse, nay, against them both, then I dare affirm there will
be found in the Contents of this Booke, that which may concern us all. You it concerns chiefly, Worthies in Parlament, on
whom, as on our deliverers, all our grievances and cares, by the
merit of your eminence and fortitude are devolv'd: Me it concerns next, having with much labour and faithfull diligence
first found out, or at least with a fearlesse and communicative
candor first publisht to the manifest good of Christendome,
that which calling to witnesse every thing mortall and immortall, I beleeve unfainedly to be true. Let not other men thinke
their conscience bound to search continually after truth, to
pray for enlightning from above, to publish what they think
they have so obtaind, & debarr me from conceiving my self
ty'd by the same duties. Yee have now, doubtlesse by the
favour and appointment of God, yee have now in your hands
a great and populous Nation to Reform; from what corruption,
what blindnes in Religion yee know well; in what a degenerat
and fal'n spirit from the apprehension of native liberty, and
true manlines, I am sure ye find: with what unbounded licence
rushing to whordoms and adulteries needs not long enquiry:
insomuch that the fears which men have of too strict a disci-

---

11. Legislated to.
12. Cf. Thessalonians 2:3–4.

pline, perhaps exceed the hopes that can bee in others, of ever introducing it with any great successe. What if I should tell yee now of dispensations and indulgences, to give a little the rains, to let them play and nibble with the bait a while; a people as hard of heart as that Egyptian Colony that went to *Canaan*.[13] This is the common doctrine that adulterous and injurious divorces were not conniv'd only, but with eye open allow'd of old for hardnesse of heart.[14] But that opinion, I trust, by then this following argument hath been well read, will be left for one of the mysteries of an indulgent Antichrist, to farm out incest by, and those his other tributary pollutions. What middle way can be tak'n then, may some interrupt, if we must neither turne to the right nor to the left, and that the people hate to be reform'd: Mark then, Judges and Lawgivers, and yee whose Office is to be our teachers, for I will utter now a doctrine, if ever any other, though neglected or not understood, yet of great and powerfull importance to the governing of mankind. He who wisely would restrain the reasonable Soul of man within due bounds, must first himself know perfectly, how far the territory and dominion extends of just and honest liberty. As little must he offer to bind that which God hath loos'n'd, as to loos'n that which he hath bound. The ignorance and mistake of this high point, hath heapt up one huge half of all the misery that hath bin since *Adam*. In the Gospel we shall read a supercilious crew of masters, whose holinesse, or rather whose evill eye, grieving that God should be so facil to man, was to set straiter limits to obedience, then God had set; to inslave the dignity of man, to put a garrison upon his neck of empty and over-dignifi'd precepts: And we shall read our Saviour never more greev'd and troubl'd, then to meet with such a peevish mad-nesse among men against their own freedome. How can we expect him to be lesse offended with us, when much of the same folly shall be found yet remaining where it lest ought, to the perishing of thousands. The greatest burden in the world is superstition; not onely of Ceremonies in the Church, but of imaginary and scarcrow sins at home. What greater weakning,

---

13. i.e. the Israelites.
14. Matthew 19:8. Mark 10:5.

what more suttle stratagem against our Christian warfare when besides the grosse body of real transgressions to encounter; wee shall bee terrify'd by a vain and shadowy menacing of faults that are not: When things indifferent shall be set to over-front us, under the banners of sin, what wonder if wee bee routed, and by this art of our Adversary, fall into the subjection of worst and deadliest offences. The superstition of the Papist is, *touch not, taste not,* when *God* bids both: and ours is, *part not, separat not,* when God and charity both permits and commands. *Let all your things be done with charity* saith St. *Paul*: and his Master saith, *Shee is the fulfilling of the Law.*[15] Yet now a civil, an indifferent, a somtime diswaded Law of mariage, must be forc't upon us to fulfill, not onely without charity, but against her. No place in Heav'n or Earth, except Hell, where charity may not enter: yet mariage the Ordinance of our solace and contentment, the remedy of our lonelinesse will not admit now either of charity or mercy to come in and mediate or pacifie the fiercnes of this gentle Ordinance, the unremedied lonelinesse of this remedy. Advise yee well, supreme Senat, if charity be thus excluded and expulst, how yee will defend the untainted honour of your own actions and proceedings: He who marries, intends as little to conspire his own ruine, as he that swears Allegiance: and as a whole people is in proportion to an ill Government, so is one man to an ill mariage. If they against any authority, Covnant or Statute, may by the soveraign edict of charity, save not only their lives, but honest liberties from unworthy bondage, as well may he against any private Covnant, which hee never enter'd to his mischief, redeem himself from unsupportable disturbances to honest peace, and just contentment: And much the rather, for that to resist the highest Magistrat though tyrannizing, God never gave us expresse allowance, only he gave us reason, charity, nature and good example to bear us out; but in this economical[16] misfortune, thus to demean our selves, besides the warrant of those foure great directors, which doth as justly belong hither, we have an expresse law of *God*, and such a law, as

15. 1 Corinthians 16:14 and Romans 13:10.
16. Domestic.

wherof our Saviour with a solemn threat forbid the abrogating.[17] For no effect of tyranny can sit more heavy on the Commonwealth, then this household unhappines on the family. And farewell all hope of true Reformation in the state, while such an evill as this lies undiscern'd or unregarded in the house. On the redresse wherof depends, not only the spiritfull and orderly life of our grown men, but the willing, and carefull education of our children. Let this therefore be new examin'd, this tenure and free-hold of mankind, this native and domestick Charter giv'n us by a greater Lord then that *Saxon* King the Confessor.[18] Let the statutes of God be turn'd over, be scann'd a new, and consider'd; not altogether by the narrow intellectuals of quotationists and common placers, but (as was the ancient right of Counsels) by men of what liberall profession soever, of eminent spirit and breeding joyn'd with a diffuse and various knowledge of divine human things; able to ballance and define good and evill, right and wrong, throughout every state of life; able to shew us the waies of the Lord, strait and faithfull as they are, not full of cranks and contradictions, and pit falling dispenses, but with divine insight and benignity measur'd out to the proportion of each mind and spirit, each temper and disposition, created so different each from other, and yet by the skill of wise conducting, all to become uniform in vertue. To expedite these knots were worthy a learned and memorable Synod; while our enemies expect to see the expectation of the Church tir'd out with dependencies and independencies[19] how they will compound, and in what Calends. Doubt not, worthy Senators to vindicate the sacred honour and judgment of *Moses* your predecessor, from the shallow commenting of Scholasticks and Canonists. Doubt not after him to reach out your steddy hands to the mis-inform'd and wearied life of man; to restore this his lost heritage into the houshold state; wherwith be sure that peace and love the best subsistence of a Christian family will return home from whence they are now banisht; places

---

17. Matthew 5:17–19 – quoted in part below, Note 41. The 'expresse law' is Deuteronomy 24:1 (above, Note 3).

18. The widely admired Edward the Confessor (1002–66).

19. i.e. Presbyterians and Independents.

of prostitution wil be lesse haunted, the neighbours bed lesse attempted, the yoke of prudent and manly discipline will be generally submitted to, sober and well order'd living will soon spring up in the Common-wealth. Ye have an author great beyond exception, *Moses*; and one yet greater, he who hedg'd in from abolishing every smallest jot and tittle of precious equity contain'd in that Law, with a more accurate and lasting Masoreth, then either the Synagogue of *Ezra*, or the *Galilean* School at *Tiberias* hath left us.[20] Whatever els ye can enact, will scarce concern a third part of the Brittish name : but the benefit and good of this your magnanimous example, will easily spread beyond the banks of *Tweed* and the *Norman* Iles.[21] It would not be the first, or second time, since our ancient *Druides*, by whom this Island was the Cathedrall of Philosophy to *France*,[22] left off their pagan rites, that England hath had this honour vouchsaft from Heav'n, to give out reformation to the World. Who was it but our English *Constantine* that baptiz'd the Roman Empire ? who but the *Northumbrian Willibrode*, and *Winifride* of *Devon* with their followers, were the first Apostles of *Germany* ? who but *Alcuin* and *Wicklef* our Country men open'd the eyes of *Europe*, the one in arts, the other in Religion.[23] Let not England, forget her precedence of teaching nations how to live.

Know, Worthies, know and exercise the privilege of your honour'd Country. A greater title I heer bring ye, then is either in the power or in the policy of *Rome* to give her

20. Masorah ('tradition') is the corpus of commentary on the text of the Hebrew Bible, not the exegetical activities of the rabbis as Milton appears to think. On the assembly convened in the time of Ezra, see Nehemiah 8–10; a similarly celebrated centre of rabbinical studies existed in Tiberias on the Sea of Galilee.

21. The Channel Islands.

22. As much was claimed by Julius Caesar, *Commentaries*, VI, 13.

23. Constantine the Great was erroneously thought to have been born in England; he was nevertheless proclaimed Emperor in York. The other names are of the learned St. Willibrorde and of Winfride (i.e. St. Boniface) – alike of the eighth century – and lastly of the great scholar Alcuin (736–804) and John Wycliffe (above, p. 81, Note 11).

Monarchs; this glorious act will stile ye the defenders of Charity. Nor is this yet the highest inscription that will adorne so religious and so holy a defence as this; behold heer the pure and sacred Law of God, and his yet purer and more sacred name offring themselvs to you first, of all Christian reformers to be acquitted from the long suffer'd ungodly attribute of patronizing Adultery. Deferre not to wipe off instantly these imputative blurrs and stains cast by rude fancies upon the throne and beauty it selfe of inviolable holines: lest some other people more devout and wise then wee, bereav us this offer'd immortal glory, our wonted prerogative, of being the first asserters in every great vindication. For me, as farre as my part leads me, I have already my greatest gain, assurance and inward satisfaction to have don in this nothing unworthy of an honest life, and studies well employ'd. With what event among the wise and right understanding handfull of men, I am secure. But how among the drove of Custom and Prejudice this will be relisht, by such whose capacity, since their youth run ahead into the easie creek of a System or a Medulla,[24] sayls there at will under the blown physiognomy of their unlabour'd rudiments, for them, what their tast will be, I have also surety sufficient, from the entire league that hath bin ever between formal ignorance and grave obstinacie. Yet when I remember the little that our Saviour could prevail about this doctrine of Charity against the crabbed textuists of his time, I make no wonder, but rest confident that who so preferrs either Matrimony, or other Ordinance before the good of man and the plain exigence of Charity, let him professe Papist, or Protestant, or what he will, he is no better then a Pharise, and understands not the Gospel: whom as a misinterpreter of Christ I openly protest against; and provoke him to the trial of this truth before all the world: and let him bethink him withall how he will soder up the shifting flaws of his ungirt permissions, his venial and unvenial dispences, wherwith the Law of God pardoning and unpardoning hath bin shamefully branded, for want of heed in glossing, to have eluded and baffl'd out all Faith and chastity from the

---

24. Compendium of knowledge.

mariagebed of that holy seed, with politick and judicial adulteries. I seek not to seduce the simple and illiterat; my errand is to find out the choisest and the learnedest, who have this high gift of wisdom to answer solidly, or to be convinc't. I crave it from the piety, the learning and the prudence which is hous'd in this place. It might perhaps more fitly have bin writt'n in another tongue:[25] and I had don so, but that the esteem I have of my Countries judgement, and the love I beare to my native language to serv it first with what I endeavour, made me speak it thus, ere I assay the verdit of outlandish readers. And perhaps also heer I might have ended nameles, but that the addresse of these lines chiefly to the Parlament of *England* might have seem'd ingratefull not to acknowledge by whose Religious care, unwearied watchfulnes, couragious and heroick resolutions, I enjoy the peace and studious leisure to remain,

> *The Honourer and Attendant of their Noble*
> *worth and vertues,*

John Milton.

25. i.e. Latin, still the international language that Milton was to use in his three *Defences* and the theological treatise *De doctrina christiana*.

THE
DOCTRINE AND DISCIPLINE OF DIVORCE;

Restor'd to the good of both Sexes.

I. BOOKE.

The Preface.

That Man is the occasion of his owne miseries, in most of those evills which hee imputes to Gods inflicting. The absurdity of our canonists in their decrees about divorce. The Christian imperiall Lawes fram'd with more Equity. The opinion of Hugo Grotius, *and* Paulus Fagius: *And the purpose in generall of this Discourse.*

MANY men, whether it be their fate, or fond opinion, easily perswade themselves, if God would but be pleas'd a while to withdraw his just punishments from us, and to restrain what power either the devill, or any earthly enemy hath to work us woe, that then mans nature would find immediate rest and releasement from all evils. But verily they who think so, if they be such as have a mind large enough to take into their thoughts a generall survey of human things, would soon prove themselves in that opinion farre deceiv'd. For though it were granted us by divine indulgence to be exempt from all that can be harmfull to us from without, yet the perversenesse of our folly is so bent, that we should never lin[26] hammering out of our owne hearts, as it were out of a flint, the seeds and sparkles of new misery to our selves, till all were in a blaze againe. And no marvell if out of our own hearts, for they are evill; but ev'n out of those things which God meant us, either for a principall good, or a pure contentment, we are still hatching and contriving upon our selves matter of continuall sorrow and perplexitie. What greater good to man then that revealed rule, whereby God vouchsafes to shew us how he would be worship? And yet that not rightly understood, became the cause that once a famous man in *Israel*[27] could not but oblige his conscience

---

26. Stop.
27. Jephthah; see Judges 11:30-40.

to be the sacrificer, or if not, the jaylor of his innocent and only daughter. And was the cause oft-times that Armies of valiant men have given up their throats to a heathenish enemy on the Sabbath day :[28] fondly thinking their defensive resistance to be as then a work unlawfull. What thing more instituted to the solace and delight of man then marriage? and yet the misinterpreting of some Scripture directed mainly against the abusers of the Law for divorce giv'n by *Moses*,[29] hath chang'd the blessing of matrimony not seldome into a familiar and coinhabiting mischiefe; at least into a drooping and disconsolate household captivity, without refuge or redemption. So ungovern'd and so wild a race doth superstition run us from one extreme of abused liberty into the other of unmercifull restraint. For although God in the first ordaining of marriage, taught us to what end he did it, in words expresly implying the apt and cheerfull conversation[30] of man with woman, to comfort and refresh him against the evill of solitary life, not mentioning the purpose of generation till afterwards, as being but a secondary end in dignity, though not in necessity; yet now, if any two be but once handed in the Church, and have tasted in any sort the nuptiall bed, let them find themselves never so mistak'n in their dispositions through any error, concealment, or misadventure, that through their different tempers, thoughts, and constitutions, they can neither be to one another a remedy against lonelines, nor live in any union or contentment all their dayes, yet they shall, so they be but found suitably weapon'd to the least possibility of sensuall enjoyment, be made, spight of *antipathy*[31] to fadge together, and combine as they may to

28. As the followers of Mattathias did, when attacked on a Sabbath by Antiochus (1 Maccabees 2 : 31 ff.).

29. Matthew (5 : 31-2 (partly quoted below, p. 153, Note 85), which in a later section (not reprinted here) Milton termed 'a Pharisaical tradition falsly grounded upon that law' – i.e. Deuteronomy 24 : 1 (above, p. 114, Note 3). See further below, pp. 155 ff.

30. Association, living with, companionship, society (Halkett, below, p. 415). Marriage was understood to have been ordained in Eden (cf. Genesis 2 : 18, quoted below, p. 131).

31. Natural incompatibility.

their unspeakable wearisomnes and despaire of all sociable delight in the ordinance which God establisht to that very end.
What a calamity is this, and as the Wise-man,[32] if he were
alive, would sigh out in his own phrase, what a *sore evill is
this under the Sunne*! All which we can referre justly to no
other author then the Canon Law[33] and her adherents, not consulting with charitie, the interpreter and guide of our faith,
but resting in the meere element of the Text; doubtles by the
policy of the devill to make that gracious ordinance become
unsupportable, that what with men not daring to venture upon
wedlock, and what with men wearied out of it, all inordinate
licence might abound. It was for many ages that mariage lay
in disgrace with most of the ancient Doctors, as a work of the
flesh, almost a defilement, wholly deny'd to Priests, and the
second time disswaded to all, as he that reads *Tertullian* or
Jerom may see at large.[34] Afterwards it was thought so Sacra-
mentall, that no adultery or desertion could dissolve it; and
this is the sense of our Canon Courts in *England* to this day, but
in no other reformed Church els:[35] yet there remains in them
also a burden on it as heavie as the other two were disgracefull or superstitious, and of as much iniquity, crossing a Law
not onely writt'n by *Moses*,[36] but character'd in us by nature, of
more antiquity and deeper ground then marriage it selfe; which
Law is to force nothing against the faultles proprieties of
nature : yet that this may be colourably done, our Saviours
words touching divorce, are as it were congeal'd into a stony
rigor, inconsistent both with his doctrine and his office, and that

---

32. King Solomon, believed to have been the author of Ecclesiastes.
On the quotation cf. 5 : 13.

33. Ecclesiastical law, as formulated in papal decrees and conciliar
statutes.

34. Tertullian (*c*. 160–*c*. 220) and St. Jerome (*c*. 342–420) persistently
praised virginity – but not always at the expense of marriage.

35. Milton contrasts the Roman Catholic view of marriage as a
sacrament – and therefore indissoluble – which Anglicans implicitly
accepted; and the tolerance of Continental Protestants for divorce
on the grounds of adultery as well as of desertion.

36. See above, Note 3.

which he preacht onely to the conscience, is by Canonicall tyranny snatcht into the compulsive censure of a judiciall Court; where Laws are impos'd even against the venerable and secret power of natures impression, to love what ever cause be found to loath. Which is a hainous barbarisme both against the honour of mariage, the dignity of man and his soule, the goodnes of Christianitie, and all the humane respects of civilitie. Notwithstanding that some of the wisest and gravest among the Christian Emperours, who had about them, to consult with, those of the Fathers then living, who for their learning and holines of life are still with us in great renowne, have made their statutes and edicts concerning this debate, far more easie and relenting in many necessary cases, wherein the Canon is inflexible. And *Hugo Grotius,* a man of these times, one of the best learned,[37] seems not obscurely to adhere in his perswasion to the equity of those Imperiall decrees, in his notes upon the *Evangelists,* much allaying the outward roughnesse of the Text, which hath for the most part been too immoderately expounded; and excites the diligence of others to enquire further in to this question, as containing many points that have not yet been explain'd. Which ever likely to remain intricate and hopelesse upon the suppositions commonly stuck to, the autority of *Paulus Fagius,* one so learned and so eminent in *England* once,[38] if it might perswade, would strait acquaint us with a solution of these differences, no lesse prudent then compendious. He in his comment on the *Pentateuch* doubted not to maintain that divorces might be as lawfully permitted by the Magistrate to Christians, as they were to the Jewes. But because he is but briefe, and these things of great consequence not to be kept obscure, I shall conceave it nothing above my duty either for the difficulty or the censure that may passe thereon, to communicate such thoughts as I also have had, and

---

37. See above, p. 68, Note 4. Milton's subsequent reference is to Grotius's *Annotationes in Libros Evangeliorum* (Amsterdam, 1641).

38. The German Protestant divine Fagius (1504–49) had been invited to England by Archbishop Cranmer and became Reader in Hebrew at Cambridge. Milton's subsequent reference is to Fagius's annotations on the Pentateuch in *Thargum* (Strassburg, 1546).

do offer them now in this generall labour of reformation, to the candid view both of Church and Magistrate; especially because I see it the hope of good men, that those irregular and unspirituall Courts have spun their utmost date in this Land; and some beter course must now be constituted. This therefore shall be the task and period of this discourse to prove, first that other reasons of divorce besides adultery, were by the Law of *Moses*, and are yet to be allow'd by the Christian Magistrate as a peece of justice, and that the words of Christ are not hereby contraried. Next, that to prohibit absolutely any divorce whatsoever except those which *Moses* excepted, is against the reason of Law, as in due place I shall shew out of *Fagius* with many additions. He therefore who by adventuring shall be so happy as with successe to light the way of such an expedient liberty and truth as this, shall restore the much wrong'd and over-sorrow'd state of matrimony, not onely to those mercifull and life-giving remedies of *Moses*, but, as much as may be, to that serene and blissfull condition it was in at the beginning; and shall deserv of all aprehensive men (considering the troubles and distempers which for want of this insight have bin so oft in Kingdomes, in States, and Families) shall deserve to be reck'n'd among the publick benefactors of civill and humane life; above the inventors of wine and oyle; for this is a far dearer, far nobler, and more desirable cherishing to mans life, unworthily expos'd to sadnes and mistake, which he shall vindicate. Not that licence and levity and unconsented breach of faith should herein be countnanc't, but that some conscionable and tender pitty might be had of those who have unwarily in a thing they never practiz'd before, made themselves the bondmen of a luckles and helples matrimony. In which Argument he whose courage can serve him to give the first onset, must look for two severall oppositions: the one from those who having sworn themselves to long custom and the letter of the Text, will not out of the road: the other from those whose grosse and vulgar apprehensions conceit but low of matrimoniall purposes, and in the work of male and female think they have all. Neverthelesse, it shall be here sought by due wayes to be made appeare, that those words of God in the institution, promising a meet help against lonelines;[39] and those words of Christ *That his yoke is easie and his burden light*,[40] were not spoken in vain; for if the knot of marriage may in no case be dissolv'd but for adultery, all the burd'ns and services of the Law are not so intolerable. This onely is desir'd of them who are minded to judge hardly of thus maintaining, that they would be still and heare all out, nor think it equall to answer deliberate reason with sudden heat and noise; remembring this, that many truths now of reverend esteem and credit, had their birth and beginning once from singular and private thoughts; while the most of men were otherwise possest; and had the fate at first to be generally exploded and exclaim'd on by many violent opposers; yet I may erre perhaps in soothing my selfe that this present truth reviv'd, will deserve on all hands to be not sinisterly receiv'd, in that it undertakes the cure of an inveterate disease crept into the best part of humane societie; and to doe this with no smarting corrosive, but with a smooth and pleasing lesson, which receiv'd hath the vertue to soften and dispell rooted and knotty sorrowes: and without inchantment if that be fear'd, or spell us'd, hath regard at once both to serious pitty, and upright honesty; that tends to be the redeeming and restoring of none but such as are the object of compassion; having in an ill houre hamper'd themselves to the utter dispatch of all their most beloved comforts and repose for this lives term. But if we shall obstinately dislike this new overture of unexpected ease and recovery, what remains but to deplore the frowardnes of our hopeles condition, which neither can endure the estate we are in, nor admit of remedy either sharp or sweet. Sharp we our selves distast; and sweet under whose hands we are, is scrupl'd and suspected as too lushious. In such a posture Christ found the *Jews*, who were neither won with the austerity of *John the Baptist*, and thought it too much licence to follow freely the charming pipe of him who sounded and proclaim'd liberty and reliefe to all distresses yet Truth in some age or other will find her witnes, and shall be justify'd at last by her own children.

---

39. Cf. Genesis 2 : 18 (quoted below, p. 131).
40. Matthew 11 : 30.

CHAP. I. *The Position. Prov'd by the Law of Moses. That Law expounded and asserted to a morall and charitable use, first by* Paulus Fagius; *next with other additions.*

To remove therfore if it be possible, this great and sad oppression which through the strictnes of a literall interpreting hath invaded and disturb'd the dearest and most peaceable estate of houshold society, to the over-burdening, if not the overwhelming of many Christians better worth then to be so deserted of the Churches considerate care, this position shall be laid down; first proving, then answering what may be objected either from Scripture or light of reason.

That indisposition, unfitnes, or contrariety of mind, arising from a cause in nature unchangeable, hindring and ever likely to hinder the main benefits of conjugal society, which are solace and peace, is a greater reason of divorce then naturall frigidity, especially if there be no children, and that there be mutuall consent.

This I gather from the Law in Deut. 24. 1. *When a man hath tak'n a wife and married her, and it come to passe that she find no favour in his eyes, because he hath found some uncleanesse in her, let him write her a bill of divorcement, and give it in her hand, and send her out of his house, &c.* This Law, if the words of Christ may be admitted into our beleef, shall never while the world stands, for him be abrogated.[41] First therfore I here set down what learned *Fagius* hath observ'd on this Law; *The Law of God,* saith he, *permitted divorce for the help of human weaknes. For every one that of necessity separats, cannot live single. That Christ deny'd divorce to his own, hinders not; for what is that to the unregenerate, who hath not attain'd such perfection? Let not the remedy be despis'd which was giv'n to weaknes. And when Christ saith, who marries the divorc't, commits adultery, it is to be understood if he had any plot in the divorce.* The rest I reserve untill it be disputed, how the Magistrate is to doe herein.[42] From hence

---

41. Cf. Matthew 5:18 ('Till heaven and earth pass, one jot or one tittle shall in no wise pass from the law, till all be fulfilled').

42. See below, pp. 169–72.

we may plainly discern a two-fold consideration in this Law. First the end of the Lawgiver, and the proper act of the Law to command or to allow somthing just and honest, or indifferent. Secondly, his sufferance from some accidental result of evill by this allowance, which the Law cannot remedy. For if this Law have no other end or act but onely the allowance of a sin, though never to so good intention, that Law is no Law but sin muffl'd in the robe of Law, or Law disguis'd in the loose garment of sin. Both which are too foule *Hypotheses* to save the *Phænomenon* of our Saviours answer to the Pharises about this matter. And I trust anon by the help of an infallible guide to perfet such *Prutenick* tables[43] as shall mend the *Astronomy* of our wide expositors.

The cause of divorce mention'd in the Law is translated *some uncleannesse*; but in the Hebrew it sounds *nakednes of ought, or any reall nakednes* : which by all the learned interpreters is refer'd to the mind, as well as to the body. And what greater nakednes or unfitnes of mind then that which hinders ever the solace and peacefull society of the maried couple, and what hinders that more then the unfitnes and defectivenes of an unconjugal mind. The cause therfore of divorce expres't in the position cannot but agree with that describ'd in the best and equalest sense of *Moses* Law. Which being a matter of pure charity, is plainly moral, and more now in force then ever : therfore surely lawfull. For if under the Law such was Gods gracious indulgence, as not to suffer the ordinance of his goodnes and favour, through any error to be ser'd and stigmatiz'd upon his servants to their misery and thraldome, much lesse will he suffer it now under the covenant of grace, by abrogating his former grant of remedy and releef. But the first institution will be objected to have ordain'd mariage inseparable. To that a little patience untill this first part have amply discours't the grave and pious reasons of this divorsive Law; and then I doubt not but with one gentle stroking to wipe away ten thousand teares out of the life of

---

43. The *Tabulae Prutenicae* (1551) of the astronomer Erasmus Reinhold were superseded by Kepler's *Rudolphine Tables* (1627).

man. Yet thus much I shall now insist on, that what ever the institution were, it could not be so enormous, nor so rebellious against both nature and reason as to exalt it selfe above the end and person for whom it was instituted.

CHAP. II. *The first reason of this Law grounded on the prime reason of matrimony. That no cov'nant whatsoever obliges against the main end both of it self, and of the parties cov'nanting.*

For all sense and equity reclaims that any Law or Cov'nant how solemne or strait soever, either between God and man, or man and man, though of Gods joyning, should bind against a prime and principall scope of its own institution, and of both or either party covnanting: neither can it be of force to ingage a blameles creature to his own perpetuall sorrow, mistak'n for his expected solace, without suffering charity to step in and do a confest good work of parting those whom nothing holds together, but this of Gods joyning, falsly suppos'd against the expresse end of his own ordinance. And what his chiefe end was of creating woman to be joynd with man, his own instituting words declare, and are infallible to informe us what is mariage and what is no mariage: unlesse we can think them set there to no purpose: *It is not good*, saith he, *that man should be alone; I will make him a help meet for him.*[44] From which words so plain, lesse cannot be concluded, nor is by any learned Interpreter, then that in Gods intention a meet and happy conversation[45] is the chiefest and the noblest end of mariage: for we find here no expression so necessarily implying carnall knowledge, as this prevention of lonelines to the mind and spirit of man. To this *Fagius, Calvin, Pareus, Rivetus,* as willingly and largely assent as can be wisht.[46] And indeed it is

---

44. Genesis 2 : 18.

45. See above, p. 124, Note 30.

46. The relevant statements in the Biblical commentaries of Fagius (above, Note 38) as well as of the authoritative Calvin (1509–64) and the widely respected exegetes David Pareus (1548–1622) and André Rivet (1572–1621), are quoted in the Yale edn, II, 246.

a greater blessing from God, more worthy so excellent a creature as man is, and a higher end to honour and sanctifie the league of marriage, whenas the solace and satisfaction of the mind is regarded and provided for before the sensitive pleasing of the body. And with all generous persons maried thus it is, that where the mind and person pleases aptly, there some unaccomplishment of the bodies delight may be better born with, then when the mind hangs off in an unclosing disproportion, though the body be as it ought; for there all corporall delight will soon become unsavoury and contemptible. And the solitarines of man, which God had namely and principally order'd to prevent by mariage, hath no remedy, but lies under a worse condition then the loneliest single life; for in single life the absence and remotenes of a helper might inure him to expect his own comforts out of himselfe or to seek with hope; but here the continuall sight of his deluded thoughts without cure, must needs be to him, if especially his complexion incline him to melancholy, a daily trouble and pain of losse in som degree like that which Reprobats feel. Lest therfore so noble a creature as man should be shut up incurably under a worse evill by an easie mistake in that ordinance which God gave him to remedy a lesse evill, reaping to himselfe sorrow while he went to rid away solitarines, it cannot avoid to be concluded, that if the woman be naturally so of disposition, as will not help to remove, but help to increase that same God-forbidd'n lonelines which will in time draw on with it a generall discomfort and dejection of mind, not beseeming either Christian profession or morall conversation, unprofitable and dangerous to the Commonwealth, when the household estate, out of which must flourish forth the vigor and spirit of all publick enterprizes, is so ill contented and procur'd at home, and cannot be supported; such a mariage can be no mariage whereto the most honest end is wanting : and the agrieved person shall doe more manly, to be extraordinary and singular in claiming the due right whereof he is frustrated, then to piece up his lost contentment by visiting the Stews, or stepping to his neighbours bed, which is the common shift in this mis-fortune; or els by suffering his usefull life to wast away, and be lost under a secret affliction of n unconscionable size to humane strength. Against all which evills the mercy of this Mosaick Law was graciously exhibited.

CHAP. III. *The ignorance and iniquity of Canon Law, providing for the right of the body in mariage, but nothing for the wrongs and greevances of the mind. An objection, that the mind should be better lookt to before contract, answered.*

How vain therfore is it, and how preposterous in the Canon Law to have made such carefull provision against the impediment of carnall performance, and to have had no care about the unconversing inability of mind, so defective to the purest and most sacred end of matrimony : and that the vessell of voluptuous enjoyment must be made good to him that has tak'n it upon trust without any caution, when as the mind from whence must flow the acts of peace and love, a far more pretious mixture then the quintessence of an excrement, though it be found never so deficient and unable to performe the best duty of marriage in a cheerfull and agreeable conversation, shall be thought good anough, how ever flat and melancholious it be, and must serve, though to the eternall disturbance and languishing of him that complains him. Yet wisdom and charity waighing Gods own institution, would think that the pining of a sad spirit wedded to lonelines should deserve to be free'd, aswell as the impatience of a sensuall desire so providently reliev'd. Tis read to us in the Liturgy, that *we must not marry to satisfie the fleshly appetite, like brute beasts that have no understanding;*[47] but the Canon so runs, as if it dreamt of no other matter then such an appetite to be satisfy'd; for if it happen that nature hath stopt or extinguisht the veins of sensuality, that mariage is annull'd. But though all the faculties of the understanding and conversing part after triall appeare to be so ill and so aversly met through natures unalterable working, as that neither peace, nor any sociable contentment can follow, tis as nothing, the contract shall stand as firme as ever, betide what will. What is this but secretly to instruct us, that how-

47. Faithfully adapted from *The Book of Common Prayer* (1552).

ever many grave reasons are pretended to the maried life, yet that nothing indeed is thought worth regard therein, but the prescrib'd satisfaction of an irrationall heat; which cannot be but ignominious to the state of mariage, dishonourable to the undervalu'd soule of man, and even to Christian doctrine it selfe. While it seems more mov'd at the disappointing of an impetuous nerve, then at the ingenuous grievance of a mind unreasonably yoakt; and to place more of mariage in the channell of concupiscence, then in the pure influence of peace and love, whereof the souls lawfull contentment is the onely fountain.

But some are ready to object, that the disposition ought seriously to be consider'd before. But let them know again, that for all the warinesse can be us'd, it may yet befall a discreet man[48] to be mistak'n in his choice, and we have plenty of examples. The sobrest and best govern'd men are least practiz'd in these affairs; and who knowes not that the bashfull mutenes of a virgin may oft-times hide all the unlivelines and naturall sloth which is really unfit for conversation; nor is there that freedom of accesse granted or presum'd, as may suffice to a perfect discerning till too late : and where any indisposition is suspected, what more usuall then the perswasion of friends, that acquaintance, as it increases, will amend all. And lastly, it is not strange though many who have spent their youth chastly, are in some things not so quick-sighted, while they hast too eagerly to light the nuptiall torch; nor is it therefore that for a modest error a man should forfeit so great a happines, and no charitable means to release him. Since they who have liv'd most loosely by reason of their bold accustoming, prove most successfull in their matches, because their wild affections unsetling at will, have been as so many divorces to teach them experience. When as the sober man honouring the appearance of modesty, and hoping well of every sociall vertue under that veile, may easily chance to meet, if not with a body impenetrable, yet

48. The energetic phrasing throughout this paragraph may appear to argue an allusion to Milton's own predicament. He nevertheless manages to reach beyond his personal involvement to the principles underlying the entire treatise. See the Introduction, above, pp. 26 ff.

often with a mind to all other due conversation inaccessible, and to all the more estimable and superior purposes of matrimony uselesse and almost liveles: and what a solace, what a fit help such a consort would be through the whole life of a man, is lesse pain to conjecture then to have experience.

CHAP. IV. *The Second Reason of this Law, because without it, mariage as it happ'ns oft is not a remedy of that which it promises, as any rationall creature would expect. That mariage, if we pattern from the beginning as our Saviour bids, was not properly the remedy of lust, but the fulfilling of conjugall love and helpfulnes.*

And that we may further see what a violent and cruell thing it is to force the continuing of those together, whom God and nature in the gentlest end of mariage never joynd, divers evils and extremities that follow upon such a compulsion, shall here be set in view. Of evils the first and greatest is, that hereby a most absurd and rash imputation is fixt upon God and his holy Laws, of conniving and dispensing with open and common adultery among his chosen people; a thing which the rankest politician would think it shame and disworship, that his Laws should countenance; how and in what manner this comes to passe, I shall reserve, till the course of method brings on the unfolding of many Scriptures. Next the Law and Gospel are hereby made liable to more then one contradiction, which I referre also thither. Lastly, the supreme dictate of charitie is hereby many wayes neglected and violated. Which I shall forthwith addresse to prove. First we know St. *Paul* saith, *It is better to marry then to burn.*[49] Mariage therfore was giv'n as a remedy of that trouble: but what might this burning mean? Certainly not the meer motion of carnall lust, not the meer goad of a sensitive desire; God does not principally take care for such cattell.[50] What is it then but that desire which God put into *Adam* in Paradise before he knew the sin of incontinence; that

---

49. 1 Corinthians 7:9.

50. Cf. Raphael's admonition to Adam in *Paradise Lost*, VIII, 579 ff.

desire which God saw it was not good that man should be left alone to burn in; the desire and longing to put off an unkindly solitarines by uniting another body, but not without a fit soule to his in the cheerfull society of wedlock. Which if it were so needfull before the fall, when man was much more perfect in himselfe, how much more is it needfull now against all the sorrows and casualties of this life to have an intimate and speaking help, a ready and reviving associate in marriage : whereof who misses by chancing on a mute and spiritles mate, remains more alone then before, and in a burning lesse to be contain'd then that which is fleshly and more to be consider'd; as being more deeply rooted even in the faultles innocence of nature. As for that other burning, which is but as it were the venom of a lusty and over-abounding concoction, strict life and labour, with the abatement of a full diet may keep that low and obedient enough : but this pure and more inbred desire of joyning to it selfe conjugall fellowship a fit conversing soul (which desire is properly call'd love) *is stronger then death,* as the spouse of Christ thought, *many waters cannot quench it, neither can the floods drown it.*[51] This is that rationall burning that mariage is to remedy, not to be allay'd with fasting, nor with any penance to be subdu'd, which how can he asswage who by mis-hap hath met the most unmeetest and unsutable mind? Who hath the power to struggle with an intelligible flame, not in paradice to be resisted, become now more ardent, by being fail'd of what in reason it lookt for; and even then most unquencht, when the importunity of a provender[52] burning is well anough appeas'd; and yet the soule hath obtained nothing of what it justly desires. Certainly such a one forbidd'n to divorce, is in effect forbidd'n to marry, and compell'd to greater difficulties then in a single life; for if there be not a more human burning which mariage must satisfie, or els may be dissolv'd, then that of copulation, mariage cannot be honorable for the meet reducing and terminating of lust between two : seeing many beasts in voluntary and chosen couples, live together as unadulterously, and are as truly maried in that respect. But

---

51. Cf. Song of Solomon 8 : 6–7.
52. Provendered?

all ingenuous men will see that the dignity & blessing of mariage is plac't rather in the mutual enjoyment of that which the wanting soul needfully seeks, then of that which the plenteous body would joyfully give away. Hence it is that *Plato* in his festival discours brings in *Socrates* relating what he fain'd to have learnt from the Prophetesse *Diotima*, how *Love* was the sonne of *Penury*, begot of *Plenty* in the garden of *Jupiter*.[53] Which divinely sorts with that which in effect *Moses* tells us, that *Love* was the son of *Lonelines*, begot in Paradise by that sociable and helpfull aptitude which God implanted between man and woman toward each other. The same also is that burning mention'd by *S. Paul*, whereof mariage ought to be the remedy; the Flesh hath other mutuall and easie curbs which are in the power of any temperate man. When therefore this originall and sinles *Penury* or *Lonelines* of the soul cannot lay it selfe down by the side of such a meet and acceptable union as God ordain'd in marriage, at least in some proportion, it cannot conceive and bring forth *Love*, but remains utterly unmarried under a formall wedlock, and still burnes in the proper meaning of S. *Paul*. Then enters *Hate*, not that Hate that sins, but that which onely is naturall dissatisfaction and the turning aside from a mistaken object: if that mistake have done injury, it fails not to dismisse with recompence; for to retain still, and not be able to love, is to heap up more injury. Thence this wise and pious Law of dismission now defended took beginning: He therfore who lacking of his due in the most native and human end of mariage, thinks it better to part then to live sadly and injuriously to that cheerfull covnant (for not to be belov'd & yet retain'd, is the greatest injury to a gentle spirit) he I say who therfore seeks to part, is one who highly honours the maried life, and would not stain it: and the reasons which now move him to divorce, are equall to the best of those that could first warrant him to marry; for, as was plainly shewn, both the hate which now diverts him and the lonelinesse which leads him still powerfully to seek a fit help, hath not the least grain of a sin in it, if he be worthy to understand himselfe.

---

53. The generation of Love from Poverty and Plenty is related in the *Symposium*, 203.

CHAP. V. *The Third Reason of this Law, because without it,*
he who hath happn'd where he finds nothing but remediles
offences and discontents, is in more and greater temptations
then ever before.

Thirdly, Yet it is next to be fear'd, if he must be still bound
without reason by a deafe rigor, that when he perceives the just
expectance of his mind defeated, he will begin even against Law
to cast about where he may find his satisfaction more compleat,
unlesse he be a thing heroically vertuous, and that are not the
common lump of men for whom chiefly the Laws ought to be
made, though not to their sins yet to their unsinning weaknesses,
it being above their strength to endure the lonely estate, which
while they shun'd, they are fal'n into. And yet there follows
upon this a worse temptation; for if he be such as hath spent
his youth unblamably, and layd up his chiefest earthly comforts in the enjoyment of a contented mariage, nor did neglect
that furderance which was to be obtain'd therein by constant
prayers, when he shall find himself bound fast to an uncom-
plying discord of nature, or, as it oft happens, to an image of
earth and fleam,[54] with whom he lookt to be the copartner of a
sweet and gladsome society and sees withall that his bondage
is now inevitable, though he be almost the strongest Christian,
he will be ready to dispair in vertue, and mutin against divine
providence: and this doubtles is the reason of those lapses and
that melancholy despair which we see in many wedded persons,
though they understand it not, or pretend other causes, because
they know no remedy, and is of extreme danger; therfore when
human frailty surcharg'd, is at such a losse, charity ought to
venture much, and use bold physick, lest an over-tost faith endanger to shipwrack.

---

54. Phlegm, which according to ancient medicine occasioned
sluggishness.

CHAP. VI. *The Fourth Reason of this Law, that God regards Love and Peace in the family, more then a compulsive performance of mariage, which is more broke by a grievous continuance, then by a needfull divorce.*

Fourthly, Mariage is a cov'nant the very beeing wherof consists, not in a forc't cohabitation, and counterfet performance of duties, but in unfained love and peace. And of matrimoniall love no doubt but that was chiefly meant, which by the ancient Sages was thus parabl'd, That Love, if he be not twin-born, yet hath a brother wondrous like him, call'd *Anteros*:[55] whom while he seeks all about, his chance is to meet with many fals and faining Desires that wander singly up and down in his likenes. By them in their borrow'd garb, Love, though not wholly blind, as Poets wrong him, yet having but one eye, as being born an Archer aiming, and that eye not the quickest in this dark region here below, which is not Loves proper sphere, partly out of the simplicity, and credulity which is native to him, often deceiv'd, imbraces and consorts him with these obvious and suborned[56] striplings, as if they were his Mothers own Sons, for so he thinks them, while they suttly keep themselves most on his blind side. But after a while, as his manner is, when soaring up into the high Towr of his *Apogæum*,[57] above the shadow of the earth, he darts out the direct rayes of his then most piercing eyesight upon the impostures, and trim disguises that were us'd with him, and discerns that this is not his genuin brother, as he imagin'd, he has no longer the power to hold fellowship with such a personated mate. For strait his arrows loose their golden heads, and shed their purple feathers, his silk'n breades[58]

---

55. Milton uses the commonplace myth of Eros and Anteros to suggest 'the responsive fire of love between mutually compliable souls ... Eros, in order to love, must find his true soul mate. Love, therefore, is conditional power, possible only in "the reflection of a coequal & *homogeneal* [homogeneous] fire" ' (Boyette, below, p. 452).

56. Frequently met and counterfeit.

57. Highest point. 'Apogee' is the point in the orbit of any planet farthest from the earth.

58. Braids (of his bowstring).

untwine, and slip their knots and that original and firie vertue giv'n him by Fate, all on a sudden goes out and leaves him un-deifi'd, and despoil'd of all his force: till finding *Anteros* at last, he kindles and repairs the almost faded ammunition of his Deity by the reflection of a coequal & *homogeneal*[59] fire. Thus mine author sung it to me;[60] and by the leave of those who would be counted the only grave ones, this is no meer amatorious novel (though to be wise and skilful in these matters, men heretofore of greatest name in vertue, have esteemed it one of the highest arks that human contemplation circling upward, can make from the glassy Sea wheron she stands) but this is a deep and serious verity, shewing us that Love in marriage cannot live nor subsist, unlesse it be mutual; and where love cannot be, there can be left of wedlock nothing, but the empty husk of an out-side matrimony; as undelightfull and unpleasing to God, as any other kind of hypocrisie. So farre is his command from tying men to the observance of duties, which there is no help for, but they must be dissembl'd. If *Salomons* advice be not over-frolick, *Live joyfully*, saith he, *with the wife whom thou lovest, all thy dayes, for that is thy portion*.[61] How then, where we finde it impossible to rejoyce or to love, can we obey this precept? how miserably do we defraud our selves of that com-fortable portion which God gives us, by striving vainly to glue an error together which God and nature will not joyn; adding but more vexation and violence to that blisfull society by our importunate superstition, that will not heark'n to St. *Paul*, I *Cor*. 7. who speaking of mariage and divorce, determines plain enough in generall, that God therein *hath call'd us to peace* and not *to bondage*.[62] Yea God himself commands in his Law more then once, and by his Prophet *Malachy*, as *Calvin* and the best translations read, that *he who hates let him divorce*;[63] that is, he

59. See above, Note 55.

60. Milton's own imagination?

61. Ecclesiastes 9:9.

62. I Corinthians 7:15.

63. Malachi 2:16. Neither Milton's rendering nor that of the Authorized Version ('the Lord ... saith that he hateth putting away' i.e. divorcing) is reliable.

who cannot love: hence is it that the Rabbins and *Maimonides* famous among the rest in a Book of his set forth by *Buxtorfius*, tells us that *Divorce was permitted by* Moses *to preserve peace in mariage, and quiet in the family.*[64] Surely the Jewes had their saving peace about them, aswell as we, yet care was tak'n that this wholsom provision for houshold peace should also be allow'd them; and must this be deny'd to Christians? O perversnes! that the Law should be made more provident of peace-making then the Gospel! that the Gospel should be put to beg a most necessary help of mercy from the Law, but must not have it: and that to grind in the mill of an undelighted and servil copulation, must be the only forc't work of a Christian mariage, oft times with such a yokefellow, from whom both love and peace, both nature and Religion mourns to be separated. I cannot therfore be so diffident, as not securely to conclude, that he who can receive nothing of the most important helps in mariage, being therby disinabl'd to return that duty which is his, with a clear and hearty countnance; and thus continues to grieve whom he would not, and is no lesse griev'd, that man ought even for loves sake and peace to move Divorce upon good and liberall conditions to the divorc't. And it is a lesse breach of wedlock to part with wise and quiet consent betimes, then still to soile and profane that mystery of joy and union with a polluting sadnes and perpetuall distemper; for it is not the outward continuing of mariage that keeps whole that cov'-nant, but whosoever does most according to peace and love, whether in mariage, or in divorce, he it is that breaks mariage least; it being so often written, that *Love only is the fullfilling of every Commandment.*[65]

---

64. From the *Guide to the Perplexed* by the Jewish philosopher Maimonides (1135–1204) as translated into Latin by the Hebraist Johann Buxtorf in 1629.

65. Cf. Romans 13:10 (as above, Note 15).

CHAP. VII. *The Fifth Reason, that nothing more hinders and disturbs the whole life of a Christian, then a matrimony found to be uncurably unfit, and doth the same in effect that an Idolatrous match.*

Fifthly, as those Priests of old were not to be long in sorrow, or if they were, they could not rightly execute their function;[66] so every true Christian in a higher order of Priesthood is a person dedicate to joy and peace, offering himself a lively sacrifice of praise and thanksgiving, and there is no Christian duty that is not to be season'd and set off with cheerfulnes; which in a thousand outward and intermitting crosses may yet be done well, as in this vale of tears, but in such a bosome affliction as this, crushing the very foundation of his inmost nature, when he shall be forc't to love against a possibility, and to use dissimulation against his soule in the perpetuall and ceaseles duties of a husband, doubtles his whole duty of serving God must needs be blurr'd and tainted with a sad unpreparednesse and dejection of spirit, wherin God has no delight. Who sees not therfore how much more Christianity it would be to break by divorce that which is more broken by undue and forcible keeping, rather then *to cover the Altar of the Lord with continuall teares, so that he regardeth not the offering any more,*[67] rather then that the whole worship of a Christian mans life should languish and fade away beneath the weight of an immeasurable griefe and discouragement. And because some think the childr'n of a second matrimony succeeding a divorce would not be a holy seed, it hinder'd not the Jews from being so, and why should we not think them more holy then the off-spring of a former ill-twisted wedlock, begott'n only out of a bestiall necessitie without any true love or contentment, or joy to their parents, so that in some sense we may call them the *children of wrath* and anguish, which will as little conduce to their sanctifying, as if they had been bastards; for nothing more then disturbance of mind suspends us from ·approaching to God. Such a disturbance especially as both assaults our faith

66. Cf. Leviticus 21 : 1–6.
67. Malachi 2 : 13.

and trust in Gods providence, and ends, if there be not a miracle of vertue on either side, not onely in bitternes and wrath, the canker of devotion, but in a desperate and vitious carelesnes; when he sees himselfe without fault of his, train'd by a deceitfull bait into a snare of misery, betrai'd by an alluring ordinance, and then made the thrall of heavines and discomfort by an undivorcing Law of God, as he erroneously thinks, but of mans iniquitie, as the truth is; for that God preferres the free and cheerfull worship of a Christian, before the grievous and exacted observance of an unhappy marriage, besides that the generall maximes of Religion assure us, will be more manifest by drawing a parallell argument from the ground of divorcing an Idolatresse, which was, lest she should alienate his heart from the true worship of God: and what difference is there whether she pervert him to superstition by her enticing sorcery, or disinable him in the whole service of God through the disturbance of her unhelpfull and unfit society; and so drive him at last through murmuring and despair to thoughts of Atheisme; neither doth it lessen the cause of separating in that the one willingly allures him from the faith, the other perhaps unwillingly drives him; for in the account of God it comes all to one that the wife looses him a servant; and therfore by all the united force of the *Decalogue* she ought to be disbanded, unlesse we must set mariage above God and charity, which is a doctrine of devils no lesse then forbidding to marry.[68]

· · · · · · · · · · · ·

CHAP. IX. *That adultery is not the greatest breach of matrimony, that there may be other violations as great.*

Now whether Idolatry or Adultery be the greatest violation of marriage, if any demand, let him thus consider, that among Christian Writers touching matrimony there be three chiefe ends thereof agreed on; Godly society, next civill, and thirdly, that of the mariage-bed. Of these the first in name to be the

---

68. Chapter VIII, here omitted, discusses the related question of 'whether an idolatrous heretick ought to be divorc't'. Milton replies in the affirmative (cf. below, Note 73).

highest and most excellent, no baptiz'd man can deny; nor that Idolatry smites directly against this prime end, nor that such as the violated end is, such is the violation: but he who affirms adultery to be the highest breach, affirms the bed to be the highest of mariage, which is in truth a grosse and borish opinion, how common soever; as farre from the countnance of Scripture, as from the light of all clean philosophy, or civill nature. And out of question the cheerfull help that may be in mariage toward sanctity of life, is the purest, and so the noblest end of that contract: but if the particular of each person be consider'd, then of those three ends which God appointed, that to him is greatest which is most necessary: and mariage is then most brok'n to him, when he utterly wants the fruition of that which he most sought therin, whether it were religious, civill, or corporall society. Of which wants to do him right by divorce only for the last and meanest, is a perverse injury, and the pretended reason of it as frigid as frigidity it selfe, which the *Code*[69] and Canon are only sensible of. Thus much of this controversie. I now return to the former argument.[70] And having shewn that disproportion, contrariety, or numnesse of minde may justly be divorc't, by proving already that the prohibition therof opposes the expresse end of Gods institution, suffers not mariage to satisfie that intellectuall and innocent desire which God himself kindl'd in man to be the bond of wedlock, but only to remedy a sublunary and bestial burning, which frugal diet without mariage would easily chast'n. Next that it drives many to transgresse the conjugall bed, while the soule wanders after that satisfaction which it had hope to find at home, but hath mis't. Or els it sits repining even to Atheism; finding it self hardly dealt with, but misdeeming the cause to be in Gods Law, which is in mans unrighteous ignorance. I have shew'n also how it unties the inward knot of mariage, which is peace and love (if that can be unti'd which was never knit) while it aimes to keep fast the outward form-

---

69. Civil law generally, or else Justinian's *Code* in particular. Cf. below, p. 161, Note 106.

70. i.e. 'whether an idolatrous heretick ought to be divorc't' (above, Note 68).

alitie; how it lets perish the Christian man, to compel imposs-
ibly the maried man.

CHAP. X. *The Sixth Reason of this Law, that to prohibit divorce
sought for natural causes is against nature.*

The sixt place declares this prohibition to be as respectlesse of
human nature as it is of religion, and therfore is not of God. He
teaches that an unlawful mariage may be lawfully divorc't. And
that those who having throughly discern'd each others disposition which oft-times cannot be till after matrimony, shall then
find a powerful reluctance[71] and recoile of nature on either side
blasting all the content of their mutuall society, that such persons are not lawfully maried (to use the Apostles words) *Say I
these things as a man, or saith not the Law also the same? for
it is writt'n,* Deut. 22. *Thou shalt not sowe thy vineyard with
divers seeds, lest thou defile both. Thou shalt not plow with
an Oxe and an Asse together,* and the like. I follow the pattern
of St. *Pauls* reasoning; *Doth God care for Asses and Oxen; how
ill they yoke together, or is it not said altogether for our sakes?
for our sakes no doubt this is writt'n.*[72] Yea the Apostle himself
in the forecited 2 *Cor.* 6. 14.[73] alludes from that place of
Deut[eronomy] to forbid mis-yoking mariage; as by the Greek
word is evident, though he instance but in one example of mis-
matching with an Infidell: yet next to that what can be a
fouler incongruity, a greater violence to the reverend secret of
nature, then to force a mixture of minds that cannot unite, and
to sowe the furrow of mans nativity with seed of two incoher-
ent and uncombining dispositions; which act being kindly and
voluntarie, as it ought, the Apostle in the language he wrote
call'd *Eunoia,* and the Latines *Benevolence,*[74] intimating the

---

71. Resistance.

72. 1 Corinthians 9:8–10, which in its allegorical interpretation
of Deuteronomy 25:4 allows Milton to attempt as much with
Deuteronomy 22:9–10.

73. 'Be yet not unequally yoked together with unbelievers' –
cited by Milton in the chapter here omitted (above, Note 68).

74. I Corinthians 7:3.

original therof to be in the understanding and the will; if not, surely there is nothing which might more properly be call'd a malevolence rather; and is the most injurious and unnaturall tribute that can be extorted from a person endew'd with reason, to be made pay out the best substance of his body, and of his soul too, as some think, when either for just powerfull causes he cannot like, or from unequall causes finds not recompence. And that there is a hidden efficacie of love and hatred in man as wel as in other kinds, not morall, but naturall, which though not alwayes in the choyce, yet in the successe of mariage wil ever be most predominant, besides daily experience, the author of *Ecclesiasticus*, whose wisedom hath set him next the Bible,[75] acknowledges, 13. 16. *A man*, saith he, *will cleave to his like*. But what might be the cause, whether each ones alotted *Genius* or proper Starre, or whether the supernall influence of Schemes and angular aspects or this elementall *Crasis*[76] here below, whether all these jointly or singly meeting friendly, or unfriendly in either party, I dare not, with the men I am likest to clash, appear so much a Philosopher as to conjecture. The ancient proverb in *Homer* lesse abstruse intitles this worke of leading each like person to his like, peculiarly to God himselfe:[77] which is plain anough also by his naming of a meet or like help in the first espousall instituted; and that every woman is meet for every man, none so absurd as to affirm. Seeing then there is indeed a twofold Seminary or stock in nature, from whence are deriv'd the issues of love and hatred distinctly flowing through the whole masse of created things, and that Gods doing ever is to bring the due likenesses and harmonies of his workes together, except when out of two contraries met to their own destruction, he moulds a third existence, and that it is error, or some evil Angel which either blindly or maliciously hath drawn together in two persons ill imbarkt in wedlock the sleeping discords and enmities of nature lull'd on purpose with

---

75. Neither Ecclesiasticus nor the other books of the Apocrypha were regarded by Protestants as canonical.

76. Blending of elements.

77. Cf. *Odyssey*, XVII, 218: 'god is bringing like and like together' (trans. A. T. Murray).

some false bait, that they may wake to agony and strife, later then prevention could have wisht, if from the bent of just and honest intentions beginning what was begun, and so continuing, all that is equall, all that is fair and possible hath been tri'd, and no accommodation likely to succeed, what folly is it still to stand combating and battering against invincible causes and effects, with evill upon evill, till either the best of our dayes be linger'd out, or ended with some speeding sorrow. The wise *Ecclesiasticus* advises rather, 37. 27. *My sonne, prove thy soule in thy life, see what is evill for it, and give not that unto it.* Reason he had to say so; for if the noysomnesse or disfigurement of body can soon destroy the sympathy of mind to wedlock duties, much more wil the annoyance and trouble of mind infuse it selfe into all the faculties and acts of the body, to render them invalid, unkindly, and even unholy against the fundamentall law book of nature, which *Moses* never thwarts, but reverences: therefore he commands us to force nothing against sympathy[78] or naturall order, no not upon the most abject creatures; to shew that such an indignity cannot be offer'd to man without an impious crime. And certainly those divine meditating words of finding out a meet and like help to man, have in them a consideration of more then the indefinite likenesse of womanhood; nor are they to be made waste paper on, for the dulnesse of Canon divinity: no nor those other allegorick precepts of beneficence fetcht out of the closet of nature to teach us goodnes and compassion in not compelling together unmatchable societies, or if they meet through mischance, by all consequence to dis-joyn them, as God and nature signifies and lectures to us not onely by those recited decrees, but ev'n by the first and last of all his visible works; when by his divorcing command the world first rose out of Chaos, nor can be renewed again out of confusion but by the separating of unmeet consorts.

----

78. Cf. 'antipathy', above, p. 124.

CHAP. XI. *The seventh reason, That sometimes continuance in mariage may be evidently the shortning or endangering of life to either party, both Law and divinitie concluding, that life is to be prefer'd before mariage the intended solace of life.*

Seventhly, The Canon Law and Divines consent, that if either party be found contriving against anothers life, they may be sever'd by divorce; for a sin against the life of mariage, is greater then a sin against the bed: the one destroyes, the other but defiles. The same may be said touching those persons who being of a pensive nature and cours of life, have sum'd up all their solace in that free and lightsome conversation which God and man intends in marriage: wherof when they see themselves depriv'd by meeting an unsociable consort, they oft-times resent one anothers mistake so deeply, that long it is not ere griefe end one of them. When therfore this danger is fore-seen, that the life is in perill by living together, what matter is it whether helples griefe, or wilfull practice be the cause; This is certain, that the preservation of life is more worth then the compulsory keeping of mariage; and it is no lesse then crueltie to force a man to remain in that state as the solace of his life, which he and his friends know will be either the undoing or the disheartning of his life. And what is life without the vigor and spiritfull exercise of life? how can it be usefull either to private or publick employment? shall it therfore be quite dejected, though never so valuable, and left to moulder away in heavines for the superstitious and impossible performance of an ill-driv'n bargain? Nothing more inviolable then vowes made to God, yet we read in *Numbers*[79] that if a wife had made such a vow, the meer will and authoritie of her husband might break it; how much more may he breake the error of his own bonds with an unfit and mistak'n wife, to the saving of his welfare, his life, yea his faith and vertue from the hazard of over-strong temptations; for if man be Lord of the Sabbath, to the curing of

---

79. Numbers 30:6-15.

Fevor,[80] can he be lesse then Lord of mariage in such important causes as these?

CHAP. XII. *The eighth reason, It is probable, or rather certain,
that every one who happ'ns to marry, hath not the calling,
and therefore upon unfitnesse found and consider'd, force
ought not to be us'd.*

Eightly, It is most sure that some ev'n of those who are not
plainly defective in body, yet are destitut of all other mariage-
able gifts, and consequently have not the calling to marry; unlesse nothing be requisite therto but a meer instrumentall body;
which to affirm, is to that unanimous Covenant a reproach: yet
it is as sure that many such, not of their own desire, but by the
perswasion of friends, or not knowing themselves, doe often
enter into wedlock; where finding the difference at length
between the duties of a married life, and the gifts of a single
life; what unfitnes of mind, what wearisomnesse, what scruples
and doubts to an incredible offence and displeasure are like to
follow between, may be soon imagin'd: whom thus to shut up
and immure and shut up together, the one with a mischosen
mate, the other in a mistak'n calling, is not a cours that Christian wisedome and tendernesse ought to use. As for the custome that some parents and guardians have of forcing mariages,
it will be better to say nothing of such a savage inhumanity,
but only thus, that the Law which gives not all freedom of
divorce to any creature endu'd with reason so assasinated, is
next in cruelty.

---

80. The parallel is with the miracles Christ performed even on
the Sabbath (Matthew 12:8–13).

CHAP. XIII. *The ninth reason, Because mariage is not a meer carnall coition, but a human Society, where that cannot reasonably be had, there can be no true matrimony. Mariage compar'd with all other cov'nants and vowes warrantably broken for the good of man. Mariage the Papists Sacrament and unfit mariage the Protestants Idoll.*

Ninthly, I suppose it will be allow'd us that mariage is a human Society, and that all human society must proceed from the mind rather than the body, els it would be but a kind of animal or beastish meeting; if the mind therfore cannot have that due company by mariage, that it may reasonably and humanly desire, that mariage can be no human society, but a certain formality; or guilding over of little better than a brutish congresse, and so in very wisdome and purenesse to be dissolv'd.

But mariage is more then human, *the Covnant of God*, Prov 2. 17. therfore man cannot dissolve it. I answer, if it be more then human, so much the more it argues the chiefe society thereof to be in the soule rather than in the body, and the greatest breach therof to be unfitnesse of mind rather then defect of body: for the body can have least affinity in a covnant more then human, so that the reason of dissolving holds good the rather. Again, I answer, that the Sabbath is a higher institution, a command of the first Table,[81] for the breach wherof God hath farre more and oftner testify'd his anger, ther for divorces, which from *Moses* to *Malachy*[82] he never took displeasure at, nor then neither, if we mark the Text; and yet as oft as the good of man is concern'd, he not onely permits, but commands to break the Sabbath. What covnant more contracted with God, and lesse in mans power, then the vow which hath once past his lips? yet if it be found rash, if offensive, if unfruit

---

81. 'Remember the Sabbath day, to keep it holy' (Exodus 20:8) The Decalogue here quoted exists in two versions, one expressly religious ('the first Table' in Exodus 20:1–17), the other distinctly more humanitarian ('the second Table' in Deuteronomy 5:6–18).

82. Malachi 2:16, quoted above, p. 140.

full either to Gods glory or the good of man, our doctrine forces not error and unwillingnes irksomly to keep it, but counsels wisedome and better thoughts boldly to break it; therfore to enjoyn the indissoluble keeping of a mariage found unfit against the good of man both soul and body, as hath bin evidenc't, is to make an Idol of mariage, to advance it above the worship of God and the good of man, to make it a transcendent command, above both the second and the first Table, which is a most prodigious doctrine.

Next, wheras they cite out of the *Proverbs*, that it is the *Covnant of God*, and therfore more then human, that consequence is manifestly false: for so the covnant which *Zedechiah* made with the Infidell King of *Babel*, is call'd the *Covnant of God*, Ezek. 17. 19. which would be strange to heare counted more then a human covnant. So every covnant between man and man, bound by oath, may be call'd the covnant of God, because God therin is attested. So of mariage he is the authour and the witnes; yet hence will not follow any divine astriction more then what is subordinate to the glory of God and the main good of either party; for as the glory of God and their esteemed fitnesse one for the other, was the motive which led them both at first to think without other revelation that God had joynd them together. So when it shall be found by their apparent unfitnesse, that their continuing to be man and wife is against the glory of God and their mutuall happinesse, it may assure them that God never joyn'd them; who hath reveal'd his gracious will not to set the ordinance above the man for whom it was ordain'd: not to canonize mariage either as a tyrannesse or a goddesse over the enfranchiz'd life and soul of man: for wherin can God delight, wherin be worshipt, wherein be glorify'd by the forcible continuing of an improper and ill-yoking couple? He that lov'd not to see the disparity of severall cattell at the plow, cannot be pleas'd with any vast unmeetnesse in mariage. Where can be the peace and love which must invite God to such a house, may it not be fear'd that the not divorcing of such a helplesse disagreement, will be the divorcing of God finally from such a place? But it is a triall of our patience they say: I grant it: but which of *Jobs* afflictions were sent him with that law, that he might not use means to remove any of them if he could? And what if it subvert our patience and our faith too? Who shall answer for the perishing of all those soules perishing by stubborn expositions of particular and inferior precepts against the generall and supreme rule of charity? They dare not affirm that mariage is either a Sacrament, or a mystery, though all those sacred things give place to man, and yet they invest it with such an awfull sanctity, and give it such adamantine chains to bind with, as if it were to be worshipt like some Indian deity, when it can conferre no blessing upon us, but works more and more to our misery. To such teachers the saying of S. *Peter* at the Councell of *Jerusalem* will doe well to be apply'd :[83] *Why tempt ye God to put a yoke upon the necks* of Christian men, which neither the *Jews,* Gods ancient people, *nor we are able to bear*: and nothing but unwary expounding hath brought upon us.[84]

* * * * * * * * * * * * *

THE SECOND BOOK.

CHAP. I. *The Ordinance of Sabbath and mariage compar'd. Hyperbole no unfrequent figure in the Gospel. Excesse cur'd by contrary excesse. Christ neither did, nor could abrogat the Law of divorce, but only reprove the abuse therof.*

Hitherto the Position undertaken hath bin declar'd, and prov'd by Law of God, that Law prov'd to be moral, and unabolishable for many reasons equal, honest, charitable, just, annext therto. It follows now that those places of Scripture which have a seeming to revoke the prudence of *Moses,* or rather that mercifull decree of God, be forthwith explain'd and reconcil'd. For what are all these reasonings worth will some reply, whenas the words of Christ are plainly against all divorce, except *in*

---

83. Cf. Acts 15:6–11.

84. Chapter XIV, here omitted, glances at those individuals who, unduly 'addicted to Religion', impose limitations on 'the blamelesse nature of man' – with predictable results.

case of fornication.[85] To whom he whose minde were to answer no more but this, *except also in case of charity*, might safely appeal to the more plain words of Christ in defence of so excepting. *Thou shalt doe no manner of worke* saith the commandment of the Sabbath.[86] Yes saith Christ works of charity. And shall we be more severe in paraphrasing the considerat and tender Gospel, then he was in expounding the rigid and peremptory Law ? What was ever in all appearance lesse made for man, and more for God alone then the Sabbath ? yet when the good of man comes into the scales, we hear that voice of infinite goodnesse and benignity that *Sabbath was made for man, not man for Sabbath.*[87] What thing ever was more made for man alone and lesse for God then mariage ? And shall we load it with a cruel and senceles bondage utterly against both the good of man and the glory of God ? Let who so will now listen, I want neither pall nor mitre, I stay neither for ordination nor induction, but in the firm faith of a knowing Christian, which is the best and truest endowment of the keyes,[88] I pronounce, the man who shall bind so cruelly a good and gracious ordinance of God, hath not in that the Spirit of Christ. Yet that every text of Scripture seeming opposite may be attended with a due exposition, this other part ensues, and makes account to find no slender arguments for this assertion out of those very Scriptures, which are commonly urg'd against it.

First therfore let us remember as a thing not to be deny'd, that all places of Scripture wherin just reason of doubt arises from the letter, are to be expounded by considering upon what occasion every thing is set down : and by comparing other Texts. The occasion which induc't our Saviour to speak of divorce was either to convince the extravagance of the Pharises in that point, or to give a sharp and vehement answer to a tempting question. And in such cases that we are not to repose

---

85. Milton has reached the major obstacle to this thesis, Christ's apparent restriction of divorce 'saving for the cause of fornication' (Matthew 5:32; cf. below, Notes 90 and 94).

86. Cf. Exodus 20:10.

87. Mark 2:27.

88. i.e. the keys given to St. Peter (Matthew 16:19).

all upon the literall terms of so many words, many instances
will teach us: Wherin we may plainly discover how Christ
meant not to be tak'n word for word, but like a wise Physician,
administring one excesse against another to reduce us to a
perfect mean: Where the Pharises were strict, there Christ
seems remisse; where they were too remiss, he saw it needfull
to seem most severe: in one place he censures an unchast look
to be adultery already committed: another time he passes over
actuall adultery with lesse reproof then for an unchast look;
not so heavily condemning secret weaknes, as open malice: So
heer he may be justly thought to have giv'n this rigid sentence
against divorce, not to cut off all remedy from a good man
who finds himself consuming away in a disconsolate and unin-
joy'd matrimony, but to lay a bridle upon the bold abuses of
those over weening *Rabbies*; which he could not more effectually
doe, then by a countersway of restraint curbing their wild
exorbitance almost into the other extreme; as when we bow
things the contrary way, to make them come to their naturall
straitnesse. And that this was the only intention of Christ is
most evident; if we attend but to his own words and protestation made in the same Sermon, not many verses before he
treats of divorcing, that he came not to abrogate from the Law
one jot or tittle,[89] and denounces against them that shall so
teach.

But S. *Luke*, the verse immediately before going that of
divorce inserts the same caveat,[90] as if the latter could not be
understood without the former; and as a witnesse to produce
against this our wilful mistake of abrogating, which must needs
confirm us that what ever els in the political law of more
special relation to the Jews might cease to us, yet that of those
precepts concerning divorce, not one of them was repeal'd by
the doctrine of Christ, unlesse we have vow'd not to beleeve
his own cautious and immediat profession; for if these our
Saviours words inveigh against all divorce, and condemn it as
adultery, except it be for adultery, and be not rather understood
against the abuse of those divorces permitted in the Law, then

89. Matthew 5:18, quoted above, Note 41.
90. Luke 16:17–18.

is that Law of *Moses*, Deut. 24. 1. not onely repeal'd and wholly annull'd against the promise of Christ and his known profession, not to meddle in matters Judicial, but that which is more strange, the very substance and purpose of that Law is contradicted and convinc't both of injustice and impurity, as having authoriz'd and maintain'd legall adultery by statute. *Moses* also cannot scape to be guilty of unequall and unwise decrees, punishing one act of secret adultery by death,[91] and permitting a whole life of open adultery by Law. And albeit Lawyers write that some politicall edicts, though not approv'd, are yet allow'd to the scum of the people and the necessity of the times; these excuses have but a weak pulse: for first, we read, not that the scoundrel people, but the choicest, the wisest, the holiest of that nation have frequently us'd these lawes, or such as these in the best and holiest times. Secondly, be it yeelded, that in matters not very bad or impure, a human law giver may slacken something of that which is exactly good, to the disposition of the people and the times: but if the perfect, the pure, the righteous law of God, for so are all his statutes and his judgements, be found to have allow'd smoothly without any certain reprehension, that which Christ afterward declares to be adultery, how can we free this Law from the horrible endightment of being both impure, unjust, and fallacious.[92]

. . . .

CHAP. XVII. *The sentence of Christ concerning divorce how to be expounded. What* Grotius *hath observ'd. Other additions.*

Having thus unfolded those ambiguous reasons, wherewith Christ, as his wont was, gave to the Pharises that came to

---

91. Cf. Leviticus 20:10, Deuteronomy 22:22.

92. Chapters II–XVI, here omitted, set forth the detailed arguments supporting Milton's ambitious efforts to qualify the common view that 'the words of Christ are plainly against all divorce, except *in case of fornication*' (above, pp. 152–3). The common denominator remains the constant plea to heed 'the all-interpreting voice of charity'.

sound him, such an answer as they deserv'd, it will not be uneasie[93] to explain the sentence it selfe that now follows; *Whosoever shall put away his wife, except it be for fornication, and shall marry another, committeth adultery.*[94] First therfore I will set down what is observ'd by *Grotius* upon this point, a man of generall learning. Next I produce what mine own thoughts gave me, before I had seen his annotations. *Origen*,[95] saith he, notes that Christ nam'd adultery rather as one example of other like cases, then as one only exception. And that it is frequent, not only in human but in divine Laws, to expresse one kind of fact, wherby other causes of like nature may have the like plea : as *Exod.* 21. 18, 19, 20, 26. *Deut.* 19. 5. And from the maxims of civil Law he shews that ev'n in sharpest penal laws, the same reason hath the same right : and in gentler Lawes, that from like causes to like the Law interprets rightly. But it may be objected, saith hee, that nothing destroyes the end of wedlock so much as adultery. To which he answers, that mariage was not ordaind only for copulation, but for mutuall help and comfort of life; and if we mark diligently the nature of our Saviours commands, wee shall finde that both their beginning and their end consists in charity : whose will is that wee should so be good to others, as that wee bee not cruell to our selves. And hence it appeares why *Marke*, and *Luke*, and S. *Paul* to the *Cor[inthians]* mentioning this precept of Christ, adde no exception : because exceptions that arise from naturall equity, are included silently under generall terms : it would bee consider'd therfore whether the same equity may not have place in other cases lesse frequent. Thus farre he.[96] From hence, is what I adde : first, that this saying of Christ, as it is usually expounded, can be no law at all, that a man for

93. Difficult.

94. Matthew 19:9 – a variant of Matthew 5:32 (quoted above, p. 153, Note 85) – follows the verse cited earlier still (p. 117, Note 14).

95. One of the most learned of the Church Fathers, the philosopher Origen (*c.* 185–*c.* 254) was eliciting favorable response throughout the Renaissance.

96. Milton has borrowed from Grotius's *Annotationes* (above, Note 37).

no cause should separate but for adultery, except it bee a supernaturall law, not binding us as we now are: had it bin the law of nature, either the Jews, or some other wise and civill nation would have pres't it: or let it be so; yet that law *Deut.* 24. 1. wherby a man hath leave to part, when as for just and naturall cause discover'd he cannot love, is a law ancienter, and deeper ingrav'n in blameles nature then the other: therfore the inspired Law-giver Moses took care that this should be specify'd and allowed: the other he let vanish in silence, not once repeated in the volume of his law, ev'n as the reason of it vanisht with Paradise. Secondly, this can be no new command, for the Gospel enjoyns no new morality, save only the infinit enlargement of charity, which in this respect is call'd the *new commandement* by S. *John*; as being the accomplishment of every command.[97] Thirdly, It is no command of perfection further then it partakes of charity, which is *the bond of perfection*.[98] Those commands therfore which compell us to self cruelty above our strength, so hardly will help forward to perfection, that they hinder and set backward in all the common rudiments of Christianity, as was prov'd. It being thus clear, that the words of Christ can be no kind of command, as they are vulgarly tak'n, we shall now see in what sence they may be a command, and that an excellent one, the same with that of *Moses*, and no other. Moses had granted that only for a natural annoyance, defect, or dislike, whether in body or mind for so the Hebrew words plainly note)[99] which a man could not force himselfe to live with, he might give a bill of divorce, therby forbidding any other cause wherin amendment or reconciliation might have place. This Law the Pharises depraving, extended to any slight contentious cause whatsoever. Christ therfore seeing where they halted,[100] urges the negative part of that law, which is necessarily understood (for the determinate permission of *Moses* binds them from further licence) and checking their supercilious drift, declares that no accidental,

---

97. John 13:34.
98. Colossians 3:14.
99. See above, p. 130.
100. Fell short.

temporary, or reconcileable offence, except fornication, can justifie a divorce: he touches not here those natural and perpetual hindrances of society, whether in body or mind, which are not to be remov'd: for such, as they are aptest to cause an unchangeable offence, so are they not capable of reconcilement because not of amendment; they do not break indeed, but they annihilate the bands of mariage more then adultery. For that fault committed argues not alwaies a hatred either natural or incidental against whom it is committed; neither does it inferre a disability of all future helpfulnes, or loyalty, or loving agreement, being once past, and pardon'd, where it can be pardon'd: but that which naturally distasts and *finds no favour in the eyes* of matrimony, can never be conceal'd, never appeas'd, never intermitted, but proves a perpetuall nullity of love and contentment, a solitude, and dead vacation[101] of all acceptable conversing. *Moses* therfore permits divorce, but in cases only that have no hands to joyn, and more need separating then adultery. Christ forbids it, but in matters only that may accord, and those lesse then fornication. Thus is *Moses* Law here plainly confirm'd, and those causes which he permitted, not a jot gainsaid. And that this is the true meaning of this place I prove also by no lesse an Author then S. *Paul* himself, 1 *Cor.* 7. 10, 11. upon which text Interpreters agree that the Apostle only repeats the precept of Christ: where while he speaks of *the wives reconcilement to her husband,* he puts it out of controversie, that our Saviour meant chiefly matters of strife and reconcilement; of which sort he would not that any difference should be the occasion of divorce, except fornication. And that we may learn better how to value a grave and prudent law of *Moses,* and how unadvisedly we smatter with our lips, when we talk of Christs abolishing any Judiciall law of his great Father, except in some circumstances which are Judaicall rather than Judicial, and need no abolishing but cease of themselvs, I say again, that this recited law of *Moses* contains a cause of divorce greater beyond compare then that for adultery; and whoso cannot so conceive it, errs and wrongs exceedingly a law

---

101. Cessation.

of deep wisdom for want of well fadoming. For let him mark no man urges the just divorcing of adultery, as it is a sin, but as it is an injury to mariage; and though it be but once committed, and that without malice, whether through importunity or opportunity, the Gospel does not therfore disswade him who would therfore divorce; but that natural hatred whenever it arises, is a greater evil in mariage, then the accident of adultery, a greater defrauding, a greater injustice, and yet not blameable, he who understands not after all this representing, I doubt his will like a hard spleen draws faster then his understanding can well sanguifie.[102] Nor did that man ever know or feel what it is to love truly, nor ever yet comprehend in his thoughts what the true intent of marriage is. And this also will be somwhat above his reach, but yet no lesse a truth for lack of his perspective, that as no man apprehends what vice is, so well as he who is truly vertuous, no man knows hel like him who converses most in heav'n, so there is none that can estimate the evil and the affliction of a naturall hatred in matrimony, unlesse he have a soul gentle anough, and spacious anough to contemplate what is true love.

And the reason why men so disesteem this wise judging Law of God, and count hate, or *the not finding of favour*, as it is there term'd, a humorous,[103] a dishonest, and slight cause of divorce, is because themselves apprehend so little of what true concord means: for if they did, they would be juster in their ballancing between natural hatred and casuall adultery; this being but a transient injury, and soon amended, I mean as to the party against whom the trespasse is: but that other being an unspeakable and unremitting sorrow and offence, wherof no amends can be made, no cure, no ceasing but by divorce, which like a divine touch in one moment heals all; and like the word of God, in one instant hushes outrageous tempests into a sudden stilnesse and peacefull calm. Yet all this so great a good of Gods own enlarging to us, is by the hard rains of them that fit us wholly diverted and imbezzl'd from us. Maligners of mankind! But who hath taught you to mangle thus, and make

102. Produce blood.
103. Capricious.

more gashes in the miseries of a blamelesse creature, with the
leaden daggers of your literall decrees, to whose ease you
cannot adde the tithe of one small atome, but by letting alone
your unhelpfull Surgery. As for such as think wandring con
cupiscence to bee here newly and more precisely forbidd'n
then it was before, if the Apostle can convince them; we know
that we are to *know lust by the law*,[104] and not by any new dis
covery of the Gospel. The Law of *Moses* knew what it per
mitted, and the Gospel knew what it forbid; hee that under a
peevish conceit of debarring concupiscence, shall goe about
to make a novice of *Moses*, (not to say a worse thing for rever
ence sake) and such a one of God himselfe, as is a horror to
think, to bind our Saviour in the default of a down-right promise
breaking, and to bind the disunions of complaining nature in
chains together, and curb them with a canon bit, tis he that
commits all the whordom and adultery, which himselfe ad
judges, besides the former guilt so manifold that lies upon
him. And if none of these considerations with all their wait
and gravity, can avail to the dispossessing him of his pretiou
literalism, let some one or othér entreat him but to read on in
the same 19. of *Math[ew]* till he come to that place that saye
*Some make themselves Eunuchs for the kingdom of heavn
sake.* And if then he please to make use of *Origens* knife, h
may doe well to be his own carver.[105]

CHAP. XVIII. *Whether the words of our Saviour be rightly
expounded only of actual fornication to be the cause of
divorce. The opinion of* Grotius *with other reasons.*

But because we know that Christ never gave a Judiciall Law, and
that the word *fornication* is variously significant in Scripture
it wil be much right done to our Saviours words, to conside
diligently, whether it be meant heer, that nothing but actual
fornication, prov'd by witnes, can warrant a divorce, for so our
cannon law judges. Neverthelesse as I find that *Grotius* on this

---

104. Cf. Romans 7:7.

105. Origen (above, Note 95), on literally interpreting the verse here
quoted (Matthew 19:12), castrated himself.

place hath observ'd, the Christian Emperours, *Theodosius* the second, and *Justinian*, men of high wisdom and reputed piety,[106] decreed it to bee a divorsive fornication, if the wife attempted either against the knowledge, or obstinatly against the will of her husband, such things as gave open suspition of adulterizing: as the wilfull haunting of feasts, and invitations with men not of her neer kindred, the lying forth of her house without probable cause, the frequenting of Theaters against her husbands mind, her endeavour to prevent or destroy conception. Hence that of *Jerom*, *Where fornication is suspected, the wife may be lawfully divorc't*; not that every motion of a jealous mind should be regarded, but that it should not be exacted to prove all things by the visibility of Law witnessing, or els to hood-wink the mind: for the law is not able to judge of these things but by the rule of equity, and by permitting a wise man to walk the middle way of prudent circumspection, neither wretchedly jealous, nor stupidly and tamely patient. To this purpose hath *Grotius* in his notes.[107] He shews also that fornication is tak'n in Scripture for such a continual headstrong behaviour, as tends to plain contempt of the husband: and proves it out of *Judges* 19. 2. where the Levites wife is said to have plaid the whoor against him; which *Josephus* and the *Septuagint*, with the *Chaldean*, interpret onely of stubbornesse and rebellion against her husband: and to this I adde that *Kimchi* and the two other Rabbies who glosse the text, are in the same opinion. *Ben Gersom* reasons, that had it bin whoordom, a Jew and a Levit would have disdain'd to fetch her again.[108] And this I shall contribute, that had it been whoordom,

---

106. The Byzantine emperor Theodosius II (401–50), celebrated for his piety, convened the Council of Ephesus in 431 and enacted the Theodosian Code. The eminently orthodox Justinian the Great (483–565) not only built several churches including Constantinople's Hagia Sophia but issued an enlargement and rearrangement of the Theodosian Code.

107. Milton has again borrowed from Grotius's *Annotationes* (above, Note 37).

108. The references are to the Jewish historian Josephus (c. 37–c. 100); to the Greek version of the Old Testament made in the

she would have chosen any other place to run to, then to her fathers house, it being so infamous for an Hebrew woman to play the harlot, and so opprobrious to the parents. Fornication then in this place of the *Judges* is understood for stubborn disobedience against her husband, and not adultery. A sin of that sudden activity as to be already committed, when no more is done, but onely lookt unchastly: which yet I should bee loath to judge worthy a divorce, though in our Saviours language it bee call'd adultery. Neverthelesse when palpable and frequent signes are giv'n, the law of God, *Numb. 5.* so far gave way to the jealousie of a man as that the woman set before the Sanctuary with her head uncover'd, was adjur'd by the Priest to swear whether she were false or no; and constrain'd to drink that *bitter water* with an undoubted *curse of rottennesse and tympany* to follow, unlesse she were innocent.[109] And the jealous man had not bin guiltles before God, as seems by the last verse, if having such a suspition in his head, he should neglect this triall; which if to this day it be not to be us'd, or be thought as uncertain of effect, as our antiquated law of *Ordalium*,[110] yet all equity will judge that many adulterous demeanors which are of lewd suspicion and example, may be held sufficient to incurre a divorce, though the act it selfe hath not been prov'd. And seeing the generosity of our Nation is so, as to account no reproach more abominable, then to bee nicknam'd the husband of an adultresse, that our law should not be as ample as the Law of God to vindicate a man from that ignoble sufferance, is our barbarous unskilfulnesse, not considering that the law should be exasperated according to our estimation of the injury. And if it must be suffer'd till the act be visibly prov'd, *Salomon* himselfe whose judgement will be granted to surpasse the acutenesse of any Canonist, confesses, *Pro. 30. 19. 20* that for the act of adultery, it is as difficult to be found as the *track*

---

third century B.C. by seventy-two scholars (hence 'Septuagint'); to the Chaldaic (Syriac) version; to the exegete Rabbi David Kimchi (1160–1235); and to the profoundly learned Rabbi Gersonides (1288 c. 1344).

109. Cf. Numbers 5 : 11–31.

110. Trial by ordeal, abolished by the early thirteenth century.

of an Eagle in the aire, or the way of a ship in the Sea: so that a man may be put to unmanly indignities, ere it be found out. This therfore may bee anough to inform us, that divorsive adultery is not limited by our Saviour to the utmost act, and that to be attested alwayes by eye witnesse, but may bee extended also to divers obvious actions, which either plainly lead to adultery, or give such presumption, wherby sensible men may suspect the deed to bee already don. And this the rather may bee thought, in that our Saviour chose to use the word *Fornication*, which word is found to signifie other matrimoniall transgressions of main breach to that covnant besides actuall adultery. For that sinne needed not the riddance of divorce, but of death by the Law, which was active ev'n till then by the examples of the woman tak'n in adultery;[111] or if the law had been dormant, our Saviour was more likely to have told them of their neglect, then to have let a capitall crime silently scape into a divorce: or if it bee said his businesse was not to tell them what was criminall in the civill Courts, but what was sinfull at the barre of conscience, how dare they then having no other ground then these our Saviours words, draw that into triall of law, which both by *Moses* and our Saviour was left to the jurisdiction of conscience? But wee take from our Saviour, say they, only that it was adultery and our Law of it selfe applies the punishment. But by their leave that so argue, the great Law-giver of all the world who knew best what was adultery both to the Jew and to the Gentile appointed no such applying, and never likes when mortall men will be vainly presuming to out-strip his justice.

---

111. Cf. John 8:3–11.

CHAP. XIX. *Christs manner of teaching. S. Paul addes to this matter of divorce without command, to shew the matter to be of equity, not of rigor. That the bondage of a Christian may be as much, and his peace as little in some other mariages besides idolatrous: If those arguments therfore be good in that one case, why not in those other: therfore the Apostle himselfe adds, ἐν τοῖς τοιούτοις.*[112]

Thus at length wee see both by this and by other places, that there is scarce any one saying in the Gospel, but must bee read with limitations and distinctions, too bee rightly understood; for Christ gives no full comments or continued discourses, but as *Demetrius* the Rhetoritian phrase it,[113] speaks oft in Monosyllables, like a maister, scattering the heavenly grain of his doctrine like pearl heer and there, which requires a skilfull and laborious gatherer, who must compare the words he findes, with other precepts, with the end of every ordinance, and with the generall *analogie* of Evangelick doctrine: otherwise many particular sayings would bee but strange repugnant riddles; and the Church would offend in granting divorce for frigidity, which is not here excepted with adultery, but by them added. And this was it undoubtedly which gave reason to S. *Paul* of his own authority, as hee professes, and without command from the Lord, to enlarge the seeming construction of those places in the Gospell; by adding a case wherin a person deserted, which is somthing lesse then divorc't, may lawfully marry again. And having declar'd his opinion in one case, he leaves a furder liberty for Christian prudence to determine in cases of like importance; using words so plain as are not to be shifted off, *that a brother or a sister is not under bondage in such cases,* adding also, that *God hath call'd us to peace* in mariage.[114]

Now if it be plain that a Christian may be brought into unworthy *bondage,* and his religious *peace* not onely interrupted now and then, but perpetually and finally hinder'd in wedlock

---

112. 'In such cases' (1 Corinthians 7:15).

113. In *On Style*, a treatise of the early fourth-century B.C. often attributed to him.

114. See above, Note 62.

by mis-yoking with a diversity of nature as well as of religion, the reasons of S. *Paul* cannot be made speciall to that one case of infidelity, but are of equal moment to a divorce, wherever Christian liberty and peace are without fault equally obstructed. That the ordinance which God gave to our comfort, may not be pinn'd upon us to our undeserved thraldom; to be coopt up as it were in mockery of wedlock, to a perpetual betrothed lonelines and discontent, if nothing worse ensue. There being nought els of marriage left between such, but a displeasing and forc't remedy against the sting of a bruit desire: which fleshly accustoming[115] without the souls union and commixture of intellectual delight, as it is rather a soiling then a fulfilling of mariage-rites, so is it anough to imbase the mettle of a generous spirit, and sinks him to a low and vulgar pitch of endeavour in all his actions, or, which is wors, leavs him in a dispairing plight of abject & hardn'd thoughts: which condition rather then a good man should fal into, a man usefull in the service of God and mankind, Christ himself hath taught us to dispence with the most sacred ordinance of his worship, even for a bodily healing to dispence with that holy and speculative rest of Sabbath,[116] much more then with the erroneous observance of an ill-knotted mariage, for the sustaining of an overcharg'd faith and perseverance.

CHAP. XX. *The meaning of S. Paul, that Charity beleeveth all things. What is to be said to the licence which is vainly fear'd will grow hereby. What to those who never have don prescribing patience in this case. The Papist most severe against divorce: yet most easie to all licence. Of all the miseries in mariage God is to be clear'd, and the fault to be laid on mans unjust laws.*

And though bad causes would take licence by this pretext, if that cannot be remedied, upon their conscience be it, who shall so doe. This was that hardnes of heart, and abuse of a good law which *Moses* was content to suffer, rather then good

_____

115. Intimacy.
116. Cf. above, p. 153.

men should not have it at all to use needfully. And he who to run after one lost sheep, left ninety nine of his own flock at random in the wildernes,[117] would little perplex his thought for the obduring of nine hunder'd and ninety such as will daily take worse liberties, whether they have permission or not. To conclude, as without charity God hath giv'n no commandment to men, so without it, neither can men rightly beleeve any commandment giv'n. For every act of true faith, as well that wherby we beleeve the law, as that wherby wee endeavour the law, is wrought in us by charity, according to that in the divine hymne of St. *Paul*, 1 *Cor.* 13. *Charity beleeveth all things*: not as if she were so credulous, which is the exposition hitherto current, for that were a trivial praise; but to teach us that charity is the high governesse of our beleefe, and that we cannot safely assent to any precept writt'n in the Bible, but as charity commends it to us. Which agrees with that of the same Apostle to the *Ephes.* 4. 14. 15. where he tells us that the way to get a sure undoubted knowledge of things, is to hold that for truth, which accords most with charity. Whose unerring guidance and conduct having follow'd as a load-starre with all diligence and fidelity in this question, I trust, through the help of that illuminating Spirit which hath favour'd me, to have done no every dayes work: in asserting after many ages the words of Christ with other Scriptures of great concernment from burdensom & remorseles obscurity, tangl'd with manifold repugnances, to their native lustre and consent between each other: hereby also dissolving tedious and *Gordian* difficulties, which have hitherto molested the Church of God, and are now decided, not with the sword of *Alexander*, but with the immaculate hands of charity, to the unspeakable good of Christendome. And let the extreme literalist sit down now and revolve[118] whether this in all necessity be not the due result of our Saviours words: or if he persist to be otherwise opinion'd, let him well advise, lest thinking to gripe fast the Gospel, he be found in stead with the canon law in his fist: whose boisterous edicts tyrannizing the blessed ordinance of mariage into the quality of a most unnatural and

117. Cf. Matthew 18 : 12–13, Luke 15 : 4–6.
118. Consider.

unchristianly yoke, have giv'n the flesh this advantage to hate it, and turn aside, oft times unwillingly, to all dissolute un-cleannesse, even till punishment it self is weary, and overcome by the incredible frequency of trading lust, and uncontroull'd adulteries. Yet men whose Creed is custom,[119] I doubt not but wil still be endeavouring to hide the sloth of their own timorous capacities with this pretext, that for all this tis better to endure with patience and silence this affliction which God hath sent. And I agree tis true; if this be exhorted and not enjoyn'd; but withall it will be wisely don to be as sure as may be, that what mans iniquity hath laid on, be not imputed to Gods sending, least under the colour of an affected patience we detain our selves at the gulphs mouth of many hideous temptations, not to be withstood without proper gifts, which, as *Perkins* well notes, God gives not ordinarily, no not to most earnest prayer.[120] Therfore we pray, *Lead us not into temptation*, a vain prayer, if having led our selves thither, we love to stay in that perilous condition. God sends remedies, as well as evills; under which he who lies and groans, that may lawfully acquit himselfe, is accessory to his own ruin: nor will it excuse him, though he suffer through a sluggish fearfulnes to search throughly what is lawfull, for feare of disquieting the secure falsity of an old opinion. Who doubts not but that it may be piously said, to him who would dismiss frigidity, bear your trial, take it, as if God would have you live this life of continence: if he exhort this, I hear him as an Angel, though he speak without warrant: but if he would compell me, I know him for Satan. To him who divorces an adulteresse, Piety might say; Pardon her; you may shew much mercy, you may win a soul: yet the law both of God and man leaves it freely to him. For God loves not to plow out the heart of our endeavours with over-hard and sad tasks. God delights not to make a drudge of vertue, whose actions must be al elective & unconstrain'd. Forc't *vertue* is

---

119. Within sight of the end of his treatise, Milton describes full circle to his initial censure of custom (above, p. 112).

120. William Perkins (1558–1602), a widely respected and liberal Calvinist, had among other influential works written *Christian Oeconomie* (1609) from which Milton quotes.

as a *bolt* overshot, it goes neither forward nor backward, and does no good as it stands. Seeing therfore that neither Scripture nor reason hath laid this unjust austerity upon divorce, we may resolve that nothing else hath wrought it, but that letter-bound servility of the Canon Doctors, supposing mariage to be a Sacrament, and out of the art they have to lay unnecessary burdens upon all men, to make a fair shew in the fleshly observance of matrimony, though peace and love with all other conjugall respects fare never so ill. And indeed the Papists who are the strictest forbidders of divorce, are the easiest libertines to admit of grossest uncleannesse; as if they had a designe by making wedlock a supportlesse[121] yoke, to violate it most, under colour of preserving it most inviolable: and withall delighting, as their mystery[122] is, to make men the day-labourers of their own afflictions, as if there were such a scarcity of miseries from abroad, that we should be made to melt our choycest home blessings, and coin them into crosses, for want wherby to hold commerce with patience. If any therfore who shall hap to read this discourse, hath been through misadventure ill ingag'd in this contracted evill here complain'd of, and finds the fits and workings of a high impatience frequently upon him, of all those wild words which men in misery think to ease themselves by uttering, let him not op'n his lips against the providence of heav'n, or tax the wayes of God and his divine truth: for they are equal, easie, and not burdensome; nor doe they ever crosse the just and reasonable desires of men, nor involve this our portion of mortall life, into a necessity of sadnesse and malcontent, by laws commanding over the unreducible *antipathies* of nature sooner or later found: but allow us to remedy and shake off those evills into which human error hath led us through the midst of our best intentions; and to support our incident extremities by that authentick precept of soveran charity; whose grand commision is to doe and to dispose over all the ordinances of God to man; that love & truth may advance each other to everlasting. While we literally superstitious through customary faintnesse

---

121. Insupportable.
122. Secret policy.

of heart, not venturing to pierce with our free thoughts into the full latitude of nature and religion, abandon our selves to serve under the tyranny of usurpt opinions, suffering those ordinances which were allotted to our solace and reviving, to trample over us and hale us into a multitude of sorrowes which God never meant us. And where he set us in a fair allowance of way, with honest liberty and prudence to our guard, we never leave subtilizing and casuisting till we have straitn'd and par'd that liberal path into a razors edge to walk on, between a precipice of unnecessary mischief on either side : and starting at every false Alarum, we doe not know which way to set a foot forward with manly confidence and Christian resolution, through the confused ringing in our eares of *panick* scruples and amazements.

CHAP. XXI. *That the matter of divorce is not to be try'd by law, but by conscience, as many other sins are. The Magistrate can only see that the condition of divorce be just and equall. The opinion of Fagius, and the reasons of this assertion.*

Another act of papall encroachment it was, to pluck the power and arbitrement of divorce from the master of family, into whose hands God and the law of all Nations had put it, and Christ so left it, preaching onely to the conscience, and not authorizing a judiciall Court to tosse about and divulge the unaccountable and secret reasons of disaffection between man and wife, as a thing most improperly answerable to any such kind of triall. But the Popes of *Rome* perceiving the great revenue and high authority it would give them ev'n over Princes, to have the judging and deciding of such a main consequence in the life of man as was divorce, wrought so upon the superstition of those ages, as to divest them of that right which God from the beginning had entrusted to the husband : by which meanes they subjected that ancient and naturally domestick prerogative to an externall and unbefitting Judicature. For although differences in divorce about Dowries, Jointures, and the like, besides the punishing of adultery, ought not to passe without referring, if need be, to the Magistrate;

yet that the absolute and final hindring of divorce cannot belong to any civil or earthly power, against the will and consent of both parties, or of the husband alone, some reasons will be here urg'd as shall not need to decline the touch. But first I shall recite what hath bin already yeilded by others in favour of this opinion. *Grotius* and many more agree that notwithstanding what Christ spake therin to the conscience, the Magistrate is not therby enjoyn'd ought against the preservation of civil peace, of equity, and of convenience. Ámong these *Fagius* is most remarkable, and gives the same liberty of pronouncing divorce to the Christian Magistrate, as the Mosaick had. *For whatever* said he, *Christ spake to the regenerat, the Judge hath to deal with the vulgar: if therfore any through hardnesse of heart will not be a tolerable wife or husband, it will be lawfull as well now as of old to passe the bill of divorce, not by privat, but by publicke authority. Nor doth man separate them then, but God by his law of divorce giv'n by* Moses. *What can hinder the Magistrate from so doing, to whose government all outward things are subject, to separate and remove from perpetual vexation and no small danger those bodies whose minds are already separate: it being his office to procure peacable and convenient living in the Common-wealth; and being as certain also, that they so necessarily separated cannot all receive a single life.*[123] And this I observe that our divines doe generally condemn separation of bed and board, without the liberty of second choice:[124] if that therfore in some cases be most purely necessary, as who so blockish to deny, then is this also as needfull. Thus farre by others is already well stept, to inform us that divorce is not a matter of Law but of Charity: if there remain a furlong yet to end the question, these following reasons may serve to gain it with any apprehension not too unlearned, or too wayward. First because ofttimes the causes of seeking divorce reside so deeply in the radical and innocent affections of nature, as is not within the diocese of Law to tamper with. Other rela-

---

123. The quotation is from Fagius's *Thargum* (above, Note 38).

124. Mere 'separation of bed and board' was not favored by Protestant writers.

tions may aptly anough be held together by a civil and vertuous love. But the duties of man and wife are such as are
chiefly conversant in that love, which is most ancient and
meerly[125] naturall; whose two prime statutes are to joyn it self
to that which is good and acceptable and friendly; and to turn
aside and depart from what is disagreeable, displeasing and
unlike: of the two this latter is the strongest, and most equal
to be regarded: for although a man may often be unjust in
seeking that which he loves, yet he can never be unjust or
blamable in retiring from his endles trouble and distast, whenas
his tarrying can redound to no true content on either side. Hate
is of all things the mightiest divider, nay, is division it self. To
couple hatred therfore though wedlock try all her golden links,
and borrow to her aid all the iron manacles and fetters of Law,
it does but seek to twist a rope of sand, which was a task,
they say, that pos'd the divell. And that sluggish feind in hell
Ocnus, whom the Poems tell of, brought his idle cordage to as
good effect, which never serv'd to bind with, but to feed the
Asse that stood at his elbow.[126] And that the restrictive Law
against divorce, attains as little to bind any thing truly in a
disjoynted mariage, or to keep it bound, but servs only to feed
the ignorance, and definitive impertinence of a doltish Canon,
were no absurd allusion. To hinder therfore those deep and
serious regresses of nature in a reasonable soul parting from that
mistak'n help which he justly seeks in a person created for
him, recollecting[127] himself from an unmeet help which was
never meant, and to detain him by compulsion in such a unpre-
destin'd misery as this, is in diameter against both nature and
institution: but to interpose a jurisdictive power upon the
inward and irremediable disposition of man, to command love
and sympathy, to forbid dislike against the guiltles instinct of
nature, is not within the Province of any Law to reach, and
were indeed an uncommodious rudeness, not a just power: for
that Law may bandy with nature, and traverse her sage
motions, was an error in *Callicles* the Rhetorician, whom

125. Entirely.
126. Ocnus wove a rope of straw which an ass promptly consumed.
127. Withdrawing.

Socrates from high principles confutes in *Plato's Gorgias*.[128] If therfore divorce may be so natural, and that law and nature are not to goe contrary, then to forbid divorce compulsively, is not only against nature, but against law.

Next it must be remember'd that all law is for some good that may be frequently attain'd, without the admixture of a worse inconvenience; and therfore many grosse faults, as ingratitude and the like, which are too farre within the soul, to be cur'd by constraint of law, are left only to be wrought on by conscience and perswasion. Which made *Aristotle* in the 10th of his *Ethicks* to *Nicomachus*, aim at a kind of division of law into private or perswasive, and publick or cumpulsive.[129] Hence it is that the law forbidding divorce, never attains to any good end of such prohibition, but rather multiplies evil. For if natures resistlesse sway in love or hate bee once compell'd, it grows carelesse of it selfe, vitious, uselesse to friend, unserviceable and spiritlesse to the Commonwealth. Which Moses rightly forsaw, and all wise Lawgivers that ever knew man, what kind of creature he was. The Parlament also and Clergy of England were not ignorant of this, when they consented that *Harry* the eighth might put away his Queen *Anne* of *Cleve*, whom he could not like after he had been wedded halfe a yeare;[130] unlesse it were that contrary to the proverb, they made a necessity of that which might have been a vertue in them to doe. For even the freedome and eminence of mans creation gives him to be a Law in this matter to himselfe, being the head of the other Sex which was made for him:[131] whom therefore though he ought not to injure, yet neither should he be forc't to retain in society to his own overthrow, nor to heare any judge therin above himself. It being also an unseemly affront to the sequestr'd and vail'd modesty of that sex, to have her unpleasingnesse and other concealments bandied up

128. *Gorgias*, 482– 510.

129. *Ethics*, X, 9.

130. The marriage of Henry VIII to Anne of Cleves, his fourth wife, was annulled six months later, in July 1540.

131. Cf. St Paul's resolute claim that 'the head of the woman is the man' (1 Corinthians 11 : 3); also above, p. 64, Note 8.

and down, and aggravated in open Court by those hir'd masters of tongue-fence. Such uncomely exigences it befell no lesse a Majesty then *Henry* the eighth to be reduc't to; who finding just reason in his conscience to forgoe his brothers wife, after many indignities of being deluded, and made a boy of by those his two Cardinall Judges,[132] was constrain'd at last for want of other proof that she had been carnally known by Prince *Arthur*, ev'n to uncover the nakednesse of that vertuous Lady, and to recite openly the obscene evidence of his brothers Chamberlain. Yet it pleas'd God to make him see all the tyranny of *Rome*, by discovering this which they exercis'd over divorce; and to make him the beginner of a reformation to this whole Kingdome by first asserting into his *familiary*[133] power the right of just divorce. Tis true, an adultresse cannot be sham'd anough by any publick proceeding: but that woman whose honour is not appeach't,[134] is lesse injur'd by a silent dismission, being otherwise not illiberally dealt with, then to endure a clamouring debate of utterlesse things, in a busines of that civill secrecy and difficult discerning, as not to bee over-much question'd by neerest friends. Which drew that answer from the greatest and worthiest *Roman* of his time *Paulus Emilius*, being demanded why hee would put away his wife for no visible reason, *This Shoo*, said he, and held it out on his foot, *is a neat shoo, a new shoo, and yet none of you know where it wrings me*:[135] much lesse by the unfamiliar cognisance of a fee'd gamester can such a private difference be examin'd, neither ought it.

Again, if Law aim at the firm establishment and preservation of matrimoniall faith, wee know that cannot thrive under violent means, but is the more violated. It is not when two unfortunately met are by the Canon forc'd to draw in that yoke an unmercifull dayes work of sorrow till death unharnesse 'em,

---

132. Campeggio and Wolsey, who deliberated on Henry's request to have his marriage to Catherine of Aragon annulled. The case rested on the claim that she had been 'carnally known' by Henry's elder brother Prince Arthur.

133. Domestic.

134. Impeached.

135. Thus Plutarch, *Aemilius Paulus*, V, 1–2.

that then the Law keeps mariage most unviolated and unbrok'n :
but when the Law takes order that mariage be accountant and
responsible to perform that society, whether it be religious,
civill, or corporal, which may be conscionably requir'd and
claim'd therein, or else to be dissolv'd if it cannot be undergone :
This is to make mariage most indissoluble, by making it a just
and equall dealer, a performer of those due helps which instituted the covnant, being otherwise a most unjust contract, and
no more to be maintain'd under tuition[136] of law, then the vilest
fraud, or cheat, or theft that may be committed. But because
this is such a secret kind of fraud or theft, as cannot bee
discern'd by law, but only by the plaintife himself, therfore
to divorce was never counted a politicall or civill offence neither
to *Jew* nor *Gentile*, nor by any judicial intendment of Christ,
further then could be discern'd to transgresse the allowance
of *Moses*, which was of necessity so large, that it doth all one
as if it sent back the matter undeterminable at law, and intractable by rough dealing, to have instructions and admonitions bestow'd about it by them whose spirituall office is to
adjure and to denounce, and so left to the conscience. The Law
can onely appoint the just and equall conditions of divorce,
and is to look how it is an injury to the divorc't, which in truth
it can be none, as a meer separation ; for if she consent, wherin
has the Law to right her ? or consent not ; then is it either just,
and so deserv'd ; or if unjust, such in all likelihood was the
divorcer, and to part from an unjust man is a happinesse, and
no injury to bee lamented. But suppose it be an injury, the law
is not able to amend it, unles she think it other then a miserable redress to return back from whence she was expell'd, or
but intreated to be gone, or else to live apart still maried without mariage, a maried widow. Last, if it be to chast'n the
divorcer, what Law punishes a deed which is not morall, but
natural, a deed which cannot certainly be found to be an
injury, or how can it be punisht by prohibiting the divorce,
but that the innocent must equally partake both in the shame
and in the smart. So that which way soever we look the

---

136. Protection.

Law can to no rationall purpose forbid divorce, it can only take care that the conditions of divorce be not injurous. Thus then we see the trial of law how impertinent it is to this question of divorce, how helplesse next, and then how hurtfull.

CHAP. XXII. *The last Reason, why divorce is not to be re-strain'd by Law, it being against the Law of nature and of Nations. The larger proof wherof referr'd to Mr.* Seldens *Book* De jure naturali & gentium. *An objection of* Paræus *answer'd. How it ought to be order'd by the Church. That this will not breed any worse inconvenience nor so bad as is now suffere'd.*

Therfore the last reason why it should not be, is the example we have, not only from the noblest and wisest Common-wealths, guided by the clearest light of human knowledge, but also from the divine testimonies of God himself, lawgiving in person to a sanctify'd people. That all this is true, who so desires to know at large with least pains, and expects not heer overlong rehersals of that which is by others already so judici-ously gather'd, let him hast'n to be acquainted with that noble volume written by our learned *Selden, Of the law of nature & of Nations,*[137] a work more useful and more worthy to be perus'd, whosoever studies to be a great man in wisdom, equity, and justice, then all those *decretals, and sumles sums,*[138] which the *Pontificial Clerks* have doted on, ever since that unfortunat mother famously[139] sinn'd thrice, and dy'd impenitent of her bringing into the world those two misbegott'n infants, & for ever infants, *Lombard & Gratian,*[140] him the compiler of Canon in iniquity, [the] other the *Tubalcain* of scholastick Sophistry,

---

137. *De jure naturali* was first published in 1640.

138. Endless digests.

139. Notoriously.

140. Peter Lombard (c. 1100–60) compiled the encyclopedic *Sen-tences*, a standard text of medieval theology; his contemporary Johannes Gratian may be regarded as the father of canon law. Milton likens Gratian to Tubal-cain whom Genesis 4:22 describes as 'an instructer of every artificer in brass and iron'.

whose overspreading *barbarism* hath not only infus'd their own bastardy upon the fruitfullest part of human learning; not only dissipated and dejected the clear light of nature in us, & of nations, but hath tainted also the fountains of divine doctrine, & render'd the pure and solid Law of God unbeneficial to us by their calumnious dunceries. Yet this Law which their unskilfulnesse hath made liable to all ignominy, the purity and wisdom of this Law shall be the buckler of our dispute. Liberty of divorce we claim not, we think not but from this Law; the dignity, the faith, the authority therof is now grown among Christians, O astonishment! a labour of no mean difficulty and envy[141] to defend. That it should not be counted a faltring dispence; a flattring permission of sin, the bil of adultery, a snare, is the expence of all this apology. And all that we solicite is, that it may be suffer'd to stand in the place where God set it amidst the firmament of his holy Laws to shine, as it was wont, upon the weaknesses and errors of men perishing els in the sincerity of their honest purposes: for certain there is no memory of whordoms and adulteries left among us now, when this warranted freedom of Gods own giving is made dangerous and discarded for a scrowle of licence. It must be your suffrages and Votes, O English men, that this exploded decree of God and *Moses* may scape, and come off fair without the censure of a shamefull abrogating: which, if yonder Sun ride sure, and mean not to break word with us tomorrow, was never yet abrogated by our Saviour. Give sentence, if you please, that the frivolous Canon may reverse the infallible judgement of *Moses* and his great director. Or if it be the reformed writers, whose doctrine perswades this rather, their reasons I dare affirm are all silenc't, unlesse it be only this. *Parœus* on the Corinthians[142] would prove that hardnes of heart in divorce is no more now to be permitted, but to be amerc't with fine and imprisonment. I am not willing to discover the forgettings of reverend men, yet here I must. What article or clause of the whole new Cov'nant can Parœus bring to exasperat the judicial

141. Unpopularity, opprobrium.

142. i.e. the *Commentarius* on that epistle by David Pareus (above, Note 46).

Law, upon any infirmity under the Gospel? (I say infirmity, for if it were the high hand of sin, the Law as little would have endur'd it as the Gospel) it would not stretch to the dividing of an inheritance; it refus'd to condemn adultery, not that these things should not be don at Law, but to shew that the Gospel hath not the least influence upon judicial Courts, much lesse to make them sharper, and more heavy; lest of all to arraine before a temporal Judge that which the Law without summons acquitted. But saith he, the law was the time of youth, under violent affections, the Gospel in us is mature age, and ought to subdue affections. True, and so ought the Law too, if they be found inordinat, and not meerly natural and blameless. Next I distinguish that the time of the Law is compar'd to youth, and pupillage in respect of the ceremonial part, which led the Jewes as children through corporal and garish rudiments, untill the fulnes of time should reveal to them the higher lessons of faith and redemption. This is not meant of the moral part, therin it soberly concern'd them not to be babies, but to be men in good earnest: the sad and awfull majesty of that Law was not to be jested with; to bring a bearded nonage with lascivious dispensations before that throne, had bin a leud affront, as it is now a grosse mistake. But what discipline is this Paræus to nourish violent affections in youth, by cockring and wanton indulgences, and to chastise them in mature age with a boyish rod of correction. How much more coherent is it to Scripture, that the Law as a strict Schoolmaster should have punisht every trespasse without indulgence so banefull to youth, and that the Gospel should now correct that by admonition and reproof only, in free and mature age, which was punisht with stripes in the childhood and bondage of the Law.[143] What therfore it allow'd then so fairly, much lesse is to be whipt now, especially in penal Courts: and if it ought now to trouble the conscience, why did that angry accuser and condemner Law repreev it? So then, neither from *Moses* nor from Christ hath the Magistrate any authority to proceed against it. But what? Shall then the disposal of that power return again

---

143. Cf. Galatians 3:24–25.

to the maister of family? Wherfore not? Since God there put it
and the presumptuous Canon thence bereft it. This only must
be provided, that the ancient manner be observ'd in presence of
the Minister and other grave selected Elders; who after they
shall have admonisht and prest upon him the words of our
Saviour, and he shall have protested in the faith of the eternal
Gospel, and the hope he has of happy resurrection, that otherwise then thus he cannot doe, and thinks himself, and this his
case not contain'd in that prohibition of divorce which Christ
pronounc't, the matter not being of malice, but of nature, and
so capable of reconciling, to constrain him furder were to
unchristen him, to unman him, to throw the mountain of
Sinai upon him, with the weight of the whole Law to boot
flat against the liberty and essence of the Gospel, and yet nothing
available either to the sanctity of mariage, the good of husband
wife, or children, nothing profitable either to Church or Common-wealth; but hurtfull and pernicious to all these respects.
But this will bring in confusion. Yet these cautious mistrusters
might consider, that what they thus object, lights not upon
this book, but upon that which I engage against them, the book
of God, and of *Moses*, with all the wisdome and providence
which had forecast the worst of confusion that could succeed,
and yet thought fit of such a permission. But let them be of good
cheer, it wrought so little disorder among the Jews, that from
Moses till after the captivity, not one of the Prophets thought
it worth rebuking; for that of *Malachy*[144] well lookt into, will
appeare to be, not against divorcing, but rather against keeping
strange Concubines, to the vexation of their *Hebrew* wives. If
therefore we Christians may be thought as good and tractable as
the Jews were, and certainly the prohibiters of divorce presume
us to be better, then lesse confusion is to bee fear'd for this
among us, then was among them. If wee bee worse, or but as
bad, which lamentable examples confirm we are, then have we
more, or at least as much need of this permitted law, as they to
whom God therfore gave it (as they say) under a harsher covnant. Let not therfore the frailty of man goe on thus inventing

---

144. As above, Note 63.

needlesse troubles to it self, to groan under the fals imagination of a strictnes never impos'd from above; enjoyning that for duty which is an impossible & vain supererogating. *Be not righteous overmuch,* is the counsell of *Ecclesiastes, why shouldst thou destroy thy selfe?*[145] Let us not be thus over-curious to strain at *atoms,*[146] and yet to stop every vent and cranny of permissive liberty; lest nature wanting those needfull pores, and breathing places which God hath not debar'd our weaknesse, either suddenly break out into some wide rupture of open vice, and frantick heresie, or else inwardly fester with repining and blasphemous thoughts, under an unreasonable and fruitless rigor of unwarranted law. Against which evills nothing can more beseem the religion of the Church, or the wisedom of the State, then to consider timely and provide. And in so doing, let them not doubt but they shall vindicate the misreputed honour of God and his great Lawgiver, by suffering him to give his own laws according to the condition of mans nature best known to him, without the unsufferable imputation of dispencing legally with many ages of ratify'd adultery. They shall recover the misattended words of Christ to the sincerity of their true sense from manifold contradictions, and shall open them with the key of charity. Many helples Christians they shall raise from the depth of sadnes and distresse, utterly unfitted, as they are, to serve God or man: many they shall reclaime from obscure and giddy sects, many regain from dissolute and brutish licence, many from desperate hardnes, if ever that were justly pleaded. They shall set free many daughters of *Israel,* not wanting much of her sad plight *whom Satan had bound eighteen years.*[147] Man they shall restore to his just dignity, and prerogative in nature, preferring the souls free peace before the promiscuous draining of a carnall rage. Mariage from a perilous hazard and snare, they shall reduce to bee a more certain hav'n and retirement of happy society; when they shall judge according to God and *Moses,* and how not then according to

145. Ecclesiastes 7:16.

146. Motes. Cf. Matthew 23:24 ('Ye blind guides, which strain at a gnat').

147. Cf. Luke 13:16.

179

Christ? when they shall judge it more wisdom and goodnes to break that covnant seemingly and keep it really, then by compulsion of law to keep it seemingly, and by compulsion of blameles nature to break it really, at least if it were ever truly joyn'd The vigor of discipline they may then turn with better successe upon the prostitute loosenes of the times, when men finding in themselves the infirmities of former ages, shall not be constrain'd above the gift of God in them, to unprofitable and impossible observances never requir'd from the civilest, the wisest the holiest Nations, whose other excellencies in morall vertue they never yet could equall. Last of all, to those whose mind still is to maintain textuall restrictions, wherof the bare sound cannot consist sometimes with humanity, much lesse with charity, I would ever answer by putting them in remembrance of a command above all commands, which they seem to have forgot, and who spake it; in comparison wherof this which they so exalt, is but a petty and subordinate precept. *Let them goe* therfore with whom I am loath to couple them, yet they will needs run into the same blindnes with the Pharises, *let them goe therfore* and consider well what this lesson means, *I will have mercy and not sacrifice*;[148] for on that *saying all the Law and Prophets depend*,[149] much more the Gospel whose end and excellence is mercy and peace: Or if they cannot learn that, how will they hear this, which yet I shall not doubt to leave with them as a conclusion: That God the Son hath put all other things under his own feet; but his Commandments hee hath left all under the feet of Charity.

---

148. Matthew 9:13; cf. Hosea 6:6.
149. Matthew 22:40.

OF EDUCATION.

TO MASTER SAMUEL HARTLIB.

(1644)

Of Education was first published in 1644 (see above, p. 29); a
second edition, issued in 1673, was appended to a much augmented
edition of the 'Minor Poems'. The Yale edition provides the text of
1644 (II, 362–415); the Columbia edition reprinted here provides the
text of 1673 (IV, 275–91; ed. Allan Abbott).]

Mr. *Hartlib*,[1]

I AM long since perswaded, that to say, or do ought worth
memory and imitation, no purpose or respect should sooner
move us, then simply the love of God, and of mankind. Nevertheless to write now the reforming of Education, though it be
one of the greatest and noblest designs that can be thought on,
and for the want whereof this Nation perishes, I had not yet at
this time been induc't, but by your earnest entreaties, and
serious conjurements; as having my mind for the present half
diverted in the pursuance of some other assertions, the knowledge and the use of which, cannot but be a great furtherance
both to the enlargement of truth, and honest living, with much
more peace. Nor should the laws of any private friendship have
prevail'd with me to divide thus, or transpose my former
thoughts, but that I see those aims, those actions which have
won you with me the esteem of a person sent hither by some
good providence from a far country[2] to be the occasion and
the incitement of great good to this Island. And, as I hear, you
have obtain'd the same repute with men of most approved
wisdom, and some of highest authority among us. Not to mention the learned correspondence which you hold in forreign

---

1. Samuel Hartlib was directly involved in the education reforms
centered on Comenius (above, p. 30). He had met Milton by 1643.

2. Comenius, who visited England in 1641.

parts, and the extraordinary pains and diligence which you have us'd in this matter both here, and beyond the Seas; either by the definite will of God so ruling, or the peculiar sway o nature, which also is Gods working. Neither can I think that so reputed, and so valu'd as you are, you would to the forfeit o your own discerning ability, impose upon me an unfit and over ponderous argument, but that the satisfaction which you pro fess to have receiv'd from those incidental Discourses which we have wander'd into, hath prest and almost constrain'd you into a perswasion, that what you require from me in this point I neither ought, nor can in conscience deferre beyond this time both of so much need at once, and so much opportunity to try what God hath determin'd. I will not resist therefore, whatever it is either of divine, or humane obligement that you lay upon me; but will forthwith set down in writing, as you request me that voluntary *Idea*,[3] which hath long in silence presented it self to me, of a better Education, in extent and comprehension far more large, and yet of time far shorter, and of attainmen far more certain, then hath been yet in practice. Brief I shall endeavour to be, for that which I have to say, assuredly this Nation hath extream need should be done sooner then spoken To tell you therefore what I have benefited herein among old renowned Authors, I shall spare; and to search what many modern *Janua's* and *Didactics*[4] more then ever I shall read, have projected, my inclination leads me not. But if you can accept of these few observations which have flowr'd off, and are, as it were, the burnishing of many studious and contemplative years altogether spent in the search of religious and civil knowledge and such as pleas'd you so well in the relating, I here give you them to dispose of.

The end then of Learning is to repair the ruines of our firs Parents by regaining to know God aright, and out of tha knowledge to love him, to imitate him, to be like him, as w

3. In the Platonic sense? Or in the sense of an objective presenta tion of a thesis (as Ong suggests, below, p. 454)?

4. Cf. Comenius's *Janua linguarum reserata* and *Didactica magna* the first was published in 1631, the second not until 1657 althougl its thesis was widely known through Hartlib's abstract in 1639.

may the neerest by possessing our souls of true vertue, which being united to the heavenly grace of faith makes up the highest perfection.[5] But because our understanding cannot in this body found it self but on sensible things, nor arrive so clearly to the knowledge of God and things invisible, as by orderly conning over the visible and inferior creature, the same method is necessarily to be follow'd in all discreet teaching. And seeing every Nation affords not experience and tradition enough for all kind of Learning, therefore we are chiefly taught the Languages of those people who have at any time been most industrious after Wisdom; so that Language is but the Instrument conveying to us things usefull to be known. And though a Linguist should pride himself to have all the Tongues that *Babel* cleft the world into, yet, if he have not studied the solid things in them as well as the Words & Lexicons, he were nothing so much to be esteem'd a learned man, as any Yeoman or Tradesman competently wise in his Mother Dialect only. Hence appear the many mistakes which have made Learning generally so unpleasing and so unsuccessful; first we do amiss to spend seven or eight years meerly in scraping together so much miserable Latine and Greek, as might be learnt otherwise easily and delightfully in one year. And that which casts our proficiency therein so much behind, is our time lost partly in too oft idle vacancies[6] given both to Schools and Universities, partly in a preposterous exaction, forcing the empty wits of Children to compose Theams, Verses and Orations, which are the acts of ripest judgment and the final work of a head fill'd by long reading and observing, with elegant maxims, and copious invention. These are not matters to be wrung from poor striplings, like blood out of the Nose, or the plucking of untimely fruit: besides the ill habit which they get of wretched barbarizing against the Latin and Greek *idiom*, with their untutor'd *Anglicisms*, odious to be read, yet not to be avoided without a well continu'd and judicious conversing among[7] pure Authors di-

5. Milton's 'comptemplative' definition of education will be followed by the 'active' one (see p. 185; thus Rajan, below, p. 463).

6. Vacations.

7. Associating with. Cf. 'conversation', above, p. 124, Note 30.

gested, which they scarce taste, whereas, if after some prepar-
atory grounds of speech by their certain forms got into memory,
they were led to the praxis thereof in some chosen short book
lesson'd throughly to them, they might then forthwith proceed to learn the substance of good things, and Arts in due order,
which would bring the whole language quickly into their
power. This I take to be the most rational and most profitable
way of learning Languages, and whereby we may best hope
to give account to God of our youth spent herein: And for the
usual method of teaching Arts,[8] I deem it to be an old errour of
Universities not yet well recover'd from the Scholastick gross-
ness of barbarous ages, that in stead of beginning with Arts
most easie, and those be such as are most obvious to the sence,
they present their young unmatriculated[9] Novices at first comming with the most intellective abstractions of Logick and
Metaphysicks: So that they having but newly left those Gram-
matick flats and shallows where they stuck unreasonably to
learn a few words with lamentable construction, and now on
the sudden transported under another climate to be tost and
turmoil'd with their unballasted wits in fadomless and unquiet
deeps of controversie, do for the most part grow into hatred
and contempt of Learning, mockt and deluded all this while
with ragged Notions and Babblements, while they expected
worthy and delightful knowledge; till poverty or youthful
years call them importunately their several wayes, and hasten
them with the sway of friends either to an ambitious and mercenary, or ignorantly zealous Divinity; Some allur'd to the
trade of Law, grounding their purposes not on the prudent and
heavenly contemplation of justice and equity which was never
taught them, but on the promising and pleasing thoughts of
litigious terms, fat contentions, and flowing fees; others betake
them to State affairs, with souls so unprincipl'd in vertue, and
true generous breeding, that flattery, and Court shifts and tyrannous Aphorisms appear to them the highest points of wisdom;
instilling their barren hearts with a conscientious slavery, if,

8. i.e. the Seven Liberal Arts: the 'trivium' (grammar, logic,
rhetoric) and the 'quadrivium' (arithmetic, geometry, astronomy
and music).   9. Inexperienced.

as I rather think, it be not fain'd. Others lastly of a more delicious and airie[10] spirit, retire themselves knowing no better, to the enjoyments of ease and luxury, living out their daies in feast and jollity; which indeed is the wisest and the safest course of all these, unless they were with more integrity undertaken. And these are the fruits of mispending our prime youth at the Schools and Universities as we do, either in learning meer words or such things chiefly, as were better unlearnt.

I shall detain you no longer in the demonstration of what we should not do, but strait conduct ye to a hill side, where I will point ye out the right path of a vertuous and noble Education; laborious indeed at the first ascent, but else so smooth, so green, so full of goodly prospect, and melodious sounds on every side, that the Harp of *Orpheus* was not more charming. I doùbt not but ye shall have more adoe to drive our dullest and laziest youth, our stocks and stubbs from the infinite desire of such a happy nurture, then we have now to hale and drag our choisest and hopefullest Wits to that asinine feast of sowthistles and brambles which is commonly set before them, as all the food and entertainment of their tenderest and most docible age. I call therefore a compleat and generous Education that which fits a man to perform justly, skilfully and magnanimously all the offices both private and publick of Peace and War.[11] And how all this may be done between twelve, and one and twenty, less time then is now bestow'd in pure trifling at Grammar and *Sophistry*, is to be thus order'd.

First to find out a spatious house and ground about it fit for an *Academy*, and big enough to lodge a hundred and fifty persons, whereof twenty or thereabouts may be attendants, all under the government of one, who shall be thought of desert sufficient, and ability either to do all, or wisely to direct, and oversee it done. This place should be at once both School and University, not needing a remove to any other house of Schollership, except it be some peculiar Colledge of Law, or Physick,[12]

---

10. Dainty and superficial.

11. Milton's 'active' definition of education completes the 'contemplative' one (above, Note 5).

12. Medicine.

where they mean to be practitioners; but as for those general studies which take up all our time from *Lilly*[13] to the commencing, as they term it, Master of Art, it should be absolute. After this pattern, as many Edifices may be converted to this use, as shall be needful in every City throughout this Land, which would tend much to the encrease of Learning and Civility every where. This number, less or more thus collected, to the convenience of a foot Company, or interchangeably two Troops of Cavalry, should divide their daies work into three parts, as it lies orderly. Their Studies, their Exercise, and their Diet.

For their Studies, First they should begin with the chief and necessary rules of some good Grammar, either that now us'd, or any better: and while this is doing, their speech is to be fashion'd to a distinct and clear pronuntiation, as near as may be to the *Italian*, especially in the Vowels. For we *Englishmen* being far Northerly, do not open our mouths in the cold air, wide enough to grace a Southern Tongue; but are observ'd by all other Nations to speak exceeding close and inward: So that to smatter Latine with an English mouth, is as ill a hearing as Law-French. Next to make them expert in the usefullest points of Grammar, and withall to season them, and win them early to the love of vertue and true labour, ere any flattering seducement, or vain principle seise them wandering, some easie and delightful Book of Education would be read to them; whereof the Greeks have store, as *Cebes*, *Plutarch*, and other Socratic discourses.[14] But in Latin we have none of classic authority extant, except the two or three first Books of *Quintilian*,[15] and some select pieces elsewhere. But here the main skill and

---

13. William Lily (1468?–1522), the first headmaster of St. Paul's, author of a Latin grammar still used in the seventeenth century.

14. The first reference is to the allegorizing Table of Cebes (Cebes is erroneously identified here with Socrates's friend); the second is to the treatise 'On the Education of Children' in Plutarch's *Moralia*; while the 'Socratic discourses' probably refer to parts of Plato's *Republic* and *Laws*.

15. i.e. of the *Institutio oratoria* by Quintilian (first century A.D.).

groundwork will be, to temper them such Lectures and Explanations upon every opportunity, as may lead and draw them in willing obedience, enflam'd with the study of Learning, and the admiration of Vertue; stirr'd up with high hopes of living to be brave men, and worthy Patriots, dear to God, and famous to all ages. That they may despise and scorn all their childish, and ill-taught qualities, to delight in manly, and liberal Exercises: which he who hath the Art, and proper Eloquence to catch them with, what with mild and effectual perswasions, and what with the intimation of some fear, if need be, but chiefly by his own example, might in a short space gain them to an incredible diligence and courage: infusing into their young brests such an ingenuous and noble ardor, as would not fail to make many of them renowned and matchless men. At the same time, some other hour of the day, might be taught them the rules of Arithmetick, and soon after the Elements of Geometry even playing, as the old manner was.[16] After evening repast, till bed-time their thoughts will be best taken up in the easie grounds of Religion, and the story of Scripture. The next step would be to the Authors [on] *Agriculture, Cato, Varro,* and *Columella,*[17] for the matter is most easie, and if the language be difficult, so much the better, it is not a difficulty above their years. And here will be an occasion of inciting and inabling them hereafter to improve the tillage of their Country, to recover the bad Soil, and to remedy the waste that is made of good: for this was one of *Hercules* praises.[18] Ere half these Authors be read (which will soon be with plying hard, and daily) they cannot chuse but be masters of any ordinary prose. So that it will be then seasonable for them to learn in any modern Author, the use of the Globes, and all the Maps; first with the old names, and then with the new: or they might be then capable to read any compendious method of natural Philosophy. And at the same time might be

---

16. As counselled by Quintilian (I, x, 39).

17. The treatises of Cato and Varro (second century B.C.) as well as Columella (first century A.D.) were still regarded as pragmatic guides to agriculture.

18. Hercules's cleansing of the Augean stables was sometimes seen as suggestive of the use of animal fertilizers.

entring into the Greek tongue, after the same manner as was before prescrib'd in the Latin; whereby the difficulties of Grammar being soon overcome, all the Historical Physiology of *Aristotle* and *Theophrastus*[19] are open before them, and as I may say, under contribution. The like access will be to *Vitruvius*, to *Seneca's* natural questions, to *Mela, Celsus, Pliny,* or *Solinus*.[20] And having thus past the principles of *Arithmetick, Geometry, Astronomy,* and *Geography* with a general compact of Physicks, they may descend in *Mathematicks* to the instrumental science of *Trigonometry,* and from thence to Fortification, Architecture, Enginry, or Navigation. And in natural Philosophy they may proceed leisurely from the History of Meteors, Minerals, plants and living Creatures as far as Anatomy. Then also in course might be read to them out of some not tedious Writer the Institution of Physick; that they may know the tempers, the humours,[21] the seasons, and how to manage a crudity:[22] which he who can wisely and timely do, is not only a great Physitian to himself, and to his friends, but also may at some time or other, save an Army by this frugal and expenseless means only; and not let the healthy and stout bodies of young men rot away under him for want of this discipline; which is a great pity, and no less a shame to the Commander. To set forward all these proceedings in Nature and Mathematicks, what hinders, but that they may procure, as oft as shal be needful, the helpful experiences of Hunters, Fowlers, Fishermen, Shepherds, Gardeners,

---

19. Aristotle's *Natural History of Animals* was often published together with extracts from the botanical works of his pupil Theophrastus (third century B.C.).

20. The references are to the treatises on architecture by Vitruvius (first century B.C.), astronomy and meteorology by Seneca (first century A.D.), geography by Pomponius Mela (first century A.D.), pharmacy by Celsus (first century A.D.), natural science by Pliny the Elder (second century A.D.), and the edition of the latter by Solinus (third century A.D.).

21. The body's four 'humours' – blood, phlegm, choler, melancholy – were in ancient medicine thought to yield health if harmoniously blended, and sickness if not.

22. Indigestion.

Apothecaries; and in the other sciences, Architects, Engineers, Mariners, Anatomists; who doubtless would be ready some for reward, and some to favour such a hopeful Seminary. And this will give them such a real tincture of natural knowledge, as they shall never forget, but daily augment with delight. Then also those Poets which are now counted most hard, will be both facil and pleasant, *Orpheus, Hesiod, Theocritus, Aratus, Nicander, Oppian, Dionysius,* and in Latin *Lucretius, Manilius,* and the rural part of *Virgil.*[23]

By this time, years and good general precepts will have furnisht them more distinctly with that act of reason which in *Ethics* is call'd *Proairesis* :[24] that they may with some judgement contemplate upon moral good and evil. Then will be requir'd special reinforcement of constant and sound endoctrinating to set them right and firm, instructing them more amply in the knowledge of Vertue and the hatred of Vice: while their young and pliant affections are led through all the moral works of *Plato, Xenophon, Cicero, Plutarch, Laertius,*[25] and those *Locrian* remnants;[26] but still to be reduc't[27] in their nightward studies wherewith they close the dayes work, under the determinate sentence of *David* or *Salomon,* or the Evangels[28] and Apostolic scriptures. Being perfect in the knowledge of personal duty, they

---

23. The references are first to the poems attributed to the legendary Orpheus, and next to Hesiod's *Works and Days* (eighth century B.C.), Theocritus's idyls (third century B.C.), Aratus's *Prognostica* (third century B.C.), Nicander's poems on natural science (second century B.C.) and Oppian's on fishing and hunting (third century A.D.), Dionysus of Alexandria's *Periegesis* (second century A.D.), Lucretius's *De rerum natura* (first century B.C.), Manilius's *Astronomica* (first century A.D.), and Virgil's 'rural part' – i.e. the *Eclogues* and *Georgics.*

24. Choice between right and wrong, as defined in Aristotle's *Nicomachean Ethics* (II, vi, 15).

25. Diogenes Laertius, reputed author of the *Lives and Opinions of Eminent Philosophers* (third century A.D.?).

26. i.e. 'On the Soul of the World', attributed to the Pythagorean philosopher Timaeus of Locri (cf. Plato's *Timaeus*).

27. Led back.

28. Gospels.

may then begin the study of Economics.[29] And either now, or before this, they may have easily learnt at any odd hour the *Italian* Tongue. And soon after, but with wariness and good antidote, it would be wholsome enough to let them taste some choice Comedies, Greek, Latin, or *Italian*: Those Tragedies also that treat of Household matters, as *Trachiniæ, Alcestis*,[30] and the like. The next remove must be to the study of *Politicks*; to know the beginning, end, and reasons of Political Societies; that they may not in a dangerous fit of the Common-wealth be such poor, shaken, uncertain Reeds, of such a tottering Conscience as many of our great Counsellers have lately shewn themselves, but stedfast pillars of the State. After this they are to dive into the grounds of Law, and legal Justice; deliver'd first, and with best warrant by *Moses*; and as far as humane prudence can be trusted, in those extoll'd remains of Grecian Law-givers, *Licurgus, Solon, Zaleucus, Charondas*, and thence to all the Roman *Edicts* and Tables with their *Justinian*;[31] and so down to the *Saxon* and common Laws of *England*, and the Statutes. Sundayes also and every evening may be now understandingly spent in the highest matters of *Theology*, and Church History ancient and modern: and ere this time the Hebrew Tongue at a set hour might have been gain'd, that the Scriptures may be now read in their own original; whereto it would be no impossibility to add the *Chaldey*, and the *Syrian* Dialect.[32] When all these employments are well conquer'd, then will the choise Histories, *Heroic Poems*, and *Attic* Tragedies of stateliest and most regal argument, with all the famous Political Orations offer themselves; which if they were not only read; but some of them got by memory, and solemnly pronounc't with right accent, and grace, as might be taught, would endue them even

29. Management of a household.

30. i.e. the plays by Sophocles and Euripides, respectively.

31. The references are to four lawgivers: the Spartan Lycurgus (ninth century B.C.?), the Athenian Solon (seventh century B.C.), and the Sicilians Zaleucus (eighth century B.C.) and Charondas (fifth century B.C.). Roman law was codified by Justinian (see above p. 161, Note 106).

32. Dialects of Aramaic.

with the spirit and vigor of *Demosthenes* or *Cicero*, *Euripides*, or *Sophocles*. And now lastly will be the time to read with them those organic[33] arts which inable men to discourse and write perspicuously, elegantly, and according to the fitted stile of lofty, mean, or lowly.[34] Logic therefore so much as is useful, is to be referr'd to this due place withall her well coucht Heads and Topics, untill it be time to open her contracted palm into a gracefull and ornate Rhetorick taught out of the rule of *Plato*, *Aristotle*, *Phalereus*, *Cicero*, *Hermogenes*, *Longinus*.[35] To which *Poetry* would be made subsequent, or indeed rather precedent, as being less suttle and fine, but more simple, sensuous and passionate. I mean not here the prosody of a verse, which they could not but have hit on before among the rudiments of Grammar; but that sublime Art which *Aristotles Poetics*, in *Horace*, and the *Italian* Commentaries of *Castelvetro, Tasso, Mazzoni*,[36] and others, teaches what the laws are of a true *Epic* Poem, what of a *Dramatic*, what of a *Lyric*, what Decorum is, which is the grand master-piece to observe. This would make them soon perceive what despicable creatures our common Rimers and Play-writers be, and shew them, what religious, what glorious and magnificent use might be made of Poetry both in divine and humane things. From hence and not till now[37] will be the right season of forming them to be able Writers and Composers in every excellent matter, when they shall be thus fraught with an universal insight into things. Or whether they be to speak in

---

33. More practical.

34. The accepted three modes of composition, approximately 'formal, informal, and colloquial'.

35. The references are, *inter alia*, to the treatise *On Style* attributed to Demetrius Phalereus (fourth century B.C.), the rhetorical works of Hermogenes (second century A.D.), and the treatise *On the Sublime* attributed to Longinus (first century A.D.).

36. Ludovico Castelvetro translated Aristotle's *Poetics* in 1570; Tasso published his *Discourses on Epic Poetry* in 1594; and Jacopo Mazzoni defended Dante in 1573 and 1587.

37. The final year in the programme of studies here outlined will be devoted to a single activity, composition (as Parker emphasizes, below, p. 454).

Parliament or Counsel, honour and attention would be waiting
on their lips. There would then also appear in Pulpits other
Visages, other gestures, and stuff otherwise wrought then what
we now sit under, oft times to as great a trial of our patience as
any other that they preach to us. These are the Studies wherein
our noble and our gentle Youth ought to bestow their time in
a disciplinary way from twelve to one and twenty; unless they
rely more upon their ancestors dead, then upon themselves living. In which methodical course it is so suppos'd they must proceed by the steddy pace of learning onward, as at convenient
times for memories sake to retire back into the middle ward, and
sometimes into the rear[38] of what they have been taught, until
they have confirm'd, and solidly united the whole body of their
perfeted knowledge, like the last embattelling of a Roman
Legion. Now will be worth the seeing what Exercises and
Recreations may best agree, and become these Studies.

Their Exercise.

The course of Study hitherto briefly describ'd, is, what I can
guess by reading, likest to those ancient and famous Schools of
Pythagoras, Plato, Isocrates, Aristotle[39] and such others, out of
which were bred up such a number of renowned Philosophers,
Orators, Historians, Poets and Princes all over *Greece, Italy*
and *Asia*, besides the flourishing Studies of *Cyrene* and *Alexandria*.[40] But herein it shall exceed them, and supply a defect as
great as that which *Plato* noted in the Common-wealth of
Sparta;[41] whereas that City train'd up their Youth most for War,
and these in their Academies and *Lycæum*, all for the Gown, th
institution of breeding which I here delineate, shall be equally
good both for Peace and War. Therefore about an hour and

38. Rear-ward is the third line in a military engagement; mid-ward
the second; foreward, the first.

39. Pythagoras's school at Crotona in Sicily was founded in the
sixth century B.C. The other schools are Plato's Academy, Aristotle
Lyceum, and Isocrates's school of oratory.

40. i.e. the medical school in Cyrene and the institutions of learning in Alexandria.

41. Cf. *Laws*, I, 626 ff., 634 ff.

half ere they eat at Noon should be allow'd them for exercise and due rest afterwards: But the time for this may be enlarg'd at pleasure, according as their rising in the morning shall be early. The Exercise which I commend first, is the exact use of their Weapon,[42] to guard and to strike safely with edge, or point; this will keep them healthy, nimble, strong, and well in breath, is also the likeliest means to make them grow large and tall, and to inspire them with a gallant and fearless courage, which being temper'd with seasonable Lectures and Precepts to them of true Fortitude and Patience, will turn into a native and heroick valour, and make them hate the cowardise of doing wrong. They must be also practiz'd in all the Locks and Gripes of Wrastling, wherein English men were wont to excell, as need may often be in fight to tugg or grapple, and to close. And this perhaps will be enough, wherein to prove and heat their single strength. The interim of unsweating themselves regularly, and convenient rest before meat may both with profit and delight be taken up in recreating and composing their travail'd spirits with the solemn and divine harmonies of Musick heard or learnt; either while the skilful *Organist* plies his grave and fancied descant,[43] in lofty fugues, or the whole Symphony with artful and unimaginable touches adorn and grace the well studied chords of some choice Composer; sometimes the Lute, or soft Organ stop waiting on elegant Voices either to Religious, martial, or civil Ditties; which if wise men and Prophets be not extreamly out, have a great power over dispositions and manners, to smooth and make them gentle from rustick harshness and distemper'd passions. The like also would not be unexpedient after Meat to assist and cherish Nature in her first concoction,[44] and send their minds back to study in good tune and satisfaction. Where having follow'd it close under vigilant eyes till about two hours before supper, they are by a sudden alarum or watch word, to be call'd out to their military motions, under skie or covert, according to the season, as was the Roman wont; first on foot, then as their age permits, on Horseback, to

---

42. Sword.
43. Fanciful improvisation.
44. Digestion.

all the Art of Cavalry; That having in sport, but with much exactness, and daily muster, serv'd out the rudiments of their Souldiership in all the skill of Embatteling, Marching, Encamping, Fortifying, Besieging and Battering, with all the helps of ancient and modern stratagems, *Tacticks* and war-like maxims, they may as it were out of a long War come forth renowned and perfect Commanders in the service of their Country. They would not then, if they were trusted with fair and hopeful armies, suffer them for want of just and wise discipline to shed away from about them like sick feathers, though they be never so oft suppli'd: they would not suffer their empty and unrecrutible[45] Colonels of twenty men in a Company to quaff out, or convey into secret hoards, the wages of a delusive list, and a miserable remnant: yet in the mean while to be over-master'd with a score or two of drunkards, the only souldery left about them, or else to comply with all rapines and violences. No certainly, if they knew ought of that knowledge that belongs to good men or good Governours, they would not suffer these things. But to return to our own institute, besides these constant exercises at home, there is another opportunity of gaining experience to be won from pleasure it self abroad; In those vernal seasons of the year, when the air is calm and pleasant, it were an injury and sullenness against nature not to go out, and see her riches, and partake in her rejoycing with Heaven and Earth. I should not therefore be a perswader to them of studying much then, after two or three years that they have well laid their grounds, but to ride out in Companies with prudent and staid Guides, to all the quarters of the Land: learning and observing all places of strength, all commodities[46] of building and of soil, for Towns and Tillage, Harbours and Ports for Trade. Sometimes taking Sea as far as to our Navy, to learn there also what they can in the practical knowledge of sailing and of Seafight. These ways would try all their peculiar gifts of Nature, and if there were any secret excellence among them, would fetch it out, and give it fair opportunities to advance it self by, which could not but mightily redound to the good of this Nation,

45. Unable to obtain recruits.
46. Conveniences.

194

and bring into fashion again those old admired Vertues and Excellencies, with far more advantage now in this purity of Christian knowledge. Nor shall we then need the *Monsieurs* of *Paris* to take our hopefull Youth into their slight and prodigal custodies and send them over back again transform'd into Mimicks, Apes and Kickshoes.[47] But if they desire to see other Countries at three or four and twenty years of age, not to learn Principles but to enlarge Experience, and make wise observation, they will by that time be such as shall deserve the regard and honour of all men where they pass, and the society and friendship of those in all places who are best and most eminent. And perhaps then other Nations will be glad to visit us for their Breeding, or else to imitate us in their own Country.

Now lastly for their Diet there cannot be much to say, save only that it would be best in the same House; for much time else would be lost abroad, and many ill habits got; and that it should be plain, healthful, and moderate I suppose is out of controversie. Thus Mr. *Hartlib*, you have a general view in writing, as your desire was, of that which at several times I had discourst with you concerning the best and Noblest way of Education; not beginning as some have done from the Cradle, which yet might be worth many considerations, if brevity had not been my scope, many other circumstances also I could have mention'd, but this to such as have the worth in them to make trial, for light and direction may be enough. Only I believe that this is not a Bow for every man to shoot in[48] that counts himself a Teacher; but will require sinews almost equal to those which *Homer* gave *Ulysses*,[49] yet I am withall perswaded that it may prove much more easie in the assay, then it now seems at distance, and much more illustrious: howbeit not more difficult then I imagine, and that imagination presents me with nothing but very happy and very possible according to best wishes; if God have so decreed, and this age have spirit and capacity enough to apprehend.

---

47. Kickshaws: fantastic persons.
48. With.
49. Cf. *Odyssey*, XXI.

AREOPAGITICA;

A SPEECH OF MR. JOHN MILTON
FOR THE LIBERTY OF VNLICENC'D PRINTING
TO THE PARLAMENT OF ENGLAND.

(1644)

[The title is an allusion to the Areopagus near the Acropolis at Athens, the seat of the Council of State which the legislators Draco and Solon later reorganized as a judicial tribunal (seventh–sixth centuries B.C.). Later still, probably about 355 B.C., the Athenian orator Isocrates pleaded for a resuscitation of the tribunal in his *Areopagiticus*.

The immediate occasion of Milton's oration was the Parliamentary ordinance of 14 June 1643 'to prevent and suppress the licence of printing' (cf. below, Notes 4 and 9). Itself unlicensed, *Areopagitica* understandably fails to mention its printer or bookseller; but Milton inscribed his name on the title page boldly, and pointedly.

The title page also quotes the words which in Euripides's *The Suppliant Women* (ll. 436–41) form part of Theseus's paean to Athens. In Milton's version:

> This is true Liberty when free born men
> Having to advise the public may speak free,
> Which he who can, and will, deserv's high praise,
> Who neither can nor will, may hold his peace;
> What can be juster in a State then this?

The first edition of *Areopagitica* (see above, pp. 30 ff.) was the only one to appear in Milton's lifetime. It is here reprinted from the Columbia edition (IV, 293–354; ed. William Haller).]

THEY who to States and Governours of the Commonwealth direct their Speech, High Court of Parlament, or wanting such accesse in a private condition, write that which they foresee may advance the publick good; I suppose them as at the beginning of no meane endeavour, not a little alter'd and mov'd inwardly in their mindes: Some with doubt of what will be the successe, others with feare of what will be the censure; some with hope, others with confidence of what they have to speake. And me perhaps each of these dispositions, as the subject was whereon I enter'd,[1] may have at other times variously affected; and likely might in these formost expressions now also disclose which of them sway'd most, but that the very attempt of this addresse thus made, and the thought of whom it hath recourse to, hath got the power within me to a passion, farre more welcome then incidentall to a Preface. Which though I say not to confesse ere any aske, I shall be blamelesse, if it be no other, then the joy and gratulation which it brings to all who wish and promote their Countries liberty; whereof this whole Discourse propos'd will be a certaine testimony, if not a Trophey. For this is not the liberty which wee can hope, that no grievance ever should arise in the Commonwealth, that let no man in this World expect; but when complaints are freely heard, deeply consider'd, and speedily reform'd, then is the utmost bound of civill liberty attain'd, that wise men looke for. To which if I now manifest by the very sound of this which I shall utter, that wee are already in good part arriv'd, and yet from such a steepe disadvantage of tyranny and superstition grounded into our principles as was beyond the manhood of a *Roman* recovery,[2] it will bee attributed first, as is most due, to the strong assistance of God our deliverer, next to your faithfull guidance and undaunted Wisdome, Lords and Commons of *England*. Neither is it in Gods esteeme the diminution of his glory, when honourable things are spoken of good men and worthy Magistrates; which if I now first should begin to doe, after so fair a progresse of your laudable deeds, and such a long obligement upon the whole Realme to your indefatigable vertues, I might be justly reckn'd among the tardiest, and the unwillingest of them that praise yee. Neverthelesse there being three principal things, without which all praising is but Courtship and flattery, First, when that only is prais'd which is solidly worth praise : next when greatest likelihoods are brought that

---

1. i.e. the anti-episcopal controversy.

2. i.e. beyond Rome's manhood to recover from Rome's misfortunes.

such things are truly and really in those persons to whom they are ascrib'd, the other, when he who praises, by shewing that such his actuall perswasion is of whom he writes, can demonstrate that he flatters not; the former two of these I have heretofore endeavour'd, rescuing the employment from him who went about to impaire your merits with triviall and malignant *Encomium*[3]; the latter as belonging chiefly to mine owne acquittall, that whom I so extoll'd I did not flatter, hath been reserv'd opportunely to this occasion. For he who freely magnifies what hath been nobly done, and fears not to declare as freely what might be done better, gives ye the best cov'nant of his fidelity; and that his loyalest affection and his hope waits on your proceedings. His highest praising is not flattery, and his plainest advice is a kinde of praising; for though I should affirme and hold by argument, that it would fare better with truth, with learning, and the Commonwealth, if one of your publisht Orders which I should name,[4] were call'd in, yet at the same time it could not but much redound to the lustre of your milde and equall Government, when as private persons are hereby animated to thinke ye better pleas'd with publick advice, then other statists have been delighted heretofore with publicke flattery. And men will then see what difference there is between the magnanimity of a trienniall Parlament,[5] and that jealous hautiness of Prelates and cabin[6] Counsellours that usurpt of late, when as they shall observe yee in the midd'st of your Victories and successes more gently brooking writt'n exceptions against a voted Order, then other Courts, which had produc't nothing worth memory but the weake ostentation of wealth, would have endur'd the least signifi'd dislike at any sudden Proclamation. If I should thus farre presume upon the

---

3. The *Humble Remonstrance* (1641) of Joseph Hall, Milton's antagonist in the anti-episcopal controversy (cf. above, p. 22).

4. i.e. the Parliamentary ordinance cited in the headnote (above, p. 196), which Milton later denounces as 'a discipline imitated from the Prelats' (below, p. 230).

5. An Act of February 1641 required that a new Parliament should meet every three years.

6. Cabinet.

meek demeanour of your civill and gentle greatnesse, Lords and Commons, as what your publisht Order hath directly said, that to gainsay, I might defend my selfe with ease, if any should accuse me of being new or insolent, did they but know how much better I find ye esteem it to imitate the old and elegant humanity of Greece, then the barbarick pride of a *Hunnish* and *Norwegian* statelines. And out of those ages, to whose polite wisdom and letters we ow that we are not yet *Gothes* and *Jutlanders*, I could name him[7] who from his private house wrote that discourse to the Parlament of *Athens*, that perswades them to change the forme of *Democraty* which was then establisht. Such honour was done in those dayes to men who profest the study of wisdome and eloquence, not only in their own Country, but in other Lands, that Cities and Siniories heard them gladly, and with great respect, if they had ought in publick to admonish the State. Thus did *Dion Prusæus* a stranger and a privat Orator counsell the *Rhodians* against a former Edict:[8] and I abound with other like examples, which to set heer would be superfluous. But if from the industry of a life wholly dedicated to studious labours, and those naturall endowments haply not the worse for two and fifty degrees of northern latitude, so much must be derogated, as to count me not equall to any of those who had this priviledge, I would obtain to be thought not so inferior, as your selves are superior to the most of them who receiv'd their counsell: and how farre you excell them, be assur'd, Lords and Commons, there can be no greater testimony appear, then when your prudent spirit acknowledges and obeyes the voice of reason from what quarter soever it be heard speaking; and renders ye as willing to repeal any Act of your own setting forth, as any set forth by your Predecessors.

If ye be thus resolv'd, as it were injury to thinke ye were not, I know not what should withhold me from presenting ye with a fit instance wherein to shew both that love of truth

---

7. Isocrates; see headnote (above, p. 196).

8. The Greek rhetorician Dion Prusaeus (first century A.D.) counselled the Rhodians not to displace the names from public statutes with those of more recent rulers.

which ye eminently professe, and that uprightnesse of your judgement which is not wont to be partiall to your selves; by judging over again that Order[9] which ye have ordain'd *to regulate Printing. That no Book, pamphlet, or paper shall be henceforth Printed, unlesse the same be first approv'd and licenc't by such*, or at least one such as shall be thereto appointed. For that part which preserves justly every mans Copy[10] to himselfe, or provides for the poor, I touch not, only wish they be not made pretenses to abuse and persecute honest and painfull[11] Men, who offend not in either of these particulars. But that other clause of Licencing Books, which we thought had dy'd with his brother *quadragesimal* and *matrimonial* when the Prelats expir'd,[12] I shall now attend with such a Homily, as shall lay before ye, first the inventors of it to bee those whom ye will be loath to own; next what is to be thought in generall of reading, what ever sort the Books be; and that this Order avails nothing to the suppressing of scandalous, seditious, and libellous Books, which were mainly intended to be supprest. Last, that it will be primely to the discouragement of all learning, and the stop of Truth, not only by disexercising and blunting our abilities in what we know already, but by hindring and cropping the discovery that might bee yet further made both in religious and civill Wisdome.

I deny not, but that it is of greatest concernment in the Church and Commonwealth, to have a vigilant eye how Bookes demeane themselves as well as men; and thereafter to confine, imprison, and do sharpest justice on them as malefactors: For Books are not absolutely dead things, but doe contain a potencie of life in them to be as active as that soule was whose progeny they are; nay they do preserve as in a violl[13] the purest efficacie and extraction of that living intellect that bred them. I know

---

9. The ordinance cited in the headnote (above, p. 196).

10. Copyright.   11. Painstaking.

12. The expiry may be said to date from the Bishops Exclusion Bill of 13 February 1642, even though episcopacy was not abolished until 1646. A 'quadragesimal' licence is a dispensation from the dietary provisions for Lenten.

13. i.e. vial.

they are as lively, and as vigorously productive, as those fab-
ulous Dragons teeth; and being sown up and down, may
chance to spring up armed men.[14] And yet on the other hand
unlesse warinesse be us'd, as good almost kill a Man as kill a
good Book; who kills a Man kills a reasonable creature, Gods
Image; but hee who destroyes a good Booke, kills reason it
selfe, kills the Image of God, as it were in the eye. Many a man
lives a burden to the Earth; but a good Booke is the pretious
life-blood of a master spirit, imbalm'd and treasur'd up on purpose to a life beyond life. 'Tis true, no age can restore a life,
whereof perhaps there is no great losse; and revolutions of ages
doe not oft recover the losse of a rejected truth, for the want
of which whole Nations fare the worse. We should be wary
therefore what persecution we raise against the living labours
of publick men, how we spill that season'd life of man preser-
v'd and stor'd up in Books; since we see a kinde of homicide
may be thus committed, sometimes a martyrdome, and if it
extend to the whole impression, a kinde of massacre, whereof
the execution ends not in the slaying of an elementall life, but
strikes at that ethereall and fift essence, the breath of reason it
selfe, slaies an immortality rather then a life. But lest I should
be condemn'd of introducing licence, while I oppose Licencing,
I refuse not the paines to be so much Historicall, as will serve
to shew what hath been done by ancient and famous Commonwealths, against this disorder, till the very time that this
project of licencing crept out of the *Inquisition*, was catcht
up by our Prelates, and hath caught some of our Presbyters.

In *Athens* where Books and Wits were ever busier then in
any other part of *Greece*, I finde but only two sorts of writings which the Magistrate car'd to take notice of; those either
blasphemous and Atheisticall, or Libellous. Thus the Books
of *Protagoras* were by the Judges of *Areopagus* commanded
to be burnt, and himselfe banisht the territory for a discourse
begun with his confessing not to know *whether there were*

---

14. Two fables refer to the sowing of dragon's teeth: Cadmus's,
under the direction of Athena; and Jason's, under that of Medea.
Milton's allusion is most likely to the former. Cf. Ovid, *Metamorphoses*, III, 101–30; VII, 121–42.

gods, or whether not: [15]//And against defaming, it was decreed
that none should be traduc'd by name, as was the manner of
Vetus Comœdia,[16] whereby we may guesse how they censur'd
libelling: And this course was quick enough, as *Cicero* writes,[17]
to quell both the desperate wits of other Atheists, and the open
way of defaming, as the event shew'd. Of other sects and
opinions though tending to voluptuousnesse, and the denying
of divine providence they tooke no heed. Therefore we do not
read that either *Epicurus*, or that libertine school of *Cyrene*,
or what the *Cynick* impudence utter'd,[18] was ever question'd
by the Laws. Neither is it recorded that the writings of those
old Comedians were supprest, though the acting of them were
forbid; and that *Plato* commended the reading of *Aristophanes*
the loosest of them all, to his royall scholler *Dionysius*, is commonly known, and may be excus'd, if holy *Chrysostome*,[19] as is
reported, nightly studied so much the same Author and had the
art to cleanse a scurrilous vehemence into the stile of a rousing
Sermon. That other leading City of *Greece*, *Lacedæmon*, considering that *Lycurgus* their Law-giver was so addicted to elegant learning, as to have been the first that brought out of
Ionia the scatter'd workes of *Homer*, and sent the Poet *Thales*
from *Creet* to prepare and mollifie the *Spartan* surlinesse with
his smooth songs and odes, the better to plant among them
law and civility,[20] it is to be wonder'd how museless and un-

---

15. As Cicero reports in *De natura deorum*, I, 23. Protagoras, the
first of the Sophists, is best known for his dictum that 'man is
a measure of all things'.

16. The Old (i.e. Aristophanic) Comedy.

17. As above, Note 15.

18. Epicurus (341–270 B.C.) was traditionally if erroneously regarded as a mere hedonist, a label more appropriate to the school
of Aristippus in Cyrene (fourth century B.C.). The Cynics, on the
other hand, upheld the self-sufficiency of virtue – but often at the
expense of social graces, witness the 'impudent' behavior of
Diogenes.

19. The great theologian of the Eastern Church St. John Chrysostom (347–407). On Aristophanes cf. below, p. 218, Note 84.

20. As Plutarch reports in *Lives* ('Lycurgus', IV).

bookish they were, minding nought but the feats of Warre. There needed no licencing of Books among them for they dislik'd all, but their owne *Laconick Apothegms*,[21] and took a slight occasion to chase *Archilochus*[22] out of their City, perhaps for composing in a higher straine then their owne souldierly ballats and roundels could reach to: Or if it were for his broad verses, they were not therein so cautious, but they were as dissolute in their promiscuous conversing; whence *Euripides* affirmes in *Andromache*, that their women were all unchaste.[23] Thus much may give us light after what sort of Bookes were prohibited among the Greeks. The Romans also for many ages train'd up only to a military roughnes, resembling most the *Lacedæmonian* guise, knew of learning little but what their twelve Tables,[24] and the *Pontifick* College with their *Augurs* and *Flamins*[25] taught them in Religion and Law, so unacquainted with other learning, that when *Carneades* and *Critolaus*, with the *Stoick Diogenes* comming Embassadors to *Rome*, tooke thereby occasion to give the City a tast of their Philosophy, they were suspected for seducers by no lesse a man then *Cato* the Censor, who mov'd it in the Senat to dismisse them speedily, and to banish all such *Attick* bablers out of *Italy*.[26] But *Scipio* and others of the noblest Senators withstood him and his old *Sabin* austerity;[27] honour'd and admir'd the men; and the Censor himself at last in his old age fell to the study of that whereof

21. Cf. Milton's censure of the apophthegms favored by Anglicans (above, p. 97, Note 53).

22. The lyric poet of the seventh century B.C., from Paros.

23. Cf. *Andromache*, ll. 590–93.

24. i.e. of jurisprudence.

25. The Pontific College was the ultimate religious authority in ancient Rome; 'augurs' interpreted the signs; and 'flamins' officiated at sacrifices (cf. above, p. 78, Note 3).

26. The Stoic Carneades on visiting Rome in 155 B.C. lectured on justice but promptly refuted his own arguments. (His companion Diogenes should not be confused with the Cynic, above, Note 18.) Cato's resentment of Greek influence was notorious.

27. The opposition to Cato ('Sabine' because brought up in that territory) by the philhellene Scipio the Younger is related by Cicero, *De senectute*, VIII, 26.

before hee was so scrupulous. And yet at the same time *Nævius* and *Plautus* the first Latine comedians had fill'd the City with all the borrow'd Scenes of *Menander* and *Philemon*.[28] Then began to be consider'd there also what was to be don to libellous books and Authors; for *Nævius* was quickly cast into prison for his unbridl'd pen, and releas'd by the *Tribunes* upon his recantation: We read also that libels were burnt, and the makers punisht by *Augustus*.[29] The like severity no doubt was us'd if ought were impiously writt'n against their esteemed gods. Except in these two points, how the world went in Books, the Magistrat kept no reckning. And therefore *Lucretius* without impeachment versifies his Epicurism to *Memmius*, and had the honour to be set forth the second time by *Cicero* so great a father of the Commonwealth; although himselfe disputes against that opinion in his own writings.[30] Nor was the Satyricall sharpnesse, or naked plainnes of *Lucilius*, or *Catullus*, or *Flaccus*,[31] by any order prohibited. And for matters of State, the story of *Titus Livius*, though it extoll'd that part which *Pompey* held,[32] was not therefore supprest by *Octavius Cæsar* of the other Faction. But that *Naso*[33] was by him banisht in his old age, for the wanton Poems of his youth, was but a meer covert of State over some secret cause: and besides, the Books were neither banisht nor call'd in. From hence we shall meet with little else but tyranny in the Roman Empire, that we may not marvell, if not so often bad, as good Books were silenc't. I shall therefore deem to have bin large anough in producing what among the ancients was punishable to write, save only which, all other arguments were free to treat on.

28. The four comic dramatists helped to displace Old Comedy (above, Note 16) in the fourth and third centuries B.C. Cf. 'scurrill Plautus', below, p. 210.   29. Cf. Tacitus, *Annals*, I, 72.

30. Lucretius 'versified' Epicurus (above, Note 18) in *De rerum natura* which Cicero is said to have edited later.

31. i.e. the satirist Lucilius in the second century B.C., and Catullus and Ovid in the first century B.C.

32. In several books of Livy's *History* now lost.

33. i.e. Ovid (Publius Ovidius Naso), who was not necessarily banished because of the 'wanton Poems' of his *Ars amatoria*.

By this time the Emperors were become Christians,[34] whose discipline in this point I doe not finde to have bin more severe then what was formerly in practice. The Books of those whom they took to be grand Hereticks were examin'd, refuted, and condemn'd in the generall Councels; and not till then were prohibited, or burnt by autority of the Emperor. As for the writings of Heathen authors, unlesse they were plaine invectives against Christianity, as those of *Porphyrius* and *Proclus*,[35] they met with no interdict that can be cited, till about the year 400. in a *Carthaginian* Councel, wherein Bishops themselves were forbid to read the Books of Gentiles, but Heresies they might read : while others long before them on the contrary scrupl'd more the Books of Hereticks, then of Gentiles. And that the primitive Councels and Bishops were wont only to declare what Books were not commendable, passing no furder, but leaving it to each ones conscience to read or to lay by, till after the yeare 800. is observ'd already by *Padre Paolo* the great unmasker of the *Trentine* Councel.[36] After which time the Popes of *Rome* engrossing what they pleas'd of Politicall rule into their owne hands, extended their dominion over mens eyes, as they had before over their judgements, burning and prohibiting to be read, what they fansied not; yet sparing in their censures, and the Books not many which they so dealt with : till *Martin* the 5.[37] by his Bull not only prohibited, but was the first that excommunicated the reading of hereticall Books; for about that time *Wicklef* and *Husse* growing terrible, were they who first drove the Papall Court to a stricter policy of prohibiting. Which cours *Leo* the 10, and his successors follow'd, untill

---

34. i.e. from the time of Constantine the Great in the early fourth century.

35. Alike opponents of Christianity, in the third and fifth centuries respectively.

36. Paolo Sarpi (as above, p. 102, Note 62), from whose *Historie of the Councel of Trent* Milton borrows extensively (see Yale edn, II, 500).

37. Pope Martin V reigned 1417-31 in the wake of the reformers Wycliffe (above, p. 81, Note 11) and John Huss of Bohemia (*c.* 1373-1415).

the Councell of Trent, and the Spanish Inquisition engendring together brought forth, or perfected those Catalogues, and expurging Indexes that rake through the entralls of many an old good Author, with a violation wors then any could be offer'd to his tomb.[38] Nor did they stay in matters Hereticall, but any subject that was not to their palat, they either condemn'd in a prohibition, or had it strait into the new Purgatory of an Index. To fill up the measure of encroachment, their latest invention was to ordain that no Book, pamphlet, or paper should be Printed (as if S. *Peter* had bequeath'd them the keys of the Presse also out of Paradise) unlesse it were approv'd and licenc't under the hands of 2 or 3 glutton Friers. For example :

Let the Chancellor *Cini* be pleas'd to see if in this present work be contain'd ought that may withstand the Printing,
                    Vincent Rabatta Vicar of *Florence.*

I have seen this present work, and finde nothing athwart the Catholick faith and good manners: In witnesse whereof I have given, &c.
                    Nicolò Cini Chancellor of *Florence.*

Attending the precedent relation, it is allow'd that this present work of *Davanzati* may be Printed,
                    Vincent Rabatta, &c.

It may be Printed, *July* 15.
            Friar *Simon Mompei d' Amelia* Chancellor of the holy office in *Florence.*

Surely they have a conceit, if he of the bottomlesse pit had not long since broke prison, that this quadruple exorcism would barre him down. I feare their next designe will be to get into their custody the licencing of that which they say *Claudius*[39]

38. Censorship of books, tightened by Pope Leo X in 1515 as by the Council of Trent in 1562 and 1563, was enforced by the Inquisition from 1542 (cf. below, Note 92). The *Index of Prohibited Books* was first issued by Pope Paul IV in 1557.

39. Milton tactfully cites Suetonius's report in a margin: 'Quo veniam daret flatum crepitumque ventris in convivio emittendi'.

intended, but went not through with. Voutsafe to see another
of their forms the Roman stamp:

Imprimatur,[40] If it seem good to the reverend Master of the
    holy Palace,   *Belcastro* Vicegerent.

Imprimatur
                Friar *Nicolò Rodolphi* Master of the holy Palace.

Sometimes 5 *Imprimaturs* are seen together dialogue-wise in the
Piatza of one Title page, complimenting and ducking each to
other with their shav'n reverences, whether the Author, who
stands by in perplexity at the foot of his Epistle, shall to the
Presse or to the spunge. These are the prety responsories, these
are the deare Antiphonies that so bewitcht of late our Prelats,
and their Chaplaines with the goodly Eccho they made; and
besotted us to the gay imitation of a lordly *Imprimatur*, one
from Lambeth house, another from the West end of *Pauls*;[41] so
apishly Romanizing, that the word of command still was set
downe in Latine; as if the learned Grammaticall pen that wrote
it, would cast no ink without Latine: or perhaps, as they thought
because no vulgar tongue was worthy to expresse the pure
conceit of an *Imprimatur*; but rather, as I hope, for that our
English, the language of men ever famous, and formost in the
atchievements of liberty, will not easily finde servile letters
anow to spell such a dictatorie presumption English. And thus
yet have the Inventors and the originall of Book-licencing ript
up, and drawn as lineally as any pedigree. We have it not, that
can be heard of, from any ancient State, or politie, or Church,
nor by any Statute left us by our Ancestors elder or later; nor
from the moderne custom of any reformed Citty, or Church
abroad; but from the most Antichristian Councel, and the most
tyrannous Inquisition that ever inquir'd. Till then Books were
ever as freely admitted into the World as any other birth; the
issue of the brain was no more stifl'd then the issue of the

---

40. Literally, 'Let it be printed'.

41. i.e. the London residence of the Archbishop of Canterbury and
the palace of the Bishop of London, respectively.

womb: no envious *Juno* sate cros-leg'd[42] over the nativity of any mans intellectuall off-spring; but if it prov'd a Monster, who denies, but that it was justly burnt, or sunk into the Sea. But that a Book in wors condition then a peccant soul, should be to stand before a Jury ere it be borne to the World, and undergo yet in darknesse the judgement of *Radamanth* and his Collegues,[43] ere it can passe the ferry backward into light, was never heard before, till that mysterious iniquity provokt and troubl'd at the first entrance of Reformation, sought out new limbo's and new hells wherein they might include our Books also within the number of their damned. And this was the rare morsell so officiously snatcht up, and só ilfavourdly imitated by our inquisiturient Bishops, and the attendant minorites[44] their Chaplains. That ye like not now these most certain Authors of this licencing order, and that all sinister intention was farre distant from your thoughts, when ye were importun'd the passing it, all men who know the integrity of your actions, and how ye honour Truth, will clear yee readily.

But some will say, What though the Inventors were bad, the thing for all that may be good? It may so; yet if that thing be no such deep invention, but obvious, and easie for any man to light on, and yet best and wisest Commonwealths through all ages, and occasions have forborne to use it, and falsest seducers, and oppressors of men were the first who tooke it up, and to no other purpose but to obstruct and hinder the first approach of Reformation; I am of those who beleeve, it will be a harder alchymy then *Lullius*[45] ever knew, to sublimat any good use out of such an invention. Yet this only is what I request to gain from this reason, that it may be held a dangerous and suspicious fruit, as certainly it deserves, for the tree that bore it, untill I can dissect one by one the properties it has.

42. As she is said to have done when Hercules was born of the union of Jupiter and Alcmena (Ovid, *Metamorphoses*, IX, 281–323).

43. Radamanthus, Minos and Aeacus were the judges of the dead in Hades.

44. i.e. the Franciscan Friars Minor.

45. Raymond Lully (c. 1234–1315), author of books on logic, medicine, chemistry, and alchemy.

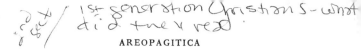

1st generation Christians — what did they read?

But I have first to finish, as was propounded, what is to be thought in generall of reading Books, what ever sort they be, and whether be more the benefit, or the harm that thence proceeds?

Not to insist upon the examples of *Moses, Daniel* & *Paul*, who were skilfull in all the learning of the Ægyptians, Caldeans, and Greeks,[46] which could not probably be without reading their Books of all sorts, in *Paul* especially, who thought it no defilement to insert into holy Scripture the sentences of three Greek Poets, and one of them a Tragedian,[47] the question was, notwithstanding sometimes controverted among the Primitive Doctors, but with great odds on that side which affirm'd it both lawfull and profitable, as was then evidently perceiv'd, when *Julian* the Apostate, and suttlest enemy to our faith, made a decree forbidding Christians the study of heathen learning: for, said he, they wound us with our own weapons, and with our owne arts and sciences they overcome us.[48] And indeed the Christians were put so to their shifts by this crafty means, and so much in danger to decline into all ignorance, that the two *Apollinarii* were fain as a man may say, to coin all the seven liberall Sciences out of the Bible, reducing it into divers forms of Orations, Poems, Dialogues, ev'n to the calculating of a new Christian Grammar.[49] But saith the Historian *Socrates*, The providence of God provided better then the industry of *Apollinarius* and his son, by taking away that illiterat law with the life of him who devis'd it. So great an injury they then held it to be depriv'd of *Hellenick* learning; and

---

46. On the skill of Moses and Daniel 'in all learning and wisdom', see Acts 7:22 and Daniel 1:17. On Paul cf. next note.

47. Acts 17:28 ('we are also his [God's] offspring') is said to derive from Aratus; Titus 1:12 ('the Cretans are always liars'), from Epimenides; and I Corinthians 15:33 (quoted below, p. 407, Note 11), from Euripides.

48. The Emperor Julian's resolution in 361 is reported in Theodoret's fifth-century ecclesiastical history (III, 8).

49. The shrewd conduct of Appolinares and his son is reported in the fifth-century ecclesiastical history of Socrates Scholasticus (III, 16). On the seven 'sciences' see above, p. 184, Note 8.

thought it a persecution more undermining, and secretly decaying the Church, then the open cruelty of *Decius* or *Dioclesian*.[50]
And perhaps it was the same politick drift that the Divell
whipt St. *Jerom* in a lenten dream, for reading *Cicero*; or else
it was a fantasm bred by the feaver which had then seis'd him.[51]
For had an Angel bin his discipliner, unlesse it were for dwelling
too much upon Ciceronianism, & had chastiz'd the reading, not
the vanity, it had bin plainly partiall; first to correct him for
grave *Cicero*, and not for scurrill *Plautus*[52] whom he confesses to
have bin reading not long before; next to correct him only,
and let so many more ancient Fathers wax old in those pleasant and florid studies without the lash of such a tutoring
apparition; insomuch that *Basil* teaches how some good use may
be made of *Margites* a sportfull Poem, not now extant, writ by
Homer; and why not then of *Morgante* an Italian Romanze
much to the same purpose.[53] But if it be agreed we shall be try'd
by visions, there is a vision recorded by *Eusebius* far ancienter
then this tale of *Jerom* to the Nun *Eustochium*, and besides has
nothing of a feavor in it.[54] *Dionysius Alexandrinus* was about
the year 240, a person of great name in the Church for piety
and learning, who had wont to avail himself much against
hereticks by being conversant in their Books; untill a certain
Presbyter laid it scrupulously to his conscience, how he durst
venture himselfe among those defiling volumes. The worthy
man loath to give offence fell into a new debate with himselfe
what was to be thought; when suddenly a vision sent from
God, it is his own Epistle that so averrs it, confirm'd him in
these words : Read any books what ever come to thy hands,

---

50. The Emperors Trajan (249–51) and Diocletian (284–305).

51. The experience is related by St. Jerome himself (Epistle XVIII,
to the nun Eustochium).

52. Cf. above, p. 204.

53. Cf. the essay 'The Right Use of Greek Literature' by St. Basil
the Great (*c.* 330–379), and the mock-romance *Il Morgante Maggiore*
by Luigi Pulci (1431–87).

54. The references are to Jerome's epistle (as above, Note 51) and
Eusebius's ecclesiastical history (VII, 7). Dionysius was Bishop of
Alexandria in 247–65.

even bad books are good to read.

for thou art sufficient both to judge aright, and to examine each matter. To this revelation he assented the sooner, as he confesses, because it was answerable to that of the Apostle to the Thessalonians, Prove all things, hold fast that which is good.[55] And he might have added another remarkable saying of the same Author; To the pure all things are pure,[56] not only meats and drinks, but all kinds of knowledge whether of good or evill; the knowledge cannot defile, nor consequently the books, if the will and conscience be not defil'd. For books are as meats and viands are; some of good, some of evill substance; and yet God in that unapocryphall vision,[57] said without exception, Rise *Peter*, kill and eat, leaving the choice to each mans discretion. Wholesome meats to a vitiated stomack differ little or nothing from unwholesome; and best books to a naughty mind are not unappliable to occasions of evill. Bad meats will scarce breed good nourishment in the healthiest concoction;[58] but herein the difference is of bad books, that they to a discreet and judicious Reader serve in many respects to discover, to confute, to forewarn, and to illustrate. Wherof what better witnes can ye expect I should produce, then one of your own now sitting in Parlament, the chief of learned men reputed in this Land, Mr. *Selden*, whose volume of naturall & national laws[59] proves, not only by great autorities brought together, but by exquisite reasons and theorems almost mathematically demonstrative, that all opinions, yea errors, known, read, and collated, are of man's service & assistance toward the speedy attainment of what is truest. I conceive therefore, that when God did enlarge the universall diet of mans body, saving ever the rules of temperance, he then also, as before, left arbitrary the dyeting and repasting of our minds; as wherein every mature man might have to exercise his owne leading capacity. How great a vertue is temperance, how much of moment through the whole life of man? yet God committs the managing

---

55. I Thessalonians 5:21.

56. Titus 1:15.

57. Acts 10:9-16.

58. Digestion (as above, p. 193, Note 44).

59. *De jure naturali* (as above, p. 175, Note 137).

so great a trust, without particular Law or prescription, wholly to the demeanour of every grown man. And therefore when he himself tabl'd the Jews from heaven, that Omer which was every mans daily portion of Manna,[60] is computed to have bin more then might have well suffic'd the heartiest feeder thrice as many meals. For those actions which enter into a man, rather then issue out of him, and therefore defile not,[61] God uses not to captivat under a perpetuall childhood of prescription, but trusts him with the gift of reason to be his own chooser; there were but little work left for preaching, if law and compulsion should grow so fast upon those things which hertofore were govern'd only by exhortation. *Salomon* informs us that much reading is a wearines to the flesh;[62] but neither he, nor other inspir'd author tells us that such, or such reading is unlawfull: yet certainly had God thought good to limit us herein, it had bin much more expedient to have told us what was unlawfull, then what was wearisome. As for the burning of those Ephesian books by St. *Pauls* converts, tis reply'd the books were magick, the Syriack so renders them.[63] It was a privat act, a voluntary act, and leaves us to a voluntary imitation: the men in remorse burnt those books which were their own; the Magistrat by this example is not appointed: these men practiz'd the books, another might perhaps have read them in some sort usefully. Good and evill we know in the field of this World grow up together almost inseparably; and the knowledge of good is so involv'd and interwoven with the knowledge of evill, and in so many cunning resemblances hardly to be discern'd, that those confused seeds which were impos'd on *Psyche*[64] as an incessant labour to cull out, and sort asunder, were not more intermixt. It was from out the rinde of one

---

60. Cf. Exodus 16:16 ff. ('the Lord hath commanded, Gather of it [the manna] every man according to his eating, an omer for every man').

61. Cf. Matthew 15:17-20.

62. Ecclesiastes 12:12.

63. Acts 19:19.

64. i.e. imposed by Venus, as related by Apuleius in *The Golden Ass* (IV-VI).

apple tasted, that the knowledge of good and evill as two
twins cleaving together leapt forth into the World. And perhaps
this is that doom which *Adam* fell into of knowing good and
evill, that is to say of knowing good by evill.[65] As therefore the //
state of man now is; what wisdome can there be to choose, what
continence to forbeare without the knowledge of evill? He
that can apprehend and consider vice with all her baits and
seeming pleasures, and yet abstain, and yet distinguish, and yet
prefer that which is truly better, he is the true warfaring[66]
Christian. I cannot praise a fugitive and cloister'd vertue, un-
exercis'd & unbreath'd, that never sallies out and sees her
adversary, but slinks out of the race, where that immortall
garland is to be run for, not without dust and heat. Assuredly
we bring not innocence into the world, we bring impurity
much rather: that which purifies us is triall, and triall is
by what is contrary. That vertue therefore which is but a
youngling in the contemplation of evill, and knows not the
utmost that vice promises to her followers, and rejects it, is
but a blank vertue, not a pure; her whitenesse is but an excre-
mentall[67] whitenesse; Which was the reason why our sage and
serious Poet *Spencer*, whom I dare be known to think a better
teacher than *Scotus* or *Aquinas*,[68] describing true temperance
under the person of *Guion*, brings him in with his palmer
through the cave of Mammon, and the bowr of earthly blisse
that he might see and know, and yet abstain.[69] Since therefore
the knowledge and survay of vice is in this world so necessary

---

65. Cf. *Paradise Lost*, IV, 222: 'Knowledge of Good bought dear
by knowing ill'.

66. The Columbia edn reads 'wayfaring'; but I have adopted the
emendation (made by hand, possibly Milton's own) in several
extant copies. The Yale edn agrees (II, 515); but cf. Kivette, below,
p. 455.   67. Superficial.

68. Less a direct reference to Duns Scotus and St. Thomas Aquinas
(alike of the thirteenth century) than an allusion to medieval
theology and philosophy generally.

69. Sir Guyon's visit to the Cave of Mammon was *not* in the
company of the Palmer (*The Faerie Queene*, II, vii, 2, and viii, 3;
cf. Sirluck, below, p. 456).

to the constituting of human vertue, and the scanning of error
to the confirmation of truth, how can we more safely, and
with lesse danger scout into the regions of sin and falsity then
by reading all manner of tractats, and hearing all manner of
reason? And this is the benefit which may be had of books pro-
miscuously read. But of the harm that may result hence three
kinds are usually reckn'd. First, is fear'd the infection that may
spread; but then all human learning and controversie in religious
points must remove out of the world, yea the Bible it selfe; for
that oftimes relates blasphemy not nicely, it describes the carnall sense of wicked men not unelegantly, it brings in holiest
men passionately murmuring against providence through all the
arguments of *Epicurus*: in other great disputes it answers dubi-
ously and darkly to the common reader: And ask a Talmudist[70]
what ails the modesty of his marginal Keri, that *Moses* and all
the Prophets cannot perswade him to pronounce the textuall
Chetiv. For these causes we all know the Bible it selfe put by the
Papist into the first rank of prohibited books. The ancientest
Fathers must be next remov'd, as *Clement* of *Alexandria*, and
that *Eusebian* book of Evangelick preparation,[71] transmitting our
ears through a hoard of heathenish obscenities to receive the
Gospel. Who finds not that *Irenæus, Epiphanius, Jerom*,[72] and
others discover more heresies then they well confute, and that
oft for heresie which is the truer opinion. Nor boots it to say for
these, and all the heathen Writers of greatest infection, if it
must be thought so, with whom is bound up the life of human
learning, that they writ in an unknown tongue, so long as
we are sure those languages are known as well to the worst of

70. A student of the Talmud, the great depository of the accumu-
lated Jewish commentaries on the Bible. The actual text ('Chetiv')
often carries emendations in the margin ('Keri').

71. The early apologist of the Christian faith St. Clement of
Alexandria (second century) and the ecclesiastical historian Eusebius
of Caesarea (*c.* 264–*c.* 340) who also wrote the *Evangelical Preparation.*

72. St. Irenaeus in the second century, Epiphanius in the fourth,
and St. Jerome in the early fifth. alike catalogue heresies in profuse
detail.

men, who are both most able, and most diligent to instill the
poison they suck, first into the Courts of Princes, acquainting
them with the choicest delights, and criticisms of sin. As perhaps did that *Petronius* whom *Nero* call'd his *Arbiter*, the Master
of his revels; and that notorious ribald of *Arezzo*, dreaded, and
yet dear to the Italian Courtiers.[73] I name not him for posterities
sake, whom *Harry* the 8. nam'd in merriment his Vicar of hell.[74]
By which compendious way all the contagion that foreine
books can infuse, will finde a passage to the people farre easier
and shorter then an Indian voyage, though it could be sail'd
either by the North of *Cataio*[75] Eastward, or of *Canada* West-
ward, while our Spanish licencing gags the English Presse never
so severely. But on the other side that infection which is from
books of controversie in Religion, is more doubtfull and dangerous to the learned, then to the ignorant; and yet those books
must be permitted untoucht by the licencer. It will be hard to
instance where any ignorant man hath bin ever seduc't by
Papisticall book in English, unlesse it were commended and
expounded to him by some of that Clergy : and indeed all such
tractats whether false or true are as the Prophesie of *Isaiah* was
to the *Eunuch*, not to be *understood without a guide*.[76] But of
our Priests and Doctors how many have bin corrupted by
studying the comments of Jesuits and *Sorbonists*,[77] and how
fast they could transfuse that corruption into the people, our
experience is both late and sad. It is not forgot, since the acute
and distinct *Arminius* was perverted meerly by the perusing of
a namelesse discours writt'n at *Delf*, which at first he took in
hand to confute.[78] Seeing therefore that those books; & those

---

73. Pietro Aretino of Arezzo (sixteenth century) was noted for
his obscene writings. Petronius, of course, is the author of the
Satyricon.

74. Sir Francis Brian, often said to have been amusingly ungodly
(cf. Fletcher, below, p. 456).

75. i.e. Cathay (China).   76. Acts 8 : 27–35.

77. i.e. the theologians of the Sorbonne.

78. The Dutch theologian Arminius (1560–1609) abandoned
Calvinism on reading an anti-Calvinist treatise he was asked to
answer.

in great abundance which are likeliest to taint both life and doctrine, cannot be supprest without the fall of learning, and of all ability in disputation, and that these books of either sort are most and soonest catching to the learned, from whom to the common people what ever is hereticall or dissolute may quickly be convey'd, and that evill manners are as perfectly learnt without books a thousand other ways which cannot be stopt, and evill doctrine not with books can propagate, except a teacher guide, which he might also doe without writing, and so beyond prohibiting, I am not able to unfold, how this cautelous[79] enterprise of licencing can be exempted from the number of vain and impossible attempts. And he who were pleasantly dispos'd, could not well avoid to lik'n it to the exploit of that gallant man who thought to pound up the crows by shutting his Parkgate. Besides another inconvenience, if learned men be the first receivers out of books, & dispredders both of vice and error, how shall the licencers themselves be confided in, unlesse we can conferr upon them, or they assume to themselves above all others in the Land, the grace of infallibility, and uncorruptednesse? And again, if it be true, that a wise man like a good refiner can gather gold out of the drossiest volume, and that a fool will be a fool with the best book, yea or without book, there is no reason that we should deprive a wise man of any advantage to his wisdome, while we seek to restrain from a fool, that which being restrain'd will be no hindrance to his folly. For if there should be so much exactnesse always us'd to keep that from him which is unfit for his reading, we should in the judgement of *Aristotle* not only, but of *Salomon*, and of our Saviour,[80] not voutsafe him good precepts, and by consequence not willingly admit him to good books; as being certain that a wise man will make better use of an idle pamphlet, then a fool will do of a sacred Scripture. 'Tis next alleg'd we must not expose our selves to temptations without necessity, and next to that, not imploy our time in vain things. To both these objections one answer will serve, out of the grounds already laid, that to all men such books are not temp-

---

79. Deceitful.

80. Aristotle, *Ethics*, I, 3; Proverbs 23:9; and Matthew 7:6.

tations, nor vanities; but usefull drugs and materialls wherewith to temper and compose effective and strong med'cins,
which mans life cannot want.[81] The rest, as children and
childish men, who have not the art to qualifie and prepare these
working minerals, well may be exhorted to forbear, but hinder'd
forcibly they cannot be by all the licencing that Sainted Inquisition could ever yet contrive; which is what I promis'd to deliver next, That this order of licencing conduces nothing to the
end for which it was fram'd; and hath almost prevented me
by being clear already while thus much hath bin explaining.
See the ingenuity[82] of Truth, who when she gets a free and
willing hand, opens her self faster, then the pace of method and
discours can overtake her. It was the task which I began with,
To shew that no Nation, or well instituted State, if they valu'd
books at all, did ever use this way of licencing; and it might
be answer'd, that this is a piece of prudence lately discover'd.
To which I return, that as it was a thing slight and obvious to
think on, so if it had bin difficult to finde out, there wanted
not among them long since, who suggested such a cours; which
they not following, leave us a pattern of their judgement, that
it was not the not knowing, but the not approving, which was
the cause of their not using it. *Plato*, a man of high autority
indeed, but least of all for his Commonwealth, in the book of
his laws, which no City ever yet receiv'd, fed his fancie[83] with
making many edicts to his ayrie Burgomasters, which they
who otherwise admire him, wish had bin rather buried and
excus'd in the *genial* cups of an *Academick* nightsitting. By
which laws he seems to tolerat no kind of learning, but by
unalterable decree, consisting most of practicall traditions, to
the attainment whereof a Library of smaller bulk then his own
dialogues would be abundant. And there also enacts that no
Poet should so much as read to any privat man, what he had
writt'n, untill the Judges and Law-keepers had seen it, and

81. Be without.

82. Ingenuousness.

83. Milton rejects the ideal commonwealths of Plato and, later,
of Sir Thomas More in *Utopia* and Bacon in *New Atlantis* (below,
p. 219).

allow'd it: But that *Plato* meant this Law peculiarly to that Commonwealth which he had imagin'd, and to no other, is evident. Why was he not else a Law-giver to himself, but a transgressor, and to be expell'd by his own Magistrats; both for the wanton epigrams and dialogues which he made, and his perpetuall reading of *Sophron Mimus*, and *Aristophanes*, books of grossest infamy,[84] and also for commending the latter of them though he were the malicious libeller of his chief friends, to be read by the Tyrant *Dionysius*, who had little need of such trash to spend his time on? But that he knew this licencing of Poems had reference and dependence to many other proviso's there set down in his fancied republic, which in this world could have no place: and so neither he himself, nor any Magistrat, or City ever imitated that cours, which tak'n apart from those other colaterall injunctions must needs be vain and fruitlesse. For if they fell upon one kind of strictnesse, unlesse their care were equall to regulat all other things of like aptness to corrupt the mind, that single endeavour they knew would be but a fond labour; to shut and fortifie one gate against corruption, and be necessitated to leave others round about wide open. If we think to regulat Printing, thereby to rectifie manners, we must regulat all recreations and pastimes, all that is delightfull to man. No musick must be heard, no song be set or sung, but what is grave and *Dorick*.[85] There must be licencing dancers, that no gesture, motion, or deportment be taught our youth but what by their allowance shall be thought honest; for such *Plato* was provided of; It will ask more then the work of twenty licencers to examin all the lutes, the violins, and the ghittars in every house; they must not be suffer'd to prattle as they doe, but must be licenc'd what they may say. And who shall silence all the airs and madrigalls, that whisper softnes in chambers? The Windows also, and the *Balcone's* must be thought on, there are shrewd books, with dangerous Frontis-

---

84. The Sicilian Sophron 'Mimus' (fifth century B.C.) authored several coarse mimes. Aristophanes, of course, hardly belongs to the same category.

85. Plato's *Republic* (III, 398–9) praises the 'manly' Doric and Phrygian styles of music, and condemns the Lydian and Ionic.

pices set to sale; who shall prohibit them, shall twenty licencers? The villages also must have their visitors to enquire what lectures the bagpipe and rebbeck[86] reads ev'n to the ballatry, and the gammuth of every *municipal* fidler, for these are the Countryman's *Arcadia's* and his *Monte Mayors*.[87] Next, what more Nationall corruption, for which England hears ill abroad, then houshold gluttony; who shall be the rectors of our daily rioting? and what shall be done to inhibit the multitudes that frequent those houses where drunk'nes is sold and harbour'd? Our garments also should be referr'd to the licencing of some more sober work-masters to see them cut into a lesse wanton garb. Who shall regulat all the mixt conversation of our youth, male and female together, as is the fashion of this Country, who shall still appoint what shall be discours'd, what presum'd, and no furder? Lastly, who shall forbid and separat all idle resort, all evill company? These things will be, and must be; but how they shall be lest hurtfull, how lest enticing, herein consists the grave and governing wisdom of a State. To sequester out of the world into *Atlantick* and *Eutopian* polities,[88] which never can be drawn into use, will not mend our condition; but to ordain wisely as in this world of evill, in the midd'st whereof God hath plac't us unavoidably. Nor is it *Plato's* licencing of books will doe this, which necessarily pulls along with it so many other kinds of licencing, as will make us all both ridiculous and weary, and yet frustrat; but those unwritt'n, or at least unconstraining laws of vertuous education, religious and civill nurture, which *Plato* there mentions, as the bonds and ligaments of the Commonwealth, the pillars and the sustainers of every writt'n Statute; these they be which will bear chief sway in such matters as these, when all licencing will be easily eluded. Impunity and remissenes, for certain are the bane of a Commonwealth, but here the great art lyes to discern in what the law is to bid restraint and punishment, and in what things perswasion only is to work. If every action which is good,

---

86. The predecessor of the violin.

87. The prose romances of Sir Philip Sidney (*Arcadia*, 1590) and orge de Montemayor (*Diana enamorada*, c. 1559).

88. See above, Note 83.

or evill in man at ripe years, were to be under pittance, and prescription, and compulsion, what were vertue but a name, what praise could be then due to well-doing, what grammercy to be sober, just or continent? many there be that complain of divin Providence for suffering *Adam* to transgresse, foolish tongues! when God gave him reason, he gave him freedom to choose, for reason is but choosing; he had bin else a meer artificiall *Adam*, such an *Adam* as he is in the motions.[89] We our selves esteem not of that obedience, or love, or gift, which is of force: God therefore left him free, set before him a provoking object, ever almost in his eyes; herein consisted his merit, herein the right of his reward, the praise of his abstinence. Wherefore did he creat passions within us, pleasures round about us, but that these rightly temper'd are the very ingredients of vertu? They are not skilfull considerers of human things who imagin to remove sin by removing the matter of sin; for besides that it is a huge heap increasing under the very act of diminishing, though some part of it may for a time be withdrawn from some persons, it cannot from all, in such a universall thing as books are; and when this is done, yet the sin remains entire. Though ye take from a covetous man all his treasure, he has yet one jewell left, yet cannot bereave him of his covetousnesse. Banish all objects of lust, shut up all youth into the severest discipline that can be exercis'd in any hermitage, ye cannot make them chaste, that came not thither so: such great care and wisdom is requir'd to the right managing of this point. Suppose we could expell sin by this means; look how much we thus expell of sin, so much we expell of vertue: for the matter of them both is the same; remove that, and ye remove them both alike. This justifies the high providence of God, who though he command us temperance, justice, continence, yet powrs out before us ev'n to a profusenes all desirable things, and gives us minds that can wander beyond all limit and satiety.[90] Why should we then affect a rigor contrary to the manner of God and of nature, by abridging or scanting those means, which

89. Puppet shows. With this entire statement, cf. *Paradise Lost*, III. 107 ff.

90. Cf. the Lady's speech in *Comus*, ll. 762 ff.

books freely permitted are, both to the triall of vertue, and the exercise of truth. It would be better done to learn that the law must needs be frivolous which goes to restrain things, uncertainly and yet equally working to good, and to evill. And were I the chooser, a dram of well-doing should be preferr'd before many times as much the forcible hindrance of evill-doing. For God sure esteems the growth and compleating of one vertuous person, more then the restraint of ten vitious. And albeit what ever thing we hear or see, sitting, walking, travel-ling, or conversing may be fitly call'd our book, and is of the same effect that writings are, yet grant the thing to be pro-hibited were only books, it appears that this order hitherto is far insufficient to the end which it intends. Do we not see, not once or oftner, but weekly that continu'd Court-libell[91] against the Parlament and City, Printed, as the wet sheets can witnes, and dispers't among us, for all that licencing can doe? yet this is the prime service a man would think, wherein this order should give proof of it self. If it were executed, you'l say. But certain, if execution be remisse or blindfold now, and in this particular, what will it be hereafter, and in other books. If then the order shall not be in vain and frustrat, behold a new labour, Lords and Commons, ye must repeal and proscribe all scanda-lous and unlicenc't books already printed and divulg'd; after ye have drawn them up into a list, that all may know which are condemn'd, and which not; and ordain that no forrein books be deliver'd out of custody, till they have bin read over. This office will require the whole time of not a few overseers, and those no vulgar men. There be also books which are partly usefull and excellent, partly culpable and pernicious; this work will ask as many more officials, to make expurgations, and ex-punctions, that the Commonwealth of learning be not dam-nify'd. In fine, when the multitude of books encrease upon their hands, ye must be fain to catalogue all those Printers who are found frequently offending, and forbidd the importation of their whole suspected *typography*. In a word, that this your order may be exact, and not deficient, ye must reform it per-

91. Most likely a reference to the royalist newspaper *Mercurius aulicus* ('Court Mercury').

fectly according to the model of *Trent* and *Sevil*,[92] which I know ye abhorre to doe. Yet though ye should condiscend to this, which God forbid, the order still would be but fruitlesse and defective to that end whereto ye meant it. If to prevent sects and schisms, who is so unread or so uncatechis'd in story, that hath not heard of many sects refusing books as a hindrance, and preserving their doctrine unmixt for many ages, only by unwritt'n traditions. The Christian faith, for that was once a schism, is not unknown to have spread all over *Asia*,[93] ere any Gospel or Epistle was seen in writing. If the amendment of manners be aym'd at, look into Italy and Spain, whether those places be one scruple the better, the honester, the wiser, the chaster, since all the inquisitionall rigor that hath bin executed upon books.

Another reason, whereby to make it plain that this order will misse the end it seeks, consider by the quality which ought to be in every licencer. It cannot be deny'd but that he who is made judge to sit upon the birth, or death of books whether they may be wafted into this world, or not, had need to be a man above the common measure, both studious, learned, and judicious; there may be else no mean mistakes in the censure of what is passable or not; which is also no mean injury. If he be of such worth as behoovs him, there cannot be a more tedious and unpleasing journey-work, a greater losse of time levied upon his head, then to be made the perpetuall reader of un-chosen books and pamphlets, oftimes huge volumes. There is no book that is acceptable unlesse at certain seasons; but to be enjoyn'd the reading of that at all times, and in a hand scars legible, whereof three pages would not down at any time in the fairest Print, is an imposition which I cannot beleeve how he that values times, and his own studies, or is but of a sensible[94] nostrill should be able to endure. In this one thing I crave leave of the present licencers to be pardon'd for so thinking: who

92. The Inquisition was reorganized, with papal approval, by Ferdinand V and Isabella in 1479; the first Grand Inquisitor was Torquemada. On the Council of Trent see above, p. 206, Note 38.

93. i.e. Asia Minor and the Near East.

94. Sensitive.

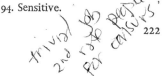

doubtlesse took this office up, looking on it through their obedience to the Parlament, whose command perhaps made all things seem easie and unlaborious to them; but that this short triall hath wearied them out already, their own expressions and excuses to them who make so many journeys to sollicit their licence, are testimony anough. Seeing therefore those who now possesse the imployment, by all evident signs wish themselves well ridd of it, and that no man of worth, none that is not a plain unthrift of his own hours is ever likely to succeed them, except he mean to put himself to the salary of a Presse-corrector, we may easily foresee what kind of licencers we are to expect hereafter, either ignorant, imperious, and remisse, or basely pecuniary. This is what I had to shew wherein this order cannot conduce to that end, whereof it bears the intention.

I lastly proceed from the no good it can do, to the manifest hurt it causes, in being first the greatest discouragement and affront, that can be offer'd to learning and to learned men. It was the complaint and lamentation of Prelats, upon every least breath of a motion to remove pluralities, and distribute more equally Church revennu's, that then all learning would be for ever dasht and discourag'd. But as for that opinion, I never found cause to think that the tenth part of learning stood or fell with the Clergy: nor could I ever but hold it for a sordid and unworthy speech of any Churchman who had a competency left him. If therefore ye be loath to dishearten utterly and discontent, not the mercenary crew of false pretenders to learning, but the free and ingenuous sort of such as evidently were born to study, and love lerning for it self, not for lucre, or any other end, but the service of God and of truth, and perhaps that lasting fame and perpetuity of praise which God and good men have consented shall be the reward of those whose publisht labours advance the good of mankind, then know, that so far to distrust the judgement & the honesty of one who hath but a common repute in learning, and never yet offended, as not to count him fit to print his mind without a tutor and examiner, lest he should drop a scism, or something of corruption, is the greatest displeasure and indignity to a free and knowing spirit that can be put upon him. What advantage is it to be a man over it is to be a boy at school, if we have only scapt the ferular,[95] to come under the fescu[96] of an *Imprimatur*? if serious and elaborat writings, as if they were no more then the theam of a Grammar lad under his Pedagogue must not be utter'd without the cursory eyes of a temporizing and extemporizing licencer. He who is not trusted with his own actions, his drift not being known to be evill, and standing to the hazard of law and penalty, has no great argument to think himself reputed in the Commonwealth wherin he was born, for other then a fool or a foreiner. When a man writes to the world, he summons up all his reason and deliberation to assist him; he searches, meditats, is industrious, and likely consults and conferrs with his judicious friends; after all which done he takes himself to be inform'd in what he writes, as well as any that writ before him; if in this the most consummat act of his fidelity and ripenesse, no years, no industry, no former proof of his abilities can bring him to that state of maturity, as not to be still mistrusted and suspected, unlesse he carry all his considerat diligence, all his midnight watchings, and expence of *Palladian*[97] oyl, to the hasty view of an unleasur'd licencer perhaps much his younger, perhaps far his inferiour in judgement, perhaps one who never knew the labour of book-writing, and if he be not repulst, or slighted, must appear in Print like a punie[98] with his guardian, and his censors hand on the back of his title to be his bayl and surety, that he is no idiot, or seducer, it cannot be but a dishonor and derogation to the author, to the book, to the priviledge and dignity of Learning. And what if the author shall be one so copious of fancie, as to have many things well worth the adding, come into his mind after licencing while the book is yet under the Presse, which not seldom happ'ns to the best and diligentest writers; and that perhaps a dozen times in one book. The Printer dares not go beyond his licenc't copy; so often then must the author trudge to his leav-giver, that those his new insertions may be viewd; and

---

95. Cane (ferula).
96. Twig; here the pointer used in a classroom.
97. Referring to Pallas Athena, the goddess of wisdom.
98. A minor (the French *puis-né*).

many a jaunt will be made, ere that licencer, for it must be the same man, can either be found, or found at leisure; mean while either the Presse must stand still, which is no small damage, or the author loose his accuratest thoughts, & send the book forth wors then he had made it, which to a diligent writer is the greatest melancholy and vexation that can befall. And how can a man teach with autority, which is the life of teaching, how can he be a Doctor in his book as he ought to be, or else had better be silent, whenas all he teaches, all he delivers, is but under the tuition, under the correction of his patriarchal[99] licencer to blot or alter what precisely accords not with the hidebound humor which he calls his judgement. When every acute reader upon the first sight of a pedantick licence, will be ready with these like words to ding[100] the book a coits distance from him, I hate a pupil teacher, I endure not an instructer that comes to me under the wardship of an overseeing fist. I know nothing of the licencer, but that I have his own hand here for his arrogance; who shall warrant me his judgement? The State Sir, replies the Stationer,[101] but has a quick return, The State shall be my governours, but not my criticks; they may be mistak'n in the choice of a licencer, as easily as this licencer may be mistak'n in an author: This is some common stuffe; and he might adde from Sir *Francis Bacon*, That *such authoriz'd books are but the language of the times*.[102] For though a licencer should happ'n to be judicious more then ordnary, which will be a great jeopardy of the next succession, yet his very office, and his commission enjoyns him to let passe nothing but what is vulgarly receiv'd already. Nay, which is more lamentable, if the work of any deceased author, though never so famous in his life time, and even to this day, come to their hands for licence to be Printed, or Reprinted, if there be found in his book one sentence of a ventrous edge, utter'd in the height of zeal, and who knows whether it might not be the dictat of a divine

---

99. A reference to Archbishop Laud, accused of aspiring to be Patriarch of the Western Church.

100. Hurl.   101. Printer.

102. From Bacon's 'An Advertisement touching the Controversies of the Church of England'.

Spirit, yet not suiting with every low decrepit humor of their own, though it were *Knox* himself, the Reformer of a Kingdom that spake it, they will not pardon him their dash : the sense of that great man shall to all posterity be lost, for the fearfulnesse, or the presumptuous rashnesse of a perfunctory licencer. And to what an author[103] this violence hath bin lately done, and in what book of greatest consequence to be faithfully publisht, I could now instance, but shall forbear till a more convenient season. Yet if these things be not resented seriously and timely by them who have the remedy in their power, but that such iron moulds[104] as these shall have autority to knaw out the choisest periods of exquisitest books, and to commit such a treacherous fraud against the orphan remainders of worthiest men after death, the more sorrow will belong to that haples race of men, whose misfortune it is to have understanding. Henceforth let no man care to learn, or care to be more then worldly wise; for certainly in higher matters to be ignorant and slothfull, to be a common stedfast dunce will be the only pleasant life, and only in request.

And as it is a particular disesteem of every knowing person alive, and most injurious to the writt'n labours and monuments of the dead, so to me it seems an undervaluing and vilifying of the whole Nation. I cannot set so lightly by all the invention, the art, the wit, the grave and solid judgement which is in England, as that it can be comprehended in any twenty capacities how good soever, much lesse that it should not passe except their superintendence be over it, except it be sifted and strain'd with their strainers, that it should be uncurrant without their manuall stamp. Truth and understanding are not such wares as to be monopoliz'd and traded in by tickets and statutes, and standards. We must not think to make a staple commodity of all the knowledge in the Land, to mark and licence it like our broad cloath, and our wooll packs. What is it but a servitude like that impos'd by the Philistims, not to be allow'd the sharpning of our own axes and coulters,[105] but we must repair from all quarters to twenty licencing forges. Had any one writt'n

103. Identity unknown.   104. Rust.

105. 1 Samuel 13 : 19–20.

and divulg'd erroneous things & scandalous to honest life, mis-using and forfeiting the esteem had of his reason among men, if after conviction this only censure were adjudg'd him, that he should never henceforth write, but what were first examin'd by an appointed officer, whose hand should be annext to passe his credit for him, that now he might be safely read, it could not be apprehended lesse then a disgracefull punishment. Whence to include the whole Nation, and those that never yet thus offended, under such a diffident and suspectfull prohibition, may plainly be understood what a disparagement it is. So much the more, when as dettors and delinquents may walk abroad without a keeper, but unoffensive books must not stirre forth without a visible jaylor in thir title. Nor is it to the common people lesse then a reproach; for if we be so jealous over them, as that we dare not trust them with an English pamphlet, what doe we but censure them for a giddy, vitious, and ungrounded people; in such a sick and weak estate of faith and discretion, as to be able to take nothing down but through the pipe of a licencer. That this is care or love of them, we cannot pretend, whenas in those Popish places where the Laity are most hated and dispis'd the same strictnes is us'd over them. Wisdom we cannot call it, because it stops but one breach of licence, nor that neither; whenas those corruptions which it seeks to prevent, break in faster at other dores which cannot be shut.

And in conclusion it reflects to the disrepute of our Ministers also, of whose labours we should hope better, and of the pro-ficiencie which thir flock reaps by them, then that after all this light of the Gospel which is, and is to be, and all this continuall preaching, they should be still frequented with such an un-princip'd, unedify'd, and laick rabble, as that the whiffe of every new pamphlet should stagger them out of thir catechism, and Christian walking. This may have much reason to dis-courage the Ministers when such a low conceit is had of all their exhortations, and the benefiting of their hearers, as that they are not thought fit to be turn'd loose to three sheets of paper without a licencer, that all the Sermons, all the Lectures preacht, printed, vented in such numbers, and such volumes, as have now well-nigh made all other books unsalable, should not be armor anough against one single *enchiridion*,[106] without the castle St. *Angelo*[107] of an *Imprimatur*.

And lest som should perswade ye, Lords and Commons, that these arguments of lerned mens discouragement at this your order, are meer flourishes, and not reall, I could recount what I have seen and heard in other Countries, where this kind of inquisition tyrannizes; when I have sat among their lerned men, for that honor I had, and bin counted happy to be born in such a place of *Philosophic* freedom, as they suppos'd England was, while themselvs did nothing but bemoan the servil condition into which lerning amongst them was brought; that this was it which had dampt the glory of Italian wits; that nothing had bin there writt'n now these many years but flattery and fustian. There it was that I found and visited the famous *Galileo* grown old, a prisner to the Inquisition, for thinking in Astronomy otherwise then the Franciscan and Dominican licencers thought.[108] And though I knew that England then was groaning loudest under the Prelaticall yoak, neverthelesse I took it as a pledge of future happines, that other Nations were so perswaded of her liberty. Yet was it beyond my hope that those Worthies were then breathing in her air, who should be her leaders to such a deliverance, as shall never be forgott'n by any revolution of time that this world hath to finish. When that was once begun, it was as little in my fear, that what words of complaint I heard among lerned men of other parts utter'd against the Inquisition, the same I should hear by as lerned men at home utterd in time of Parlament against an order of licencing; and that so generally, that when I had disclos'd my self a companion of their discontent, I might say, if without envy, that he whom an honest *quæstorship* had indear'd to the *Sicilians*, was not more by them importun'd against *Verres*,[109] then the favourable

106. Both 'hand-book' and 'hand-knife'.

107. On the left bank of the Tiber in Rome: in Milton's time, a papal prison.

108. For the other personalities Milton met on the Continent, see above, pp. 19 f. and 68.

109. Cicero while quaestor in Sicily (75 B.C.) had denounced the corrupt government of the praetor Verres.

opinion which I had among many who honour ye, and are known and respected by ye, loaded me with entreaties and perswasions, that I would not despair to lay together that which just reason should bring into my mind, toward the removal of an undeserved thraldom upon lerning. That this is not therefore the disburdning of a particular fancie, but the common grievance of all those who had prepar'd their minds and studies above the vulgar pitch to advance truth in others, and from others to entertain it, thus much may satisfie. And in their name I shall for neither friend nor foe conceal what the generall murmur is; that if it come to inquisitioning again, and licencing, and that we are so timorous of our selvs, and so suspicious of all men, as to fear each book, and the shaking of every leaf, before we know what the contents are, if some who but of late were little better then silenc't from preaching, shall come now to silence us from reading, except what they please, it cannot be guest what is intended by som but a second tyranny over learning: and will soon put it out of controversie that Bishops and Presbyters are the same to us both name and thing. That those evills of Prelaty which before from five or six and twenty Sees were distributivly charg'd upon the whole people, will now light wholly upon learning, is not obscure to us: whenas now the Pastor of a small unlearned Parish, on the sudden shall be exalted Archbishop over a large dioces of books, and yet not remove, but keep his other cure too, a mysticall pluralist.[110] He who but of late cry'd down the sole ordination of every novice Batchelor of Art, and deny'd sole jurisdiction over the simplest Parishioner, shall now at home in his privat chair assume both these over worthiest and excellentest books and ablest authors that write them. This is not, Yee Covnants and Protestations[111] that we have made, this is not to put down Prelaty, this is but to chop an Episcopacy, this is but to translate the Palace *Metropolitan*[112] from one kind of dominion into another, this

---

110. One who enjoys several benefices at once.

111. The Solemn League and Covenant (1643) upheld Presbyterian-ism against Laud's efforts to impose episcopacy; the Protestation (1641) upheld civil liberties against Charles's effort to curtail them.

112. i.e. Archbishop Laud.

is but an old canonicall slight of *commuting* our penance. To startle thus betimes at a meer unlicenc't pamphlet will after a while be afraid of every conventicle, and a while after will make a conventicle of every Christian meeting. But I am certain that a State govern'd by the rules of justice and fortitude, or a Church built and founded upon the rock of faith and true knowledge, cannot be so pusillanimous. While things are yet not constituted in Religion, that freedom of writing should be restrain'd by a discipline imitated from the Prelats, and learnt by them from the Inquisition to shut us up all again into the brest of a licencer, must needs give cause of doubt and discouragement to all learned and religious men. Who cannot but discern the finenes of this politic drift, and who are the contrivers; that while Bishops were to be baited down, then all Presses might be open; it was the peoples birthright and priviledge in time of Parlament, it was the breaking forth of light. But now the Bishops abrogated and voided out of the Church, as if our Reformation sought no more, but to make room for others into their seats under another name, the Episcopall arts begin to bud again, the cruse of truth must run no more oyle, liberty of Printing must be enthrall'd again under a Prelaticall commission of twenty, the privilege of the people nullify'd, and which is wors, the freedom of learning must groan again, and to her old fetters; all this the Parlament yet sitting. Although their own late arguments and defences against the Prelats might remember them that this obstructing violence meets for the most part with an event utterly opposite to the end which it drives at : instead of suppressing sects and schisms, it raises them and invests them with a reputation : *The punishing of wits enchaunces their autority*, saith the Vicount St. Albans,[113] *and a forbidd'n writing is thought to be a certain spark of truth that flies up in the faces of them who seeke to tread it out.* This order therefore may prove a nursing mother to sects, but I shall easily shew how it will be a step-dame to Truth : and first by disinabling us to the maintenance of what is known already.

Well knows he who uses to consider, that our faith and

---

113. Bacon; see above, p. 225, Note 102.

knowledge thrives by exercise, as well as our limbs and complexion. Truth is compar'd in Scripture to a streaming fountain;[114] if her water flow not in a perpetuall progression, they sick'n into a muddy pool of conformity and tradition. A man may be a heretick in the truth; and if he beleeve things only because his Pastor sayes so, or the Assembly so determins, without knowing other reason, though his belief be true, yet the very truth he holds, becomes his heresie. There is not any burden that som would gladlier post off to another, then the charge and care of their Religion. There be, who knows not that there be of Protestants and professors[115] who live and dye in as arrant an implicit faith, as any lay Papist of Loretto.[116] A wealthy man addicted to his pleasure and to his profits, finds Religion to be a traffick so entangl'd, and of so many piddling accounts, that of all mysteries[117] he cannot skill to keep a stock going upon that trade. What should he doe? fain he would have the name to be religious, fain he would bear up with his neighbours in that. What does he therefore, but resolvs to give over toyling, and to find himself out som factor, to whose care and credit he may commit the whole managing of his religious affairs; som Divine of note and estimation that must be. To him he adheres, resigns the whole warehouse of his religion, with all the locks and keyes into his custody; and indeed makes the very person of that man his religion; esteems his associating with him a sufficient evidence and commendatory of his own piety. So that a man may say his religion is now no more within himself, but is becom a dividuall movable,[118] and goes and comes neer him, according as that good man frequents the house. He entertains him, gives him gifts, feasts him, lodges him; his religion comes home at night, praies, is liberally supt, and sumptuously laid to sleep, rises, is saluted, and after the malmsey, or some well spic't bruage, and better breakfasted then he[119]

---

114. Cf. Psalms 85:11.
115. i.e. those who profess religion.
116. The shrine near Ancona.
117. Trades, crafts.
118. Separable and removable.
119. Christ; see Mark 11:12-14.

whose morning appetite would have gladly fed on green figs between *Bethany* and *Ierusalem*, his Religion walks abroad at eight, and leavs his kind entertainer in the shop trading all day without his religion.

Another sort there be who when they hear that all things shall be order'd, all things regulated and setl'd; nothing writt'n but what passes through the custom-house of certain Publicans[120] that have the tunaging and the poundaging of all free spok'n truth, will strait give themselves up into your hands, mak'em & cut'em out what religion ye please; there be delights, there be recreations and jolly pastimes that will fetch the day about from sun to sun, and rock the tedious year as in a delightfull dream. What need they torture their heads with that which others have tak'n so strictly, and so unalterably into their own pourveying. These are the fruits which a dull ease and cessation of our knowledge will bring forth among the people. How goodly, and how to be wisht were such an obedient unanimity as this, what a fine conformity would it starch us all into? doubtles a stanch and solid peece of frame-work, as any January could freeze together.

Nor much better will be the consequence ev'n among the Clergy themselvs; it is no new thing never heard of before, for a *parochiall* Minister, who has his reward, and is at his *Hercules* pillars[121] in a warm benefice, to be easily inclinable, if he have nothing else that may rouse up his studies, to finish his circuit in an English concordance and a *topic folio*,[122] the gatherings and savings of a sober graduatship, a *Harmony* and a *Catena*,[123] treading the constant round of certain common doctrinall heads, attended with their uses, motives, marks and means, out of which as out of an alphabet or sol fa[124] by forming and transforming, joyning and dis-joyning variously a little book-craft,

120. Collectors of taxes.

121. The straits of Gibraltar, and so 'the utmost limit'.

122. Commonplace book.

123. The first harmonizes divergent readings of the four Gospels; the second arranges extracts in a 'chain' as commentaries on the Scriptures.

124. Musical scale.

and two hours meditation might furnish him unspeakably to the performance of more then a weekly charge of sermoning: not to reck'n up the infinit helps of interlinearies, breviaries, synopses, and other loitering gear. But as for the multitude of Sermons ready printed and pil'd up, on every text that is not difficult, our London trading St. *Thomas* in his vestry, and adde to boot St. *Martin*, and St. *Hugh*,[125] have not within their hallow'd limits more vendible ware of all sorts ready made: so that penury he never need fear of Pulpit provision, having where so plenteously to refresh his magazin. But if his rear and flanks be not impal'd,[126] if his back dore be not secur'd by the rigid licencer, but that a bold book may now and then issue forth, and give the assault to some of his old collections in their trenches, it will concern him then to keep waking, to stand in watch, to set good guards and sentinells about his receiv'd opinions, to walk the round and counter-round with his fellow inspectors, fearing lest any of his flock be seduc't, who also then would be better instructed, better exercis'd and disciplin'd. And God send that the fear of this diligence which must then be us'd, doe not make us affect the lazines of a licencing Church.

For if we be sure we are in the right, and doe not hold the truth guiltily, which becomes not, if we our selves condemn not our own weak and frivolous teaching, and the people for an untaught and irreligious gadding rout, what can be more fair, then when a man judicious, learned, and of a conscience, for ought we know, as good as theirs that taught us what we know, shall not privily from house to house, which is more dangerous, but openly by writing publish to the world what his opinion is, what his reasons, and wherefore that which is now thought cannot be sound. Christ urg'd it as wherewith to justifie himself, that he preacht in publick;[127] yet writing is more publick then preaching; and more easie to refutation, if need be, there being so many whose businesse and profession meerly it is, to be the champions of Truth; which if they neglect, what can be imputed but their sloth, or unability?

---

125. Churches surrounded by bookshops.
126. Protected.
127. John 18:19–20.

Thus much we are hinder'd and dis-inur'd[128] by this cours of licencing toward the true knowledge of what we seem to know. For how much it hurts and hinders the licencers themselves in the calling of their Ministery, more then any secular employment, if they will discharge that office as they ought, so that of necessity they must neglect either the one duty or the other, I insist not, because it is a particular, but leave it to their own conscience, how they will decide it there.

There is yet behind of what I purpos'd to lay open, the incredible losse, and detriment that this plot of licencing puts us to, more then if som enemy at sea should stop up all our hav'ns and ports, and creeks, it hinders and retards the importation of our richest Marchandize, Truth: nay it was first establisht and put in practice by Antichristian malice and mystery on set purpose to extinguish, if it were possible, the light of Reformation, and to settle falshood; little differing from that policie wherewith the Turk upholds his *Alcoran*, by the prohibition of Printing. 'Tis not deny'd, but gladly confest, we are to send our thanks and vows to heav'n, louder then most of Nations, for that great measure of truth which we enjoy, especially in those main points between us and the Pope, with his appertinences the Prelats: but he who thinks we are to pitch our tent here, and have attain'd the utmost prospect of reformation, that the mortall glasse wherein we contemplate, can shew us, till we come to *beatific* vision,[129] that man by this very opinion declares, that he is yet farre short of Truth.

Truth indeed came once into the world with her divine Master, and was a perfect shape most glorious to look on: but when he ascended, and his Apostles after him were laid asleep, then strait arose a wicked race of deceivers, who as that story goes of the *Ægyptian Typhon* with his conspirators, how they dealt with the good *Osiris*,[130] took the virgin Truth, hewd her

128. Disaccustomed.

129. Cf. I Corinthians 13:12 ('For we now see through a glass, darkly; but then face to face').

130. Osiris's body, torn asunder and scattered by Typhon, was collected by his wife Isis and their son Horus. Cf. Plutarch's allegorical interpretation in 'Isis and Osiris'.

lovely form into a thousand peeces, and scatter'd them to the four winds. From that time ever since, the sad friends of Truth, such as durst appear, imitating the carefull search that *Isis* made for the mangl'd body of *Osiris*, went up and down gathering up limb by limb still as they could find them. We have not yet found them all, Lords and Commons, nor ever shall doe, till her Masters second comming; he shall bring together every joynt and member, and shall mould them into an immortall feature of lovelines and perfection. Suffer not these licencing prohibitions to stand at every place of opportunity forbidding and disturbing them that continue seeking, that continue to do our obsequies to the torn body of our martyr'd Saint. We boast our light; but if we look not wisely on the Sun it self, it smites us into darknes. Who can discern those planets that are oft *Combust*,[131] and those stars of brightest magnitude that rise and set with the Sun, untill the opposite motion of their orbs bring them to such a place in the firmament, where they may be seen evning or morning. The light which we have gain'd, was giv'n us, not to be ever staring on, but by it to discover onward things more remote from our knowledge. It is not the unfrocking of a Priest, the unmitring of a Bishop, and the removing him from off the *Presbyterian* shoulders that will make us a happy Nation, no, if other things as great in the Church, and in the rule of life both economicall and politicall be not lookt into and reform'd, we have lookt so long upon the blaze that *Zuinglius*[132] and *Calvin* hath beacon'd up to us, that we are stark blind. There be who perpetually complain of schisms and sects, and make it such a calamity that any man dissents from their maxims. 'Tis their own pride and ignorance which causes the disturbing, who neither will hear with meeknes, nor can convince, yet all must be supprest which is not found in their *Syntagma*.[133] They are the troublers, they are the dividers of unity, who neglect and permit not others to unite those dissever'd peeces which are yet wanting to the body of Truth. To be still searching what we know not, by what we

---

131. Burnt up (used of planets coming within 8° 30′ of the sun).
132. The Zurich reformer Huldreich Zwingli (1484–1531).
133. Systematic doctrinal treatise.

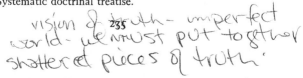

vision of truth – unperfect world – we must put together shattered pieces of truth.

know, still closing up truth to truth as we find it (for all her body is *homogeneal*,[134] and proportionall) this is the golden rule in *Theology* as well as in Arithmetick, and makes up the best harmony in a Church; not the forc't and outward union of cold, and neutrall, and inwardly divided minds.

Lords and Commons of England, consider what Nation it is wherof ye are, and wherof ye are the governours: a Nation not slow and dull, but of a quick, ingenious, and piercing spirit, acute to invent, suttle and sinewy to discours, not beneath the reach of any point the highest that human capacity can soar to. Therefore the studies of learning in her deepest Sciences have bin so ancient, and so eminent among us, that Writers of good antiquity, and ablest judgement have bin perswaded that ev'n the school of *Pythagoras*, and the *Persian* wisdom took beginning from the old Philosophy of this Iland.[135] And that wise and civill Roman, *Julius Agricola*, who govern'd once here for *Cæsar*, preferr'd the naturall wits of Britain, before the labour'd studies of the French.[136] Nor is it for nothing that the grave and frugal *Transilvanian*[137] sends out yearly from as farre as the mountanous borders of *Russia*, and beyond the *Hercynian* wildernes,[138] not their youth, but their stay'd men, to learn our language, and our *theologic* arts. Yet that which is above all this, the favour and the love of heav'n we have great argument to think in a peculiar manner propitious and propending towards us. Why else was this Nation chos'n before any other, that out of her as out of *Sion* should be proclam'd and sounded forth the first tidings and trumpet of Reformation of all *Europ*.[139] And had it not bin the obstinat perversnes of our Prelats against the divine and admirable spirit of *Wicklef*, to suppresse him as

---

134. Homogeneous (as above, p. 139, Note 55).

135. Actually, the other way around; vestiges of Pythagorean and Zoroastrian concepts were often associated with the Druids, as by Pliny the Elder (*Natural History*, XXX, 2).

136. Cf. Tacitus, *Agricola*, XXI.

137. Seventeenth-century Transylvania was both independent and Protestant.

138. i.e. south and central Germany.

139. Cf. above, p. 81, Note 11.

a schismatic and *innovator*, perhaps neither the *Bohemian Husse* and *Jerom*,[140] no nor the name of *Luther*, or of *Calvin* had bin ever known: the glory of reforming all our neighbours had bin compleatly ours. But now, as our obdurat Clergy have with violence demean'd the matter, we are become hitherto the latest and the backwardest Schollers, of whom God offer'd to have made us the teachers. Now once again by all concurrence of signs, and by the generall instinct of holy and devout men, as they daily and solemnly expresse their thoughts, God is decreeing to begin some new and great period in his Church, ev'n to the reforming of Reformation it self: what does he then but reveal Himself to his servants, and as his manner is, first to his English-men; I say as his manner is, first to us, though we mark not the method of his counsels, and are unworthy. Behold now this vast City; a City of refuge, the mansion house of liberty, encompast and surrounded with his protection; the shop of warre hath not there more anvils and hammers waking, to fashion out the plates and instruments of armed Justice in defence of beleaguer'd Truth, then there be pens and heads there, sitting by their studious lamps, musing, searching, revolving new notions and idea's wherewith to present, as with their homage and their fealty the approaching Reformation: others as fast reading, trying all things, assenting to the force of reason and convincement. What could a man require more from a Nation so pliant and so prone to seek after knowledge. What wants there to such a towardly[141] and pregnant soile, but wise and faithfull labourers, to make a knowing people, a Nation of Prophets, of Sages, and of Worthies. We reck'n more then five months yet to harvest; there need not be five weeks, had we but eyes to lift up, the fields are white already. Where there is much desire to learn, there of necessity will be much arguing, much writing, many opinions; for opinion in good men is but knowledge in the making. Under these fantastic terrors of sect and schism, we wrong the earnest and zealous thirst after knowledge and understanding which God

---

140. Jerome of Prague (*c.* 1365–1416) was a disciple of Wycliffe and Huss (above, p. 205, Note 37).

141. Promising.

hath stirr'd up in this City. What some lament of, we rather should rejoyce at, should rather praise this pious forwardnes among men, to reassume the ill deputed care of their Religion into their own hands again. A little generous prudence, a little forbearance of one another, and som grain of charity might win all these diligences to joyn, and unite into one generall and brotherly search after Truth; could we but forgoe this Prelaticall tradition of crowding free consciences and Christian liberties into canons and precepts of men. I doubt not, if some great and worthy stranger should come among us, wise to discern the mould and temper of a people, and how to govern it, observing the high hopes and aims, the diligent alacrity of our extended thoughts and reasonings in the pursuance of truth and freedom, but that he would cry out as *Pirrhus* did, admiring the Roman docility and courage, if such were my *Epirots*, I would not despair the greatest design that could be attempted to make a Church or Kingdom happy.[142] Yet these are the men cry'd out against for schismaticks and sectaries; as if, while the Temple of the Lord was building, some cutting, some squaring the marble, others hewing the cedars, there should be a sort of irrationall men who could not consider there must be many schisms and many dissections made in the quarry and in the timber, ere the house of God can be built. And when every stone is laid artfully together, it cannot be united into a continuity, it can but be contiguous in this world; neither can every peece of the building be of one form; nay rather the perfection consists in this, that out of many moderat varieties and brotherly dissimilitudes that are not vastly disproportionall arises the goodly and the graceful symmetry that commends the whole pile and structure. Let us therefore be more considerat builders, more wise in spirituall architecture, when great reformation is expected. For now the time seems come, wherein *Moses* the great Prophet may sit in heav'n rejoycing to see that memorable and glorious wish of his fulfill'd, when not only our sev'nty Elders, but all the Lords people are become Prophets.[143] No marvell then though some

142. King Pyrrhus of Epirus defeated the Romans at Heraclea in 280 B.C.   143. Numbers 11 : 27-29.

men, and some good men too perhaps, but young in goodnesse, as *Joshua* then was, envy them. They fret, and out of their own weaknes are in agony, lest these divisions and subdivisions will undoe us. The adversarie again applauds, and waits the hour, when they have brancht themselves out, saith he, small anough into parties and partitions, then will be our time. Fool! he sees not the firm root, out of which we all grow, though into branches: nor will beware untill he see our small divided maniples[144] cutting through at every angle of his ill united and unweildy brigade. And that we are to hope better of all these supposed sects and schisms, and that we shall not need that solicitude honest perhaps though over timorous of them that vex in this behalf, but shall laugh in the end, at those malicious applauders of our differences, I have these reasons to perswade me.

First, when a City shall be as it were besieg'd and blockt about, her navigable river infested, inrodes and incursions round, defiance and battell oft rumor'd to be marching up ev'n to her walls, and suburb trenches, that then the people, or the greater part, more then at other times, wholly tak'n up with the study of highest and most important matters to be reform'd, should be disputing, reasoning, reading, inventing, discoursing, ev'n to a rarity, and admiration, things not before discourst or writt'n of, argues first a singular good will, contentednesse and confidence in your prudent foresight, and safe government, Lords and Commons; and from thence derives it self to a gallant bravery and well grounded contempt of their enemies, as if there were no small number of as great spirits among us, as his was, who when Rome was nigh besieg'd by *Hanibal*, being in the City, bought that peece of ground at no cheap rate, whereon *Hanibal* himself encampt his own regiment.[145] Next it is a lively and cherfull presage of our happy successe and victory. For as in a body, when the blood is fresh, the spirits pure and vigorous, not only to vital, but to rationall faculties, and those in the acutest, and the pertest operations of wit and suttlety, it argues in what good plight and constitution the body is, so when the

144. Platoons (from the Roman military unit 'manipulus').
145. Thus Livy, XXVI, 11.

239

cherfulnesse of the people is so sprightly up, as that it has, not only wherewith to guard well its own freedom and safety, but to spare, and to bestow upon the solidest and sublimest points of controversie, and new invention, it betok'ns us not degenerated, nor drooping to a fatall decay, but casting off the old and wrincl'd skin of corruption to outlive these pangs and wax young again, entring the glorious waies of Truth and prosperous vertue destin'd to become great and honourable in these latter ages. Methinks I see in my mind a noble and puissant Nation rousing herself like a strong man after sleep, and shaking her invincible locks:[146] Methinks I see her as an Eagle muing[147] her mighty youth, and kindling her undazl'd eyes at the full midday beam; purging and unscaling her long abused sight at the fountain it self of heav'nly radiance; while the whole noise of timorous and flocking birds, with those also that love the twilight, flutter about, amaz'd at what she means, and in their envious gabble would prognosticat a year of sects and schisms.

What should ye doe then, should ye suppresse all this flowry crop of knowledge and new light sprung up and yet springing daily in this City, should ye set an *Oligarchy* of twenty ingrossers[148] over it, to bring a famin upon the minds again, when we shall know nothing but what is measur'd to us by their bushel? Beleeve it, Lords and Commons, they who counsell ye to such a suppressing, doe as good as bid ye suppresse your selves; and I will soon shew how. If it be desir'd to know the immediat cause of all this free writing and free speaking, there cannot be assign'd a truer then your own mild, and free, and human government; it is the liberty, Lord and Commons, which your own valorous and happy counsels have purchast us, liberty which is the nurse of all great wits; this is that which hath rarify'd and enlightn'd our spirits like the influence of heav'n; this is that which hath enfranchis'd, enlarg'd and lifted up our apprehensions degrees above themselves. Ye cannot make us now lesse capable, lesse knowing, lesse eagerly pur-

146. Possibly an allusion to Samson (as Daniels claims, below, p. 454)?

147. Moulting; renewing.

148. Monopolists.

240

suing of the truth, unlesse ye first make your selves, that made us so, lesse the lovers, lesse the founders of our true liberty. We can grow ignorant again, brutish, formall, and slavish, as ye found us; but you then must first become that which ye cannot be, oppressive, arbitrary, and tyrannous, as they were from whom ye have free'd us. That our hearts are now more capacious, our thoughts more erected to the search and expectation of greatest and exactest things, is the issue of your owne vertu propagated in us; ye cannot suppresse that unlesse ye reinforce an abrogated and mercilesse law, that fathers may dispatch at will their own children. And who shall then stick closest to ye, and excite others? not he who takes up armes for cote and conduct, and his four nobles of Danegelt.[149] Although I dispraise not the defence of just immunities, yet love my peace better, if that were all. Give me the liberty to know, to utter, and to argue freely according to conscience, above all liberties.

What would be best advis'd then, if it be found so hurtfull and so unequall to suppresse opinions for the newnes, or the unsutablenes to a customary acceptance, will not be my task to say; I only shall repeat what I have learnt from one of your own honourable number, a right noble and pious Lord, who had he not sacrific'd his life and fortunes to the Church and Commonwealth, we had not now mist and bewayl'd a worthy and undoubted patron of this argument. Ye know him I am sure; yet I for honours sake, and may it be eternall to him, shall name him, the Lord *Brook*.[150] He writing of Episcopacy, and by the way treating of sects and schisms, left Ye his vote, or rather now the last words of his dying charge, which I know will ever be of dear and honour'd regard with Ye, so full of meeknes and breathing charity, that next to his last testament, who bequeath'd love and peace to his Disciples,[151] I cannot call to mind where I have read or heard words more mild and

---

149. Various forms of taxation.

150. The Parliamentary leader and general Robert Greville, 2nd Lord Brooke – author of the *Discourse of Episcopacie* (1641) to which Milton refers – was killed during an engagement at Lichfield (1643).

151. John 14:15–31.

peacefull. He there exhorts us to hear with patience and humility those, however they be miscall'd, that desire to live purely, in such a use of Gods Ordinances, as the best guidance of their conscience gives them, and to tolerat them, though in some disconformity to our selves. The book it self will tell us more at large being publisht to the world, and dedicated to the Parlament by him who both for his life and for his death deserves, that what advice he left be not laid by without perusall.

And now the time in speciall is, by priviledge to write and speak what may help to the furder discussing of matters in agitation. The Temple of *Janus*[152] with his two *controversal* faces might now not unsignificantly be set open. And though all the windes of doctrin were let loose to play upon the earth, so Truth be in the field, we do injuriously by licencing and prohibiting to misdoubt her strength. Let her and Falshood grapple, who ever knew Truth put to the wors, in a free and open encounter. Her confuting is the best and surest suppressing. He who hears what praying there is for light and clearer knowledge to be sent down among us, would think of other matters to be constituted beyond the discipline of *Geneva*, fram'd and fabric't[153] already to our hands. Yet when the new light which we beg for shines in upon us, there be who envy, and oppose, if it comes not first in at their casements. What a collusion is this, whenas we are exhorted by the wise man to use diligence, *to seek for wisdom as for hidd'n treasures*[154] early and late, that another order shall enjoyn us to know nothing but by statute. When a man hath bin labouring the hardest labour in the deep mines of knowledge, hath furnisht out his findings in all their equipage, drawn forth his reasons as it were a battell raung'd, scatter'd and defeated all objections in his way, calls out his adversary into the plain, offers him the advantage of wind and sun, if he please; only that he may try the matter by dint of argument, for his opponents then to sculk, to lay ambushments, to keep a narrow bridge of licencing where the challenger should passe,

152. The Roman god of gateways. His two heads faced in opposite directions; the temple's doors remained open in wartime.

153. Fabricated. The reference is, of course, to Calvinism.

154. Cf. Matthew 13:44.

though it be valour anough in shouldiership, is but weaknes and cowardise in the wars of Truth. For who knows not that Truth is strong next to the Almighty; she needs no policies, nor stratagems, nor licencings to make her victorious, those are the shifts and the defences that error uses against her power : give her but room, & do not bind her when she sleeps, for then she speaks not true, as the old *Proteus* did, who spake oracles only when he was caught & bound,[155] but then rather she turns herself into all shapes, except her own, and perhaps tunes her voice according to the time, as *Micaiah* did before *Ahab*,[156] untill she be adjur'd into her own likenes. Yet is it not impossible that she may have more shapes then one. What else is all that rank of things indifferent, wherein Truth may be on this side, or on the other, without being unlike her self. What but a vain shadow else is the abolition of *those ordinances, that hand writing nayl'd to the crosse*,[157] what great purchase is this Christian liberty which *Paul* so often boasts of. His doctrine is, that he who eats or eats not, regards a day, or regards it not, may doe either to the Lord.[158] How many other things might be tolerated in peace, and left to conscience, had we but charity, and were it not the chief strong hold of our hypocrisie to be ever judging one another. I fear yet this iron yoke of outward conformity hath left a slavish print upon our necks; the ghost of a linnen decency[159] yet haunts us. We stumble and are impatient at the least dividing of one visible congregation from another, though it be not in fundamentalls; and through our forwardnes to suppresse, and our backwardnes to recover any enthrall'd peece of truth out of the gripe of custom, we care not to keep truth separated from truth, which is the fiercest rent and disunion of all. We doe not see that while we still affect by all means a rigid externall formality, we may as soon fall again into a grosse conforming stupidity, a stark and dead

---

155. Cf. *Odyssey*, IV, 384–93.

156. I Kings 22.

157. Colossians 2 : 14.

158. Cf. Romans 14 : 1–13.

159. A sarcastic allusion to the controversy about ecclesiastical vestments etc.

congealment of *wood and hay and stubble*[160] forc't and frozen together, which is more to the sudden degenerating of a Church then many *subdichotomies*[161] of petty schisms. Not that I can think well of every light separation, or that all in a Church is to be expected *gold and silver and pretious stones*:[162] it is not possible for man to sever the wheat from the tares, the good fish from the other frie; that must be the Angels Ministery at the end of mortall things.[163] Yet if all cannot be of one mind, as who looks they should be? this doubtles is more wholsome, more prudent, and more Christian that many be tolerated, rather then all compell'd. I mean not tolerated Popery, and open superstition, which as it extirpats all religions and civill supremacies, so it self should be extirpat, provided first that all charitable and compassionat means be us'd to win and regain the weak and misled: that also which is impious or evil absolutely either against faith or maners no law can possibly permit, that intends not to unlaw it self: but those neighbouring differences or rather indifferences, are what I speak of, whether in some point of doctrine or of discipline, which though they may be many, yet need not interrupt *the unity of Spirit*, if we could but find among us *the bond of peace*.[164] In the mean while if any one would write, and bring his helpfull hand to the slow-moving Reformation which we labour under, if Truth have spok'n to him before others, or but seem'd at least to speak, who hath so bejesuited us that we should trouble that man with asking licence to doe so worthy a deed? and not consider this, that if it come to prohibiting, there is not ought more likely to be prohibited then truth it self; whose first appearance to our eyes blear'd and dimm'd with prejudice and custom, is more unsightly and unplausible then many errors, ev'n as the person is of many a great man slight and contemptible to see to. And what doe they tell us vainly of new opinions, when this very opinion of theirs, that none must be heard, but whom they like

---

160. 1 Corinthians 3:12.
161. Inconsequential divisions.
162. As above, Note 160.
163. Matthew 13:24 ff.
164. Ephesians 4:3.

is the worst and newest opinion of all others; and is the chief cause why sects and schisms doe so much abound, and true knowledge is kept at distance from us; besides yet a greater danger which is in it. For when God shakes a Kingdome with strong and healthfull commotions to a generall reforming, 'tis not untrue that many sectaries and false teachers are then busiest in seducing; but yet more true it is, that God then raises to his own work men of rare abilities, and more then common industry not only to look back and revise what hath bin taught heretofore, but to gain furder and goe on, some new enlightn'd steps in the discovery of truth. For such is the order of Gods enlightning his Church, to dispense and deal out by degrees his beam, so as our earthly eyes may best sustain it. Neither is God appointed and confin'd, where and out of what place these his chosen shall be first heard to speak; for he sees not as man sees, chooses not as man chooses, lest we should devote our selves again to set places, and assemblies, and outward callings of men; planting our faith one while in the old Convocation house, and another while in the Chappell at Westminster;[165] when all the faith and religion that shall be there canoniz'd, is not sufficient without plain convincement, and the charity of patient instruction to supple the least bruise of conscience, to edifie the meanest Christian, who desires to walk in the Spirit, and not in the letter of human trust, for all the number of voices that can be there made; no though *Harry* the 7. himself there,[166] with all his leige tombs about him, should lend them voices from the dead, to swell their number. And if the men be erroneous who appear to be the leading schismaticks, what witholds us but our sloth, our self-will, and distrust in the right cause, that we doe not give them gentle meetings and gentle dismissions, that we debate not and examin the matter throughly with liberall and frequent audience; if not for their sakes, yet for our own? seeing no man who hath tasted learning, but will confesse the many waies of profiting by those who not contented with stale receits are able to manage, and set forth

---

165. Anglicans used to meet in the Chapter House, Westminster Abbey; Presbyterians from 1643 met in Henry VII's Chapel.

166. i.e. buried in the Chapel referred to (previous note).

new positions to the world. And were they but as the dust and cinders of our feet, so long as in that notion they may yet serve to polish and brighten the armoury of Truth, ev'n for that respect they were not utterly to be cast away. But if they be of those whom God hath fitted for the speciall use of these times with eminent and ample gifts, and those perhaps neither among the Priests, nor among the Pharisees, and we in the hast of a precipitant zeal shall make no distinction, but resolve to stop their mouths, because we fear they come with new and dangerous opinions, as we commonly forejudge them ere understand them, no lesse then woe to us, while thinking thus to defend the Gospel, we are found the persecutors.

There have bin not a few since the beginning of this Parlament, both of the Presbytery and others who by their unlicenc't books to the contempt of an *Imprimatur* first broke that triple ice clung about our hearts, and taught the people to see day: I hope that none of those were the perswaders to renew upon us this bondage which they themselves have wrought so much good by contemning. But if neither the check that *Moses* gave to young *Joshua*, nor the countermand which our Saviour gave to young *John*, who was so ready to prohibit those whom he thought unlicenc't,[167] be not anough to admonish our Elders how unacceptable to God their testy mood of prohibiting is, if neither their own remembrance what evill hath abounded in the Church by this lett[168] of licencing, and what good they themselves have begun by transgressing it, be not anough, but that they will perswade, and execute the most *Dominican* part of the Inquisition[169] over us, and are already with one foot in the stirrup so active at suppressing, it would be no unequall distribution in the first place to suppresse the suppressors themselves; whom the change of their condition hath puft up, more then their late experience of harder times hath made wise.

And as for regulating the Presse, let no man think to have the honour of advising ye better than your selves have done in that Order publisht next before this, that no book be Printed,

---

167. Luke 9:49–50; also above, Note 143.

168. Obstruction.

169. The Inquisition's licensers were usually Dominicans.

unlesse the Printers and the Authors name, or at least the Printers be register'd.[170] Those which otherwise come forth, if they be found mischievous and libellous, the fire and the execu-tioner will be the timeliest and the most effectuall remedy, that mans prevention can use. For this *authentic* Spanish policy[171] of licencing books, if I have said ought, will prove the most unlicenc't book it self within a short while; and was the im-mediat image of a Star-chamber decree[172] to that purpose made in those very times when that Court did the rest of those her pious works, for which she is now fall'n from the Starres with *Lucifer.* Whereby ye may guesse what kind of State prudence, what love of the people, what care of Religion, or good man-ners there was at the contriving, although with singular hypoc-risie it pretended to bind books to their good behaviour. And how it got the upper hand of your precedent Order so well constituted before, if we may beleeve those men whose pro-fession gives them cause to enquire most, it may be doubted there was in it the fraud of some old *patentees* and *monopolizers* in the trade of book-selling; who under pretence of the poor in their Company not to be defrauded, and the just retaining of each man his severall copy, which God forbid should be gain-said, brought divers glosing colours to the House, which were indeed but colours, and serving to no end except it be to exercise a superiority over their neighbours, men who doe not therefore labour in an honest profession to which learning is indetted, that they should be made other mens vassalls. Another end is thought was aym'd at by some of them in procuring by petition this Order, that having power in their hands, malignant books might the easier scape abroad, as the event shews. But of these *Sophisms* and *Elenchs*[173] of marchandize I skill not: This I know, that errors in a good government and in a bad are equally almost incident; for what Magistrate may not be mis-inform'd,

---

170. The order was passed on 29 January 1642.

171. i.e. in the sense that censorship descends from the Inquisition, especially its Spanish variety (above, p. 222, Note 92).

172. Issued by Charles I on 11 July 1637. (The Court of Star Chamber was abolished on 5 July 1641.)

173. Fallacious arguments.

and much the sooner, if liberty of Printing be reduc't into the power of a few; but to redresse willingly and speedily what hath bin err'd, and in highest autority to esteem a plain advertisement[174] more then others have done a sumptuous bribe, is a vertue (honour'd Lords and Commons) answerable to Your highest actions, and whereof none can participat but greatest and wisest men.

---

174. Notification.

THE TENURE OF KINGS
AND MAGISTRATES

(1649)

Milton's exposition of the voluntary contract between free men and their governors (see above, p. 32) is described on the title page as *The Tenure of Kings and Magistrates: proving, that it is Lawfull, and hath been held so through all Ages, for any, who have the Power, to call to account a Tyrant, or wicked King, and after due conviction, to depose, and put him to death; if the ordinary Magistrate have neglected, or deny'd to doe it. And that they, who of late, so much blame Deposing, are the Men that did it themselves.* 13

First published in February 1649, the treatise was amended a year later. Like the Yale edition (III, 189–258), the Columbia edition reprinted here provides the text of 1650 (V, 1–59, with textual notes in 315–22; ed. William Haller).]

I F men within themselves would be govern'd by reason, and not generally give up thir understanding to a double tyrannie, of Custom from without, and blind affections within, they would discerne better, what it is to favour and uphold the Tyrant of a Nation.[1] But being slaves within doors, no wonder that they strive so much to have the public State conformably govern'd to the inward vitious rule, by which they govern themselves. For indeed none can love freedom heartilie, but good men; the rest love not freedom, but licence; which never hath more scope or more indulgence then under Tyrants. Hence is it that Tyrants are not oft offended, nor stand much in doubt of bad men, as being all naturally servile; but in whom vertue and true worth most is eminent, them they feare in earnest, as by right thir Maisters, against them lies all thir hatred and suspicion. Consequentlie neither doe bad men hate Tyrants, but have been

---

1. Cf. the censure of custom at the outset of *The Doctrine and Discipline of Divorce*, above, pp. 112 f.

always readiest with the falsifi'd names of *Loyalty*, and *Obedience*, to colour over thir base compliances. And although somtimes for shame, and when it comes to thir owne grievances, of purse especially, they would seeme good Patriots, and side with the better cause, yet when others for the deliverance of thir Countrie, endu'd with fortitude and Heroick vertue to feare nothing but the curse writt'n against those *That doe the worke of the Lord negligently*,[2] would goe on to remove, not only the calamities and thraldoms of a People, but the roots and causes whence they spring, streight these men,[3] and sure helpers at need, as if they hated only the miseries but not the mischiefs, after they have juggl'd and palter'd with the world, bandied and born armes against thir King, devested him, dis-annointed him, nay curs'd him all over in thir Pulpits and thir Pamphlets, to the ingaging of sincere and real men, beyond what is possible or honest to retreat from, not only turne revolters from those principles, which only could at first move them, but lay the staine of disloyaltie, and worse, on those proceedings, which are the necessary consequences of thir own former actions; nor dislik'd by themselves, were they manag'd to the intire advantages of thir own Faction; not considering the while that he toward whom they boasted thir new fidelitie counted them accessory; and by those Statutes and Lawes which they so impotently brandish against others, would have doom'd them to a Traytors death, for what they have don alreadie. 'T is true, that most men are apt anough to civill Wars and commotions as a noveltie, and for a flash hot and active; but through sloth or inconstancie, and weakness of spirit either fainting, ere thir own pretences, though never so just, be half attain'd, or through an inbred falshood and wickednes, betray oft times to destruction with themselves, men of noblest

---

2. Jeremiah 48:10.

3. i.e. the Presbyterians, 'those who now of late would seem so much to abhorr deposing [the King]' (below, p. 273). See also Milton's account of the circumstances (above, p. 73) as well as his poem 'On the New Forcers of Conscience under the Long Parliament'. Cf. below, p. 350, Note 64.

:emper joyn'd with them for causes, whereof they in their rash
undertakings were not capable.

If God and a good cause give them Victory, the prosecution
wherof for the most part, inevitably draws after it the alteration
of Lawes, change of Government, downfal of Princes and thir
families; then comes the task to those Worthies which are the
soule of that enterprize, to be swett and labour'd out amidst
the throng and noises of Vulgar and irrational men. Some con-
testing for privileges, customs, forms, and that old entanglement
of Iniquity, thir gibrish Lawes, though the badge of thir ancient
slavery. Others who have beene fiercest against thir Prince,
under the notion of a Tyrant, and no mean incendiaries of the
Warr against him, when God out of his providence and high
disposal hath deliver'd him into the hand of thir brethren, on
a suddain and in a new garbe of Allegiance, which thir doings
have long since cancell'd; they plead for him, pity him, extoll
him, protest against those that talk of bringing him to the tryal
of Justice, which is the Sword of God, superior to all mortal
things, in whose hand soever by apparent signes his testified will
is to put it. But certainly if we consider who and what they are,
on a suddain grown so pitifull, wee may conclude, thir pitty can
be no true, and Christian commiseration, but either levitie and
shallowness of minde, or else a carnal admiring of that worldly
pomp and greatness, from whence they see him fall'n; or rather
lastly a dissembl'd and seditious pity, fain'd of industry to begett
new discord. As for mercy, if it be to a Tyrant, under which
Name they themselves have cited him so oft in the hearing of
God, of Angels, and the holy Church assembl'd, and there
charg'd him with the spilling of more innocent blood by farr,
then ever *Nero* did,[4] undoubtedly the mercy which they pretend, is the mercy of wicked men; and their mercies, wee read
are cruelties;[5] hazarding the welfare of a whole Nation, to have
sav'd one, whom so oft they have tearm'd *Agag*;[6] and vilifying
the blood of many *Jonathans*, that have sav'd *Israel*;[7] insisting

---

4. i.e. in the persecutions of the mid first century.

5. Proverbs 12 : 10.

6. Cf. 1 Samuel 15 : 32–33.

7. Cf. 1 Samuel 14 : 1 ff.

with much niceness on the unnecessariest clause of thir Covnant[8] wrested, wherein the feare of change, and the absurd contradiction of a flattering hostilitie had hampered them, but not scrupling to give away for complements, to an implacable revenge, the heads of many thousand Christians more.

Another sort there is, who comming in the cours of these affaires, to have thir share in great actions, above the form of Law or Custom, at least to give thir voice and approbation begin to swerve, and almost shiver at the Majesty and grandeur of som noble deed, as if they were newly enter'd into a great sin; disputing presidents,[9] forms, and circumstances, when the Commonwealth nigh perishes for want of deeds in substance don with just and faithfull expedition. To these I wish better instruction, and vertue equal to thir calling; the former of which, that is to say Instruction, I shall indeavour, as my dutie is, to bestow on them; and exhort them not to startle[10] from the just and pious resolution of adhering with all thir strength & assistance to the present Parlament & Army, in the glorious way wherin Justice and Victory hath set them; the only warrants through all ages, next under immediat Revelation, to excercise supream power, in those proceedings which hitherto appeare equal to what hath been don in any age or Nation heretofore, justly or magnanimouslie. Nor let them be discourag'd or deterr'd by any new Apostate Scarcrowes, who under show of giving counsel, send out their barking monitories and *memento's*,[11] empty of ought else but the spleene of a frustrated Faction. For how can that pretended counsel bee either sound or faithfull, when they that give it, see not for madness and vexation of thir ends lost, that those Statutes and Scriptures which both falsly and scandalously, they wrest against thir Friends and Associates, would by sentence of the common adversarie, fall first and heaviest upon thir own heads.

---

8. i.e. 'to preserve [the King's] person, Crown and dignity' (below p. 274).

9. Precedents.

10. Deviate.

11. As William Prynne did, in his vitriolic *Briefe Memento* of January 1649.

Neither let milde and tender dispositions be foolishly softn'd from thir duty and perseverance, with the unmaskuline Rhetorick of any pulling Priest or Chaplain, sent as a friendly Letter of advice, for fashion sake in privat, and forthwith publisht by the Sender himself, that wee may know how much of friend there was in it, to cast an odious envie upon them, to whom it was pretended to be sent in charitie. Nor let any man be deluded by either the ignorance or the notorious hypocrisie and self-repugnance of our dancing Divines, who have the conscience and the boldness, to come with Scripture in thir mouthes, gloss'd and fitted for thir turnes with a double contradictory sense, transforming the sacred verity of God, to an Idol with two Faces, looking at once two several ways;[12] and with the same quotations to charge others, which in the same case they made serve to justifie themselves. For while the hope to bee made Classic and Provincial Lords[13] led them on, while pluralities[14] greas'd them thick and deep, to the shame and scandal of Religion, more then all the Sects and Heresies they exclaim against, then to fight against the Kings person, and no less a Party of his Lords and Commons, or to put force upon both the Houses, was good, was lawfull, was no resisting of Superior powers; they onely were powers not to be resisted, who countenanc'd the good, and punish't the evil. But now that thir censorious domineering is not suffer'd to be universal, truth and conscience to be freed, Tithes and Pluralities to be no more, though competent allowance provided, and the warme experience of large gifts, and they so good at taking them; yet now to exclude & seize upon impeach't Members,[15] to bring Delinquents without exemption to a faire Tribunal by the common National Law against murder, is now to be no less than *Corah*, *Dathan*, and *Abiram*.[16] He who but erewhile in the Pulpits was a cursed Tyrant, an enemie to God and Saints,

---

12. i.e. like Janus (as above, p. 242, Note 152).

13. Referring to the proposed organization of Presbyterians into provinces and, in turn, classes.

14. Multiple benefices; cf. 'pluralist', above, p. 229, Note 110.

15. As it happened to eleven members of Parliament in July 1647.

16. The three rebels against Moses and Aaron (Numbers 16:1 ff.).

lad'n with all the innocent blood spilt in three Kingdoms, and so to be fought against, is now, though nothing penitent or alter'd from his first principles, a lawfull Magistrate, a Sovran Lord, the Lords anointed, not to be touch'd, though by themselves imprison'd. As if this onely were obedience, to preserve the meere useless bulke of his person, and that onely in prison, not in the field, and to disobey his commands, deny him his dignity and office, every where to resist his power but where they thinke it onely surviving in their own faction.

But who in particular is a Tyrant cannot be determin'd in a general discours, otherwise then by supposition; his particular charge, and the sufficient proof of it must determin that: which I leave to Magistrates, at least to the uprighter sort of them, and of the people, though in number less by many, in whom faction least hath prevaild above the Law of nature and right reason, to judge as they find cause. But this I dare owne as part of my faith, that if such a one there be, by whose Commission, whole massachers have been committed on his faithfull Subjects, his Provinces offerd to pawn or alienation, as the hire of those whom he had sollicited to come in and destroy whole Citties and Countries; be he King, or Tyrant, or Emperour, the Sword of Justice is above him; in whose hand soever is found sufficient power to avenge the effusion, and so great a deluge of innocent blood. For if all human power to execute, not accidentally but intendedly, the wrath of God upon evil doers without exception, be of God; then that power, whether ordinary, or if that faile, extraordinary so executing that intent of God, is lawfull, and not to be resisted. But to unfold more at large this whole Question, though with all expedient brevity, I shall here set downe from first beginning, the original of Kings; how and wherfore exalted to that dignitie above thir Brethren; and from thence shall prove, that turning to Tyranny they may bee as lawfully depos'd and punish'd, as they were at first elected: This I shall doe by autorities and reasons, not learnt in corners among Scisms and Heresies, as our doubling Divines are ready to calumniat, but fetch't out of the midst of choicest and most authentic learning, and no prohibited Authors, nor many Heathen, but Mosaical, Christian, Orthodoxal, and which must needs be more convincing to our Adversaries, Presbyterial.[17]

No man who knows ought, can be so stupid to deny that all men naturally were borne free, being the image and resemblance of God himself, and were by privilege above all the creatures, born to command and not to obey : and that they liv'd so. Till from the root of *Adams* transgression, falling among themselves to doe wrong and violence, and foreseeing that such courses must needs tend to the destruction of them all, they agreed by common league to bind each other from mutual injury, and joyntly to defend themselves against any that gave disturbance or opposition to such agreement. Hence came Citties, Townes and Common-wealths. And because no faith in all was found sufficiently binding, they saw it needfull to ordaine som authoritie, that might restrain by force and punishment what was violated against peace and common right. This autoritie and power of self-defence and preservation being originally and naturally in every one of them, and unitedly in them all, for ease, for order, and least each man should be his own partial judge, they communicated and deriv'd to one, whom for the eminence of his wisdom and integritie they chose above the rest, or to more then one whom they thought of equal deserving : the first was call'd a King; the other Magistrates. Not to be thir Lords and Maisters (though afterward those names in som places were giv'n voluntarily to such as had been Authors of inestimable good to the people) but, to be thir Deputies and Commissioners, to execute, by vertue of thir intrusted power, that justice which else every man by the bond of nature and of Cov'nant must have executed for himself, and for one another. And to him that shall consider well why among free Persons, one man by civil right should beare autority and jurisdiction over another, no other end or reason can be imaginable. These for a while govern'd well, and with much equity decided all things at thir own arbitrement : till the temptation of such a power left absolute in thir hands, perverted them at length to injustice and partialitie. Then did they who now by tryal had

---

17. See above, Note 3.

found the danger and inconveniences of committing arbitrar,
power to any, invent Laws either fram'd, or consented to by al
that should confine and limit the autority of whom they chos
to govern them: that so man, of whose failing they had proo1
might no more rule over them, but law and reason abstracte
as much as might be from personal errors and frailties. Whil
as the Magistrate was set above the people, so the Law was se
above the Magistrate. When this would not serve, but that th
Law was either not executed, or misapply'd, they were col
strain'd from that time, the onely remedy left them, to put col
ditions and take Oaths from all Kings and Magistrates at thi
first instalment to doe impartial justice by Law: who upo
those termes and no other, receav'd Allegeance from the peopl
that is to say, bond or Covnant to obey them in execution c
those Lawes which they the people had themselves made, c
assented to. And this ofttimes with express warning, that if th
King or Magistrate prov'd unfaithfull to his trust, the peopl
would be disingag'd. They added also Counselors and Parla
ments, nor to be onely at his beck, but with him or withou
him, at set times. or at all times, when any danger threatn'd t
have care of the public safety. Therefore saith *Claudius Sese*
a French Statesman, *The Parliament was set as a bridle to th
King;*[18] which I instance rather, not because our English Lawyer
have not said the same long before, but because that Frenc
Monarchy is granted by all to be a farr more absolute the
ours. That this and the rest of what hath hitherto been spok"
is most true, might be copiously made appeare throughout a
Stories Heathen and Christian; ev'n of those Nations wher
Kings and Emperours have sought meanes to abolish all ancier
memory of the Peoples right by thir encroachments and usu1
pations. But I spare long insertions, appealing to the know
constitutions of both the latest Christian Empires in Europe, th
Greek[19] and German, besides the French, Italian, Arragonian
English, and not least the Scottish Histories: not forgetting th

18. From Claude de Seissel's *La Grand Monarchie de Franc*
(1519).   19. i.e. Byzantine.

20. The Kings of Aragon were sometimes said not to hav
espoused absolutism.

onely by the way, that *William* the Norman though a Conqueror, and not unsworn at his Coronation, was compell'd the second time to take oath at *S. Albanes*, ere the people would be brought to yield obedience.

It being thus manifest that the power of Kings and Magistrates is nothing else, but what is only derivative, transferr'd and committed to them in trust from the People, to the Common good of them all, in whom the power yet remaines fundamentally, and cannot be taken from them, without a violation of thir natural birthright, and seeing that from hence *Aristotle* and the best of Political writers have defin'd a King, him who governs to the good and profit of his People, and not for his own ends,[21] it follows from necessary causes, that the Titles of Sov'ran Lord, natural Lord, and the like, are either arrogancies, or flatteries, not admitted by Emperours and Kings of best note, and dislikt by the Church both of Jews, *Isai.* 26. 13. and ancient Christians, as appears by *Tertullian*[22] and others. Although generally the people of Asia, and with them the Jews also, especially since the time they chose a King against the advice and counsel of God,[23] are noted by wise Authors much inclinable to slavery.

Secondly, that to say, as is usual, the King hath as good right to his Crown and dignitie, as any man to his inheritance, is to make the Subject no better then the Kings slave, his chattell, or his possession that may be bought and sould. And doubtless if hereditary title were sufficiently inquir'd, the best foundation of it would be found either but in courtesie or convenience. But suppose it to be of right hereditarie, what can be more just and legal, if a subject for certain crimes be to forfet by Law from himself, and posterity, all his inheritance to the King, then that a King for crimes proportional, should forfet all his title and inheritance to the people: unless the people must be thought created all for him, he not for them, and they all in one body inferior to him single, which were a kinde of treason against the dignitie of mankind to affirm.

21. *Nicomachean Ethics*, VIII, xi, 1.

22. In the conclusion of his treatise *On the Crown* (early third century).

23. Cf. 1 Samuel 8. The matter is further discussed below, pp. 259 f.

Thirdly it follows, that to say Kings are accountable to none but God, is the ouerturning of all Law and government. For if they may refuse to give account, then all cov'nants made with them at Coronation; all Oathes are in vaine, and meer mockeries, all Lawes which they sweare to keep, made to no purpose; for if the King feare not God, as how many of them doe not? we hold then our lives and estates, by the tenure of his meer grace and mercy, as from a God, not a mortal Magistrate, a position that none but Court Parasites or men besotted would maintain. *Aristotle* therefore, whom we commonly allow for one of the best interpreters of nature and morality, writes in the fourth of his politics chap. 10. that Monarchy unaccountable, is the worst sort of Tyranny; and least of all to be endur'd by free born men. And surely no Christian Prince, not drunk with high mind, and prouder then those Pagan *Cæsars* that deifi'd themselves, would arrogate so unreasonably above human condition, or derogate so basely from a whole Nation of men his Brethren, as if for him only subsisting, and to serve his glory; valuing them in comparison of his owne brute will and pleasure, no more then so many beasts, or vermin under his Feet, not to be reasond with, but to be trod on; among whom there might be found so many thousand Men for wisdom, vertue, nobleness of mind, and all other respects, but the fortune of his dignity, farr above him. Yet some would perswade us, that this absurd opinion was King *Davids*; because in the 51 *Psalm* he cries out to God, *Against thee onely have I sinn'd*;[24] as if *David* had imagin'd that to murder *Uriah* and adulterate his Wife,[25] had bin no sinn against his Neighbour, when as that Law of *Moses* was to the King expresly, *Deut.* 17 [.20] not to think so highly of himself above his Brethren. *David* therfore by those words could mean no other, then either that the depth of his guiltiness was known to God onely, or to so few as had not the will or power to question him, or that the sin against God was greater beyond compare then against *Uriah.* Whatever his meaning were, any wise man will see that the pathetical words of a Psalme can be no certaine decision to a poynt that hath

24. Psalm 51:4.
25. Bathsheba, as related in 2 Samuel 11:2 ff.

abundantly more certain rules to goe by. How much more rationally spake the Heathen King *Demophoon* in a Tragedy of *Euripides* then these Interpreters would put upon King *David*, *I rule not my people by Tyranny, as if they were Barbarians, but am my self liable, if I doe unjustly, to suffer justly.*[26] Not unlike was the speech of *Trajan* the worthy Emperor, to one whom he made General of his Prætorian Forces. Take this drawn sword, saith he, to use for me, if I reigne well, if not, to use against me. Thus *Dion* relates.[27] And not *Trajan* onely, but *Theodosius* the yonger a Christian Emperor and one of the best, causd it to be enacted as a rule undenyable and fit to be acknowledg'd by all Kings and Emperors, that a Prince is bound to the Laws; that on the autority of Law the autority of a Prince depends, and to the Lawes ought submitt. Which Edict of his remains yet in the *Code* of *Justinian. l. 1. tit.* 24. as a sacred constitution to all the succeeding Emperors.[28] How then can any King in Europe maintain and write himself account-able to none but God when Emperors in thir own imperial Statutes have writt'n and decreed themselves accountable to Law. And indeed where such account is not fear'd, he that bids a man reigne over him above Law, may bid as well a savage Beast.

It follows lastly, that since the King or Magistrate holds his autoritie of the people, both originaly and naturally for their good in the first place, and not his own, then may the people as oft as they shall judge it for the best, either choose him or reject him, retaine him or depose him though no Tyrant, meerly by the liberty and right of free born Men, to be govern'd as seems to them best. This, though it cannot but stand with plain reason, shall be made good also by Scripture. *Deut.* 17. 14. *When thou art come into the Land which the Lord thy God giveth thee, and shalt say I will set a King over mee, like as all the Nations about mee.* These words confirme us that the right of choosing, yea of changing thir own Goverment is by the grant of God himself in the People. And therfore when they desir'd

---

26. *The Heraclidae*, ll. 418–21.

27. Dion Cassius, *Roman History*, LXVIII, 16.

28. See above, p. 161, Note 106.

a King, though then under another form of government, and
though thir changing displeas'd him, yet he that was himself
thir King,[29] and rejected by them, would not be a hindrance to
what they intended, furder then by perswasion, but that they
might doe therein as they saw good, 1 Sam. 8. onely he reserv'd
to himself the nomination of who should reigne over them.
Neither did that exempt the King, as if he were to God onely
accountable, though by his especial command anointed. Therfore *David first made a Covnant with the Elders of Israel, and
so was by them anointed King,* 2 Sam. 5. 3. 1 Chron. 11. [3.]
And *Jehoiada* the Priest making *Jehoash* King, made a Cov'nant
between him and the People, 2 *Kings* 11. 17. Therfore when
R[eh]oboam at his comming to the Crown, rejected those conditions which the Israelites brought him, heare what they answer
him, *What portion have we in David, or Inheritance in the son
of Jesse? See to thine own House David.*[30] And for the like
conditions not perform'd, all Israel before that time depos'd
Samuel; not for his own default, but for the misgoverment of
his Sons. But som will say to both these examples, it was evilly
done. I answer, that not the latter, because it was expressly
allow'd them in the Law to set up a King if they pleas'd; and
God himself joyn'd with them in the work; though in som sort
it was at that time displeasing to him, in respect of old *Samuel*
who had govern'd them uprightly. As *Livy* praises the Romans
who took occasion from *Tarquinius* a wicked Prince to gaine
thir libertie, which to have extorted, saith hee, from *Numa*,
or any of the good Kings before, had not bin seasonable.[31] Nor
was it in the former example don unlawfully; for when
R[eh]oboam had prepar'd a huge Army to reduce the Israelites,
he was forbidd'n by the Prophet, 1 *Kings* 12. 24. *Thus saith the
Lord yee shall not goe up, nor fight against your brethren, for
this thing is from me.* He calls them thir Brethren, not Rebels,
and forbidds to be proceeded against them, owning the thing
himself, not by single providence, but by approbation, and that
not onely of the act, as in the former example, but of the fit

---

29. i.e. God.
30. 1 Kings 12:16.
31. *Roman History,* II.

season also; he had not otherwise forbidd to molest them. And those grave and wise Counselors whom *Rehoboam* first advis'd with, spake no such thing, as our old gray headed Flatterers now are wont, stand upon your birth-right, scorn to capitulate, you hold of God, not of them; for they knew no such matter, unless conditionally, but gave him politic counsel, as in a civil transaction. Therfore Kingdom and Magistracy, whether supreme or subordinat, is without difference, call'd *a human ordinance*, 1 *Pet.* 2. 13. &c. which we are there taught is the will of God wee should alike submitt to, so farr as for the punishment of evil doers, and the encouragement of them that doe well. *Submitt* saith he, *as free men.*[32] But to any civil power unaccountable, unquestionable, and not to be resisted, no not in wickedness, and violent actions, how can we submit as free men? *There is no power but of God*, saith *Paul, Rom.* 13. [1.] as much as to say, God put it into mans heart to find out that way at first for common peace and preservation, approving the exercise therof; els it contradicts *Peter* who calls the same autority an Ordinance of man. It must be also understood of lawfull and just power, els we read of great power in the affaires and Kingdoms of the World permitted to the Devil: for saith he to Christ, *Luke* 4. 6. *All this power will I give thee and the glory of them, for it is deliver'd to me, & to whomsoever I will, I give it*: neither did he ly, or Christ gainsay what he affirm'd; for in the thirteenth of the *Revelation* wee read how the Dragon gave to the beast *his power, his seate, and great autority*: which beast so autoriz'd most expound to be the tyrannical powers and Kingdoms of the earth.[33] Therfore Saint *Paul* in the forecited Chapter tells us that such Magistrates he meanes, as are, not a terror to the good but to the evil; such as beare not the sword in vaine, but to punish offenders, and to encourage the good.[34] If such onely be mentioned here as powers

---

32. 1 Peter 2 : 16.

33. Revelation 13 : 2. Interpretations of historical events by appealing to this Book was commonplace in Milton's time; he was more temperate than most.

34. Romans 13 : 3, 4.

to be obeyd, and our submission to them onely requir'd, then doubtless those powers that doe the contrary, are no powers ordain'd of God, and by consequence no obligation laid upon us to obey or not to resist them. And it may bee well observed that both these Apostles, whenever they give this precept express it in termes not *concrete* but *abstract*, as Logicians are wont to speake, that is, they mention the ordinance, the power, the autoritie before the persons that execute it; and what that power is, least we should be deceav'd, they describe exactly. So that if the power be not such, or the person execute not such power, neither the one nor the other is of God, but of the Devil, and by consequence to bee resisted. From this exposition *Chrysostome* also on the same place dissents not; explaining that these words were not writt'n in behalf of a tyrant.[35] And this is verify'd by *David*, himself a King, and likeliest to bee Author of the *Psalm* 94. 20. which saith *Shall the throne of iniquity have fellowship with thee?* And it were worth the knowing, since Kings in these dayes, and that by Scripture, boast the justness of thir title, by holding it immediately of God, yet cannot show the time when God ever set on the throne them or thir forefathers, but onely when the people chose them, why by the same reason, since God ascribes as oft to himself the casting down of Princes from the throne, it should not be thought as lawful, and as much from God, when none are seen to do it but the people, and that for just causes. For if it needs must be a sin in them to depose, it may as likely be a sin to have elected. And contrary if the peoples act in election be pleaded by a King, as the act of God, and the most just title to enthrone him, why may not the peoples act of rejection, bee as well pleaded by the people as the act of God, and the most just reason to depose him? So that we see the title and just right of raigning or deposing, in reference to God, is found in Scripture to be all one; visible onely in the people and depending meerly upon justice and demerit. Thus farr hath bin considered briefly the power of Kings and Magistrates; how

---

35. St. John Chrysostom (cf. above, p. 202, Note 19), *Homily XXIII on the Book of Genesis.*

it was and is originally the peoples, and by them conferr'd in trust onely to bee imployed to the common peace and benefit; with liberty therfore and right remaining in them to reassume it to themselves, if by Kings or Magistrates it be abus'd; or to dispose of it by any alteration, as they shall judge most conducing to the public good.

Wee may from hence with more ease, and force of argument determin what a Tyrant is, and what the people may doe against him. A Tyrant whether by wrong or by right comming to the Crown, is he who regarding neither Law nor the common good, reigns for himself and his faction: Thus St. *Basil* among others defines him.[36] And because his power is great, his will boundless and exorbitant, the fulfilling whereof is for the most part accompanied with innumerable wrongs and oppressions of the people, murders, massachers, rapes, adulteries, desolation, and subversion of Citties and whole Provinces, look how great a good and happiness a just King is, so great a mischeife is a Tyrant; as hee the public father of his Countrie, so this the common enemie. Against whom what the people lawfully may doe, as against a common pest, and destroyer of mankinde, I suppose no man of cleare judgement need goe furder to be guided then by the very principles of nature in him. But because it is the vulgar folly of men to desert thir own reason, and shutting thir eyes to think they see best with other mens, I shall show by such examples as ought to have most waight with us, what hath bin don in this case heretofore. The *Greeks* and *Romans*, as thir prime Authors witness, held it not onely lawfull, but a glorious and Heroic deed, rewarded publicly with Statues and Garlands, to kill an infamous Tyrant at any time without tryal: and but reason, that he who trod down all Law, should not be voutsaf'd the benefit of Law. Insomuch that *Seneca* the Tragedian brings in *Hercules* the grand suppressor of Tyrants, thus speaking,

---

36. In his Commonplace Book, Milton quoted from the fourth-century Father of the Church St. Basil the Great: 'In this respect a tyrant differs from a king; the one considers at every point his own advantage, the other provides what is helpful to his subjects' (Yale edn, I, 453).

> *Victima haud ulla amplior*
> *Potest, magisque opima mactari Jovi*
> *Quam Rex iniquus*

> *There can be slaine*
> *No sacrifice to God more acceptable*
> *Then an unjust and wicked King.*[37]

But of these I name no more, lest it bee objected they were Heathen; and come to produce another sort of men that had the knowledge of true Religion. Among the Jews this custom of tyrant-killing was not unusual. First *Ehud*, a man whom God had raysed to deliver Israel from *Eglon* King of *Moab*, who had conquerd and rul'd over them eighteene years, being sent to him as an Ambassador with a present, slew him in his own house.[38] But hee was a forren Prince, an enemie, and *Ehud* besides had special warrant from God. To the first I answer, it imports not whether forren or native: For no Prince so native but professes to hold by Law; which when he himself overturns, breaking all the Covnants and Oaths that gave him title to his dignity, and were the bond and alliance between him and his people, what differs he from an outlandish King, or from an enemie? For look how much right the King of *Spaine* hath to govern us at all, so much right hath the King of *England* to govern us tyranically. If he, though not bound to us by any League, comming from *Spaine* in person to subdue us or to destroy us, might lawfully by the people of *England* either bee slaine in fight, or put to death in capitivity, what hath a native King to plead, bound by so many Covnants, benefits and honours to the welfare of his people, why he through the contempt of all Laws and Parlaments, the onely tie of our obedience to him, for his own wills sake, and a boasted prerogative unaccountable, after sev'n years warring and destroying of his best Subjects,[39] overcom, and yielded prisoner, should think to scape

---

37. *Hercules furens*, ll. 822–4.

38. Judges 3 : 14–15.

39. i.e. since Charles raised his standard on 22 August 1642. Milton further remarks on the 'sev'n years Warr' below, pp. 274 f.

unquestionable, as a thing divine, in respect of whom so many thousand Christians destroy'd, should lie unaccounted for, polluting with their slaughtered carcases all the Land over, and crying for vengeance against the living that should have righted them. Who knows not that there is a mutual bond of amity and brother-hood between man and man over all the World, neither is it the English Sea that can sever us from that duty and relation : a straiter bond yet there is between fellow-subjects, neighbours, and friends; But when any of these doe one to another so as hostility could doe no worse, what doth the Law decree less against them, then op'n enemies and invaders? or if the Law be not present, or too weake, what doth it warrant us to less then single defence, or civil warr? and from that time forward the Law of civil defensive warr differs nothing from the Law of forren hostility. Nor is it distance of place that makes enmitie, but enmity that makes distance. He therfore that keeps peace with me, neer or remote, of whatsoever Nation, is to mee as farr as all civil and human offices an Englishman and a neighbour : but if an Englishman forgetting all Laws, human, civil and religious, offend against life and liberty, to him offended and to the Law in his behalf, though born in the same womb, he is no better than a Turk, a Sarasin, a Heathen. This is Gospel, and this was ever Law among equals; how much rather then in force against any King whatever, who in respect of the people is confessed inferior and not equal : to distinguish therfore of a Tyrant by outlandish, or domestic is a weak evasion. To the second that he was an enemie, I answer, what Tyrant is not? yet *Eglon* by the Jewes had bin acknowledgd as thir Sovran; they had serv'd him eighteen yeares, as long almost as we our *William* the Conqueror, in all which time he could not be so unwise a Statesman but to have tak'n of them Oaths of Fealty and Allegeance, by which they made themselves his proper Subjects, as thir homage and present sent by *Ehud* testify'd. To the third, that he had special warrant to kill *Eglon* in that manner, it cannot bee granted, because not expressd; tis plain that he was raysed by God to be a Deliverer, and went on just principles, such as were then and ever held allowable, to deale so by a Tyrant that could not otherwise be dealt with. Neither did

Samuel though a Profet, with his own hand abstain from *Agag;* a forren enemie no doubt; but mark the reason. *As thy Sword hath made women childless;*[40] a cause that by the sentence of Law it self nullifies all relations. And as the Law is between Brother and Brother, Father and Son, Maister and Servant, wherfore not between King or rather Tyrant and People? And whereas *Jehu* had special command to slay *Jehoram* a successive and hereditarie Tyrant,[41] it seems not the less imitable for that; for where a thing grounded so much on natural reason hath the addition of a command from God, what does it but establish the lawfulness of such an act. Nor is it likely that God who had so many wayes of punishing the house of *Ahab* would have sent a subject against his Prince, if the fact in it self, as don to a Tyrant, had bin of bad example. And if *David* refus'd to lift his hand against the Lords anointed,[42] the matter between them was not tyranny, but privat enmity, and *David* as a privat person had bin his own revenger, not so much the peoples. But when any tyrant at this day can shew to be the Lord's anointed, the onely mention'd reason why *David* withheld his hand, he may then but not till then presume on the same privilege.

Wee may pass therfore hence to Christian times. And first our Saviour himself, how much he favour'd Tyrants, and how much intended they should be found or honourd among Christians, declares his mind not obscurely; accounting thir absolute autority no better than Gentilism, yea though they flourish'd it over with the splendid name of Benefactors;[43] charging those that would be his Disciples to usurp no such dominion; but that they who were to bee of most autoritie among them, should esteem themselves Ministers and Servants to the public. *Matt.* 20. 25. *The Princes of the Gentiles excercise Lordship over them,* and *Mark* 10. 42. *They that seem to rule,* saith he, either slighting or accounting them no lawful rulers, *but yee shall not be so, but the greatest among you shall be your Servant.* And although hee

---

40. 1 Samuel 15:33.

41. Jehoram was Ahab's son; the command to Jehu is given in 2 Kings 9:7.

42. i.e. Saul; see 1 Samuel 24:6, 26:9.

43. Luke 22:25.

himself were the meekest, and came on earth to be so, yet to a Tyrant we hear him not voutsafe an humble word: but *Tell that Fox, Luc.* 13. [31–32.] So farr we ought to be from thinking that Christ and his Gospel should be made a Sanctuary for Tyrants from justice, to whom his Law before never gave such protection. And wherfore did his Mother the Virgin *Mary* give such praise to God in her profetic song, that he had now by the comming of Christ *Cutt down Dynasta's or proud Monarchs from the throne*,[44] if the Church, when God manifests his power in them to doe so, should rather choose all miserie and vassalage to serve them, and let them stil sit on their potent seats to bee ador'd for doing mischief. Surely it is not for nothing that tyrants by a kind of natural instinct both hate and feare none more than the true Church and Saints of God, as the most dangerous enemies and subverters of Monarchy, though indeed of tyranny; hath not this bin the perpetual cry of Courtiers, and Court Prelats? whereof no likelier cause can be alleg'd, but that they well discern'd the mind and principles of most devout and zealous men, and indeed the very discipline of Church, tending to the dissolution of all tyranny. No marvel then if since the faith of Christ receav'd, in purer or impurer times, to depose a King and put him to death for Tyranny, hath bin accounted so just and requisite, that neighbour Kings have both upheld and tak'n part with subjects in the action. And *Ludovicus Pius*, himself an Emperor, and Son of *Charles* the great, being made Judge, *Du Haillan* is my author,[45] between *Milegast* King of the *Vultzes* and his Subjects who had depos'd him, gave his verdit for the Subjects, and for him whom they had chos'n in his room. Note here that the right of electing whom they please is by the impartial testimony of an Emperor in the people. For, said he, *A just Prince ought to be prefer'd before an unjust, and the end of goverment before the prerogative.* And *Constantinus Leo*, another Emperor, in the *Byzantine* Laws saith, *that the end of a King is for the general good, which he not performing is but the*

44. Luke 1:52.

45. Bernard de Girard, Sieur du Haillan, *L'Histoire de France* (1576). Louis the Pious was Holy Roman Emperor 818–40.

counterfet of a King.[46] And to prove that som of our own Monarchs have acknowledg'd that thir high office exempted them not from punishment, they had the Sword of St. *Edward*[47] born before them by an officer who was call'd Earle of the Palace, eev'n at the times of thir highest pomp and solemnities, to mind them, saith *Matthew Paris*, the best of our Historians,[48] that if they erred, the Sword had power to restraine them. And what restraint the Sword comes to at length, having both edge and point, if any *Sceptic* will doubt, let him feel. It is also affirm'd from diligent search made in our ancient books of Law, that the Peers and Barons of England had a legal right to judge the King: which was the cause most likely, for it could be no slight cause, that they were call'd his Peers, or equals. This however may stand immovable, so long as man hath to deale with no better then man; that if our Law judge all men to the lowest by thir Peers, it should in all equity ascend also, and judge the highest. And so much I find both in our own and forren Storie, that Dukes, Earles, and Marqueses were at first not hereditary, not empty and vain titles, but names of trust and office, and with the office ceasing, as induces me to be of opinion, that every worthy man in Parlament, for the word Baron imports no more, might for the public good be thought a fit Peer and judge of the King; without regard had to petty caveats, and circumstances, the chief impediment in high affaires, and ever stood upon most by circumstantial men. Whence doubtless our Ancestors who were not ignorant with what rights either Nature or ancient Constitution had endowed them, when Oaths both at Coronation, and renewed in Parlament would not serve, thought it no way illegal to depose and put to death thir tyrannous Kings. Insomuch that the Parlament drew up a charge against *Richard the second*, and the Commons requested to have judgement decree'd against him, that the realme might not bee endangered. And *Peter Martyr* a Divine of formost rank, on the

---

46. From the *Eclogue* (740) of the Byzantine Emperor Leo III.

47. The Curtano of King Edward the Confessor (1042–66).

48. Paris (c. 1199–1259) compiled the *Chronica maiora* in part by drawing on the *Flores historiarum* of Roger of Wendover.

third of *Judges* approves thir doings.[49] Sir *Thomas Smith* also a
Protestant and a Statesman, in his Commonwelth of *England*,[50]
putting the question whether it be lawfull to rise against a Tyrant, answers that the vulgar judge of it according to the event,
and the lerned according to the purpose of them that do it. But
far before these days, *Gildas* the most ancient of all our Historians,[51] speaking of those times wherein the Roman Empire
decaying quitted and relinquished what right they had by Conquest to this Iland, and resign'd it all into the peoples hands,
testifies that the people thus re-invested with thir own original
right, about the year 446, both elected them Kings, whom they
thought best (the first Christian Brittish Kings that ever raign'd
heer since the Romans) and by the same right, when they apprehended cause, usually depos'd and put them to death. This is
the most fundamental and ancient tenure that any King of
England can produce or pretend to; in comparison of which, all
other titles and pleas are but of yesterday. If any object that
Gildas condemns the Britans for so doing, the answer is as
ready; that he condemns them no more for so doing, then hee
did before for choosing such, for saith he, *They anointed them
Kings, not of God, but such as were more bloody then the rest.*
Next hee condemns them not at all for deposing or putting them
to death, but for doing it over hastily, without tryal or well
examining the cause, and for electing others wors in thir room.
Thus we have heer both domestic and most ancient examples
that the people of Britain have depos'd and put to death thir
Kings in those primitive Christian times. And to couple reason
with example, if the Church in all ages, Primitive, Romish, or
Protestant, held it ever no less thir duty then the power of thir
Keyes,[52] though without express warrant of Scripture, to bring
indifferently both King and Peasant under the utmost rigor of
thir Canons and Censures Ecclesiastical, eev'n to the smiting
him with a final excommunion, if he persist impenitent, what

---

49. Pietro Martire Vermigli, *In librum Iudicum* (1571).

50. As above, p. 88, Note 30.

51. St. Gildas (516?–570), author of *De excidio et conquestu Britanniae.*

52. The keys given to St.Peter (Matthew 16:18–19).

hinders but that the temporal Law both may and ought, though without a special Text or precedent, extend with like indifference the civil Sword, to the cutting off without exemption him that capitally offends. Seeing that justice and Religion are from the same God, and works of justice ofttimes more acceptable. Yet because that some lately, with the tongues and arguments of Malignant backsliders, have writt'n that the proceedings now in Parlament against the King, are without precedent from any Protestant State or Kingdom, the examples which follow shall be all Protestant and chiefly Presbyterian.

In the yeare 1546. The *Duke of Saxonie, Lantgrave of Hessen*, and the whole Protestant league raysd op'n Warr against *Charles the fifth* thir Emperor, sent him a defiance, renounc'd all faith and allegeance towards him, and debated long in Councel whither they should give him so much as the title of *Cæsar. Sleidan. l. 17.*[53] Let all men judge what this wanted of deposing or of killing, but the power to doe it.

In the year 1559. The Scotch Protestants claiming promise of thir Queen Regent for libertie of conscience, she answering that promises were not to be claim'd of Princes beyond what was commodious for them to grant, told her to her face in the Parlament then at *Sterling*, that if it were so, they renounc'd thir obedience; and soon after betook them to Armes. *Buchanan Hist. l. 16.*[54] Certainly when allegeance is renounc'd, that very hour the King or Queen is in effect depos'd.

In the yeare 1564. *John Knox* a most famous Divine and the reformer of *Scotland* to the Presbyterian discipline, at a general Assembly maintained op'nly in a dispute against *Lethington* the Secretary of State, that Subjects might & ought execute Gods judgements upon thir King; that the fact of *Jehu* and others against thir King having the ground of Gods ordinary command to put such and such offenders to death was not extraordinary, but to bee imitated of all that preferr'd the honour of God to

---

53. From *The General History of the Reformation* by Johann Philippson surnamed Sleidanus (1506–56).

54. From *Rerum scoticarum historia* (1582) of George Buchanan. The Queen Regent is Mary of Guise, mother of Mary Queen of Scots.

the affection of flesh and wicked Princes; that Kings, if they offend, have no privilege to be exempted from the punishments of Law more then any other subject; so that if the King be a Murderer, Adulterer, or Idolater, he should suffer, not as a King, but as an offender; and this position he repeats again and again before them. Answerable was the opinion of *John Craig* another learned Divine,[55] and that Lawes made by the tyranny of Princes, or the negligence of people, thir posterity might abrogate, and reform all things according to the original institution of Common-welths. And *Knox* being commanded by the Nobilitie to write to *Calvin* and other lerned men for thir judgement in that question, refus'd; alleging that both himself was fully resolv'd in conscience, and had heard thir judgements, and had the same opinion under handwriting of many the most godly and most lerned that he knew in Europe; that if he should move the question to them againe, what should he doe but shew his own forgetfulness or inconstancy. All this is farr more largely in the Ecclesiastic History of *Scotland l.* 4.[56] with many other passages to this effect all the Book over; set out with diligence by Scotchmen of best repute among them at the beginning of these troubles, as if they laboured to inform us what wee were to doe, and what they intended upon the like occasion.

And to let the world know that the whole Church and Protestant State of *Scotland* in those purest times of reformation were of the same beleif, three years after, they met in the feild *Mary* thir lawful and hereditary Queen, took her prisoner yielding before fight, kept her in prison, and the same yeare depos'd her. *Buchan. Hist. l.* 18.

And four years after that, the Scots in justification of thir deposing Queen *Mary*, sent Ambassadors to Queen *Elizabeth*, and in a writt'n Declaration alleg'd that they had us'd toward her more lenity then shee deserv'd, that thir Ancestors had heretofore punish'd thir Kings by death or banishment; that the Scots were a free Nation, made King whom they freely chose, and with the same freedom unkingd him if they saw cause, by right of ancient laws and Ceremonies yet remaining, the old

55. A supporter of Knox (1512–1600).

56. John Knox's *History of the Reformation in Scotland* (1560 ff.).

customs yet among the High-landers in choosing the head of thir Clanns, or Families; all which with many other arguments bore witness that regal power was nothing else but a mutual Covnant or stipulation between King and people. *Buch. Hist. l.* 20. These were Scotchmen and Presbyterians; but what measure then have they lately offerd, to think such liberty less beseeming us then themselves, presuming to put him upon us for a Maister whom thir law scarce allows to be thir own equal? If now then we heare them in another strain then heretofore in the purest times of thir Church, we may be confident it is the voice of Faction speaking in them, not of truth and Reformation. Which no less in *England* then in *Scotland*, by the mouthes of those faithful witnesses commonly call'd Puritans, and Nonconformists, spake as clearly for the putting down, yea the utmost punishing of Kings, as in thir several Treatises may be read; eev'n from the first raigne of *Elizabeth* to these times. Insomuch that one of them, whose name was *Gibson*, foretold K. *James*, he should be rooted out, and conclude his race, if he persisted to uphold Bishops.[57] And that very inscription stampt upon the first Coines at his Coronation, a naked Sword in a hand with these words, *Si mereor in me, Against me, if I deserve,* not only manifested the judgement of that State, but seem'd also to presage the sentence of Divine justice in this event upon his Son.

In the yeare 1581. the States of *Holland* in a general Assembly at the *Hague*, abjur'd all obedience and subjection to *Philip* King of *Spaine*; and in a Declaration justifie thir so doing; for that by his tyrannous government against faith so many times giv'n & brok'n he had lost his right to all the Belgic Provinces; that therfore they depos'd him and declar'd it lawful to choose another in his stead. *Thuan. l.* 74.[58] From that time, to this, no State or Kingdom in the world hath equally prosperd: But let them remember not to look with an evil and prejudicial eye upon thir Neighbours walking by the same rule.[59]

---

57. James Gibson's warning to James VI was delivered in 1586.

58. From Jacques-Auguste de Thou's *History of his Own Times* (1604).

59. The Dutch had formally protested against the trial of Charles I.

But what need these examples to Presbyterians, I mean to those who now of late would seem so much to abhorr deposing, when as they to all Christendom have giv'n the latest and the liveliest example of doing it themselves. I question not the lawfulness of raising Warr against a Tyrant in defence of Religion, or civil libertie; for no Protestant Church from the first *Waldenses*[60] of *Lyons*, and *Languedoc* to this day but have don it round, and maintain'd it lawful. But this I doubt not to affirme, that the Presbyterians, who now so much condemn deposing, were the men themselves that deposd the King, and cannot with all thir shifting and relapsing, wash off the guiltiness from thir own hands. For they themselves, by these thir late doings have made it guiltiness, and turn'd thir own warrantable actions into Rebellion.

There is nothing that so actually makes a King of *England*, as rightful possession and Supremacy *in all causes both civil and Ecclesiastical*: and nothing that so actually makes a Subject of *England*, as those two Oaths of Allegeance and Supremacy observ'd *without equivocating, or any mental reservation*. Out of doubt then when the King shall command things already constituted in Church, or State, obedience is the true essence of a subject, either to doe, if it be lawful, or if he hold the thing unlawful, to submitt to that penaltie which the Law imposes, so long as he intends to remaine a Subject. Therfore when the people or any part of them shall rise against the King and his autority executing the Law in any thing establish'd civil or Ecclesiastical, I doe not say it is rebellion, if the thing commanded though establish'd be unlawful, and that they sought first all due means of redress (and no man is furder bound to Law) but I say it is an absolute renouncing both of Supremacy and Allegeance, which in one word is an actual and total deposing of the King, and the setting up of another supreme autority over them. And whether the Presbyterians have not don all this and much more, they will not put mee, I suppose, to reck'n up a seven years story fresh in the memory of all

60. The sect which in the twelfth century broke from the Papacy. Their massacre by the House of Savoy in 1655 was to occasion one of Milton's greatest sonnets.

men.[61] Have they not utterly broke the Oath of Allegeance, rejecting the Kings command and autority sent them from any part of the Kingdom whether in things lawful or unlawful? Have they not abjur'd the Oath of Supremacy by setting up the Parlament without the King, supreme to all thir obedience, and though thir Vow and Covnant bound them in general to the Parlament, yet somtimes adhering to the lesser part of Lords and Commons that remain faithful, as they terme it, and eev'n of them, one while to the Commons without the Lords, another while to the Lords without the Commons?[62] Have they not still declar'd thir meaning, whatever thir Oath were, to hold them onely for supreme whom they found at any time most yeilding to what they petition'd? Both these Oaths which were the straitest bond of an English subject in reference to the King, being thus broke & made voide, it follows undeny-ably that the King from that time was by them in fact abso-lutely depos'd, and they no longer in reality to be thought his subjects, notwithstanding thir fine clause in the Covnant to preserve his person, Crown, and dignity, set there by some dodg-ing Casuist with more craft then sincerity to mitigate the matter in case of ill success and not tak'n I suppose by any honest man, but as a condition subordinat to every the least particle that might more concerne Religion, liberty, or the public peace. To prove it yet more plainly that they are the men who have depos'd the King, I thus argue. We know that King and Subject are relatives, and relatives have no longer being then in the rela-tion; the relation between King and Subject can be no other then regal autority and subjection. Hence I inferr past their defend-ing, that if the Subject who is one relative, take away the relation, of force he takes away also the other relative; but the Presbyterians who were one relative, that is to say Subjects, have for this sev'n years tak'n away the relation, that is to say the Kings autority, and thir subjection to it, therfore the Presby-

---

61. See above, p. 264, Note 39.

62. The Presbyterians, wont to vote with the minority party of the Independents ('the lesser part'), approved in the Lords the pro-posals of Charles I for an episcopal settlement, but rejected them in the Commons.

erians for these sev'n years have remov'd and extinguishd the
other relative, that is to say the King, or to speak more in brief
have depos'd him; not onely by depriving him the execution of
his autoritie, but by conferring it upon others. If then thir
Oaths of subjection brok'n, new Supremacy obey'd, new Oaths
and Covnants tak'n, notwithstanding frivolous evasions, have
in plaine termes unking'd the King, much more then hath thir
sev'n years Warr; not depos'd him onely but outlaw'd him, and
defi'd him as an alien, a rebell to Law, and enemie to the State.
It must needs be clear to any man not avers from reason, that
hostilitie and subjection are two direct and positive contraries;
and can no more in one subject stand together in respect of the
same King, then one person at the same time can be in two
remote places. Against whom therfore the Subject is in act of
hostility we may be confident that to him he is in no subjection :
and in whom hostility takes place of subjection, for they can
by no meanes consist together, to him the King can be not
onely no King, but an enemie. So that from hence we shall not
need dispute whether they have depos'd him, or what they have
defaulted towards him as no King, but shew manifestly how
much they have done toward the killing him. Have they not
levied all these Warrs against him whether offensive or defensive (for defence in Warr equally offends, and most prudently
before hand) and giv'n Commission to slay where they knew
his person could not be exempt from danger? And if chance
or flight had not sav'd him, how oft'n had they killd him,
directing thir Artillery without blame or prohibition to the very
place where they saw him stand? Have they not Sequester'd
him, judg'd or unjudgd, and converted his revenew to other
uses, detaining from him as a grand Delinquent, all meanes of
livelyhood, so that for them long since he might have perisht,
or have starv'd? Have they not hunted and pursu'd him round
about the Kingdom with sword and fire? Have they not formerly
deny'd to Treat with him, and thir now recanting Ministers
preach'd against him, as a reprobate incurable, an enemy to
God and his Church markt for destruction, and therfore not to
be treated with? Have they not beseig'd him, & to thir power
forbidd him Water and Fire, save what they shot against him to

the hazard of his life? Yet while they thus assaulted and endangered it with hostile deeds, they swore in words to defend it
with his Crown and dignity; not in order, as it seems now, to
a firm and lasting peace, or to his repentance after all this
blood; but simply, without regard, without remorse, or any
comparable value of all the miseries and calamities sufferd by
the poore people, or to suffer hereafter through his obstinacy
or impenitence. No understanding man can bee ignorant that
Covnants are ever made according to the present state of persons
and of things; and have ever the more general laws of nature
and of reason included in them, though not express'd. If I make
a voluntary Covnant as with a man, to doe him good, and he
prove afterward a monster to me, I should conceave a dis-
obligement. If I covnant, not to hurt an enemie, in favour of
him & forbearance, & hope of his amendment, & he, after that,
shall doe me tenfould injury and mischief, to what he had don
when I so Covnanted, and stil be plotting what may tend to
my destruction, I question not but that his after actions release
me; nor know I Covnant so sacred that withholds me from
demanding justice on him. Howbeit, had not thir distrust in a
good cause, and the fast and loos of our prevaricating Divines
oversway'd, it had bin doubtless better not to have inserted in
a Covnant unnecessary obligations, and words not works of a
supererogating Allegeance[63] to thir enemy; no way advantageous
to themselves, had the King prevail'd, as to thir cost many
would have felt; but full of snare and distraction to our friends,
usefull onely, as we now find, to our adversaries, who under
such a latitude and shelter of ambiguous interpretation have
ever since been plotting and contriving new opportunities to
trouble all again. How much better had it bin, and more becom-
ming an undaunted vertue, to have declar'd op'nly and boldly
whom and what power the people were to hold Supreme; as
on the like occasion Protestants have don before, and many
conscientious men now in these times have more then once
besought the Parlament to doe, that they might goe on upon a
sure foundation, and not with a ridling Covnant in thir mouths,

63. i.e. 'the unnecessariest clause of thir Covnant' mentioned earlier
(above, p. 252).

276

seeming to sweare counter almost in the same breath Allegeance and no Allegeance; which doubtless had drawn off all the minds of sincere men from siding with them, had they not discern'd thir actions farr more deposing him then thir words upholding him; which words made now the subject of cavillous interpretations, stood ever in the Covnant, by judgement of the more discerning sort, an evidence of thir feare, not of thir fidelity. What should I return to speak on, of those attempts for which the King himself hath oft'n charg'd the Presbyterians of seeking his life, when as in the due estimation of things, they might without a fallacy be sayd to have don the deed outright. Who knows not that the King is a name of dignity and office, not of person: Who therfore kills a King, must kill him while he is a King. Then they certainly who by deposing him have long since tak'n from him the life of a King, his office and his dignity, they in the truest sence may be said to have killd the King: nor onely by thir deposing and waging Warr against him, which besides the danger to his personal life, sett him in the fardest opposite point from any vital function of a King, but by thir holding him in prison, vanquishd and yeilded into thir absolute and *despotic* power, which brought him to the lowest degradement and incapacity of the regal name. I say not by whose matchless valour[64] next under God, lest the story of thir ingratitude thereupon carry me from the purpose in hand, which is to convince them that they, which I repeat againe, were the men who in the truest sense killd the King, not onely as is prov'd before, but by depressing him thir King farr below the rank of a subject to the condition of a Captive, without intention to restore him, as the Chancellour of *Scotland* in a speech told him plainly at *Newcastle*,[65] unless hee granted fully all thir demands, which they knew he never meant. Nor did they Treat or think of Treating with him, till thir hatred to the Army that deliverd them, not thir love or duty to the King, joyn'd them secretly with men sentenc'd so oft for Reprobats in thir own mouthes, by whose suttle inspiring- they grew madd upon a

---

64. Cromwell.

65. Where Charles was imprisoned in May 1646. The Scottish Chancellor was John Campbell, Earl of London.

most tardy and improper Treaty.[66] Whereas if the whole bent of thir actions had not bin against the King himself, but only against his evil counselers, as they faind, & published, wherfore did they not restore him all that while to the true life of a King, his office, Crown, and Dignity, when he was in thir power, & they themselves his neerest Counselers. The truth therfore is, both that they would not, and that indeed they could not without thir own certain destruction; having reduc'd him to such a final pass, as was the very death and burial of all in him that was regal, and from whence never King of *England* yet reviv'd, but by the new re-inforcement of his own party, which was a kind of resurrection to him. Thus having quite extinguisht all that could be in him of a King, and from a total privation clad him over, like another specifical[67] thing, with formes and habitudes destructive to the former, they left in his person, dead as to Law, and all the civil right either of King or Subject, the life onely of a Prisner, a Captive and a Malefactor. Whom the equal and impartial hand of justice finding, was no more to spare then another ordnary man; not onely made obnoxious to the doom of Law by a charge more then once drawn up against him, and his own confession to the first Article at *Newport*,[68] but summond and arraign'd in the sight of God and his people, curst & devoted to perdition worse then any Ahab, or Antiochus,[69] with exhortation to curse all those in the name of God that made not Warr against him, as bitterly as *Meroz* was to be curs'd, that went not out against a Canaanitish King,[70] almost in all the Sermons, Prayers, and Fulminations that have bin utterd this sev'n yeares by those clov'n tongues of falshood and dissention; who now, to the

---

66. The Treaty of Newport negotiated in the latter part of 1648 in the Isle of Wight.

67. Kind of.

68. The Treaty (above, Note 66) had specified that the war espoused by Parliament was 'just and lawful'.

69. The tyrannical Ahab (1 Kings 16:29 ff.) and Antiochus IV Epiphanes (1 Maccabees 1).

70. The inhabitants of Meroz were cursed for failing to help Barak against the Canaanite king Jabin (Judges 5:23).

stirring up of new discord, acquitt him; and against thir own disciplin, which they boast to be the throne and scepter of Christ, absolve him, unconfound him, though unconverted, unrepentant, unsensible of all thir pretious Saints and Martyrs whose blood they have so oft laid upon his head : and now againe with a new sovran anointment can wash it all off, as if it were as vile, and no more to be reckn'd for, then the blood of so many Dogs in a time of Pestilence : giving the most opprobrious lye to all the acted zeale that for these many yeares hath filld thir bellies, and fed them fatt upon the foolish people. Ministers of sedition, not of the Gospel, who while they saw it manifestly tend to civil Warr and blood shed, never ceasd exasperating the people against him; and now that they see it likely to breed new commotion, cease not to incite others against the people that have sav'd them from him, as if sedition were thir onely aime, whether against him or for him. But God, as we have cause to trust, will put other thoughts into the people, and turn them from giving care or heed to these Mercenary noise-makers, of whose fury, and fals prophecies we have anough experience; and from the murmurs of new discord will incline them to heark'n rather with erected minds to the voice of our Supreme Magistracy, calling us to liberty and the flourishing deeds of a reformed Common-wealth; with this hope that as God was heretofore angry with the Jews who rejected him and his forme of Government to choose a King, so that he will bless us, and be propitious to us who reject a King to make him onely our leader and supreme governour in the conformity as neer as may be of his own ancient goverment; if we have at least but so much worth in us to entertaine the sense of our future happiness, and the courage to receave what God voutsafes us : wherein we have the honour to precede other Nations who are now labouring to be our followers. For as to this question in hand what the people by thir just right may doe in change of goverment, or of governour, we see it cleerd sufficiently; besides other ample autority eev'n from the mouths of Princes themselves. And surely they that shall boast, as we doe, to be a free Nation, and not have in themselves the power to remove, or to abolish any governour supreme, or subordinat,

with the goverment it self upon urgent causes, may please thir
fancy with a ridiculous and painted freedom, fit to coz'n babies;
but are indeed under tyranny and servitude; as wanting that
power, which is the root and sourse of all liberty, to dispose and
œconomize[71] in the Land which God hath giv'n them, as
Maisters of Family in thir own house and free inheritance.
Without which natural and essential power of a free Nation,
though bearing high thir heads, they can in due esteem be
thought no better then slaves and vassals born, in the tenure
and occupation of another inheriting Lord. Whose goverment,
though not illegal, or intolerable, hangs over them as a Lordly
scourge, not as a free goverment; and therfore to be abrogated.
How much more justly then may they fling off tyranny, or
tyrants; who being once depos'd can be no more then privat
men, as subject to the reach of Justice and arraignment as any
other transgressors. And certainly if men, not to speak of
Heathen, both wise and Religious have don justice upon Tyrants
what way they could soonest, how much more milde & human
then is it, to give them faire and op'n tryal? To teach lawless
Kings, and all who so much adore them, that not mortal man,
or his imperious will, but Justice is the onely true sovran and
supreme Majesty upon earth. Let men cease therfore out of
faction & hypocrisie to make out-cries and horrid things of
things so just and honorable. Though perhaps till now no protestant State or kingdom can be alleg'd to have op'nly put to
death thir King, which lately some have writt'n, and imputed
to thir great glory; much mistaking the matter. It is not, neither
ought to be the glory of a Protestant State, never to have put
thir King to death; It is the glory of a Protestant King never to
have deserv'd death. And if the Parlament and Military Councel
doe what they doe without precedent, if it appeare thir duty,
it argues the more wisdom, vertue, and magnanimity, that they
know themselves able to be a precedent to others. Who perhaps
in future ages, if they prove not too degenerat, will look up
with honour, and aspire toward these exemplary, and matchless
deeds of thir Ancestors, as to the highest top of thir civil glory

---

71. Administer household affairs.

and emulation. Which heretofore, in the persuance of fame and forren dominion, spent it self vain-gloriously abroad; but henceforth may learn a better fortitude, to dare execute highest Justice on them that shall by force of Armes endeavour the oppressing and bereaving of Religion and thir liberty at home: that no unbridl'd Potentate or Tyrant, but to his sorrow for the future, may presume such high and irresponsible licence over mankinde, to havock and turn upside-down whole Kingdoms of men, as though they were no more in respect of his perverse will then a Nation of Pismires. As for the party calld Presbyterian, of whom I believe very many to be good and faithfull Christians, though misledd by som of turbulent spirit, I wish them earnestly and calmly not to fall off from thir first principles; nor to affect rigor and superiority over men not under them; not to compell unforcible things, in Religion especially, which if not voluntary, becomes a sin; nor to assist the clamor and malicious drifts of men whom they themselves have judg'd to be the worst of men, the obdurat enemies of God and his Church : nor to dart against the actions of thir brethren, for want of other argument, those wrested Lawes and Scriptures thrown by Prelats and Malignants against thir own sides, which though they hurt not otherwise, yet tak'n up by them to the condemnation of thir own doings, give scandal to all men, and discover in themselves either extreame passion, or apostacy. Let them not oppose thir best friends and associats, who molest them not at all, infringe not the least of thir liberties; unless they call it thir liberty to bind other mens consciences, but are still seeking to live at peace with them and brotherly accord. Let them beware an old and perfet enemy,[72] who though he hope by sowing discord to make them his instruments, yet cannot forbeare a minute the op'n threatning of his destind revenge upon them, when they have servd his purposes. Let them, feare therfore if they be wise, rather what they have don already, then what remaines to doe, and be warn'd in time they put no confidence in Princes whom they have provok'd, lest they be added to the examples of those that miserably have

---

72. Charles; but cf. 'that old serpent, called the Devil, and Satan, which deceiveth the whole world' (Revelation 12:9).

tasted the event. Stories[73] can informe them how *Christiern*
the second, King of *Denmark* not much above a hundred years
past, driv'n out by his Subjects, and receav'd againe upon new
Oaths and conditions, broke through them all to his most
bloody revenge; slaying his chief opposers when he saw his
time, both them and thir children invited to a feast for that purpose. How *Maximilian*[74] dealt with those of *Bruges*, though by
mediation of the *German* Princes reconcil'd to them by solem
and public writings drawn and seald. How the massacre at
Paris[75] was the effect of that credulous peace which the French
Protestants made with *Charles* the ninth thir King: and that
the main visible cause which to this day hath sav'd the *Netherlands* from utter ruin, was thir final not beleiving the perfidious
cruelty which, as a constant maxim of State, hath bin us'd by
the Spanish Kings on their Subjects that have tak'n Armes and
after trusted them; as no later age but can testifie, heretofore
in *Belgia* it self, and this very yeare in *Naples*.[76] And to conclude with one past exception, though farr more ancient, *David*,
whose sanctify'd prudence might be alone sufficient, not to warrant us only, but to instruct us, when once he had tak'n Armes,
never after that trusted *Saul*, though with tears and much
relenting he twise promis'd not to hurt him.[77] These instances,
few of many, might admonish them both English and Scotch not
to let thir own ends, and the driving on of a faction betray
them blindly into the snare of those enemies whose revenge
looks on them as the men who first begun, fomented and
carri'd on, beyond the cure of any sound or safe accommodation, all the evil which hath since unavoidably befall'n them
and thir King.

I have somthing also to the Divines, though brief to what
were needfull; not to be disturbers of the civil affairs, being
in hands better able and more belonging to manage them; but
to study harder, and to attend the office of good Pastors, know-

---

73. Histories.

74. The Holy Roman Emperor Maximilian I (1459–1519).

75. On St. Bartholomew's Eve in 1572.

76. i.e. 1648, when the Spanish crushed a revolt in Naples.

77. 1 Samuel 19:6 and 26:21.

ing that he whose flock is least among them hath a dreadfull charge, not performd by mounting twise into the chair[78] with a formal preachment huddl'd up at the odd hours of a whole lazy week, but by incessant pains and watching *in season and out of season,*[79] *from house to house* over the soules of whom they have to feed. Which if they ever well considered, how little leasure would they find to be the most pragmatical Sidesmen[80] of every popular tumult and Sedition? And all this while are to learn what the true end and reason is of the Gospel which they teach; and what a world it differs from the censorious and supercilious lording over conscience. It would be good also they liv'd so as might perswade the people they hated covetousness, which worse then heresie, is idolatry; hated pluralities[81] and all kind of Simony; left rambling from Benefice to Benefice, like rav'nous Wolves seeking where they may devour the biggest. Of which if som, well and warmely seated from the beginning, be not guilty, twere good they held not conversation with such as are: let them be sorry that being call'd to assemble about reforming the Church, they fell to progging[82] and solliciting the Parlament, though they had renounc'd the name of Priests, for a new setling of thir Tithes and Oblations; and double lin'd themselves with spiritual places of commoditie beyond the possible discharge of thir duty. Let them assemble in Consistory[83] with thir Elders and Deacons, according to ancient Ecclesiastical rule, to the preserving of Church-discipline, each in his several charge, and not a pack of Clergiemen by themselves to belly-cheare in their presumptuous Sion,[84] or to promote designes, abuse and gull the simple Laity, and stirr up tumult, as the Prelats did, for the maintenance of thir pride and avarice. These things if they observe, and waite with patience, no doubt but all things will goe well without their importunities or exclamations: and the Printed letters

---

78. Pulpit.

79. Cf. 2 Timothy 4:2.

80. Active partisans.

81. As above, Note 14.

82. Importuning.

83. Low diocesan court in the Calvinist discipline.

84. Sion College, the seat of the Presbyterian provincial assembly from 1647.

which they send subscrib'd with the ostentation of great Characters[85] and little moment, would be more considerable then now they are. But if they be the Ministers of Mammon in stead of Christ, and scandalize his Church with the filthy love of gaine, aspiring also to sit the closest & the heaviest of all Tyrants, upon the conscience, and fall notoriously into the same sinns, wherof so lately and so loud they accus'd the Prelates, as God rooted out those wicked ones immediately before, so will he root out them thir imitators: and to vindicate his own glory and Religion, will uncover thir hypocrisie to the op'n world; and visit upon thir own heads that *curse ye Meroz*,[86] the very *Motto* of thir Pulpits, wherwith so frequently, not as *Meroz*, but more like Atheists they have blasphem'd the vengeance of God, and traduc'd the zeale of his people. And that they be not what they goe for, true Ministers of the Protestant doctrine, taught by those abroad, famous and religious men, who first reformd the Church, or by those no less zealous, who withstood corruption and the Bishops heer at home, branded with the name of Puritans and Nonconformists, wee shall abound with testimonies to make appeare: that men may yet more fully know the difference between Protestant Divines, and these Pulpit-firebrands.[87]

---

85. The unduly large capitals on the title pages of Presbyterian tracts.

86. Cf. above, p. 278, Note 70.

87. The fourteen 'testimonies' of Continental divines that follow are taken, *seriatim*, from Luther (as reported in the *Commentaries* of Sleidanus – cf. above, Note 53 – and the *Miscellanies* of the Catholic polemicist Johannes Cochlaeus), Zwingli (from his *Opera*, 1545), Calvin (from his *Praelectiones in librum prophetiarum Danielis*, 1561), Bucer (from his *Sacra quattuor evangelica*, 6th edn, 1555), and Paraeus (from his *Commentarius* on the Epistle of the Romans, 1647). On Pareus see above, p. 131, Note 46; and on Zwingli, p. 235, Note 132. Milton was intimately acquainted with another work by the German reformer Bucer, *De regno Christi* (1550), part of which he translated as *The Judgement of Martin Bucer concerning Divorce* (1644).

Luther. *Lib. contra Rusticos apud Sleidan. l. 5.*

Is est hodie rerum status, &c. *Such is the state of things at this day, that men neither can, nor will, nor indeed ought to endure longer the domination of you Princes.*

Neque vero Cæsarem, &c. *Neither is Cæsar to make Warr as head of Christ'ndom, Protector of the Church, Defender of the Faith; these Titles being fals and Windie, and most Kings being the greatest Enemies to Religion. Lib: De bello contra Turcas. apud Sleid. l.* 14. What hinders then, but that we may depose or punish them?

These also are recited by *Cochlæus* in his *Miscellanies* to be the words of *Luther*, or some other eminent Divine, then in Germany, when the Protestants there entred into solemn Covnant at *Smalcaldia*. Ut ora ijs obturem &c. *That I may stop thir mouthes, the Pope and Emperor are not born but elected, and may also be depos'd as hath bin oft'n don.* If *Luther*, or whoever els thought so, he could not stay there; for the right of birth or succession can be no privilege in nature to let a Tyrant sit irremoveable over a Nation free born, without transforming that Nation from the nature and condition of men born free, into natural, hereditary, and successive slaves. Therfore he saith furder; *To displace and throw down this Exactor, this Phalaris,*[88] *this Nero, is a work well pleasing to God;* Namely, for being such a one: which is a moral reason. Shall then so slight a consideration as his happ to be not elective simply, but by birth, which was a meer accident, overthrow that which is moral, and make unpleasing to God that which otherwise had so well pleasd him? certainly not: for if the matter be rightly argu'd, Election much rather then chance, bindes a man to content himself with what he suffers by his own bad Election. Though indeed neither the one nor other bindes any man, much less any people to a necessary sufferance of those wrongs and evils, which they have abilitie and strength anough giv'n them to remove.

---

88. The cruel tyrant of Agrigentum (565–549 B.C.).

Zwinglius. tom. 1. articul. 42.

Quando vero perfidè, &c. *When Kings raigne perfidiously, and against the rule of Christ, they may according to the word of God be depos'd.*

Mihi ergo compertum non est, &c. *I know not how it comes to pass that Kings raigne by succession, unless it be with consent of the whole people.* ibid.

Quum vero consensu, &c : *But when by suffrage and consent of the whole people, or the better part of them, a Tyrant is depos'd or put to death, God is the chief leader in that action.* ibid.

Nunc cum tam tepidi sumus, &c. *Now that we are so luke warm in upholding public justice, we indure the vices of Tyrants to raigne now a dayes with impunity; justly therfore by them we are trod underfoot, and shall at length with them be punisht. Yet ways are not wanting by which Tyrants may be remoov'd, but there wants public justice.* ibid.

Cavete vobis ô tyranni. *Beware yee Tyrants for now the Gospell of Jesus Christ spreading farr and wide, will renew the lives of many to love innocence and justice; which if yee also shall doe, yee shall be honoured. But if yee shall goe on to rage and doe violence, yee shall be trampl'd on by all men.* ibid.

Romanum imperium imò quodq; &c. *When the Roman Empire or any other shall begin to oppress Religion, and wee negligently suffer it, wee are as much guilty of Religion so violated, as the Oppressors themselvs.* Idem Epist. ad Conrad. Somium.

Calvin on Daniel. c. 4. v. 25.

Hodie Monarchæ semper in suis titulis, &c. *Now adays Monarchs pretend alwayes in thir Titles, to be Kings by the grace of God: but how many of them to this end onely pretend it, that they may raigne without controule; for to what purpose is the grace of God mentioned in the Title of Kings, but that they may acknowledge no Superiour? In the meane while God, whose name they use, to support themselves, they willingly would* read under thir feet. It is therfore a meer cheat when they boast to raigne by the grace of God.

Abdicant se terreni principes, &c. *Earthly Princes depose themselves while they rise against God, yea they are unworthy to be numberd among men: rather it behooves us to spitt upon thir heads then to obey them.* On Dan: c. 6. v. 22.

Bucer on Matth. c. 5.

Si princeps superior, &c. *If a Sovran-Prince endeavour by armes to defend transgressors, to subvert those things which are taught in the word of God, they who are in autority under him, ought first to disswade him; if they prevaile not, and that he now beares himself not as a Prince, but as an enemie, and seekes to violate privileges and rights granted to inferior Magistrates or commonalities, it is the part of pious Magistrates, imploring first the assistance of God, rather to try all ways and means, then to betray the flock of Christ, to such an enemie of God: for they also are to this end ordain'd, that they may defend the people of God, and maintain those things which are good and just. For to have supreme power less'ns not the evil committed by that power, but makes it the less tolerable, by how much the more generally hurtful. Then certainly the less tolerable, the more unpardonably to be punish'd.*

Of *Peter Martyr* we have spoke before.[89]
Parœus in Rom. 13.

Quorum est constituere Magistratus, &c. *They whose part it is to set up Magistrates, may restrain them also from outragious deeds, or pull them down; but all Magistrates are set up either by Parlament, or by Electors, or by other Magistrates; they therfore who exalted them, may lawfully degrade and punish them.*

Of the Scotch Divines I need not mention others then the famousest among them, *Knox,* & and his fellow Labourers in the Reformation of *Scotland;* whose large Treatises on this subject, defend the same Opinion. To cite them sufficiently, were to

---

89. Above, p. 269, Note 49.

insert thir whole Books, writt'n purposely on this argument *Knox Appeal;* and to the Reader; where he promises in a Post script that the Book which he intended to set forth, call'd, *The* second blast of the Trumpet, should maintain more at large, that the same men most justly may depose, and punish him whom unadvisedly they have elected, notwithstanding birth, succession, or any Oath of Allegeance. Among our own Divines, *Cart wright* and *Fenner*, two of the Lernedest, may in reason satisfy us what was held by the rest. *Fenner* in his Book of *Theologie* maintaining, That *they who have power, that is to say a Parla ment, may either by faire meanes or by force depose a Tyrant* whom he defines to be him, that wilfully breakes all, or the principal conditions made between him and the Common wealth. *Fen. Sac: Theolog. c.* 13. and *Cartwright* in a prefix't Epistle testifies his approbation of the whole Book.[90]

Gilby de obedientiâ. p. 25. & 105.

Kings have thir autoritie of the people, who may upon occa sion reassume it to themselves.

Englands Complaint against the Canons.

The people may kill wicked Princes as monsters and crue beasts.

Christopher Goodman of Obedience.

When Kings or Rulers become blasphemers of God, oppressor and murderers of thir Subjects, they ought no more to be ac counted Kings or lawfull Magistrates, but as privat men to be examind, accus'd, condemn'd and punisht by the Law of God and being convicted and punisht by that law, it is not man but Gods doing, *C.* 10. *p.* 139.

---

90. From Dudley Fenner's *Sacra theologia* (1586) and, earlier Thomas Cartwright's *Admonition to Parliament* (1572). Of the seven testimonies that follow, the first two are neither by Anthony Gilby nor from *Englands Complaint* (1640) but indirectly from John Ponet's *Short Treatise of Politike Power* (1556; thus Sonia Miller, below p. 456). The remaining five quotations are from Christopher Good man's *How Superior Powers Oght to be Obeyed* (1558).

By the civil laws a foole or Idiot born, and so prov'd shall loose the lands and inheritance wherto he is born, because he is not able to use them aright. And especially ought in no case be sufferd to have the goverment of a whole Nation; But there is no such evil can come to the Commonwealth by fooles and idiots as doth by the rage and fury of ungodly Rulers; Such therfore being without God ought to have no autority over Gods people, who by his Word requireth the contrary. *C.* 11. *p.* 143, 144.

No person is exempt by any Law of God from this punishment, be he King, Queene, or Emperor, he must dy the death, for God hath not plac'd them above others, to transgress his laws as they list, but to be subject to them as well as others, and if they be subject to his laws, then to the punishment also, so much the more as thir example is more dangerous. *C.* 13. *p.* 184.

When Magistrates cease to doe thir Duty, the people are as it were without Magistrates, yea worse, and then God giveth the sword into the peoples hand, and he himself is become immediatly thir head. *p.* 185.

If Princes doe right and keep promise with you, then doe you owe to them all humble obedience: if not, yee are discharg'd, and your study ought to be in this case how ye may depose and punish according to the Law such Rebels against God and oppressors of thir Country. *p.* 190.

This *Goodman* was a Minister of the *English* Church at *Geneva*, as *Dudley Fenner* was at *Middleburrough*, or some other place in that Country. These were the Pastors of those Saints and Confessors who flying from the bloudy persecution of Queen *Mary*, gather'd up at length thir scatterd members into many Congregations; wherof som in upper, some in lower *Germany*, part of them settl'd at *Geneva*; where this Author having preachd on this subject to the great liking of certain lerned and godly men who heard him, was by them sundry times & with much instance requir'd to write more fully on that point. Who therupon took it in hand, and conferring with the best lerned in those parts (among whom *Calvin* was then living in the same City) with their special approbation he publisht this treatise, aiming principally, as is testify'd by *Whitting-ham* in the Preface, that his Brethren of *England*, the Protestants, might be perswaded in the truth of that Doctrine concerning obedience to Magistrates. *Whittingham in Prefat.*[91]

These were the true Protestant Divines of *England*, our fathers in the faith we hold; this was their sense, who for so many yeares labouring under Prelacy, through all stormes and persecutions kept Religion from extinguishing; and deliverd it pure to us, till there arose a covetous and ambitious genera-tion of Divines (for Divines they call themselves) who feining on a sudden to be new converts and proselytes from Episcopacy, under which they had long temporiz'd, op'nd thir mouthes at length, in shew against Pluralities and Prelacy, but with intent to swallow them down both; gorging themselves like Harpy's on those simonious places and preferments of thir outed predeces-sors, as the quarry for which they hunted, not to pluralitie onely but to multiplicitie: for possessing which they had accused them thir Brethren, and aspiring under another title to the same authoritie and usurpation over the consciences of all men.

Of this faction diverse reverend and lerned Divines, as they are stil'd in the Phylactery[92] of thir own Title page, pleading the lawfulnes of defensive Armes against this King, in a Treatise call'd *Scripture and Reason*,[93] seem in words to disclaime utterly the deposing of a King; but both the Scripture and the reasons which they use, draw consequences after them, which without their bidding, conclude it lawfull. For if by Scripture, and by that especially to the *Romans*,[94] which they most insist upon, Kings, doing that which is contrary to Saint *Pauls* definition of a Magistrat, may be resisted, they may altogether with as much force of consequence be depos'd or punishd. And if by reason the unjust autority of Kings *may be forfeted in part, and his*

---

91. From William Whittingham's preface to Goodman's treatise (previous note).

92. Cf. Matthew 23:5 on the Pharisees' hypocrisy: 'all work they do for to be seen of men: they make broad their phylacteries' – i.e. amulets with Biblical texts worn by pious Jews.

93. Published by order of the Commons in April 1643.

94. Romans 13:1–2 (partly quoted above, p. 261).

power be reassum'd in part, either by the Parlament or People, *for the case in hazard and the present necessitie,* as they affirm p. 34, there can no Scripture be alleg'd, no imaginable reason giv'n, that necessity continuing, as it may alwayes, and they in all prudence and thir duty may take upon them to foresee it, why in such a case they may not finally amerce him with the loss of his Kingdom, of whose amendment they have no hope. And if one wicked action persisted in against Religion, Laws, and liberties may warrant us to thus much in part, why may not forty times as many tyrannies, by him committed, warrant us to proceed on restraining him, till the restraint become total. For the ways of justice are exactest proportion; if for one trespass of a King it require so much remedie or satisfaction, then for twenty more as hainous crimes, it requires of him twentyfold; and so proportionably, till it com to what is utmost among men. If in these proceedings against thir King they may not finish by the usual cours of justice what they have begun, they could not lawfully begin at all. For this golden rule of justice and moralitie, as well as of Arithmetic, out of three termes which they admitt, will as certainly and unavoydably bring out the fourth, as any Probleme that ever *Euclid*, or *Apollonius*[95] made good by demonstration.

And if the Parlament, being undeposable but by themselves, as is affirm'd, *p.* 37, 38, might for his whole life, if they saw cause, take all power, authority, and the sword out of his hand, which in effect is to unmagistrate him, why might they not, being then themselves the sole Magistrates in force, proceed to punish him who being lawfully depriv'd of all things that define a Magistrate, can be now no Magistrate to be degraded lower, but an offender to be punisht. Lastly, whom they may defie, and meet in battell, why may they not as well prosecute by justice? For lawfull warr is but the execution of justice against them who refuse Law. Among whom if it be lawfull (as they deny not, *p.* 19, 20.) to slay the King himself

---

95. The mathematicians Euclid and Appollonius of Perga (third and second centuries B.C.). The 'golden rule' of arithmetic, the Rule of Three, 'enables us to find the fourth term in a proportion' (Yale edn, III, 253). See also above, p. 236.

comming in front at his own peril, wherfore may not justice doe that intendedly, which the chance of a defensive warr might without blame have don casualy, nay purposely, if there it finde him among the rest. They aske p. 19. *By what rule of Conscience or God, a State is bound to sacrifice Religion, Laws and liberties, rather then a Prince defending such as subvert them, should com in hazard of his life.* And I ask by what conscience, or divinity, or Law, or reason, a State is bound to leave all these sacred concernments under a perpetual hazard and extremity of danger, rather then cutt off a wicked Prince, who sitts plotting day and night to subvert them : They tell us that the Law of nature justifies any man to defend himself, eev'n against the King in Person : let them shew us then why the same Law, may not justifie much more a State or whole people, to doe justice upon him, against whom each privat man may lawfully defend himself; seing all kind of justice don, is a defence to good men, as well as a punishment to bad; and justice don upon a Tyrant is no more but the necessary self-defence of a whole Common wealth. To Warr upon a King, that his instruments may be brought to condigne punishment, and therafter to punish them the instruments, and not to spare onely, but to defend and honour him the Author, is the strangest peece of justice to be call'd Christian, and the strangest peece of reason to be call'd human, that by men of reverence and learning, as thir stile imports them, ever yet was vented. They maintain in the third and fourth Section, that a Judge or inferior Magistrate is anointed of God, is his Minister, hath the Sword in his hand, is to be obey'd by St. *Peters* rule,[96] as well as the Supreme, and without difference any where exprest : and yet will have us fight against the Supreme till he remove and punish the inferior Magistrate (for such were greatest Delinquents) when as by Scripture, and by reason, there can no more autority be shown to resist the one then the other; and altogether as much, to punish or depose the Supreme himself, as to make Warr upon him, till he punish or deliver up his inferior Magistrates, whom in the same terms we are commanded to obey, and not to resist

96. 1 Peter 2 : 13–14 (partly quoted above, p. 261).

Thus while they, in a cautious line or two here and there stuft in, are onely verbal against the pulling down or punishing of Tyrants, all the Scripture and the reason which they bring, is in every leafe direct and rational to inferr it altogether as lawful, as to resist them. And yet in all thir Sermons, as hath by others bin well noted, they went much furder. For Divines, if ye observe them, have thir postures, and thir motions no less expertly, and wish no less variety then they that practice feats in the Artillery-ground. Sometimes they seem furiously to march on, and presently march counter; by and by they stand, and then retreat; or if need be can face about, or wheele in a whole body, with that cunning and dexterity as is almost unperceavable; to winde themselves by shifting ground into places of more advantage. And Providence onely must be the drumm, Providence the word of command, that calls them from above, but always to som larger Benefice, or acts them into such or such figures, and promotions. At thir turnes and doublings no men readier; to the right, or to the left; for it is thir turnes which they serve chiefly; heerin only singular; that with them there is no certain hand right or left; but as thir own commodity[97] thinks best to call it. But if there come a truth to be defended, which to them, and thir interest of this world seemes not so profitable, strait these nimble motionists can finde no eev'n leggs to stand upon: and are no more of use to reformation throughly performed, and not superficially, or to the advancement of Truth (which among mortal men is alwaies in her progress) then if on a sudden they were strook maime, and crippl'd. Which the better to conceale, or the more to countnance by a general conformity to thir own limping, they would have *Scripture*, they would have *reason* also made to halt with them for company; and would putt us off with impotent conclusions, lame and shorter then the premises. In this posture they seem to stand with great zeale and confidence on the wall of *Sion*;[98] but like *Jebusites*, not like *Israelites*, or *Levites*: blinde also as well as lame, they discern not *David* from *Adonibezec*: but cry him up for the Lords anointed, whose thumbs and

97. Advantage.
98. As above, p. 283, Note 84.

great toes not long before they had cut off upon thir Pulpi
cushions.[99] Therfore he who is our only King, the root of *David*
and whose Kingdom is eternal righteousness, with all those
that Warr under him, whose happiness and final hopes are laid
up in that only just & rightful kingdom (which we pray inces
santly may com soon, and in so praying wish hasty ruin and
destruction to all Tyrants) eev'n he our immortal King, and al
that love him, must of necessity have in abomination these
blind and lame Defenders of *Jerusalem*; as the soule of *David*
hated them, and forbide them entrance into Gods House
and his own.[100] But as to those before them, which I cited firs
(and with an easie search, for many more might be added) a
they there stand, without more in number, being the best and
chief of Protestant Divines, we may follow them for faithfu
Guides, and without doubting may receive them, as Witnesse
abundant of what wee heer affirme concerning Tyrants. And
indeed I find it generally the cleere and positive determination
of them all, (not prelatical, or of this late faction subprelatical
who have writt'n on this argument; that to doe justice on a law
less King, is to a privat man unlawful, to an inferior Magistrate
lawfull: or if they were divided in opinion, yet greater then
these here alleg'd, or of more autority in the Church, there can
be none produc'd. If any one shall goe about by bringing other
testimonies to disable these, or by bringing these against them
selves in other cited passages of thir Books, he will not only
faile to make good that fals and impudent assertion of those
mutinous Ministers, that the deposing and punishing of a King
or Tyrant, *is against the constant Judgement of all Protestant*
Divines, it being quite the contrary, but will prove rather
what perhaps he intended not, that the judgement of Divines
if it be so various and inconstant to it self, is not considerable
or to be esteem'd at all. Ere which be yeilded, as I hope it never
will, these ignorant assertors in thir own art will have prov'd
themselves more and more, not to be Protestant Divines, whose
constant judgement in this point they have so audaciously

99. According to Judges 1:4–7, the Israelites on invading Palestine
seized Adonibezek 'and cut off his thumbs and his great toes'.

100. 2 Samuel 5:8.

bely'd, but rather to be a pack of hungrie Churchwolves, who in the steps of *Simon Magus*[101] thir Father, following the hot sent of double Livings and Pluralities, advousons, donatives, inductions, and augmentations,[102] though uncall'd to the Flock of Christ, but by the meer suggestion of thir Bellies, like those Priests of *Bel*, whose pranks *Daniel* found out;[103] have got possession, or rather seis'd upon the Pulpit, as the strong hold and fortress of thir sedition and rebellion against the civil Magistrate. Whose friendly and victorious hand having rescu'd them from the Bishops thir insulting Lords, fed them plenteously, both in public and in privat, rais'd them to be high and rich of poore and base; onely suffer'd not thir covetousness & fierce ambition, which as the pitt that sent out their fellow locusts,[104] hath bin ever bottomless and boundless, to interpose in all things, and over all persons, thir impetuos ignorance and importunity.

---

101. According to Acts 8:9–25, Simon the magician offered Peter and John money to purchase the power of the Holy Spirit.

102. Forms of ecclesiastical preferment.

103. As related in the apocryphal book of Bel and the Dragon.

104. Cf. Revelation 9:1 ff.

A TREATISE OF CIVIL POWER
IN ECCLESIASTICAL CAUSES
(1659)

[Milton's principal work in defence of religious liberty (see above, p. 30) is described on the title page as *A Tretise of Civil Power in Ecclesiastical Causes: shewing that it is not lawfull for any power on earth to compell in matters of Religion*. The edition of February 1659 was the only one to appear in Milton's lifetime. It is here reprinted from the Columbia edition (VI, 1–41; ed. William Haller).]

TO THE PARLAMENT

of the Commonwealth of England with the dominions therof.

I have prepar'd, supream Councel, against the much expected time of your sitting, this treatise; which, though to all Christian magistrates equally belonging, and therfore to have bin written in the common language of Christendom,[1] *natural dutie and affection hath confin'd, and dedicated first to my own nation: and in a season wherin the timely reading therof, to the easier accomplishment of your great work, may save you much labor and interruption: of two parts usually propos'd, civil and ecclesiastical, recommending civil only to your proper care, ecclesiastical to them only from whom it takes both that name and nature. Yet for this cause only do I require or trust to finde acceptance, but in a two-fold respect besides: first as bringing cleer evidence of scripture and protestant maxims to the Parlament of England, who in thir late acts, upon occasion, have professd to assert only the true protestant Christian religion, as it is contained in the holy scriptures: next, in regard that your power being but for a time, and having in your selves a Christian libertie of your own, which at one time or other may be oppressd, therof truly sensible, it will concern you while you*

---

1. Latin.

are in power, so to regard other mens consciences, as you would your own should be regarded in the power of others; and to consider that any law against conscience is alike in force against any conscience, and so may one way or other justly redound upon your selves. One advantage I make no doubt of, that I shall write to many eminent persons of your number, alreadie perfet and resolvd in this important article of Christianitie. Some of whom I remember to have heard often for several years, at a councel next in autoritie to your own,[2] so well joining religion with civil prudence, and yet so well distinguishing the different power of either, and this not only voting, but frequently reasoning why it should be so, that if any there present had bin before of an opinion contrary, he might doubtless have departed thence a convert in that point, and have confessed, that then both commonwealth and religion will at length, if ever, flourish in Christendom, when either they who govern discern between civil and religious, or they only who so discern shall be admitted to govern. Till then nothing but troubles, persecutions, commotions can be expected; the inward decay of true religion among our selves, and the utter overthrow at last by a common enemy. Of civil libertie I have written heretofore by the appointment, and not without the approbation of civil power:[3] of Christian liberty I write now; which others long since having don with all freedom under heathen emperors, I should do wrong to suspect, that I now shall with less under Christian governors, and such especially as profess openly thir defence of Christian libertie; although I write this not otherwise appointed or induc'd then by an inward perswasion of the Christian dutie which I may usefully discharge herin to the common Lord and Master of us all, and the certain hope of his approbation, first and chiefest to be sought: In the hand of whose providence I remain, praying all success and good event on your publick councels to the defence of true religion and our civil rights.

JOHN MILTON.

---

2. The Council of State.

3. The first *Defence* (1651) had been written at the order of the republican government.

A TREATISE OF CIVIL POWER
IN ECCLESIASTICAL CAUSES

Two things there be which have bin ever found working much mischief to the church of God, and the advancement of truth; force on the one side restraining, and hire on the other side corrupting the teachers thereof. Few ages have bin since the ascension of our Saviour, wherin the one of these two, or both together have not prevaild. It can be at no time therfore unseasonable to speak of these things; since by them the church is either in continual detriment and oppression, or in continual danger. The former shall be at this time my argument; the latter as I shall finde God disposing me, and opportunity inviting.[4] What I argue, shall be drawn from the scripture only; and therin from true fundamental principles of the gospel; to all knowing Christians undeniable. And if the governors of this commonwealth since the rooting out of prelats have made least use of force in religion, and most have favord Christian liberty of any in this Iland before them since the first preaching of the gospel, for which we are not to forget our thanks to God, and their due praise, they may, I doubt not, in this treatise finde that which not only will confirm them to defend the Christian liberty which we enjoy, but will incite them also to enlarge it, if in aught they yet straiten it. To them who perhaps herafter, less experienc'd in religion, may come to govern or give us laws, this or other such, if they please, may be a timely instruction: however to the truth it will be at all times no unneedfull testimonie; at least some discharge of that general dutie which no Christian but according to what he hath receivd, knows is requir'd of him if he have aught more conducing to the advancement of religion then what is usually endeavourd, freely to impart it.

It will require no great labor of exposition to unfold what is here meant by matters of religion; being as soon apprehended as defin'd, such things as belong chiefly to the knowledge and service of God; and are either above the reach and light of nature

---

4. Later in 1659, Milton was to publish *Considerations touching the likeliest means to remove hirelings out of the Church.*

without revelation from above, and therfore liable to be variously understood by humane reason, or such things as are enjoind or forbidden by divine precept, which els by the light of reason would seem indifferent to be don or not don; and so likewise must needs appeer to everie man as the precept is understood. Whence I here mean by conscience or religion, that full perswasion whereby we are assur'd that our beleef and practise, as far as we are able to apprehend and probably make appeer, is according to the will of God & his Holy Spirit within us, which we ought to follow much rather then any law of man, as not only his word every where bids us, but the very dictate of reason tells us. *Act. 4. 19. whether it be right in the sight of God, to hearken to you more then to God, judge ye.* That for beleef or practise in religion according to this conscientious perswasion no man ought to be punished or molested by any outward force on earth whatsoever, I distrust not, through Gods implor'd assistance, to make plane by these following arguments.

First it cannot be deni'd, being the main foundation of our protestant religion, that we of these ages, having no other divine rule or autoritie from without us warrantable to one another as a common ground but the holy scripture, and no other within us but the illumination of the Holy Spirit so interpreting that scripture as warrantable only to our selves and to such whose consciences we can so perswade, can have no other ground in matters of religion but only from the scriptures. And these being not possible to be understood without this divine illumination, which no man can know at all times to be in himself, much less to be at any time for certain in any other, it follows cleerly, that no man or body of men in these times can be the infallible judges or determiners in matters of religion to any other mens consciences but thir own. And therfore those Beroeans[5] are commended, *Acts* 17. 11, who after the preaching even of S. *Paul, searchd the scriptures daily, whether those things were so.* Nor did they more then what God himself in many places commands us by the same apostle,

---

5. The citizens of Berea in northern Greece.

to search, to try, to judge of these things our selves: And gives us reason also, *Gal. 6. 4, 5. let every man prove his own work, and then shall he have rejoicing in himself alone, and not in another: for every man shall bear his own burden.* If then we count it so ignorant and irreligious in the papist to think himself dischargd in Gods account, beleeving only as the church beleevs, how much greater condemnation will it be to the protestant his condemner, to think himself justified, beleeving only as the state beleevs? With good cause therfore it is the general consent of all sound protestant writers, that neither traditions, councels nor canons of any visible church, much less edicts of any magistrate or civil session, but the scripture only can be the final judge or rule in matters of religion, and that only in the conscience of every Christian to himself. Which protestation made by the first publick reformers of our religion against the imperial edicts of *Charls* the fifth, imposing church-traditions without scripture, gave first beginning to the name of *Protestant;*[6] and with that name hath ever bin receivd this doctrine, which preferrs the scripture before the church, and acknowledges none but the Scripture sole interpreter of it self to the conscience. For if the church be not sufficient to be implicitly beleeved, as we hold it is not, what can there els be nam'd of more autoritie then the church but the conscience; then which God only is greater, 1 *Joh.* 3. 20? But if any man shall pretend, that the scripture judges to his conscience for other men, he makes himself greater not only then the church, but also then the scripture, then the consciences of other men; a presumption too high for any mortal; since every true Christian able to give a reason of his faith, hath the word of God before him, the promisd Holy Spirit, and the minde of Christ within him, 1 *Cor.* 2. 16; a much better and safer guide of conscience, which as far as concerns himself he may far more certainly know then any outward rule impos'd upon him by others whom he inwardly neither knows nor can know; at least knows nothing of them more sure then this one thing, that they cannot be his judges in religion. 1. *Cor.* 2. 15. *the spirituall man judgeth*

6. The protest had emanated from the princes of the League of Schmalkald to the ambassador of the Emperor Charles V in 1537.

all things, but he himself is judg'd of no man. Chiefly for this cause do all true protestants account the pope antichrist,[7] for that he assumes to himself this infallibilitie over both the conscience and the scripture; *siting in the temple of God,* as it were opposite to God, *and exalting himself above all that is called god, or is worshipd,* 2 Thess. 2. 4. That is to say not only above all judges and magistrates, who though they be calld gods, are far beneath infallible, but also above God himself, by giving law both to the scripture, to the conscience, and to the spirit it self of God within us. Whenas we finde, *James* 4. 12, *there is one lawgiver, who is able to save and to destroy: who art thou that judgest another?* That Christ is the only lawgiver of his church and that it is here meant in religious matters, no well grounded Christian will deny. Thus also S. *Paul,* Rom. 14. 4. *who art thou that judgest the servant of another? to his own Lord he standeth or falleth: but he shall stand; for God is able to make him stand.* As therfore of one beyond expression bold and presumptuous, both these apostles demand, *who art thou* that presum'st to impose other law or judgment in religion then the only lawgiver and judge Christ, who only can save and can destroy, gives to the conscience? And the forecited place to the *Thessalonians* by compar'd effects resolvs us, that be he or they who or wherever they be or can be, they are of far lesse autoritie then the church, whom in these things as protestants they receive not, and yet no less antichrist in this main point of antichristianism, no less a pope or popedom then he at *Rome,* if not much more; by setting up supream interpreters of scripture either those doctors whom they follow, or, which is far worse, themselves as a civil papacie assuming unaccountable supremacie to themselves not in civil only but ecclesiastical causes. Seeing then that in matters of religion, as hath been prov'd, none can judge or determin here on earth, no not church-governors themselves against the consciences of other beleevers, my inference is, or rather not mine but our Saviours own, that in those matters they neither can command nor use

7. Not Milton's exaggeration. For one reason or another, the equation was accepted by 'all the *Reformed* Churches' (as Bishop Thomas Barlow remarked in his *Genuine Remains,* 1693, p. 228).

constraint; lest they run rashly on a pernicious consequence, forewarnd in that parable *Mat.* 13. from the 26 to the 31 verse: *least while ye gather up the tares, ye root up also the wheat with them. Let both grow together until the harvest: and in the time of harvest I will say to the reapers, Gather ye together first the tares &c.* whereby he declares that this work neither his own ministers nor any els can discerningly anough or judgingly perform without his own immediat direction, in his own fit season; and that they ought till then not to attempt it. Which is further confirmd 2 *Cor.* 1. 24. *not that we have dominion over your faith, but are helpers of your joy.* If apostles had no dominion or constraining powr over faith or conscience, much less have ordinary ministers. 1 *Pet.* 5. 2, 3. *Feed the flock of God not by constraint &c. neither as being lords over Gods heritage.* But some will object, that this overthrows all church-discipline, all censure of errors, if no man can determin. My answer is, that what they hear is plane scripture; which forbids not church-sentence or determining, but as it ends in violence upon the conscience unconvinc'd. Let who so will interpret or determin, so it be according to true church-discipline; which is exercis'd on them only who have willingly joind themselves in that covnant of union, and proceeds only to a separation from the rest, proceeds never to any corporal inforcement or forfeture of monie; which in spiritual things are the two arms of Antichrist, not of the true church; the one being inquisition, the other no better then a temporal indulgence of sin for monie, whether by the church exacted or by the magistrate; both the one and the other a temporal satisfaction for what Christ hath satisfied eternally; a popish commuting of penaltie, corporal for spiritual; a satisfaction to man especially to the magistrate, for what and to whom we owe none: these and more are the injustices of force and fining in religion, besides what I most insist on, the violation of Gods express commandment in the gospel, as hath bin shewn. Thus then if church-governors cannot use force in religion, though but for this reason, because they cannot infallibly determin to the conscience without convincement, much less have civil magistrates autoritie to use force where they can much less judge; unless they mean only to be the civil executioners of them who have no civil power to give them such commission, no nor yet ecclesiastical to any force or violence in religion. To summe up all in brief, if we must beleeve as the magistrate appoints, why not rather as the church! if not as either without convincement, how can force be lawful? But some are ready to cry out, what shall then be don to blasphemie? Them I would first exhort not thus to terrifie and pose the people with a Greek word: but to teach them better what it is; being a most usual and common word in that language to signifie any slander, any malitious or evil speaking, whether against God or man or any thing to good belonging: blasphemie or evil speaking against God malitiously, is far from conscience in religion; according to that of *Marc 9. 39. there is none who doth a powerfull work in my name, and can likely speak evil of me.* If this suffice not, I referre them to that prudent and well deliberated act *August 9.* 1650; where the Parlament defines blasphemie against God, as far as it is a crime belonging to civil judicature, *pleniùs ac meliùs Chrysippo & Crantore;*[8] in plane English more warily, more judiciously, more orthodoxally then twice thir number of divines have don in many a prolix volume: although in all likelihood they whose whole studie and profession these things are should be most intelligent and authentic therin, as they are for the most part, yet neither they nor these unnerring always or infallible. But we shall not carrie it thus; another Greek apparition stands in our way, *heresie* and *heretic*; in like manner also rail'd at to the people as in a tongue unknown. They should first interpret to them, that heresie, by what it signifies in that language, is no word of evil note; meaning only the choise or following of any opinion good or bad in religion or any other learning: and thus not only in heathen authors, but in the New testament it self without censure or blame. *Acts 15. 5. certain of the heresie of the Pharises which beleevd,* and 26. 5. *after the exactest heresie of our religion I livd a Pharise.* In which sense Presbyterian or Independent may without reproach be calld a heresie. Where it is mentioned with

_____

8. So Horace (*Epistles* I, ii, 4) upholds Homer's poems as 'better and more complete' guides than either the Stoic Chrysippus or the Academic Crantor.

blame, it seems to differ little from schism 1 *Cor.* 11. 18, 19. *I hear that there be schisms among you* &c. *for there must also heresies be among you* &c; though some who write of heresie after their own heads, would make it far worse than schism; whenas on the contrarie, schism signifies division, and in the worst sense; heresie, choise only of one opinion before another, which may bee without discord. In apostolic times therfore ere the scripture was written, heresie was a doctrin maintaind against the doctrin by them deliverd : which in these times can be no otherwise defin'd then a doctrin maintaind against the light, which we now only have, of the scripture. Seeing therfore that no man, no synod, no session of men, though calld the church, can judge definitively the sense of scripture to another mans conscience, which is well known to be a general maxim of the Protestant religion, it follows planely, that he who holds in religion that beleef or those opinions which to his conscience and utmost understanding appeer with most evidence or probabilitie in the scripture, though to others he seem erroneous, can no more be justly censur'd for a heretic then his censurers; who do but the same thing themselves while they censure him for so doing. For ask them, or any Protestant, which hath most autoritie, the church or the scripture? they will answer, doubtless, that the scripture: and what hath most autoritie, that no doubt but they will confess is to be followd. He then who to his best apprehension follows the scripture, though against any point of doctrine by the whole church receivd, is not the heretic; but he who follows the church against his conscience and perswasion grounded on the scripture. To make this yet more undeniable, I shall only borrow a plane similie, the same which our own writers, when they would demonstrate planest that we rightly preferre the scripture before the church, use frequently against the Papist in this manner. As the Samaritans beleevd Christ, first for the womans word, but next and much rather for his own,[9] so we the scripture; first on the churches word, but afterwards and much more for its own, as the word of God; yea the church it

----

9. John 4:7 ff.

self we beleeve then for the scripture. The inference of it self follows: if by the Protestant doctrine we beleeve the scripture not for the churches saying, but for its own as the word of God, then ought we to beleeve what in our conscience we apprehend the scripture to say, though the visible church with all her doctors gainsay; and being taught to beleeve them only for the scripture, they who so do are not heretics, but the best protestants: and by their opinions, whatever they be, can hurt no protestant, whose rule is not to receive them but from the scripture: which to interpret convincingly to his own conscience none is able but himself guided by the Holy Spirit; and not so guided, none then he to himself can be a worse deceiver. To protestants therfore whose common rule and touchstone is the scripture, nothing can with more conscience, more equitie, nothing more protestantly can be permitted then a free and lawful debate at all times by writing, conference or disputation of what opinion soever, disputable by scripture: concluding, that no man in religion is properly a heretic at this day, but he who maintains traditions or opinions not probable by scripture; who, for aught I know, is the papist only; he the only heretic, who counts all heretics but himself. Such as these, indeed, were capitally punishd by the law of *Moses*, as the only true heretics, idolaters, plane and open deserters of God and his known law:[10] but in the gospel such are punished by excommunion only. *Tit. 3. 10. an heretic, after the first and second admonition, reject.* But they who think not this heavie anough and understand not that dreadfull aw and spiritual efficacie which the apostle hath expressed so highly to be in church-discipline, 2 *Cor.* 10. [4 ff.]. of which anon, and think weakly that the church of God cannot long subsist but in a bodilie fear, for want of other prooff will needs wrest that place of S. *Paul Rom.* 13. [1 ff.]. to set up civil inquisition, and give power to the magistrate both of civil judgment and punishment in causes ecclesiastical. But let us see with what strength of argument. *Let every soul be subject to the higher powers.*[11] First, how prove they that the apostle means other powers then such as they to

---

10. e.g. Exodus 32:22 ff., etc.

11. Romans 13:1 ff.; also discussed above, pp. 261 ff.

whom he writes were then under; who medld not at all in ecclesiasticall causes, unless as tyrants and persecuters; and from them, I hope, they will not derive either the right of magistrates to judge in spiritual things, or the dutie of such our obedience. How prove they next, that he intitles them here to spiritual causes, from whom he witheld, as much as in him lay, the judging of civil; 1 *Cor.* 6. 1, &c. If he himself appeald to *Cesar,* it was to judge his innocence, not his religion. *For rulers are not a terror to good works, but to the evil;* then are they not a terror to conscience, which is the rule or judge of good works grounded on the scripture. But heresie, they say, is reck'nd among evil works *Gal. 5.* 20: as if all evil works were to be punished by the magistrate; wherof this place, thir own citation, reck'ns up besides heresie a sufficient number to confute them; *uncleanness, wantonness, enmitie, strife, emulations, animosities, contentions, envyings;* all which are far more *manifest* to be judgd by him then heresie, as they define it; and yet I suppose they will not subject these evil works nor many more such like to his cognisance and punishment. *Wilt thou then not be affraid of the power? do that which is good and thou shalt have praise of the same.* This shews that religious matters are not here meant; wherin from the power here spoken of they could have no praise. *For he is the minister of God to thee for good;*[12] true; but in that office and to that end and by those means which in this place must be cleerly found, if from this place they intend to argue. And how for thy good by forcing, oppressing and insnaring thy conscience? Many are the ministers of God, and thir offices no less different then many; none more different then state and church-government. Who seeks to govern both must needs be worse then any lord prelat or church-pluralist:[13] for he in his own facultie and profession, the other not in his own and for the most part not throughly understood makes himself supream lord or pope of the church as far as his civil jurisdiction stretches, and all the ministers of God therin, his ministers, or his curates rather in the function onely, not in the government: while he himself assumes to

---

12. Romans 13 : 3–4.
13. As above, p. 229, Note 110.

rule by civil power things to be rul'd only by spiritual: when as this very chapter v. 6 appointing him his peculiar office, which requires utmost attendance, forbids him this worse then church-plurality from that full and waightie charge, wherein alone he is *the minister of God, attending continually on this very thing.* To little purpose will they here instance *Moses,* who did all by immediate divine direction, no nor yet *Asa, Jehosaphat,* or *Josia,*[14] who both might when they pleasd receive answer from God, and had a commonwealth by him deliverd them, incorporated with a national church exercis'd more in bodily then in spiritual worship, so as that the church might be calld a commonwealth and the whole commonwealth a church: nothing of which can be said of Christianitie, deliverd without the help of magistrates, yea in the midst of thir opposition; how little then with any reference to them or mention of them, save onely of our obedience to thir civil laws, as they countnance good and deterr evil: which is the proper work of the magistrate, following in the same verse, and shews distinctly wherin he is the minister of God, *a revenger to execute wrath on him that doth evil.* But we must first know who it is that doth evil: the heretic they say among the first. Let it be known then certainly who is a heretic: and that he who holds opinions in religion professdly from tradition or his own inventions and not from Scripture but rather against it, is the only heretic; and yet though such, not alwaies punishable by the magistrate, unless he do evil against a civil Law, properly so calld, hath been already prov'd without need of repetition. *But if thou do that which is evil, be affraid.*[15] To do by scripture and the gospel according to conscience is not to do evil; if we therof ought not to be affraid, he ought not by his judging to give cause; causes therfore of Religion are not here meant. *For he beareth not the sword in vain.* Yes altogether in vain, if it smite he knows not what; if that for heresie which not the church it self, much less he, can determine absolutely to be so; if truth for error, being himself so often fallible, he bears the

14. The restorers of worship in accordance with Mosaic precepts (2 Chronicles 14, 19, and 34).

15. Romans 13:4.

sword not in vain only, but unjustly and to evil. *Be subject no*
only for wrath, but for conscience sake: how for sake against
conscience? By all these reasons it appeers planely that the
apostle in this place gives no judgment or coercive power to
magistrates, neither to those then nor these now in matters of
religion; and exhorts us no otherwise then he exhorted those
Romans. It hath now twice befaln me to assert, through God
assistance, this most wrested and vexd place of scripture; hereto
fore against *Salmasius* and regal tyranie over the state;[16] now
against *Erastus* and state-tyranie over the church.[17] If from such
uncertain or rather such improbable grounds as these they endue
magistracie with spiritual judgment, they may as well invest him
in the same spiritual kinde with power of utmost punishment
excommunication; and then turn spiritual into corporal, as no
worse authors did then *Chrysostom*, *Jerom* and *Austin*, whom
Eramus and others in thir notes on the New Testament have cited
to interpret that *cutting off* which S. *Paul* wishd to them who had
brought back the Galatians to circumcision, no less then the
amercement of thir whole virilitie;[18] and *Grotius* addes that thi
concising punishment of circumcisers became a penal law then
upon among the *Visigothes*:[19] a dangerous example of beginning
in the spirit to end so in the flesh: wheras that cutting of
much likelier seems meant a cutting off from the church, no
unusually so termd in scripture, and a zealous imprecation, no
a command. But I have mentiond this passage to shew how
absurd they often prove who have not learnd to distinguish

16. The first *Defence* against Salmasius (see the Introduction
above, p. 34) explicated Romans 13:1 ff. in a fashion similar to the
discussion in *The Tenure* (see Note 11).

17. The German theologian Thomas Erastus (1524–83) upheld the
supremacy of civil authority in ecclesiastical matters.

18. Erasmus in 1522 summarized several interpretations of Gala
tians 5:12 ('I would that they were even *cut off* which trouble you'
as ventured by St. Augustine ('Austin') and others. The interpretation
ranged from excommunication to castration (!).

19. Grotius (cf. above, p. 68, Note 4) in quoting the views of St
Jerome and St. John Chrysostom mentioned also that the Visigoth
punished apostasy by mutilation.

rightly between civil power and ecclesiastical. How many persecutions then, imprisonments, banishments, penalties and
stripes; how much bloodshed have the forcers of conscience to
answer for, and protestants rather then papists! For the papist,
judging by his principles, punishes them who beleeve not as
the church beleevs though against the scripture: but the protestant, teaching every one to beleeve the scripture though
against the church, counts heretical and persecutes, against his
own principles, them who in any particular so beleeve as he
in general teaches them; them who most honor and beleeve
divine scripture, but not against it any humane interpretation
though universal; them who interpret scripture only to themselves, which by his own position none but they to themselves
can interpret; them who use the scripture no otherwise by his
own doctrine to thir edification, then he himself uses it to thir
punishing: and so whom his doctrine acknowledges a true
beleever, his discipline persecutes as a heretic. The papist exacts
our beleef as to the church due above scripture; and by the
church, which is the whole people of God, understands the
pope, the general councels prelatical only and the surnam'd
fathers: but the forcing protestant though he deny such beleef
to any church whatsoever, yet takes it to himself and his
teachers, of far less autorite then to be calld the church and
above scripture beleevd; which renders his practice both contrarie to his beleef, and far worse then that beleef which he
condemns in the papist. By all which well considerd, the more
he professes to be a true protestant, the more he hath to answer
for his persecuting then a papist. No protestant therfore of
what sect soever following scripture only, which is the common
sect wherin they all agree, and the granted rule of everie mans
conscience to himself, ought, by the common doctrine of protestants, to be forc'd or molested for religion. But as for poperie
and idolatrie, why they also may not hence plead to be tolerated, I have much less to say. Their religion the more considerd,
the less can be acknowledgd a religion; but a Roman principalitie rather, endevouring to keep up her old universal
dominion under a new name and meer shaddow of a catholic
religion; being indeed more rightly nam'd a catholic heresie

against the scripture; supported mainly by a civil, and, except in *Rome*, by a forein power: justly therfore to be suspected, not tolerated by the magistrate of another countrey. Besides, of an implicit faith, which they profêss, the conscience also becoms implicit; and so by voluntarie servitude to mans law, forfets her Christian libertie. Who then can plead for such a conscience as being implicitly enthrald to man instead of God, almost becoms no conscience, as the will not free, becoms no will. Nevertheless if they ought not to be tolerated, it is for just reason of state more then of religion; which they who force though professing to be protestants, deserve as little to be tolerated themselves, being no less guiltie of poperie in the most popish point. Lastly, for idolatrie, who knows it not to be evidently against all scripture both of the Old and New Testament, and therfore a true heresie, or rather an impietie; wherin a right conscience can have naught to do; and the works therof so manifest, that a magistrate can hardly err in prohibiting and quite removing at least the publick and scandalous use therof.

From the riddance of these objections I proceed yet to another reason why it is unlawfull for the civil magistrate to use force in matters of religion; which is, because to judge in those things, though we should grant him able, which is prov'd he is not, yet as a civil magistrate he hath no right. Christ hath a government of his own, sufficient of it self to all his ends and purposes in governing his church; but much different from that of the civil magistrate; and the difference in this verie thing principally consists, that it governs not by outward force, and that for two reasons. First because it deals only with the inward man and his actions, which are all spiritual and to outward force not lyable: secondly to shew us the divine excellence of his spirituall kingdom, able without worldly force to subdue all the powers and kingdoms of this world, which are upheld by outward force only. That the inward man is nothing els but the inward part of man, his understanding and his will, and that his actions thence proceeding, yet not simply thence but from the work of divine grace upon them, are the whole matter of religion under the gospel, will appeer planely by considering what that religion is; whence we shall perceive yet more planely that it cannot be forc'd. What evangelic religion is, is told in two words, faith and charitie; or beleef and practise.[20] That both these flow either the one from the understanding, the other from the will, or both jointly from both, once indeed naturally free, but now only as they are regenerat and wrought on by divine grace, is in part evident to common sense and principles unquestiond, the rest by scripture: concerning our beleef, *Mat.* 16. 17. *flesh and blood hath not reveald it unto thee, but my father which is in heaven*: concerning our practise, as it is religious and not meerly civil, *Gal.* 5. 22, 23 and other places declare it to be the fruit of the spirit only. Nay our whole practical dutie in religion is contained in charitie, or the love of God and our neighbour, no way to be forc'd, yet the fulfilling of the whole law;[21] that is to say, our whole practise in religion. If then both our beleef and practise, which comprehend our whole religion, flow from faculties of the inward man, free and unconstrainable of themselves by nature, and our practise not only from faculties endu'd with freedom, but from love and charitie besides, incapable of force, and all these things by transgression lost, but renewd and regenerated in us by the power and gift of God alone, how can such religion as this admit of force from man, or force be any way appli'd to such religion, especially under the free offer of grace in the gospel, but it must forthwith frustrate and make of no effect both the religion and the gospel? And that to compell outward profession, which they will say perhaps ought to be compelld though inward religion cannot, is to compell hypocrisie not to advance religion, shall yet, though of it self cleer anough, be ere the conclusion further manifest. The other reason why Christ rejects outward force in the government of his church, is, as I said before, to shew us the divine excellence of his spiritual kingdom, able without worldly force to subdue all the powers and kingdoms of this world, which are upheld by outward force only: by which to uphold religion otherwise then to defend

---

20. Cf. Donne: 'love God, and love thy Neighbour, that is, faith and works' (*Sermons*, ed. E. M. Simpson and G. R. Potter, Berkeley, 1955, II, 256).

21. Cf. Romans 13:10; *Paradise Lost*, XII, 403-4.

the religious from outward violence, is no service to Christ or his kingdom, but rather a disparagement, and degrades it from a divine and spiritual kingdom to a kingdom of this world : which he denies it to be, – because it needs not force to confirm it : *Joh.* 18. 36. *if my kingdom were of this world, then would my servants fight, that I should not be delivered to the Jewes.* This proves the kingdom of Christ not governed by outward force; as being none of this world, whose kingdoms are maintained all by force onely : and yet disproves not that a Christian commonwealth may defend it self against outward force in the cause of religion as well as in any other; though Christ himself, coming purposely to dye for us, would not be so defended. 1 *Cor.* 1. 27. *God hath chosen the weak things of the world to confound the things which are mighty.* Then surely he hath not chosen the force of this world to subdue conscience and conscientious men, who in this world are counted weakest; but rather conscience, as being weakest, to subdue and regulate force, his adversarie, not his aide or instrument in governing the church. 2 *Cor.* 10. 3, 4, 5, 6. *for though we walk in the flesh, we do not warre after the flesh: for the weapons of our warfare are not carnal; but mightie through God to the pulling down of strong holds; casting down imaginations and everie high thing that exalts it self against the knowledge of God; and bringing into captivitie everie thought to the obedience of Christ: and having in a readiness to aveng all disobedience.* It is evident by the first and second verses of this chapter, that the apostle here speaks of that spiritual power by which Christ governs his church, how allsufficient it is, how powerful to reach the conscience and the inward man with whom it chiefly deals and whom no power els can deal with. In comparison of which as it is here thus magnificently describ'd, how uneffectual and weak is outward force with all her boistrous tooles, to the shame of those Christians and especially those churchmen, who to the exercising of church discipline never cease calling on the civil magistrate to interpose his fleshlie force; an argument that all true ministerial and spiritual power is dead within them : who think the gospel, which both began and spread over the whole world for above three hundred years

nder heathen and persecuting emperors, cannot stand or con-
inue, supported by the same divine presence and protection
o the worlds end, much easier under the defensive favor onely
f a Christian magistrate, unless it be enacted and settled, as
hey call it, by the state, a statute or a state-religion: and
nderstand not that the church itself cannot, much less the state,
ettle or impose one tittle of religion upon our obedience im-
licit, but can only recommend or propound it to our free
nd conscientious examination: unless they mean to set the
tate higher then the church in religion, and with a grosse
ontradiction give to the state in thir settling petition that com-
nand of our implicit beleef, which they deny in thir setled
onfession both to the state and to the church. Let them cease
hen to importune and interrupt the magistrate from attending
o his own charge in civil and moral things, the settling of
hings just, things honest, the defence of things religious settled
y the churches within themselves; and the repressing of thir
ontraries determinable by the common light of nature; which
s not to constrain or to repress religion, probable by scripture,
ut the violaters and persecuters therof: of all which things
e hath anough and more then anough to do, left yet undon;
or which the land groans and justice goes to wrack the while:
et him also forbear force where he hath no right to judge;
or the conscience is not his province: least a worse *woe* arrive
im, for worse offending, then was denounc'd by our Saviour
Matt. 23. 23. against the Pharises: ye have forc'd the conscience,
which was not to be forc'd; but judgment and mercy ye have
not executed: this ye should have don, and the other let alone.
And since it is the councel and set purpose of God in the gospel
by spiritual means which are counted weak, to overcom all
power which resists him;[22] let them not go about to do that by
worldly strength which he hath decreed to do by those means
which the world counts weakness, least they be again obnoxious
to that saying which in another place is also written of the
Pharises, *Luke* 7. 30. *that they frustrated the councel of God.*
The main plea is, and urgd with much vehemence to thir imita-

---

22. Cf. *Paradise Lost*, XII, 567–9.

tion, that the kings of *Juda*, as I touched before,[23] and especially *Josia* both judged and us'd force in religion. 2 *Chr.* 34. 33. *h made all that were present in Israel to serve the Lord thir God* an argument, if it be well weighed, worse then that us'd by the false prophet *Shemaia* to the high priest, that in imitation o *Jehoiada* he ought to put *Jeremie* in the stocks, *Jer.* 29. 24, 26 &c. for which he receivd his due denouncement from God. But to this besides I return a threefold answer : first, that the state of religion under the gospel is far differing from what it was under the law : then was the state of rigor, childhood, bondage and works, to all which force was not unbefitting; now i the state of grace, manhood, freedom and faith; to all which belongs willingness and reason, not force : the law was then written on tables of stone, and to be performd according to the letter, willingly or unwillingly; the gospel, our new covnant upon the heart of every beleever, to be interpreted only by the sense of charitie and inward perswasion : the law had no distinct government or governors of church and commonwealth, but the Priests and Levites judg'd in all causes not ecclesiastical only but civil, *Deut.* 17. 8, &c. which under the gospel is for bidden to all church-ministers, as a thing which Christ thir master in his ministerie disclam'd *Luke* 12, 14; as a thing beneathe them 1 *Cor.* 6. 4; and by many of our statutes, as to them who have a peculiar and far differing government o thir own. If not, why different the governors? why not church ministers in state-affairs, as well as state-ministers in church affairs? If church and state shall be made one flesh again as under the law, let it be withall considerd, that God who then joind them hath now severd them; that which, he so ordaining was then a lawfull conjunction, to such on either side as join again what he hath severd, would be nothing now but thir own presumptuous fornication. Secondly, the kings of *Juda* and those magistrates under the law might have recours, as I said before, to divine inspiration; which our magistrates under the gospel have not, more then to the same spirit, which those whom they force have oft times in greater measure then them

---

23. Above, p. 307.

selves: and so, instead of forcing the Christian, they force the Holy Ghost; and, against that wise forewarning of *Gamaliel*,[24] fight against God. Thirdly, those kings and magistrates us'd force in such things only as were undoubtedly known and forbidden in the law of *Moses*, idolatrie and direct apostacie from that national and strict enjoind worship of God; wherof the corporal punishment was by himself expressly set down: but magistrates under the gospel, our free, elective and rational worship, are most commonly busiest to force those things which in the gospel are either left free, nay somtimes abolishd when by them compelld, or els controverted equally by writers on both sides, and somtimes with odds on that side which is against them. By which means they either punish that which they ought to favor and protect, or that with corporal punishment and of thir own inventing, which not they but the church hath receivd command to chastise with a spiritual rod only. Yet some are so eager in thir zeal of forcing, that they refuse not to descend at length to the utmost shift of that parabolical prooff *Luke* 14. 16, &c. *compell them to come in*; therfore magistrates may compell in religion. As if a parable were to be straind through every word or phrase, and not expounded by the general scope therof: which is no other here then the earnest expression of Gods displeasure on those recusant Jewes, and his purpose to preferre the gentiles on any terms before them; expressd here by the word *compell*. But how compells he? doubtless no otherwise then he draws, without which no man can come to him, *Joh.* 6. 44: and that is by the inward perswasive motions of his spirit and by his ministers; not by the outward compulsions of a magistrate or his officers. The true people of Christ, as is foretold *Psal.* 110. 3, *are a willing people in the day of his power*; then much more now when he rules all things by outward weakness, that both his inward power and their sinceritie may the more appeer. *God loveth a chearfull giver*: then certainly is not pleasd with an unchearfull

---

24. The advice was meant to dissuade the Council of the High Priest from restraining the apostles: 'for if ... this work be of men, it will come to nought: but if it be of God, ye cannot overthrow it' (Acts 5:38–9).

worshiper; as the verie words declare of his evangelical invitations. *Esa. 55. 1. ho, everie one that thirsteth, come. Joh. 7. 37. if any man thirst. Rev. 3. 18. I counsel thee.* and 22, 17. *whosoever will, let him take the water of life freely.* And in that grand commission of preaching to invite all nations *Marc* 16. 16, as the reward of them who come, so the penaltie of them who come not is only spiritual. But they bring now some reason with thir force, which must not pass unanswered; that the church of *Thyatira* was blam'd *Rev.* 2. 20 for suffering the false *prophetess to teach and to seduce.* I answer, that seducement is to be hinderd by fit and proper means ordaind in church-discipline; by instant and powerfull demonstration to the contrarie; by opposing truth to error, no unequal match; truth the strong to error the weak though slie and shifting. Force is no honest confutation; but uneffectual, and for the most part unsuccessfull, oft times fatal to them who use it : sound doctrine diligently and duely taught, is of herself both sufficient, and of herself (if some secret judgment of God hinder not) alwaies prevalent against seducers. This the *Thyatirians* had neglected, suffering, against Church-discipline, that woman to teach and seduce among them : civil force they had not then in thir power; being the Christian part only of that citie, and then especially under one of those ten great persecutions, wherof this the second was raisd by *Domitian* : [25] force therfore in these matters could not be requir'd of them, who were then under force themselves.

I have shewn that the civil power hath neither right nor can do right by forcing religious things : I will now shew the wrong it doth; by violating the fundamental privilege of the gospel, the new-birthright of everie true beleever, Christian libertie. *2 Cor. 3. 17. where the spirit of the Lord is, there is libertie. Gal. 4. 26. Jerusalem which is above, is free; which is the mother of us all.* and 31. *we are not children of the bondwoman but of the free.* It will be sufficient in this place to say no more of Christian libertie, then that it sets us free not only from the bondage of those ceremonies, but also from the forcible imposi-

---

25. Roman emperor, A.D. 81–96.

tion of those circumstances, place and time in the worship of God: which though by him commanded in the old law, yet in respect of that veritie and freedom which is evangelical, S. Paul comprehends both kindes alike, that is to say, both ceremonie and circumstance, under one and the same contemtuous name of *weak and beggarly rudiments, Gal.* 4. 3. 9, 10. *Col.* 2. 8. with 16: conformable to what our Saviour himself taught *John* 4. 21, 23. *neither in this mountain nor yet at Jerusalem. In spirit and in truth: for the father seeketh such to worship him*; that is to say, not only sincere of heart, for such he sought ever, but also, as the words here chiefly import, not compelld to place, and by the same reason, not to any set time; as his apostle by the same spirit hath taught us *Rom.* 14. 6, &c. *one man esteemeth one day above another, another* &c. *Gal.* 4. 10. *Ye observe dayes, and moonths* &c. *Coloss.* 2. 16. These and other such places of scripture the best and learnedest reformed writers have thought evident anough to instruct us in our freedom not only from ceremonies but from those circumstances also, though impos'd with a confident perswasion of moralitie in them, which they hold impossible to be in place or time. By what warrant then our opinions and practises herin are of late turnd quite against all other Protestants, and that which is to them orthodoxal, to us become scandalous and punishable by statute, I wish were once again better considerd; if we mean not to proclame a schism in this point from the best and most reformed churches abroad. They who would seem more knowing, confess that these things are indifferent, but for that very cause by the magistrate may be commanded. As if God of his special grace in the gospel had to this end freed us from his own commandments in these things, that our freedom should subject us to a more greevous yoke, the commandments of men. As well may the magistrate call that common or unclean which God hath cleansed, forbidden to S. *Peter Acts* 10. 15; as well may he loos'n that which God hath strait'nd, or strait'n that which God hath loos'nd, as he may injoin those things in religion which God hath left free, and lay on that yoke which God hath taken off. For he hath not only given us this gift as a special privilege and excellence of the free gospel above the servile law, but strictly also hath commanded us to keep it and enjoy it. *Gal. 5. 13. you are calld to libertie. 1 Cor. 7. 23. be not made the servants of men. Gal. 5. 14. stand fast therfore in the libertie wherwith Christ hath made us free; and be not intangl'd again with the yoke of bondage.* Neither is this a meer command, but for the most part in these forecited places accompanied with the verie waightiest and inmost reasons of Christian religion : *Rom.* 14. 9, 10. *for to this end Christ both dy'd and rose and reviv'd, that he might be Lord both of the dead and living. But why doest thou judge thy brother? &c.* how presum'st thou to be his lord, to be whose only Lord, at least in these things, Christ both dy'd and rose and livd again ? *We shall all stand before the judgment seat of Christ;* why then dost thou not only judge, but persecute in these things for which we are to be accountable to the tribunal of Christ only, our Lord and lawgiver? 1 *Cor.* 7. 23. *ye are bought with a price; be not made the servants of men;* some trivial price belike, and for some frivolous pretences paid in their opinion, if bought and by him redeemd who is God from what was once the service of God, we shall be enthrald again and forc'd by men to what now is but the service of men. *Gal.* 4. 31, with 5. 1. *we are not children of the bond-woman &c. stand fast therfore &c. Col.* 2. 8. *beware least any man spoil you, &c. after the rudiments of the world, and not after Christ.* Solid reasons wherof are continu'd through the whole chapter. *v.* 10. *ye are complete in him, which is the head of all principalitie and power:* not completed therfore or made the more religious by those ordinances of civil power, from which Christ thir head hath dischargd us; *blotting out the handwriting of ordinances, that was against us, which was contrarie to us; and took it out of the way, nailing it to his cross, v.* 14: blotting out ordinances written by God himself, much more those so boldly written over again by men, ordinances which were against us, that is, against our frailtie, much more those which are against our conscience. *Let no man therfore judge you in respect of &c. v.* 16. *Gal.* 4. 3, &c. *even so we, when we were children, were in bondage under the rudiments of the world: but when the fullness of time was come, God sent forth his son &c. to redeem them that were under the law, that we*

*ight receive the adoption of sons &c. Wherfore thou art no
*ore a servant, but a son &c. But now &c. how turn ye again
* the weak and beggarly rudiments, wherunto ye desire again
* be in bondage? ye observe dayes &c.* Hence it planely appeers,
hat if we be not free we are not sons, but still servants un-
*a*dopted; and if we turn again to those weak and beggarly rudi-
*m*ents, we are not free; yea though willingly and with a mis-
*g*uided conscience we desire to be in bondage to them; how
*m*uch more then if unwillingly and against our conscience? Ill
*w*as our condition chang'd from legal to evangelical, and small
*a*dvantage gotten by the gospel, if for the spirit of adoption to
*f*reedom, promisd us, we receive again the spirit of bondage
*t*o fear; if our fear which was then servile towards God only,
*m*ust be now servile in religion towards men : strange also and
*p*reposterous fear, if when and wherin it hath attaind by the
*r*edemption of our Saviour to be filial only towards God, it
*m*ust be now servile towards the magistrate. Who by subjecting
*u*s to his punishment in these things, brings back into religion
*t*hat law of terror and satisfaction, belonging now only to civil
*c*rimes; and thereby in effect abolishes the gospel by establish-
*in*g again the law to a far worse yoke of servitude upon us then
*b*efore. It will therfore not misbecome the meanest Christian
*t*o put in minde Christian magistrates, and so much the more
*fr*eely by how much the more they desire to be thought Christ-
*ia*n (for they will be thereby, as they ought to be in these things,
*t*he more our brethren and the less our lords) that they meddle
*n*ot rashly with Christian libertie, the birthright and outward
*te*stimonie of our adoption : least while they little think it, nay
*t*hink they do God service, they themselves like the sons of that
*b*ondwoman be found persecuting them who are freeborne of
*th*e spirit; and by a sacrilege of not the least aggravation bereav-
*in*g them of that sacred libertie which our Saviour with his own
*b*lood purchas'd for them.

A fourth reason why the magistrate ought not to use force in
*r*eligion, I bring from the consideration of all those ends which
*h*e can likely pretend to the interposing of his force therin :
*a*nd those hardly can be other then first the glorie of God;
*n*ext either the spiritual good of them whom he forces, or the

temporal punishment of their scandal to others. As for th
promoting of Gods glory, none, I think, will say that his glori
ought to be promoted in religious things by unwarrantabl
means, much less by means contrarie to what he hath com
manded. That outward force is such, and that Gods glory i
the whole administration of the gospel according to his own
will and councel ought to be fulfilld by weakness, at least s
refuted, not by force; or if by force, inward and spiritual, no
outward and corporeal, is already prov'd at large. That outwar
force cannot tend to the good of him who is forc'd in religion
is unquestionable. For in religion what ever we do under th
gospel, we ought to be therof perswaded without scruple; an
are justified by the faith we have, not by the work we d
Rom. 14. 5. *Let every man be fully perswaded in his own min*
The other reason which follows necessarily, is obvious *Gal.*
16, and in many other places of St. *Paul*, as the groundwork an
foundation of the whole gospel, that we are *justified by th
faith of Christ, and not by the works of the law*; if not by th
works of Gods law, how then by the injunctions of mans law
Surely force cannot work perswasion, which is faith; canno
therfore justifie nor pacifie the conscience; and that whic
justifies not in the gospel, condemns; is not only not good, bu
sinfull to do. *Rom.* 14. 23. *Whatsoever is not of faith, is sir*
It concerns the magistrate then to take heed how he forces i
religion conscientious men: least by compelling them to d
that wherof they cannot be perswaded, that wherin they canno
finde themselves justified, but by thir own consciences cor
demnd, instead of aiming at thir spiritual good, he force ther
to do evil; and while he thinks himself *Asa, Josia, Nehemia,* h
be found *Jeroboam*, who causd Israel to sin;[26] and thereb
draw upon his own head all those sins and shipwracks of im
plicit faith and conformitie, which he hath forc'd, and all th
wounds given to those *little ones*, whom to offend he wi
finde worse one day then that violent drowning mentione
Matt. 18. 6. Lastly as a preface to force, it is the usual pretenc
that although tender consciences shall be tolerated, yet scanda

26. King *Jeroboam* was punished for introducing idolatrou
worship (1 Kings 12:26 ff. and 14:10 ff.).

thereby given shall not be unpunishd, prophane and licentious men shall not be encourag'd to neglect the performance of religious and holy duties by color of any law giving libertie to tender consciences. By which contrivance the way lies ready open to them heerafter who may be so minded, to take away by little and little, that liberty which Christ and his gospel, not any magistrate, hath right to give: though this kinde of his giving be but to give with one hand and take away with the other, which is a deluding not a giving. As for scandals, if any man be offended at the conscientious liberty of another, it is a taken scandal not a given. To heal one conscience we must not wound another: and men must be exhorted to beware of scandals in Christian libertie, not forc'd by the magistrate; least while he goes about to take away the scandal, which is uncertain whether given or taken, he take away our liberty, which is the certain and the sacred gift of God, neither to be touchd by him, nor to be parted with by us. None more cautious of giving scandal then St. *Paul*. Yet while he made himself *servant to all*, that he *might gain the more*, he made himself so of his own accord, was not made so by outward force, testifying at the same time that he *was free from all men*, 1 *Cor.* 9. 19: and therafter exhorts us also *Gal.* 5. 13. *ye were calld to libertie* &c. *but by love serve one another*: then not by force. As for that fear least prophane and licentious men should be encourag'd to omit the performance of religious and holy duties, how can that care belong to the civil magistrate, especially to his force? For if prophane and licentious persons must not neglect the performance of religious and holy duties, it implies, that such duties they can perform; which no Protestant will affirm. They who mean the outward performance, may so explane it; and it will then appeer yet more planely, that such performance of religious and holy duties especialy by prophane and licentious persons, is a dishonoring rather then a worshiping of God; and not only by him not requir'd but detested: *Prov.* 21. 27. *the sacrifice of the wicked is an abomination: how much more when he bringeth it with a wicked minde?* To compell therfore the prophane to things holy in his prophaneness, is all one under the gospel, as to have compelld the unclean to sacrifise in his uncleanness under the law. And I adde withall, that to compell the licentious in his licentiousness, and the conscientious against his conscience, coms all to one; tends not to the honor of God, but to the multiplying and the aggravating of sin to them both. We read not that Christ ever exercis'd force but once; and that was to drive prophane ones out of his temple, not to force them in:[27] and if thir beeing there was an offence, we finde by many other scriptures that thir praying there was an abomination: and yet to the Jewish law that nation, as a servant, was oblig'd, but to the gospel each person is left voluntarie, calld only, as a son, by the preaching of the word; not to be driven in by edicts and force of arms. For if by the apostle, *Rom.* 12. 1, we are *beseechd as brethren by the mercies of God to present our bodies a living sacrifice, holy, acceptable to God, which is our reasonable service* or worship, then is no man to be forc'd by the compulsive laws of men to present his body a dead sacrifice and so under the gospel most unholy and unacceptable, because it is his unreasonable service, that is to say, not only unwilling but unconscionable. But if prophane and licentious persons may not omit the performance of holy duties, why may they not partake of holy things? why are they prohibited the Lords supper; since both the one and the other action may be outward; and outward performance of dutie may attain at least an outward participation of benefit? The church denying them that communion of grace and thanksgiving, as it justly doth, why doth the magistrate compell them to the union of performing that which they neither truly can, being themselves unholy, and to do seemingly is both hatefull to God, and perhaps no less dangerous to perform holie duties irreligiously then to receive holy signes or sacraments unworthily. All prophane and licentious men, so known, can be considerd but either so without the church as never yet within it, or departed thence of thir own accord, or excommunicate: if never yet within the church whom the apostle, and so consequently the church have naught to do to judge, as he professes 1 *Cor.* 5. 12, then by what autoritie does the magistrate judge, or, which is worse, compell

27. John 2:14-16.

in relation to the church? if departed of his own accord, like that lost sheep *Luke* 15. 4, &c. the true church either with her own or any borrowd force worries him not in again, but rather in all charitable manner sends after him; and if she finde him, layes him gently on her shoulders; bears him, yea bears his burdens; his errors, his infirmities any way tolerable, *so fulfilling the law of Christ, Gal.* 6. 2: if excommunicate, whom the church hath bid go out, in whose name doth the magistrate compell to go in? The church indeed hinders none from hearing in her publick congregation, for the doors are open to all: nor excommunicates to destruction, but, as much as in her lies, to a final saving. Her meaning therfore must needs bee, that as her driving out brings on no outward penaltie, so no outward force or penaltie of an improper and only a destructive power should drive in again her infectious sheep; therfore sent out because infectious, and not driven in but with the danger not only of the whole and sound, but also of his own utter perishing. Since force neither instructs in religion nor begets repentance or amendment of life, but, on the contrarie, hardness of heart, formalitie, hypocrisie, and, as I said before, everie way increase of sin; more and more alienates the minde from a violent religion expelling out and compelling in, and reduces it to a condition like that which the *Britains* complain of in our storie, driven to and fro between the *Picts* and the sea.[28] If after excommunion he be found intractable, incurable, and will not hear the church, he becoms as one never yet within her pale, *a heathen or a publican, Mat.* 18. 17; not further to be judgd, no not by the magistrate, unless for civil causes; but left to the final sentence of that judge, whose coming shall be in flames of fire; that *Maran athà*,[29] 1 *Cor.* 16. 22; then which to him so left nothing can be more dreadful and ôfttimes to him particularly nothing more speedie, that is to say, the Lord cometh: In the mean while deliverd up to Satan, 1 *Cor.* 5. 5. 1 *Tim.* 1. 20.

---

28. The Britons had complained to the Roman consul Aetius, 'The barbarians drive us to the Sea, the Sea drives us to the barbarians; ... we perish, either by the Sword or by the Sea.' The story is related in Milton's *History of Britain*, Book III.

29. 'Our Lord, come' (in Aramaic).

that is, from the fould of Christ and kingdom of grace to the world again which is the kingdom of Satan; and as he was receivd *from darkness to light, and from the power of Satan to God, Acts* 26, 18, so now deliverd up again from light to darkness, and from God to the power of Satan; yet so as is in both places manifested, to the intent of saving him, brought sooner to contrition by spiritual then by any corporal severitie. But grant it belonging any way to the magistrate, that prophane and licentious persons omit not the performance of holy duties, which in them were odious to God even under the law, much more now under the gospel, yet ought his care both as a magistrate and a Christian, to be much more that conscience be not inwardly violated, then that licence in these things be made outwardly conformable: since his part is undoubtedly as a Christian, which puts him upon this office much more then as a magistrate, in all respects to have more care of the conscientious then of a prophane; and not for their sakes to take away (while they pretend to give) or to diminish the rightfull libertie of religious consciences.

On these four scriptural reasons as on a firm square this truth, the right of Christian and evangelic liberty, will stand immoveable against all those pretended consequences of license and confusion which for the most part men most licentious and confus'd themselves, or such as whose severitie would be wiser then divine wisdom, are ever aptest to object against the waies of God: as if God without them when he gave us this libertie, knew not of the worst which these men in thir arrogance pretend will follow: yet knowing all their worst, he gave us this liberty as by him judgd best. As to those magistrates who think it their work to settle religion, and those ministers or others, who so oft call upon them to do so, I trust, that having well considerd what hath bin here argu'd, neither they will continue in that intention, nor these in that expectation from them: when they shall finde that the settlement of religion belongs only to each particular church by perswasive and spiritual means within it self, and that the defence only of the church belongs to the magistrate. Had he once learnt not further to concern himself with church affairs, half his labor

might be spar'd, and the commonwealth better tended. To
which end, that which I premis'd in the beginning, and in due
place treated of more at large, I desire now concluding, that
they would consider seriously what religion is: and they will
find it to be in summe, both our beleef and our practise depending upon God only. That there can be no place then left for the
magistrate or his force in the settlement of religion, by appointing either what we shall beleeve in divine things or practise in
religious (neither of which things are in the power of man
either to perform himself or to enable others) I perswade me
in the Christian ingenuitie of all religious men, the more they
examin seriously, the more they will finde cleerly to be true:
and finde how false and deceivable that common saying is,
which is so much reli'd upon, that the Christian Magistrate is
custos utriusque tabulæ, keeper of both tables;[30] unless is meant
by keeper the defender only: neither can that maxim be maintaind by any prooff or argument which hath not in this discours
first or last bin refuted. For the two tables, or ten commande-
ments, teach our dutie to God and our neighbour from the
love of both; give magistrates no authoritie to force either:
they seek that from the judicial law; though on false grounds,
especially in the first table, as I have shewn; and both in first
and second execute that autoritie for the most part not according to Gods judicial laws but thir own. As for civil crimes and
of the outward man, which all are not, no not of those against
the second table, as that of coveting; in them what power they
have, they had from the beginning, long before *Moses* or the
two tables were in being. And whether they be not now as little
in being to be kept by any Christian as they are two legal
tables, remanes yet as undecided, as it is sure they never were
yet deliverd to the keeping of any Christian magistrate. But
of these things perhaps more some other time; what may serve
the present hath bin above discourst sufficiently out of the
scriptures: and to those produc'd might be added testimonies,
examples, experiences of all succeeding ages to these times
asserting this doctrine: but having herin the scripture so copious

30. The two versions of the ten commandments (see above, p. 150,
Note 81).

and so plane, we have all that can be properly calld true strength and nerve; the rest would be but pomp and incumbrance. Pomp and ostentation of reading is admir'd among the vulgar : but doubtless in matters of religion he is learnedest who is planest. The brevitie I use, not exceeding a small manual, will not therfore, I suppose, be thought the less considerable, unless with them perhaps who think that great books only can determin great matters. I rather chose the common rule, not to make much ado where less may serve. Which in controversies and those especially of religion, would make them less tedious, and by consequence read ofter, by many more, and with more benefit.

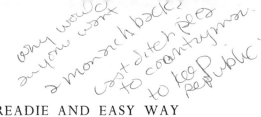

handwritten annotations: why would anyone want a monarch back? / last ditch plea to countrymen to keep republic

THE READIE AND EASY WAY
TO ESTABLISH A FREE COMMONWEALTH
(1660) *courageous*

Milton's plea shortly before the restoration of the monarchy (see above, pp. 32 ff.) is described on the title page as *The Readie & Easie Way to Establish a Free Commonwealth, and the Excellence herof compar'd with the inconveniences and dangers of readmitting kingship in this nation.*

First published in February (?) 1660, the treatise was amended within two months. The Columbia edition reprinted here provides the revised text (VI, 111-49, with textual notes in 359-67; ed. William Haller).]

ALTHOUGH since the writing of this treatise,[1] the face of things hath had some change, writs for new elections have bin recall'd, and the members at first chosen, readmitted from exclusion, yet not a little rejoicing to hear declar'd the resolution of those who are in power, tending to the establishment of a free Commonwealth, and to remove, if it be possible, this noxious humor of returning to bondage, instilld of late by som deceivers, and nourishd from bad principles and fals apprehensions among too many of the people, I thought best not to suppress what I had written, hoping that it may now be of much more use and concernment to be freely publishd, in the midst of our Elections to a free Parlament, or their sitting to consider freely of the Government; whom it behoves to have all things represented to them that may direct thir judgment therin; and I never read of any State, scarce of any tyrant grown so incurable, as to refuse counsel from any in a time of public deliberation; much less to be offended. If thir absolute determination be to enthrall

1. i.e. two months earlier, when the treatise was first published. Milton's warning of 'returning to bondage' is of course an allusion to the restoration of the monarchy – an imminent reality after the elections of 26 April 1660.

us, before so long a Lent of Servitude, they may permitt us a little Shroving-time first,[2] wherin to speak freely, and take our leaves of Libertie. And because in the former edition through haste, many faults escap'd, and many books were suddenly dispersd, ere the note to mend them could be sent, I took the opportunitie from this occasion to revise and somwhat to enlarge the whole discourse, especially that part which argues for a perpetual Senat. The treatise thus revis'd and enlarg'd, is as follows.

The Parliament of *England*, assisted by a great number of the people who appeerd and stuck to them faithfullest in defence of religion and thir civil liberties, judging kingship by long experience a government unnecessarie, burdensom and dangerous,[3] justly and magnanimously abolishd it; turning regal bondage into a free Commonwealth, to the admiration and terrour of our emulous neighbours. They took themselves not bound by the light of nature or religion, to any former covnant, from which the King himself by many forfeitures of a latter date or discoverie, and our own longer consideration theron had more & more unbound us, both to himself and his posteritie; as hath bin ever the justice and the prudence of all wise nations that have ejected tyrannie. They covnanted *to preserve the Kings person and autoritie in the preservation of the true religion and our liberties*;[4] not in his endeavoring to bring in upon our consciences a Popish religion,[5] upon our liberties thraldom, upon our lives destruction, by his occasioning, if not complotting, as was after discovered, the *Irish* massacre,[6] his fomenting and arming the rebellion, his covert leaguing with

---

2. Befòre the advent of Lent, Shrove Tuesday permitted amusements like carnivals etc.

3. The very words of the parliamentary resolution of February 1649 abolishing the monarchy.

4. From the Solemn League and Covenant of 1643.

5. Episcopacy.

6. While Charles I was not responsible for the massacres mounted by the Irish (also mentioned earlier, p. 254), he nevertheless endeavored to secure Irish military support.

the rebels against us, his refusing more then seaven times, pro-positions most just and necessarie to the true religion and our liberties, tenderd him by the Parlament both of *England* and *Scotland*.[7] They made not thir covnant concerning him with no difference between a king and a god, or promisd him as *Job* did to the Almightie, *to trust in him, though he slay us*:[8] they understood that the solemn ingagement, wherin we all forswore kingship, was no more a breach of the covnant, then the cov-nant was of the protestation before[9] but a faithful and prudent going on both in the words, well weighd, and in the true sense of the covnant, *without respect of persons*,[10] when we could not serve two contrary maisters, God and the king, or the king and that more supreme law, sworn in the first place to maintain, our safetie and our libertie. They knew the people of *England* to be a free people, themselves the representers of that freedom; & although many were excluded, & as many fled (so they pre-tended) from tumults to *Oxford*,[11] yet they were left a sufficient number to act in Parlament; therefor not bound by any statute of preceding Parlaments, but by the law of nature only, which is the only law of laws truly and properly to all mankinde fundamental; the beginning and the end of all Government; to which no Parlament or people that will throughly reforme, but may and must have recourse; as they had and must yet have in church reformation (if they throughly intend it) to evangelic rules; not to ecclesiastical canons, though never so ancient, so ratifi'd and established in the land by Statutes, which for the most part are meer positive laws, neither natural nor moral, & so by any Parlament for just and serious considerations, with-

---

7. The seven sets of propositions were submitted to Charles periodically from 1642 to 1648.

8. Job 13:15.

9. The 'Engagement' or oath of loyalty to the Commonwealth (October 1649), and the parliamentary protest against the levying of a Catholic army in Ireland (May 1641).

10. As before, Note 4.

11. Royalist members of both Houses whose Parliament was opened by Charles in Oxford in January 1644. But most Members stayed at Westminster.

out scruple to be at any time repeal'd. If others of thir number, in these things were under force, they were not, but under free conscience; if others were excluded by a power which they could not resist, they were not therefore to leave the helm of government in no hands, to discontinue thir care of the public peace and safetie, to desert the people in anarchie and confusion; no more then when so many of thir members left them, as made up in outward formalitie a more legal Parlament of three estates against them.[12] The best affected also and best principl'd of the people, stood not numbring or computing on which side were most voices in Parlament, but on which side appeerd to them most reason, most safetie, when the house divided upon main matters : what was well motiond and advis'd, they examind not whether fear or perswasion carried it in the vote; neither did they measure votes and counsels by the intentions of them that voted; knowing that intentions either are but guessd at, or not soon anough known; and although good, can neither make the deed such, nor prevent the consequence from being bad : suppose bad intentions in things otherwise welldon; what was welldon, was by them who so thought, not the less obey'd or followd in the state; since in the church, who had not rather follow *Iscariot* or *Simon* the magician,[13] though to covetous ends, preaching, then *Saul,* though in the uprightness of his heart persecuting the gospell ?[14] Safer they therefor judgd what they thought the better counsels, though carried on by some perhaps to bad ends, then the wors, by others, though endevord with best intentions : and yet they were not to learn that a greater number might be corrupt within the walls of a Parlament as well as of a citie; wherof in matters of neerest concernment all men will be judges; nor easily permitt, that the odds of voices in thir greatest councel, shall more endanger them by corrupt or credulous votes, then the odds of enemies by open assaults; judging that most voices ought not alwaies to prevail where main matters are in question; if others hence will

12. The 'estates' of bishops, lords, and commons, in the Parliament at Oxford (previous note).

13. i.e. Judas and Simon Magus (as above, p. 295, Note 101).

14. As Saul (St. Paul) did, before his conversion (Acts 22 : 3 ff.).

pretend to disturb all counsels, what is that to them who pretend not, but are in real danger; not they only so judging, but a great though not the greatest, number of thir chosen Patriots, who might be more in waight, then the others in number; there being in number little vertue, but by weight and measure wisdom working all things: and the dangers on either side they seriously thus waighd: from the treatie,[15] short fruits of long labours and seaven years warr; securitie for twenty years, if we can hold it; reformation in the church for three years: then put to shift again with our vanquishd maister. His justice, his honour, his conscience declar'd quite contrarie to ours; which would have furnishd him with many such evasions, as in a book entitl'd *an inquisition for blood*,[16] soon after were not conceald: bishops not totally remov'd, but left as it were in ambush, a reserve, with ordination in thir sole powr; thir lands alreadie sold, not to be alienated, but rented, and the sale of them call'd *sacrilege*; delinquents few of many brought to condigne punishment; accessories punishd;[17] the chief author, above pardon, though after utmost resistance, vanquish'd; not to give, but to receive laws; yet besought, treated with, and to be thankd for his gratious concessions, to be honourd, worshipd, glorifi'd. If this we swore to do, with what righteousness in the sight of God, with what assurance that we bring not by such an oath the whole sea of blood-guiltiness upon our own heads? If on the other side we preferr a free government, though for the present not obtain, yet all those suggested fears and difficulties, as the event will prove, easily overcome, we remain finally secure from the exasperated regal power, and out of

---

15. The 'most tardy and improper Treaty' of Newport (above, p. 278, Note 66), rejected by Parliament as having failed to provide the twenty years' control of the army and the minimum of three years' Presbyterian form of ecclesiastical government they had demanded of Charles. The 'seven years warr' covers the period 1642–9 as above, p. 264, Note 39).

16. By James Howell (1649), who argued that Charles was not bound by the Treaty of Newport since he had acted 'in his politic capacity'.

17. Strafford and Laud (see above, p. 103, Note 64).

snares; shall retain the best part of our libertie, which is our religion, and the civil part will be from these who deferr us, much more easily recoverd, being neither so suttle nor so awefull as a King reinthron'd. Nor were thir actions less both at home and abroad then might become the hopes of a glorious rising Commonwealth : nor were the expressions both of armie and people, whether in thir publick declarations or several writings other then such as testifi'd a spirit in this nation no less noble and well fitted to the liberty of a Commonwealth, then in the ancient *Greeks* or *Romans*. Nor was the heroic cause unsuccesfully defended to all Christendom against the tongue of a famous and thought invincible adversarie; nor the constancie and fortitude that so nobly vindicated our liberty, our victory at once against two the most prevailing usurpers over mankinde, superstition and tyrannie unpraisd or uncelebrated in a written monument, likely to outlive detraction, as it hath hitherto convinc'd or silenc'd not a few of our detractors, especially in parts abroad.[18] After our liberty and religion thus prosperously fought for, gaind and many years possessd, except in those unhappie interruptions, which God hath remov'd, now that nothing remains, but in all reason the certain hopes of a speedie and immediat settlement for ever in a firm and free Commonwealth, for this extolld and magnifi'd nation, regardless both of honour wonn or deliverances voutsaf't from heaven, to fall back or rather to creep back so poorly as it seems the multitude would to thir once abjur'd and detested thraldom of Kingship, to be our selves the slanderers of our own just and religious deeds, though don by som to covetous and ambitious ends, yet not therefor to be staind with their infamie, or they to asperse the integritie of others, and yet these now by revolting from the conscience of deeds welldon both in church and state, to throw away and forsake, or rather to betray a just and noble cause for the mixture of bad men who have ill manag'd and abus'd it (which had our fathers don heretofore, and on the same pretence deserted true religion, what had long ere this become of our gospel and all protestant reformation so much

18. The 'adversarie' is Salmasius; the 'monument', Milton's first *Defence* of 1651. See the account of Edward Phillips, below, p. 391.

intermixt with the avarice and ambition of some reformers?) and by thus relapsing, to verifie all the bitter predictions of our triumphing enemies, who will now think they wisely discernd and justly censur'd both us and all our actions as rash, rebellious, hypocritical and impious, not only argues a strange degenerate contagion suddenly spread among us fitted and prepar'd for new slaverie, but will render us a scorn and derision to all our neighbours. And what will they at best say of us and of the whole *English* name, but scoffingly as of that foolish builder, mentiond by our Saviour, who began to build a tower, and was not able to finish it.[19] Where is this goodly tower of a Commonwealth, which the English boasted they would build to overshaddow kings, and be another *Rome* in the west? The foundation indeed they laid gallantly; but fell into a wors confusion, not of tongues, but of factions, then those at the tower of *Babel*; and have left no memorial of thir work behinde them remaining, but in the common laughter of *Europ*. Which must needs redound the more to our shame, if we but look on our neighbours the United Provinces,[20] to us inferior in all outward advantages; who notwithstanding, in the midst of great difficulties, courageously, wisely, constantly went through with the same work, and are setl'd in all the happie enjoiments of a potent and flourishing Republic to this day.

Besides this, if we returne to Kingship, and soon repent, as undoubtedly we shall, when we begin to finde the old encroachments coming on by little and little upon our consciences, which must necessarily proceed from king and bishop united inseparably in one interest, we may be forc'd perhaps to fight over again all that we have fought, and spend over again all that we have spent, but are never like to attain thus far as we are now advanc'd to the recoverie of our freedom, never to have it in possession as we now have it, never to be voutsaf't heerafter the like mercies and signal assistances from heaven in our cause, if by our ingratefull backsliding we make these fruitless; flying now to regal concessions from his divine condescensions and gratious answers to our once importuning

---

19. Luke 14:28–30.
20. i.e. the Netherlands.

praiers against the tyrannie which we then groand under: making vain and viler then dirt the blood of so many thousand faithfull and valiant *English* men, who left us in this libertie, bought with thir lives; losing by a strange aftergame of folly, all battels we have wonn, together with all *Scotland* as to our conquest,[21] hereby lost, which never any of our kings could conquer, all the treasure we have spent, not that corruptible treasure only, but that far more precious of all our late miraculous deliverances; treading back again with lost labour all our happie steps in the progress of reformation; and most pittifully depriving our selves the instant fruition of that free government which we have so dearly purchased, a free Commonwealth, not only held by wisest men in all ages the noblest, the manliest, the equallest, the justest government, the most agreeable to all due libertie and proportioned equalitie, both human, civil, and Christian, most cherishing to vertue and true religion, but also (I may say it with greatest probabilitie) planely commended, or rather enjoind by our Saviour himself, to all Christians, not without remarkable disallowance, and the brand of *gentilism* upon kingship.[22] God in much displeasure gave a king to the *Israelites,* and imputed it a sin to them that they sought one:[23] but *Christ* apparently forbids his disciples to admitt of any such heathenish government: *the kings of the gentiles,* saith he, *exercise lordship over them*; and they that *exercise authoritie upon them, are call'd benefactors: but ye shall not be so; but he that is greatest among you, let him be as the younger; and he that is chief, as he that serveth.*[24] The occasion of these his words was the ambitious desire of *Zebede's* two sons, to be exalted above thir brethren in his kingdom, which they thought was to be ere long upon earth. That he speaks of civil government, is manifest by the former part of the comparison, which inferrs the other part to be alwaies in the same kinde. And what government coms neerer to this precept of Christ, then a free Common-

---

21. Cromwell had defeated the Scots at Dunbar and Worcester.

22. 'Christ ... hath expressly declar'd, that such regal domination is from the gentiles, not from him' (below, p. 338). Cf. Note 24.

23. Cf. 1 Samuel 8:11–18.

24. Luke 22:25–6. Cf. above, Note 22.

wealth; wherin they who are greatest, are perpetual servants and drudges to the public at thir own cost and charges, neglect thir own affairs; yet are not elevated above thir brethren; live soberly in thir families, walk the streets as other men, may be spoken to freely, familiarly, friendly, without adoration. Wheras a king must be ador'd like a Demigod, with a dissolute and haughtie court about him, of vast expence and luxurie, masks and revels, to the debaushing of our prime gentry both male and female; not in thir passetimes only, but in earnest, by the loos imploiments of court service, which will be then thought honorable. There will be a queen also of no less charge; in most likelihood outlandish and a Papist; besides a queen mother such alreadie;[25] together with both thir courts and numerous train : then a royal issue, and ere long severally thir sumptuous courts; to the multiplying of a servile crew, not of servants only, but of nobility and gentry, bred up then to the hopes not of public, but of court offices; to be stewards, chamberlains, ushers, grooms, even of the close-stool;[26] and the lower thir mindes debas'd with court opinions, contrarie to all vertue and reformation, the haughtier will be thir pride and profuseness : we may well remember this not long since at home; or need but look at present into the *French* court, where enticements and preferments daily draw away and pervert the Protestant Nobilitie. As to the burden of expence, to our cost we shall soon know it; for any good to us, deserving to be termd no better then the vast and lavish price of our subjection and their debausherie; which we are now so greedily cheapning,[27] and would so fain be paying most inconsideratly to a single person; who for any thing wherin the public really needs him, will have little els to do, but to bestow the eating and drinking of excessive dainties, to set a pompous face upon the superficial actings of State, to pageant himself up and down in progress among the perpetual bowings and cringings of an

25. i.e. Queen Henrietta Maria. Two years later Charles II was also to marry a Catholic, Catherine of Braganza.

26. Grooms 'of the king's stool' were a reality in the fifteenth and sixteenth centuries.

27. Bargaining about.

abject people, on either side deifying and adoring him for nothing don that can deserve it. For what can hee more then another man? who even in the expression of a late court-poet,[28] sits only like a great cypher set to no purpose before a long row of other significant figures. Nay it is well and happy for the people if thir King be but a cypher, being oft times a mischief, a pest, a scourge of the nation, and which is wors, not to be remov'd, not to be contrould, much less accus'd or brought to punishment, without the danger of a common ruin, without the shaking and almost subversion of the whole land. Wheras in a free Commonwealth, any governor or chief counselor offending, may be remov'd and punishd without the least commotion. Certainly then that people must needs be madd or strangely infatuated, that build the chief hope of thir common happiness or safetie on a single person:[29] who if he happen to be good, can do no more then another man, if to be bad, hath in his hands to do more evil without check, then millions of other men. The happiness of a nation must needs be firmest and certainest in a full and free Councel of thir own electing, where no single person, but reason only swaies. And what madness is it, for them who might manage nobly thir own affairs themselves, sluggishly and weakly to devolve all on a single person; and more like boyes under age then men, to committ all to his patronage and disposal, who neither can performe what he undertakes, and yet for undertaking it, though royally paid, will not be thir servant, but thir lord? how unmanly must it needs be, to count such a one the breath of our nostrils, to hang all our felicity on him, all our safetie, our well-being, for which if we were aught els but sluggards or babies, we need depend on none but God and our own counsels, our own active vertue and industrie; *Go to the Ant, thou sluggard*, saith *Solomon; consider her waies, and be wise; which having no prince, ruler, or lord, provides her meat in the summer, and gathers her food in the harvest.*[30] Which evidently shews us,

---

28. Not identified.   29. Cf. the Introduction, above, pp. 32–3.

30. Proverbs 6:6. Milton like many republicans appealed to the commonwealth of the ants, just as royalists invoked the monarchy of the bees.

that they who think the nation undon without a king, though they look grave or haughtie, have not so much true spirit and understanding in them as a pismire: neither are these diligent creatures hence concluded to live in lawless anarchie, or that commended, but are set the examples to imprudent and ungovernd men, of a frugal and selfgoverning democratie or Commonwealth; safer and more thriving in the joint providence and counsel of many industrious equals, then under the single domination of one imperious Lord. It may be well wonderd that any Nation styling themselves free, can suffer any man to pretend hereditarie right over them as thir lord; when as by acknowledging that right, they conclude themselves his servants and his vassals, and so renounce thir own freedom. Which how a people and thir leaders especially can do, who have fought so gloriously for liberty, how they can change thir noble words and actions, heretofore so becoming the majesty of a free people, into the base necessitie of court flatteries and prostrations, is not only strange and admirable,[31] but lamentable to think on. That a nation should be so valorous and courageous to winn thir liberty in the field, and when they have wonn it, should be so heartless[32] and unwise in thir counsels, as not to know how to use it, value it, what to do with it or with themselves; but after ten or twelve years prosperous warr and contestation with tyrannie, basely and besottedly to run their necks again into the yoke which they have broken, and prostrate all the fruits of thir victorie for naught at the feet of the vanquishd, besides our loss of glorie, and such an example as kings or tyrants never yet had the like to boast of, will be an ignominie if it befall us, that never yet befell any nation possessd of thir libertie; worthie indeed themselves, whatsoever they be, to be for ever slaves: but that part of the nation which consents not with them, as I perswade me of a great number, far worthier then by their means to be brought into the same bondage. Considering these things so plane, so rational, I cannot but yet furder admire on the other side, how any man who hath the true principles of justice and religion in him, can presume

---

31. Astonishing.
32. Lacking in courage.

or take upon him to be a king and lord over his brethren, whom he cannot but know whether as men or Christians, to be for the most part every way equal or superior to himself: how he can display with such vanitie and ostentation his regal splendor so supereminently above other mortal men; or being a Christian, can assume such extraordinarie honour and worship to himself while the kingdom of Christ our common King and Lord, is hid to this world, and such *gentilish*[33] imitation forbid in express words by himself to all his disciples. All Protestants hold that Christ in his church hath left no vicegerent of his power, but himself without deputie, is the only head therof, governing it from heaven: how then can any Christian-man derive his kingship from Christ, but with wors usurpation then the Pope his headship over the church, since Christ not only hath not left the least shaddow of a command for any such vicegerence from him in the State, as the Pope pretends for his in the Church, but hath expressly declar'd, that such regal dominion is from the gentiles, not from him, and hath strictly charg'd us, not to imitate them therin.

I doubt not but all ingenuous and knowing men will easily agree with me, that a free Commonwealth without single person or house of lords, is by far the best government, if it can be had; but we have all this while say they bin expecting[34] it, and cannot yet attain it. Tis true indeed, when monarchie was dissolvd, the form of a Commonwealth should have forthwith bin fram'd; and the practice therof immediatly begun; that the people might have soon bin satisfi'd and delighted with the decent order, ease and benefit therof: we had bin then by this time firmly rooted past fear of commotions or mutations, & now flourishing: this care of timely setling a new government instead of ye old, too much neglected, hath bin our mischief. Yet the cause therof may be ascrib'd with most reason to the frequent disturbances, interruptions and dissolutions which the Parlament hath had partly from the impatient or disaffected people, partly from som ambitious leaders in the

33. See above, Notes 22 and 24.
34. Waiting for.

rmie;[35] much contrarie, I beleeve, to the mind and approbation
f the Armie it self and thir other Commanders, once undeceivd,
r in thir own power. Now is the opportunitie, now the very
eason wherein we may obtain a free Commonwealth and
stablish it for ever in the land, without difficulty or much delay.
Vrits are set out for elections, and which is worth observing
1 the name, not of any king, but of the keepers of our libertie,
o summon a free Parlament:[36] which then only will indeed be
ree, and deserve the true honor of that supreme title, if they
reserve us a free people. Which never Parlament was more
ree to do; being now call'd, not as heretofore, by the summons
f a king, but by the voice of libertie: and if the people, laying
side prejudice and impatience, will seriously and calmly now
onsider thir own good both religious and civil, thir own libertie
nd the only means thereof, as shall be heer laid before them,
nd will elect thir Knights and Burgesses[37] able men, and
ccording to the just and necessarie qualifications (which for
ught I hear, remain yet in force unrepeald, as they were
ormerly decreed in Parlament)[38] men not addicted to a single
erson or house of lords, the work is don; at least the founda-
ion firmly laid of a free Commonwealth, and good part also
rected of the main structure. For the ground and basis of
very just and free government (since men have smarted so oft
or commiting all to one person) is a general councel of ablest
nen, chosen by the people to consult of public affairs from
ime to time for the common good. In this Grand Councel must
he sovrantie, not transferrd, but delegated only, and at it were
eposited, reside; with this caution they must have the forces
y sea and land committed to them for preservation of the
ommon peace and libertie; must raise and manage the public
evenue, at least with som inspectors deputed for satisfaction

---

35. Parliament was in 1659 twice dissolved under pressure from
rmy leaders.

36. The writs of March 1660 were issued 'in the name of the
Keepers of the Liberties of England'.

37. Representatives of the counties on the one hand, and of the
owns, boroughs and universities on the other.

38. The anti-royalist decrees of January and February 1660.

of the people, how it is imploid; must make or propose, a
more expressly shall be said anon, civil laws; treat of commerce
peace, or warr with forein nations, and for the carrying o
som particular affairs with more secrecie and expedition, mus
elect, as they have alreadie out of thir own number and other
a Councel of State.[39]

And although it may seem strange at first hearing, by reason
that mens mindes are prepossessed with the notion of successiv
Parlaments, I affirme that the Grand or General Councel bein
well chosen, should be perpetual: for so thir business is or ma
be, and oft times urgent; the opportunitie of affairs gaind c
lost in a moment. The day of counsel cannot be set as the da
of a festival; but must be readie alwaies to prevent or answe
all occasions. By this continuance they will become everie wa
skilfullest, best provided of intelligence from abroad, best a
quainted with the people at home, and the people with then
The ship of the Commonwealth is alwaies under sail; they s
at the stern; and if they stear well, what need is ther t
change them; it being rather dangerous? Add to this, that th
Grand Councel is both foundation and main pillar of the whol
State; and to move pillars and foundations, not faultie, canno
be safe for the building. I see not therefor, how we can b
advantag'd by successive and transitorie Parlaments; but tha
they are much likelier continually to unsettle rather then 1
settle a free government; to breed commotions, changes, nove
ties and uncertainties; to bring neglect upon present affairs an
opportunities, while all mindes are suspense[40] with expectatio
of a new assemblie, and the assemblie for a good space take
up with the new setling of it self. After which, if they finde n
great work to do, they will make it, by altering or repealin
former acts, or making and multiplying new; that they ma
seem to see what thir predecessors saw not, and not to hav
assembld for nothing: till all law be lost in the multitude c

39. Not Cromwell's Council of State in which Milton himse
had served, but the council of twenty-one M.P.s and eleven ou
siders set up in May 1659.

40. In suspense.

clashing statutes. But if the ambition of such as think themselves injur'd that they also partake not of the government, and are impatient till they be chosen, cannot brook the perpetuitie of others chosen before them, or if it be feard that long continuance of power may corrupt sincerest men, the known expedient is, and by som lately propounded,[41] that annually (or if the space be longer, so much perhaps the better) the third part of Senators may go out according to the precedence of thir election, and the like number be chosen in thir places, to prevent the setling of too absolute a power, if it should be perpetual: and this they call *partial rotation*. But I could wish that this wheel or partial wheel in State, if it be possible, might be avoided; as having too much affinitie with the wheel of fortune. For it appeers not how this can be don, without danger and mischance of putting out a great number of the best and ablest: in whose stead new elections may bring in as many raw, unexperienc'd and otherwise affected, to the weakning and much altering for the wors of public transactions. Neither do I think a perpetual Senat, especially chosen and entrusted by the people, much in this land to be feard, where the well-affected either in a standing armie, or in a setled militia have thir arms in thir own hands. Safest therefor to me it seems and of least hazard or interruption to affairs, that none of the Grand Councel be mov'd, unless by death or just conviction of some crime: for what can be expected firm or stedfast from a floating foundation? however, I forejudge not any probable expedient, any temperament that can be found in things of this nature so disputable on either side. Yet least this which I affirme, be thought my single opinion, I shall add sufficient testimonie. Kingship it self is therefor counted the more safe and durable, because the king and, for the most part, his councel, is not chang'd during life: but a Commonwealth is held immortal; and therin firmest, safest and most above fortune: for the death of a king, causeth

---

41. e.g. James Harrington, whose *Oceana* (1656) argued for a parliament with a rotating Senate to propose matters, and a larger body to vote on them. Milton regarded the scheme as unduly complicated (see below, pp. 343 ff.).

ofttimes many dangerous alterations; but the death now and then of a Senator is not felt; the main bodie of them still continuing permanent in greatest and noblest Commonwealths, and as it were eternal. Therefor among the *Jews*, the supreme councel of seaventie, call'd the *Sanhedrim*, founded by *Moses*, in *Athens*, that of *Areopagus*, in *Sparta*, that of the Ancients, in *Rome*, the Senat, consisted of members chosen for term of life; and by that means remaind as it were still the same to generations.[42] In *Venice* they change indeed ofter then every year som particular councels of State, as that of six, or such other; but the true Senat, which upholds and sustains the government, is the whole aristocracie immovable.[43] So in the United Provinces, the States General, which are indeed but a councel of state deputed by the whole union, are not usually the same persons for above three or six years; but the States of every citie, in whom the sovrantie hath bin plac'd time out of minde, are a standing Senat, without succession, and accounted chiefly in that regard the main prop of thir liberty. And why they should be so in every well ordered Commonwealth, they who write of policie, give these reasons; 'That to make the Senat successive, not only impairs the dignitie and lustre of the Senat, but weakens the whole Commonwealth, and brings it into manifest danger; while by this means the secrets of State are frequently divulgd, and matters of greatest consequence committed to inexpert and novice conselors, utterly to seek in the full and intimate knowledge of affairs past.'[44] I know not therefor what should be peculiar in *England* to make successive Parlaments thought safest, or convenient here more then in other nations, unless it be the fickl'ness which is attributed to

42. On the Sanhedrin, see Numbers 11 : 16 ff.; and on the Areopagus, the headnote to *Areopagitica* (above, p. 196). In Sparta, under the constitution of Lycurgus, the thirty 'ancients' were elected for life – as were the members of the Roman Senate.

43. Venice's self-perpetuating Great Council superseded the authority of the short-term Doge and the members of the executive Council of Six.

44. Adapted from the Latin of Jean Bodin, *The Six Bookes of a Commonweale* (English trans., 1606).

us as we are Ilanders:[45] but good education and acquisit[46] wisdom ought to correct the fluxible fault, if any such be, of our watry situation. It will be objected, that in those places where they had perpetual Senats, they had also popular remedies against thir growing too imperious: as in *Athens*, besides *Areopagus*, another Senat of four or five hunderd; in *Sparta* the *Ephori*; in *Rome*, the Tribunes of the people. But the event tels us, that these remedies either little availd the people, or brought them to such a licentious and unbridl'd democratie, as in fine ruind themselves with thir own excessive power. So that the main reason urg'd why popular assemblies are to be trusted with the peoples libertie, rather than a Senat of principal men, because great men will be still endeavoring to inlarge thir power, but the common sort will be contented to maintain thir own libertie, is by experience found false; none being more immoderat and ambitious to amplifie thir power, then such popularities; which was seen in the people of *Rome*; who at first contented to have thir Tribunes, at length contended with the Senat that one Consul, then both; soon after, that the Censors and Prætors also should be created Plebeian, and the whole empire put into their hands; adoring lastly those, who most were advers to the Senat, till *Marius* by fulfilling thir nordinat desires, quite lost them all the power for which they had so long bin striving, and left them under the tyrannie of *Sylla*:[47] the ballance therefor must be exactly so set, as to preserve and keep up due autoritie on either side, as well in the Senat as in the people. And this annual rotation of a Senat to consist of three hunderd, as is lately propounded,[48] requires also another popular assembly upward of a thousand, with an answerable rotation. Which besides that it will be liable to all those inconveniencies found in the foresaid remedies, cannot

45. Bodin (previous note) based his view of island dwellers as deceitfull and treacherous' on Plato's remarks in *Laws*, IV, 704.

46. Acquired.

47. The plebeian general Caius Marius (155–86 B.C.), having conspired with demagogues, was displaced by the dictator Cornelius Sulla (138–78 B.C.).

48. By Harrington (as before, Note 41).

but be troublesom and chargeable, both in thir motion[49] and thir session, to the whole land; unweildie with thir own bulk, unable in so great a number to mature thir consultations as they ought, if any be allotted them, and that they meet not from so many parts remote to sit a whole year lieger[50] in one place, only now and then to hold up a forrest of fingers, or to convey each man his bean or ballot into the box, without reason shewn or common deliberation; incontinent of secrets if any be imparted to them, emulous and always jarring with the other Senat. The much better way doubtless will be in this wavering condition of our affairs, to deferr the changing or circumscribing of our Senat, more then may be done with ease, till the Commonwealth be thoroughly setl'd in peace and safetie, and they themselves give us the occasion. Militarie men hold it dangerous to change the form of battel in view of an enemie: neither did the people of *Rome* bandie with thir Senat while any of the *Tarquins* livd, the enemies of thir libertie,[51] nor sought by creating Tribunes to defend themselves against the fear of thir Patricians, till sixteen years after the expulsion of thir kings, and in full securitie of thir state, they had or thought they had just cause given them by the Senat. Another way will be, to wel-qualifie and refine elections: not committing all to the noise and shouting of a rude multitude, but permitting only those of them who are rightly qualifi'd, to nominat as many as they will; and out of that number others of a better breeding, to chuse a less number more judiciously, till after a third or fourth sifting and refining of exactest choice, they only be left chosen who are the due number, and seem by most voices the worthiest. To make the people fittest to chuse, and the chosen fittest to govern, will be to mend our corrupt and faulty education, to teach the people faith not without vertue, temperance, modestie, sobrietie, parsimonie, justice; not to admire wealth or honour; to hate turbulence and ambition; to place every one his privat welfare and happiness in the public

---

49. Commuting to and from Westminster.

50. Stationary.

51. The Roman Republic was established after the last of the Tarquins was banished (late sixth century B.C.).

peace, libertie and safetie. They shall not then need to be much mistrustfull of thir chosen Patriots in the Grand Councel; who will be then rightly call'd the true keepers of our libertie, though the most of thir business will be in forein affairs. But to prevent all mistrust, the people then will have thir several ordinarie assemblies (which will henceforth quite annihilate the odious power and name of Committies)[52] in the chief town of every countie, without the trouble, charge, or time lost of summoning and assembling from far in so great a number, and so long residing from thir own houses, or removing of thir families, to do as much at home in thir several shires, entire or subdivided, toward the securing of thir libertie, as a numerous assembly of them all formd and conven'd on purpose with the wariest rotation. Wherof I shall speak more ere the end of this discourse: for it may be referrd to time, so we be still going on by degrees to perfection. The people well weighing and performing these things, I suppose would have no cause to fear, though the *Parlament* abolishing that name, as originally signifying but the *parlie* of our Lords and Commons with thir *Norman* king when he pleasd to call them,[53] should, with certain limitations of thir power, sit perpetual, if thir ends be faithfull and for a free Commonwealth, under the name of a Grand or General Councel. Till this be done, I am in doubt whether our State will be ever certainly and throughly setl'd; never likely till then to see an end of our troubles and continual changes or at least never the true settlement and assurance of our libertie. The Grand Councel being thus firmly constituted to perpetuitie, and still, upon the death or default of any member, suppli'd and kept in full number, ther can be no cause alleag'd why peace, justice, plentifull trade and all prosperitie should not thereupon ensue throughout the whole land; with as much assurance as can be of human things, that they shall so continue (if God favour us, and our wilfull sins provoke him not) even to the coming of our true and rightfull and only to

---

52. The local committees which during the Protectorate enforced loyalty to Cromwell.

53. The hardly warranted assumption is that the Commonwealth existed before the Norman conquest.

be expected King, only worthie as he is our only Saviour, the Messiah, the Christ, the only heir of his eternal father, the only by him anointed and ordaind since the work of our redemption finishd, Universal Lord of all mankinde. The way propounded is plane, easie and open before us; without intricacies, without the introducement of new or obsolete forms, or terms, or exotic models; idea's that would effect nothing, but with a number of new injunctions to manacle the native liberty of mankinde; turning all vertue into prescription, servitude, and necessitie, to the great impairing and frustrating of Christian libertie: I say again, this way lies free and smooth before us; is not tangl'd with inconveniencies; invents no new incumbrances; requires no perilous, no injurious alteration or circumscription of mens lands and proprieties; secure, that in this Commonwealth, temporal and spiritual lords remov'd, no man or number of men can attain to such wealth or vast possession, as will need the hedge of an Agrarian law[54] (never succesful, but the cause rather of sedition, save only where it began seasonably with first possession) to confine them from endangering our public libertie; to conclude, it can have no considerable objection made against it, that it is not practicable: least it be said hereafter, that we gave up our libertie for want of a readie way or distinct form propos'd of a free Commonwealth. And this facilitie we shall have above our next neighbouring Commonwealth (if we can keep us from the fond conceit of somthing like a duke of *Venice*, put lately into many mens heads, by som one or other sutly driving on under that notion his own ambitious ends to lurch a crown)[55] that our liberty shall not be hamperd or hoverd over by any ingagement to such a potent familie as the house of *Nassaw*[56] of whom to stand in perpetual doubt and suspicion, but we shall live the cleerest and absolutest free nation in the world. On the contrarie, if ther be a king, which the inconsiderate multitude are

---

54. In Harrington's elaborate scheme (above, Note 41).

55. Richard Cromwell and others were said to have been considered for a position analogous to that of the Doge in Venice.

56. The Princes of Orange-Nassau, heirs of the Stadtholder William of Orange (assassinated, 1584).

now so madd upon, mark how far short we are like to com of all those happinesses, which in a free state we shall immediately be possessd of. First, the Grand Councel, which, as I shewd before, should sit perpetually (unless thir leisure give them now and then som intermissions or vacations, easilie manageable by the Councel of State left sitting) shall be call'd, by the kings good will and utmost endeavor as seldom as may be. For it is only the kings right, he will say, to call a parlament; and this he will do most commonly about his own affairs rather then the kingdom's, as will appeer planely so soon as they are call'd. For what will thir business then be and the chief expence of thir time, but an endless tugging between petition of right and royal prerogative, especially about the negative voice,[57] militia, or subsidies, demanded and oft times extorted without reasonable cause appeering to the Commons, who are the only true representatives of the people, and thir libertie, but will be then mingl'd with a court-faction; besides which within thir own walls, the sincere part of them who stand faithfull to the people, will again have to deal with two troublesom counterworking adversaries from without, meer creatures of the king, spiritual, and the greater part, as is likeliest, of temporal lords, nothing concernd with the peoples libertie. If these prevail not in what they please, though never so much against the peoples interest, the Parlament shall be soon dissolvd, or sit and do nothing; not sufferd to remedie the least greevance, or enact aught advantageous to the people. Next, the Councel of State shall not be chosen by the Parlament, but by the king, still his own creatures, courtiers and favorites; who will be sure in all thir counsels to set thir maister's grandure and absolute power, in what they are able, far above the peoples libertie. I denie not but that ther may be such a king, who may regard the common good before his own, may have no vitious favorite, may hearken only to the wisest and incorruptest of his Parlament: but this rarely happens in a monarchie not elective; and it behoves not a wise nation to commit the summ of thir welbeing, the whole state of thir safetie to fortune. What need they; and how absurd

---

57. i.e. the royal veto.

would it be, when as they themselves to whom his chief vertue
will be but to hearken, may with much better management
and dispatch, with much more commendation of thir own
worth and magnanimitie govern without a maister. Can the
folly be paralleld, to adore and be the slaves of a single person
for doing that which it is ten thousand to one whether he can
or will do, and we without him might do more easily, more
effectually, more laudably our selves? Shall we never grow
old anough to be wise to make seasonable use of gravest
autorities, experiences, examples? Is it such an unspeakable
joy to serve, such felicitie to wear a yoke? to clink our
shackles, lockt on by pretended law of subjection more intolerable and hopeless to be ever shaken off, then those which are
knockt on by illegal injurie and violence? *Aristotle*, our chief
instructer in the Universities, least this doctrine be thought
Sectarian, as the royalist would have it thought, tels us in the
third of his Politics, that certain men at first, for the matchless
excellence of thir vertue above others. or som great public
benifit, were created kings by the people; in small cities and
territories, and in the scarcitie of others to be found like them:
but when they abus'd thir power and governments grew larger,
and the number of prudent men increased, that then the people
soon deposing thir tyrants, betook them, in all civilest places, to
the form of a free Commonwealth.[58] And why should we thus
disparage and prejudicate our own nation, as to fear a scarcitie
of able and worthie men united in counsel to govern us, if we
will use diligence and impartiality to finde them out and chuse
them, rather yoking our selves to a single person, the natural
adversarie and oppressor of libertie, though good, yet far easier
corruptible by the excess of his singular power and exaltation,
or at best, not comparably sufficient to bear the weight of
government, nor equally dispos'd to make us happie in the
enjoyment of our libertie under him.

But admitt, that monarchie of it self may be convenient to
som nations; yet to us who have thrown it out, receivd back
again, it cannot but prove pernicious. For kings to com, never

---

58. *Politics*, III, 15.

forgetting thir former ejection, will be sure to fortifie and arm themselves sufficiently for the future against all such attempts hereafter from the people: who shall be then so narrowly watchd and kept so low, that though they would never so fain and at the same rate of thir blood and treasure, they never shall be able to regain what they now have purchasd and may enjoy, or to free themselves from any yoke impos'd upon them: nor will they dare to go about it; utterly disheartn'd for the future, if these thir highest attempts prove unsuccesfull; which will be the triumph of all tyrants heerafter over any people that shall resist oppression; and thir song will then be, to others, how sped the rebellious *English*? to our posteritie, how sped the rebells your fathers? This is not my conjecture, but drawn from God's known denouncement against the gentilizing *Israelites;* who thought they were governd in a Commonwealth of God's own ordaining, he only thir king, they his peculiar people, yet affecting rather to resemble heathen, but pretending the misgovernment of *Samuel's* sons,[59] no more a reason to dislike thir Commonwealth, then the violence of *Eli's* sons[60] was imputable to that priesthood or religion, clamourd for a king. They had thir longing; but with this testimonie of God's wrath; *ye shall cry out in that day because of your king whom ye shall have chosen, and the Lord will not hear you in that day.*[61] Us if he shall hear now, how much less will he hear when we cry heerafter, who once deliverd by him from a king, and not without wondrous acts of his providence, insensible and unworthie of those high mercies, are returning precipitantly, if he withhold us not, back to the captivitie from whence he freed us. Yet neither shall we obtain or buy at an easie rate this new guilded yoke which thus transports us: a new royal-revenue must be found, a new episcopal; for those are individual:[62] both which being wholly dissipated or bought by privat persons or assign'd for service don, and especially to the Armie, cannot be recoverd without a general detriment and confusion to mens estates, or a heavie imposition on all mens

---

59. 1 Samuel 8:5–18 (as above, p. 260).
60. 1 Samuel 2:12–17.
61. 1 Samuel 8:18. Cf. above, Note 23.
62. Privately owned.

purses; benifit to none, but the worst and ignoblest sort of men, whose hope is to be either the ministers of court riot and excess, or the gainers by it: But not to speak more of losses and extra-ordinarie levies on our estates, what will then be the revenges and offences rememberd and returnd, not only by the chief person, but by all his adherents; accounts and reparations that will be requir'd, suites, inditements, inquiries, discoveries, complaints, informations, who knows against whom or how many, though perhaps neuters,[63] if not to utmost infliction, yet to imprisonment, fines, banishment, or molestation; if not these, yet disfavor, discountnance, disregard and contempt on all but the known royalist or whom he favors, will be plenteous: nor let the new royaliz'd presbyterians[64] perswade themselves that thir old doings, though now recanted, will be forgotten; whatever conditions be contriv'd or trusted on. Will they not beleeve this; nor remember the pacification,[65] how it was kept to the *Scots*; how other solemn promises many a time to us? Let them but now read the diabolical forerunning libells,[66] the faces the gestures that now appeer foremost and briskest in all public places; as the harbingers of those that are in expectation to raign over us; let them but hear the insolencies, the menaces, the insultings of our newly animated common enemies crept lately out of thir holes, thir hell, I might say, by the language of thir infernal pamphlets, the spue of every drunkard, every ribald nameless, yet not for want of licence, but for very shame of thir own vile persons, not daring to name themselves, while they traduce others by name; and give us to foresee that they intend to second thir wicked words, if ever they have power

---

63. Not committed to either side in the Civil War.

64. The inconsistent Presbyterians had first endeavored to limit the monarchy, then 'tried to their utmost to raise a tumult' against the regicide (above, p. 73, but especially pp. 250, 273 ff.), next upheld the Commonwealth – and now favor Charles II.

65. The Treaty of Newport (as before, p. 331, Note 15).

66. The 'libells', like the 'infernal pamphlets' mentioned next, are the acrimonious royalist denunciations of republicans. They included Sir Roger L'Estrange's attack on Milton in the pointedly entitled *No Blinde Guides* (April 1660).

with more wicked deeds. Let our zealous backsliders forethink now with themselves, how thir necks yok'd with these tigers of Bacchus, these new fanatics of not the preaching but the sweating-tub, inspir'd with nothing holier then the Venereal pox,[67] can draw one way under monarchie to the establishing of church discipline with these new-disgorg'd atheismes: yet shall they not have the honor to yoke with these, but shall be yok'd under them; these shall plow on their backs. And do they among them who are so forward to bring in the single person, think to be by him trusted or long regarded? So trusted they shall be and so regarded, as by kings are wont reconcil'd enemies; neglected and soon after discarded, if not prosecuted for old traytors; the first inciters, beginners, and more then to the third part actors of all that followd; it will be found also, that there must be then as necessarily as now (for the contrarie part will be still feard) a standing armie; which for certain shall not be this, but of the fiercest Cavaliers, of no less expence, and perhaps again under *Rupert*:[68] but let this armie be sure they shall soon be disbanded, and likeliest without arrear or pay; and being disbanded, not be sure but they may as soon be questiond for being in arms against thir king: the same let them fear, who have contributed monie; which will amount to no small number that must then take thir turn to be made delinquents and compounders.[69] They who past reason and recoverie are devoted to kingship, perhaps will answer, that a greater part by far of the Nation will have it so; the rest therefor must yield. Not so much to convince these, which I little hope, as to confirm them who yield not, I reply; that this greatest part have both in reason and the trial of just battel, lost the right of their election what the government shall be: of them who have not

---

67. The preaching tub was the pulpit of street preachers; the sweating tub was used in treating venereal diseases.

68. Prince Rupert (1619–82), son of Queen Elizabeth of Bohemia and nephew of Charles I, had mounted spectacular cavalry charges during the Civil War.

69. Royalist landowners, declared 'delinquents' by the Long Parliament, had their estates confiscated; but they were 'compounders' if they could instead pay a specified sum of money.

lost that right, whether they for kingship be the greater num
ber, who can certainly determin? Suppose they be; yet of
freedom they partake all alike, one main end of government:
which if the greater part value not, but will degeneratly forgoe
is it just or reasonable, that most voices against the main end
of government should enslave the less number that would
be free? More just it is doubtless, if it com to force, that a less
number compell a greater to retain, which can be no wrong
to them, thir libertie, then that a greater number for the
pleasure of their baseness, compell a less most injuriously to be
thir fellow slaves. They who seek nothing but thir own just
libertie, have alwaies right to winn it and to keep it, when
ever they have power, be the voices never so numerous that
oppose it. And how much we above others are concernd to
defend it from kingship, and from them who in pursuance
therof so perniciously would betray us and themselves to most
certain miserie and thraldom, will be needless to repeat.

Having thus far shewn with what ease we may now obtain
a free Commonwealth, and by it with as much ease all the free
dom, peace, justice, plentie that we can desire, on the other
side the difficulties, troubles, uncertainties, nay rather impossi
bilities to enjoy these things constantly under a monarch,
will now proceed to shew more particularly wherin our free
dom and flourishing condition will be more ample and secure to
us under a free Commonwealth then under kingship.

The whole freedom of man consists either in spiritual or
civil libertie. As for spiritual, who can be at rest, who can
enjoy any thing in this world with contentment, who hath no
libertie to serve God and to save his own soul, according to
the best light which God hath planted in him to that purpose
by the reading of his reveal'd will and the guidance of his holy
spirit? That this is best pleasing to God, and that the whole
Protestant Church allows no supream judge or rule in matter
of religion, but the scriptures, and these to be interpreted by
the scriptures themselves, which necessarily inferrs liberty of
conscience, I have heretofore prov'd at large in another treatise,[70]

---

70. *A Treatise of Civil Power in Ecclesiastical Causes*, above, pp
296 ff.

and might yet furder by the public declarations, confessions and admonitions of whole churches and states, obvious in all historie since the Reformation.

This liberty of conscience which above all other things ought to be to all men dearest and most precious, no government more inclinable not to favor only but to protect, then a free Commonwealth; as being most magnanimous, most fearless and confident of its own fair proceedings. Wheras kingship, though looking big, yet indeed most pusillanimous, full of fears, full of jealousies, startl'd at every ombrage,[71] as it hath bin observd of old to have ever suspected most and mistrusted them who were in most esteem for vertue and generositie of minde, so it is now known to have most in doubt and suspicion them who are most reputed to be religious. Queen *Elizabeth* though her self accounted so good a Protestant, so moderate, so confident of her Subjects love would never give way so much as to Presbyterian reformation in this land, though once and again besought, as *Camden*[72] relates, but imprisoned and persecuted the very proposers therof; alleaging it as her minde & maxim unalterable, that such reformation would diminish regal autoritie. What liberty of conscience can we expect of others, far wors principl'd from the cradle, traind up and governd by *Popish* and *Spanish* counsels, and on such depending hitherto for subsistence?[73] Especially what can this last Parlament expect, who having reviv'd lately and publishd the covnant, have reingag'd themselves, never to readmitt Episcopacie: which no son of *Charls* returning, but will most certainly bring back with him, if he regard the last and strictest charge of his father, *to persevere in not the doctrin only, but the government of the church of* England; *not to neglect the speedie and effectual suppressing of errors and schisms;*[74] among which he accounted

---

71. Shadow.

72. The historian William Camden (as above, p. 88, Note 29).

73. Milton alludes to Charles II's upbringing by a Catholic mother (above, Note 25) and his participation with the Spaniards in the battle of Flanders (1658).

74. Quoted from *Eikon Basilike* ('The Royal Image'), attributed to the martyred Charles I; Milton had already replied to it in

Presbyterie one of the chief: or if notwithstanding that charge of his father, he submitt to the covnant, how will he keep faith to us with disobedience to him; or regard that faith given, which must be founded on the breach of that last and solemnest paternal charge, and the reluctance, I may say the antipathie which is in all kings against Presbyterian and Independent discipline? for they hear the gospel speaking much of libertie; a word which monarchie and his bishops both fear and hate, but a free Commonwealth both favors and promotes; and not the word only, but the thing it self. But let our governors beware in time, least thir hard measure to libertie of conscience be found the rock wheron they shipwrack themselves as others have now don before them in the cours wherin God was directing thir stearage to a free Commonwealth, and the abandoning of all those whom they call *sectaries*, for the detected falshood and ambition of som, be a wilfull rejection of thir own chief strength and interest in the freedom of all Protestant religion, under what abusive name soever calumniated.

The other part of our freedom consists in the civil rights and advancements of every person according to his merit: the enjoyment of those never more certain, and the access to these never more open, then in a free Commonwealth. Both which in my opinion may be best and soonest obtain, if every countie in the land were made a kinde of subordinate Commonaltie or Commonwealth, and one chief town or more, according as the shire is in circuit, made cities, if they be not so call'd alreadie; where the nobilitie and chief gentry from a proportionable compas of territorie annexd to each citie, may build, houses or palaces, befitting thir qualitie, may bear part in the government, make thir own judicial laws, or use these that are, and execute them by thir own elected judicatures and judges without appeal, in all things of civil government between man and man. So they shall have justice in thir own hands, law executed fully and finally in thir own counties and precincts, long wishd, and spoken of, but never yet obtain; they shall have none then to blame but themselves, if it be not well administerd; and fewer

Eikonoklastes ('The Image Breaker'). The covenant referred to, had been reaffirmed by Parliament in March 1660.

laws to expect or fear from the supreme autoritie; or to those that shall be made, of any great concernment to public libertie, they may without much trouble in these commonalties or in more general assemblies call'd to thir cities from the whole territorie on such occasion, declare and publish thir assent or dissent by deputies within a time limited sent to the Grand Councel: yet so as this thir judgment declar'd shal submitt to the greater number of other counties or commonalties, and not avail them to any exemption of themselves, or refusal of agreement with the rest, as it may in any of the United Provinces, being sovran within it self, oft times to the great disadvantage of that union.[75] In these imploiments they may much better then they do now, exercise and fit themselves, till thir lot fall to be chosen into the Grand Councel, according as thir worth and merit shall be taken notice of by the people. As for controversies that shall happen between men of several counties, they may repair, as they do now, to the capital citie, or any other more commodious, indifferent place and equal judges. And this I finde to have bin practisd in the old *Athenian* Commonwealth, reputed the first and ancientest place of civilitie in all *Greece*; that they had in thir several cities, a peculiar; in *Athens*, a common government; and thir right, as it befell them, to the administration of both.[76] They should have heer also schools and academies at thir own choice, wherin thir children may be bred up in thir own sight to all learning and noble education not in grammar only, but in all liberal arts and exercises. This would soon spread much more knowledge and civilitie, yea religion through all parts of the land, by communicating the natural heat of government and culture more distributively to all extreme parts, which now lie numm and neglected, would soon make the whole nation more industrious, more ingenuous at home, more potent, more honorable abroad. To this a free Commonwealth will easily assent; (nay the Parlament

75. The absence of a centralized authority in the Netherlands was a severe handicap, made evident in their loss of the naval war with England in 1652–3.

76. Cleisthenes in 510 B.C. had decentralized the government of Attica by the creation of ten relatively autonomous tribes.

hath had alreadie som such thing in designe) for of all governments a Commonwealth aims most to make the people flourishing, vertuous, noble and high spirited. Monarchs will never
permitt: whose aim is to make the people, wealthie indeed
perhaps and well fleec't, for thir own shearing and the supplie
of regal prodigalitie; but otherwise softest, basest, vitiousest,
servilest, easiest to be kept under; and not only in fleece, but
in minde also sheepishest; and will have all the benches of
judicature annexd to the throne, as a gift of royal grace that
we have justice don us; whenas nothing can be more essential
to the freedom of a people, then to have the administration of
justice and all public ornaments in thir own election and within
thir own bounds, without long travelling or depending on remote places to obtain thir right or any civil accomplishment;
so it be not supreme, but subordinate to the general power
and union of the whole Republic. In which happy firmness as
in the particular above mentioned, we shall also far exceed
the United Provinces, by having, not as they (to the retarding
and distracting oft times of thir counsels or urgentest occasions) many Sovranties united in one Commonwealth, but
many Commonwealths under one united and entrusted Sovrantie. And when we have our forces by sea and land, either
of a faithful Armie or a setl'd Militia, in our hands to the firm
establishing of a free Commonwealth, publick accounts under
our own inspection, general laws and taxes with thir causes in
our own domestic suffrages, judicial laws, offices and ornaments
at home in our own ordering and administration, all distinction
of lords and commoners, that may any way divide or sever
the publick interest, remov'd, what can a perpetual senat have
then wherin to grow corrupt, wherin to encroach upon us or
usurp; or if they do, wherin to be formidable? Yet if all this
avail not to remove the fear or envie of a perpetual sitting,
it may be easilie provided, to change a third part of them
yearly or every two or three years, as was above mentioned;
or that it be at those times in the peoples choice, whether they
will change them, or renew thir power, as they shall finde
cause.

I have no more to say at present: few words will save us, well

considerd; few and easie things, now seasonably don. But if
the people be so affected, as to prostitute religion and libertie
to the vain and groundless apprehension, that nothing but kingship can restore trade, not remembering the frequent plagues
and pestilences that then wasted this citie, such as through
God's mercie we never have felt since,[77] and that trade flourishes
no where more then in the free Commonwealths of *Italie*,
Germanie, and the Low-Countries before thir eyes at this day,
yet if trade be grown so craving and importunate through the
profuse living of tradesmen, that nothing can support it, but
the luxurious expences of a nation upon trifles or superfluities,
so as if the people generally should betake themselves to
frugalitie, it might prove a dangerous matter, least tradesmen
should mutinie for want of trading, and that therefor we must
forgoe & set to sale religion, libertie, honor, safetie, all concernments Divine or human to keep up trading, if lastly, after all
this light among us, the same reason shall pass for current to
put our necks again under kingship, as was made use of by the
Jews to returne back to *Egypt* and to the worship of thir idol
queen, because they falsly imagind that they then livd in more
plentie and prosperitie,[78] our condition is not sound but rotten,
both in religion and all civil prudence; and will bring us soon,
the way we are marching, to those calamities which attend
alwaies and unavoidably on luxurie, all national judgments
under forein or domestic slaverie: so far we shall be from
mending our condition by monarchizing our government, whatever new conceit now possesses us. However with all hazard
I have ventur'd what I thought my duty to speak in season,
and to forewarne my countrey in time: wherin I doubt not but
ther be many wise men in all places and degrees, but am sorrie
the effects of wisdom are so little seen among us. Many circumstances and particulars I could have added in those things
wherof I have spoken; but a few main matters now put speedily
in execution, will suffice to recover us, and set all right: and
ther will want at no time who are good at circumstances; but

77. The last major outbreak of the plague was in 1625; the next
was to be in 1665.

78. Cf. the longing of the Jews for Egypt in Numbers 11 : 5.

men who set thir mindes on main matters and sufficiently urge them, in these most difficult times I finde not many. What I have spoken, is the language of that which is not call'd amiss *the good Old Cause*:[79] if it seem strange to any, it will not seem more strange, I hope, then convincing to backsliders. Thus much I should perhaps have said though I were sure I should have spoken only to trees and stones; and had none to cry to, but with the Prophet, *O earth, earth, earth!* to tell the very soil it self, what her perverse inhabitants are deaf to.[80] Nay though what I have spoke, should happ'n (which Thou suffer not, who didst create mankinde free; nor Thou next, who didst redeem us from being servants of men!) to be the last words of our expiring libertie. But I trust I shall have spoken perswasion to abundance of sensible and ingenuous men: to som perhaps whom God may raise of these stones to become children of reviving libertie;[81] and may reclaim, though they seem now chusing them a captain back for *Egypt*,[82] to bethink themselves a little and consider whether they are rushing; to exhort this torrent also of the people, not to be so impetuos, but to keep thir due channell; and at length recovering and uniting thir better resolutions, now that they see alreadie how open and unbounded the insolence and rage is of our common enemies, to stay these ruinous proceedings; justly and timely fearing to what a precipice of destruction the deluge of this epidemic madness would hurrie us through the general defection of a misguided and abus'd multitude.

---

79. The term was deployed ironically, and often sarcastically, by opponents of the Commonwealth.

80. Jeremiah 22:29.

81. Cf. the vision in Ezekiel 37 of the dry bones which revive as the prophet preaches to them.

82. The argument reverts to the intially posited warning of 'returning to bondage' (above, p. 327, Note 1).

DE DOCTRINA CHRISTIANA

(discovered 1823; first published 1825)

Milton's Latin treatise on Christian doctrine (see above, pp. 40 ff.) was most likely written sometime during the decade 1655–1665; the required materials began to be collected, no doubt, at an earlier period. Massive as the treatise is, only some of its more substantive or representative sections could be accommodated here; but the titles of the omitted chapters are given as a constant reminder of the work's aspiration after unity of argument.

Theoretically, Milton's principal approach is by way of the Bible. "I have chosen," he declares in his prefatory address, "to fill my pages even to redundance with quotations from Scripture, that so as little space as possible might be left for my own words, even when they arise from the context of revelation itself." The principle is often applied with relentless vigor, even if the exposition of controversial subjects like the subordinationism of the Son to the Father (pp. 373 ff.) or polygamy (pp. 385 ff.) necessarily involves discourses beyond the biblical passages dutifully invoked.

The Yale edition (vol. VI) provides a translation by John Carey; the Columbia edition reprinted here in part (from vols. XIV–XVII) provides the translation by Charles R. Sumner in 1825, ed. James H. Hanford and Waldo H. Dunn. Sumner's translation will most likely fail to please; but then *any* translation of a theological treatise is wont to prove inadequate, in that a theological discourse in one language can hardly ever be matched in another. The ensuing pages must therefore be deemed suggestive, not definitive. The committed reader will wish to consult Milton's Latin as a matter of priority.]

THE MAJOR PREMISES

JOHN MILTON ENGLISHMAN:

To all the churches of Christ, and to all who profess the Christian Faith throughout the world, Peace, and the Recognition of the Truth, and Eternal Salvation in God the Father, and in our Lord Jesus Christ.

Since the commencement of the last century, when religion began to be restored from the corruptions of more than thirteen hundred years to something of its original purity,[1] many treatises of theology have been published, conducted according to sounder principles, wherein the chief heads of Christian doctrine are set forth sometimes briefly, sometimes in a more enlarged and methodical order. I think myself obliged, therefore, to declare in the first instance why, if any works have already appeared as perfect as the nature of the subject will admit, I have not remained contented with them; or, if all my predecessors have treated it unsuccessfully, why their failure has not deterred me from attempting an undertaking of a similar kind.

If I were to say that I had devoted myself to the study of the Christian religion because nothing else can so effectually rescue the lives and minds of men from those two detestable curses, slavery and superstition, I should seem to have acted rather from a regard to my highest earthly comforts, than from a religious motive. But since it is only to the individual faith of each that the Deity has opened the way of eternal salvation, and as he requires that he who would be saved should have a personal belief of his own, I resolved not to repose on the faith or judgment of others in matters relating to God; but on the one hand, having taken the grounds of my faith from divine revelation alone, and on the other, having neglected nothing which depended on my own industry, I thought fit to scrutinize and ascertain for myself the several points of my religious belief, by the most careful perusal and meditation of the Holy Scriptures themselves . . .

1. The Reformation initiated by Luther in the "last century"—the sixteenth—is viewed by Milton as a return to the purity of early Christianity before the advent of the "corruptions" of medieval Catholicism

If I communicate the result of my inquiries to the world at large; if, as God is my witness, it be with a friendly and benignant feeling towards mankind, that I readily give as wide a circulation as possible to what I esteem my best and richest possession, I hope to meet with a candid reception from all parties, and that none at least will take unjust offence, even though many things should be brought to light which will at once be seen to differ from certain received opinions. I earnestly beseech all lovers of truth, not to cry out that the Church is thrown into confusion by that freedom of discussion and inquiry which is granted to the schools, and ought certainly to be refused to no believer, since we are ordered "to prove all things," and since the daily progress of the light of truth is productive far less of disturbance to the Church, than of illumination and edification. Nor do I see how the Church can be more disturbed by the investigation of truth, than were the Gentiles by the first promulgation of the gospel; since so far from recommending or imposing anything on my own authority, it is my particular advice that every one should suspend his opinion on whatever points he may not feel himself fully satisfied, till the evidence of Scripture prevail, and persuade his reason into assent and faith. Concealment is not my object; it is to the learned that I address myself, or if it be thought that the learned are not the best umpires and judges of such things, I should at least wish to submit my opinions to men of a mature and manly understanding, possessing a thorough knowledge of the doctrines of the gospel; on whose judgments I should rely with far more confidence, than on those of novices in these matters. And whereas the greater part of those who have written most largely on these subjects have been wont to fill whole pages with explanations of their own opinions, thrusting into the margin the texts in support of their doctrine with a summary reference to the chapter and verse, I have chosen, on the contrary, to fill my pages even to redundance with quotations from Scripture, that so as little space as possible might be left for my own words, even when they arise from the context of revelation itself.

It has also been my object to make it appear from the opinions I shall be found to have advanced, whether new or old, of how much consequence to the Christian religion is the liberty not only of winnowing and sifting every doctrine, but also of thinking and even writing respecting it, according to our individual faith and persuasion; an inference which will be stronger in proportion to the weight and importance of those opinions, or rather in proportion to the authority of Scripture, on the abundant testimony of which they rest. Without this liberty there is neither religion nor gosepl—force alone prevails—by which it is disgraceful for the Christian religion to be supported. Without this liberty we are still enslaved, not indeed, as formerly, under the divine law, but, what is worst of all, under the law of man, or to speak more truly, under a barbarous tyranny. But I do not expect from candid and judicious readers a conduct so unworthy of them, that like certain unjust and foolish men, they should stamp with the invidious name of heretic or heresy whatever appears to them to differ from the received opinions, without trying the doctrine by a comparison with Scripture testimonies. According to their notions, to have branded any one at random with this opprobrious mark, is to have refuted him without any trouble, by a single word. By the simple imputation of the name of heretic, they think that they have despatched their man at one blow. To men of this kind I answer, that in the time of the apostles, ere the New Testament was written, whenever the charge of heresy was applied as a term of reproach, that alone was considered as heresy which was at variance with their doctrine orally delivered, and that those only were looked upon as heretics, who according to Romans 16:17, 18, "caused divisions and offences contrary to the doctrine" of the apostles, "serving not our Lord Jesus Christ, but their own belly." By parity of reasoning therefore, since the compilation of the New Testament, I maintain that nothing but what is in contradiction to it can properly be called heresy.

For my own part, I adhere to the Holy Scriptures alone; I follow no other heresy or sect. I had not even read any of the works of heretics, so called, when the mistakes of those who are reckoned for orthodox, and their incautious handling of Scripture, first taught me to agree with their opponents whenever those opponents agreed with Scripture. If this be heresy, I confess with St. Paul, Acts 24:14, "that after the way which they call heresy, so worship I the God of my fathers, believing all things which are written in the law and the prophets"; to which I add, whatever is written in the New Testament. Any other judges or paramount interpreters of the Christian belief, together with all implicit faith, as it is called, I, in common with the whole Protestant Church, refuse to recognize.

For the rest, brethren, cultivate truth with brotherly love. Judge of my present undertaking according to the admonishing of the Spirit of God, and neither adopt my sentiments, nor reject them, unless every doubt has been removed from your belief by the clear testimony of relevation. Finally, live in the faith of our Lord and Savior Jesus Christ. Farewell.

J.M.

. . . .

BOOK ONE

CHAP. I. *Of the Definition of Christian Doctrine, and the Several Parts Thereof.*

The Christian Doctrine is that Divine Revelation disclosed in various ages by Christ (though he was not known under that name in the beginning) [2] concerning the nature and worship of the Deity, for the promotion of the glory of God, and the salvation of mankind . . .

Christian doctrine is comprehended under two divisions: *Faith, or the knowledge of God*; and *Love, or the worship of God* . . .

2. Christ (the Anointed One) is understood to be a stage in the gradual revelation of the Divine Purpose to man.

CHAP. II. *Of God.*

Though there be not a few who deny the existence of God, yet the Deity has imprinted upon the human mind so many unquestionable tokens of himself, and so many traces of him are apparent throughout the whole of nature, that no one in his senses can remain ignorant of the truth . . . There can be no doubt that every thing in the world, by the beauty of its order, and the evidence of a determinate and beneficial purpose which pervades it, testifies that some supreme efficient Power must have preexisted, by which the whole was ordained for a specific end.

There are some who pretend that nature or fate is this supreme Power: but the very name of nature implies that it must owe its birth to some prior agent, or, to speak properly, signifies in itself nothing; but means either the essence of a thing, or that general law which is the origin of every thing, and under which every thing acts; on the other hand, fate can be nothing but a divine decree emanating from some almighty power.

Further, those who attribute the creation of every thing to nature, must necessarily associate chance with nature as a joint divinity; so that they gain nothing by this theory, except that in the place of that one God, whom they cannot tolerate, they are obliged, however reluctantly, to substitute two sovereign rulers of affairs, who must almost always be in opposition to each other. In short, many visible proofs, the verification of numberless predictions, a multitude of wonderful works have compelled all nations to believe, either that God, or that some evil power whose name was unknown, presided over the affairs of the world. Now that evil should prevail over good, and be the true supreme power, is as unmeet as it is incredible. Hence it follows as a necessary consequence, that God exists.

Again: the existence of God is further proved by that feeling, whether we term it conscience, or right reason, which even in the worst of characters is not altogether extinguished. If there were no God, there would be no distinction between right and wrong; the estimate of virtue and vice would entirely depend on the blind opinion of men; none would follow virtue, none would be restrained from vice by any sense of shame, or fear of the laws, unless conscience or right reason did from time to time convince every one, however unwilling, of the existence of God, the Lord and ruler of all things, to whom, sooner or later, each must give an account of his own actions, whether good or bad.

The whole tenor of Scripture proves the same thing; and the disciples of the doctrine of Christ may fairly be required to give assent to this truth before all others, according to Hebrews 11 :6, "he that cometh to God, must believe that he is." It is proved also by the dispersion of the ancient nation of the Jews throughout the whole world, conformably to what God often forewarned them would happen on account of their sins. Nor is it only to pay the penalty of their own guilt that they have been reserved in their scattered state, among the rest of the nations, through the revolution of successive ages, and even to the present day; but also to be a perpetual and living testimony to all people under heaven, of the existence of God, and of the truth of the Holy Scriptures.

No one, however, can have right thoughts of God, with nature or reason alone as his guide, independent of the word, or message of God. Romans 10 : 14, "how shall they believe in him of whom they have not heard?"

God is known, so far as he is pleased to make us acquainted with himself, either from his own nature, or from his efficient power.

When we speak of knowing God, it must be understood with reference to the imperfect comprehension of man; for to know God as he really is, far transcends the powers of man's thoughts, much more of his perception. 1 Timothy 6 : 16, "dwelling in the light which no man can approach unto." God therefore has made as full a revelation of himself as our minds can conceive, or the weakness of our nature can bear. Exodus 33 : 20, 23, "there shall no man see me, and live . . . but thou shalt see my back parts." Isaiah 6 : 1, "I saw the Lord sitting upon a throne, high and lifted up, and his train filled the temple." John 1:18, "no man hath seen God at any time." 6:46, "not that any man hath seen the Father, save he which is of God, he hath seen the Father." 5:37, "ye have neither heard his voice at any time." 1 Corinthians 13:12, "we see through a glass, darkly . . . in part."

Our safest way is to form in our minds such a conception of God, as shall correspond with his own delineation and representation of himself in the sacred writings. For granting that both in the literal and figurative descriptions of God, he is exhibited not as he really is, but in such a manner as may be within the scope of our comprehensions, yet we ought to entertain such a conception of him, as he, in condescending to accommodate himself to our capacities, has shown that he desires we should conceive. For it is on this very account that he has lowered himself to our level, lest in our flights above the reach of human understanding, and beyond the written word of Scripture, we should be tempted to indulge in vague cogitations and subtleties . . .[3]

Chap. III. *Of the Divine Decrees*

. . . The decrees of God are general or special. God's general decree is that whereby he has decreed from all eternity of his own most free and wise and holy purpose, whatever he himself willed, or was about to do . . .

To comprehend the whole matter in a few words, the sum of the argument may be thus stated in strict conformity with reason. God of his wisdom determined to create men and angels reasonable beings, and therefore free agents; foreseeing at the same time which way the bias of their will would incline, in the exercise of their own uncontrolled liberty. What then? shall we say that this foresight or foreknowledge on the part of God imposed on them the necessity of acting in any definite way? No more than if the future event had been foreseen by

3. The rest of the chapter collects a series of biblical quotations in order to delineate God's names and attributes.

any human being. For what any human being has foreseen as certain to happen, will not less certainly happen than what God himself has predicted. Thus Elisha foresaw how much evil Hazael would bring upon the children of Israel in the course of a few years, 2 Kings 8:12. Yet no one would affirm that the evil took place necessarily on account of the fore-knowledge of Elisha; for had he never foreknown it, the event would have occurred with equal certainty, through the free will of the agent. In like manner nothing happens of necessity because God has foreseen it; but he foresees the event of every action, because he is acquainted with their natural causes, which, in pursuance of his own decree, are left at liberty to exert their legitimate influence. Consequently the issue does not depend on God who foresees it, but on him alone who is the object of his foresight. Since therefore, as has before been shown, there can be no absolute decree of God regarding free agents, undoubtedly the prescience of the Deity (which can no more bias free agents than the prescience of man, that is, not at all, since the action in both cases is intransitive, and has no external influence) can neither impose any necessity of itself, nor can it be considered at all as the cause of free actions. If it be so considered, the very name of liberty must be altogether abolished as an unmeaning sound; and that not only in matters of religion, but even in questions of morality and indifferent things. There can be nothing but what will happen necessarily, since there is nothing but what is fore-known by God.

That this long discussion may be at length concluded by a brief summary of the whole matter, we must hold that God foreknows all future events, but that he has not decreed them all absolutely: lest the consequence should be that sin in general would be imputed to the Deity, and evil spirits and wicked men exempted from blame. Does my opponent avail himself of this, and think the concession enough to prove either that God does not foreknow every thing, or that all future events must therefore happen necessarily, because God has foreknown them? I allow that future events which God has foreseen, will happen certainly, but not of necessity. They will happen certainly, because the divine prescience cannot be deceived, but they will not happen necessarily, because prescience can have no influence on the object foreknown; inasmuch as it is only an intransitive action. What therefore is to happen according to contingency and the free will of man, is not the effect of God's prescience, but is produced by the free agency of its own natural causes, the future spontaneous inclination of which is perfectly known to God. Thus God foreknew that Adam would fall of his own free will; his fall was therefore certain, but not necessary, since it proceeded from his own free will, which is incompatible with necessity. Thus also God foreknew that the Israelites would turn from the true worship to strange gods, Deuteronomy 31 : 16. If they were to be led to revolt necessarily on account of this prescience on the part of God, it was unjust to threaten them with the many evils which he was about to send upon them, 31:17, it would have been to no purpose that a song was ordered to be written, which should be a witness for him against the children of Israel, because their sin would have been of necessity. The truth is that the prescience of God, like that of Moses, 31:27, had no extraneous influence, and God testifies, 31:16, that he foreknew they would sin from their own voluntary impulse, and of their own accord—"this people will rise up," &c. and 31:18, "I will surely hide my face in that day . . . in that they are turned unto other gods." Hence the subsequent revolt of the Israelites was not the consequence of God's foreknowledge, but his foreknowledge led him to know that, although they were free agents, they would certainly revolt, owing to causes with which he was well acquainted. 31:20, 21, "when they shall have eaten and filled themselves, and waxen fat, then will they turn unto other gods . . . I know their imagination which they go about, even now before I have brought them into the land which I sware."

From what has been said it is sufficiently evident, that free causes are not impeded by any law of necessity arising from the decree or prescience of God. There are some who in their zeal to oppose this doctrine, do not hesitate even to assert that God is himself the cause and origin of sin. Such men, if they are not to be looked upon as misguided rather than mischievous, should be ranked among the most abandoned of all blasphemers. An attempt to refute them, would be nothing more than an argument to prove that God was not the evil spirit . . .

CHAP. IV. *Of Predestination*

The principal special decree of God relating to man is termed Predestination, whereby God in pity to mankind, though foreseeing that they would fall of their own accord, predestinated to eternal salvation before the foundation of the world those who should believe and continue in the faith; for a manifestation of the glory of his mercy, grace, and wisdom, according to his purpose in Christ.

It has been the practice of the schools to use the word predestination, not only in the sense of election, but also of reprobation. This is not consistent with the caution necessary on so momentous a subject, since wherever it is mentioned in Scripture, election alone is uniformly intended . . .[4]

It was not simply man as a being who was to be created, but man as a being who was to fall of his own accord, that was the matter or object of predestination; for that manifestation of divine grace and mercy which God designed as the ultimate purpose of predestination, presupposes the existence of sin and misery in man, originating from himself alone. That the fall of man was not necessary is admitted on all sides; but if such, nevertheless, was the nature of the divine decree, that his fall became really inevitable, both which opinions, however contradictory, are sometimes held by the same persons, then the restoration of man, after he had lapsed of necessity, became no longer a matter of grace on the part of God, but of simple justice. For if it be granted that he lapsed, though not against his own will, yet of necessity, it will be impossible not

4. Here as before, the claim advanced is promptly supported by a number of biblical quotations.

to think that the admitted necessity must have overruled or influenced his will by some secret force or guidance. But if God foresaw that man would fall of his own free will, there was no occasion for any decree relative to the fall itself, but only relative to the provision to be made for man, whose future fall was foreseen. Since then the apostasy of the first man was not decreed, but only foreknown by the infinite wisdom of God, it follows that predestination was not an absolute decree before the fall of man; and even after his fall, it ought always to be considered and defined as arising, not so much from a decree itself, as from the immutable condition of a decree . . .

Scripture . . . offers salvation and eternal life equally to all, under the condition of obedience in the Old Testament, and of faith in the New. There can be no doubt that the tenor of the decree as promulgated was in conformity with the decree itself, otherwise the integrity of God would be impugned, as expressing one intention, and concealing another within his breast . . . God originally foreknew those who should believe; that is, he decreed or announced it as his pleasure that it should be those alone who should find grace in his sight through Christ, that is, all men, if they would believe. These he predestinated to salvation, and to this end he, in various ways, called all mankind to believe, or in other words, to acknowledge God in truth; those who actually thus believed he justified; and those who continued in the faith unto the end he finally glorified . . . Those therefore who were about to love, that is, to believe in God, God foreknew or approved; or in general all men, if they should believe; those whom he thus foreknew, he predestinated, and called them that they might believe; those who believed, he justified. But if God justified believers, and believers only, inasmuch as it is faith alone that justifieth, he foreknew those only who would believe, for those whom he foreknew he justified; those therefore whom he justified he also foreknew, namely, those alone who were about to believe. So Romans 11 : 2, "God hath not cast away his people which he foreknew," that is, believers, as appears from

11 : 20. 2 Timothy 2 : 19, "the Lord knoweth them that are his," that is, "all who name the name of Christ, and depart from iniquity"; or in other words, all believers. 1 Peter 1 : 2, "elect according to the foreknowledge of God the Father, through sanctification of the Spirit, unto obedience and sprinkling of the blood of Jesus Christ." This can be applicable to none but believers, whom the Father has chosen, according to his foreknowledge and approbation of them, through the sanctification of the Spirit and faith, without which the sprinkling of the blood of Christ would avail them nothing. Hence it seems that the generality of commentators are wrong in interpreting the foreknowledge of God in these passages in the sense of prescience; since the prescience of God seems to have no connection with the principle or essence of predestination; for God has predestinated and elected whoever believes and continues in the faith. Of what consequence is it to us to know whether the prescience of God foresees who will, or will not, subsequently believe? for no one believes because God has foreseen his belief, but God foresees his belief because he was about to believe. Nor is it easy to understand how the prescience or foreknowledge of God with regard to particular persons can be brought to bear at all upon the doctrine of predestination, except for the purpose of raising a number of useless and utterly inapplicable questions. For why should God foreknow particular individuals, or what could he foreknow in them which should induce him to predestinate them in particular, rather than all in general, when the condition of faith, which was common to all mankind, had been once laid down. Without searching deeper into this subject, let us be contented to know nothing more than that God, out of his infinite mercy and grace in Christ, has predestinated to salvation all who should believe . . .

But an objection of another kind may perhaps be made. If God be said to have predestinated men only on condition that they believe and continue in the faith, predestination will not be altogether of grace, but must depend on the will and belief of mankind; which is derogatory to the exclusive efficacy of divine grace. I maintain on the contrary that, so far from the doctrine of grace being impugned, it is thus placed in a much clearer light than by the theory of those who make the objection. For the grace of God is seen to be infinite, in the first place, by his showing any pity at all for man whose fall was to happen through his own fault. Secondly, by his "so loving the world, that he gave his only begotten Son" for its salvation. Thirdly, by his granting us again the power of volition, that is, of acting freely, in consequence of recovering the liberty of the will by the renewing of the Spirit. It was thus that he opened the heart of Lydia, Acts 16:14. Admitting, however, that the condition whereon the decree depends (that is to say, the will enfranchised by God himself, and that faith which is required of mankind) is left in the power of free agents, there is nothing in the doctrine either derogatory to grace, or inconsistent with justice; since the power of willing and believing is either the gift of God, or, so far as it is inherent in man, partakes not of the nature of merit or good works, but only of a natural faculty. Nor does this reasoning represent God as depending upon the human will, but as fulfilling his own pleasure, whereby he has chosen that man should always use his own will with a regard to the love and worship of the Deity, and consequently with a regard to his own salvation. If this use of the will be not admitted, whatever worship or love we render to God is entirely vain and of no value; the acceptableness of duties done under a law of necessity is diminished, or rather is annihilated altogether, inasmuch as freedom can no longer be attributed to that will over which some fixed decree is inevitably suspended.

The objections, therefore, which some urge so vehemently against this doctrine, are of no force whatever; namely, that the repentance and faith of the predestinated having been foreseen, predestination becomes posterior in point of time to works, that it is rendered dependent on the will of man, that God is defrauded of part of the glory of our salvation, that man is puffed up with pride, that the foundations of all Christian consolation in life and in death are shaken, that gratuitous ustification is denied. On the contrary, the scheme, and consequently the glory, not only of the divine grace, but also of the divine wisdom and justice, is thus displayed in a clearer manner than on the opposite hypothesis; and consequently the principal end is effected which God proposed to himself in predestination . . .

Thus much, therefore, may be considered as a certain and irrefragable truth: that God excludes no one from the pale of repentance and eternal salvation, till he has despised and rejected the propositions of sufficient grace, offered even to a late hour, for the sake of manifesting the glory of his long-suffering and justice . . .

CHAP. V. [Of the Son of God]

PREFATORY REMARKS

I cannot enter upon subjects of so much difficulty as the Son of God and the Holy Spirit, without again premising a few introductory remarks. If indeed I were a member of the Church of Rome, which requires implicit obedience to its creed on all points of faith, I should have acquiesced from education or habit in its simple decree and authority, even though it denies that the doctrine of the Trinity, as now received, is capable of being proved from any passage of Scripture. But since I enroll myself among the number of those who acknowledge the word of God alone as the rule of faith, and freely advance what appears to me much more clearly deducible from the Holy Scriptures than the commonly received opinion, I see no reason why any one who belongs to the same Protestant or Reformed Church, and professes to acknowledge the same rule of faith as myself, should take offence at my freedom, particularly as I impose my authority on no one, but merely propose what I think more worthy of belief than the creed in general acceptation. I only entreat that my readers will ponder and examine my statements in a spirit which desires to discover nothing but the truth, and with a mind free from prejudice. For without intending to oppose the authority of Scripture, which I consider inviolably sacred, I only take upon myself to refute human interpretations as often as the occasion requires, conformably to my right, or rather to my duty as a man. If indeed those with whom I have to contend were able to produce direct attestation from heaven to the truth of the doctrine which they espouse, it would be nothing less than impiety to venture to raise, I do not say a clamor, but so much as a murmur against it. But inasmuch as they can lay claim to nothing more than human powers, assisted by that spiritual illumination which is common to all, it is not unreasonable that they should on their part allow the privileges of diligent research and free discussion to another inquirer, who is seeking truth through the same means and in the same way as themselves, and whose desire of benefiting mankind is equal to their own.

In reliance, therefore, upon divine assistance, let us now enter upon the subject itself.

OF THE SON OF GOD

Hitherto I have considered the internal efficiency of God, as manifested in his decrees. His external efficiency, or the execution of his decrees, whereby he carries into effect by external agency whatever decrees he has purposed within himself may be comprised under the heads of Generation, Creation and Government of the Universe.

First, Generation, whereby God, in pursuance of his decree has begotten his only Son; whence he chiefly derives his appelation of Father.

Generation must be an external efficiency, since the Father and Son are different persons; and the divines themselves acknowledge this, who argue that there is a certain emanation of the Son from the Father (which will be explained when the doctrine concerning the Holy Spirit is under examination) for though they teach that the Spirit is co-essential with the Father, they do not deny its emanation, procession, spiration and issuing from the Father, which are all expressions denoting external efficiency. In conjunction with this doctrine they hold that the Son is also co-essential with the Father, and generated from all eternity. Hence this question, which is naturally very obscure, becomes involved in still greater difficulties if the received opinion respecting it be followed; for though the Father be said in Scripture to have begotten the Son in a double sense, the one literal, with reference to the production of the Son, the other metaphorical, with reference to his exaltation, many commentators have applied the passages which allude to the exaltation and mediatorial functions of Christ as proof of his generation from all eternity. They have indeed this excuse, if any excuse can be received in such a case, that it is impossible to find a single text in all Scripture to prove the eternal generation of the Son. Certain, however, it is, whatever some of the moderns[5] may allege to the contrary, that the Son existed in the beginning, under the name of the logos or word, and was the first of the whole creation, by whom afterwards all other things were made both in heaven and earth. John 1:1-3, "in the beginning was the Word, and the Word was with God, and the Word was God," &c. 17:5, "and now, O Father, glorify me with thine own self with the glory which I had with thee before the world was." Colossians 1:15, 18, "the first-born of every creature." Revelation 3:14, "the beginning of the creation of God." 1 Corinthians 8:6, "Jesus Christ, by whom are all things." Ephesians 3:9, "who created all things by Jesus Christ." Colossians 1:16, "all things were created by him and for him." Hebrews 1:2, "by whom also he made the worlds," whence it is said, 1:10, "thou, Lord, in the beginning hast laid the foundation of the earth"; respecting which more will be said in the seventh chapter, on the Creation.

All these passages prove the existence of the Son before the world was made, but they conclude nothing respecting his generation from all eternity. The other texts which are pro-

5. In opposing himself to the "moderns," Milton aligns himself with those Patristic writers who upheld "subordinationism" or the differentiation between the Father and the Son argued here. On the theological background, consult *Bright Essence* (as below, p. 461).

duced relate only to his metaphorical generation, that is, to his resuscitation from the dead, or to his unction to the mediatorial office, according to St. Paul's own interpretation of the second Psalm: "I will declare the decree; Jehovah hath said unto me, Thou are my Son; this day have I begotten thee," which the apostle thus explains, Acts 13:32, 33, "God hath fulfilled the promise unto us their children, in that he hath raised up Jesus again; as it is also written in the second Psalm Thou art my Son; this day have I begotten thee." Romans 1:4 "declared to be the Son of God with power, according to the Spirit of holiness, by the resurrection from the dead." Hence Colossians 1:18, Revelation 1:4, "the first begotten of the dead." Hebrews 1:5, speaking of the exaltation of the Son above the angels; "for unto which of the angels said he at any time, Thou art my Son, this day have I begotten thee? and again, I will be to him a Father, and he shall be to me a Son." Again, 5:5, 6, with reference to the priesthood of Christ; "so also Christ glorified not himself to be made an High Priest but he that said unto him, Thou art my Son, this day have I begotten thee: as he saith also in another place, Thou art a priest for ever," &c. Further, it will be apparent from the second Psalm, that God has begotten the Son, that is, has made him a king: 2:6, "yet have I set my King upon my holy hill of Sion"; and then in the next verse, after having anointed his King, whence the name of *Christ* is derived, he says, "this day have I begotten thee." Hebrews 1:4, 5, "being made so much better than the angels, as he hath by inheritance obtained a more excellent name than they." No other name can be intended but that of Son, as the following verse proves: "for unto which of the angels said he at any time, Thou art my Son; this day have I begotten thee?" The Son also declares the same of himself. John 10:35, 36, "say ye of Him whom the Father hath sanctified, and sent into the world, Thou blasphemest, because I said, I am the Son of God?" By a similar figure of speech though in a much lower sense, the saints are also said to be begotten of God.

It is evident however upon a careful comparison and examination of all these passages, and particularly from the whole of the second Psalm, that however the generation of the Son may have taken place, it arose from no natural necessity, as is generally contended, but was no less owing to the decree and will of the Father than his priesthood or kingly power, or his resuscitation from the dead. Nor is it any objection to this that he bears the title of begotten, in whatever sense that expression is to be understood, or of God's *own Son*, Romans 8:32. For he is called the own Son of God merely because he had no other Father besides God, whence he himself said, that *God was his Father*, John 5:18. For to Adam God stood less in the relation of Father, than of Creator, having only formed him from the dust of the earth; whereas he was properly the Father of the Son made of his own substance. Yet it does not follow from hence that the Son is co-essential with the Father, for then the title of Son would be least of all applicable to him, since he who is properly the Son is not coeval with the Father, much less of the same numerical essence, otherwise the Father and the Son would be one person; nor did the Father beget him from any natural necessity, but of his own free will, a mode more perfect and more agreeable to the paternal dignity; particularly since the Father is God, all whose works, and consequently the works of generation, are executed freely according to his own good pleasure, as has been already proved from Scripture.

For questionless, it was in God's power consistently with the perfection of his own essence not to have begotten the Son, inasmuch as generation does not pertain to the nature of the Deity, who stands in no need of propagation; but whatever does not pertain to his own essence or nature, he does not effect like a natural agent from any physical necessity. If the generation of the Son proceeded from a physical necessity, the Father impaired himself by physically begetting a co-equal; which God could no more do than he could deny himself; therefore the generation of the Son cannot have proceeded otherwise than from a decree, and of the Father's own free will.

Thus the Son was begotten of the Father in consequence of his decree, and therefore within the limits of time, for the decree itself must have been anterior to the execution of the decree . . .

The Son is also called *only begotten*. John 1 : 14, "and we beheld his glory, the glory as of the only begotten of the Father." 1 : 18, "the only begotten Son which is in the bosom of the Father." 3 : 16, 18, "he gave his only begotten Son." 1 John 4 : 9, "God sent his only begotten Son." Yet he is not called one with the Father in essence, inasmuch as he was visible to sight, and given by the Father, by whom also he was sent, and from whom he proceeded; but he enjoys the title of only begotten by way of superiority, as distinguished from many others who are also said to have been born of God. John 1 : 13, "which were born of God." 1 John 3 : 9, "whosoever is born of God, doth not commit sin." James 1 : 18, "of his own will begat he us with the word of truth." 1 John 5 : 1, "whosoever believeth," &c. "is born of God." 1 Peter 1 : 3, "which according to his abundant mercy hath begotten us again unto a lively hope." But since throughout the Scriptures the Son is never said to be begotten, except, as above, in a metaphorical sense, it seems probable that he is called *only begotten* principally because he is the one mediator between God and man.

So also the Son is called the *first born*. Romans 8 : 29, "that he might be the first born among many brethren." Colossians 1 : 15, "the first born of every creature." 1 : 18, "the first born from the dead." Hebrews 1 : 6, "when he bringeth in the first begotten into the world." Revelation 3 : 14, "the beginning of the creation of God"—all which passages preclude the idea of his coessentiality with the Father, and of his generation from all eternity. Thus it is said of Israel, Exodus 4 : 22, "thus saith Jehovah, Israel is my son, even my first born"; and of Ephraim, Jeremiah 31 : 9, "Ephraim is my first born"; and of all the saints, Hebrews 12 : 23, "to the general assembly of the first born."

Hitherto only the metaphorical generation of Christ has

been considered; but since to generate another who had no previous existence, is to give him being, and that if God generate by a physical necessity, he can generate nothing but a co-equal Deity, which would be inconsistent with self-existence, an essential attribute of Divinity; (so that according to the one hypothesis there would be two infinite Gods, or according to the other the *first* or *efficient* cause would become the *effect*, which no man in his senses will admit) it becomes necessary to inquire how or in what sense God the Father can have begotten the Son. This point also will be easily explained by reference to Scripture. For when the Son is said to be *the first born of every creature*, and *the beginning of the creation of God*, nothing can be more evident than that God of his own will created, or generated, or produced the Son before all things, endued with the divine nature, as in the fulness of time he miraculously begat him in his human nature of the Virgin Mary. The generation of the divine nature is described by no one with more sublimity and copiousness than by the apostle to the Hebrews, 1:2, 3, "whom he hath appointed heir of all things, by whom also he made the worlds; who being the brightness of his glory, and the express image of his person," &c. It must be understood from this, that God imparted to the Son as much as he pleased of the divine nature, nay of the divine substance itself, care being taken not to confound the substance with the whole essence, which would imply, that the Father had given to the Son what he retained numerically the same himself; which would be a contradiction of terms instead of a mode of generation. This is the whole that is revealed concerning the generation of the Son of God. Whoever wishes to be wiser than this, becomes foiled in his pursuit after wisdom, entangled in the deceitfulness of vain philosophy, or rather of sophistry, and involved in darkness . . .[6]

6. Expectations to the contrary, Milton's longest single chapter does not end here. Anticipating a chorus of disapprobation, he went on to argue at even greater length the premises set forth in the pages reprinted to this point.

CHAP. VI. *Of the Holy Spirit*

CHAP. VII. *Of the Creation*

The second species of external efficiency is commonly called
Creation . . . Creation is that act whereby God the Father
produced every thing that exists by his Word and Spirit, that
is, by his will, for the manifestation of the glory of his power
and goodness . . .

Thus far it has appeared that God the Father is the primary
and efficient cause of all things. With regard to the original
matter of the universe, however, there has been much difference of opinion. Most of the moderns contend that it was
formed from nothing, a basis as unsubstantial as that of their
own theory. In the first place, it is certain that neither the
Hebrew verb בָּרָא nor the Greek χτίζειν, nor the Latin *creare*
can signify to create out of nothing. On the contrary, these
words uniformly signify to create out of matter. Genesis 1:21
27, "God created . . . every living creature which the waters
brought forth abundantly . . . male and female created he
them." Isaiah 54:16, "behold, I have created the smith . . .
have created the waster to destroy." To allege, therefore, that
creation signifies production out of nothing, is, as logicians
say, to lay down premises without a proof; for the passages of
Scripture commonly quoted for this purpose, are so far from
confirming the received opinion, that they rather imply the
contrary; namely, that all things were not made out of nothing,
2 Corinthians 4:6, "God, who commanded the light to shine
out of darkness." That this darkness was far from being a mere
negation, is clear from Isaiah 45:7, "I am Jehovah; I form the
light, and create darkness." If the darkness be nothing, God in
creating darkness created nothing, or in other words, he created and did not create, which is a contradiction. Again, what
we are required "to understand through faith" respecting "the
worlds," is merely this, that "the things which were seen were
not made of things which do appear," Hebrews 11:3. Now
"the things which do not appear" are not to be considered as
synonymous with nothing, for nothing does not admit of a

plural, nor can a thing be made and compacted together out of nothing, as out of a number of things, but the meaning is, that they do not appear as they now are. The apocryphal writers, whose authority may be considered as next to that of the Scriptures, speak to the same effect. Wisdom 11:17, "thy almighty hand that made the world of matter without form." 2 Maccabees 7:28, "God made the earth and all that is therein of things that were not." The expression in Matthew 2:18 may be quoted, "the children of Rachel are not." This, however, does not mean properly that they are nothing, but that, according to a common Hebraism, they are no longer among the living.

It is clear then that the world was framed out of matter of some kind or other. For since action and passion are relative terms, and since, consequently, no agent can act externally, unless there be some patient, such as matter, it appears impossible that God could have created this world out of nothing; not from any defect of power on his part, but because it was necessary that something should have previously existed capable of receiving passively the exertion of the divine efficacy. Since, therefore, both Scripture and reason concur in pronouncing that all these things were made, not out of nothing, but out of matter, it necessarily follows, that matter must either have always existed independently of God, or have originated from God at some particular point of time. That matter should have been always independent of God, seeing that it is only a passive principle, dependent on the Deity, and subservient to him; and seeing, moreover, that, as in number, considered abstractedly, so also in time or eternity there is no inherent force or efficacy; that matter, I say, should have existed of itself from all eternity, is inconceivable. If on the contrary it did not exist from all eternity, it is difficult to understand from whence it derives its origin. There remains, therefore, but one solution of the difficulty, for which moreover we have the authority of Scripture, namely, that all things are of God. Romans 11:36, "for of him, and through him, and to him are all things." 1 Corinthians 8:6, "there is but one God, the Fa-

ther, of whom are all things": where the same Greek preposi
tion is used in both cases. Hebrews 2:11, "for both he tha
sanctifieth, and they who are sanctified, are all of one."

In the first place, there are, as is well known to all, fou
kinds of causes, *efficient*, *material*, *formal*, and *final*. Inas
much then as God is the primary, and absolute, and sole caus
of all things, there can be no doubt but that he comprehend
and embraces within himself all the causes above mentioned
Therefore the material cause must be either God, or nothing
Now nothing is no cause at all; and yet it is contended tha
forms, and above all, that human forms, were created out o
nothing. But matter and form, considered as internal causes
constitute the thing itself; so that either all things must hav
had two causes only, and those external, or God will not hav
been the perfect and absolute cause of every thing. Secondly
it is an argument of supreme power and goodness, that suc
diversified, multiform, and inexhaustible virtue should exis
and be *substantially* inherent in God (for that virtue canno
be *accidental* which admits of degrees, and of augmentatio
or remission, according to his pleasure) and that this d
versified and substantial virtue should not remain dormar
within the Deity, but should be diffused and propagated an
extended as far and in such manner as he himself may wil
For the original matter of which we speak, is not to be looke
upon as an evil or trivial thing, but as intrinsically good, an
the chief productive stock of every subsequent good. It was
substance, and derivable from no other source than from th
fountain of every substance, though at first confused an
formless, being afterwards adorned and digested into order b
the hand of God.

Those who are dissatisfied because, according to this view
substance was imperfect, must also be dissatisfied with Go
for having originally produced it out of nothing in an impe
fect state, and without form. For what difference does
make, whether God produced it in this imperfect state out o
nothing, or out of himself? By this reasoning, they only tran
fer that imperfection to the divine efficiency, which they a
unwilling to admit can properly be attributed to substanc

considered as an efflux of the Deity. For why did not God create all things out of nothing in an absolutely perfect state at first? It is not true, however, that matter was in its own nature originally imperfect; it merely received embellishment from the accession of forms, which are themselves material. And if it be asked how what is corruptible can proceed from incorruption, it may be asked in return how the virtue and efficacy of God can proceed out of nothing. Matter, like the form and nature of the angels itself, proceeded incorruptible from God; and even since the fall it remains incorruptible as far as concerns its essence . . .

CHAP. VIII. *Of the Providence of God, or of his General Government of the Universe*

The remaining species of God's external efficiency, is his government of the whole creation. His general government is that whereby God the Father regards, preserves, and governs the whole of creation with infinite wisdom and holiness according to the conditions of his decree . . .

The providence of God is either ordinary or extraordinary. His ordinary providence is that whereby he upholds and preserves the immutable order of causes appointed by him in the beginning. This is commonly, and indeed too frequently, described by the name of nature; for nature cannot possibly mean anything but the mysterious power and efficacy of that divine voice which went forth in the beginning, and to which, as to a perpetual command, all things have since paid obedience . . . The extraordinary providence of God is that whereby God produces some effect out of the usual order of nature, or gives the power of producing the same effect to whomsoever he may appoint. This is what we call a miracle. Hence God alone is the primary author of miracles, as he only is able to invert that order of things which he has himself appointed . . .

CHAP. IX. *Of the Special Government of Angels*

CHAP. X. *Of the Special Government of Man before the Fall, in-*
cluding the Institutions of the Sabbath and of Marriage

The Providence of God as regards mankind relates to man either in his state of rectitude or since his fall.

With regard to that which relates to man in his state of rectitude, God, having placed him in the garden of Eden, and furnished him with whatever was calculated to make life happy,
commanded him, as a test of his obedience, to refrain from
eating of the single tree of knowledge of good and evil, under
penalty of death if he should disregard the injunction. Genesis
1:28, "subdue the earth, and have dominion—." 2:15–17, "he
put him into the garden of Eden . . . of every tree in the garden thou mayest freely eat; but in the day that thou eatest of
the tree of the knowledge of good and evil, thou shalt surely
die."

This is sometimes called "the covenant of works," though it
does not appear from any passage of Scripture to have been
either a covenant, or of works. No works whatever were required of Adam; a particular act only was forbidden. It was
necessary that something should be forbidden or commanded
as a test of fidelity, and that an act in its own nature indifferent, in order that man's obedience might be thereby manifested. For since it was the disposition of man to do what was
right, as a being naturally good and holy, it was not necessary
that he should be bound by the obligation of a covenant to perform that to which he was of himself inclined; nor would he
have given any proof of obedience by the performance of works
to which he was led by a natural impulse, independent
of the divine command. Not to mention, that no command,
whether proceeding from God or from a magistrate, can properly be called a covenant, even where rewards and punishments are attached to it; but rather an exercise of jurisdiction.

The tree of knowledge of good and evil was not a sacrament,
as it is generally called; for a sacrament is a thing to be used,
not abstained from: but a pledge, as it were, and memorial of
obedience.

It was called the tree of knowledge of good and evil from the event; for since Adam tasted it, we not only know evil, but we know good only by means of evil. For it is by evil that virtue is chiefly exercised, and shines with greater brightness . . .

[Of Marriage]

Marriage is a most intimate connection of man with woman, ordained by God, for the purpose either of the procreation of children, or of the relief and solace of life. Hence it is said, Genesis 2:24, "therefore shall a man leave his father and his mother, and shall cleave unto his wife, and they shall be one flesh." This is neither a law nor a commandment, but an effect or natural consequence of that most intimate union which would have existed between them in the perfect state of man; nor is the passage intended to serve any other purpose, than to account for the origin of families.

In the definition which I have given, I have not said, in compliance with the common opinion, "of one man with one woman," lest I should by implication charge the holy patriarchs and pillars of our faith, Abraham, and the others who had more than one wife at the same time, with habitual fornication and adultery; and lest I should be forced to exclude from the sanctuary of God as spurious, the holy offspring which sprang from them, yea, the whole of the sons of Israel, for whom the sanctuary itself was made. For it is said, Deuteronomy 23:2, "a bastard shall not enter into the congregation of Jehovah, even to his tenth generation." Either therefore polygamy is a true marriage, or all children born in that state are spurious; which would include the whole race of Jacob, the twelve holy tribes chosen by God. But as such an assertion would be absurd in the extreme, not to say impious, and as it is the height of injustice, as well as an example of most dangerous tendency in religion, to account as sin what is not such in reality; it appears to me, that, so far from the question respecting the lawfulness of polygamy being trivial, it is of the highest importance that it should be decided . . .

[Milton at this point argues against three biblical passages presumably opposed to polygamy (Genesis 2:24, Leviticus 18:18, and Deuteronomy 17:17), collects other passages favorable to his point of view, and concludes:]

It appears to me sufficiently established by the above arguments that polygamy is allowed by the law of God; lest however any doubt should remain, I will subjoin abundant examples of men whose holiness renders them fit patterns for imitation, and who are among the lights of our faith. Foremost I place Abraham, the father of all the faithful, and of the holy seed, Genesis 16:1, &c. Jacob, chap. 3, and, if I mistake not, Moses, Numbers 12:1, "for he had married [a Cushite, marginal translation, or] an Ethiopian woman." It is not likely that the wife of Moses, who had been so often spoken of before by her proper name of Zipporah, should now be called by the new title of a Cushite; or that the anger of Aaron and Miriam should at this time be suddenly kindled, because Moses forty years before had married Zipporah; nor would they have acted thus scornfully towards one whom the whole house of Israel had gone out to meet on her arrival with her father Jethro. If then he married the Cushite during the lifetime of Zipporah, his conduct in this particular received the express approbation of God himself, who moreover punished with severity the unnatural opposition of Aaron and his sister. Next I place Gideon, that signal example of faith and piety, Judges 8:30, 31, and Elkanah, a rigid Levite, the father of Samuel; who was so far from believing himself less acceptable to God on account of his double marriage, that he took with him his two wives every year to the sacrifices and annual worship, into the immediate presence of God; nor was he therefore reproved, but went home blessed with Samuel, a child of excellent promise, 1 Samuel 2:10. Passing over several other examples, though illustrious, such as Caleb, 1 Chronicles 2:46, 48, 7:1, 4, the sons of Issachar, in number "six and thirty thousand men, for they had many wives and sons," contrary to the modern European practice, where in many places the land is suffered to remain uncultivated for want of population;

and also Manasseh, the son of Joseph, 1 Chronicles 7:14. I come to the prophet David, whom God loved beyond all men, and who took two wives, besides Michal; and this not in a time of pride and prosperity, but when he was almost bowed down by adversity, and when, as we learn from many of the psalms, he was entirely occupied in the study of the word of God, and in the right regulation of his conduct. 1 Samuel 25:42, 43, and afterwards, 2 Samuel 5:12, 13, "David perceived that Jehovah had established him king over Israel, and that he had exalted his kingdom for his people Israel's sake: and David took him more concubines and wives out of Jerusalem." Such were the motives, such the honorable and holy thoughts whereby he was influenced, namely, by the consideration of God's kindness towards him for his people's sake. His heavenly and prophetic understanding saw not in that primitive institution what we in our blindness fancy we discern so clearly; nor did he hesitate to proclaim in the supreme council of the nation the pure and honorable motives to which, as he trusted, his children born in polygamy owed their existence. 1 Chronicles 28:5, "of all my sons, for Jehovah hath given me many sons, he hath chosen," &c. I say nothing of Solomon, notwithstanding his wisdom, because he seems to have exceeded due bounds; although it is not objected to him that he had taken many wives, but that he had married strange women; 1 Kings 11:1, Nehemiah 13:26. His son Rehoboam "desired many wives," not in the time of his iniquity, but during the three years in which he is said to have walked in the way of David, 2 Chronicles 11:17, 21, 23. Of Joash mention has already been made; who was induced to take two wives, not by licentious passion, or the wanton desires incident to uncontrolled power, but by the sanction and advice of a most wise and holy man, Jehoiada the priest. Who can believe, either that so many men of the highest character should have sinned through ignorance for so many ages; or that their hearts should have been so hardened; or that God should have tolerated such conduct in his people? Let therefore the rule received among theologians have the same weight here as in other cases: "The practice of the saints is the best interpretation of the commandments" . . .

CHAP. XI. *Of the Fall of our First Parents, and of Sin*

. . . Sin is distinguished into that which is common to all men, and the personal sin of each individual. The sin which is common to all men is that which our first parents, and in them all their posterity committed, when, casting off their obedience to God, they tasted the fruit of the forbidden tree . . . This sin originated, first, in the instigation of the devil, as is clear from the narrative in Genesis 3 and from 1 John 3:8, "he that committeth sin is of the devil, for the devil sinneth from the beginning." Secondly, in the liability to fall with which man was created, whereby he, as the devil had done before him, "abode not in the truth" (John 8:44) nor "kept his first estate, but left his own habitation" (Jude 6). If the circumstances of this crime are duly considered, it will be acknowledged to have been a most heinous offence, and a transgression of the whole law. For what sin can be named, which was not included in this one act? It comprehended at once distrust in the divine veracity, and a proportionate credulity in the assurances of Satan; unbelief; ingratitude; disobedience; gluttony; in the man excessive uxoriousness, in the woman a want of proper regard for her husband, in both an insensibility to the welfare of their offspring, and that offspring the whole human race; parricide, theft, invasion of the rights of others, sacrilege, deceit, presumption in aspiring to divine attributes, fraud in the means employed to attain the object, pride, and arrogance . . .

The personal sin of each individual is that which each in his own person has committed independently of the sin which is common to all. Here likewise all men are guilty. Job 9:20, "if I justify myself, mine own mouth shall condemn me." 10:15, "if I be righteous, yet will I not lift up my head." Psalm 143:2, "in thy sight shall no man living be justified." Proverbs 20:9, "who can say, I am pure from my sin?" Ecclesiastes 7:20, "there is not a just man upon earth that doeth good, and sinneth not." Romans 3:23, "all have sinned."

Both kinds of sin, as well that which is common to all, as that which is personal to each individual, consist of the two following parts, whether we term them gradations, or divisions, or modes of sin, or whether we consider them in the light of cause and effect; namely, evil concupiscence, or the desire of sinning, and the act of sin itself . . . Evil concupiscence is that of which our original parents were first guilty, and which they transmitted to their posterity, as sharers in the primary transgression, in the shape of an innate propensity to sin . . . The second thing in sin, after evil concupiscence, is the crime itself, or the act of sinning, which is commonly called Actual Sin. This may be incurred, not only by actions commonly so called, but also by words and thoughts, and even by the omission of good actions . . .

Chap. XII. *Of the Punishment of Sin*

Chap. XIII. *Of the Death of the Body*

. . . The death of the body is to be considered in the light of a punishment for sin, no less than the other degrees of death, notwithstanding the contrary opinion entertained by some. Romans 5:13, 14, "until the law sin was in the world . . . death reigned from Adam to Moses." 1 Corinthians 15:21, "since by man came death"; that is to say, temporal as well as eternal death; as is clear from the corresponding member of the sentence, "by man came also the resurrection from the dead"; therefore that bodily death from which we are to rise again, originated in sin, and not in nature; contrary to the opinion of those who maintain that temporal death is the result of natural causes, and that eternal death alone is due to sin.

The death of the body is the loss or extinction of life. The common definition, which supposes it to consist in the separation of soul and body, is inadmissible. For what part of man is it that dies when this separation takes place? Is it the soul? This will not be admitted by the supporters of the above definition. Is it then the body? But how can that be said to die, which never had any life of itself? Therefore the separation of soul and body cannot be called the death of man.

Here then arises an important question, which, owing to the prejudice of divines in behalf of their preconceived opinions, has usually been dismissed without examination, instead of being treated with the attention it deserves. Is it the whole man, or the body alone, that is deprived of vitality? And as this is a subject which may be discussed without endangering our faith or devotion, whichever side of the controversy we espouse, I shall declare freely what seems to me the true doctrine, as collected from numberless passages of Scripture; without regarding the opinion of those, who think that truth is to be sought in the schools of philosophy, rather than in the sacred writings.

Inasmuch then as the whole man is uniformly said to consist of body, spirit, and soul (whatever may be the distinct provinces severally assigned to these divisions), I shall first show that the whole man dies, and, secondly, that each component part suffers privation of life. It is to be observed, first of all, that God denounced the punishment of death against the whole man that sinned, without excepting any part. For what could be more just, than that he who had sinned in his whole person, should die in his whole person? Or, on the other hand, what could be more absurd than that the mind, which is the part principally offending, should escape the threatened death; and that the body alone, to which immortality was equally allotted, before death came into the world by sin, should pay the penalty of sin by undergoing death, though not implicated in the transgression?

[Milton's procedure at this point is much the same as elsewhere: he collects the relevant biblical passages and annotates them in the light of the stated premise.]

CHAP. XIV. *Of Man's Restoration and of Christ as Redeemer*

. . . The restoration of man is the act whereby man, being delivered from sin and death by God the Father through Jesus Christ, is raised to a far more excellent state of grace and glory than that from which he had fallen . . . In this restoration are comprised the redemption and renovation of man. Redemption is that act whereby Christ, being sent in the fulness of time, redeemed all believers at the price of his own blood, by his own voluntary act, conformable to the eternal counsel and grace of God the Father . . .

Two points are to be considered in relation to Christ's character as Redeemer: his nature and office.

His nature is twofold, divine and human. Matthew 16:16, "the Christ, the Son of the living God." Genesis 3:15, "the seed of the woman." John 1:1, 14, "the Word of God . . . and the Word was made flesh." John 3:13, "he that came down from heaven, even the Son of man that is in heaven." John 5:31, "he that cometh from above . . . he that cometh from heaven." Acts 2:30, "of the fruit of the loins of David, according to the flesh." See also Romans 1:3, 8:3, "God sending his own Son in the likeness of sinful flesh." Romans 9:5, "of whom as concerning the flesh Christ came, who is over all, God." 1 Corinthians 15:47, "the second man is the Lord from heaven." Galatians 4:4, "God sent forth his Son, made of a woman." Philippians 2:7, 8, "but made himself of no reputation, and took upon him the form of a servant, and was made in the likeness of men, and being found in fashion as a man." Hebrews 2:14, 16, "he also himself took part of flesh and blood . . . he took not on him the nature of angels, but he took on him the seed of Abraham." Hebrews 14:5, etc., "wherefore when he cometh into the world, he saith, Sacrifice and offering thou wouldest not, but a body hast thou prepared me . . . then said I, Lo, I come." 1 John 1:7, "the blood of Jesus Christ his Son." 1 John 4:2, "every spirit that confesseth that Jesus Christ is come in the flesh, is of God." Colossians 2:9, "in him dwelleth all the fulness of the Godhead bodily" . . . John 3:34, "God giveth not the spirit by measure unto him." John 1:17, "grace and truth came by Jesus Christ." 1 Timothy 3:16, "God was manifest in the flesh," that is, in the incarnate Son, his own image. With regard to Christ's divine nature, the reader is referred to what was proved in a former chapter concerning the Son of God; from whence it follows, that he by whom all things were made both in heaven and earth, even the angels themselves, he who in the beginning was the Word, and God with God, and although not supreme, yet the first born of every creature, must necessarily have existed previous to his incarnation, whatever subtleties may have been invented to evade this conclusion by those who contend for the merely human nature of Christ.

This incarnation of Christ, whereby he, being God, took upon him the human nature, and was made flesh, without thereby ceasing to be numerically the same as before, is generally considered by theologians as, next to the Trinity in Unity, the greatest mystery of our religion. Of the mystery of the Trinity, however, no mention is made in Scripture; whereas the incarnation is frequently spoken of as a mystery. 1 Timothy 3:16, "without controversy great is the mystery of godliness; God was manifest in the flesh." Colossians 2:2, 3, "to the acknowledgment of the mystery of God, and of the Father, and of Christ; in which (namely, in this mystery) are hid all the treasures of wisdom." Ephesians 1:9, 10, "having made known unto us the mystery of his will . . . that he might gather together in one all things in Christ." Ephesians 3:4, "in the mystery of Christ." See also Colossians 4:3, Ephesians 3:9, "the fellowship of the mystery which from the beginning of the world hath been hid in God, who created all things by Jesus Christ." Colossians 1:26, 27, "the riches of the glory of this mystery . . . which is Christ" . . .

CHAP. XV. *Of the Office of the Mediator and of his Threefold Functions*

. . . The mediatorial office of Christ is that whereby, at the special appointment of God the Father, he voluntarily performed, and continues to perform, on behalf of man, whatever is requisite for obtaining reconciliation with God, and eternal salvation . . .

In treating of the office of the Mediator, we are to consider his threefold functions as prophet, priest, and king, and his manner of administering the same. His function as a prophet is to instruct his Chruch in heavenly truth, and to declare the whole will of his Father . . . [This] prophetical function began with the creation of the world, and will continue till the end of all things . . .

Christ's sacerdotal function is what whereby he once offered himself to God the Father as a sacrifice for sinners, and has always made, and still continues to make intercession for us . . . The kingly function of Christ is that whereby being made king by God the Father, he governs and preserves, chiefly by an inward law and spiritual power, the Church which he has purchased for himself, and conquers and subdues its enemies . . .

CHAP. XVI. *Of the Ministry of Redemption*

CHAP. XVII. *Of Man's Renovation, including his Calling*

CHAP. XVIII. *Of Regeneration*

CHAP. XIX. *Of Repentance*

CHAP. XX. *Of Saving Faith*

CHAP. XXI. *Of being ingrafted in Christ, and its Effects*

CHAP. XXII. *Of Justification*

. . . Justification is the gratuitous purpose of God, whereby those who are regenerate and ingrafted in Christ are absolved from sin and death through his most perfect satisfaction, and accounted just in the sight of God, not by the works of the law, but through faith . . .

An important question here arises, which is discussed with much vehemence by the advocates on both sides; namely, whether faith alone justifies? Our divines answer in the affirmative; adding, that works are the effects of faith, not the cause of justification, Romans 3:24, 27, 28, Galatians 2:16, as above. Others contend that justification is not by faith alone, on the authority of James 2:24, "by works a man is justified, and not by faith only." As however the two opinions appear at first sight inconsistent with each other, and incapable of being maintained together, the advocates of the former, to obviate the difficulty arising from the passage of St. James, allege that the apostle is speaking of justification in the sight of men, not in the sight of God. But whoever reads attentively from the fourteenth verse to the end of the chapter, will see that the apostle is expressly treating of justification in the sight of God. For the question there at issue relates to the faith which profits, and which is a living and a saving faith; consequently it cannot relate to that which justifies only in the sight of men, inasmuch as this latter may be hypocritical. When therefore the apostle says that we are justified by works, and not by faith only, he is speaking of the faith which profits, and which is a true, living, and saving faith. Considering then that the apostles, who treat this point of our religion with particular attention, nowhere, in summing up their doctrine, use words implying that a man is justified by faith alone, but generally conclude as follows, that "man is justified by faith without the deeds of the law," Romans 3:28. I am at a loss to conjecture why our divines should have narrowed the terms of the apostolical conclusion. Had they not so done, the declaration in the one text, that "by faith man is justified without the deeds of the law," would have appeared perfectly consistent with that in the other, "by works man is justified, and not by faith only." For St. Paul does not say simply that a man is justified without works, but "without the works of the law"; nor yet by faith alone, but "by faith which worketh by love," Galatians 5:6. Faith has its own works, which may be different from the works of the law. We are justified therefore by faith, but by a living, not a dead faith; and that faith alone which acts is counted living; James 2:17, 20, 26. Hence we are justified by faith without the works of the law, but not without the works of faith; inasmuch as a living and true faith cannot consist without works, though these latter may differ from the works of the written law . . .

The writings of the prophets, apostles, and evangelists, composed under divine inspiration, are called the Holy Scriptures. . . . The Scriptures, partly by reason of their own simplicity, and partly through divine illumination, are plain and perspicuous in all things necessary to salvation, and adapted to the instruction even of the most unlearned, through the medium of diligent and constant reading . . .

The requisites for the public interpretation of Scripture have been laid down by divines with much attention to usefulness, although they have not been observed with equal fidelity. They consist in knowledge of languages; inspection of the originals; examination of the context; care in distinguishing between literal and figurative expressions; consideration of cause and circumstance, of antecedents and consequents; mutual comparison of texts; and regard to the analogy of faith. Attention must also be paid to the frequent anomalies of syntax . . . Lastly, no inferences from the text are to be admitted, but such as follow necessarily and plainly from the words themselves; lest we should be constrained to receive what is not written for what is written, the shadow for the substance, the fallacies of human reasoning for the doctrines of God: for it is by the declarations of Scripture, and not by the conclusions of the schools, that our consciences are bound.

Every believer has a right to interpret the Scriptures for himself, inasmuch as he has the Spirit for his guide, and the mind of Christ is in him; nay, the expositions of the public interpreter can be of no use to him, except so far as they are confirmed by his own conscience . . . If however there be any difference among professed believers as to the sense of Scripture, it is their duty to tolerate such difference in each other, until God shall have revealed the truth to all. Philippians 3:15, 16, "let us therefore, as many as be perfect, be thus minded; and if in anything ye be otherwise minded, God shall reveal even this unto you: nevertheless, whereto we have already attained, let us walk by the same rule, let us mind the same thing." Romans 14:4, "to his own master he standeth or falleth: yea, he shall be holden up."

The rule and canon of faith, therefore, is Scripture alone. Psalm 19:9, "the judgments of Jehovah are true and righteous altogether." Scripture is the sole judge of controversies; or rather, every man is to decide for himself through its aid, under the guidance of the Spirit of God . . .

CHAP. XXXI. *Of Particular Churches*

CHAP. XXXII. *Of Church Discipline*

CHAP. XXXIII. *Of Perfect Glorification, including the Second Advent of Christ, the Resurrection of the Dead, and the General Conflagration*

BOOK TWO:

OF THE WORSHIP OF GOD

CHAP. I. *Of Good Works*

III

EXTRACTS, MAINLY ON LITERATURE

from a letter to Charles Diodati,
23 September 1637[1]

What besides God has resolved concerning me I know not, but this at least: He has instilled into me, if into any one, a vehement love of the beautiful.[2] Not with so much labour, as the fables have it, is Ceres said to have sought her daughter Prosperina as it is my habit day and night to seek for this idea of the beautiful, as for a certain image of supreme beauty, through all the forms and faces of things (for many are the shapes of things divine) and to follow it as it leads me on by some sure traces which I seem to recognize. Hence it is that, when any one scorns what the vulgar opine in their depraved estimation of things, and dares to feel and speak and be that which the highest wisdom throughout all ages has taught to be best, to that man I attach myself forthwith by a kind of real necessity, wherever I find him.

from a letter to Benedetto Bonmattei,
10 September 1638[3]

whoever in a state knows how to form wisely the manners of men and to rule them at home and in war with excellent institutes, him in the first place, above others, I should esteem worthy of all honour; but next to him the man who strives to establish in maxims and rules the method and habit of speaking and writing received from a good age of the nation, and, as it were, to fortify the same round with a kind of wall, any attempt to overleap which ought to be prevented by a law only short of that of Romulus. Should we compare the two in respect of utility, it is the former alone that can make the social exis-

---

1. Source: Columbia edn, XII, 27; trans. David Masson.

2. The Latin original provides here a Greek phrase which specifies 'the beautiful' as τὸ καλόν, which Milton realized implies both an aesthetic and a moral judgment.

3. Source: Columbia edn, XII, 31 and 33; trans. David Masson.

tence of the citizens just and holy, but it is the latter alone that can make it splendid and beautiful, – which is the next thing to be wished. The one, as I believe, supplies a noble courage and intrepid counsels against an enemy invading the territory; the other takes to himself the task of extirpating and defeating, by means of a learned detective police of ears and a light cavalry of good authors, that barbarism which makes large inroads upon the minds of men, and is a destructive intestine enemy to genius. Nor is it to be considered of small consequence what language, pure or corrupt, a people has, or what is their customary degree of propriety in speaking it, – a matter which oftener than once involved the salvation of Athens: nay, while it is Plato's opinion that by a change in the manner and habit of dressing serious commotions and mutations are portended in a commonwealth, I, for my part, would rather believe that the fall of that city and its low and obscure condition were consequent on the general vitiation of its usage in the matter of speech. For, let the words of a country be in part unhandsome and offensive in themselves, in part debased by wear and wrongly uttered, and what do they declare but, by no light indication, that the inhabitants of that country are an indolent, idly-yawning race, with minds already long prepared for any amount of servility? On the other hand, we have never heard that any empire, any state, did not flourish moderately at least as long as liking and care for its own language lasted.

from *Pro populo anglicano defensio*
$(1651)^4$

From the philosophers you now appeal to the poets, and I am very willing to follow you. 'Aeschylus by himself is enough to inform us,' you say, 'that kings in Greece held a power not liable to any laws or any judicature; for in the tragedy of *The Suppliants* he calls the king of the Argives "a ruler not subject to judgment".' Know you (for the greater the variety of your arguments, the more I discern how recklessly uncritical you are),

---

4. *The First Defence*. Source: Columbia edn, VII, 307; trans. Samuel L. Wolff.

know then, I say, that we must not regard the poet's words
as his own, but consider who it is that speaks in the play, and
what that person says; for different persons are introduced,
sometimes good, sometimes bad, sometimes wise men, sometimes fools, and they speak not always the poet's opinion, but
what is most fitting to each character.

from a letter to Henry de Brass,
15 July 1657[5]

In the matter of Sallust, which you refer to me, I will say
freely, since you wish me to tell plainly what I do think, that I
prefer Sallust to any other Latin historian; which also was the
almost uniform opinion of the Ancients. Your favourite Tacitus
has his merits; but the greatest of them, in my judgment, is
that he imitated Sallust with all his might. As far as I can gather
from what you write, it appears that the result of my discourse
with you personally on this subject has been that you are
now nearly of the same mind with me respecting that most
admirable writer; and hence it is that you ask me, with reference to what he has said, in the introduction to his *Catilinarian
War* – as to the extreme difficulty of writing History, from the
obligation that the expressions should be proportional to the
deeds – by what method I think a writer of History might
attain that perfection. This, then, is my view : that he who
would write of worthy deeds worthily must write with mental
endowments and experience of affairs not less than were in
the doer of the same, so as to be able with equal mind to
comprehend and measure even the greatest of them, and when
he has comprehended them, to relate them distinctly and gravely
in pure and chaste speech. That he should do so in ornate
style, I do not much care about; for I want a Historian, not an
Orator. Nor yet would I have frequent maxims, or criticisms
on the transactions, prolixly thrown in, lest, by interrupting
the thread of events, the Historian should invade the office of
the Political Writer : for, if the Historian, in explicating coun-

---

5. Source : Columbia edn, XII, 93 and 95; trans. David Masson.

sels and narrating facts, follows truth most of all, and not his own fancy or conjecture, he fulfils his proper duty. I would add also that characteristic of Sallust, in respect of which he himself chiefly praised Cato, – to be able to throw off a great deal in few words: a thing which I think no one can do without the sharpest judgment and a certain temperance at the same time. There are many in whom you will not miss either elegance of style or abundance of information; but for conjunction of brevity with abundance, i.e., for the despatch of much in few words, the chief of the Latins, in my judgment, is Sallust. Such are the qualities that I think should be in the Historian that would hope to make his expressions proportional to the facts he records.

The Verse of *Paradise Lost* (1668)[6]

The measure is *English* Heroic Verse without Rime, as that of *Homer* in *Greek*, and of *Virgil* in *Latin*; Rime being no necessary Adjunct or true Ornament of Poem or good Verse, in longer Works especially, but the Invention of a barbarous Age, to set off wretched matter and lame Meeter; grac't indeed since by the use of some famous modern Poets, carried away by Custom, but much to thir own vexation, hindrance, and constraint to express many things otherwise, and for the most part worse then else they would have exprest them. Not without cause therefore some both *Italian* and *Spanish* Poets of prime note have rejected Rime both in longer and shorter Works, as have also long since our best *English* Tragedies, as a thing of it self, to all judicious ears, triveal and of no true musical delight; which consists onely in apt Numbers, fit quantity of Syllables,

---

6. This note was added not in the poem's first edition of 1667 but in its fifth issue of 1668. S. Simmons, the printer, provided an explanation: 'Courteous Reader, There was no Argument at first intended to the Book, but for the satisfaction of many that have desired it, I procur'd it, and withal a reason of that which stumbled many others, why the Poem Rimes not.' Source: Columbia edn, II, 6; ed. Frank A. Patterson.

nd the sense variously drawn out from one Verse into another, ot in the jingling sound of like endings, a fault avoyded by he learned Ancients both in Poetry and all good Oratory. This eglect then of Rime so little is to be taken for a defect, though t may seem so perhaps to vulgar Readers, that it rather is to e esteem'd an example set, the first in *English*, of ancient iberty recover'd to Heroic Poem from the troublesom and nodern bondage of Rimeing.

from *The History of Britain*
(1670)[7]

.. worthy deeds are not often destitute of worthy relaters: as y a certain Fate great Acts and great Eloquence have most ommonly gon hand in hand, equalling and honouring each ther in the Same Ages. 'Tis true that in obscurest times, by hallow and unskilfull Writers, the indistinct noise of many attels, and devastations, of many Kingdoms over-run and lost, ath come to our Eares. For what wonder, if in all Ages, Ambition and the love of rapine hath stirr'd up greedy and iolent men to bold attempts in wasting and ruining Warrs, vhich to posterity have left the work of Wild Beasts and Destroyers, rather then the Deeds and Monuments of men and Conquerours. But he whose just and true valour uses the ecessity of Warr and Dominion, not to destroy but to prevent estruction, to bring in liberty against Tyrants, Law and Civil- ty among barbarous Nations, knowing that when he Conquers ll things else, he cannot Conquer *Time*, or *Detraction*, wisely onscious of this his want as well as of his worth not to be orgott'n or conceal'd, honours and hath recourse to the aid f Eloquence, his freindliest and best supply; by whose im- nortall Record his noble deeds, which else were transitory, ecoming fixt and durable against the force of Yeares and Generations, he fails not to continue through all Posterity, ver *Envy*, *Death*, and *Time*, also victorious. Therfore when

---

7. Source: Columbia edn, X, 32–3; ed. George P. Krapp.

the esteem of Science, and liberal study waxes low in th
Common-wealth, wee may presume that also there all civi
Vertue, and worthy action is grown as low to a decline: an
then Eloquence, as it were consorted in the same destiny
with the decrease and fall of vertue corrupts also and fades; a
least resignes her office of relating to illiterat and frivolou
Historians; such as the persons themselvs both deserv, and ar
best pleas'd with; whilst they want either the understandin;
to choose better, or the innocence to dare invite the examin
ing, and searching stile of an intelligent, and faithfull Write
to the survay of thir unsound exploits, better befreinded b
obscurity then Fame.

'Of that sort of Dramatic Poem which is call'd Tragedy' (1671)[8]

Tragedy, as it was antiently compos'd, hath been ever hel
the gravest, moralest, and most profitable of all other Poems
therefore said by *Aristotle* to be of power by raising pity an
fear, or terror, to purge the mind of those and such lik
passions, that is to temper and reduce them to just measur
with a kind of delight, stirr'd up by reading or seeing thos
passions well imitated.[9] Nor is Nature wanting in her ow
effects to make good his assertion: for so in Physic things o
melancholic hue and quality are us'd against melancholy
sowr against sowr, salt to remove salt humours.[10] Hence Philo
sophers and other gravest Writers, as *Cicero*, *Plutarch* an
others, frequently cite out of Tragic Poets, both to adorn an
illustrate thir discourse. The Apostle *Paul* himself thought i
not unworthy to insert a verse of *Euripides* into the Text o

---

8. The preface to *Samson Agonistes*. Source: Columbia edn,
331–3; ed. Frank A. Patterson.

9. Aristotle's celebrated statement in the *Poetics* (Ch. VI) is als
quoted, in both Greek and Latin, on the title page of *Samso
Agonistes*.

10. The medical terminology, implicit in Aristotle's own formula
tion, had been much belabored by his Renaissance interpreters.

Holy Scripture, 1 *Cor.* 15. 33.[11] and *Parœus* commenting on the *Revelation*, divides the whole Book as a Tragedy, into Acts distinguisht each by a Chorus of Heavenly Harpings and Song between.[12] Heretofore Men in highest dignity have labour'd not a little to be thought able to compose a Tragedy. Of that honour *Dionysius* the elder was no less ambitious, then before of his attaining to the Tyranny.[13] *Augustus Cæsar* also had begun his *Ajax*, but unable to please his own judgment with what he had begun, left it unfinisht.[14] *Seneca* the Philosopher is by some thought the Author of those Tragedies (at lest the best of them) that go under that name.[15] *Gregory Nazianzen* a Father of the Church, thought it not unbeseeming the sanctity of his person to write a Tragedy, which he entitl'd, *Christ suffering*.[16] This is mention'd to vindicate Tragedy from the small esteem, or rather infamy, which in the account of many it undergoes at this day with other common Interludes; hap'ning through the Poets error of intermixing Comic stuff with Tragic sadness and gravity; or introducing trivial and vulgar persons, which by all judicious hath bin counted absurd; and brought in without discretion, corruptly to gratifie the people. And though antient Tragedy use no Prologue,[17] yet using sometimes, in case of self defence, or explanation, that which *Martial* calls an Epistle; in behalf of this Tragedy coming forth after the antient manner, much different from what among us passes for best, thus much before-hand may be Epistl'd; that *Chorus* is here introduc'd

---

11. The proverbial 'evil communications corrupt good manners' s also attributed to Euripides in *Areopagitica* (above, p. 209, Note 47).

12. On David Pareus see above, p. 131, Note 46. His treatise on the Book of Revelation was translated into English in 1644.

13. Dionysius, tyrant of Syracuse, wrote several plays; one won the first prize in Athens.

14. Thus Suetonius, II, 85.

15. i.e. the ten tragedies which Thomas Newton had translated in 1581.

16. Milton accepts the usual attribution of the tragedy to St. Gregory of Nazianzus (325?–390?).

17. i.e. apology for a play.

after the Greek manner, not antient only but modern, and stil in use among the *Italians*.[18] In the modelling therefore of thi Poem, with good reason, the Antients and the *Italians* are rathe follow'd, as of much more autority and fame. The measure o Verse us'd in the Chorus is of all sorts, call'd by the Greek *Monostrophic*, or rather *Apolelymenon*,[19] without regard had to *Strophe*, *Antistrophe* or *Epod*, which were a kind of Stanza' fram'd only for the Music, then us'd with the Chorus that sung not essential to the Poem, and therefore not material; or being divided into Stanza's or Pauses, they may be call'd *Allæo- stropha*.[20] Division into Act and Scene referring chiefly to the Stage (to which this work never was intended) is here omitted.

It suffices if the whole Drama be found not produc't be yond the fift Act, of the style and uniformitie, and that com monly call'd the Plot, whether intricate or explicit,[21] which i nothing indeed but such œconomy, or disposition of the fabl as may stand best with versimilitude and decorum; they only will best judge who are not unacquainted with *Æschulus Sophocles*, and *Euripides*, the three Tragic Poets unequall'd ye by any, and the best rule to all who endeavour to write Tragedy The circumscription of time wherein the whole Drama begin and ends, is according to antient rule, and best example, within the space of 24 hours.[22]

See also the passages quoted in the Introduction (above, pp. 24 and 44–5) and the statements in *Of Education* (pp. 183–4, 191, 193 but especially in *The Reason of Church–Government* (pp. 55 ff.) Consult also the passages collected by Ida Langdon, *Milton's Theory of Poetry and Fine Art* (New Haven, 1924).

---

18. Cf. Milton's statement on Castelvetro *et al.*, above, p. 191.

19. i.e. 'free', as Milton's context suggests.

20. i.e. strophes of various lengths.

21. Complex or simple – as in Aristotle's discussion of plot (*Poetics*, Ch. X).

22. Not an Aristotelian notion but a deduction of later critics.

APPENDIX
TWO EARLY BIOGRAPHIES

JOHN AUBREY

JOHN MILTON
(1681)

[John Aubrey (1626–97) prepared the following notes in 1681 for his fellow antiquary Anthony à Wood, who used them in his biography of Milton in *Fasti Oxoniensis* (1691). They are invaluable as the testimony of a man who was personally acquainted with Milton ('He was scarce so tall as I am').

Aubrey's notes are reprinted from *Aubrey's Brief Lives*, ed. O. L. Dick, 3rd edn (1960), pp. 199–203; the original manuscript is transcribed in *The Early Lives of Milton*, ed. Helen Darbishire (1932), pp. 1–15.]

MR. JOHN MILTON was of an Oxfordshire familie. His Grandfather was a Roman Catholic of Holton, in Oxfordshire, near Shotover.

His father was brought-up in the University of Oxon, at Christ Church, and his grandfather disinherited him because he kept not to the Catholique Religion (he found a Bible in English, in his Chamber). So therupon he came to London, and became a Scrivener (brought up by a friend of his; was not an Apprentice) and gott a plentifull estate by it, and left it off many yeares before he dyed. He was an ingeniose man; delighted in musique; composed many Songs now in print, especially that of *Oriana*. I have been told that the Father composed a Song of fourscore parts for the Lantgrave of Hess, for which his Highnesse sent a meddall of gold, or a noble present. He dyed about 1647; buried in Cripple-gate-church, from his house in the Barbican.

His son John was borne the 9th of December 1608, *die Veneris*, half an hour after 6 in the morning, in Bread Street, in

London, at the Spread Eagle, which was his house (he had also in that street another howse, the Rose; and other houses in other places). Anno Domini 1619, he was ten yeares old; and was then a Poet. His school-master then was a Puritan, in Essex, who cutt his haire short.

He went to Schoole to old Mr. Gill,[1] at Paule's Schoole. Went at his owne Chardge only, to Christ's College in Cambridge at fifteen, where he stayed eight yeares at least. Then he travelled into France and Italie (had Sir H. Wotton's commendatory letters[2]). At Geneva he contracted a great friendship with the learned Dr. Deodati of Geneva.[3] He was acquainted with Sir Henry Wotton, Ambassador at Venice, who delighted in his company. He was severall yeares beyond Sea, and returned to England just upon the breaking-out of the Civill Warres.

From his brother, Christopher Milton: – when he went to Schoole, when he was very young, he studied very hard, and sate-up very late, commonly till twelve or one a clock at night, and his father ordered the mayde to sitt-up for him, and in those yeares (10) composed many Copies of Verses which might well become a riper age. And was a very hard student in the University, and performed all his exercises there with very good Applause. His first Tutor there was Mr. Chapell;[4] from whom receiving some unkindnesse (whipt him) he was afterwards (though it seemed contrary to the Rules of the College) transferred to the Tuition of one Mr. Tovell,[5] who dyed Parson of Lutterworth. He went to travell about the year 1638 and was abroad about a year's space, chiefly in Italy.

Immediately after his return he took a lodging at Mr. Russell's a Taylour, in St. Bride's Churchyard, and took into his tuition

---

1. Alexander Gill, the elder (1564–1635), whose son Milton befriended.

2. Cf. Milton's account, above, p. 67, and that of Phillips, below, p. 420.

3. On Giovanni Diodati, see above, p. 70, Note 8.

4. William Chappell, later Bishop of Cork (1582–1649).

5. Nathaniel Tovey (1597?–1658), Fellow of Christ's College, Cambridge, 1621–34.

his sister's two sons, Edward and John Philips,[6] the first 10, the other 9 years of age; and in a yeare's time made them capable of interpreting a Latin authour at sight. And within three years they went through the best of Latin and Greek Poetts – Lucretius and Manilius, of the Latins (and with him the use of the Globes, and some rudiments of Arithmetic and Geometry.) Hesiod, Aratus, Dionysius Afer, Oppian, Apollonii *Argonautica*, and Quintus Calaber. Cato, Varro and Columella *De re rustica* were the very first Authors they learn't. As he was severe on the one hand, so he was most familiar and free in his conversation to those to whome most sowre in his way of education. N.B. he mad his Nephews Songsters, and sing, from the time they were with him.

His first wife (Mrs. Powell, a Royalist) was brought up and lived where there was a greate deale of company and merriment, dancing, etc. And when she came to live with her husband, at Mr. Russell's, in St. Bride's Churchyard, she found it very solitary; no company came to her; oftimes heard his Nephews beaten and cry. This life was irkesome to her, and so she went to her Parents as Fo[re]st-hill. He sent for her, after some time; and I thinke his servant was evilly entreated : but as for matter of wronging his bed, I never heard the least suspicions; nor had he, of that, any Jealousie.

Two opinions doe not well on the same Boulster; she was a Royalist, and went to her mother to the King's quarters, neer Oxford. I have perhaps so much charity to her that she might not wrong his bed : but what man, especially contemplative, would like to have a young wife environ'd and storm'd by the Sons of Mars, and those of the enemi partie ? He parted from her, and wrote the Triplechord about divorce.[7]

He had a middle wife, whose name was Katharin Woodcock. No child living by her.

He maried his third wife, Elizabeth Minshull, the year before the Sicknesse : a gent. person, a peacefull and agreable humour. Hath two daughters living : Deborah was his amanuensis

6. For Edward Phillips's biography of Milton, see below, pp. 415 ff.
7. The three treatises : *The Doctrine and Discipline of Divorce* (see above, pp. 112 ff.), *Tetrachordon* (1645, and *Colasterion* (1645).

(he taught her Latin, and to reade Greeke to him when he had lost his eie-sight.)

His sight began to faile him at first upon his writing against Salmasius,[8] and before 'twas full compleated one eie absolutely failed. Upon the writing of other bookes, after that, his other eie decayed. His eie-sight was decaying about 20 yeares before his death. His father read without spectacles at 84. His mother had very weake eies, and used spectacles presently after she was thirty yeares old.

His harmonicall and ingeniose Soul did lodge in a beautifull and well proportioned body. He was a spare man. He was scarce so tall as I am (*quaere*, quot feet I am high: *resp.*, of middle stature).

He had abroun hayre. His complexion exceeding faire – he was so faire that they called him *the Lady of Christ's College*. Ovall face. His eie a darke gray.

He was very healthy and free from all diseases: seldome tooke any physique (only sometimes he tooke manna): only towards his latter end he was visited with the Gowte, Spring and Fall.

He had a delicate tuneable Voice, and had a good skill. His father instructed him. He had an Organ in his howse; he played on that most. Of a very cheerfull humour. He would be chearfull even in his Gowte-fitts, and sing.

He had a very good Memorie; but I believe that his excellent Method of thinking and disposing did much to helpe his Memorie.

His widowe haz his picture, drawne very well and like when a Cambridge-schollar, which ought to be engraven; for the Pictures before his bookes are not at all like him.

His exercise was chiefly walking. He was an early riser (*scil* at 4 a clock *manè*) yea, after he lost his sight. He had a man to read to him. The first thing he read was the Hebrew bible and that was at 4 h. *manè*, ½h. plus. Then he contemplated.

At 7 his man came to him again, and then read to him again and wrote till dinner; the writing was as much as the reading

---

8. See above, p. 34.

His daughter, Deborah, could read to him in Latin, Italian and French, and Greeke. Maried in Dublin to one Mr. Clarke (sells silke, etc.) very like her father. The other sister is Mary, more like her mother.

After dinner he used to walke 3 or four houres at a time (he always had a Garden where he lived) went to bed about 9.

Temperate man, rarely dranke between meales. Extreme pleasant in his conversation, and at dinner, supper, etc.; but satyricall. (He pronounced the letter R (*littera canina*) very hard – a certain signe of a Satyricall Witt – from John Dreyden.)

All the time of writing his *Paradise Lost*, his veine began at the Autumnall Aequinoctiall, and ceased at the Vernall or thereabouts (I believe about May) and this was 4 or 5 yeares of his doeing it. He began about 2 yeares before the King came-in, and finished about three yeares after the King's restauracion.

In the 4th booke of *Paradise Lost* there are about six verses of Satan's Exclamation to the Sun, which Mr. E. Philips remembers about 15 or 16 yeares before ever his Poem was thought of, which verses were intended for the Beginning of a Tragoedie which he had designed, but was diverted from it by other businesse.[9]

He was visited much by the learned; more then he did desire. He was mightily importuned to goe into France and Italie. Foraigners came much to see him, and much admired him, and offer'd to him great preferments to come over to them; and the only inducement of severall foreigners that came over into England, was chiefly to see Oliver Protector, and Mr. John Milton; and would see the hous and chamber wher he was borne. He was much more admired abrode then at home.

His familiar learned Acquaintance were Mr. Andrew Marvell, Mr. Skinner, Dr. Pagett, M.D.[10]

John Dreyden, Esq., Poet Laureate, who very much admires him, went to him to have leave to putt his *Paradise Lost* into

---

9. The verses are also quoted by Edward Phillips, below, p. 433.

10. Marvell (1621–78), Cyriack Skinner (1627–1700), Dr Nathan Paget (1615–79). Phillips (below, p. 434) adds two more 'particular friends': Henry Lawrence the younger and Marchamont Needham.

a Drame in rythme. Mr. Milton recieved him civilly, and told him *he would give him leave to tagge his Verses.*[11]

His widowe assures me that Mr. T. Hobbs was not one of his acquaintance, that her husband did not like him at all, but he would acknowledge him to be a man of great parts, and a learned man. Their Interests and Tenets did run counter to each other.[12]

Whatever he wrote against Monarchie was out of no animosity to the King's person, or owt of any faction or interest, but out of a pure Zeale to the Liberty of Mankind, which he thought would be greater under a free state than under a Monarchial government. His being so conversant in Livy and the Roman authors, and the greatness he saw donne by the Roman common wealth, and the vertue of their great Commanders induc't him to.

Mr. John Milton made two admirable Panegyricks, as to Sublimitie of Witt, one on Oliver Cromwel, and the other on Thomas, Lord Fairfax, both which his nephew Mr. Philip hath But he hath hung back these two yeares, as to imparting copies to me for the Collection of mine.[13] Were they made in commendation of the Devill, 'twere all one to me: 'tis the ὕψος[14] that I looke after. I have been told that 'tis beyond Waller's[15] or anything in that kind.

---

11. The result was Dryden's 'opera', *The State of Innocence and Fall of Man* (1677).

12. See above, pp. 34–5.

13. The sonnets were finally published by Phillips himself (see below, p. 438, Note 15).

14. 'Sublimity'; a reference to Longinus's treatise *On the Sublime*

15. Edmund Waller (1606–87) managed to celebrate Cromwell in one poem, and denounce him in another.

EDWARD PHILLIPS

THE LIFE OF MR. JOHN MILTON
(1694)

[Edward Phillips (1630–96), the son of Milton's sister Anne and
Edward Phillips the elder, was not only tutored by the poet but 'was
ut to Board with him also' (below, p. 425). The *Life* of his uncle is
he single most important early biography of Milton, despite its
requent errors in chronology. It was originally prefixed to Phillips's
ranslation of Milton's *Letters of State* (1694), from where it is now
eprinted (pp. i-xliii).]

Of all the several parts of History, that which sets forth the
ives, and Commemorates the most remarkable Actions, Sayings,
r Writings of Famous and Illustrious Persons, whether in War
r Peace; whether many together, or any one in particular, as
. is not the least useful in it self, so it is in highest Vogue and
steem among the Studious and Reading part of Mankind. The
host Eminent in this way of History were among the Ancients,
Plutarch and *Diogenes Laertius* of the *Greeks*; the first wrote the
ives, for the most part, of the most Renowned Heroes and
Warriours of the *Greeks* and *Romans*; the other the Lives of
he Ancient *Greek* Philosophers. And *Cornelius Nepos* (or as
ome will have it *Aemilius Probus*) of the *Latins*, who wrote the
ives of the most illustrious *Greek* and *Roman* Generals. Among
he Moderns, *Machiavel* a Noble *Florentine*, who Elegantly wrote
he Life of *Castrucio Castracano*, Lord of Luca. And of our
ation, Sir Fulk Grevil, who wrote the life of his most intimate
riend Sir *Philip Sidney*: Mr. *Thomas Stanly* of *Cumberlo
reen*, who made a most Elaborate improvement to the foresaid
Laertius, by adding to what he found in him, what by diligent
earch and enquiry he Collected from other Authors of best
uthority. *Isaac Walton*, who wrote the Lives of Sir *Henry
Wotton*, Dr. *Donne*; and for his Divine Poems, the admired Mr.
George Herbert. Lastly, not to mention several Biographers of
onsiderable Note, the Great *Gassendus* of *France*, the worthy

Celebrator of two no less worthy Subjects of his impartial Pen
viz. The Noble Philosopher *Epicurus*, and the most politely
Learned Virtuoso of his Age, his Country-man, Monsieur *Periesk*
And pitty it is the Person whose memory we have here under
taken to perpetuate by recounting the most memorable Trans
actions of his Life, (though his Works sufficiently recommen
him to the World) finds not a well-informed Pen able to se
him forth, equal with the best of those here mentioned; fo
doubtless had his Fame been as much spread through *Europe*
in *Thuanus*'s time as now it is, and hath been for several Years
he had justly merited from that Great Historian, an Eulog
not inferiour to the highest, by him given to all the Learne
and Ingenious that liv'd within the compass of his History. Fo
we may safely and justly affirm, that take him in all respects, fo
Acumen of Wit, Quickness of Apprehension, Sagacity of Judge
ment, Depth of Argument, and Elegancy of Style, as well in *Lati*
as *English*, as well in Verse as Prose, he is scarce to be parallel'd b
any the best of Writers our Nation hath in any Age brought forth.

He was born in *London*, in a House in *Breadstreet*, the Leas
whereof, as I take it, but for certain it was a House in *Bread
street*, became in time part of his Estate in the Year of our Lord
1606.[1] His Father *John Milton*, an Honest, Worthy, and Sub
stantial Citizen of *London*, by Profession a Scrivener, to whic
Profession he voluntarily betook himself, by the advice an
assistance of an intimate Friend of his, Eminent in that Calling
upon his being cast out by his Father, a bigotted *Roma
Catholick*, for embracing, when Young, the Protestant Faith
and abjuring the Popish Tenets; for he is said to have bee
Descended of an Ancient Family of the *Miltons*, of *Milton*, nea
Abington in *Oxfordshire*; where they had been a long tim
seated, as appears by the Monuments still to be seen in *Milto*
Church, till one of the Family having taken the wrong side, i
the Contests between the Houses of *York* and *Lancaster*, wa
sequestred of all his Estate, but what he held by his Wif
However, certain it is, that this Vocation he followed for man
Years, at his said House in *Breadstreet*, with success suitab

---

1. The correct date is 1608.

o his Industry, and prudent conduct of his Affairs; yet did he not so far quit his own Generous and Ingenious Inclinations, as to make himself wholly a Slave to the World; for he sometimes found vacant hours to the Study (which he made his recreation) of the Noble Science of Musick, in which he advanc'd to that perfection, that as I have been told, and as I take it, by our Author himself, he Composed an *In Nomine* of Forty Parts : for which he was rewarded with a Gold Medal and Chain by a *Polish* Prince, to whom he presented it. However, this is a Truth not to be denied, that for several Songs of his Composition, after the way of these times, three or four of which are still to be seen in Old *Wilby*'s set of Ayres, besides some Compositions of his in *Ravenscrofs* Psalms, he gained the Reputation of a considerable Master in this most charming of all the Liberal Sciences : Yet all this while, he managed his Grand Affair of this World with such Prudence and Diligence, that by the assistance of Divine Providence favouring his honest endeavours, he gained a Competent Estate, whereby he was enabled to make a handsom Provision both for the Education and Maintenance of his Children; for three he had, and no more, all by one Wife, *Sarah*, of the Family of the *Castons*, derived originally from *Wales*. A Woman of Incomparable Vertue and Goodness; *John* the Eldest, the Subject of our present Work, *Christopher*, and an onely Daughter *Ann*.

Christopher being principally designed for the Study of the Common-Law of *England*, was Entered Young a Student of the *Inner-Temple*, of which House he lived to be an Ancient Bencher, and keeping close to that Study and Profession all his Life time, except in the time of the Civil Wars of *England*; when being a great favourer and assertor of the King's Cause, and Obnoxious to the Parliament's side, by acting to his utmost power against them, so long as he kept his Station at *Reading*; and after that Town was taken by the Parliament Forces, being forced to quit his House there, he steer'd his course according to the Motion of the King's Army. But when the War was ended with Victory and Success to the Parliament Party, by the Valour of General *Fairfax*, and the craft and Conduct of *Cromwell*; and his composition made by

the help of his Brother's Interest, with the then prevaili[
Power; he betook himself again to his former Study and P[
fession, following Chamber-Practice every Term, yet came
no Advancement in the World in a long time, except so[
small Employ in the Town of *Ipswich*, where (and near it)
lived all the latter time of his Life. For he was a person o[
modest quiet temper, preferring Justice and Vertue before
Worldly Pleasure or Grandeur: but in the beginning of t[
Reign of K. *James* the II. for his known Integrity and Abil[
in the Law, he was by some Persons of Quality recommended
the King, and at a Call of Serjeants received the Coif, and t[
same day was Sworn one of the Barons of the Exchequer, a[
soon after made one of the Judges of the Common Pleas; [
his Years and Indisposition not well brooking the Fatigue
publick Imployment, he continued not long in either of th[
Stations, but having his *Quietus est*, retired to a Country Li[
his Study and Devotion.

Ann, the onely Daughter of the said *John Milton* the Eld[
had a considerable Dowry given her by her Father, in Marria[
with *Edward Philips*, (the Son of *Edward Philips* of *Shrewsbur*
who coming up Young to Town, was bred up in the Crov[
Office in Chancery, and at length came to be Secondary
the Office under Old Mr. *Bembo*; by him she had, besi[
other Children that dyed Infants, two Sons yet surviv[
of whom more hereafter; and by a second Husband, [
Thomas Agar, who (upon the Death of his Intimate Frie[
Mr. *Philips*) worthily Succeeded in the place, which exc[
some time of Exclusion before and during the *Interregnum*,
held for many Years, and left it to Mr. *Thomas Milton* (the S[
of the aforementioned Sir *Christopher*) who at this day execu[
it with great Reputation and Ability; Two Daughters, *Mary* w[
died very Young, and *Ann* yet surviving.

But to hasten back to our matter in hand; *John* our Auth[
who was destin'd to be the Ornament and Glory of his Countr[
was sent, together with his Brother, to *Paul's* School, wher[
Dr. *Gill* the Elder[2] was then Chief Master; where he was ente[

2. See above, p. 410, Note 1.

into the first Rudiments of Learning, and advanced therin with that admirable Success, not more by the Discipline of the School and good Instructions of his Masters, (for that he had another Master possibly at his Father's house, appears by the Fourth Elegy of his Latin Poems written in his 18th year, to *Thomas Young* Pastor of the *English* Company of Merchants at *Hamborough*,[3] wherein he owns and stiles him his Master) than by his own happy Genius, prompt Wit and Apprehension, and insuperable Industry; for he generally sate up half the Night, and well in voluntary Improvements of his own choice, as the exact perfecting of his School-Exercises: So that at the Age of 15 he was full ripe for Academick Learning, and accordingly was sent to the University of *Cambridge*; where in *Christ's College*, under the Tuition of a very Eminent Learned man, whose Name I cannot call to mind,[4] he Studied Seven years, and took his Degree of Master of Arts; and for the extraordinary Wit and Reading he had shown in his Performances to attain his Degree, (some whereof spoken at a Vacation-Exercise in his 19th. year of Age, are to be yet seen in his Miscellaneous Poems) he was lov'd and admir'd by the whole University, particularly by the Fellows and most Ingenious Persons of his House. Among the rest there was a Young Gentleman, one Mr. *King*, with whom, for his great Learning and Parts, he had contracted a particular Friendship and Intimacy; whose death (for he was drown'd on the *Irish* Seas in his passage from *Chester* to *Ireland*) he bewails in that most excellent Monody in his forementioned Poems, Intituled *Lycidas*. Never was the loss of Friend so Elegantly lamented; and among the rest of his Juvenile Poems, some he wrote at the Age of 15, which contain a Poetical Genius scarce to be parallel'd by any *English* Writer. Soon after he had taken his Master's Degree, he thought fit to leave the University: Not upon any disgust or discontent for want of Preferment, as some Ill-willers have reported; nor upon any cause whatsoever forc'd to flie, as his Detractors maliciously feign; but from which aspersion he sufficiently clears himself in his Second Answer to

3. Thomas Young (1587?–1655) was one of the Smectymnuans (see above, p. 22).

4. But see Aubrey, above, p. 410.

Alexander Morus,[5] the Author of a Book call'd *Clamor Regi Sanguinis ad Cœlum*, the chief of his Calumniators; in which he plainly makes it out, that after his leaving the University, to the no small trouble of his Fellow-Collegiates, who in general regretted his Absence, he for the space of Five years lived for the most part with his Father and Mother at their house at *Horton* near *Colebrook* in *Barkshire*; whither his Father, having got an Estate to his content, and left off all business, was retir'd from the Cares and Fatigues of the world. After the said term of Five years, his Mother then dying, he was willing to add to his acquired Learning the observation of Foreign Customs, Manners and Institutions; and thereupon took a resolution to Travel more especially designing for *Italy*;[6] and accordingly, with his Father's Consent and Assistance; he put himself into an Equipage suitable to such a Design; and so intending to go by the way of *France*, he set out for *Paris* accompanied onely with one Man, who attended him through all his Travels; for his Prudence was his Guide, and his Learning his Introduction and Presentation to Persons of most Eminent Quality. However, he had also a most Civil and Obliging Letter of Direction and Advice from Sir *Henry Wootton* then Provost of *Eaton*, and formerly Resident Embassador from King *James* the First to the State of *Venice* which Letter is to be seen in the First Edition of his Miscellaneous Poems. At *Paris* being Recommended by the said Sir *Henry* and other Persons of Quality, he went first to wait upon my Lord *Scudamore*, then Embassador in *France* from King *Charles* the First. My Lord receiv'd him with wonderful Civility and understanding he had a desire to make a Visit to the great *Hugo Grotius*, he sent several of his Attendants to wait upon him, and to present him in his Name to that Renowned Doctor and Statesman, who was at that time Embassador from *Christina* Queen of *Sweden*, to the *French* King. *Grotius* took the Visit kindly, and gave him Entertainment suitable to his Worth, and the high Commendations he had heard of him. After a few days not intending to make the usual Tour of *France*, he took his leave of my Lord, who at his departure from Paris, gave him

5. See above, p. 37.

6. See Milton's account, above, pp. 67–70.

Letters to the *English* Merchants residing in any part through which he was to Travel, in which they were requested to shew him all the Kindness, and do him all the Good Offices that lay in their Power.

From *Paris* he hastened on his Journey to *Nicæa*, where he took Shipping, and in a short space arrived at *Genoa*; from whence he went to *Leghorn*, thence to Pisa, and to *Florence*; In this City he met with many charming Objects, which Invited him to stay a longer time then he intended; the pleasant Scituation of the Place, the Nobleness of the Structures, the exact Humanity and Civility of the Inhabitants, the more Polite and Refined sort of Language there, then elsewhere. During the time of his stay here, which was about Two Months, he Visited all the private Academies of the City, which are Places establish'd for the improvement of Wit and Learning, and maintained a Correspondence and perpetual Friendship among Gentlemen fitly qualified for such an Institution : and such sort of Academies there are in all or most of the most noted Cities in *Italy*. Visiting these Places, he was soon taken notice of by the most Learned and Ingenious of the Nobility, and the Grand Wits of *Florence*, who caress'd him with all the Honours and Civilities imaginable, particularly *Jacobo Gaddi, Carolo Dati, Antonio Francini, Frescobaldo, Cultelino, Bonmatthei* and *Clementillo* : Whereof *Gaddi* hath a large Elegant *Italian Canzonet* in his Praise; *Dati*, a Latin Epistle; both Printed before his Latin Poems, together with a Latin Distich of the Marquess of *Villa*, and another of *Selvaggi*, and a Latin *Tetrastick* of *Giovanni Salsilli* a *Roman*.

From *Florence* he took his Journey to *Siena*, from thence to *Rome*; where he was detain'd much about the same time he had been at *Florence*; as well by his desire of seeing all the Rarities and Antiquities of that most Glorious and Renowned City, as by the Conversation of *Lucas Holstenius*, and other Learned and Ingenious men who highly valued his Acquaintance, and treated him with all possible Respect.

From *Rome* he Travelled to *Naples*, where he was introduced by a certain Hermite, who accompanied him in his Journey from *Rome* thither, into the Knowledge of *Giovanni Baptista Manso*, Marquess of *Villa*, a *Neapolitan* by Birth, a Person of high

Nobility, Vertue, and Honour, to whom the famous *Italian* Poet, *Torquato Tasso*, Wrote his Treatise *de Amicitia*; and moreover mentions him with great Honour in that Illustrious Poem of his, Intituled, *Gierusalemme Liberata*: This Noble Marquess received him with extraordinary Respect and Civility, and went with him himself to give him a sight of all that was of Note and Remark in the City, particularly the Viceroys Palace, and was often in Person to Visit him at his Lodging. Moreover, this Noble Marquess honoured him so far, as to make a Latin Distich in his Praise, as hath been already mentioned; which being no less pithy then short, though already in Print, it will not be unworth the while here to repeat.

> *Ut Mens, Forma, Decor, Facies, [mos,] fi Pietas,[7] sic,*
> *Non Anglus Verum Hercle Angelus ipse foret.*

In return of this Honour, and in gratitude for the many Favours and Civilities received of him, he presented him at his departure with a large Latin Eclogue, Intituled, *Mansus*, afterward's Published among his Latin Poems. The Marquess at his taking leave of him gave him this Complement, That he would have done him many more Offices of Kindness and Civility, but was therefore rendered incapable in regard he had been over-liberal in his speech against the Religion of the Country.

He had entertain'd some thoughts of passing over into *Sicily* and *Greece*, but was diverted by the News he receiv'd from *England*, that Affairs there were tending towards a Civil War; thinking it a thing unworthy in him to be taking his Pleasure in Foreign Parts, while his Countreymen at home were Fighting for their Liberty: But first resolved to see *Rome* once more; and though the Merchants gave him a caution that the Jesuits were hatching designs against him, in case he should return thither, by reason of the freedom he took in all his discourses of Religion; nevertheless he ventured to prosecute his Resolution, and to *Rome* the second time he went, determining with himself not industriously to begin to fall into any

---

7. 'This word relates to his being a Protestant not a *Roman-Catholick*' (Phillips's note).

Discourse about Religion; but, being ask'd, not to deny or
endeavour to conceal his own Sentiments; Two months he staid
at *Rome;* and in all that time never flinch'd, but was ready to
defend the Orthodox Faith against all Opposers; and so well he
succeeded therein, that Good Providence guarding him, he went
safe from *Rome* back to *Florence,* where his return to his
friends of that City was welcomed with as much Joy and
Affection, as had it been to his Friends and Relations in his
own Countrey, he could not have come a more joyful and welcome Guest. Here, having staid as long as at his first coming,
excepting an excursion of a few days to *Luca,* crossing the
Apennine, and passing through *Bononia* and *Ferrara,* he arriv'd
at *Venice,* where when he had spent a Month's time in view-
ing of that Stately City, and Shipp'd up a Parcel of curious and
rare Books which he had pick'd up in his Travels; particularly a
Chest or two of choice Musick-books of the best Masters
flourishing about that time in *Italy,* namely, *Luca Marenzo,*
Monte Verde, Horatio Vecchi, Cifa, the Prince of *Venosa* and
several others, he took his course through *Verona, Milan,* and
the *Pœnine Alps,* and so by the Lake *Leman* to *Geneva,* where
he staid for some time, and had daily converse with the most
learned *Giovanni Deodati,* Theology-Professor in that City, and
so returning through *France,* by the same way he had passed it
going to *Italy,* he, after a Peregrination of one compleat Year
and about Three Months, arrived safe in *England,* about the
time of the Kings making his second Expedition against the
Scots.

Soon after his return, and visits paid to his Father and other
friends, he took him a Lodging in St. *Brides* Church-yard, at
the House of one *Russel* a Taylor, where he first undertook the
Education and Instruction of his Sister's two Sons, the Younger
whereof had been wholly committed to his Charge and Care.
And here by the way, I judge it not impertinent to mention the
many Authors both of the Latin and Greek, which through his
excellent judgement and way of Teaching, far above the Pedantry of common publick Schools (where such Authors are scarce
ever heard of) were run over within no greater compass of time,
then from Ten to Fifteen or Sixteen Years of Age. Of the Latin

the four Grand Authors, *De Re Rustica, Cato, Varro, Columella,* and *Palladius; Cornelius Celsus,* an Ancient Physician of the *Romans;* a great part of *Pliny's* Natural History, *Vitruvius* his Architecture, *Frontinus* his Stratagems, with the two Egregious Poets, *Lucretius,* and *Manilius.* Of the Greek; *Hesiod,* a Poet equal with *Homer; Aratus* his *Phænomena,* and *Diosemeia, Dionysius Afer de situ Orbis,* Oppian's *Cynegeticks & Halieuticks. Quintus Calaber* his Poem of the *Trojan* War, continued from *Homer; Apollonius Rhodius* his Argonaticks, and in Prose, Plutarch's *Placita Philosophorum* & Περι Παιδων 'Αγογιας, Geminus's Astronomy; *Xenophon's Cyri Institutio & Anabasis, Aelians Tacticks,* and *Polyænus* his Warlike Stratagems; thus by teaching he in some measure increased his own knowledge, having the reading of all these Authors as it were by Proxy; and all this might possibly have conduced to the preserving of his Eye-sight, had he not, moreover, been perpetually busied in his own Laborious Undertakings of the Book or Pen. Nor did the time thus Studiously imployed in conquering the *Greek* and *Latin* Tongues, hinder the attaining to the chief Oriental Languages, *viz.* The *Hebrew, Caldee* and *Syriac,* so far as to go through the *Pentateuch,* or Five Books of *Moses* in *Hebrew,* to make a good entrance into the *Targum* or *Chaldee* Paraphrase, and to understand several Chapters of St. *Matthew* in the *Syriac* Testament, besides an introduction into several Arts and sciences, by Reading *Urstisius* his Arithmetick, *Riffs* Geometry, *Petiscus* his *Trigonometry, Joannes de Sacro Bosco de Sphæra;* and into the *Italian* and *French* Tongues, by reading in *Italian, Giovan Villani's* History of the Transactions between several petty States of *Italy;* and in *French* a great part of *Pierre Davity,* the famous Geographer of *France* in his time. The *Sunday's* work was for the most part the Reading each day a Chapter of the *Greek* Testament, and hearing his Learned Exposition upon the same, (and how this savoured of Atheism in him, I leave to the courteous Backbiter to judge). The next work after this, was the writing from his own dictation, some part, from time to time, of a Tractate which he thought fit to collect from the ablest of Divines, who had written of that Subject; *Amesius, Wollebius, &c. viz.* A perfect System of Divinity, of which more hereafter.[8] Now persons so far Manuducted into the highest paths of Literature both Divine and Human, had they received his documents with the same Acuteness of Wit and Apprehension, the same Industry, Alacrity, and Thirst after Knowledge, as the Instructor was indued with, what Prodigies of Wit and Learning might they have proved! the Scholars might in some degree have come near to the equalling of the Master, or at last have in some sort made good what he seems to predict in the close of an Elegy he made in the Seventeenth Year of his Age, upon the Death of one of his Sister's Children (a Daughter) who died in her Infancy.

> *Then thou the Mother of so sweet a Child,*
> *Her false Imagin'd Loss cease to Lament,*
> *And Wisely learn to curb thy Sorrows Wild;*
> *This if thou do, he will an Offspring give,*
> *That to the Worlds last end, shall make thy*
> *Name to live.*[9]

But to return to the Thread of our Discourse; he made no long stay in his Lodgings in St. *Brides* Church-yard; necessity of having a place to dispose his Books in, and other Goods fit for the furnishing of a good handsome House, hastning him to take one; and accordingly a pretty Garden-House he took in *Aldersgate*-Street, at the end of an Entry; and therefore the fitter for his turn, by the reason of the Privacy, besides that there are few Streets in *London* more free from Noise then that.

Here first it was that his Academick Erudition was put in practice, and Vigorously proceeded, he himself giving an Example to those under him, (for it was not long after his taking this House, e're his Elder Nephew[10] was put to Board with him also) of hard Study, and spare Diet; only this advantage he had, that once in three Weeks or a Month, he would drop into the Society of some Young Sparks of his Acquaintance, the chief whereof were Mr. *Alphry*, and Mr. *Miller*, two Gentlemen of

---

8. On this solitary reference to *De doctrina christiana*, see above, ρ. 41. Phillips failed to return to the subject.

9. 'On the Death of a Fair Infant dying of a Cough', ll. 71–3, 76–7.

10. Edward Phillips.

Gray's-Inn, the *Beau*'s of those Times, but nothing near so bad as those now-a-days; with these Gentlemen he would so far make bold with his Body, as now and then to keep a Gawdy-day.

In this House he continued several Years, in the one or two first whereof, he set out several Treatises, *viz.* That of *Reformation* [see above, pp. 77 ff.]; that against *Prelatical Episcopacy*; The *Reason of Church-Government* [pp. 49 ff.]; The *Defence of Smectimnuus* [pp. 61 ff.], at least the greatest part of them, but as I take it, all; and some time after, one Sheet of Education, which he dedicated to Mr. *Samuel Hartlib*, he that wrote so much of Husbandry; this Sheet is Printed at the end of the Second Edition of his Poems; and lastly, *Areopagitica*. During the time also of his continuance in this House, there fell out several Occasions of the Increasing of his Family. His Father, who till the taking of *Reading* by the Earl of *Essex* his Forces, had lived with his other Son at his House there, was upon that Son's dissettlement necessitated to betake himself to this his Eldest Son, with whom he lived for some Years, even to his Dying Day. In the next place he had an Addition of some Scholars, to which may be added, his entring into Matrimony; but he had his Wife's company so small a time, that he may well be said to have become a single man again soon after.

About *Whitsuntide* it was, or a little after, that he took a Journey into the Country; no body about him certainly knowing the Reason, or that it was any more than a Journey of Recreaation: after a Month's stay, home he returns a Married-man, that went out a Batchelor; his Wife being *Mary* the Eldest Daugher of Mr. *Richard Powell*, then a Justice of Peace, of *Forresthill*, near *Shotover* in *Oxfordshire;* some few of her nearest Relations accompanying the Bride to her new Habitation; which by reason the Father nor anybody else were yet come, was able to receive them; where the Feasting held for some days in Celebration of the Nuptials, and for entertainment of the Bride's Friends. At length they took their leave, and returning to *Forresthill*, left the Sister behind; probably not much to her satisfaction; as appeared by the Sequel; by that time she had for a Month or thereabout led a Philosophical Life (after having been used to a great House, and much Company and Joviality). Her Friends, possibly incited by her own desire, made earnest suit by Letter, to have her Company the remaining part of the Summer, which was granted, on condition of her return at the time appointed, *Michalemas*, or thereabout: In the mean time came his Father, and some of the foremention'd Disciples. And now the Studies went on with so much the more Vigour, as there were more Hands and Heads employ'd; the Old Gentleman living wholly retired to his Rest and Devotion, without the least trouble imaginable: Our Author, now as it were a single man again, made it his chief diversion now and then in an Evening to visit the Lady *Margaret Lee*, Daughter to the — *Lee*, Earl of *Marlborough*, Lord High Treasurer of *England*, and President of the Privy Council to King *James* the First. This Lady being a Woman of great Wit and Ingenuity, had a particular Honour for him, and took much delight in his Company, as likewise her Husband Captain *Hobson*, a very Accomplish'd Gentleman; and what Esteem he at the same time had for Her, appears by a Sonnet he made in praise of her, to be seen among his other Sonnets in his extant Poems. *Michalemas* being come, and no news of his Wife's return, he sent for her by Letter, and receiving no answer, sent several other Letters, which were also unanswered; so that at last he dispatch'd down a Foot-Messenger with a Letter, desiring her return; but the Messenger came back not only without an answer, at least a satisfactory one, but to the best of my remembrance, reported that he was dismissed with some sort of Contempt; this proceeding, in all probability, was grounded upon no other Cause but this, namely, That the Family being generally addicted to the Cavalier Party, as they called it, and some of them possibly ingaged in the King's Service, who by this time had his Head Quarters at *Oxford*, and was in some Prospect of Success, they began to repent them of having Matched the Eldest Daughter of the Family to a Person so contrary to them in Opinion; and thought it would be a blot in their Escutcheon, when ever that Court should come to Flourish again; however, it so incensed our Author, that he thought it would be dishonourable ever to receive her again, after such a repulse; so that he forthwith prepared to Fortify himself with Arguments for such a Resolution and accordingly wrote two Treatises, by which he undertook to maintain, That it was against Reason (and the enjoyment of it not proveable by Scripture) for any Married Couple disagreeable in Humour and Temper, or having an aversion to each, to be forc'd to live yok'd together all their Days. The first was, His Doctrine and Discipline of Divorce; of which there was Printed a Second Edition, with some Additions [see above pp. 112 ff.]. The other in prosecution of the first, was styled, *Tetrachordon*. Then the better to confirm his own Opinion, by the attestation of others, he set out a Piece called the Judgement of *Martin Bucer*, a Protestant Minister, being a Translation, out of that Reverend Divine, of some part of his Works, exactly agreeing with him in Sentiment. Lastly, he wrote in answer to a Pragmatical Clerk, who would needs give himself the Honour of Writing against so great a Man, His Colasterion or Rod of Correction for a Sawcy Impertinent. Not very long after the setting forth of these Treatises, having application made to him by several Gentlemen of his acquaintance, for the Education of their Sons, as understanding haply the Progress he had infixed by his first undertakings of that nature, he laid out for a large House, and soon found it out; but in the interim before he removed, there fell out a passage, which though it altered not the whole Course he was going to Steer, yet it put a stop or rather an end to a grand Affair, which was more than probably thought to be then in agitation : It was indeed a design of Marrying one of Dr. *Davis*'s Daughters, a very Handsome and Witty Gentlewoman, but averse as it is said to this Motion; however, the Intelligence hereof, and the then declining State of the King's Cause, and consequently of the Circumstances of Justice *Powell*'s Family, caused them to set all Engines on Work, to restore the late Married Woman to the Station wherein they a little before had planted her; at last this device was pitch'd upon. There dwelt in the Lane of St. *Martins-L-Grand*, which was hard by, a Relation of our Author's, one *Blackborough*, whom it was known he often visited, and upon this occasion the visits were the more narrowly observ'd, and possibly there might be a Combination between both Parties; the Friends on both sides concentring in the same action though on different behalfs. One time above the rest, he making his usual visit, the Wife was ready in another Room, and on a sudden he was surprised to see one whom he thought to have never seen more, making Submission and begging Pardon on her Knees before him; he might probably at first make some shew of aversion and rejection; but partly his own generous nature, more inclinable to Reconciliation than to perseverance in Anger and Revenge; and partly the strong intercession of Friends on both sides, soon brought him to an Act of Oblivion, and a firm League of Peace for the future; and it was at length concluded, That she should remain at a Friend's house, till such time as he was settled in his New house at *Barbican*, and all things for her reception in order; the place agreed on for her present abode, was the Widow *Webber's* house in St. *Clement's* Church-yard, whose Second Daughter had been Married to the other Brother many years before; the first fruits of her return to her Husband was a brave Girl, born within a year after; though, whether by ill Constitution, or want of Care, she grew more and more decrepit. But it was not only by Children that she increas'd the number of the Family, for in no very long time after her coming, she had a great resort of her Kindred with her in the House, *viz.* her Father and Mother, and several of her Brothers and Sisters, which were in all pretty Numerous; who upon his Father's Sickning and Dying soon after went away. And now the House look'd again like a House of the Muses only, tho the accession of Scholars was not great. Possibly his proceeding thus far in the Education of Youth may have been the occasion of some of his Adversaries calling him Pædagogue and Schoolmaster: Whereas it is well known he never set up for a Publick School to teach all the young Fry of a Parish, but only was willing to impart his Learning and Knowledge to Relations, and the Sons of some Gentlemen that were his intimate Friends; besides, that neither his Converse, nor his Writings, nor his maner of Teaching ever savour'd in the least any thing of Pedantry; and probably he might have some prospect of putting in Practice his Academical Institution, according to the Model laid down in his Sheet of Education [see above pp. 181 ff.]. The Pro-

gress of which design was afterwards diverted by a Series of
Alteration in the Affairs of State; for I am much mistaken, if
there were not about this time a design in Agitation of making
him Adjutant-General in Sir *William Waller's* Army; but the
new modelling of the Army soon following, prov'd an obstruction to that design; and Sir *William*, his Commission being laid
down, began, as the common saying is, to turn *Cat in Pan*.

It was not long after the March of *Fairfax* and *Cromwell*
through the City of *London* with the whole Army, to quell the
Insurrectionists *Brown* and *Massy*, now Malecontents also, were
endeavouring to raise in the City against the Armies proceedings, ere he left his great House in *Barbican*, and betook himself to a smaller in *High Holbourn*, among those that open
backward into *Lincolns-Inn*-Fields, here he liv'd a private and
quiet Life, still prosecuting his Studies and curious Search into
Knowledge, the grand Affair perpetually of his Life; till such
time as the War being now at an end, with compleat Victory
to the Parliament's side, as the Parliament then stood purg'd
of all its Dissenting Members, and the King after some Treatie
with the Army, *re Infecta*, brought to his Tryal; the form of
Government being now chang'd into a Free State, he was hereupon oblig'd to Write a Treatise, call'd the *Tenure of Kings and
Magistrates* [see above pp. 249 ff.] After which his thoughts
were bent upon retiring again to his own private Studies, and
falling upon such Subjects as his proper Genius prompted him to
Write of, among which was the History of our own Nation
from the Beginnning till the *Norman* Conquest, wherein he had
made some progress. When for this his last Treatise, reviving
the fame of other things he had formerly Published, being more
and more taken notice of his excellency of Stile, and depth of
Judgement, he was courted into the Service of this new Commonwealth, and at last prevail'd with (for he never hunted
after Preferment, nor affected the Tintamar and Hurry of Publick business) to take upon him the Office of *Latin* Secretary
to the Counsel of State for all their Letters to Foreign Princes
and States : for they stuck to this Noble and Generous Resolution, not to write to any, or receive Answers from them, but in
a Language most proper to maintain a Correspondence among

the Learned of all Nations in this part of the World; scorning to carry on their Affairs in the Wheedling Lisping Jargon of the Cringing *French*, especially having a Minister of State able to cope with the ablest any Prince or state could imploy for the Latin Tongue; and so well he acquitted himself in this station, that he gain'd from abroad both Reputation to himself, and Credit to the State that Employed him; and it was well the business of his Office came not very fast upon him, for he was scarce well warm in his Secretaryship before other work flow'd in upon him, which took him up for some considerable time.

In the first place there came out a Book said to have been written by the King, and finished a little before his Death, Entituled, Εἰκων Βασιλικη, that is, *The Royal Image*; a Book highly cryed up for it's smooth Style, and pathetical Composure; wherefore to obviate the impression it was like to make among the *Many*, he was obliged to Write an Answer, which he Entituled Εἰκονοκλαετης, of *Image-Breaker*; and upon the heels of that, out comes in Publick the great Kill-cow of *Christendom*,[11] with his *Defensio Regis contra Populum Anglicanum*; a Man so Famous and cryed up for his *Plinian Exercitations*, and other Pieces of reputed Learning, that there could no where have been found a Champion that durst lift up the Pen against so formidable an Adversary, had not our little *English David* had the Courage to undertake this great *French Goliath*, to whom he gave such a hit in the Forehead, that he presently staggered, and soon after fell; for immediately upon the coming out of the Answer, Entituled, *Defensio Populi Anglicani, contra Claudium Anonymum*, &c. he that till then had been Chief Minister and Superintendent in the Court of the Learned *Christina* Queen of *Sweden*, dwindled in esteem to that degree, that he at last vouchsafed to speak to the meanest Servant. In short, he was dismiss'd with so cold and sighting an Adieu, that after a faint dying Reply, he was glad to have recourse to Death, the remedy of Evils, and ender of Controversies.

And now I presume our Author had some breathing space; but it was not long; for though *Salmasius* was departed, he left

---

11. Salmasius; see above, p. 36–7.

some things behind, new Enemies started up, Barkers, though no
great Biters; who the first Assertor of *Salmasius* his Cause was
is not certainly known, but variously conjectur'd at, some
supposing it to be one *Janus* a Lawyer of *Grays-Inn*, some Dr
Bramhal, made by King *Charles* the Second after his Restauration
Archbishop of *Armagh* in *Ireland*; but whoever the Author was
the Book was thought fit to be taken into correction, and our
Author not thinking it worth his own undertaking, to the dis
turbing the progress of whatever more chosen work he had
then in hands, committed this task to the youngest of his
Nephews, but with such exact Emendations before it went to
Press, that it might have very well have passed for his, but that
he was willing the person that took the pains to prepare it for his
Examination and Polishment, should have the Name and Credit
of being Author; so that it came forth under this Title, *Joannis
Philippi Angli Defensio pro Populo Anglicano contra*, &c. Dur
ing the Writing and Publishing of this Book, he lodg'd at one
Thomson's next door to the *Bull-head* Tavern at *Charing-Cross*
opening into the *Spring-Garden*, which seems to have been only
a Lodging taken, till his designed Apartment in *Scotland-Yard*
was prepared for him; for hither he soon removed from the fore
said place; and here his third Child, a Son was born, which
through ill usage, or bad Constitution of an ill chosen Nurse
died an Infant; from this Apartment, whether he thought it
not healthy, or otherwise convenient for his use, or whatver else
was the reason, he soon after took a pretty Garden-house in
Petty-France in *Westminster*, next door to the Lord *Scudamore's*
and opening into St. *James's* Park; here he remain'd no less than
Eight years, namely, from the year 1652, till within a few weeks
of King *Charles* the 2d's Restoration. In this House his first
Wife dying in Childbed, he Married a Second, who after a
Year's time died in Childbed also; this his Second marriage
was about Two or Three years after his being wholly de
priv'd of Sight, which was just going, about the time of his
Answering *Salmasius*; whereupon his Adversaries gladly take
occasion of imputing his blindness as a Judgment upon him
for his answering the King's Book, &c. whereas it is most cer
tainly known, that his Sight, what with his continual Study

his being subject to the Head-ake, and perpetual tampering with Physick to preserve it, had been decaying for above a dozen years before, and the sight of one for a long time clearly lost. Here he wrote, by his *Amanuensis*, his Two Answers to *Alexander More*; who upon the last Answer quitted the field. So that being now quiet from State-Adversaries and publick Contests, he had leisure again for his own Studies and private Designs; which were his foresaid *History* of England, and a New *Thesaurus Linguæ Latinæ*, according to the manner of *Stephanus*; a work he had been long since Collecting from his own Reading, and still went on with it at times, even very near to his dying day; but the Papers after his death were so dis-composed and deficient, that it could not be made fit for the Press; However, what there was of it, was made use of for another Dictionary.

But the Heighth of his Noble Fancy and Invention began now to be seriously and mainly imployed in a Subject worthy of such a Muse, viz. A Heroick Poem, Entituled, *Paradise Lost*; the Noblest in the general Esteem of Learned and Judicious Persons, of any yet written by any either Ancient or Modern: This Subject was first designed a Tragedy, and in the Fourth Book of the Poem there are Ten Verses, which several Years before the Poem was begun, were shewn to me, and some others, as designed for the very beginning of the said Tragedy. The Verses are These;

> O Thou that with surpassing Glory Crown'd!
> Look'st from thy sole Dominion, like the God
> Of this New World; at whose sight all the Stars
> Hide their diminish'd Heads; to thee I call,
> But with no friendly Voice; and add thy Name,
> O Sun! to tell thee how I hate thy Beams
> That bring to my remembrance, from what State
> I fell, how Glorious once above thy Sphere;
> Till Pride and worse Ambition threw me down,
> Warring in Heaven, against Heaven's Glorious King.[12]

---

12. *Paradise Lost*, IV, 32–41.

There is another very remarkable Passage in the Composure of this Poem, which I have particular occasion to remember; for whereas I had the perusal of it from the very beginning; for some years as I went from time to time to Visit him, in a Parcel of Ten, Twenty, or Thirty Verses at a Time, which being Written by whatever hand came next, might possibly want Correction as to the Orthography and Pointing; having as the Summer came on, not been shewed any for a considerable while, and desiring the reason thereof, was answered, That his Vein never happily flow'd, but from the *Autumnal Equinoctial* to the *Vernal*, and that whatever he attempted was never to his satisfaction, though he courted his fancy never so much; so that in all the years he was about this Poem, he may be said to have spent but half his time therein.

It was but a little before the King's Restoration that he Wrote and Published his Book in *Defence of a Commonwealth* [see above, pp. 327 ff.]; so undaunted he was in declaring his true Sentiments to the world; and not long before, his Power of the *Civil Magistrate in Ecclesiastical affairs* [see above, pp. 296 ff.]; and his *Treatise against Hirelings*, just upon the King's coming over; having a little before been sequestred from his Office of *Latin* Secretary, and the Salary thereunto belonging, he was forc'd to leave his House also, in *Petty France*, where all the time of his abode there, which was eight years, as above-mentioned, he was frequently visited by persons of Quality, particularly my Lady *Ranala*, whose son for some time he instructed; all Learned Foreigners of Note, who could not part out of this City, without giving a visit to a person so Eminent; and lastly, by particular Friends that had a high esteem for him, *viz.* Mr. *Andrew Marvel*, young *Laurence* (the Son of him that was President of *Oliver's* Council) to whom there is a Sonnet among the rest, in his Printed Poems; Mr. *Marchamont Needham*, the Writer of *Politicus*; but above all, Mr. *Cyriak Skinner* whom he honoured with two Sonnets, one long since publick among his Poems; the other but newly Printed.

His next removal was, by the advice of those that wisht him well, and had a concern for his preservation, into a place of retirement and abscondence, till such time as the current of affairs for the future should instruct him what farther course to take; it was a Friend's House in *Bartholomew-Close*, where he liv'd till the Act of Oblivion came forth; which it pleased God, prov'd as favourable to him as could be hop'd or expected, through the intercession of some that stood his Friends both in Council and Parliament; particularly in the House of Commons, Mr. *Andrew Marvel*, a Member for *Hull*, acted vigorously in his behalf, and made a considerable party for him; so that, together with *John Goodwin* of *Coleman-Street*, he was only so far excepted as not to bear any Office in the Commonwealth. Soon after appearing again in publick, he took a House in *Holborn* near *Red Lyon Fields*, where he stayed not long before his Pardon having pass'd the Seal, he remov'd to *Jewin Street*; there he liv'd when he married his 3d. Wife, recommended to him by his old friend Dr. *Paget* in *Coleman-street*; but he stay'd not long after his new Marriage, ere he remov'd to a House in the *Artillery*-walk leading to *Bunhill Fields*. And this was his last Stage in this World, but it was of many years continuance, more perhaps than he had had in any other place besides. Here he finisht his noble Poem, and publisht it in the year 1666.[13] The first Edition was Printed in Quarto by one *Simons* a Printer in *Aldersgate-Street*, the other in a large Octavo by *Starky* near *Temple-Bar*, amended, enlarg'd, and differently dispos'd as to the Number of Books, by his own Hand, that is by his own appointment; the last set forth many years since his death in a large Folio with Cuts added by *Jacob Tonson*. Here it was also that he finisht and publisht his History of our Nation till the Conquest, all compleat so far as he went, some Passages only excepted, which being thought too sharp against the Clergy, could not pass the Hand of the Licencer, were in the Hands of the late Earl of *Anglesey* while he liv'd; where at present is uncertain.

It cannot certainly be concluded when he wrote his excellent Tragedy entitled *Samson Agonistes*, but sure enough it is that it came forth after his publication of *Paradice lost*, together with

---

13. The correct date is 1667.

his other Poem call'd *Paradice regain'd* which doubtless was begun and finisht and Printed after the other was publisht, and that in a wonderful short space considering the sublimeness of it; however it is generally censur'd to be much inferiour to the other, though he could not hear with patience any such thing when related to him; possibly the Subject may not afford such variety of Invention, but it is thought by the most judicious to be little or nothing inferiour to the other, for stile and decorum. The said Earl of *Anglesy* whom he presented with a Copy of the unlicens'd Papers of his History, came often here to visit him, as very much coveting his society and converse; as likewise others of the Nobility, and many persons of eminent quality; nor were the visits of Foreigners ever more frequent than in this place, almost to his dying day. His Treatise of true Religion, Heresy, Schism and Toleration, &c. was doubtless the last thing of his writing that was publisht before his Death. He had, as I remember, prepared for the Press an answer to some little scribing Quack in *London*; who had written a Scurrilous Libel against him, but whether by the disswasion of Friends, as thinking him a Fellow not worth his notice, or for what other cause I know not, this Answer was never publisht.

He died in the year 1673,[14] towards the latter end of the Summer, and had a very decent interment according to his Quality, in the Church of St. *Giles Cripplegate*, being attended from his House to the Church by several Gentlemen then in Town, his principal wellwishers and admirers.

He had three Daughters who surviv'd him many years (and a Son) all by his first Wife (of whom sufficient mention hath been made.) *Anne* his Eldest as abovesaid, and *Mary* his Second, who were both born at his House in *Barbican*; and *Debora* the youngest, who is yet living, born at his House in *Petty-France* between whom and his Second Daughter, the Son, named *John* was born as above-mention'd, at his Apartment in *Scotland Yard*. By his Second Wife, *Catherine* the Daughter of Captain *Woodcock* of *Hackney*, he had only one Daughter, of which the Mother the first year after her Marriage died in Child bed

---

14. The correct date is 1674.

nd the Child also within a Month after. By his Third Wife
lizabeth the Daughter of one Mr. *Minshal* of *Cheshire*, (and
inswoman to Dr. *Paget*) who surviv'd him, and is said to be
et living, he never had any Child; and those he had by the First
e made serviceable to him in that very particular in which he
ost wanted their Service, and supplied his want of Eye-sight
y their Eyes and Tongue; for though he had daily about him
ne or other to Read to him; some persons of Man's Estate, who
f their own accord greedily catch'd at the opportunity of
eing his Readers, that they might as well reap the benefit of
what they Read to him, as oblige him by the benefit of their
eading; others of younger years sent by their Parents to the
ame end, yet excusing only the Eldest Daughter by reason
f her bodily Infirmity, and difficult utterance of Speech, (which
o say truth I doubt was the Principal cause of excusing her)
he other two were Condemn'd to the performance of Reading,
nd exactly pronouncing of all the Languages of what ever
ook he should at one time or other think fit to peruse, *Viz.*
he *Hebrew* (and I think the *Syriac*), the *Greek*, the *Latin*, the
talian, *Spanish* and *French*. All which sorts of Books to be con-
ned to Read, without understanding one word, must needs be
Tryal of Patience, almost beyond endurance; yet it was en-
ured by both for a long time, yet the irksomeness of this
mployment could not be always concealed, but broke out
nore and more into expressions of uneasiness; so that at length
hey were all (even the Eldest also) sent out to learn some
Curious and Ingenious sorts of Manufacture, that are proper
or Women to learn, particularly Imbroideries in Gold or Silver.
t had been happy indeed if the Daughters of such a person had
een made in some measure Inheritrixes of their Father's
earning; but since Fate otherwise decreed, the greatest Honour
hat can be ascribed to this now living (and so would have been
o the others had they lived) is to be Daughter to a man of his
extraordinary Character.

He is said to have dyed worth 1500 *l.* in Money (a considerable
state, all things considered) besides Household Goods; for he
ustained such losses as might well have broke any person less
rugal and temperate then himself; no less then 2000 *l.* which

he had put for Security and improvement into the Excise Office, but neglecting to recal it in time, could never after get it out with all the Power and Interest he had in the Great ones of those Times; besides another great Sum, by mismanagement and for want of good advice.

Thus I have reduced into form and order what ever I have been able to rally up, either from the recollection of my own memory, of things transacted while I was with him, or the Information of others equally conversant afterwards, or from his own mouth by frequent visits to the last.[15]

---

15. Phillips appended at this point 'two material passages, which ... relate not immediately to our concerns', as well as Milton's sonnets to Cromwell, Fairfax, Vane, and Skinner.

BIBLIOGRAPHY

CONTENTS

ABBREVIATIONS

The place of publication is given only if it is other than London or New York. For the abbreviations "Columbia ed." and "Yale ed.," see above, p. 10.

ALH	*Achievements of the Left Hand*, ed. Michael Lieb and John T. Shawcross (Amherst, 1974)
AN&Q	*American Notes and Queries*
CE	*College English*
EA	*Études anglaises*
ELH	*Journal of English Literary History*
ELN	*English Language Notes*
ELR	*English Literary Renaissance*

BIBLIOGRAPHY

ES	English Studies
HLQ	Huntington Library Quarterly
HTR	Harvard Theological Review
JEGP	Journal of English and Germanic Philology
JHI	Journal of the History of Ideas
JWCI	Journal of the Warburg and Courtauld Institutes
MLN	Modern Language Notes
MLQ	Modern Language Quarterly
MLR	Modern Language Review
MP	Modern Philology
MQ	Milton Quarterly
MS	Milton Studies
N&Q	Notes and Queries
PBSA	Proceedings of the Bibliographical Society of America
PMLA	Publications of the Modern Language Association
PQ	Philological Quarterly
QJS	Quarterly Journal of Speech
RES	Review of English Studies
SEL	Studies in English Literature
SP	Studies in Philology
TLS	Times Literary Supplement
TSLL	Texas Studies in Language and Literature
UTQ	University of Toronto Quarterly

A BIBLIOGRAPHICAL NOTE

For a general guide to studies on Milton, see the chapter by Douglas Bush in *English Poetry: Select Bibliographical Guides*, ed. A. E. Dyson (1971); for more comprehensive guides, consult C. A. Patrides's compilation for the *New Cambridge Bibliography of English Literature*, ed. George Watson (1974), I, 1237–95, and J. H. Hanford's Goldentree Bibliography on Milton (revised 1979). The standard bibliographical works are: John T. Shawcross, *Milton: A Bibliography for the Years 1624–1700* (Binghamton, N.Y., 1984); D. H. Stevens, *Reference Guide to Milton: 1800–1930* (Chicago, 1930); Harris F. Fletcher, *Contributions to a Milton Bibliography: 1800–1930* (Urbana, 1931); and Calvin Huckabay, *John Milton: An Annotated Bibliography, 1929–1968* (Pittsburgh, rev. ed., 1969). On Milton's "critical heritage," see Shawcross's companion volumes for the years 1624–1731 and 1731–1801 (published 1970 and 1972, respectively).

A Milton Encyclopedia, gen. ed. William B. Hunter, Jr. (Lewisburg

Pa., 1978–1983), 9 vols., is necessarily of central importance. Also very useful is *The Age of Milton*, ed. C. A. Patrides and Raymond B. Waddington (New York, 1980), which contains eleven chapters on the period's various dimensions (history, politics, education, theology, science, music, the visual arts, etc.) as well as an important guide through the primary sources and a wide-ranging bibliography of secondary sources (pp. 370–427).

Annual bibliographies include: the English Association's *The Year's Work in English Studies* (1919 ff.); the Modern Humanities Research Association's *Annual Bibliography of English Language and Literature* (1920 ff.); *PMLA* (1922 ff.); *SP* (1922 ff.); and *SEL* (1961 ff.).

STUDIES OF THE BACKGROUND

[See also the fuller lists in the *Milton Encyclopedia* and *The Age of Milton*, as above.]

Ashley, Maurice. *The Golden Century: Europe 1598–1715.* 1969.

———. *Life in Stuart England.* 1964.

Ashton, Trevor, ed. *Crisis in Europe 1560–1660.* 1965.

Atkins, J. W. H. *English Literary Criticism: The Renascence.* 2d ed. 1951.

Aylmer, G. E. *The Struggle for the Constitution 1603–1689.* 1963. American ed., *A Short History of Seventeenth-Century England.*

Aylmer, G. E., ed. *The Interregnum: The Quest for Settlement 1646–60.* 1972.

———. *The Levellers in the English Revolution.* 1975.

Baker, Herschel. *The Image of Man* and *The Wars of Truth.* 1961; 1952. On Christian humanism.

———. *The Race of Time: Three Lectures on Renaissance Historiography.* Toronto, 1967.

Baldwin, C. S. *Renaissance Literary Theory and Practice: Classicism in the Rhetoric and Poetic of Italy, France, and England, 1400–1600.* 1939.

Baldwin, Thomas W. *William Shakespeare's Small Latine and Lesse Greeke.* 2 vols. Urbana, 1944.

Bamborough, J. B. *The Little World of Man.* 1952. On Renaissance psychological theory.

Bennett, H. S. *English Books and Readers 1603 to 1640.* Cambridge, 1970.

Bush, Douglas. *English Literature in the Earlier Seventeenth Century.* 2d rev. ed. Oxford, 1962.

———. *The Renaissance and English Humanism*. Toronto, 1939.

Cassirer, Ernst. *The Platonic Renaissance in England*, trans. J. P. Pettegrove. 1953.

Charlton, Kenneth. *Education in Renaissance England*. 1965.

Christianson, Paul K. *Reformers and Babylon: Apocalyptic Visions in England from the Reformation to the Outbreak of the Civil War*. Toronto, 1977.

Clark, Donald L. *John Milton at St. Paul's School: A Study of Ancient Rhetoric in English Renaissance Education*. 1948.

Cochrane, Eric, ed. *The Late Italian Renaissance 1525–1630*. 1970.

Collinson, Patrick. *The Elizabethan Puritan Movement*. 1967.

Cragg, G. R. *From Puritanism to the Age of Reason: A Study of Changes in Religious Thought within the Church of England 1660 to 1700*. Cambridge, 1950.

Cruickshank, John, ed. *French Literature and Its Background*, vol. II: *The Seventeenth Century*. Oxford, 1969.

Curtis, Mark H. *Oxford and Cambridge in Transition, 1558–1642*. Oxford, 1959.

Elliott, J. H. *Imperial Spain 1469–1716*. 1963.

Farmer, David L. *Britain and the Stuarts*. 1965.

Fisch, Harold. *Jerusalem and Albion: The Hebraic Factor in Seventeenth-Century Literature*. 1964.

Friedrich, Carl J. *The Age of the Baroque 1610–1660*. 1952.

Fussner, F. Smith. *The Historical Revolution: English Historical Writing and Thought 1580–1640*. 1962.

Garin, Eugenio. *Italian Humanism*. Trans. Peter Munz. 1965.

Geyl, Peter. *The Netherlands in the Seventeenth Century*. 1936–1964.

Grierson, Sir Herbert. *Cross-Currents in English Literature of the Seventeenth Century*. 1929.

Hall, A. Rupert. *From Galileo to Newton, 1630–1720*. 1963.

Hall, Marie Boas. *The Scientific Renaissance 1450–1630*. 1962.

Haller, William. *Liberty and Reformation in the Puritan Revolution*. 1955.

———. *The Rise of Puritanism*. 1938.

Hardison, O. B., ed. *English Literary Criticism: The Renaissance*. 1963.

Hathaway, Baxter. *Marvels and Commonplaces: Renaissance Literary Criticism*. 1968.

Heppe, Heinrich, ed. *Reformed Dogmatics, set out and illustrated from the sources*. Ed. Ernest Bizer, trans. G. T. Thomson. 1950.

Herrick, Marvin T. *The Poetics of Aristotle in England*. New Haven, 1930.

Hill, Christopher. *The Century of Revolution 1603–1714*. Edinburgh, 1961.

———. *Intellectual Origins of the English Revolution*. Oxford, 1965.

———. *The World Turned Upside Down: Radical Ideas during the English Revolution*. 1972.

Howell, Wilbur S. *Logic and Rhetoric in England, 1500–1700*. Princeton, 1956.

Johnson, Francis R. *Astronomical Thought in Renaissance England*. Baltimore, 1937.

Jonas, Leah. *The Divine Science: The Aesthetic of Some Representative Seventeenth-Century English Poets*. 1940.

Jones, J. R. *Britain and Europe in the Seventeenth Century*. 1966.

Jones, Richard F. *Ancients and Moderns: A Study of the Rise of the Scientific Movement in Seventeenth-Century England*. 2d ed. 1961.

Jordan, Wilbur K. *The Development of Religious Toleration in England*. Esp. vols. II–IV. 1932–1940.

Knappen, M. M. *Tudor Puritanism*. Chicago, 1939.

Knott, John R., Jr. *The Sword of the Spirit: Puritan Responses to the Bible*. Chicago, 1980.

Koyré, Alexandre. *From the Closed World to the Infinite Universe*. Baltimore, 1957.

Kristeller, Paul O. *Renaissance Thought: I* and *II*. 1961; 1965.

———. *Studies in Renaissance Thought and Letters*. Rome, 1956.

Kristeller, Paul O., and Philip P. Wiener, eds. *Renaissance Essays*. 1968.

Lanham, Richard A. *The Motives of Eloquence: Literary Rhetoric in the Renaissance*. New Haven, 1976.

le Huray, Peter. *Music and the Reformation in England*. 1967.

Levy, F. J. *Tudor Historical Thought*. San Marino, Calif., 1967.

Lewis, C. S. *The Discarded Image: An Introduction to Medieval and Renaissance Literature*. Cambridge, 1964.

Lockyer, Roger. *Tudor and Stuart Britain 1471–1714*. 1964.

Lutaud, Olivier. *Les deux Révolutions d'Angleterre: Documents politiques, sociaux, religieux*. Paris, 1978.

McAdoo, H. R. *The Spirit of Anglicanism*. 1965.

Macpherson, C. B. *The Political Theory of Possessive Individualism: Hobbes to Locke*. Oxford, 1962.

Mazzeo, Joseph A. *Renaissance and Revolution: Backgrounds to Seventeenth-Century English Literature*. 1965.

Mintz, Samuel I. *The Hunting of Leviathan: Seventeenth-Century Reactions to the Materialism and Moral Philosophy of Thomas Hobbes*. Cambridge, 1962.

More, Paul E., and Frank L. Cross, eds. *Anglicanism: The Thought and Practice of the Church of England*. 1935.

Morris, Christopher. *Political Thought in England: Tyndale to Hooker*. 1953.

Mulder, John R. *The Temple of the Mind: Education and Literary Taste in Seventeenth-Century England*. 1969.

Nelson, Norman. *Peter Ramus and the Confusion of Logic, Rhetoric and Poetry*. Ann Arbor, 1947.

The New Cambridge Modern History, III: *The Counter-Reformation and the Price Revolution, 1559–1610*, ed. R. B. Wernham. 1968. IV: *The Decline of Spain and the Thirty Years War, 1609–1648/59*, ed. J. P. Cooper. 1970. V: *The Ascendancy of France, 1648–1688*, ed. F. L. Carsten. 1961.

Notestein, Wallace. "The English Woman, 1580 to 1650." In *Studies in Social History*, ed. J. H. Plumb, chap. III. 1955.

Nuttall, Geoffrey F. *The Holy Spirit in Puritan Faith and Experience*. Oxford, 1946.

Ong, Walter J., S.J. *Ramus, Method, and the Decay of Dialogue*. Cambridge, Mass., 1958.

Parks, George B. "The Decline and Fall of the English Renaissance Admiration of Italy." *HLQ* 31 (1968) : 341–57.

Patrides, C. A. *Premises and Motifs in Renaissance Thought and Literature*. Princeton, 1982.

Patrides, C. A., ed. *The Cambridge Platonists*. 1969.

Patrides, C. A., and Raymond B. Waddington, eds. *The Age of Milton: Backgrounds to Seventeenth-Century Literature*. 1980.

Patrides, C. A., and Joseph Wittreich, eds. *The Apocalypse in English Renaissance Thought and Literature*. Ithaca, N.Y., 1984.

Pennington, D. H. *Seventeenth Century Europe*. 1970.

Powell, Chilton L. *English Domestic Relations 1487–1653*. 1917.

Raab, Felix. *The English Face of Machiavelli: A Changing Interpretation 1500–1700*. 1964.

Robb, Nesca. *Neoplatonism of the Italian Renaissance*. 1935.

Rogers, P. G. *The Fifth Monarchy Men*. 1966.

Russell, Conrad. *The Crisis of Parliaments: English History 1500–1660*. Oxford, 1971.

Scholem, Gershom G. *Major Trends in Jewish Mysticism*. Rev. ed. 1946.

Schücking, Levin L. *The Puritan Family*. Trans. B. Battershaw. 1969.

Sells, Arthur L. *The Paradise of Travellers: The Italian Influence on Englishmen in the Seventeenth Century*. 1964.

Shumaker, Wayne. *The Occult Sciences in the Renaissance*. Berkeley, 1972.

Skinner, Quentin. *Foundations of Modern Political Thought*. 2 vols. Cambridge, 1978.

Spingarn, Joel E. *A History of Literary Criticism in the Renaissance*. 2d ed. 1908.

Spingarn, Joel E., ed. *Critical Essays of the Seventeenth Century*. 3 vols. Oxford, 1908–1909.

Stone, Lawrence. *The Causes of the English Revolution 1529–1642*. 1972.

Strauss, Leo. *The Political Philosophy of Hobbes*. Trans. E. M. Sinclair. Oxford, 1936.

Tawney, R. H. *Religion and the Rise of Capitalism*. 1926.

Thomas, Keith. *Religion and the Decline of Magic*. 1971.

Tulloch, John. *Rational Theology and Christian Philosophy in England in the Seventeenth Century*. Rev. ed. 2 vols. Edinburgh, 1874. Still a reliable account.

Walker, D. P. "Orpheus the Theologian and Renaissance Platonism." *JWCI* 16 (1953) : 100–120. On Orphism.

Walzer, Michael. *The Revolution of the Saints: A Study in the Origins of Radical Politics*. Cambridge, Mass., 1965.

Webster, Charles, ed. *Samuel Hartlib and the Advancement of Learning*. Cambridge, 1970.

Wedgwood, C. V. *The King's Peace: 1637–1641*. 1955.

———. *The King's War: 1641–1647*. 1959.

Weinberg, Bernard. *A History of Literary Criticism in the Italian Renaissance*. 2 vols. Chicago, 1961.

Wiener, Philip P., ed. *Dictionary of the History of Ideas*. 3 vols. 1973.

Willey, Basil. *The Seventeenth Century Background*. 1934.

Williamson, George. *Seventeenth Century Contexts*. 1960.

Wilson, Charles. *England's Apprenticeship 1603–1763*. 1965.

Wilson, F. P. *Elizabethan and Jacobean*. Oxford, 1945.

Woodward, William H. *Studies in Education during the Age of the Renaissance, 1400–1600*. Cambridge, 1906.

Wright, Louis B. *Middle-Class Culture in Elizabethan England*. Chapel Hill, 1935.

Yates, Frances A. *Giordano Bruno and the Hermetic Tradition*. 1964. On Renaissance hermetic thought.

Zagorin, Perez. *The Court and the Country: The Beginnings of the English Revolution*. 1969.

THE PROSE OF THE ENGLISH RENAISSANCE

General Studies

[The following list includes general as well as particular studies of representative figures from the late sixteenth to the late seventeenth centuries.]

Adolph, Robert. *The Rise of Modern Prose Style.* Cambridge, Mass., 1968.

Anselment, Raymond A. "Rhetoric and the Dramatic Satire of Martin Marprelate." *SEL* 10 (1970) : 103–19.

Babb, Lawrence. *Sanity in Bedlam: A Study of Robert Burton's "Anatomy of Melancholy."* East Lansing, 1959.

Barish, Jonas A. "Baroque Prose in the Theater: Ben Jonson." *PMLA* 73 (1958) : 184–95.

———. "The Prose Style of John Lyly." *ELH* 23 (1956) : 14–35.

Brinkley, Roberta F., ed. *Coleridge on the Seventeenth Century,* pp. 411–500. Durham, N.C., 1955. Extensive comments on prose style in general, but also on Browne, Bunyan, Burton, Donne, Milton, et al.

Chandos, John, ed. *In God's Name: Examples of Preaching in England 1534–1662.* 1971.

Crane, William G. *Wit and Rhetoric in the Renaissance: The Formal Basis of Elizabethan Prose Style.* 1937.

Croll, Morris W. *Style, Rhetoric and Rhythm.* Ed. J. Max Patrick et al. Princeton, 1966. On Renaissance prose and rhetoric.

Crook, Margaret B., et al. *The Bible and Its Literary Associations.* 1937.

Daiches, David. *The King James Version of the English Bible.* Chicago, 1941.

Eliot, T. S. "Lancelot Andrewes." 1926. In his *Selected Essays,* pp. 299–310. 1932.

Gordon, Ian A. *The Movement of English Prose,* chaps. VII–XII. 1966.

Hill, W. Speed. "The Authority of Hooker's Style." *SP* 67 (1970) : 328–38.

Huntley, Frank L. *Sir Thomas Browne: A Bibliographical and Critical Study.* Ann Arbor, 1962.

Jones, Richard F. *The Seventeenth Century.* Stanford, 1951. With four essays on prose style.

Knights, L. C. "Hooker and Milton: A Contrast of Styles." In his *Public Voices,* chap. III. 1971.

Miner, Earl. "Patterns of Stoicism in Thought and Prose Styles, 1530–1700." *PMLA* 85 (1970) : 1023–34.

Mitchell, W. Fraser. *English Pulpit Oratory from Andrewes to Tillotson*. 1932.

Mueller, William R. *John Donne: Preacher*. Princeton, 1962.

Myrick, Kenneth. "The *Defence of Poesie* as a Classical Oration." In his *Sir Philip Sidney as a Literary Craftsman*, 2d ed., chap. II. Lincoln, 1965.

Novarr, David. *The Making of Walton's "Lives."* Ithaca, N.Y., 1958.

Patrides, C. A., ed. *Approaches to Sir Thomas Browne*. Columbia, Mo., 1982.

Salzman, Paul. *English Prose Fiction 1558–1700*. Oxford, 1984.

Sharrock, Roger. *John Bunyan*. 1954.

Stedmont, J. M. "English Prose of the Seventeenth Century." *Dalhousie Review* 30 (1950) : 269–78.

Vickers, Brian. *Francis Bacon and Renaissance Prose*. Cambridge, 1968.

Webber, Joan. *Contrary Music: The Prose Style of John Donne*. Madison, 1963.

———. *The Eloquent "I": Style and Self in Seventeenth-Century Prose*. Madison, 1968.

White, Helen C. *English Devotional Literature, Prose, 1600–1640*. Madison, 1931.

Williamson, George. *The Senecan Amble: A Study in Prose from Bacon to Collier*. 1951.

Wilson, F. P. *Seventeenth Century Prose*. Berkeley, 1960. Lectures on Burton, Browne, biography, and the sermon.

STUDIES OF MILTON'S PROSE

Of the two complete editions of Milton's prose, the Columbia and the Yale (above, p. 10), only the latter is fully annotated. Editions of selections include the World's Classics (1931) and the Everyman (revised 1958) but especially the annotated editions by Merritt Y. Hughes (1947, 1957) and J. Max Patrick (1967). There is also a facsimile of selected prose works (Scolar Press, 1967–1968, 3 vols.) and an indispensable *Concordance to the English Prose of John Milton*, gen. ed. Harold Kollmeier (Binghamton, N.Y., 1985).

The Life Records of John Milton have been edited by J. Milton French (New Brunswick, N.J., 1949–1958), 5 vols.; and the *Early Lives of Milton*, by Helen Darbishire (1932, repr. 1965). Noteworthy modern critical biographies have been written by James H. Hanford (1949),

David Daiches (1957), Douglas Bush (1964, 1965), and A. N. Wilson (1983). The most ambitious modern biography is by William R. Parker, *Milton* (Oxford, 1968), 2 vols.

General Studies

Arthos, John. *Milton and the Italian Cities*. 1968. The background to Milton's visit (above, pp. 19 ff.).

Banks, Theodore H. *Milton's Imagery*. 1950. On the prose works, *passim*.

Barker, Arthur E. *Milton and the Puritan Dilemma 1641–1660*. Toronto, 1942.

Bennett, Joan S. "God, Satan, and King Charles: Milton's Royal Portraits." *PMLA* 92 (1977) : 441–57.

Broadbent, J. B. "Links between Poetry and Prose in Milton." *ES* 37 (1956) : 1–14.

Bryant, Joseph A., Jr. "Milton's Views on Universal and Civil Decay." In *SAMLA Studies in Milton*, ed. J. Max Patrick, pp. 1–19. Gainesville, Fla., 1953.

Christopher, Georgia B. *Milton and the Science of the Saints*. Princeton, 1982.

Clavering, Rose, and J. T. Shawcross. "Milton's European Itinerary and His Return Home." *SEL* 5 (1965) : 49–59.

Corns, Thomas N. *The Development of Milton's Prose Style*. Oxford, 1982.

———. "Obscenity, Slang and Indecorum in Milton's English Prose." *Prose Studies* 3 (1980) : 5–14.

Diekhoff, John S., ed. *Milton on Himself: Milton's Utterances upon Himself and His Works*. 1939.

Egan, James. *The Inward Teacher: Milton's Rhetoric of Christian Liberty*. University Park, Pa., 1980.

———. "The Satiric Wit of Milton's Prose Controversies." *Studies in the Literary Imagination* 10 (1977) : ii, 97–104.

Ekfelt, Fred E. "The Graphic Diction of Milton's English Prose." *PQ* 25 (1946) : 269–76.

———. "Latinate Diction in Milton's English Prose." *PQ* 28 (1949) : 53–71.

Emerson, Everett H. "A Note on Milton's Early Puritanism." In *Essays in Honor of E. L. Marilla*, ed. Thomas A. Kirby and William John Olive, pp. 127–34. Baton Rouge, 1970.

Evans, G. Blakemore. "The State of Milton's Text: The Prose 1643–48." *JEGP* 59 (1960) : 497–505.

Fallon, Robert T. "Filling the Gaps: New Perspectives on Mr. Secretary Milton." *MS* 12 (1978) : 165–95.

———. "Milton in the Anarchy, 1659–60." *SEL* 21 (1981) : 123–46.

Fink, Zera S. "The Theory of the Mixed State and the Development of Milton's Political Thought." *PMLA* 57 (1942) : 705–36. Revised in his *The Classical Republicans*, chap. IV. Evanston, 1945.

Fixler, Michael. *Milton and the Kingdoms of God.* 1964.

Fletcher, Harris F. *The Use of the Bible in Milton's Prose.* Urbana, 1929.

French, J. Milton. "Milton as Satirist." *PMLA* 51 (1936) : 414–29.

Frye, Roland M. *Milton's Imagery and the Visual Arts.* Princeton, 1978.

Gilman, Wilbur E. *Milton's Rhetoric: Studies in His Defense of Liberty.* Columbia, Mo., 1939.

Grierson, Sir Herbert. "Milton and Political Liberty." In his *Criticism and Creation*, pp. 71–91. 1949.

Grose, Christopher. "The Greatest Decency: Poetry, Images, and Discourse in Milton's Prose." In his *Milton's Epic Process*, chap. II. New Haven, 1973.

Hamilton, K. G. "The Structure of Milton's Prose." In *Language and Style in Milton*, ed. R. D. Emma and J. T. Shawcross, chap. X. 1967.

Hanford, James H. "Milton in Italy." *Annuale medievale* 5 (1964) : 49–63.

Hill, Christopher. *Milton and the English Revolution.* 1977.

———. "Milton and Marvell." In *Approaches to Marvell*, ed. C. A. Patrides, pp. 1–30. 1978.

Hill, John Spencer. *John Milton, Poet, Priest, and Prophet: A Study of Divine Vocation in Milton's Poetry and Prose.* Totowa, N.J., 1979.

Hughes, Merritt Y. "Milton as a Revolutionary." In his *Ten Perspectives on Milton*, chap. X. New Haven, 1965.

Kranidas, Thomas. *The Fierce Equation: A Study of Milton's Decorum.* Esp. chap. II, "Decorum from the Prose." The Hague, 1965.

———. "A View of Milton and the Traditional." *MS* 1 (1969) : 15–29.

Lamla, Max and Gertraud. *Wahlidee, Wahlrecht und Wahlpraxis in den Prosaschriften John Miltons zur Zeit der Englische Revolution.* Frankfurt, 1981.

Le Comte, Edward. "Milton as Satirist and Wit." In *Th' Upright Heart and Pure*, ed. A. P. Fiore, pp. 45–59. Pittsburgh, 1967.

———. *Milton and Sex.* 1978.

———. *Yet Once More: Verbal and Psychological Pattern in Milton.* 1954.

Major, John M. "Milton's View of Rhetoric." *SP* 64 (1967) : 685–711.

Maxey, Chester C. "Voices of Freedom." In his *Political Philosophies*, pp. 236–46. 1938.

Morkan, Joel. "Wrath and Laughter: Milton's Ideas on Satire." *SP* 69 (1972) : 475–95.

Neumann, Joshua H. "Milton's Prose Vocabulary." *PMLA* 60 (1945) : 102–20.

O'Keeffe, Timothy J. *Milton and the Pauline Tradition.* Washington, D.C., 1982.

Parker, William R. *Milton's Contemporary Reputation.* Columbus, 1940.

Patrides, C. A. *Milton and the Christian Tradition.* Oxford, 1966; repr. Hamden, Conn., 1979.

———. "'Something like prophetic strain': Apocalyptic Configurations in Milton." In *The Apocalypse in English Renaissance Thought and Literature,* ed. Patrides and Joseph Wittreich, chap. VIII. Ithaca, N.Y., 1984.

Patterson, Annabel. "The Civic Hero in Milton's Prose." *MS* 8 (1975) : 71–101.

Radzinowicz, Mary Ann. *Toward "Samson Agonistes": The Growth of Milton's Mind.* Princeton, 1978.

Rajan, Balachandra. *The Lofty Rhyme: A Study of Milton's Major Poetry.* 1970. Draws frequently on the prose.

Rosenberg, Donald M. "Satirical Techniques in Milton's Polemical Prose." *Satire Newsletter* 8 (1971) : 91–97.

———. "Theme and Structure in Milton's Autobiographies." *Genre* 2 (1969) : 314–25.

Samuel, Irene. "Milton on Comedy and Satire." *HLQ* 35 (1972) : 107–30.

———. "Milton on the Province of Rhetoric." *MS* 10 (1977) : 177–93.

Sensabaugh, George F. *Milton in Early America.* Princeton, 1964.

———. *That Grand Whig, Milton.* Stanford, 1952. On Milton's influence.

Shawcross, John T. "A Survey of Milton's Prose Works." In *ALH,* pp. 291–391.

Sirluck, Ernest. "Milton's Idle Right Hand." *JEGP* 60 (1961) : 749–85.

———. "Milton's Political Thought: The First Cycle." *MP* 61 (1964) : 209–24.

Spencer, T. J. B. "Milton, the First English Philhellene." *MLR* 47 (1952) : 533–34.

Stavely, Keith W. *The Politics of Milton's Prose Style.* New Haven, 1975.

Svendsen, Kester. *Milton and Science.* Cambridge, Mass., 1956.

Thompson, E. N. S. "Milton's Prose Style." *PQ* 14 (1935) : 1–15.

Weaver, Richard M. "Milton's Heroic Prose." In his *The Ethics of Rhetoric,* pp. 143–63. Chicago, 1953.

Webber, Joan. "John Milton: The Prose Style of God's English Poet." In her *The Eloquent "I,"* pp. 184–218. Madison, 1968.

Wittreich, Joseph. "'The Crown of Eloquence': The Figure of the Orator in Milton's Prose Works." In *ALH*, pp. 3–54.

Wolfe, Don M. "Limits of Miltonic Toleration." *JEGP* 60 (1961): 834–46.

———. "Milton and Hobbes: A Contrast in Social Temper." *SP* 41 (1944):410–26.

———. *Milton in the Puritan Revolution.* 1941.

Woodhouse, A. S. P. "Milton, Puritanism, and Liberty." *UTQ* 4 (1935): 483–513.

Woolrych, Austin. "Milton and Cromwell." In *ALH*, pp. 185–218.

———. "Milton's Political Commitment: The Interplay of Puritan and Classical Ideals." *Wascana Review* 9 (1974):166–88.

Zagorin, Perez. "John Milton." In his *A History of Political Thought in the English Revolution*, pp. 106–20. 1954.

On the antiepiscopal tracts

Allen, John W. "Milton's Writings of 1641–42." In his *English Political Thought 1603–44*, I:323–28. 1938.

Anselment, Raymond A. *"Betwixt Jest and Earnest":* . . . *the Decorum of Religious Ridicule.* Toronto, 1979.

Auksi, Peter. "Milton's 'Sanctifi'd Bitternesse': Polemical Technique in the Early Prose." *TSLL* 19 (1977):363–81.

Duvall, Robert F. "Time, Place, Persons: The Background of Milton's *Of Reformation*." *SEL* 7 (1967):107–18.

Egan, James. "Milton and the Marprelate Tradition." *MS* 8 (1975): 103–21.

Fish, Stanley. "Reason in *The Reason of Church Government*." In his *Self-Consuming Artifacts*, chap. V. Berkeley, 1972.

Gilbert, Allan H. "Milton's Defense of Bawdry." In *SAMLA Studies in Milton*, ed. J. Max Patrick, pp. 54–71. Gainesville, Fla., 1953.

Haller, William. *Liberty and Reformation in the Puritan Revolution*, chap. II (ii–iii). 1955.

———. *The Rise of Puritanism*, Chap. IX. 1938.

Hanford, James H. "The Youth of Milton." 1925. Reprinted in his *John Milton: Poet and Humanist*, esp. pp. 50 ff. Cleveland, 1966. The first to draw attention to the passage in the *Apology* (above, p. 61) as crucial to Milton's development generally, and the argument in *Comus* particularly.

Huntley, John F. "The Images of Poet and Poetry in Milton's *The Reason of Church-Government*." In *ALH*, pp. 83–120.

Kranidas, Thomas. "'Decorum' and the Style of Milton's Antiprelatical Tracts." *SP* 62 (1965) : 176–87. Revised in his *The Fierce Equation*, chap. II(a). The Hague, 1965.

———. "Milton and the Rhetoric of Zeal." *TSLL* 6 (1965) : 423–32.

———. "*Of Reformation*: The Politics of Vision." *ELH* 49 (1982) : 497–513.

———. "Style and Rectitude in Seventeenth-Century Prose: Hall, Smectymnuus, and Milton." *HLQ* 46 (1983) : 237–69.

———. "Words, Words, Words, and the Word: *Of Prelatical Episcopacy*." *MS* 16 (1982) : 153–56.

Lieb, Michael. "Milton and the Organicist Polemic." *MS* 4 (1972) : 79–99.

———. "*Of Reformation* and the Dynamics of Controversy." In *ALH*, pp. 55–82.

Limouze, Henry S. "Joseph Hall and the Prose Style of John Milton." *MS* 15 (1981) : 121–41.

Looten, C. "Les débuts de Milton pamphlétaire." *EA* 1 (1937) : 297–313.

Low, Anthony. "Plato and His Equal Xenophon." *MQ* 4 (1970) : 20–22

McCabe, Richard. "The Form and Methods of Milton's *Animadversions . . . .*" *ELN* 18 (1981) : 266–72.

Patrick, J. Max. "The Date of Milton's *Of Prelatical Episcopacy*." *HLQ* 13 (1950) : 303–11.

Rosenberg, Donald M. "Parody of Style in Milton's Polemics." *MS* 2 (1970) : 113–18.

———. "Style and Meaning in Milton's Anti-Episcopal Tracts." *Criticism* 15 (1973) : 43–57.

Sasek, Lawrence A. "Plato and His Equal Xenophon." *ELN* 7 (1970) : 260–62.

Sensabaugh, George F. "Jefferson's Use of Milton in the Ecclesiastical Controversies of 1776." *American Literature* 26 (1955) : 552–59.

Via, John A. "Milton's Antiprelatical Tracts: The Poet Speaks in Prose." *MS* 5 (1973) : 87–127.

On the divorce treatises

Barker, Arthur E. "Christian Liberty in Milton's Divorce Pamphlets." *MLR* 35 (1940) : 153–61.

Boyette, Purvis E. "Milton's Divorce Tracts and the Law of Marriage." *Tulane Studies in English* 17 (1969) : 73–92.

able, Lana. "Coupling Logic and Milton's Doctrine of Divorce." *MS* 15 (1981) : 143–59.

ye, Roland M. "The Teachings of Classical Puritanism on Conjugal Love." *Studies in the Renaissance* 2 (1955) : 148–59.

ilbert, Allan H. "Milton on the Position of Women." *MLR* 15 (1920) : 240–64.

alkett, John. *Milton and the Idea of Matrimony: A Study of the Divorce Tracts and "Paradise Lost."* New Haven, 1970.

aller, William and Malleville. "The Puritan Art of Love." *HLQ* 5 (1941–1942) : 235–72.

uquelet, Theodore L. "The Rule of Charity in Milton's Divorce Tracts." *MS* 6 (1974) : 199–214.

irson, M. A. "The Influence of Milton's Divorce Tracts on Farquhar's *Beaux' Stratagem.*" *PMLA* 39 (1924) : 174–78.

·josne, Roger. "Nature humaine et loi divine dans le *Tetrachordon.*" *EA* 27 (1974) : 415–24.

erill, R. V. "Eros and Anteros." *Speculum* 19 (1944) : 265–84. The background to the myth used by Milton (above, p. 139).

lsen, V. Norskov. *The New Testament Logia on Divorce: A Study of Their Interpretation from Erasmus to Milton.* Tübingen, 1971.

wen, Eivion. "Milton and Selden on Divorce." *SP* 43 (1946) : 233–57.

·rlette, John M. "Milton, Ascham, and the Rhetoric of the Divorce Controversy." *MS* 10 (1977) : 195–215.

·gers, Katherine M. *The Troublesome Helpmate: A History of Misogyny in Literature,* esp. pp. 151–59. Seattle, 1966.

·egel, Paul N. "Milton and the Humanist Attitude toward Women." *JHI* 11 (1950) : 42–53.

·endsen, Kester. "Science and Structure in Milton's *Doctrine of Divorce.*" *PMLA* 67 (1952) : 435–45.

hompson, Claud A. ". . . the Bibliographical Tangle of *The Doctrine and Discipline of Divorce.*" *PBSA* 68 (1974) : 297–305.

On *Of Education*

·ndy, Murray W. "Milton's View of Education in *Paradise Lost.*" *JEGP* 21 (1922) : 127–52.

·ntley, John F. "*Proairesis, Synteresis,* and the Ethical Orientation of Milton's *Of Education.*" *PQ* 43 (1964) : 40–46.

·anidas, Thomas. "Milton's 'Grand Master Peece.'" *AN&Q* 2 (1963) : 54–55. Interprets the word (above, p. 191) as "master plot."

·elczer, William. "Looking Back Without Anger: Milton's *Of Edu-*

cation." In *Milton and the Middle Ages*, ed. John Mulryan, pp. 91–102. Lewisburg, Pa., 1982.

Ong, Walter J., S.J. "'Idea' Titles in Milton's Milieu." In *Studies in Honor of D. T. Starnes*, pp. 227–39. Austin, 1967. Annotate "idea" (above, p. 182).

Parker, William R. "Education: Milton's Ideas and Ours." *CE* 24 (1962): 1–14.

Quintana, Ricardo. "Notes on English Educational Opinion during the Seventeenth Century." *SP* 27 (1930): 265–92.

Samuel, Irene. "Milton on Learning and Wisdom." *PMLA* 64 (1949): 708–23.

———. "Milton Speaks to Academe." *MQ* 4 (1970): 2–4.

Sensabaugh, George F. "Milton on Learning." *SP* 43 (1946): 258–72.

Smith, Constance I. "Some Ideas on Education before Locke." *JHI* 2 (1962): 403–6.

Spencer, T. J. B. "Longinus in English Criticism: Influences before Milton." *RES*, n.s. 8 (1957): 137–43.

Taylor, Ivan E. "John Milton's Views on the Teaching of Foreign Languages." *Modern Language Journal* 33 (1949): 528–36.

Thompson, Elbert N. S. "Milton's *Of Education*." *SP* 15 (1918): 159–75.

On *Areopagitica*

Camé, Jean F. "Images in Milton's *Areopagitica*." *Cahiers elisabéthains* 6 (1974): 23–37.

Christensen, Parley A. "On Liberty in Our Time: Milton and Mill." *Western Humanities Review* 6 (1952): 110–18.

Clyde, William M. *The Struggle for the Freedom of the Press from Caxton to Cromwell*, pp. 77–84. 1934.

Daniels, Edgar F. "Samson in *Areopagitica*." *N&Q* 209 (1964): 92–9.

Dowling, Paul M. "Milton's *Areopagitica* and Isocrates' *Areopagiticus*." *MS* 21 (1985).

———. "Milton's Use (or Abuse) of History in *Areopagitica*." *Cithara* 23 (1983): 28–37.

———. "'The Scholasticke Grosnesse of Barbarous Ages': The Question of the Humanism of Milton's Understanding of Virtue." In *Milton and the Middle Ages*, ed. John Mulryan, pp. 59–7. Lewisburg, Pa., 1982.

Evans, John X. "Imagery as Argument in *Areopagitica*." *TSLL* 8 (1966): 189–205.

Fletcher, Harris F. "Milton's Vicar of Hell." *JEGP* 47 (1948) : 387–89.

Flory, Sister Ancilla M., S.B.S. "Free Movement and Baroque Perspective in Milton's *Areopagitica*." *Xavier University Studies* 6 (1967) : 93–98.

Forster, E. M. "The Tercentenary of the *Areopagitica*." In his *Two Cheers for Democracy*, pp. 51–55. 1951.

Haller, William. "Before *Areopagitica*." *PMLA* 42 (1927) : 875–900.

———. "For the Liberty of Unlicens'd Printing." *American Scholar* 14 (1945) : 326–33.

———. "Two Early Allusions to *Areopagitica*." *HLQ* 12 (1949) : 207–12.

Hunter, G. K. "The Structure of Milton's *Areopagitica*." *ES* 39 (1958) : 117–19.

Illo, John. "The Misreading of Milton." In *Radical Perspectives in the Arts*, ed. Lee Baxandall, pp. 178–92. Penguin Books, 1972.

Kendall, Willmoore. "How to Read Milton's *Areopagitica*." *Journal of Politics* 22 (1960) : 439–73.

Kendrick, Christopher. "Ethics and the Orator in *Areopagitica*." *ELH* 50 (1983) : 655–91.

Kivette, Ruth M. "The Ways and Wars of Truth." *MQ* 6 (1972) : 81–86. Favors reading of "wayfaring" (above, p. 213, n. 66).

Le Comte, Edward S. "*Areopagitica* as a Scenario for *Paradise Lost*." In *ALH*, pp. 121–41.

Limouze, Henry S. "'The Surest Suppressing': Writer and Censor in Milton's *Areopagitica*." *Centennial Review* 24 (1980) : 103–17.

Martin, L. C. "'Muing her Mighty Youth'—a Defence." *RES* 21 (1945) : 44–46. Cf. above, p. 240, n. 147.

Mayoux, Jean-Jacques. "Un classique de la liberté." *Critique* 118 (1957) : 195–207.

Miller, Leo. "The Italian Imprimatures in Milton's *Areopagitica*." *PBSA* 65 (1971) : 345–55. Cf. above, pp. 206–7.

Morkan, Joel. "Milton's *Areopagitica*: A Reason for the Title." *N&Q* 20 (1973) : 167–68.

Noah, James E. "Oliver Cromwell, Protector, and the English Press." *Journalism Quarterly* 39 (1962) : 57–62.

Osgood, Charles G. "*Areopagitica*—1644." In his *Creed of a Humanist*, pp. 105–13. Seattle, 1963.

Ould, Hermon, ed. *Freedom of Expression: A Symposium . . . to Commemorate the Tercentenary of . . . "Areopagitica."* 1945.

Price, Alan F. "Incidental Imagery in *Areopagitica*." *MP* 49 (1952) : 217–22.

Sensabaugh, George F. "Adaptations of *Areopagitica*." *HLQ* 13 (1950) : 201–5. See also *MLN* 61 (1946) : 166–69, and *N&Q*, n.s. 2 (1955) : 212–13.

Sirluck, Ernest. "Milton's Critical Use of Historical Sources: An Illustration." *MP* 50 (1952) : 226–31. On the use of Sarpi (above, p. 205).

———. "Milton Revises the *Faerie Queene*." *MP* 48 (1950) : 90–96. The implications of Milton's careless reference (above, p. 213, n. 69)

Smallenburg, Harry R. "Contiguities and Moving Limbs: Style as Argument in *Areopagitica*." *MS* 9 (1976) : 169–84.

Spitz, David. "Milton's *Areopagitica*: Testament of Our Time." In his *Essays in the Liberal Idea of Freedom*, pp. 100–110. Tucson, 1964.

West, Michael. "'Not Without Dust and Heat': A Ciceronianism in *Areopagitica*." *RES* 29 (1978) : 181–85.

Wiley, Margaret L. *The Subtle Knot: Creative Scepticism in Seventeenth-Century England*, chap. X. 1952.

Williams, Arnold. "*Areopagitica* Revisited." *UTQ* 14 (1944) : 67–74.

Whitaker, Juanita. "'The Wars of Truth': Wisdom and Strength in *Areopagitica*." *MS* 9 (1976) : 185–201.

Wittreich, Joseph. "Milton's *Areopagitica*: Its Isocratic and Ironic Contexts." *MS* 4 (1972) : 101–15.

———. "Pico and Milton: A Gloss on *Areopagitica*." *ELN* 9 (1971) 108–10. Records a parallel to Milton's statement, above, p. 240.

On The Tenure of Kings and Magistrates *and* Eikonoklastes

Hesselberg, Arthur K. *A Comparative Study of the Political Theories of Ludovicus Molina, S.J., and John Milton*. Washington, D.C., 1952

Hughes, Merritt Y. "*Eikon Basilike*." In *Calm of Mind*, ed. Joseph Wittreich, pp. 1–24. Cleveland, 1971.

———. "Milton's Treatment of Reformation History in *The Tenure of Kings and Magistrates*." In his *Ten Perspectives on Milton*, chap. IX. New Haven, 1965.

Miller, Sonia. "Two References in Milton's *Tenure of Kings*." *JEGP* 50 (1951) : 320–25. Cf. above, p. 288, n. 90.

O'Keeffe, Timothy J. "The Imaginal Strategy of *Eikonoklastes*." *Ball State University Forum* 11 (1971) : 227–45.

Sandler, Florence. "Icon and Iconoclast." In *ALH*, pp. 160–84.

Shawcross, John T. "The Higher Wisdom of *The Tenure*." In *ALH*, pp. 142–59.

———. "Milton's *Tenure of Kings and Magistrates*: Date of Composition, Editions, and Issues." *PBSA* 60 (1966) : 1–8.

Sirluck, Ernest. "*Eikon Basilike, Eikon Ailthini,* and *Eikonoklastes.*" *MLN* 69 (1954) : 497–502. On the attribution of the first to Bishop Gauden.

Trevor-Roper, Hugh. "*Eikon Basilike:* The Problem of the King's Book." *History Today* 1 (September 1951) : 7–12.

Whiting, George W. "The Sources of *Eikonoklastes:* A Resurvey." *SP* 32 (1935) : 74–102.

On the three Defenses

Ayers, R. W. "The John Phillips—John Milton *Angli Reponsio:* Editions and Relations." *PBSA* 56 (1962) : 66–72. Also on its date, in *PQ* 38 (1959) : 95–101.

Bowers, A. Robin. "Milton and Salmasius: The Rhetorical Imperatives." *PQ* 52 (1973) : 55–68.

Bradley, S. A. J. "Ambiorix Ariovistus, Detractor of Milton's *Defensio,* Identified." *MP* 73 (1976) : 382–88.

French, J. Milton. "The Date of Milton's *First Defense.*" *Library,* 5th series, 3 (1948) : 56–58.

Grace, William J. "Milton, Salmasius, and the Natural Law." *JHI* 24 (1963) : 323–36.

Hoffman, Richard L. "The Rhetorical Structure of Milton's *Second Defence.*" *Studia Neophilologica* 43 (1971) : 227–45.

McGuire, Mary Ann. "'A Most Just Vituperation': Milton's Christian Orator in *Pro se defensio.*" *Studies in the Literary Imagination* 10 (1977) : ii, 105–14.

Madan, Francis F. "A Revised Bibliography of Salmasius' *Defensio regia* and Milton's *Pro populo anglicano defensio.*" *Library,* 5th series, 9 (1954) : 101–21.

Merrill, Harry G. "Political Drama of the Salmasian Controversy: An Essay in Perspective." In *Studies in Honor of J. C. Hodges and A. Thaler,* pp. 49–56. Knoxville, 1961.

Seaton, Ethel. *Literary Relations of England and Scandinavia in the Seventeenth Century.* Oxford, 1935. On Milton and Salmasius, pp. 107–9.

Speer, Diane P. "Milton's *Defensio Prima:* Ethos and Vituperation in a Polemic Engagement." *QJS* 56 (1970) : 277–83.

Svendsen, Kester. On Milton and Alexander More (as above, p. 37, n. 39).

Wolfe, Don M. "Milton and Cromwell: April 1653." In *English Studies Today,* 4th series, ed. Ilva Cellini and Giorgio Melchiori, pp. 311–24. Rome, 1966.

On the last pamphlets

Ayers, Robert W. "The Editions of *Readie & Easie Way*." *RES* 25 (1974) : 280–91.

Egan, James. "Public Truth and Personal Witness in Milton's Last Tracts." *ELH* 20 (1973) : 231–48.

Fink, Z. S. "Venice and English Political Thought in the Seventeenth Century." *MP* 38 (1940–1941) : 155–72.

Henry, Nathaniel H. "Milton's Last Pamphlet: Theocracy and Intolerance." In *A Tribute to G. C. Taylor*, ed. Arnold Williams, pp. 197–210. Chapel Hill, 1952. On *Of True Religion*.

Hunter, William B. "Milton and Richard Cromwell." *ELN* 3 (1966) : 252–59.

Lewalski, Barbara K. "Milton on Learning and the Learned-Ministry Controversy." *HLQ* 24 (1961) : 267–81. The context of his *Considerations*.

———. "Milton: Political Beliefs and Polemical Methods, 1659–60." *PMLA* 74 (1959) : 191–202.

Radzinowicz, Mary Ann. "*Samson Agonistes* and Milton the Politician in Defeat." *PQ* 44 (1965) : 454–71.

Smallenburg, Harry. "Government of the Spirit: Style, Structure and Theme in *Treatise of Civil Power*." In *ALH*, pp. 219–38.

Stavely, Keith W. "The Style and Structure of Milton's *Readie and Easie Way*." *MS* 5 (1973) : 269–87.

Stewart, Stanley. "Milton Revises *The Readie and Easie Way*." *MS* 20 (1984) : 205–24.

On historiography

Benjamin, Edwin B. "Milton and Tacitus." *MS* 4 (1972) : 117–40.

Berry, Lloyd E. "Giles Fletcher the Elder and Milton's *A Brief History of Moscovia*." *RES*, n.s. 11 (1960) : 150–56.

Bryant, Joseph A., Jr. "Milton and the Art of History: A Study of Two Influences on *A Brief History of Moscovia*." *PQ* 29 (1950) : 15–30. Cf. G. B. Parks, "Milton's *Moscovia* and History," *PQ* 31 (1952) 218–21, and Bryant's rejoinder, pp. 221–23.

Cawley, Robert R. *Milton's Literary Craftsmanship: A Study of "A Brief History of Moscovia," with an Edition of the Text*. Princeton, 1941.

Firth, Sir Charles. "Milton as an Historian." In his *Essays Historical and Literary*, pp. 61–102. Oxford, 1938.

Fogle, French R. "Milton as Historian." In *Milton and Clarendon*, by Fogle and H. R. Trevor-Roper, pp. 1–20. Los Angeles, 1965.

French, J. Milton. "Milton as Historian." *PMLA* 50 (1935) : 469–79.

Gleason, John B. "The Nature of Milton's *Moscovia*." *SP* 61 (1964) : 640–49.

Glicksman, Harry. "The Sources of Milton's *History of Britain*." *University of Wisconsin Studies in Language and Literature* 11 (1920) : 105–44.

Landon, Michael. "John Milton's *History of Britain*: Its Place in English Historiography." *University of Mississippi Studies in English* 6 (1965) : 59–76.

Le Comte, Edward. "Milton's Attitude toward Women in the *History of Britain*." *PMLA* 62 (1947) : 977–83.

Martinet, Marie-Madeleine. "'British Troy': . . . De l'Histoire mythique à l'histoire critique." In *Prélude au matin d'un poète*, ed. Olivier Lutaud, pp. 62–76. Paris, 1983.

Nicholas, Constance. *Introduction and Notes to Milton's "History of Britain*. Urbana, 1957.

Parks, George B. "The Occasion of Milton's *Moscovia*." *SP* 40 (1943) : 399–404. See also under Bryant, above.

Patrides, C. A. *"The Grand Design of God": The Literary Form of the Christian View of History*, pp. 84–90, 108–9. 1972.

Samuel, Irene. "Milton and the Ancients on the Writing of History." *MS* 2 (1970) : 131–48.

On grammar and logic

Campbell, Gordon. "Milton's *Accedence Commenc't Grammar*." *MQ* 10 (1976) : 39–48.

Clark, Donald L. "Milton's Rhetorical Exercises." *QJS* 46 (1960) : 297–301.

Dahl, Rolf. "The Date of Milton's *Artis logicae* and the Development of the Idea of Definition in Milton's Works." *HLQ* 43 (1979) : 25–36.

Duhamel, P. Albert. "Milton's Alleged Ramism." *PMLA* 67 (1952) : 1035–53.

Emma, Ronald D. *Milton's Grammar*. The Hague, 1964.

Fisher, Peter F. "Milton's Logic." *JHI* 23 (1962) : 37–60.

French, J. Milton. "Some Notes on Milton's *Accedence Commenc't Grammar*." *JEGP* 60 (1961) : 641–50.

Grose, Christopher. "Ramus, Metaphor, and the *Art of Logic*." In his *Milton's Epic Process*, chap. V. New Haven, 1973.

Howell, Wilbur S. *Logic and Rhetoric in England 1500–1700*, pp. 213–19. Princeton, 1956.

Miller, Leo. "Milton Edits Freigius' 'Life of Ramus.'" *Renaissance and Reformation* 8 (1972) : 112–14.

Ong, Walter J., S.J. "Logic and the Epic Muse: Reflections on Noetic Structures in Milton's Milieu." In *ALH*, pp. 239–68.

Scott-Craig, T. S. K. "The Craftsmanship and Theological Significance of Milton's *Art of Logic*." *HLQ* 17 (1953) : 1–16.

On *De doctrina christiana*

[The date of composition is not known. Of the scholars listed below, Hanford dates the work in 1655–1660; Kelley, circa 1658–1660; Sewell, in three stages: 1640 ff., 1658–1660, and after 1660.

The Columbia ed. provides the translation of the treatise by Sumner (1825); the Yale ed. (vol. VI), that by John Carey. The introduction to the latter by Maurice Kelley does not fully reflect the recent discussions of *De doctrina* and its intellectual contexts.]

Adamson, J. H. "Milton's Arianism." *HTR* 53 (1960) : 269–76; reprinted in *Bright Essence* (see under Hunter, below).

Bullough, Geoffrey. "Polygamy among the Reformers." In *Renaissance and Modern Essays*, ed. G. R. Hibbard, pp. 5–23. 1966.

Burke, Kenneth. "Words anent Logology." In *Perspectives in Literary Symbolism*, ed. Joseph Strelka, pp. 72–82. University Park, Pa., 1968.

Burns, Norman T. *Christian Mortalism from Tyndale to Milton*. Cambridge, Mass., 1972.

Campbell, Gordon. "Alleged Imperfections in Milton's *De doctrina*." *MQ* 12 (1978) :64–65.

———. "*De doctrina christiana*: Its Structural Principles and Its Unfinished State." *MS* 9 (1976) :243–60.

———. "Milton's Theological and Literary Treatments of the Creation." *Journal of Theological Studies* 30 (1979) : 128–37.

———. "The Son of God in *De doctrina* and *Paradise Lost*." *MLR* 7 (1980) : 507–14.

Conklin, George N. *Biblical Criticism and Heresy in Milton*. 1949. On the philological aspects of Milton's exegesis in *De doctrina*.

Craig, Hardin. "An Ethical Distinction by John Milton." In his *The Written Word and Other Essays*, pp. 78–88. Chapel Hill, 1953.

Gehman, Henry S. "Milton's Use of Hebrew in the *De doctrina*." *Jewish Quarterly Review* 24 (1938) : 37–44.

Hanford, James H. "The Date of Milton's *De doctrina*." *SP* 17 (1920) 309–19.

annay, Margaret. "Milton's Doctrine of the Holy Scriptures." *Christian Scholar's Review* 5 (1976) : 339–49.

askin, Dayton, S.J. "Milton's Strange Pantheon: The Apparent Tritheism of the *De doctrina*." *Heythrop Journal* 16 (1975) : 129–48.

unter, William B. "Milton's Arianism Reconsidered." *HTR* 52 (1959) : 9–35. Reprinted in *Bright Essence* (see below).

———. "Some Problems in Milton's Theological Vocabulary." *HTR* 57 (1964) : 353–65. Reprinted in *Bright Essence* (see below).

———. "The Theological Context of Milton's *Christian Doctrine*." In *ALH*, pp. 269–87.

unter, William B., C. A. Patrides, and J. H. Adamson. *Bright Essence: Studies in Milton's Theology*. Salt Lake City, 1971. A collection of thirteen essays.

lley, Maurice. *This Great Argument: A Study of Milton's "De doctrina christiana" as a Gloss upon "Paradise Lost."* Princeton, 1941. See also his "Milton's Arianism Again Reconsidered," *HTR* 54 (1961) : 195–205, and "Milton and the Trinity," *HLQ* 33 (1970) : 315–20.

acCallum, H. R. "Milton and the Figurative Interpretation of the Bible." *UTQ* 31 (1962) : 397–415.

iller, Leo. *John Milton among the Polygamophiles*. 1974.

ineka, Francis E. "The Critical Reception of Milton's *De doctrina*." *University of Texas Studies in English* 22 (1943) : 115–47.

trides, C. A. "Milton and the Arian Controversy." *Proceedings of the American Philosophical Society* 120 (1976) : 245–52.

———. "Milton and Arianism." *JHI* 25 (1964) : 423–29. Reprinted in *Bright Essence* (see under Hunter, above).

———. "*Paradise Lost* and the Language of Theology." In *Language and Style in Milton*, ed. R. D. Emma and J. T. Shawcross, pp. 102–19. Reprinted in *Bright Essence* (see under Hunter, above).

———. "An Open Letter on the Yale Edition of *De doctrina*." *MQ* 7 (1973) : 72–74.

jan, B. "*Paradise Lost* and the *De doctrina*." In his *"Paradise Lost" and the Seventeenth Century Reader*, pp. 22–38. 1948.

esing, John. "The Materiality of God in Milton's *De doctrina*." *HTR* 50 (1957) : 159–73.

ott-Craig, T. S. K. "Milton's Use of Wolleb and Ames." *MLN* 55 (1940) : 403–7.

well, Arthur. *A Study in Milton's Christian Doctrine*. 1939.

aheen, Naseeb. "Milton's Muse and the *De doctrina*." *MQ* 8 (1974) : 72–76.

Shullenberger, William. "Linguistic and Poetic Theory in Milton's *I doctrina.*" *ELN* 19 (1982) :262–78.

Stapleton, Laurence. "Milton's Conception of Time in *The Christi Doctrine.*" *HTR* 57 (1964) :9–21.

Williamson, George. "Milton and the Mortalist Heresy." *SP* 22 (1935 553–79. See further Nathaniel H. Henry, "Milton and Hobb Mortalism and the Intermediate State," *SP* 48 (1951) :234–4 and C. A. Patrides, "Psychopannychism in Renaissance Europe *SP* 60 (1963) :227–29.

On the Commonplace Book, the State Papers, and the letter

Bottkol, J. McG. "The Holograph of Milton's Letter to Holstenius *PMLA* 68 (1953) :617–27.

Hanford, James H. "The Chronology of Milton's Private Studies." In I *John Milton: Poet and Humanist*, chap. II. Cleveland, 1966.

Mohl, Ruth. *Milton and His Commonplace Book*. 1969.

Patrick, J. Max. "Significant Aspects of the Miltonic State Paper *HLQ* 33 (1970) :321–30.

Tillyard, E. M. W. "Milton's Private Correspondence and Academ Exercises." In his *Studies in Milton*, pp. 107–36. 1951.

Tillyard, Phyllis B., trans. *Private Correspondence and Academic Ex cises*. Cambridge, 1932.

On literary criticism

Bywater, Ingram. "Milton and the Aristotelian Definition of Traged *Journal of Philology* 27 (1901): 267–75.

Flower, Annette C. "The Critical Context of the Preface to *Sams Agonistes.*" *SEL* 10 (1970) :409–23.

Freedman, Morris. "Milton and Dryden on Rhyme." *HLQ* 24 (1961 337–44.

Jones, Charles E. "Milton's 'Brief Epic.'" *SP* 44 (1947) :209–27. On t allusion to the Book of Job (above, p. 56).

Koehler, G. Stanley. "Milton on Numbers, Quantity and Rime." *SP* (1958) :201–17.

Langdon, Ida. *Milton's Theory of Poetry and Fine Art*. New Haven, 192

Lewalski, Barbara K. "*Samson Agonistes* and the 'Tragedy' of t Apocalypse." *PMLA* 85 (1970) :1050–62. The context and i plications of Milton's references (above, pp. 56, 407).

Mohl, Ruth. "Milton on some of the Writing of his Day." In *Studies*

Language and Literature in Honour of M. Schlauch, pp. 261–72. Warsaw, 1966.

ueller, Martin E. "Sixteenth-Century Italian Criticism and Milton's Theory of Catharsis." *SEL* 6 (1966) : 139–50.

jan, B. "'Simple, Sensuous, and Passionate.'" In *Milton*, ed. Arthur E. Barker, pp. 3–20. 1965. The reference to poetry in *Of Education* (above, p. 183) placed within a broader context.

muel, Irene. "Milton on Style." *Cornell Library Journal* 9 (1969) : 39–58.

llin, Paul R. "Sources of Milton's Catharsis: A Reconsideration." *JEGP* 60 (1961) : 712–30.

eadman, John M. "'Passions Well Imitated': Rhetoric and Poetics in the Preface to *Samson Agonistes*." In *Calm of Mind*, ed. Joseph Wittreich, pp. 175–207. Cleveland, 1971.